E. V. Thompson Omnibus

Somewhere a Bird is Singing
Singing Spears

E. V. Thompson Omnibus

Somewhere a Bird is Singing
Singing Spears

E. V. THOMPSON

timewarner
paperbacks

A *Time Warner* Paperback

This omnibus edition first published in Great Britain by Time Warner Paperbacks in 2004
E. V. Thompson Omnibus Copyright © E. V. Thompson 2004

Previously published separately:
Somewhere a Bird is Singing first published in Great Britain
by Little, Brown and Company in 1999
Published by Warner Books in 2000
Reprinted 2000
Reprinted by Time Warner Paperbacks in 2002
Copyright © E. V. Thompson 1999

Singing Spears first published in Great Britain
by Macmillan London Ltd in 1982
First published in paperback by Pan Books Ltd in 1984
Published by Warner Books in 1999
Copyright © E. V. Thompson 1982

The moral right of the author has been asserted.

A CIP catalogue record for this book is available from the British Library

ISBN 0 7515 3654 7

Printed and bound in Great Britain by
Mackays of Chatham Ltd, Chatham

Time Warner Paperbacks
An imprint of
Time Warner Books UK
Brettenham House
Lancaster Place
London WC2E 7EN

www.TimeWarnerBooks.co.uk

Somewhere a Bird is Singing

1

'If your hand comes so close as six inches from that there pie I swear I'll cut it off, you see if I don't.'

The barbaric threat was reinforced by a bloody meat cleaver, wielded by Alfie Philpott and waved menacingly at Sally Harrup. The perspiring pie-maker was wearing a grubby, well-worn straw boater and an even dirtier blue-and-white striped butcher's apron.

'Is that another of those urchins trying to nick one of our pies, Alfie?' The disembodied voice came from beyond a doorway draped with a palm-frond curtain, half-hidden behind a long wooden counter piled high with pies and cardboard advertisements.

'I wasn't going to pinch any of your bleedin' pies,' the young girl protested indignantly. 'I was . . . I was just seeing if they was fresh, that's all.' She sniffed derisively. 'I expect they're all stale, anyway.'

'I'll have less of your cheek, young lady, or one of these nights you'll disappear and end up *inside* my pies. Then you'll find out just how fresh they are.'

'You don't frighten me, not even with that old knife.'

Despite her display of bravado, Sally took a step backwards. It brought her closer to the door, which led to the cobblestone street outside. Strange rumours occasionally circulated about Alfie Philpott and the contents of his pies.

The palm-frond curtain was pushed aside and the head of the pie-man's wife appeared. From where she was standing, the woman could see a thin, pinched-face girl, wearing a threadbare brown coat, which was far too small, over a thin gingham dress that was quite unsuitable for early December.

'Lor', bless us, Alfie! She's all tongue and very little else. She wouldn't make more'n a couple of twopenny pies – and they'd be all gristle.'

'You think so, Grace?'

'I do. Tell you what, Alfie. Give the girl a pie. It'll help put a bit of flesh on her. Add a bit of taste, like, just in case we decide to do something with her sometime.'

'I'm not sure it's worth it . . .'

Alfie Philpott tried to keep up the pretence of being fierce, but he had seen the hungry eagerness on Sally's face in response to his wife's suggestion. 'Oh well, perhaps you're right. Here, you can have a pie – but just one, mind.'

He added the rider as Sally dived towards a number of hot pies, fresh from the oven, heaped in a pyramid on a large flat dish on the counter.

'Thanks, mister . . . missus.'

Sally grabbed a pie hurriedly, afraid the pie-shop owners might change their minds about making such an unexpected and quixotic gesture.

As she turned to leave the shop, the woman called to her, 'Just a minute, young lady.'

Clutching the hot pie, Sally stopped in the doorway. Some of the earlier belligerence returned to her voice as she asked, 'What d'you want?'

Whatever it was, she was certainly not handing back the pie.

'What's your name, girl? I like to know who we're giving our pies to.'

'Sally.'

'Sally what?'

'Just Sally, that's what everyone calls me.'

She had no intention of giving this woman her full name, no matter how generous she appeared to be.

'Are you honest, Sally?'

''Course I'm honest.' Sally said indignantly. At the same time she crossed her fingers. It was not easy while holding a hot pie. 'What sort of a question's that?'

'I'm asking because, if you're honest, we can give you work sometimes. Delivering pies.'

'How much would you pay me?' Sally asked uncertainly.

'A farthing for each delivery,' Alfie said quickly, before his wife got too carried away with her own generosity.

'And a free pie when you finish work,' said his wife, ignoring her husband's frown.

'*Two* pies,' Sally said promptly. 'One for me, and one for my sister. She's in bed, sick.'

'One fresh pie, and one leftover.'

'All right,' Sally tried hard not to allow her delight to show. 'When do you think you might have some work for me?'

'You can start tomorrow. We're always busy in the weeks leading up to Christmas – but you'll need to be here early. No rolling in at midday, or whenever it suits you. And have a wash before you come to work. We don't want you putting off customers with your dirty looks.'

'Blimey! You believe in getting your money's worth, don't you? All right, I'll be here early – and I'll have a wash at home first.'

As soon as Sally had left the shop, Alfie turned to his wife. 'I don't know what you were thinking of, Grace, offering work to an urchin like that. She'll probably run off with the takings, first chance she gets.'

'I somehow don't think so, Alfie. The girl was obviously hungry but that doesn't make her a thief. Anyway, if I'm wrong it won't be the end of the world for us, will it? We can afford to make the occasional mistake. Besides, how old would our Mary be now, had she lived?'

Carefully placing the meat cleaver on the wooden butcher's block, Alfie moved to put an arm about his wife's shoulders. Giving her an affectionate hug, he said, 'I knew that's what you were thinking about. Our Mary would have been seventeen. Much the same age as that young lady, I reckon, give or take a year or so.'

'And if things had been different, would you like to think that someone who could afford it would refuse to give a pie to her, if she was hungry?'

'Of course not. But if I didn't stop you, you'd get carried away by every young urchin who put her nose inside the door. That young lady's probably off somewhere right now, trying to sell her pie to someone else. I doubt if we'll ever see her again.'

* * *

'What's that you've got stuffed inside your jumper, girl?'

'Whatever it is has nothing to do with you, Charlie Shields.'

The exchange over, Sally dodged his outstretched hand with an ease born of practice. Charlie spent much of the day sitting on the doorstep of the house where Sally and her sister rented a small back room on the first floor.

A sufferer from chronic asthma, Charlie occupied the two rooms on the ground floor. He was all right most of the time, but Sally knew from experience it was foolish to take any chances with him. Drunk or sober, Charlie's hand had a nasty habit of wandering up a girl's leg if she were foolish enough to linger as she stepped through the doorway.

Nevertheless, he was sympathetic enough towards Sally and her sister and would occasionally send up a gift of a piece of fruit, or perhaps some fish. Such delicacies were brought to him by members of his large family, some of whom worked in the Plymouth fruit and vegetable market, and others who were fishermen.

When she reached the safety of the gloomy, narrow passageway, Sally paused at the foot of the stairs and called back, 'If you really want to know, it's a meat pie. Alfie Philpott gave it to me.'

'Alfie don't give nothing away to no one. I expect you've nicked it.' Charlie gave a short, throaty laugh, which promptly led to a brief but intense bout of coughing.

'I didn't need to pinch it,' Sally retorted indignantly. 'He gave it to me. What's more, his missus wants me to work for 'em.'

'You . . . work?' Breathing with difficulty, Charlie
cuffed away the tears brought on by his coughing.
'What sort of work can you do? You ain't got enough
meat on you to do any work.'

'I do more work than you've ever done, Charlie
Shields. Enough to pay the rent, anyway.'

Turning her back on the asthmatic ground-floor ten-
ant, Sally ascended the uncarpeted stairs with all the
dignity a ragged seventeen-year-old could muster.

2

Upstairs, in a small, untidy and sparsely furnished rear room, an emaciated young woman lay beneath a blanket on a narrow bed, where, at night, she slept head-to-toe with her sister. Looking much older than her twenty-two years, the young woman's face was turned towards an open window.

The window, which was devoid of curtains, overlooked the back of a terrace of identical houses, now hidden by darkness. No more than the lengths of two tiny backyards away, the buildings were oppressively close.

At the sound of the door opening, the young woman turned her head, slowly and wearily. When she saw Sally, her tired smile gave a glimpse of the beauty she had possessed before she was ravaged by disease.

'Hello, love. What have you been up to today?' The voice was as feeble as the young woman's sick body.

'I've brought you something nice to eat, Ruth. It's still hot.'

Sally put an arm beneath her sister's wasted body to

raise her. At the same time she took the pillow from the foot of the bed and rested it against the iron bed head.

When Sally thought Ruth was comfortable, she took a chipped plate from a shelf and placed the pie on it. 'Here, eat this while it's still nice and hot. It'll put some strength in you. It's not a stale leftover, either. It's fresh from Alfie Philpott's shop, hardly out of the oven.'

'You haven't been nicking for me, have you, Sally? If you're caught they'll put you away and that'd be the end of me, for sure.'

'What's the matter with everyone?' Sally's indignation was unfeigned. 'I come in with something nice for my sister and everyone thinks I must have pinched it! Well, I haven't. It was given to me by Alfie Philpott and his wife. What's more, they've given me a job too – so there!'

'What d'you mean, a job? I thought you had one at the cardboard-box factory, over by the station.'

Sally shrugged and averted her gaze from her sister. 'I got the sack.'

'Again? What was the reason this time?'

'The foreman wanted me to work overtime – and it wasn't to make no boxes, neither. Now, eat your supper before it gets cold. You'd better enjoy it, I'll be bringing a couple of 'em home every day from now on.'

'Tell me about this new job of yours.' As she spoke, Ruth broke the pie in half and put a piece to her mouth. She ate very little these days, but the hot pie smelled delicious.

'I'll be delivering for the Philpotts. They're going to give me a farthing for each delivery and two pies to bring home at the end of each day. I'll make enough money to pay the rent and be bringing home food too. There'll probably be enough money left over at the end of the week to buy something special for you, Ruth.'

Ruth took no more than three or four bites from the piece of pie she had in her hand before putting the remainder back on the plate. Pushing it across the bed towards Sally she said, 'Here, I've not touched the one half. You eat it.'

'Are you sure . . . ?' Sally's mouth had been watering as the aroma of freshly cooked beef and gravy wafted towards her. Nevertheless, she waited until her sister nodded before reaching out for the plate.

Watching her sister eat, Ruth said wearily, 'You're a good girl, Sally. You deserve a better life than spending all your time looking after a sister who's never going to get better.'

Ruth looked sadly at Sally and the younger girl reached out with her free hand. Gripping her sister's fingers, she squeezed them hard.

'I've told you before, you mustn't talk like that. I *want* to look after you, the same as you've done for me all my life.'

It was true. Their mother had died when Sally was a small girl of seven and Ruth only twelve. The girls had never known their father.

It was not until Sally was much older that she realised *how* Ruth had earned the money to keep them both. Even so, it had not come as too much of a shock. Prostitution was a fact of life for a great many young girls in the cities of England – and Plymouth was a sailor's town.

'You sure you don't want any more of this?' Sally

had eaten the untouched portion from the plate and was eyeing the remainder hungrily.

'Quite sure. You have it.'

As Sally gulped down the rest of the pie, Ruth asked, 'What are you doing tonight?'

'Nothing. I'll stay home and keep you company.'

'No you won't. You ought to be out with girls your own age. Having a bit of fun.'

'I seem to remember you've always warned me against going out and having "a bit of fun".'

'You know very well what it is I've always warned you against – and hiring out your body to anyone with the money to pay for it ain't fun, I can tell you. They're paying you to give 'em what they want, whether you feel like it or not – and most times I didn't. No, Sally, it was never my idea of "fun".'

'Yet you did it – for me.'

'I did it because it was the only way I knew to earn a living. For both of us.'

Ruth smiled weakly at Sally. 'Go on, get out and enjoy yourself for a couple of hours. I'm not really in the mood for talking tonight. Besides, I'll be fast asleep in half an hour. Off you go.'

'Well . . . only if you're quite sure.'

'Of course I am . . . Listen! What's that?'

'It sounds like a band, although I've never heard one around the Barbican before.'

'Go and find it, then you can tell me about it tomorrow – but you'd better hurry, it's already dark out there. Before you go, open that window a bit more. I can listen to the band while I'm getting off to sleep.'

Crossing the bare-board floor, Sally heaved the window up on protesting pulley wheels. She could hear the band more clearly now. It sounded as though it was in the next street, beyond the houses visible from their window.

This was the Barbican, a crowded slum of run-down houses, adjacent to a small harbour that extended almost to the heart of late-nineteenth-century Plymouth.

Sally decided she would go and find the band. Afterwards, she might take a walk to the music hall. A young man who worked there claimed to be a distant relative. He had once been keen on Ruth and would sometimes allow Sally in without paying.

The music hall occasionally had a night when members of the audience were invited on stage to sing or tell jokes. If the audience liked the act they would throw coins on the stage.

Sally possessed a good voice and had once ventured on to the stage. The audience had liked her so much she had come away with more than three shillings clutched in her hand.

She should have had six, but the stage manager had insisted that half the takings were his 'by tradition'. He had also invited her back to sing whenever there was a similar evening, but had not suggested she would be allowed in free of charge.

Yes, she would go there. Today had been a lucky day. She had landed a promising job at the pie shop, and now she might make some extra money at the theatre – if it was the right night. Then she would be able to buy something *really* nice for Ruth. Something attractive to look at and bring pleasure to the girl who was confined to a small dark room in Plymouth's overcrowded Barbican.

A room she was unlikely ever to leave alive.

3

Outside the house, in the narrow confines of Pin's Lane, Sally paused. Charlie Shields, still seated in front of the doorway, said, 'Off to listen to the band, are you?'

'I might be,' replied Sally, determined to be non-committal. 'Then again, I might not.'

'You don't want to waste your time chasing after *them*. It's a Salvation Army band. You won't find any fun there. You'd get more laughs watching the fishermen unloading their catch on the quay and teasing the Scots herring women. Why don't you come and sit here a while and chat with me?'

'No thanks. I'd rather go and watch the fishermen on the quay.'

'You've got far too much backchat,' declared Charlie. 'One day you'll end up the same as your sister, you mark my words. It's as well your poor mother never lived to see the way the pair of you have turned out. It would have broken her poor heart.'

Sally had a retort ready but it remained unspoken as tears filled her eyes and she turned away. She would not allow Charlie to see that his words had found their mark. It would have revealed a vulnerability he would not be slow to take advantage of in the future.

In the years following her mother's death there had been many occasions when Sally had cried herself to sleep, longing for her mother. It had proved especially bad on the many occasions when life was treating the young sisters particularly harshly.

Sometimes, especially now Ruth was bedridden, the sisters would talk far into the night about the mother Sally had hardly known. With the passing of time their mother had assumed a piety she had never achieved during her lifetime.

Occasionally, too, during the quiet of the night, when only Ruth's laboured breathing broke the silence, Sally would wonder about the identity of her unknown father. It was a subject Ruth would never discuss.

She knew her mother had been 'in service' – a house servant – working for a rich family when she became pregnant with Ruth. Although she had never returned to work for the family afterwards, she had always maintained that both girls had the same father. It was all she had ever said on the subject.

As a result, Sally would occasionally allow her imagination to run riot. She wondered whether he had been a son of the rich family. Or a friend, perhaps. He might even be a titled gentleman . . . !

Rounding the corner, away from Pin's Lane, the sound of the band became much louder. It seemed the musicians were now playing on the quayside, not far from where the fishing boats landed their catches.

But she could hear another sound too. That of a crowd. A noisy crowd. Sally walked faster. This might not be the colourless entertainment Charlie had predicted after all.

There were many who did not share Charlie's view that the Salvation Army was harmless and boring. Among those most violently opposed to the teetotal Christian organisation were the breweries and the landlords of the country's inns and taverns. Disturbed that the popularity of the Salvation Army was growing, they had organised their own band of supporters. It was known as the 'Skeleton Army' – a name adopted from its skull and crossbones logo – and it attracted the hooligan element from the beer-houses and dockside taverns. Recently there had been a series of violent clashes between the Skeleton Army and the fervent but pacifist evangelists.

When the large, gas-lit cobblestone space beside the quay came into view, Sally could see the uniformed Salvation Army band formed up by the water's edge. There were about twenty of them, carrying a variety of instruments.

A number of spectators had gathered to listen, but, as was invariably the case when the band played, the Salvation Army's opponents were here too.

Sally had lived in the waterside Barbican district of Plymouth all her life and she knew its bullies and thugs by sight. She now spotted many in the crowd. Jeering the bandsmen and -women, they attempted to rival them with their discordant rendition of bawdy songs, while banners boasting the skull and crossbones logo were waved enthusiastically.

When word went around the town that the Salvation Army band was playing in the Barbican, landlords of the area's public houses urged their customers to swell the ranks of the Skeleton Army. As an incentive the drinkers were promised that their mugs would be refilled, free of charge, upon their return.

Already, the rowdy crowd of opponents was more numerous than the Salvation Army band and its numbers were increasing with every passing minute.

It was clear to Sally that there would soon be trouble. She wondered why the bandsmen did not cease playing and make their escape while it was still possible.

But the Salvation Army, created by William Booth, had not been formed only to desert its sacred duty when faced by such opposition. Booth and his followers were pledged to join battle against the devil in an all-out war aimed at winning the souls of men and women. No sacrifice was too great if it resulted in salvation for even a single sinner.

As the band played on, a young woman, wearing a simple black uniform and straw bonnet, began exhorting those in the crowd to give up their wicked ways and turn to Jesus.

By now, the Salvation Army's opponents outnumbered them by more than two to one. Those at the front of the noisy ranks of the Skeleton Army, many of them innocent bystanders who had brought their young children along to listen to the music and singing, were being forced ever closer to the band by new arrivals exerting pressure from the rear of the gathering.

One young mother had a year-old child in her arms and a pretty four-year-old daughter, who was performing a happy dance in time to the music, beside her. Not until too late did the woman realise that she and her small family were standing between the Salvation Army and their ill-intentioned opponents. Clutching the baby to her, she reached out to take her daughter's hand and lead her away.

But the young girl, who was thoroughly enjoying the music, was not yet ready to leave. Evading her mother's hand, she moved away, closer to the band – and also nearer to the quayside.

At the same moment, one of a small group of well-wishers also realised the danger posed by the Skeleton Army. Before scurrying to safety, the man took some coins from his pocket and threw them in the direction of one of the Salvation Army women. But the coins fell short, and a raggedly dressed boy from the ranks of the opposition was quick to seize the opportunity unexpectedly afforded him. Darting forward, he picked up the silver coins before dashing back to the safety of the cheering rowdies.

However, in his haste he collided with the small girl who was escaping from her mother. Knocked off balance, the child staggered backwards, arms flailing in a vain attempt to regain her footing. Then, to the horror of the suddenly hushed onlookers, she disappeared over the edge of the quay and fell into the dark waters below.

The tide was on the ebb and there was a considerable drop to the water. The splash her small body made was lost in the cries of the onlookers – but her mother's scream was not. Rushing to the edge of the quay, the woman cried, 'Mary . . . ! MARY . . . !'

For a few moments there was utter pandemonium among the horrified crowd as the mother hysterically begged for someone – *anyone* – to rescue her little girl.

To add to the confusion, the band played on uncertainly for a few more minutes, before the sound died away discordantly.

A fisherman on the fringe of the crowd ran to some stone steps a short distance away, which led down to the water. A small boat was moored here. One of the uniformed Salvation Army bandsmen abandoned band and instrument and clattered down the steps to join the fisherman. Scrambling into the boat, they cast off the mooring rope and headed out on the dark waters of the harbour.

Meanwhile, another more enterprising young Salvation Army bandsman – and certainly more courageous than any of the other watchers – flung off his hat and jacket, pulled off his shoes and plunged head first into the harbour.

By now the followers of the Salvation Army and the Skeleton Army, their differences momentarily put to one side, crowded along the edge of the harbour, blocking off what little light was available to those attempting a rescue.

The mother of the unfortunate little girl continued to wail, joined now by her thoroughly frightened young son.

Suddenly, a man's voice called from somewhere out on the waters of the harbour. 'Hello, ashore! This is the customs cutter. What's going on?'

Twenty or more men shouted explanations. Once the customs men had caught the gist of what was happening one of them called back, 'We'll come closer and see if we can help.'

Before the cheers of the crowd had fully died away, the voice of the young bandsman who had so courageously dived into the water called from the darkness, 'I've found her. I've got her here. Can someone get a boat and take her from me?'

The cheering redoubled and now many voices were calling from the harbour itself. It appeared that the small dinghy manned by the fishermen and the customs cutter had come together in the darkness.

Then one of the two men in the dinghy shouted, 'We've got her on board – and she's still breathing.'

Now Salvationists and Skeleton Army followers united in a cheer that startled all the gulls night-roosting on the roofs of buildings around the harbour. It was followed by a movement of the crowd towards the steps to which the dinghy would return.

By the time the boat bumped against the steps the small girl had recovered sufficiently to be tearfully calling for her mother. Lifted from the boat she was passed from hand to hand above the heads of the crowd until she was reunited with her sobbing parent.

Only now did one of the Salvation Army women ask, 'Where's John? Wasn't he in the boat too?' When no one replied, she explained anxiously, 'He's the one who dived in and saved the girl. Where is he now?'

'He's probably been taken on board the customs cutter,' said the Salvation Army musician who had helped to man the dinghy.

There was a confused silence before he called into the darkness, 'Ahoy there! Customs cutter. Do you have the man who rescued the girl on board?'

'No. We thought he must have been picked up by the dinghy.' The voice from the darkness called back the chilling news.

The fisherman and the Salvation Army bandsman ran back down the steps to the dinghy. A couple of minutes later the customs cutter also returned to the area.

Soon the two boats were joined by others, but although

the search continued for more than an hour, nothing was found of the missing bandsman.

While the search was being carried out, one of the Salvation Army girls hurried to the bandsman's home, in the forlorn hope that he might have slipped ashore unnoticed and gone home to change.

She returned with the grim news that he had not gone home and no one there had seen him.

There was no more music from the Salvation Army band that evening. Gradually, as hope faded and the search for the missing man was abandoned, they and the members of the Skeleton Army left the scene, their differences temporarily forgotten.

Abandoning all thoughts of going to the music hall, Sally ran home to tell Ruth about the exciting happenings of the evening.

4

The next morning, Sally told Grace and Alfie Philpott about the events of the previous evening. Grace made suitably sympathetic noises, adding, 'Perhaps the young man climbed out of the water unnoticed and went home to change out of his wet clothes.'

Sally shook her head. 'No, someone checked. Besides, on my way here this morning I spoke to one of the fisherwomen. She said a body was pulled from the harbour at first light this morning. It was probably the Salvation Army bandsman. The men who found him said it looked as though he'd been hit by a boat. He was hit by the customs boat, I expect.'

Alfie was not in a very good mood this morning and was less sympathetic, 'If this so-called "Salvation Army" hadn't been there in the first place there would have been no accident. That lot have a lot to answer for, the way they go around, stirring folk up.'

Giving Sally a warning glance, Grace said to her husband, 'I'm sure you're right, dear. I must admit though, they don't seem to do anyone any harm. But then, I don't know very much about 'em, myself.'

'You're none the worse off for that,' declared Alfie. 'There's enough trouble in the world without having hallelujah hooligans making more. Now, can we get some of these deliveries on their way? I've taken orders for ten from the brewery, another twenty-five are wanted over at Stonehouse first thing this morning and we've got a whole batch of orders for midday . . . You'd better get moving, girl. If you're going to work for us you'll need to learn you don't keep customers waiting. Without them there'd be no wages for any of us.'

By the end of the day, Sally had earned one shilling and threepence three farthings. In order to achieve this she had delivered hundreds of meat pies and estimated she must have walked at least twenty miles. Her legs were tired, she was footsore and the muscles of her arms ached from carrying the heavy basket.

Nevertheless, the coins jangling in her pocket and two hot pies clutched in her hand were sufficient compensation for her aches and pains.

She had worked hard and earned an honest day's wages.

On the way home she stopped at a corner shop close to Pin's Lane. From here, the Italian owner sold ice-cream during the day and fried chips from early evening until well into the night. She bought a pennyworth of chips for Ruth to eat with her pie.

However, when Sally reached the small back room, she saw immediately that Ruth would be eating very little.

'I'm sorry, Sally,' the sick young woman said, in response to her sister's enthusiasm. 'I've had one of my bad days. I don't think I can eat a thing. It would be wasted on me. You have both of 'em.'

Doing her best to hide her disappointment, Sally said, 'I couldn't eat *two*, not with all these chips as well. But it would be a pity to waste them. I'll take a pie and some chips down to Charlie. He wasn't sitting on the step as usual. Perhaps he's not feeling too well today, either. I'll do it now, while everything's still hot. Then I'll come back and make you comfortable.'

'I'm sorry, Sally, especially as this is your first day at your new job. I know you've bought the chips for me 'specially, but I really couldn't eat them.' Ruth managed a wan smile for her sister. 'When you come back you can tell me all about your day.'

Carrying a plate of pie and chips, Sally knocked at Charlie's door. She walked into his untidy, gloomy room, without waiting for a reply. The elderly man was not ill. In fact he was seated at the table quaffing ale from a pewter mug.

He was not alone. Sitting across the table from him was a young man whose face seemed vaguely familiar to Sally.

'I'm sorry, Charlie, I didn't know you had company. I just called in to see if you'd like this.' She put the plate of food on the table. 'I brought it home for Ruth, but she doesn't feel like eating tonight. It'd be a pity to waste it.'

'Bless you, girl. It's one of Alfie Philpott's pies, too! My mouth would water every time I walked past his shop, when I got about a bit more, but he was a bit pricey for the likes of me.'

Giving her a wink, he said, 'I know you'd prefer it if it was just me here, but come and join us anyway. This is Ethan, my youngest brother's boy. He's just come visiting and has brought me some ale. No doubt we can find a drop for you.'

'I'm not stopping, Charlie. I must go back upstairs and see what I can do for Ruth. It worries me, her not being hungry. She doesn't eat enough these days to keep a kitten alive.'

She nodded at Charlie's companion, and had reached the door when she turned suddenly and said excitedly, 'I recognise you now! You're the bandsman who brought the young girl ashore last night, after she'd fallen in the harbour.'

The young man looked embarrassed. 'I didn't do very well, did I? I let poor John Albon drown – and he was the real hero of the night.'

'That wasn't your fault. I was speaking to someone this morning who said he'd probably been run down by the customs cutter.'

'I've heard the same – but it doesn't make me feel any better.'

Ethan had a quiet, self-deprecating manner and Sally realised he was incredibly shy.

'What's all this about?' While the others had been talking, Charlie had been tucking into the pie and chips. He spoke now with his mouth full of food.

'Ethan will tell you all about it,' said Sally. 'I must go back upstairs now and see to Ruth. It was nice meeting you, Ethan. Enjoy your grub, Charlie.'

Shutting the door behind her, Sally returned upstairs to her sister. Ruth listened dutifully as Sally told of her day's work, her meeting with Ethan and his part in the events of the previous night.

As she talked, Sally ate her pie and portion of chips.

When they were gone, she made Ruth comfortable and began tidying up the room.

She was still working when there was a tentative knock on the door. Exchanging a glance with Ruth, Sally went to the door and opened it. Ethan was standing outside.

'I hope I haven't disturbed you,' he said with the same shy manner Sally had observed when she met him earlier. 'I came to the house with some fresh fish for Charlie. As you very kindly gave him some supper, he doesn't really need them all – and they won't keep. I thought your sister might fancy them. They'll be easier for her to eat than a meat pie.'

'Who is it?' Ruth called from her bed.

'It's Ethan, Charlie's nephew. He's brought some fish for you. He thought you might fancy them.'

'Well, don't leave him standing out there on the landing. Bring him in so I can see what he looks like.' As she spoke, Ruth struggled to sit up in bed and Sally hurried to her assistance.

As Sally lifted her sister, she called to Ethan, 'It's very kind of you. Won't you come in and say hello to Ruth? She doesn't have many visitors.'

Hesitantly, Ethan came inside the room, nodding a greeting to Ruth as he said, 'I thought you might find these fish tasty. They're easier eating than a pie.'

'Yes . . . yes, I think I might. Do you know, Sally, I really do fancy a mouthful or two of fish. Why don't you fry them up for me while I chat with Ethan. I can't remember the last time I had a conversation with a young man – especially one who's a hero. Come here and sit by the bed, Ethan. Tell me about what happened last night. Sally came home absolutely full of it . . .'

5

'How long has your sister been ill?'

Ethan asked the question as he and Sally walked together through the streets that led away from Plymouth's Barbican district. They were close to Union Street now, the busy thoroughfare that linked the main town with the naval dockyard areas of Stonehouse and Devonport.

Ruth had kept Ethan talking while Sally cooked the fish. She had then eaten a meal that delighted the younger girl. When it was gone, Ruth declared she wanted to sleep. She suggested that Sally should walk at least part of the way home with Ethan, to give her an opportunity to fall asleep without being disturbed.

After leaving the house with Sally, Ethan had explained that he was not going home immediately but was calling on his brother and his wife. They lived in Stonehouse, some little distance away.

At first, as they walked together, Ethan's shyness made conversation difficult, but as his tongue gradually loosened Sally learned a little of his background. He was the son and grandson of fishermen and it was a life he claimed to enjoy.

Suddenly, he blurted out, 'You . . . you don't have to walk along with me, if you'd rather not.'

'Why would I "rather not"?' Sally asked, puzzled.

'Well . . . your sister didn't ask what you wanted to do. She just told you to come and keep me company.'

Sally shrugged. 'It doesn't matter to me. I've got nothing better to do.' Aware of the condition and quality of her clothes, she added, 'Of course, if you'd rather not be seen with *me* . . .'

'That isn't what I meant,' Ethan replied quickly. 'I *like* being with you, but . . .' He made an apologetic gesture. 'I can't really talk about much except music and fishing.'

'That's all right. I don't know anything about either of them things, so whatever you say, I won't have heard it before.'

She had presented him with a chance to tell her about himself and his occupation. But when he failed to take advantage of the opportunity they walked together in silence for a while.

The knowledge that Ethan was shy intrigued Sally. She could think of no other young man of her acquaintance who had the same problem. Most were quite the opposite and would seek any opportunity to attempt far more liberties than Sally was prepared to allow them.

'Do you have any sisters?' she asked.

Ethan shook his head. 'No . . . but I've got five brothers, all older than me.'

'Five!' Sally's expression was one of undisguised envy. 'I've always wished I had brothers – as well as Ruth, of course,' she added hurriedly. 'Are they all fishermen?'

'Every one. We've got our own boat too,' he added proudly.

Sally looked at him as though he'd claimed kinship with Queen Victoria. 'Charlie's always bragging about all the people he knows, but he's never said anything about having rich relatives!'

Ethan smiled. 'We're certainly not rich. My pa needed to borrow money to buy the boat. We're still paying off the loan. I sometimes feel we'd all be better off if we were working for somebody else.'

Sally was unable to comprehend that someone who actually *owned* something did not consider himself rich. Only rich people owned things like houses or boats.

Suddenly, for no reason she could think of, she asked, 'Why are you in the Salvation Army? It's not the sort of thing rich people do.'

In truth, the only thing that Sally knew about the Salvation Army was that it claimed to be concerned for the spiritual and physical well-being of the poor. Therefore it could not possibly enjoy the support of *rich* people.

Those who had money either ignored the poor or took advantage of them at every opportunity. At least that was what she had heard Ruth and her friends say on many occasions. Nothing had occurred in Sally's life to cast doubt on such an observation.

Ethan appeared somewhat embarrassed. 'I feel a bit of a fraud, really. Years ago one of my aunts gave me a flute and I taught myself to play it. I joined the Salvation Army because I wanted to be in their band.' Even more embarrassed, he added, 'I haven't told that to anyone before.'

After they had walked in silence for a few more paces, he continued, 'Everyone else seems to have joined the Salvation Army because of a burning passion to take religion to those they feel need it most. Men and women who are the greatest sinners.'

Sally frowned. 'But they only work among the poor. Does that mean rich people don't sin as much as we do?'

'I wouldn't say that.' Ethan smiled again. 'Mind you, rich folk probably don't *need* to sin quite as much. They don't have to steal in order to survive, or don't need to drink to forget the sort of life they lead or the place in which they live.'

Sally looked at Ethan quizzically. 'You sure you just joined the Salvation to play in their band? You sound just like one of them.'

'Do I? Perhaps that's because I've just been to visit Uncle Charlie. He doesn't have very much, and . . . and then I came up to your room and saw how little you have – and you've a sick sister to look after too. Before that I called in to see the family of that little girl who fell in the harbour last night . . . one of the band knew where they lived,' he explained. 'I thought I'd take them some fish too and make sure the little girl was all right.' He hesitated, before adding, 'The bandsman also told me that the little girl's father had once joined the Salvation Army. He didn't stay for very long though. He's a drunkard and spends almost every penny he earns on drink.'

Ethan paused. When he spoke once more he chose his words very carefully in an attempt to hide the depth of his feelings. 'The house was as clean as a new pin, even though there was hardly any furniture in the room.

They didn't have a fire either, and it seems the little girl has only one dress – the one she was wearing when she fell in the harbour. Today hadn't been a good drying day, so she had nothing to wear. I only gave the woman a few fish, yet you'd think I'd handed her a fortune . . .'

He stopped speaking and Sally realised that Ethan was both kind and sensitive. He claimed to have joined the Salvation Army for purely selfish reasons, but she felt he was not out of place in its ranks.

During their conversation they had turned off Union Street. Now they heard the sound of raised voices and a small knot of brawling men spilled from a house into the road in front of them.

Ethan immediately took Sally's arm and led her to the opposite pavement. 'I think we'd better give them a wide berth.'

'Why? They've got no quarrel with us.'

'It sounds as though a couple of them are foreign sailors,' said Ethan, quickening his pace. 'They've probably been drinking so won't know who's on their side and who's against them. Besides, that's Mother Darling's house.'

'Who's Mother Darling?'

'She's someone young women shouldn't know anything about.'

'You mean . . . she runs a whore house?'

Ethan flushed scarlet and was glad the dim gas-lamps hid his hot cheeks. 'That's right, and there are some queer goings-on there, I can tell you.'

'What sort of goings-on?'

'Oh . . . all sorts of things.'

'Well, tell me *what*, exactly,' persisted Sally. She was

aware that Ethan was embarrassed but, without knowing why, she was taking a perverse pleasure in continuing to question him.

They turned the corner from the street, leaving Mother Darling's house and the fighting group behind them.

Slowing his pace a little, Ethan said, 'It's said that young country girls answer adverts in the newspapers and come to Plymouth thinking they're coming to work as servants. Many of them end up in Mother Darling's house. Then they're shipped off to France, Belgium – or even Arab countries – and are never seen again.'

Resisting an urge to look over her shoulder to ensure they were not being followed, Sally said scornfully, 'That's just talk. I don't suppose anything like that happens at all.'

'Yes it does,' Ethan persisted. 'One of my brothers saw half a dozen girls being put on board a Belgian boat not long ago. He said they all looked dopey; they needed to be helped on board, as though they'd been given something. My brother said he recognised Mother Darling's son as one of the men helping the sailors take them on board.'

'I wonder how he came to know Mother Darling's son,' Sally said provocatively.

Aware that Sally was trying to embarrass him, Ethan replied, 'I wouldn't know that, but I do know that Mary Street is no place for a young woman.'

Sally realised that Charlie could not have explained to his nephew how Ruth had earned her living before she became ill. She decided not to enlighten him, even though she told herself that what Ethan thought of her really did not matter. They would probably never meet again.

'We're almost at my brother's house now,' said Ethan. 'Will you come in with me and meet him and his wife, Sophie? You'd like her.'

'No. I don't want to be too late back or I'll disturb Ruth. Besides, I need to be up early tomorrow, for work.'

Hesitantly, Ethan asked, 'Would you mind if I called in to see you the next time I pay a visit to Uncle Charlie?'

'Of course not. It'll be nice for Ruth to have someone different to talk to.' Sally tried to sound nonchalant. She did not want him to realise he was the first man to express an interest in her. A *real* interest. She did not count Charlie or the other men like him. Their interest was not in her as a *person*.

They stopped at a door that opened directly on to the narrow pavement. 'This is where Albert and Sophie live. You're quite sure you won't come in? They'd make you very welcome.'

'No, I'll see you again. 'Bye.'

Sally walked away carrying a warm glow inside her. She decided she liked Ethan. She had taken notice of all he had told her too. When she reached the street where Mother Darling lived, she hurried past and took another road that would take her to Union Street and so back to the Barbican.

6

The next few days were busy for Sally. At times, it seemed that most of the residents of Plymouth must have taken a sudden fancy to Alfie Philpott's pies. She was hard-put to keep up with deliveries.

It was taken for granted by the Philpotts that Sally was happy to work full-time for them. Indeed, with Christmas not far away, the pie-shop owners even discussed the possibility of employing another youngster to help with the ever-increasing need for deliveries.

Sally had not seen Ethan since his visit to the Pin's Lane house, but it was hardly surprising. From discreet enquiries she made when delivering pies to the fish quay, she knew that local fishermen were taking advantage of the current good weather. They were spending all available time at sea in order to meet the huge demands of the London market.

Late one afternoon, she returned to the shop in happy anticipation of finishing work for the day and returning home to Ruth. To her surprise, she found both Alfie and Grace still busily cooking.

'Ah! There you are, Sally.' Grace looked hot and flustered. 'We were beginning to fear you wouldn't get back in time. We've got an order for you to take out right away.'

Sally's heart sank. She had been looking forward to going home. The weather had deteriorated during the previous night, with a gale sweeping in from the east, and although it had improved somewhat now, it was still too rough for fishing. All the Plymouth fishing boats would have remained in harbour today, and she had been hoping Ethan might take the opportunity to call and see her.

However, she could not refuse to make the delivery. The Philpotts were generous employers. Only the previous night they had given her more than a pound of beef, left over at the end of the day from their pie-making, to take home to Pin's Lane.

'Where are they to go to?' she asked.

'To Mary Street, just off Union Street,' replied Grace. 'I expect you know it.'

Sally's heart sank. It would take her almost forty minutes to make the return errand, but Grace said, 'I realise it's getting late in the day, but there'll be an extra threepence in it for you and you can go straight home when you've made the delivery and take the basket with you. The woman who came in and placed the order would have taken the pies with her, but we were nearly out. I said I'd make some fresh and have 'em delivered.'

As Grace was speaking, Sally had been trying to place the street in question. When realisation came, she asked in sudden concern, 'Who have I got to deliver them to?'

'Number fourteen. To a Mrs Darling.'

Sally's jaw dropped and Alfie said swiftly, 'What's the matter, girl, do you know the woman?'

'No . . . I mean . . . yes.'

'No – yes? What's that supposed to mean?'

Hesitantly, Sally gave the Philpotts a summarised version of what Ethan had told her and of the fight he and she had witnessed when they passed along Mary Street.

Grace was concerned, but Alfie said scornfully, 'There are fights right outside this shop most nights – and you don't want to believe every rumour you hear, girl. If you listened to some folk talking about what we're supposed to put in our pies you'd never dare deliver 'em, let alone eat 'em. Anyway, you're going to Mary Street to take the lady some pies, not in response to any newspaper advertisement. But I'll tell you what I'll do. If you don't turn up for work in the morning I'll go along to the police station and have them search this woman's house for you.' With that Alfie went off, shaking his head in disbelief.

But Grace was less sceptical of Sally's fears. 'I'm sure Alfie's right, dear, but you mind yourself when you get there. If there's the least sign of anything funny going on, you just cut and run. Fortunately they've paid us in advance, so you don't need to worry yourself about that.'

On the way to Mary Street with a laden basket over her arm, Sally almost convinced herself that Alfie was probably right. Barbican rumours were quite often grossly exaggerated – although this one had come, almost first-hand, from Ethan. She doubted very much whether he would have embellished such a story.

Her apprehension increased when she turned into Mary Street. Finally arriving at number fourteen, she hesitated fearfully for a moment or two. Then, telling herself the house was no different to any other in the street, she knocked resolutely on the door.

Much to her relief, the woman who opened the door was the antithesis of all she had been anticipating.

Small, plump and motherly, the woman beamed benevolently at Sally. 'Hello, my dear, and what can I do for you?'

'I'm from Alfie Philpott. Delivering the pies you ordered.'

'Why, of course! Come in, come in. I wasn't expecting you quite so soon – but that's Alfie Philpott for you. Not only does he make the best pies in Plymouth, he's reliable, too. That's right, bring them through to the kitchen and put them down on the table. You won't mind if I count them? Not that I think for a moment Alfie would try to cheat me, but he's human, same as everyone else and we all make mistakes, don't we?'

'You'll find they're all there,' said Sally, wondering why she had feared meeting such a homely and ordinary woman. 'In fact, Grace Philpott has put in an extra pie, to make up for them not being ready when you called.'

'Well, that was kind of her. Very kind indeed.'

Despite her words, Mother Darling continued to count, until she was able to confirm she had indeed received the full order – plus one.

Before she had quite finished counting, Sally said, 'It's a whole lot of pies for one household, are you having a party?'

'A party? Why, yes dear, that's exactly it. We're having a party . . .'

At that moment a man entered the room. Big and burly, he had a couple of days' growth of stubble on his face and a long thin scratch extending from the corner of his left eye down his cheek, almost to his chin.

Giving Sally a look that brought back all her earlier fears, he said, 'Well, here's a pretty little thing, and no mistake. Has she come to work for us, Mother?'

'No, Sidney, she's a local girl who's just delivered the pies I ordered from Alfie Philpott . . . for the party.'

'The party . . . ? Oh yes, the party!' Sidney chuckled. 'Perhaps she'd like to stay for it, eh?'

'She'll be kept busy enough by Alfie Philpott . . . but you're right about one thing. She *is* a pretty little thing.'

Turning to Sally, she gave her a disarming smile. 'You know, a girl like you could be earning a lot more money than you'll ever make delivering pies.'

Uncomfortably aware there was a hidden meaning in Mother Darling's words, Sally said hurriedly, 'I'm quite happy working for Alfie and Grace Philpott, thank you.'

'Well, if you ever change your mind, you come here and see me—'

At that moment there came a scream, followed by a bump on an upstairs floor.

As Sally heard someone running down the stairs, Sidney Darling darted from the kitchen, moving impressively fast for a man of his bulk.

Another scream was immediately stifled, then a muffled voice shouted, 'I want to go home. Let me go!'

Alarmed, Sally moved towards the kitchen door,

intent on discovering what was happening. She found Mother Darling blocking her way.

'I should stay here for a moment or two, dear.' Although her words were no more than a suggestion, Mother Darling made it quite clear that Sally would not be allowed past her.

Raising her voice, she called, 'Who is it, Sidney?'

From somewhere on the stairs, her son responded, 'It's that young Rachel causing trouble again.'

'Oh dear, poor girl,' Mother Darling replied with apparent sympathy. 'Put her in the front bedroom – but don't forget to turn the key. I'll come up and tend to the poor dear in a few moments.'

Shaking her head sadly, she explained to Sally, 'It's my niece, poor dear soul. She recently lost her mother – my sister – and it's quite turned her mind. We've had to call the doctor to her more than once. He's said the only thing to be done is to keep her under lock and key, in the hope she'll get her senses back one day. If she doesn't, he says she'll need to be shut away in an asylum. I can't see that happen, can I? Not to my own flesh and blood.'

Sally fervently hoped her expression of sympathy was convincing.

She breathed a big sigh of relief when, a few minutes later, she stood on the pavement in Mary Street and the door was closed behind her by the woman she was now certain was a brothel keeper.

If she needed any further proof, it came only moments later. She was still standing in the street, wondering what she could do to help the girl she was convinced was trying to escape from the house, when she heard breaking glass, the sound coming from somewhere above the spot where she stood. At the same time pieces of glass showered down about her from an upstairs window.

The same voice cried out, 'HELP! Help me . . . PLEASE! I'm being kidnapped. They've been doing things to me. Help—'

The heartfelt pleas came to an abrupt end, but they left Sally badly shaken. Not least because she had just left the house in which the girl was imprisoned.

As she stood there, undecided what she should do, Sally heard voices from inside the room. It sounded like Mother Darling and her son, cursing the girl who had shouted.

Sally did not wait to hear any more. Taking to her heels she ran from the street and did not stop until she reached the lights of Union Street.

In the house in Mary Street, Sid Darling threw open the door of the room in which the young girl was imprisoned. She was about to use her shoe to break another pane of glass when he caught hold of her upraised arm and threw her back against the wall.

Not attempting to rise to her feet, the girl scrambled for the door on all fours, but Mother Darling was standing, squat and solid, in the doorway, blocking her path.

The next moment, Sid Darling lifted the girl from the ground, an arm about her waist.

'Let . . . me . . . go!' Her arms and legs were flailing wildly but it made no impression on the big man.

'We've got a lively one here and no mistake,' said Sid. 'I think me and Wallace need to give her something else to think about, don't you?'

'I was hoping to get a higher price for this one as "untried goods", Sid, but you're right. She does need to be taught a lesson and she's young enough to fetch a decent price anyway. Take her up to the back room in the loft – and don't let her scream too much. We've disturbed the neighbours enough for one night. If we're not careful we'll be getting complaints, won't we?'

The evil old procuress went away chuckling. The residents of Mary Street knew better than to complain about anything that went on in Mother Darling's house.

The young girl's screams and sobs would go unheeded.

7

In the back room on the first floor of the Pin's Lane house, Ruth was having one of her better days and she listened in silence to the story blurted out by her excited sister.

'What do you think I should do, Ruth?' Sally asked the question anxiously when she had finished.

'Nothing,' Ruth replied firmly.

'What do you mean "nothing"? This girl's in trouble, Ruth. *Real* trouble. I can't just shrug it off as though nothing happened.'

'You will if you have any sense. You don't know for certain that what you were told by Mother Darling was a lie. Besides, you're not just dealing with her. Sid Darling's her son – and he's a man to keep well clear of, believe me. Many girls have rued the day they crossed him. You mustn't get involved in this, Sal. Life's picked up for you lately. Try to keep it that way.'

'Supposing it was *me* who was in trouble? Wouldn't you want someone to help me, if they could?'

'It's *not* you in trouble, and you can't go through life

taking everyone's troubles on your shoulders. You've got enough to put up with as it is, looking after me. Now, make me a nice cup of tea and forget you've seen or heard anything. Then you can go downstairs to Charlie's room. Your young man's down there. He came looking for you and was disappointed when he found only me here. Rather than stay and tire me with his chatter, he said he'd wait downstairs for you.'

Sally and Ethan met on the stairs. His obvious delight at seeing her again would have thrilled her on any other occasion, but she still had the fate of the girl at Mother Darling's on her mind. Choosing to disregard Ruth's advice she blurted out the story to Ethan.

Much to Sally's chagrin, Ethan's immediate response was no different to Ruth's.

'You don't want to involve yourself with any of the happenings at Mother Darling's. She and her son are a bad lot.'

'I know they're a bad lot,' said Sally, her exasperation showing. 'That's exactly why someone *has* to get involved. They've got a young girl locked up in their house. God knows what they'll do to her . . .'

Recalling the girl's last desperate words, she added, 'In fact I can't bear to think about what they've *already* done to her. All right, if you won't help then I'll go to the police.'

'You'll get no help from them,' Ethan said bitterly. 'Make a complaint to the police and you'll most likely end up being the one they arrest. The Salvation Army knows of at least eight brothels in Plymouth. They've reported them time and time again. Most of those who've made the complaints have found themselves arrested and charged with "obstruction" the very next time they've gone out on a parade. Meanwhile, the brothels carry on their business as usual.'

Sally was aware that Ethan's statement would have come as no surprise to Ruth. She had frequently complained that although the police carried out periodic purges against the prostitutes who worked on the streets or frequented the public houses, the brothels were allowed to carry on their business unhindered. Nevertheless, she was not prepared to ignore what she had witnessed that evening.

Remembering the pitiful cries of the unseen girl, she pleaded, 'There must be *something* that can be done, Ethan? I can't stop thinking about the poor girl in that house . . . !'

Ethan remained silent for some moments, then he said, 'I know someone we can talk to. Whether she can help is another matter, but it's worth a try.'

'A woman! What can a woman do?'

'As I said, I don't know. She's a Salvation Army captain who hasn't been in Plymouth very long. She was sent from London to set up a house for women who want to give up that sort of life. She'll be at the meeting in Central Hall right now. Do you want to go and speak to her?'

Sally shrugged resignedly. 'I can't see that she'll be able to do anything, but it's better than doing nothing at all.'

Captain Eva Cassington was a small, dark-haired, lively woman, but Sally was dismayed to find she was hardly older than Ruth. She had been expecting a mature, formidable woman. Someone capable of brow-beating Mother Darling and her burly son.

Nevertheless, coaxed by the Salvation Army captain, Sally told her what she had seen and the other woman listened in attentive silence.

When Sally ended her story, Eva Cassington said, 'What makes you think prostitution is involved? That the circumstances are not exactly what this woman says they are?'

Sally looked to Ethan and he repeated what his brother had told him, adding that the house in Mary Street was a notorious brothel.

'You are of the opinion the police will do nothing if we go to them?'

'Certainly not at the request of anyone in the Salvation Army,' confirmed Ethan.

'I see. Then we'll need to do something about it ourselves, won't we? How long ago is it since you were at this house, Sally?'

'It's more than two hours now.' Sally was impressed by the decisiveness of the Salvation Army captain. 'But what can we do without the police? Mother Darling's son is a big man. From all I've heard about him, he actually enjoys fighting.'

'Then we'll need to take someone with us who's even larger and enjoys fighting more than he does. I know just the man. He's on his knees in the hall right now, giving thanks to the Lord for his salvation. Wait here while I go and fetch him.'

When Captain Eva had passed from view, Sally asked Ethan anxiously, 'Do you think she knows what she's doing? Mother Darling's not going to admit what's been going on – and her son's hardly likely to let us search the house to find the girl.'

'I'm more worried about what might happen if they

recognise *you*,' said Ethan, his concern showing. 'It will be obvious you're the one who's reported them. They know you work for Alfie Philpott, so it wouldn't be hard for them to find you.'

Sally was still pondering this problem when Captain Eva returned. A giant of a man lumbered along behind her. His skin was as black as the Salvation Army captain's bonnet and he had a grin that displayed even, white teeth.

There was a gasp from Ethan and he said quickly, with awe in his voice, 'It's Zulu Joe!'

Wasting no time on introductions, Captain Eva said briskly, 'There's a girl out there in need of help. Let's go and set about the Lord's work.'

On the way to Mary Street, Ethan told the young Salvation Army captain of his fears for Sally's future safety if she were to be recognised by either of the Darlings.

'It's something that can't be ignored,' she agreed. 'Sally, tell me the story of this girl once again and explain exactly where she was when she last attracted your attention.'

When Sally had repeated her story, Eva said, 'If this Mother Darling and her son are all you say they are, then it will be better if both you and Ethan stay out of sight. I'll take Joe to the house with me and say a passer-by heard the commotion and repeated it to me.'

Mary Street was not very far and they were soon there. As agreed, Ethan and Sally remained behind in Union Street, while Eva and her large bodyguard went on to tackle the two Darlings.

Many of the shops in the busy Union Street thorough-fare were closing as the notorious area prepared to give itself over to less savoury activities. An unwritten law existed whereby respectable women passing along the street kept to the pavement on the north side. This left the south side to the women, now putting in their nightly appearance, who earned a living selling themselves to the sailors of different nationalities who frequented the public houses.

There were still enough respectable people using the street to ensure that the young couple would not be troubled.

The chill easterly wind that had been blowing all day had eased off considerably, yet it was still cold enough to make would-be revellers hurry to seek the warmth and companionship they hoped to find inside one of the street's public houses.

'That Zulu Joe doesn't say very much, does he?' commented Sally, as they gazed in the window of a pawnbroker's shop, which would remain open for business until late in the evening.

'He can't,' replied Ethan. 'It's said that when he was a small boy, he and his mother were captured by Arab slavers. He kicked up so much fuss when the slavers attacked his mother that they cut out his tongue to shut him up.'

'That's a *horrible* story!' Sally shuddered. 'But how does anyone know what happened if he can't tell them?'

'He can write in English,' replied Ethan. 'He was taught by a missionary who brought him to England some years ago. The missionary became very friendly with William Booth, the Salvation Army's general. When the missionary died, the Army looked after Zulu Joe. He came to Plymouth from London with Captain Wardle, the officer in charge of the Plymouth corps.'

Warming to his subject, he continued, 'Bits and pieces have been added to his story recently. A soldier who came to Central Hall claimed that Zulu Joe isn't really a Zulu at all, but got his name by scouting against them for the British when he and the missionary were in Africa. I don't know how true it is, but he's no stranger to a fight. When Captain Wardle first came to Plymouth he gave a talk and described how Zulu Joe would see off gangs of roughs in the East End of London. Since Captain Eva came here, Zulu Joe seems to have taken to her.'

'Well, I hope he's tough enough to rescue that girl and give Sid Darling what he deserves,' Sally said fervently.

8

When twenty minutes had passed and Captain Eva and Zulu Joe had not returned, Sally and Ethan began to grow concerned. They were greatly relieved when the pair turned the corner into Union Street – but the girl who had called to Sally for help was not with them.

In answer to Sally's question, Eva said, 'She wasn't anywhere in the house. In fact there were only two other people there, two prostitutes who seem to be sharing a back room. I know this is so because Mother Darling proved surprisingly accommodating. She allowed us to see all over the house.'

'But . . . I was telling you the truth, honest I was. The girl *was* there. I heard her. She was terrified and begging for help.'

'I don't doubt you, Sally. Mother Darling's son wasn't in the house and she made everything far too easy for me. Had she been entirely innocent she would have been filled with indignation at having me prying into her business. She certainly wouldn't have thrown the house open to me. Besides, there *had* been people in the

house – a large number of them, I'd say. How many pies
did you deliver?'

Puzzled, Sally said, 'Two dozen. Mother Darling said
they were having a party.'

'There was no sign of a party, but I estimate there had
probably been as many as twenty people in the house
recently. Whether or not they were willing guests, I
wouldn't like to say, but I did notice one thing that
struck me as very strange and which tends to confirm your story. There were keys in the locks of every
upstairs room, where I believe the girls to have been,
and all were on the outside of the doors!'

'Where can the girls have gone?' asked Sally. 'And
what's happened to the one who was so desperate
for help?'

'Again, I don't know – although I did see the broken
window pane in the upstairs front room. Perhaps Ethan
can help us. You told me your brother once saw this
Sidney Darling putting girls on board a boat. Was it a
passenger vessel?'

Ethan shook his head. 'No, it was a big deep-sea
Belgian fishing boat . . .' Suddenly realising what was
behind her questioning, he added excitedly, 'One just
like it came into the harbour yesterday – it might even
be the same one. We all noticed it especially because
it didn't come alongside the fish quay, as the foreign
fishing boats usually do. It berthed on the other side of
the harbour, at Shepherd's Wharf, which is practically
deserted right now. I can even tell you the boat's name.
It's the *Astique*.'

'You don't know if the boat's still there? Might it have
sailed this evening?'

'There's no chance of that. Nothing has left harbour

during today's gale. The wind's been strong enough to blow a boat straight back in if it tried to put to sea. Nothing will move until morning now. The tide will be against it for the next hour or so. A stranger to Plymouth would need to be desperate to try to take his boat out in the dark.'

'Then we'll go to where it's moored and try to find out whether they've taken a cargo of English girls on board. How many men are there likely to be in the crew of this Belgian fishing boat?'

'I don't know too much about the foreign fishing boats – especially one as large as this, but they usually carry more men than we do. Judging by its size, I wouldn't be surprised if there were twelve or possibly eighteen men on board. I'd say that's too many for one man to take on – even for Zulu Joe.'

'Then we'll need to find others to help us. Yet we don't want to start something that might lead to a lot of people getting injured, especially as we're not entirely certain these girls are on board. General Booth's army fights for souls, not bodies.' Deep in thought, Eva frowned. Then she added, 'However, not everyone who comes to the meetings in Central Hall has declared for the Lord. Even if they intend doing it, I don't doubt He will be content to wait a while longer for them, in a cause such as this. But before I do anything drastic, I *would* like to confirm there are English girls on board this Belgian boat . . .'

'Why don't I take our dinghy, row across the harbour to the Belgian boat and see if I can hear or see anything?' Ethan said eagerly. 'They won't see me in the dark.'

'How long will it take you?'

'Once I reach the dinghy it'll be no more than fifteen minutes. Twenty at the most.'

'And how long will it take me to reach Shepherd's Wharf by road from Central Hall?'

'That depends how fast you walk,' Ethan declared cautiously, 'but it should be no longer than half an hour.'

Eva bit her lip thoughtfully. 'That will make it a bit late for what I have in mind, but it's better than doing something without adequate investigation. We could be made to look very foolish. All right, Ethan, off you go and do what needs to be done. In the meantime, Zulu Joe and I will hurry along to Central Hall and hope the meeting hasn't already broken up.'

'I'll go with Ethan,' declared Sally.

When it seemed Captain Eva might raise an objection, she added hurriedly, 'If we do find out something, Ethan can put me ashore. Then I'll run to Central Hall to tell you what we've found while he's taking his boat back.'

To Sally's relief, Captain Eva said, 'That makes sense. I'll be on my way to Shepherd's Wharf with as many men as I can gather from Central Hall, but I'm sure you'll find us. If you tell me there are no girls on the boat we'll sing the Belgian fishermen a few hymns anyway. It will be good for their souls.'

9

Sally had difficulty keeping up with Ethan as they hurried towards the Barbican. He had long legs and every half-dozen paces she needed to break into a trot in order to catch up with him.

'Do we need to go quite so fast?' she asked breathlessly.

'Yes,' he replied unsympathetically. 'And if these girls are on board and we're to rescue them, we need to have a plan. Perhaps Captain Eva can create some sort of disturbance on the wharf so we can get close to the Belgian boat from the harbour – we might even get on board, if there's no one about. But we need to hurry. The tide will soon be high enough for the crew to set sail if they take fright. That would be dangerous for everyone involved.'

Too breathless to reply, Sally thought about what Ethan had said until they reached the gas-lit Barbican.

A strong smell of fish hung on the air and dozens of fishing boats were moored in tightly packed lines, bows on to the quayside. Many displayed lanterns and there seemed to be a surprising amount of activity.

When Sally commented, breathlessly, on this, Ethan said, 'The wind has moved around in the last couple of hours. There are signs that the weather will be much better tomorrow, so the boats are being made ready to go to sea. At this time of year we can't afford to lose any opportunity to catch fish.'

The boat owned by Ethan's family was named *Mermaid*. He pointed out the vessel to Sally and, as they clambered over other boats to reach it, explained in haste that the dinghy they needed was secured to the fishing boat's stern.

On board *Mermaid*, two men were working by the yellow light of a lantern. The light was sufficient for Sally to recognise that both bore a strong resemblance to Ethan. One of the men was perhaps thirty years older than Ethan, the other less than ten.

As she scrambled on board the boat behind Ethan, the older man looked from his son to Sally, scrutinising her thoroughly. The younger man did not immediately see her and spoke in a jocular manner to his brother.

'Hello, young Ethan. Have you come to give us a hand to get the boat ready for tomorrow?'

'No, we've come to borrow the dinghy.'

'We . . . ?' Ethan's brother suddenly saw Sally but it was his father who spoke to her first.

'Hello, young lady. I don't think we've met before.'

'This is Sally. Sally, this is my pa – and Paul, my oldest brother.'

Sally nodded to each of the men in turn. Although she said nothing she was aware they were taking a keen interest in her.

'You'll be the maid my brother Charlie was telling me about. You live upstairs in the same house as him.'

Before Sally could reply, Henry Shields turned his attention to Ethan. 'Did you say you wanted to borrow the dinghy? What do you want with it at this time of night?'

Ethan hesitated for only a few moments. His was not a family that kept secrets from one another.

His father and brother listened in silence as he told them of Sally's visit to the home of Mother Darling and of all that had transpired since.

When Ethan ended his story, Henry Shields frowned. 'What makes you think this girl might be on the Belgian boat?'

'Our Danny saw a whole lot of girls being taken on to a Belgian trawler a while ago. He said it looked as though they'd been doped. Sid Darling was with them. It's likely there's more than one girl involved. Possibly as many as a couple of dozen.'

'If Sid Darling's mixed up in this business you're probably right about what's going on. I've known him since we were both boys. He hasn't improved with the years. But what can the pair of you do about it?'

'We're going to Shepherd's Wharf in the hope we might see or hear something suspicious on the Belgian boat.'

'And if you do?'

'I'll land Sally and she'll run to tell Captain Eva Callington, one of the Salvation Army women. She's bringing some of the worshippers from Central Hall to the wharf. Hopefully they'll be able to board the boat and rescue the girls.'

Sally realised Ethan's explanation over-simplified the whole situation. So too did his father.

'You're expecting some rag, tag and bobtail from a Salvation Army meeting to risk life and limb by taking on a boatload of Belgian fisherman? All to save some girls they don't know – and who might not even *want* to be saved? At the very best, they'll succeed in convincing the Belgians they should set sail as soon as the tide's in their favour – and that will be in less than an hour if they're desperate enough to try it. Remember too, if they run into trouble on their way out to sea they won't be at all concerned about what happens to these girls.'

Waiting a few moments for his words to sink in, Henry Shields shook his head. 'No, it's not a good idea at all, young Ethan.'

'But we can't let them get away with the girls from Mother Darling's house,' Sally said passionately. 'You should have heard the cries of the girl who was trying to escape. They were pitiful.'

'I didn't say we should let them escape with the girls. Only that we need to think things out carefully before we do anything. Where is this Captain Eva right now?'

'Gathering up the men and women from Central Hall,' Ethan replied. 'We've just left her. Once she's got enough to go with her she'll start marching them off to Shepherd's Wharf.'

'It'll take her a while to get there,' Henry Shields said thoughtfully. 'All the same, we'll need to get moving. All right, Ethan, you can take the dinghy. Go to Shepherd's Wharf and see what you can find out – but don't let yourselves be seen. If you're convinced they have girls on board, drop Sally off farther along the wharf to meet up with this Captain Eva, then come back here as quickly as you can. While you're gone I'll speak to some of the fishermen. There are enough of 'em around tonight to see off the Belgians. They'll be only too happy to do it if they believe they're trying to make off with English girls.'

Turning his attention to Sally, Henry said, 'You, girl. When you find this Salvation Army captain, tell her that when she reaches Shepherd's Wharf she's to get her crowd to make as much noise as they can, alongside the boat. Create a really good diversion. We'll do the rest.'

10

Although she lived so close to the harbour, Sally had rarely been for a trip in a boat, and never after dark. It was a cold enough night to make her shiver, yet she hardly noticed. She was both excited and fearful about the mission she and Ethan were undertaking.

The harbour was quite small but it seemed that she and Ethan, in their tiny boat, were completely cut off from the people who could be seen walking about the narrow, gas-lit streets around the water's edge.

Ethan had been rowing for no more than ten minutes when Sally whispered hoarsely, 'How long will it take us to get there?'

'Shh!' he stopped rowing and whispered the admonishment. 'That's Shepherd's Wharf, just ahead.'

Peering past him, Sally was just able to make out the inadequately lit wharf, no more than ten or fifteen boat lengths in front of them.

At first she was unable to see the Belgian fishing boat. Then she made out a tall mast silhouetted against a shadowy warehouse. The tide was still low enough for the boat to be settled well below the level of the timber-faced wharf.

Now she had located the vessel she was also able to make out a faint curtain of pale light. In all probability it was escaping from a partly closed hatchway on the deck of the fishing vessel. She gained the impression that *Astique* was a large vessel. Far larger than the fishing boat belonging to the Shields family.

Ethan was using the oars with utmost caution now, slowly easing the small dinghy closer to the Belgian boat. Suddenly, Sally heard an outburst of raucous laughter from the other vessel. There was another sound, too. The cry of a young girl!

Before the sound had fully died away, it was echoed by the shrill scream of a second girl.

'There's certainly more than one girl on board,' Ethan whispered. '*And* they're in trouble. I think we've heard enough, don't you?'

'Yes,' Sally replied fiercely. 'Land me so I can go and find Captain Eva – and quickly.'

'Tell her to hurry – and remember what my pa said. She's to create as much of a diversion as she can but nothing else. We want to get as many men as possible off that boat before Pa and the others try to board it.'

'What will you do once you've told your pa what's going on?'

'I'll stay with them . . .' Ethan had been rowing hard as they talked, and abruptly they bumped against some stone steps, some distance from the Belgian fishing boat. 'Off you go – and hurry.'

'I will . . . Take care, Ethan.'

Put ashore at the steps, Sally ran between tall, dark

warehouse buildings before she reached the streets of the town. No more than five minutes later, she met up with the uniformed Salvation Army officer.

Captain Eva was accompanied by half a dozen similarly clad girls. The women, playing flutes and tambourines, marched at the head of a motley group of perhaps fifty men and women, many from the town's vagrant community.

The silent Zulu Joe was with them and the unusual group was attracting considerable attention from those it passed in the street, although no one attempted to molest it.

Sally passed on her information, telling Captain Eva what Ethan's father had said. The Salvation Army captain immediately ordered her party to increase their pace, ignoring the protests of those who were unaware of the reason for their foray on to the streets of Plymouth.

The music of the small 'band' was silenced when it reached the conglomeration of stone and ramshackle wooden buildings that formed Shepherd's Wharf.

Captain Eva brought the group to a halt at the edge of the wharf, and looked out across the dark waters of the harbour. She was unable to see anything.

'Do you think Ethan and the other fishermen will be in position yet?' she asked Sally.

'I don't know,' Sally replied anxiously. 'But I think we should do as Mr Shields asked, in case they are out there waiting.'

'You're quite right. Let's make a start.'

Captain Eva led her motley party to where the tall mast of the *Astique* rose above the edge of the wharf. She gathered her bandswomen around her, then lined up the rest of the group in front of her.

'We'll begin by singing "Storm the Forts of Darkness",' she called. 'If you don't know the words I'm quite sure you'll be familiar with the tune, so just "la-la" your way through it. Ready? One, two three . . .'

With the Salvation Army girls beating time on their jangling tambourines, and the thin notes of the flutes carrying the tune, the impromptu choir began to sing. It was immediately apparent that they possessed far more enthusiasm than musical ability.

Much to Sally's amazement the tune of the Salvationists' song was one she knew, but it was more usually sung to the words of 'Here's to Good Old Whisky'.

They had not being singing for many minutes when a head appeared above the ladder leading from the wharf to the fishing boat. For a few moments a Belgian fisherman looked at the party on the wharf, his face registering incredulity. Then, calling down to those on the boat below him, he climbed up to the wharf, closely followed by some of his fellow crew members.

When there were nine bemused Belgian fishermen standing on the wharf, Captain Eva called out gaily to them, 'Come closer. Come and join us.'

Some of the men were about to obey her, when one of their number spoke sharply to them and they stopped.

Sally felt an overwhelming urge to move closer to the edge of the wharf and see if she could detect any movement on the water, but she did not dare run the risk of alerting the Belgians. They were already beginning to show signs of boredom with the admittedly unmusical singing of the majority of those taking part in the Salvation Army's impromptu concert party.

'We must do something to keep them interested for

a while longer,' Sally said desperately. 'We don't want them returning to their boat just yet.'

'I think I know what might keep them interested.' Captain Eva beckoned to one of the two flautists and spoke to her. As the singing died away, the flautist began playing a Scottish reel.

Hitching her skirt up to a height that would have incurred the stern disapproval of the Salvation Army founder, Captain Eva began dancing, one hand holding up her skirt, the other held high in the air.

As she skipped and twirled, the tambourines took up the beat and the worshippers from Central Hall began clapping in time to the music. After hesitating uncertainly for a minute or two more, the fishermen from the Belgian boat drew nearer and joined in the clapping.

Because of the noise they were creating it was some minutes before those standing on the wharf became aware of another sound.

It came from the *Astique* – the sound of men shouting, in both English and Flemish.

The first reaction of the fishermen was to return to their vessel, belatedly aware they had been tricked. Captain Eva immediately brought her dance to an end and shouted to her followers, 'Stop them! Don't let them get back to their boat.'

There was room for no more than one man at a time to swing himself onto the narrow ladder. Only one of the fishermen succeeded in gaining it before the men who had marched with Captain Eva ran to obey her command. Zulu Joe was the first to reach the ladder and he made his presence felt immediately – but it was not only men who took part in the mêlée.

Sally saw three of the black-bonneted Salvation Army girls belabouring a Belgian fishermen with their tambourines, as he fought with one of the men from Central Hall.

Suddenly, the head of Ethan's oldest brother appeared above the ladder from the boat. Scrambling to the wharf, he was closely followed by a dishevelled young girl, who seemed terrified by what was going on about her. Then a second girl appeared – and a third.

Now another Plymouth fisherman appeared and dived among the brawling, shouting throng. During the course of the next few minutes, still more fishermen and girls climbed the ladder to the wharf.

By the time the last of the girls had reached safety, the odds had turned heavily in favour of the Englishmen. The Belgians were beating a desperate retreat towards the edge of the wharf. One or two were fortunate enough to find their way back on board via the ladder. Others swung themselves over the edge of the wharf and dropped to the deck of their boat. One, in an attempt to escape the wrath of Plymouth fishermen, took a flying leap into the darkness, hoping he would not land on anything that would cause him serious injury.

An unknown number of Belgian fishermen were thrown into the water of the harbour by the Plymouth men, enthusiastically assisted by Zulu Joe.

Meanwhile, Sally was busy searching the crowd for Ethan.

Ethan's father and brother had been prominent in the fighting, but Sally had seen no sign of the youngest member of the Shields family. She had become increasingly concerned, until she saw his head appear above the edge of the wharf, as he shinned up the ladder from the Belgian fishing boat.

Greatly relieved, Sally hurried towards him, but she was almost bowled over by one of the last of the Belgian fishermen trying to make good his escape. As the big man reached the ladder, he spotted Ethan and drew back his heavily booted foot with the intention of kicking the younger man clear.

Scarcely more than an arm's length away, Sally screamed a warning to Ethan. At the same time she flew at the Belgian fisherman, who was now balanced on one leg, in readiness for a kick to Ethan's head. Sally hit the fisherman with all her might, just as Ethan jerked his head to one side. The kick struck him only a glancing blow to the side of his head and he was able to maintain his grip on the ladder with little difficulty.

The Belgian fisherman was less fortunate. Shouting in terror and with arms flailing, he lost his balance and disappeared from view, to land with a sickening thud on the deck of the fishing boat.

Sally hardly noticed. As she helped Ethan to the safety of the wharf, she demanded anxiously, 'Are you all right? Your head . . . ?'

'His foot hardly touched me,' Ethan reassured her. 'But it would have been a very different story if you hadn't been near.'

At that moment Henry Shields hurried across to them. Putting an arm across Sally's shoulders, he said, 'I saw what you did, girl. I don't know if Ethan realises it, but you've probably saved his life. If the kick hadn't finished him, the fall certainly would have.'

Sally had known very few genuine and spontaneous

gestures of affection during her lifetime, and she experienced a strange mixture of pleasure and embarrassment.

In a bid to cover her confusion, she said, 'Should we go and find out whether the Belgian was badly hurt?'

'Not unless you want to go to Belgium in their place. He and the others deserve everything that's happened to them. Look over there.'

He pointed to where Captain Eva had gathered together the rescued girls in the shadows of a nearby warehouse. Sally counted seventeen in total. The Salvation Army women were comforting the bewildered and frightened girls, two of whom were in a state of near-hysteria.

Sally, Ethan and some of the Plymouth fishermen made their way to where Eva kneeled beside a noisily sobbing young girl. When Sally asked hesitantly whether the girl was going to be all right, Eva glanced up at her and answered, fiercely, 'No, she's never going to be "all right". Not for as long as she lives.' The anger leaving her momentarily, she added more gently, 'But, thanks to you, that's likely to be a whole lot longer than it would otherwise have been.'

Shifting her glance from Sally to Henry Shields and the Plymouth fishermen standing silently behind him, she said, 'You performed a wonderful service tonight, on the side of the Lord.' Pointing to the still weeping girl, she asked, 'Do you know how old she is?' Without waiting for a reply the vehemence returned to her voice as she said, 'She's eleven years old and has already suffered more violence than most women will experience in a lifetime.'

Her words provoked an angry murmur from the

fishermen who had heard her words. But Eva had more to say. 'Oh, don't think this is anything unusual in this great country of ours. She's the youngest of them here tonight – but only just. Two of the girls are twelve and five are thirteen years of age. Not one is older than fifteen. We've dealt with the Belgian fishermen in the way they deserve, but there are many others involved in this disgusting trade. It should really be a task for the courts to deal with. The men who have brutalised this young girl deserve to be put away in a prison for a very long time – and they're still here, in Plymouth.'

'You're already too late for that,' declared Henry Shields, looking over her shoulder. 'The Belgian crew have slipped their boat's moorings. They're on their way home. Without them you'd never get a conviction.'

'We'll see about that,' Eva said fiercely. 'Far too many young girls are suffering at the hands of these people. I'll not rest until I've put an end to this vile trade, once and for all.'

11

When Captain Eva was satisfied all the rescued girls had recovered sufficiently, she set off with them to the Salvation Army headquarters, which was close to Central Hall.

They were escorted by many of the men and women who had taken part in the battle for their freedom. The fishermen now felt a proprietorial interest in the welfare of the girls they had rescued.

The men had actually discovered twenty-one girls on board, but surprisingly four had chosen to remain on the boat. It seemed they were not entirely averse to the way of life they knew would be their lot in Belgium. One actually told her would-be rescuers that she considered it preferable to a lifetime working as a household drudge in England.

'What will happen to these girls now?' Sally asked Eva, indicating the girls who straggled along the road in comparative silence. The excitement of their dramatic rescue had given way to an appreciation of their present uncertain situation.

'They'll stay with Captain Wardle and his wife for tonight. He's the officer in charge of the Plymouth corps of the Salvation Army. He lives at the headquarters – it's really no more than a large loft in Central Street that used to be the Army's meeting place. There'll be plenty of room for everyone there, although we'll need to try to find them some bedding.'

'They won't be able to stay there forever,' said Ethan, who had been listening to the conversation.

'Of course not,' agreed Captain Eva. 'No doubt many of the girls will wish to return home. Unfortunately, some have no home they can return to. I'll try to find respectable domestic posts for them.'

'What about the eleven-year-old?' asked Sally, referring to the girl whose shoulders still heaved every few steps, as she sobbed out her pain and misery.

'Poor Rachel. She poses a considerable problem. I'll take her home to stay with me until she feels able to put this ordeal behind her. It's even possible I can use what's happened to her to benefit others.'

'How?' Sally was sceptical. 'By having Mother Darling and her son locked up for what they've done? That won't put a stop to what's happened tonight, will it? There are too many others like them, you've said so yourself.'

'You're right, of course, Sally – and not only in Plymouth, either. There are men and women just like them in Portsmouth, Exeter, Bristol – and a great many more in London. Unfortunately, no action is taken by the authorities to put an end to what is going on. One of the problems is that so many of the girls have no one to whom they can turn for help. No one who cares what happens to them. And those who have are often so ashamed of what's happened they won't talk about it – to anyone. I can't say I entirely blame them. Those very, very few who do lodge a complaint despair when the police take no action to help them. All too often the sympathies of the police seem to be with the brothel keepers. At least, that was my experience in London.'

Captain Eva's chin set in an expression that Sally would come to know well. 'I intend to change that one day – and change the age of consent too. At thirteen a girl is a mere child. Far, far too young to be dragged into the vilest trade imaginable.'

The spacious loft 'home' of Salvation Army Captain James Wardle was a huge roof space, which extended the full length of a disused warehouse. It would provide ample dormitory-type accommodation for the rescued girls.

However, as Captain Eva had anticipated, there was a desperate shortage of bedding and it was a cold night.

Despite the lateness of the hour an immediate call went out to all the Salvation Army families in the area. They were asked to donate a blanket, sheet or even a cushion to serve as a pillow.

Ethan was one of those able to help. On his way home to fetch a couple of blankets, he found the fishermen around the quay still excitedly discussing the events of the night with their colleagues.

Ethan explained to them the latest problem and within minutes men and boys were hurrying to their homes to collect contributions for the unfortunate girls.

Half an hour later, Ethan was pushing a handcart laden with a variety of bedding through the streets of Plymouth, bound for the home of Captain James Wardle.

After the delivery, he and Sally were walking back to the Barbican together, through the near-deserted early morning streets of Plymouth, discussing the events of the past few hours.

'Those girls have a great deal to thank you for, Sally,' declared Ethan. 'If you hadn't been so determined to do something about what you suspected was going on at Mother Darling's, they would all be on their way to Belgium now. I doubt if they would ever have seen England again.'

When Sally made no immediate reply, he continued, 'I'm grateful to you too. If it hadn't been for you I'd have had my head kicked in by that Belgian. My pa reckons you saved my life. He was telling Ma all about it when I went home to collect the blankets. She said I must bring you home, so she can meet you.'

'She probably won't be quite so pleased with me when she learns it was me who stirred up all the trouble in the first place,' said Sally.

'What sort of a thing is that to say? You're the heroine of the Barbican tonight – and rightly so. There's not one of us fishermen who doesn't think so.'

Sally might have been a heroine that night to the fishermen and the girls preparing for bed in the Salvation Army loft in Central Street, but there was one man in Plymouth who thought very differently.

Sid Darling had been drinking in a public house in Union Street when a rumour began to circulate about a fracas at Shepherd's Wharf, involving Plymouth and Belgian fishermen.

Sid Darling hurried off to learn the truth of what had happened but he found Shepherd's Wharf deserted and the Belgian trawler gone.

Returning to the Barbican public house, he listened to the excited chatter around him. It did not take him long to discover what had taken place.

But although he now knew the sequence of events that had occurred, he had heard nothing to explain what had led to the disruption of an arrangement that had worked smoothly on many previous occasions. He needed to talk it over with his mother, as a matter of some urgency.

His route home took him close to Central Hall. As he drew near he saw a crowd of people approaching him, talking animatedly. Among them was a number of men and women wearing Salvation Army uniforms.

In view of the events of the night, he thought it prudent to draw back into the shadows of a deep doorway and allow the group to go on their way without noticing him.

None of the party observed him as they passed by, chatting excitedly. He was about to leave the doorway when he saw two others pushing an empty handcart along the road towards him.

Remaining in the doorway as they passed by, he recognised Sally – and the answer to the question that had been troubling him all evening became immediately clear.

He now realised who had been responsible for interfering with the girls on the boat and putting him at risk of arrest. She had also cost him a great deal of money and might have put an end to a very lucrative business that had taken him a long time to set up.

Sid Darling's formidable reputation owed a great deal to the fact that he never allowed anyone who slighted him in any way to remain unpunished.

He would not let such a reputation be put at risk by a mere slip of a girl. He would teach her a lesson she would never forget.

12

At the shop the following morning, Sally told Grace
Philpott what had happened on Shepherd's Wharf,
deliberately playing down her own part in the proceedings.

The kind-hearted shopkeeper immediately insisted
that Sally's first errand of the day should be to take two
dozen pies to the Salvation Army's loft headquarters.

'*Two dozen?*' Alfie had listened to Sally's account of
the night's events with tight-lipped disapproval. His
displeasure was not aimed at Sally, but at the fact that
such a thing should have occurred in Plymouth. However, he now voiced a protest at his wife's spontaneous
generosity. 'Sally said there were only seventeen girls.
Why send two dozen?'

'Don't you think some of those Salvation Army people
who are helping the girls would appreciate something
nice to start the day with too? They've certainly done
enough to earn a treat. I tell you, Alfie, I've got a lot
of time for these people. They don't preach one thing,
then go off and do another. Nor do they look down their

noses at them poor unfortunates most other religious don't want to know about.'

Grace faced him, hands on hips, daring him to argue with her.

There were occasions when Alfie could successfully argue with Grace, and others when he could not. This was one of the latter. He retreated to the kitchen, grumbling quietly to himself.

Returning her attention to Sally, Grace said positively, 'Two dozen pies it is. When you see this Captain whatever-her-name-is, you tell her if she needs any extra blankets tonight, I've got a couple she's very welcome to.'

When Sally left the shop with a basket containing the hot pies over her arm, Alfie was still complaining that his wife's generosity would one day prove to be the ruination of their business.

Captain Eva, Captain Wardle and their helpers were delighted with Grace's gift. They and their charges tucked into them with great enthusiasm right away.

Sally remained with Captain Eva and the girls while they ate. 'They seem a lot happier this morning,' she commented, as the girls chattered noisily, many of them sitting on the floor as they ate.

'That's because half of them will be given the money to return home today.' Less cheerfully, she added, 'They're the lucky ones who have come to no harm as a result of what's happened to them. Some of the others have. Even so, by the end of the week a few of those will have decided to go home anyway, saying nothing to their friends and families about any of this. The remainder either have no homes to go back to or are too ashamed ever to face their families again.'

'What will happen to them?' Sally was genuinely concerned. Remembering what the Salvation Army captain had said the night before, she added, 'Do you think you *will* be able to find work for them?'

Captain Eva shrugged unhappily. 'That's why I've been sent to Plymouth, to take care of girls such as these. If I can only find a house for the Army to buy, or rent, I'll be able to look after them and others and put their lives back together.'

For a while, Sally said nothing. She wondered how different her own life might have been had there been someone like Captain Eva to help Ruth earn a respectable living in order to provide for them.

She was still deep in her own thoughts when Eva said, 'It's poor Rachel I'm really concerned about. She's so young. After this experience it will be a long while before she trusts anyone again. She showed a great deal of spirit when she attracted your attention, but that seems to have gone. She's been brutally treated, poor girl.'

'Where is she now?'

'She isn't here,' explained the Salvation Army captain. 'I took her home last night to the rooms I rent. I thought she needed special care. I was quite right. Twice during the night she woke screaming and her sobbing was pitiful. But she was asleep when I left her this morning. One of the Army girls who was with us last night is staying there with her.'

'Does she have a family to go back to?'

'No one close enough to care about her.' Eva was unable to keep the bitterness she felt from her voice.

'Her father was killed soldiering. When her mother died a year later, she was put in a workhouse, in Oxford. It was the workhouse master who saw the advertisement in a newspaper, asking for young girls to go into domestic service. He promptly packed her off without making any enquiries about those who had placed the advertisement.'

She had finished eating now. Standing up, she brushed a crumb from her plain black uniform dress and added, 'Not that it would have made very much difference if he had. I doubt if the advertisement can be traced to Mother Darling. Rachel and the others were taken to Mary Street from a house just outside Plymouth. It sounds to me as though the house was rented on a temporary basis and used for the sole purpose of deceiving young girls into believing they were being offered legitimate employment.'

'So there are more people than Sid and Mother Darling involved in this?'

'Oh yes, Sally. Very many more – and not only in Plymouth. The sale of young girls to brothels, especially foreign brothels, is a well-organised and highly profitable business. There is so much money involved it's proving very, very difficult to stamp out this vile trade.'

Sally would like to have learned more from the Salvation Army captain but she remembered, somewhat belatedly, that she was employed by Grace and Alfie Philpott to deliver their pies.

Standing up, she said, 'I must get back to work. Can I call and speak to Rachel after I've finished this evening?'

'Of course. There's an important meeting being held at Central Hall this evening. I'll bring Rachel with me.'

As Sally left and was clattering down the rather rickety outside wooden staircase that led from the loft, Captain Eva called after her, 'Please thank the pie-shop owners for us. Tell them they will be in our prayers today. They are truly Christian people.'

13

That evening, Sally hurried to complete her chores as Ruth picked unenthusiastically at her supper.

'You're in a great hurry tonight, our Sal. Are you meeting that young man of yours?'

'I doubt it. It's been a fine day, he'll have been out fishing. No, I'm meeting up with the girl I was telling you about. The one who caused all the fuss at Mother Darling's and started everything off last night.'

Ruth had still been awake when Sally had returned home in the early hours of the morning, and she had listened to her sister's excited account of all that had happened.

Ruth's light-hearted mood vanished and she frowned. 'You did what needed doing, Sal, but I wish to heaven you hadn't got mixed up in it in the first place. If Sid Darling ever finds out it was you who had them girls rescued, you'll be in more trouble than you've ever known before. There's no such thing as "forgive and forget" where he's concerned. No one who's crossed him has ever got away with it. All the girls on the streets are scared stiff of him – and with just cause.'

'Then we'll just have to hope he never finds out,' replied Sally, with more bravado than she felt. 'Now, is there anything else I can get you before I go?'

'No, I've got everything I want. Everything except my health. Try not to be too late tonight. I'll be lying here worrying about you.'

Although Sally had not expected to meet Ethan that evening, she was delighted to see him coming towards her as she turned out of Pin's Lane. With Ruth's warning on her mind, she was relieved too.

When she expressed surprise that he was not out fishing, he grinned happily. 'We put out early this morning and had hardly left harbour when we ran into a huge shoal of pilchards. Within a couple of hours we'd taken so many fish the *Mermaid* was in danger of sinking under the weight. We were the first boat back to the fish quay and so got a really good price for our catch. Not only that, Pa reckons we might be lucky enough to find the same shoal tomorrow if this weather holds. He says this could well be the best Christmas ever for the family.'

Realising he had not stopped talking since they had met up, he asked, 'Where are you off to now? Anywhere that I can come too?'

'Central Hall. Captain Eva is bringing Rachel there to meet me. I can't see any reason why you shouldn't come. You did as much as anyone to help her last night.'

It was a fine evening and Ethan's happy chatter made the distance from Pin's Lane to Central Hall seem far shorter than it actually was. Sally had never known

Ethan to talk quite so much before. His shyness with her seemed to have completely disappeared.

Although he made frequent references to the drama of the previous night, much of his talk was of Christmas, which was now only ten days away.

Sally listened to him without saying anything. Christmas was not a time of the year she particularly enjoyed. It always served to bring home to Ruth and Sally that they had no family with whom to share the festivities. It also tended to disrupt the routine of life about them.

'What are you doing for Christmas?'

Ethan put the unexpected question to Sally as they neared Central Hall.

'Me? I'll no doubt be working until late on Christmas Eve, but with the money I earn I should be able to buy something nice for Ruth to eat. Then I'll spend most of Christmas Day looking after her.'

Some of Ethan's effervescence seeped away. 'Oh! I'd forgotten that you have Ruth to look after.'

When Sally looked at him questioningly, he said, 'My ma said I should ask you if you'd like to come and eat with us on Christmas Day.'

The invitation took Sally by surprise. Ethan had mentioned the previous night that his mother had expressed a wish to meet her – but to go to a strange house and sit down to a meal with Mr and Mrs Shields and their six sons . . . ! The thought of it terrified her.

'I . . . I just can't, Ethan. I couldn't leave Ruth. She always looks forward to having me at home with her. Especially on a day like that.'

It wasn't quite the truth, but it was the best excuse she could think of on the spur of the moment.

'Of course. I should have realised you would have to take care of Ruth. It won't be much of a Christmas for you, though, will it?'

Sally shrugged. 'It doesn't make much difference, we never do anything special at Christmas, anyway – although this one will be better than most, now I'm earning good money.'

'Don't you ever have a Christmas tree . . . or decorations, things like that?'

'No.'

Sally had vague memories of a room festooned with decorations, but that had been when she was very small and her mother was still alive.

'Sally . . .' Ethan spoke hesitantly, 'I know you need to be at home for most of the day with Ruth, but . . . will you come to my house to meet Ma some time during the day? Even if it's only to say "Hello" and "Goodbye"? She really would like to meet you – and I'd like you to meet her, too.'

Sally thought about it for a few moments. She was aware that Ethan was deeply disappointed she would not be having a meal with his family – and she did not like hurting him.

'All right.'

Once her acceptance was out, it surprised her almost as much as it did Ethan, but there was no doubting his delight.

'You will? When? I mean . . . what time shall I tell Ma you'll be there?'

'I can't tell you that just yet. It depends on how Ruth is, really.'

'Of course, but the time doesn't matter. Ma will understand – and you needn't worry about being the only girl there. My second-oldest brother, Albert, is married. He and his wife will be at the house for most of the day. Joe's girlfriend will probably be there as well. Joe's the next youngest to me,' he explained, still hardly able to contain his delight.

Sally was not at all certain she wanted to meet other young women in the presence of his family. She was fully aware the clothes she owned would not stand comparison with those worn by most girls of her age, but she said nothing. A few minutes later they reached Central Hall.

14

'But Captain Eva asked me to come here tonight to meet her.'

Sally spoke with growing frustration. A burly, uniformed Salvation Army 'soldier' was on duty at the inner entrance to Central Hall. He refused to allow Sally and Ethan to enter.

'I'm sorry but I've already told you, Captain Cassington isn't here and you can't just walk in the hall in the middle of the talk. It's being given by a senior officer from London. He's a *very* important man. A commissioner – and a personal friend of General Booth!'

The Salvation Army man was adamant. Captain Eva was not in the hall; he did not know where she was – and he was not going to allow Sally and Ethan to enter while the important speaker was addressing his audience.

Suddenly, a young uniformed woman hurried from the hall looking flustered. She was one of the women who had been playing a tambourine on Shepherd's Wharf the previous evening. When she saw Sally, her expression showed great relief.

'I'm glad you're here. I thought I might have missed you. I was so excited at being introduced to Commissioner Hubble, I quite forgot I had a message for you from Captain Eva. I really am sorry.'

'Why isn't she here? Has something happened? Is it to do with the girls we rescued?'

'It is, but it's nothing bad. In fact, it's very, very exciting. She's been given a house to use as a refuge for them. She's spent the whole of the day moving them in. That's why she isn't here tonight, even though it's a special meeting. She felt getting the girls settled in was more important. She wants you to go there to see her.'

Handing over a scrap of paper, the Salvation Army girl said, 'Here's the address. It's on the Barbican, in Palace Lane.'

Sally knew the small street well. It was on the very edge of the Barbican. The houses there were old – very old – but also extremely large.

'Shall I come with you?' Ethan asked hopefully.

'I don't see why not,' Sally replied. 'Captain Eva was happy enough to have you around last night. I'm sure she'll be pleased to see you again.'

The house was very large indeed and, to Sally's mind, frighteningly impressive inside. When she and Ethan entered, they were immediately aware of an aroma of carbolic soap and furniture polish.

Eva looked very pleased to see them. As she held the door wide for them to enter, she said happily, 'Come in. Come in, both of you. Isn't this absolutely marvellous? Have you ever seen such a splendid house?'

'You said nothing about it last night. I thought you were still looking for a place.'

'So I was – then. But Commissioner Hubble came to see me this morning, at our headquarters. He's the man who's talking at Central Hall tonight. He arrived from London yesterday and stayed the night with a great friend of his, a member of a wealthy Methodist family. They'd heard what had happened at Shepherd's Wharf and wanted to meet the girls. When they asked what would happen to them now, I told them the reason I'd been sent here by General Booth. I said that if only I could find a suitable house I could take care of the girls, and others like them. I sincerely believe God must have been listening to my prayers and sent Commissioner Hubble's friend here to me. He owns several houses in Plymouth and this one just happened to be empty! He was so moved by the plight of the girls, he said I could have the house, rent free, for as long as I need it and we were all able to move in right away!'

Eva clapped her hands together in an expression of sheer joy. 'Isn't it absolutely wonderful? The house is only partly furnished right now, but it's a veritable palace. Of course, we're going to need one or two extra things. There aren't enough beds or chairs at the moment, but God will provide them. I just know he will. Honestly, Sally, I could sing for sheer joy.'

Sally knew very little of God, and religion had never seriously encroached upon her life. As a result, she felt vaguely uncomfortable with Captain Eva's fervour, but there was more to come.

'Of course, I realise it's not only God I have to thank for everything – but you too, Sally. If you hadn't responded to poor Rachel's cries for help, the girls wouldn't have been rescued and this magnificent house wouldn't be ours.'

'Ethan helped too,' said Sally, embarrassed at being singled out for such praise.

'He most certainly did,' agreed Eva. 'As he's here, he can help again. The owner of the house said there are more bits and pieces of furniture in the loft. Ethan can climb up there for us and see exactly what there is—'

'Where's Rachel? Is she here too?'

Sally put the questions before Captain Eva had the chance to begin eulogising about her once more.

'Yes.' Some of Eva's happiness ebbed away. 'I'd like to say she was grateful enough to want to thank you, but right now she's blaming the whole world for what's happened to her. She'll get over it, of course, but she *is* being rather difficult, poor girl.'

They were at the foot of a stout staircase, which led to the first floor of the house, and Eva called up, 'Rachel! Come on down. Sally's here to meet you.'

A few minutes later a slight but very pretty girl appeared at the top of the stairs. Her pale, drawn face was bruised, her lip was swollen and she had a particularly nasty graze on one cheekbone.

She came down the stairs slowly and uncertainly, her dark eyes never leaving Sally's face.

As soon as she reached the foot of the stairs, she blurted out, fiercely, 'Why didn't you do something to help me when you first came to Mother Darling's? Why did you leave me there so . . . so they could do things to me?'

Her eyes filled with tears and she turned away. Then, abruptly, she rushed back up the stairs, stumbling once or twice on the way so great was her hurry to escape the small crowd gathered in the hallway.

Sally was distressed by the other girl's words, but Eva

put an arm about her shoulders and hugged her. 'You mustn't take any notice, Sally. Rachel really did suffer greatly, both at the house and on the boat. She is full of anger and wants someone to blame. It will take a long time before she can get things into perspective and is able to face the world again.'

'Poor girl!' Sally was moved to tears. 'She did so much, too. She's the one everyone should be thanking for the rescue. She was determined the Darlings weren't going to get away with what they were up to and she put herself in danger by kicking up such a fuss.'

'You both played a very important part,' said Eva. 'So too did Ethan. I'll go up and speak to Rachel in a few minutes, but after all that's happened I think we deserve at least a *little* celebration.'

Calling to one of the girls who was standing nearby, she said, 'Ethel, put the kettle on, we're going to have a cup of tea. It's time to cut into that cake Mrs Wardle sent for us, too. Afterwards we'll give thanks to the Lord for the part He has played in helping us.'

15

Rachel Green did not come down from her room again that evening. After a brief prayer session with the girls and Ethan, Eva took tea and cake to Rachel in her room, and remained there with her.

Meanwhile, Sally stood chatting to some of the girls on the top-floor landing, while Ethan handed down furniture from the loft. Gradually, as the girls talked, Sally was able to build up a picture of how they had been trapped by the Darlings.

Most of the young girls were either members of large families whose parents were finding it hard to make ends meet or had lost one of their parents. The prospect of having a daughter placed in domestic service – no longer a drain on the family resources and able at some time in the near future to contribute something, however small, to the family income – was a very desirable state of affairs.

Many of the girls had been overjoyed to leave poor, overcrowded homes to make the exciting journey to Plymouth and take up new employment, hopefully in a large town.

All agreed they had been surprised when they arrived at their destination to find an isolated house in the country, neglected to the point of dereliction. Another cause for concern was the couple who were waiting to greet them. Coarse-mannered and dressed in cheap clothes, they were hardly the type of employers they had been expecting.

The couple explained this away by telling the girls that they were running an agency, supplying servants to wealthy households in the Plymouth area. They added spice to their story by declaring that some of the girls might very soon find themselves working for titled employers.

By late afternoon there were twenty-one girls in the house, and they were given a meal and some wine to drink.

Rachel did not like wine, but did not like to say so. When the couple were not looking, she gave her drink to one of the other girls.

It was soon apparent that there was something wrong with the wine. All the girls except Rachel were falling around in a state resembling a drunken stupor, unable to control their limbs or marshal their thoughts.

The woman explained their condition away to Rachel by saying the wine was from France. As well as being some of the finest that money could buy, it was also far more potent than folk in England were used to.

Rachel had not been entirely satisfied with the explanation, but she was a very young and inexperienced country girl. She could think of no reason why the woman should lie to her, or want to harm the girls.

Late that evening, an enclosed van arrived at the house to convey the girls to Mary Street, in Plymouth, where they arrived very late at night.

They remained here in the dubious care of the Darlings until the following evening. During this time they were locked in upstairs rooms and given food and drink that kept them in a state that one of the girls described as 'dopey'.

From what they overheard later, it seemed that the plan had not involved the girls going to Mary Street at all. They should have boarded the Belgian fishing boat direct from the house outside Plymouth but, unfortunately for their kidnappers, the boat had been delayed by adverse winds in the Channel.

Rather than risk the long return journey to the large house outside Plymouth, it was decided to take the girls to Mary Street.

Locked in a room at the home of the Darlings, Rachel had belatedly realised this was unlikely to be the beginning of a career in domestic service. It was now that she made the dramatic attempt to escape, which had been witnessed by Sally.

The escape attempt had cost her dearly. Carried to an upstairs room, she had been viciously beaten, then raped, by Sid Darling. A further horrific assault had been carried out by one of Sid Darling's accomplices, who was helping him to guard the girls.

But Rachel's nightmare was not over. Her ordeal had been repeated yet again when she had been taken on board the Belgian fishing boat. Some of the other girls were also raped by the Belgian sailors, most of whom had been drinking heavily since reaching Plymouth.

Their torment did not come to an end until the dramatic arrival of the Plymouth fishermen.

*   *   *

Walking home with Ethan later that evening, Sally repeated what the girls had told her, adding that she could not blame Rachel for her bitter outburst when they had been introduced.

'It's understandable,' agreed Ethan. 'But I'm sure that when she's recovered from all this, she'll realise there was nothing more you could have done. You certainly couldn't have done anything any quicker.'

'I don't know,' Sally said unhappily. 'Perhaps I should have made a fuss when I was in Mary Street. Got the neighbours to help, or something.'

'If they'd wanted to do something to help they'd have done it long ago,' Ethan declared firmly. 'They must have known what's been going on in the house. They're not blind, or stupid. The trouble is, everyone is scared of Sid Darling. So scared that he could murder someone in the middle of the street and nobody would "see" anything he could be put away for. If you'd made any sort of fuss at the time you'd have found yourself on the boat with them. Then there'd have been no rescue.'

'You're probably right,' Sally agreed reluctantly. 'But it doesn't make me feel a whole lot better. I'll go back to the house tomorrow night. Perhaps Rachel will speak to me then. I'd like to be able to help her, if I can. She's got no one else.'

'She's got Captain Eva now,' Ethan pointed out, 'and she won't give up until Rachel is all right again. Happily, all the girls are safe now. Let's talk about something happier. You *will* come to our house some time on Christmas Day? I can tell my ma tonight . . . ?'

16

Grace Philpott listened with increasing horror as Sally repeated the stories told to her by the girls the previous evening.

'It . . . it's *unbelievable*!' She almost exploded with fury when Sally had ended the tale.

Turning to her husband, her distress clear on her face, she asked, 'Can you believe such things could go on in Plymouth without there being some sort of outcry, Alfie?'

'There are a whole lot of things going on in the world you know nothing about, Grace – and you're none the worse off for that.' Alfie shrugged. 'It would be different if there was something you could do about it, but there's not.'

Grace looked at her husband for so long he began to feel uncomfortable. However, her next words indicated that he had not been the subject of her thoughts.

'That's just where you're wrong, Alfie Philpott. There *is* something I can do, and I'm going to do it. Are you forgetting that Percy Mallett is my uncle?'

Alfie's startled expression was an indication that he *had* forgotten. 'You haven't had anything to do with your uncle Percy for years!'

'All the more reason why he should take notice when I go to see him now. After all, he's an alderman and chairman of the Police Authority. It's his *duty* to do something about such goings-on.'

Alfie realised his wife was about to embark on a course of action that would most probably incur the enmity of a man as dangerous as Sid Darling.

'Now, Grace, this isn't anything you should get involved in. We're running a pie shop. The goodwill of our customers is important to us.'

'Not if the customers are like the Darlings, it's not. We can do without their sort. There are plenty of the other kind who will approve of anything that can be done to stamp out this sort of thing.'

Addressing Sally, she said, 'I want you to introduce me to this Captain Eva – and I'd like to meet the poor young girl who has suffered so much because of the Darlings, too. You and I will go along to their house this evening. I'll cook something special for the girls this afternoon. We can take it along with us. I might not be able to do anything about what's happened to the poor souls, but I'll make sure they don't go hungry.'

A few minutes later Sally left the Philpotts' shop with a laden basket, doing her best to ignore the glare directed at her by Alfie.

That evening, Grace and Sally were let in to the Barbican Refuge by one of the girls. She told them Captain Eva and the others were at prayer in the large lounge.

While Grace was being shown to the lounge, Sally

took the food they had brought to the kitchen to be reheated. Then she laid out plates in readiness for the evening meal. Had Grace not been so generous the girls would have eaten bread and cheese. They would welcome the improved menu.

As Sally made her own way to the prayer meeting, the occupants broke into a rousing hymn. When she entered the room she was astonished to see Grace singing with a gusto that rivalled Captain Eva's.

She took her place on a seat beside her employer. When the hymn came to an end, Grace whispered enthusiastically, 'That was a Wesleyan hymn. I used to sing it in chapel when I was a young girl. I'd forgotten how much I enjoyed those services.'

Captain Eva led her small congregation in a couple of simple prayers and the service came to an end. Sally introduced the two women and, while the girls rushed off to the kitchen to enjoy their unexpected treat, Grace explained to the Salvation Army officer her reasons for coming to the house.

'When Sally told me of all that had happened I found it difficult to believe such things could go on in our city. Those poor girls – especially that young Rachel! Which one is she?'

'Rachel didn't come down to the meeting,' explained Eva. 'She suffered a great deal more than any of the others. It's going to take her quite some time to get over all that's happened to her. She's in a small room of her own. I let her stay there.'

'Poor child!' Grace said, with genuine sympathy. 'I would like to meet her before I leave. But my main reason for coming here is to see if we can't make certain we have the two Darlings arrested and discuss what might be done to prevent anything like this happening again.'

'If we could have the Darlings arrested and convicted for what they've done it would be a very important step along the road to doing away with the trade in young girls,' said Eva. 'But there is an inexplicable reluctance on the part of the police to bring it to an end. We've tried on many occasions in London. I'm told things are no different here.'

'Then we must *make* them different,' Grace said positively. She told the Salvation Army captain about her uncle.

Grace's enthusiasm for the crusade she intended taking up matched that of Captain Eva. Soon the two women were in animated conversation.

Sally was on her way to join the other girls in the kitchen when Eva called after her.

'Sally, would you like to take something to eat up to Rachel in her room?'

Remembering the last occasion the two girls had met, Sally asked, 'Wouldn't it be better if one of the other girls took it up? Seeing me seems to upset her.'

Eva shook her head. 'Rachel and I have talked about that. She realises her outburst was quite out of order. In fact, I think she might like to see you and thank you for what you did, instead of blaming you for what couldn't be done.'

17

Sally tapped on the door of Rachel's room with trepidation. She needed to knock three times before receiving a reply.

'Who is it?'

'It's Sally Harrup. I've brought something for you to eat.'

After a few moments of silence, the reply came back through the closed door, 'I don't want anything.'

'You wouldn't say that if you knew what it is. Grace Philpott has cooked it 'specially with you in mind.'

It was doubtful Rachel had any idea who 'Grace Philpott' was, but Sally was correct in thinking the mention of the name would tantalise the other girl enough for her to open the door.

When Rachel stood in the doorway, the room behind her was in darkness, but there was enough light from the low-burning gaslight on the landing for Sally to see that the young girl had been crying.

'Who's this Grace Philpott – and how does she know about me?'

'Grace is the woman I work for. She knows about you because I've told her. Grace is downstairs with Captain Eva right now. They're talking about having Sid Darling arrested for what he did to you and so put a stop to what he and his friends are doing with other girls.'

'I know what I'd like to do to *him*,' Rachel said fiercely.

'No one would blame you, whatever you did,' Sally agreed, relieved that Rachel was talking to her. 'I feel the same about him, and he's only ever *looked* at me.'

Sally was standing outside the room carrying a meal that would not have disgraced the finest restaurants in the city. There were fruit tarts, too, which Grace had cooked as a special treat for the girls.

'Can I come in . . . ?'

Rachel stood to one side and Sally entered the room.

'Do you have a light in here?'

'There are some matches somewhere.'

A few moments later Sally could hear matches being rattled in a box; one was scraped into life and the gaslight fixed to a bracket on the wall burst into flame with a pop. Looking around the small room, the crumpled bedclothes indicated to Sally that Rachel had been lying on the bed fully clothed.

As Rachel straightened the bedclothes, Sally said, 'Here, eat this before it gets too cold.'

Rachel dutifully sat down and began picking at the food on the plate. Almost reluctantly, she said, 'This is nice.'

'I told you you'd enjoy it. You must tell Grace. She'll be delighted. She's a softie, really, and she can't wait to meet you. She once had a little girl of her own, but she died when she was only three. I don't think

Grace has ever got over it. She can't look at any girl who's anywhere near my age – or yours, come to that – without thinking of how her own little girl would have been, had she lived. It's very sad.'

Rachel carried on eating in silence for a few minutes until, without looking up at Sally, she said, 'I'm sorry I said you hadn't been quick enough to help me. Captain Eva has told me how much you did to help. If you hadn't gone to her I don't know where I'd be . . . Probably in Belgium, I suppose, having men do to me what Sid Darling and the others did . . .'

Rachel's lower lip began to tremble and Sally said hurriedly, 'It's all right, Rachel. Please don't get upset, or you'll upset me too. You don't know how many times I've asked myself what else I might have done to stop all those things happening to you. But . . . I just couldn't have done any more. Honest.'

'I know . . .'

Suddenly Rachel began to cry. Sally took the fork from her hand and put her arms about her, feeling desperately sorry for the distressed and abused young girl.

After Sally had been holding her for some minutes, Rachel pulled away. 'I'm sorry. That wasn't fair on you.'

'You don't have to be sorry . . . for anything. Look, eat up what you can, then we'll go and find Grace. You'll like her, I know you will.'

'All right. I . . . I'll try to finish it, but I doubt if I'll be able to swallow anything right now.'

Despite this statement, Rachel finished much of the meal. Between mouthfuls she questioned Sally about her own life.

When she heard that Sally's mother was dead and she

had never known her father, she stared at Sally with an expression of deep sympathy. 'So you're on your own too! How do you manage?'

'I'm not entirely on my own,' admitted Sally. 'I have an older sister who's looked after me since I was seven. But she's very ill and now I need to look after her.'

'Where do you live?'

'We have a room in Pin's Lane.' Remembering that Rachel did not know Plymouth, she explained, 'It's not far from here, close to Sutton harbour – that's where you were when we rescued you.'

'Could I come to see you there some time?'

'Of course you can. I'll take you there myself. Ruth will be pleased to see you – she's my sister. She doesn't have many visitors. I've told her all about you and the others.'

'I'd like that. I'd like us to be friends, too,' she added hesitantly.

Standing up, Rachel crossed the room to look at herself in a small mirror hanging on the wall in a corner of the room. She ran a brush through her hair a couple of times before turning back to Sally, her head held high. 'I'm ready to go and meet this lady now.'

18

Rachel entered the room uncertainly, coaxed by Sally. Looking up, Grace Philpott saw a small and particularly vulnerable young girl, and the shop owner's heart went out to her immediately.

Tears sprung to her eyes as she said, 'My dear soul! You hardly seem old enough to be sent off to domestic service, let alone have all this happen to you. It's too dreadful for words.' She stopped, momentarily, too overcome to say more.

'This is Mrs Philpott,' Captain Eva explained. 'She's been extremely generous in helping to feed you and the other girls. Now she wants to see this Sidney Darling brought before the courts – particularly for what he did to you. If we go ahead it might prove to be a very unpleasant ordeal for you. Because of this, I feel you should be given time to think about it—'

'I don't need any time to think about anything,' Rachel declared vehemently. 'Nothing that's said or done to me now can be as bad as what he's already done. Even hanging would be too good for him.'

'You're quite right,' Grace said emphatically. 'We may not see him hanged, but I'll not rest until he's been sent to prison for a very long time.' Turning to Captain Eva, she asked, 'What's the first thing we need to do?'

'I'll go to the police station in the morning and report what's happened. If we're lucky they'll send someone here to interview Rachel and the others. If they don't show any signs of doing anything, perhaps you'll involve your uncle?'

'I can't wait in the hope that they *might* do something,' retorted Grace. 'I want to *know* they're taking action right now.'

This was the assertiveness Sally had occasionally glimpsed in the shop when Grace was determined to gain her own way with her husband.

Grace continued, 'You go along to the police station this evening and I'll call on Uncle Percy right away. You come with me, Sally. You know as much of what went on as anyone else. You can fill in any gaps about what's happened.' Giving Rachel a sympathetic smile, she said, 'I'll not sleep tonight unless I know something's going to be done. I feel ashamed to know that such things are happening in a respectable town like ours.'

Her expression softened even more as Rachel stood wide-eyed, listening to her. 'Don't you worry, my dear. Nobody's going to harm you again. Not while you've got Captain Eva and me to look after you.'

Returning her attention to Eva, she said, 'I'll be on my way now, but we'll meet again soon. I'd like to say how much I enjoyed what little piece of your service I was able to take part in tonight. It took me back to my childhood chapel days. They were very happy days. Thinking of what these poor young girls have been through has made me realise just how lucky I've been.'

'You're very welcome to come to any of our meetings, either here or in Central Hall,' replied Eva. 'I hope that one day we'll both be able to give thanks together for our achievement in bringing these men to justice.'

The reception given to Captain Eva at the Plymouth police station was all that members of the Salvation Army had come to expect from the police.

Two policemen were behind the desk in the Charge Office. One, a sergeant, was leaning on the counter, writing laboriously in a large, leather-bound ledger, while at the rear of the office a balding constable was busily sorting paper clips, pins and short pencils into separate compartments of a wooden drawer, which had been placed upon a narrow table.

When Eva pushed her way through the double swing doors, the sergeant looked up to see who was entering. He immediately returned his attention to the ledger, ponderously writing, the pen noisily scratching its way across the broad page.

Eva was wearing her Salvation Army uniform, as she always did, no matter where she went, and she was fully aware that this was the reason for the officers' off-handed manner, which verged on rudeness.

She waited patiently for almost five minutes, during which time she was patently ignored by the two policemen. Deciding she had been tolerant for long enough, she said politely, 'I would like to be attended to, if you don't mind.'

Neither policemen replied, although the constable

seemed to find something amusing in the situation.

'Will I receive attention here, or shall I make my way along the corridor and find someone more senior to speak to?'

Without looking up, the sergeant said, 'Constable Waller, see what it is this young woman wants.'

'What this "young woman" wants is to see the officer in charge of your police station,' Eva said, more sharply than before. 'I have a serious complaint to make.'

'If it's anything to do with the violence that occurred during the last Salvation Army march through town, you're wasting your time,' said the sergeant. 'All the reports have already gone to the superintendent. Every one of them says the fault lay with the Salvation Army. If you hadn't chosen to march past a building site when the men were enjoying their midday break there would have been no trouble. No doubt the superintendent will ban any future marches. It's not before time, if you ask me.'

'I'm not asking you,' Eva retorted. 'And my coming here has nothing to do with a march. It concerns a far more serious matter – too serious for you to deal with, I should imagine. I wish to report a very serious attack on a young girl – on more than one young girl, in fact. I also have evidence of a trade in procuring young girls and shipping them off to the countries of Europe.'

The pen ceased its abrasive progress across the page and the constable forsook his time-wasting task. Both men were now giving her their full attention, but it was the sergeant who spoke.

'Are you the mother of the child you say was assaulted?'

'She has no mother – or father. She came to me for help.'

'She should have come straight to the police, not to you. Where is she now?'

'She's staying with me,' Eva said warily. She was not sure what action the police sergeant might decide to take.

'I can do nothing unless this girl comes here and makes a complaint personally. It's no good you coming in and giving me a second-hand story about something that might, or might not, have happened.'

'No one is reporting anything to *you*, Sergeant. I'll tell the full story to the officer in charge.'

'Well, seeing as there's no inspector here right now, that makes me the officer in charge – and I say there's nothing to be done until the alleged victim comes and makes a formal complaint, in person.'

'Very well, I'll return in the morning and speak to someone more senior then.'

Eva turned to go.

She had reached the door when the sergeant called to her. 'I suggest you take note of what I said to you about your marches – and about the band too. It's inciting trouble. We don't allow that sort of thing here in Plymouth. You and the others in this so-called "army" of yours can expect to be arrested the next time you take to the streets.'

19

When Eva returned to the Salvation Army house in the Barbican, she was still quietly fuming about the police sergeant's attitude and his refusal to accept the seriousness of her complaint.

Not that it surprised her. All over the country the police adopted a stance towards the Salvation Army that she found entirely incomprehensible. In London she had been present on various occasions when policemen stood doing nothing while a peaceful march of Salvation Army members was viciously broken up by hooligans and paid members of the Skeleton Army.

When faced with such attacks, Salvation Army members were under strict orders not to retaliate. While a few found such a policy impossible to sustain, most succeeded in 'turning the other cheek', even when they suffered severe injuries as a result.

Despite this, when the police finally moved in to break up disturbances, it was usually only Salvation Army members who were arrested and brought before the courts.

The charge against them was, in the main, 'obstruction', or some other trivial offence, but it did not prevent many being given prison sentences.

On the other hand, she could recall no occasion when the ruffians of the Skeleton Army and their supporters had been arrested.

Once inside the Barbican Refuge, Eva was surprised to find Grace had already returned. She was accompanied by Sally and a tall, distinguished-looking man, who was talking earnestly to Rachel.

Grace introduced the man to Eva as her uncle, Percy Mallet.

Taking Eva's hand, the man gave her a brief but friendly smile. 'I, too, briefly held the rank of captain, Miss Cassington. It was during the relief of Lucknow, when real officers were in desperately short supply. Your rank, I believe, was won in the equally unsavoury but far less publicised battlefields of the London streets?'

Releasing her hand, Percy Mallet became more solemn. 'I have just been listening to this unfortunate child's horrific story. I find it difficult to believe that such things can happen in our city.'

'It's happening in a great many cities throughout the land,' Eva replied grimly. 'While we continue to leave law and order in the hands of policemen lacking in vision and compassion I fear it will always be so.'

She told the story of her visit to Plymouth police station and the alderman frowned angrily.

'That sounds very like Sergeant Garrett. He should have been retired years ago. I think he's probably been in the force since it was founded. Plymouth has changed a great deal since then. Unfortunately,

Sergeant Garrett hasn't changed with it.' Suddenly brisk, he asked, 'Would you be available to come to police headquarters with me tomorrow morning, say . . . ten o'clock?'

Eva nodded. 'Any time to suit you, if you think it will achieve any purpose.'

'I'll bring a carriage and we'll go and speak to the superintendent who is in charge in the temporary absence of the chief constable. We won't take Rachel, or Sally. When it becomes necessary to interview them, someone can come here.'

Inclining his head at his niece, he said, 'I am most grateful to you for bringing this to my attention, Grace. We really should see more of each other. Why don't you and Alfie come to the house one Sunday evening . . . ?'

Still talking, Percy Mallett walked with Grace from the room.

As he left, Eva turned to the two girls. 'Well! Mrs Philpott has accomplished far more than I have this evening. But it doesn't matter *how* it comes about as long as something is done about Sidney Darling and his friends – and I have a feeling it will now.'

'What's going to happen to me when it's all over?' Rachel asked plaintively. 'Will I have to go away some-where?'

'Of course not,' Eva replied positively. 'You can stay here for as long as you wish. In fact, I'll be very glad of your help. I have an idea that once word of this affair gets around, we will be very busy here in Plymouth.'

20

Having someone wearing the uniform of an officer of the Salvation Army – especially when that someone was a woman – seated in his office was anathema to Police Superintendent Jeremiah Spindler.

However, he was careful not to allow his feelings to show. As well as being an alderman and chairman of the Police Authority, Percy Mallett was well respected in the Plymouth community and wielded considerable authority.

The senior policeman listened attentively to what the city elder had to say and maintained his silence until Captain Eva had told her story.

'There would appear to be a great many witnesses to the release of these girls from the Belgian fishing boat,' he said. 'Unfortunately, those on board are no longer within our jurisdiction. I presume there are no witnesses to the alleged defilement of this young girl?'

'I hardly think such attacks are carried out in public,' Eva retorted sarcastically. 'I can certainly testify to the girl's acute distress when we rescued her.'

'I have spoken to her too,' said Percy Mallett. 'I am in no doubt whatsoever that she is telling the truth.'

'No doubt you are right, Mr Mallett,' the policeman said. Observing the alderman's expression, he added hurriedly, 'Indeed, I am certain you are. However, it is essential in such matters to present a case to the court that will leave no doubt in the minds of judge or jury. Where is the girl now?'

'At a house in the Barbican that has been turned over to the Salvation Army. Some of the other girls are with her.'

'When can you bring her to the police station?'

Eva looked quickly at Percy Mallett. Correctly interpreting the message contained in the glance, he said, 'I think it would be better if you were to go along to the house and speak to her there, Superintendent. You will also have the other girls readily available to corroborate her story.'

Superintendent Spindler successfully hid his indignation at the other man's words. He was not in the habit of carrying out such duties personally.

'I'll send along my best inspector to interview these girls and to carry out an investigation of this man Darling. When we're quite certain of our facts I'll have a warrant sworn out for this man's arrest. You can rest assured I will take a personal interest in this matter and it will be pursued vigorously. Very vigorously indeed.'

'Good! We can't have such things going on in our town, can we? I'll leave it in your hands for now, Superintendent. You can be quite certain I too will be taking a keen interest in the progress you make in this disgraceful matter. I sincerely hope we might keep it from becoming public knowledge until you have made the necessary arrests.'

When Percy Mallett set Eva down at the house in Palace Lane, he said, 'I think you might find things will begin to happen now, Miss Cassington.'

'I don't doubt it, Mr Mallett – and I thank you on behalf of the girls. We shall certainly include you in our prayers tonight.'

'Your prayers will always be welcome, but the knowledge that these poor girls are in safe hands is thanks enough. Goodnight, Captain.'

Eva entered the house happy in the belief that she was beginning to succeed in the task for which she had been sent to Plymouth. She also entertained hopes that it might ultimately lead to a greater understanding between the police and the Salvation Army.

Only forty-eight hours after her meeting with Superintendent Spindler, all the hopes Eva had entertained of a change in her fortunes were effectively dashed.

A very efficient police inspector called at the Barbican Refuge and took statements from Rachel and the other girls. He expressed genuine sympathy and promised Captain Eva that Sid Darling would be arrested swiftly and brought to justice for all he had done.

A warrant was duly sworn out for Darling's arrest. However, when the police raided the house in Mary Street he was not there and Mother Darling informed them she had no knowledge of his whereabouts.

She was questioned closely about her part in the offences for which her son was wanted, but she was adamant that he was solely responsible for letting out the upstairs rooms. She claimed she suffered from arthritis in her knees, which prevented her from climbing the stairs, and she had no knowledge of anything that went on there.

Unfortunately, there was nothing in the statements the inspector had taken that would incriminate her, so Mother Darling remained free – at least, for the foreseeable future.

But worse was to come for Captain Eva and the Plymouth corps of the Salvation Army.

That Sunday, she and Captain Wardle were to lead their followers through the streets of Plymouth in what would be the biggest parade they had ever staged in the town. The event had been organised to celebrate the second anniversary of the establishment of the Plymouth movement and had been publicised well in advance.

The local Salvation band, to which Ethan belonged, would be augmented by musicians from the nearby seaside resort of Torquay. They would head a procession of Salvationists gathered from many Devon and Cornwall towns.

However, in view of the publicity the parade had received, it was doubtful it would be allowed to pass off without incident.

The Skeleton Army had become more effectively organised of late. It was even producing its own newspaper, rather unimaginatively called *The Skeleton*, which was distributed throughout the country.

The newspaper had published details of the forthcoming Plymouth march and called upon its own 'soldiers' to come to the town. They were asked to 'help clear the streets of these fanatics and blasphemers who are bringing the Christian religion into ridicule'.

Such an article was a blatant incitement to riot. As

such, it was inconceivable that the police were not aware of it. Yet the only action they took was aimed at the Salvation Army. Superintendent Spindler sent a strongly worded letter to Captain Wardle, instructing that the route taken for their march must not include any major thoroughfares. The superintendent warned that any riotous or provocative behaviour would not be tolerated.

By now there were only five girls, including Rachel, remaining at the Barbican Refuge. All asked if they might take part in the march. However, Eva refused, insisting they must remain in the house.

When one of the girls questioned her decision, Eva pointed out that they were not soldiers of the Salvation Army. Indeed they had not even asked to be considered as recruits. Furthermore, all were strangers to Plymouth, and if violence erupted – as it undoubtedly would – the parade would be forced to scatter, and not knowing the city, the girls would not know where to run and be at the mercy of the crowd. Eva felt they had suffered enough already.

Consequently, when the day arrived and the soldiers of the Salvation Army were making their way to the gathering point outside Central Hall, none of the girls was with them. For this, at least, Eva would later be grateful.

21

Some indication of what the parading members of the Salvation Army could expect came even before they formed up outside their headquarters in readiness to commence the march.

As uniformed men and women arrived at the entrance to Central Street they were heckled and jostled by a growing number of ruffians. Singing, jeering and shouting obscenities at the Salvationists, the hooligans singled out the young, uniformed girls as particular targets.

The two Salvation Army captains leading the march went among their members, doing their best to bolster morale by reminding the 'soldiers' that they were fighting the Lord's battle, on His behalf.

Meanwhile, inside Central Hall, more experienced Army colleagues were laying out bandages, salve, soap and towels, knowing all would be needed before the day was over.

Eventually, some three hundred uniformed Salvationists had gathered. They were standing about in nervous but determined groups when Captain Wardle called for them to form ranks. When this order was carried out to his satisfaction, the band struck up a suitably stirring martial tune and the celebration march got under way.

The jeering crowd at the end of the street was more than a hundred strong now. Although it was noisy, it made no attempt to prevent the procession, bound for Plymouth's famous Hoe, from leaving Central Street. Indeed, it parted to allow the Salvationists through, falling in behind them.

The Salvation Army carried banners of blue, red and gold. Held on high, the colours represented the purity of Heaven, the blood of Christ, and the fire of the Holy Ghost.

The opposition had banners too. Made from black cloth, each carried a crude painting of a skeleton.

'What are they playing at?' Eva spoke in an aside to Captain Wardle as the Skeleton Army fell in behind the marching Salvationists. The two officers were marching side by side, between the band and the uniformed marchers. 'Why did they let us through and not attack us there and then?'

'We are too close to home.' The senior captain had taken part in marches in many of Britain's towns and cities. He was no stranger to violence and the tactics of those who used it.

'Too many of us could have escaped back to the loft or the hall. They'll wait until we're too far away to scuttle back. They've planned this very carefully, Eva. They'll hit us hard when they feel they have the greatest advantage. My feeling is that they'll wait until we reach the Hoe. There's nowhere to hide there. We'll need to trust in the shelter of the Lord.'

But Captain Wardle was wrong in his surmise of where the attack from the Skeleton Army would take place.

Sally was anxious to watch and listen to Ethan and his fellow bandsmen, and she had settled Ruth down before hurrying off to follow the parade. As she watched Ethan set off from Central Hall with the others, leading the parade, she felt a proprietorial pride.

However, as the procession approached a main junction in the centre of town, Sally sensed increasing tension among the Skeleton Army.

The letter from the Plymouth police chief had warned against taking the parade along any of the town's main roads but Captain Wardle had little choice but to cross some of the main thoroughfares. It was now, as the cavalcade reached one of the town's busiest junctions, that the Skeleton Army and its followers struck.

It was a spot where four roads met, and on a weekday it would have been crowded with town traffic. Although today was Sunday, it was still busy, but not everyone on the streets was going about their lawful business. A number of heavy farm carts, pulled by patient draw-horses, were waiting close to the junction in each of the four streets, and the pavements were crowded with pedestrians. One look at them was enough for Sally to know that this was where the Skeleton Army was going to mount its attack. Among the crowd she recognised many of the rag, tag and bobtail who frequented the public houses in the Barbican.

Concerned for Ethan and the others, Sally pushed her way through the men about her in a bid to warn Captain Eva. She was already too late.

Together with those waiting at the junction, the

members of the Skeleton Army who had followed the
parade from Central Street now surged forward to
surround the men and women of the Salvation Army.

At the same time, the horses hitched to the waiting
wagons were whipped up. The heavy wagons trundled
forward in a simple but carefully planned manoeuvre.
Three wagons on each road effectively sealed off the
exits from the wide junction. The Salvation Army cavalcade was trapped inside, together with a large number
of the Skeleton Army and its supporters.

Fighting broke out immediately as the Skeleton Army
struck out indiscriminately at uniformed men and women
– and children.

At the same time, other Skeleton Army members
climbed upon the wagons from outside the hastily
formed arena, revealing another facet of the careful
planning that had gone into ambushing the Salvation
Army procession.

The wagons were loaded with a wide variety of
missiles. The more innocuous were rotten eggs and vege-
tables; far more lethal were cobblestones and chunks
of wood, some of the latter having nails hammered
through them.

As the missiles flew through the air towards the
trapped 'soldiers of Christ', Sally crawled on hands
and knees beneath one of the wagons, heading for the
spot where she had last glimpsed Ethan.

She emerged in a noisy, struggling mass of humanity,
where the screams of the younger Salvation Army girls
mingled with jubilant shouts from followers of the
Skeleton Army.

Although members of the Salvation Army were
expected to 'turn the other cheek' when faced with

violence, a number were fighting back and giving a very good account of themselves.

One of these was Ethan.

Looking furious, he was actually taking the fight to the opposition. When Sally glimpsed him amidst the mêlée, he was throwing punches at a Skeleton Army supporter, who was desperately trying to protect himself as he retreated from the angry young fisherman. But Ethan was lost to view again almost immediately as a number of Skeleton Army supporters swarmed around him.

Sally fought her way towards him, clawing, kicking and making full use of her elbows and knees.

Along the way she tripped over the broken pole of a Salvation Army banner. She picked it up and wielded it to considerable effect and eventually reached Ethan.

He was still on his feet and fighting furiously, but his face was bloody and he was hopelessly outnumbered.

Sally laid about her with renewed vigour and for a moment or two the pair held their own against their opponents. It was unlikely they would have been able to hold the Skeleton Army supporters at bay for much longer, but succour was at hand.

It arrived from a totally unexpected quarter and in a bizarre manner. A circus, which had been touring France, had landed at Plymouth's Millbay docks that morning, but no trains were available to take it on until the following day. The owner had decided to take his circus to the open fields to the north-east of the town.

The circus owner was fully aware that he would require permission from the chief constable before parading his animals through the town. However, he thought the police could hardly object if he was merely *leading* his animals through the town to the fields, where they would remain until the train was available.

It was an opportunity to give the townsfolk a preview of what they could expect when the circus returned to give a performance in the summer. It would thus provide the circus with useful free publicity.

Unaware of what was happening at the junction in the heart of the town, the circus hands were leading horses, camels and elephants, together with caged lions and tigers, in the direction of the fracas.

Along the pavements, clowns, fully painted, kept pace with the circus procession, handing out sweets from gaily painted and be-ribboned buckets, together with notices of the next year's performances, to all the children they met. Also striding along were men dressed in bright top hats and jackets, atop incredibly high stilts hidden beneath long, striped trousers.

It was the elephants that proved to be the undoing of the Skeleton Army. As the procession ambled towards the wagons fencing in the fighting mob, one of the horses spotted them – and promptly bolted. As a second startled horse followed the first, bystanders and brawlers fled from the affray and ran for safety.

When one of the elephants trumpeted in fright, causing the tigers to roar, there was no controlling the horses. Soon everyone, Salvation Army and Skeleton Army followers alike, was fleeing from the scene, all thoughts of battle at an end. On their way they took the stilt legs from beneath the balancing circus hands, engendering more mayhem.

It was now, belatedly, that the police appeared on the scene. Many men and women were too badly hurt to run away; some were sheltering in shop doorways, others simply sitting on the kerbside, nursing their injuries.

The junction was strewn with litter and missiles of all types. Salvation Army bonnets, banners, broken band instruments and every imaginable variety of rotten vegetable.

The newly arrived police made six arrests that day.

All were members of the Salvation Army and among their number were Captains Wardle and Cassington.

22

Sally witnessed the arrest of Captain Eva, but it was done with so little fuss that she did not immediately realise what was happening.

She was walking back to Central Hall with Ethan. His face was bruised and grazed and he wanted to clean up before returning home.

Along the way Sally discovered the reason for Ethan's extreme anger. One of the Skeleton Army had snatched his precious flute, flung it to the ground and stamped on it. Ethan admitted the incident had made him go berserk for a while.

Aware of what the instrument and his music meant to him, Sally was truly sympathetic.

They were walking along the pavement, part of a long, straggling procession of bedraggled and battered Salvation Army members and their sympathisers. All were making for the sanctuary of their headquarters in Central Street.

In sharp contrast to the scene immediately prior to the attack, there were many policemen in evidence now.

Walking in pairs, they kept pace with the Salvationists.

Most of the policemen maintained a disapproving silence, but a few directed jocular, albeit mocking comments at the retreating 'soldiers'.

Because of this, nobody took very much notice at first when a sergeant and two colleagues began talking to Eva. It was not until she left her companions and turned back, accompanied by the policemen, that they realised she was being arrested.

There was an immediate protest from the Salvationists but other policemen moved in to prevent Captain Eva and her escort from being followed.

A few of the uniformed Salvation Army members, frustrated by the events of the day, protested vigorously. A series of scuffles broke out and more arrests were made.

Ethan wanted to go to Eva's aid, but Sally dissuaded him. She managed to convince him that it was not what Eva would want.

When Eva passed her by, Sally called, 'What are they arresting you for?'

Tight-lipped, Eva replied, 'I don't know. You'll need to ask the sergeant.'

'That's enough of that,' the sergeant said sternly to Sally. 'Miss Cassington is under arrest. I'll have no talking to her.'

Sally was still standing looking after the departing quartet when Eva turned around. Shaking off the restraining hand of one of the policemen, she called, 'Sally, tell them at headquarters what's happened. They must send someone along to the Refuge to take care of the girls . . .'

Two policemen now took hold of her and propelled

her along the road, but she had been reassured by Sally's wave of acknowledgement and put up no resistance.

'What do you think will happen to Captain Eva?' asked Ethan.

Sally had speeded up her pace and he put the question to her as they began to overtake other Salvationists talking excitedly about this latest incident in an eventful day.

'Who knows?' Sally replied. 'It depends on the reason they've arrested her. As far as I know she's done nothing at all to break the law. The trouble back there was caused by the Skeleton Army – but I didn't see any of *them* arrested.'

'Can't we do something to try to get her released?' Ethan queried.

'I'm going to do my best,' replied Sally, 'once I've seen you treated and cleaned up and have found someone to go and take charge of the Refuge. I shall go and speak to Grace Philpott. Her uncle is chairman of the police authority and he's met Captain Eva. Perhaps he can do something to get her released.'

Grace Philpott dashed any idea of asking her uncle to help Captain Eva on this occasion.

'I know he won't be able to do anything, dear,' she said. 'It's not even worth asking him.'

Sally had called on Grace in the flat that she and Alfie occupied above the pie shop.

'He made it quite plain to me when we were discussing the problems of the Salvation Army,' Grace explained. 'He's able to take up matters that the police should be dealing with, but he can't interfere when someone's been arrested and will be appearing before a magistrate. Even so, I'll go to see him the first opportunity I get tomorrow, to let him know what's been going on.'

Standing up, she began pacing the room. 'The important thing right now is to see that the girls at the Refuge don't fly into a panic when they hear Captain Eva has been arrested. I'm especially worried about Rachel. She was just beginning to regain some confidence. I'll go and see if there's anything I can do.'

Alfie had been listening in silence to the conversation between his wife and Sally. Now he spoke for the first time. 'You don't want to go getting yourself involved in such goings on, Grace,' he cautioned. 'Leave it to the Salvation Army. They know what they're doing.'

'We're already involved,' retorted Grace. 'We have been since I took Uncle Percy around there and we met that poor little girl.' Suddenly conciliatory, she rested a hand on her husband's arm. 'I've got to go and see what I can do to help them, Alfie. You know that. If you're perfectly honest with yourself, you wouldn't want me to be any other way – and the reason I love you so much is because you *do* understand such things.'

Secretly pleased at her show of affection, Alfie said gruffly, 'Well . . . all right then, but don't forget we have a business to run. If we don't put that first you won't be able to help anyone.'

'Of course, but don't worry if I'm not home tonight. If Captain Eva isn't set free, someone will need to stay with those girls. I think I'm the best one to do it. Just get everything ready for the morning and I'll be in the shop at the usual time to begin work.'

Sally expected Alfie to be angry with Grace's decision, but he had been married to her for many years. He knew there were occasions when he might argue and win the day – and others when he needed to bow to the inevitable.

This was one of the latter occasions. He gave in graciously.

23

When Percy Mallett called at the house on the Barbican, Grace had the girls in the kitchen, trying their hand at cooking. They appeared to be enjoying themselves immensely.

He explained his presence by saying he happened to be passing. Having heard earlier in the day of the clash between the Salvation Army and its opponents, he thought he would call in to check Captain Eva was all right.

'But what are *you* doing here?' he asked his niece.

'I'm here because Captain Eva has been arrested. She's being held in the police cells. I was going to come to tell you about it later today.'

'Arrested? On what charge?' Percy Mallett was horrified.

'You'd better ask Sally. She was there.'

Sally had made her way to the Refuge after returning home and boiling a couple of eggs for Ruth's Sunday lunch. She now told the Police Authority chairman of the attack upon the Salvation Army parade by the

Skeleton Army; of its succour from an unexpected quarter – and of Captain Eva's subsequent arrest.

'I've since heard that Captain Wardle was arrested too, and some of the others. I hope there's a good doctor down at the police station. A few of the Salvation Army were quite badly hurt.'

'Where were the police while all this was going on?' Percy Mallet asked, tight-faced.

Sally said bitterly, 'I never saw one of 'em until it was all over. When they did come they arrested the wrong people. Those they should have taken in are them who belonged to the Skeleton Army. The men who were paid by the landlords of the pubs to cause trouble. But I didn't see one of *them* arrested.'

'I'm afraid I can do nothing to help Captain Eva immediately, but I'll call for a full report on the whole incident,' said Percy Mallett. 'I can assure you of that.'

Turning to his niece, he said, 'In the meantime, is there anything I can do to help you, Grace?'

'Yes.' Pointing to Sally, she said, 'You can give this young lady a ride to her home in your carriage. She has a sick sister to take care of – and she needs to be in work on time in the morning if we're not to upset Alfie. He's been very patient so far, but he won't be if we start losing business.'

It was the first time Sally had ever ridden in a carriage. It was only for a short distance, but she enjoyed the experience. On the way to Pin's Lane, Percy questioned her, establishing that she was an orphan.

'That's most sad,' he said with genuine sympathy. 'Is that how you became involved with the Salvation Army?'

'No.' Sally told him about meeting with Ethan and of his part in helping to save the small girl who had fallen in Sutton harbour. 'Ethan enjoys playing in the band,' she boasted proudly. 'At least, he *did*.'

Explaining the destruction of Ethan's flute by the Skeleton Army supporter, she added, 'I don't know what he'll do now. He really only joined the Salvation Army so he could play his flute. He loves music. I doubt if he'll stay with them if he can't be in their band.'

Warming to her subject, Sally went on to tell how Ethan and his family had played a leading part in rescuing Rachel and the other girls.

'This Ethan sounds quite an exceptional young man,' commented Percy Mallett.

'He is,' agreed Sally.

In that moment she realised she really meant it. She had grown very fond of Ethan without ever intending to allow it to happen – or even being aware that it had.

In the pie shop the next morning, Alfie was having a grumble because Grace had stayed at the Refuge overnight.

'Do you realise it's the first time we've spent a night away from each other in all the years we've been married, Grace? I rue the day you got mixed up with this Salvation Army lot – and I put the blame for that firmly on you, young lady.' Alfie glared at Sally. 'I took pity on you and gave you a job, and this is the thanks I get for it?'

'*You* gave her a job? I seem to remember that was *my* idea. At the time you were threatening to take her head off with that meat cleaver of yours. Anyway, I'm glad I've been able to help those poor young girls. You are too, Alfie Philpott, so just stop your grumbling and pass me some more of that meat when you've finished cutting it up. You'll be even more pleased this afternoon. I've asked one of the Salvation Army women to bring Rachel here. You'll like her, Alfie, *really* like her, but I don't want you grumbling at her, even if you don't mean it. She's been through a lot, that poor girl, and has no one she can turn to. No mother, or father. You just be nice to her, you hear?'

Sally felt a twinge of jealousy as she listened to Grace talk about Rachel. She too was an orphan. She wondered whether Grace had forgotten.

She felt guilty almost immediately for her feelings. Grace – and Alfie – were fully aware of her situation and they had both been very good to her because of it. They were kind and caring people. Sally told herself she was glad Rachel had found someone like the hard-working couple to take an interest in her.

After all, she had Ruth to talk to when things went wrong. Even when Ruth was having one of her bad days, she still had someone to care for and someone who cared for her.

Setting off on her first errand of the day, Sally told herself she would not be selfish and unreasonable about Rachel. Instead, she would do all she could to make the younger girl realise there were many people who cared for her.

24

With the exception of Captains Wardle and Cassington, the Salvationists arrested after the aborted parade were dealt with quickly and relatively leniently.

Found guilty of a variety of charges, which included 'obstruction' and committing a 'breach of the peace', they were either given a nominal fine or bound over to keep the peace.

However, when the two captains were placed in the dock they were jointly charged with the more serious offence of being engaged in an 'unlawful assembly'. Both Salvationists were aware they faced the prospect of imprisonment.

They pleaded 'Not Guilty' but when the time came for them to present their defence, Captain Wardle refused to say anything.

When the magistrates' clerk demanded a reason, Wardle claimed that entering a defence would be a waste of his own and everybody else's time. He pointed out that the magistrate dealing with the case was a member of a prominent family of local brewers. He would therefore be biased against a defendant belonging to an organisation dedicated to promoting teetotalism.

Angrily, the magistrate told Captain Wardle that his duty was to administer the laws of the land. The Salvationist was in court for breaking those laws. He would be dealt with accordingly, without fear or favour.

Still red-faced from what he considered to be Captain Wardle's impertinence, the magistrate asked Eva whether she had anything to say in her own defence.

'Yes, your worship. We were none of us involved in any form of unlawful assembly. Captain Wardle and I were leading a parade to the Hoe, in order to hold an open-air service.'

'I go to a church service every Sunday, Miss Cassington, but I don't take a band along with me. Why did you consider that to be necessary?'

'Music is a God-given blessing, sir. One we wish to share with everyone.'

'Nonsense! You must have known it would attract curious and idle persons who had nothing better to do than cause mischief and disturb the peace of the town.'

'They are the very people we try to attract. It gives us the opportunity to bring them to God and show them the right path to his divine grace.'

'Nevertheless, you are a minority religious group, Miss Cassington. In this world, the minority must bow to the wishes of the majority, would you not agree?'

'Most certainly not, sir! The vast majority of people in this world of ours are sinners. Should I become a sinner too? Or should I try to show them the error of their ways and bring them to God? You surely must agree my way is better, sir?'

Her words brought an outbreak of laughter from the

public gallery and a spontaneous burst of applause, which died abruptly when the magistrate turned a stern gaze upon those responsible.

'I will not have music-hall behaviour in my court. Another such outburst and I will have you all removed. Now, does either defendant have anything of relevance to add to what has already been said?'

'Only the hope that God's wisdom may guide your judgement,' said Eva. 'And to tell you that whatever your decision, I will pray for you.'

The magistrate leaned over his bench and held a low-voiced conversation with his clerk, which lasted for some minutes. There appeared to be some disagreement between the two men.

Eventually, the magistrate silenced his clerk with a dismissive wave of his hand. The clerk sat back in his chair, shaking his head in silent disapproval.

Returning his attention to the two Salvation Army officers standing in the dock, the magistrate said, 'I regret I am unable to inform you that there has been any divine intercession on your behalf. Neither did I feel it necessary to seek the Lord's guidance in this matter. The law of the land is quite clear.'

Clasping his hands together and placing his elbows on the bench in front of him, the magistrate looked sternly at the two defendants. 'You are both senior members of the organisation to which you belong. The chief constable made it perfectly clear to you in writing, through one of his senior officers, that you were to keep your parade off the main roads of this city. You flagrantly disregarded that directive. The result was that law-abiding citizens were obliged to witness the disgraceful scenes of violence that took place yesterday.

Such a blatant disregard for law and order will not be tolerated by this court. You will both go to prison for a month. I trust . . .'

The remainder of the magistrate's words were lost in a roar of protest from the public gallery.

The uniformed members of the Salvation Army who packed the public seats stood up, stamping their feet angrily and shouting their disapproval at the imposition of a prison sentence on the two popular officers.

For some minutes the magistrate and his clerk tried in vain to restore order.

The spectators continued their racket long after Captain Eva and the officer commanding the Plymouth corps of the Salvation Army had been taken off to the cells beneath the courtroom. Eventually, the angry magistrate was forced to adjourn all further proceedings for the day.

Rising to his feet and closely followed by his clerk, he retired from the courtroom via a door behind the magistrate's chair, pursued by the booing of those in the public gallery.

When the magistrate had gone, the ushers and a number of policemen began clearing the court of the angry, shocked and temporarily leaderless Salvationists.

25

Sally heard the news of Captain Eva's imprisonment as she was returning from one of her deliveries. She met a group of Salvation Army women who had just left the magistrates' court. They were now heading for the Army headquarters to break the news to Captain Wardle's wife and to arrange for someone to take over the duties of the two jailed officers.

Sally was utterly dismayed. Not because someone she knew had been sent to prison – such an occurrence was by no means unusual in the Barbican. Indeed many of her neighbours in Pin's Lane had served sentences in Plymouth's gaol. Most were criminals and it was an accepted hazard of their way of life.

Captain Eva most certainly was *not* a criminal.

Her sole aim in life was to improve the lot of those no one else would help. She did not deserve to be thrown into prison.

The very thought of Captain Eva having to spend a month in a prison cell thoroughly upset Sally. She was still fighting back tears when she reached the pie shop.

'Ah! There you are, Sally. I've got a nice order for you to deliver to Customs House. It's not very far from where you live, so, if you like, you can pop in to see that poor sister of yours. Take her one of my fruit specials. It might tempt her to eat.' Grace had learned much more about the home circumstances of her young employee, and she would occasionally give Sally small treats to take to Ruth.

She was busily kneading dough as she talked and had hardly looked up when Sally came in. Rachel was happily helping her, but she was not as preoccupied as Grace. She realised that Sally was very close to tears.

'What's the matter, Sally? Has something happened to upset you?'

Grace looked up now and immediately stopped pounding the soft mountain of dough on the table in front of her.

'What is it, girl?'

Behind her, Alfie stopped raking out ashes from the fire beneath the large oven, in order that he too might hear Sally's reply.

'It's Captain Eva. She's been sent to prison.'

The disbelieving silence that followed her words was broken by Grace. 'What are you talking about, Sally? What nonsense is this?'

Grace rested flour-whitened hands on hips and Rachel stared in ashen-faced disbelief as Sally repeated what the Salvation Army girls had told her.

'I don't believe it. People aren't sent to prison just for parading in the streets.' Grace was having great difficulty accepting what Sally had told her.

'They kept her in the police station all last night,' Rachel pointed out.

'That was different,' said Grace. 'That was just the police being spiteful. But prison . . . ! She's done nothing to be sent there. Are you certain you've got it right, Sally?'

'That's what the Salvation Army women said and they should know. They were in court when the magistrate sent Captain Eva down. Captain Wardle was sent to jail as well.'

Brushing flour and dough from her hands, Grace picked up a towel to complete the job. Unfastening her apron, she said, 'Alfie, hurry up with that fire. When you've done you can set to work on this dough and take over the baking for the rest of the day. No . . . don't argue, you can do it every bit as good as me, when you want to.'

'Where are you going, Grace?'

'To the Refuge, to see what's happening there. Those girls need someone sensible to take care of them, Alfie. Captain Eva's not there to do it, so someone else must. If they can't find anyone else, I'll take the job on myself.'

'What about me?' asked Rachel. 'What will happen to me now?'

'You'll stay here while the shop's open. If you haven't heard anything from me by this evening, Sally will bring you to the Refuge. Is that all right with you, Sally? You can leave work early, so it needn't make you late getting home.'

Sally nodded.

'Right, I'll be off then. Alfie, before you do anything else you'd better take out the pies that are already in the oven, otherwise they'll be overdone.'

After issuing this directive, Grace hurried from the kitchen. She left Alfie, his hands black with ash and coal, looking after her, thoroughly bewildered.

'It's all right, Alfie. I'll take out the pies,' said Sally. 'You be cleaning yourself up so you can get on with the cooking. Rachel will serve in the shop when I go out. I'll help her when I'm not delivering – and she can always call out to you if there's something she doesn't understand.'

'There are far too many chiefs and only one indian around here,' Alfie grumbled peevishly. 'You sure you wouldn't like me to put on a song-and-dance act while I'm doing everything else?'

Despite his sarcastic comments, Alfie hurriedly cleaned himself up and changed into a clean striped apron before taking on the task abandoned so hurriedly by Grace.

Outside in the shop, Sally helped a nervous Rachel to serve a woman customer. When she had left the shop, Sally spoke quietly to the younger girl, so that Alfie would not hear.

'You mustn't take too much notice of Alfie when he grumbles about something. Grace never does. He's as soft as butter, really – and just as generous as Grace. He doesn't want everyone to realise it, that's all.'

26

Grace returned to the shop just before it closed for the day. She had helped to draw up an 'arrangement' for the Refuge and the girls who lived there with Captain Wardle's wife.

It was agreed that for as long as Captain Eva was in prison, two or three Salvation Army girls would remain at the Refuge during daylight hours. Grace would take over from them each evening, cook an evening meal for the girls and sleep in the house overnight.

When Alfie protested that he needed feeding too, Grace retorted that he could 'feed his face' during the day. Anyway, she added, he would benefit from losing a few pounds from around his waistline.

In a kindlier vein, she added, 'It will only be for a month, Alfie. You wouldn't want to leave young Rachel and the others all night without having anyone responsible looking after them, would you now?'

Alfie's muttered reply was unintelligible, but Grace soothed his hurt feelings by giving him a warm hug. 'You won't be neglected, Alfie, I promise, but it's nice

to know you'll miss me. Some husbands would be only
too pleased to get rid of their wives for a few hours.'

Embarrassed but pleased by his wife's show of
affection, Alfie broke free and made an unnecessary
show of tidying cooking implements in the already
neat kitchen.

'You can come to the Refuge with me when I go,'
Grace said to Rachel. 'It will save Sally a walk.'

'Can I come back here with you tomorrow?' Rachel
asked eagerly.

'You're welcome to come here as often as you like,'
said Grace, beaming at the young girl. 'You can go out
with Sally sometimes when she's delivering, too. That
way you'll get to know a bit of the town. It hasn't been
a happy place for you so far, but you'll like Plymouth
when you get to know it, I know you will.'

That evening, in the room at Pin's Lane, Sally was
busily ironing the clothes she had washed the day
before. She and Ruth were talking about the prison
sentence imposed upon Captain Eva. Ruth agreed with
her sister that it was totally unjustified.

Suddenly, there was a knock at the door, startling
both girls. When Sally opened the door she was both
surprised and pleased to see Ethan outside. She invited
him in and they all discussed the events of the day for
some time before Ethan declared he did not wish to tire
Ruth by remaining talking for too long. He suggested
Sally should walk with him as far as the harbour. He
explained that he and his brothers had been painting
their fishing boat and he would like to know what Sally
thought of the new colour.

'That's a novel excuse for getting a girl to go out for

a walk with you, if ever I heard one!' Ruth gave Ethan a tired but understanding smile. 'Go along, Sally.'

'I've still got some ironing to do,' Sally said. 'And I need to be in the shop early tomorrow morning. I doubt if Grace will be back from the Refuge at the crack of dawn and I can't expect poor old Alfie to do everything by himself.'

'Don't make feeble excuses just because you feel you shouldn't be leaving me,' said Ruth. 'You want to go out with Ethan, really, and the ironing isn't going to run away. You can do it another day. Anyway, you'll only keep me awake with your chatter and I'm feeling tired. Off you go now.'

'Well . . . if you're *really* tired, I'll go.'

Sally tried to sound reluctant to leave her sister, but she had already placed the flat-iron on the hob and was stuffing the unironed clothes away in a drawer.

Two minutes later she was walking on the damp cobblestones of the sloping Pin's Lane, heading towards the harbour.

'What colour have you painted your boat?' Sally asked, as they turned the corner into Southside Street, heading for the Barbican.

'Bright blue. We've only just begun to paint it today and haven't got very far,' admitted Ethan. 'But I wanted to speak to you about something and I didn't want to mention it in front of Ruth.'

Intrigued, Sally asked what it was that was such a secret.

'I called in to see Uncle Charlie before I came up to your room,' exclaimed Ethan. 'He told me someone had been to the house earlier today, asking questions about you.'

'Why should anyone want to know about *me*?' Sally was puzzled. 'Who was it?'

'It was a woman,' Charlie said. 'She didn't give him a name – and she didn't know yours, until Charlie told her. She wanted to know if "the girl who worked at Alfie Philpott's pie shop lived in the house". When Charlie asked if she meant you – Sally – she didn't seem too sure. He said you lived there, but weren't in.'

There was a lull in the conversation as they drew back in the narrow street to allow a cart laden with fish from the harbour to rumble past.

'Charlie said she asked questions about which room you lived in, and whether your ma and pa lived there with you. By this time he was getting a bit suspicious. He told her you didn't have any parents, but he didn't mention Ruth.'

'Who'd want to know about me – and why?'

'Well, that's the reason I didn't want to say anything that might worry Ruth. Charlie said that when he was talking to the woman, he felt he'd seen her before, somewhere. It wasn't until she'd gone off that he remembered where it had been. He saw her once at the Albion, just along the road from here. She was there with Sid Darling. She's one of his women. Charlie believes she has one of the rooms in Mother Darling's house, in Mary Street.'

Sally felt her stomach contract in sudden fear. 'You mean . . . Sid Darling has found out I was the one who told on him and he sent her to find out about me?'

'Can you think of any other reason why this particular

woman should come to Pin's Lane asking so many questions about you?'

Sally shook her head. 'What do you think I ought to do?'

'I don't know, but it worries me, Sally. Couldn't you go off and stay with someone for a while? To the house run by Captain Eva, perhaps – or with the Philpotts?'

'I couldn't leave Ruth. Anyway, Grace is staying at the Refuge until Captain Eva comes out of prison. I can't go anywhere.'

'Then you'll just have to be careful when you're not working. I'll ask Uncle Charlie to keep an eye on you. He wouldn't be much good if Sid Darling came to the house, but he could shout loud enough to attract attention. That might be enough to frighten him off. He wouldn't want the police to catch up with him.'

'Do you think he's likely to come to the house?' Sally was genuinely frightened.

'I don't think anyone knows what Sid Darling is likely to do,' replied Ethan. 'What I *will* do is speak to my pa and brothers about it. Between us we should be able to call around to your place now and then, when you're home, to make sure you're all right.'

'Thank you . . . but I'd feel a lot better if the police arrested him.'

'Of course you would – and they will.' In a rare gesture of affection, Ethan reached for her hand and held it. 'In the meantime, I'll spend all the time I can with you. I'd like that, anyway.'

Retaining a hold on his hand, Sally realised that she would like that too. Life for her would be taking an upward turn if only the shadow of Sid Darling was not lurking in the background . . .

27

In the few days before Christmas, Alfie and Grace Philpott did more business than at any time the pair could remember. It seemed their pies had earned a reputation as the finest in Plymouth.

On one occasion a huge order came in for pies with which to feed the passengers of a large steamship. The vessel had put in to Plymouth Sound to shelter from a brief but fierce easterly gale.

On days such as this, Sally and Rachel helped in the shop and kitchen, while the delivery of the pies was made by Ethan and his youngest brother, Joe. Prevented from fishing by the inclement weather, they were happy to earn money in any way they could.

Grace was working very hard, her time divided between the shop and the Refuge. Then, two days before Christmas, Captain Wardle and Eva were released from prison on the orders of the Home Secretary.

Their release had been prompted by a public outcry against the harsh and frequently illogical sentences handed out to members of the Salvation Army. The

Plymouth courts were not the only ones in the land seen to be victimising them.

In an increasing number of cases, the convictions were contrary to the evidence presented to the courts.

Particular disquiet had been voiced in London about the punishment meted out to Salvation Army members in the courts of Devon towns, Plymouth being just one of them.

Percy Mallett had himself written to the Home Secretary. He protested that such blatant miscarriages of justice were bringing the law itself into disrepute. He pointed out that the law-abiding citizens of his town were losing all respect for those whose duty it was to maintain law and order.

His letter was just one of many received by the Home Secretary from persons of authority throughout the land.

Many more had aired their misgivings through the columns of national and provincial newspapers. There were a few dissenting letter writers, but a huge majority expressed support for the aims of the Salvation Army, even when they did not always approve of the methods used in achieving them.

Alfie was delighted and not a little relieved to have Grace home with him once more, day *and* night. However, she still maintained a considerable interest in the well-being of the girls in the Refuge.

She and Alfie were both very taken with young Rachel. The young orphan, in her turn, had become increasingly reliant upon Grace.

Captain Eva had been aware since their first meeting of Rachel's workhouse-induced dislike of anything that even remotely resembled an institution. Therefore, when it was suggested to Rachel by Eva and Grace that she should move in with Grace and Alfie 'on an experimental basis' she was happy to agree.

The recently released Salvation Army captain insisted, however, that Rachel must spend at least part of Christmas Day with the other girls at the Refuge. She also wanted her to accompany them to one of the Army's meetings in Central Hall on that day.

Rachel was quite happy with this arrangement. She was also delighted when Grace insisted that the girls and Captain Eva should come to the flat above the shop. Here, albeit in grossly overcrowded conditions, they would enjoy a Christmas dinner that she would prepare and cook for them.

Sally was invited too. She and Rachel had become firm friends and Rachel implored her to accept the invitation, but Sally had already agreed to visit Ethan's home. Besides, she did not want to leave Ruth alone for too long on this special day.

Ruth did not agree. She told Sally she should accept both invitations and not be tied by her.

'I'll be fine at home by myself, Sal,' she said for the third time that evening. 'I'm quite happy being at home by myself every other day. Besides, I'll spend most of the day sleeping, you know that. It will be miserable at home here, having to tiptoe around so as not to wake me. Especially when all your friends are somewhere else, enjoying themselves.'

Sally was aware of the truth of Ruth's statement. Her sister slept for much of the time now. Nevertheless, Sally had no intention of leaving her alone for too long on Christmas Day.

Ruth had grown progressively weaker in recent weeks. Although Sally was reluctant to face the truth, she realised that this might well be the last Christmas she would have with Ruth.

'I *like* being with you, Ruth,' she insisted. 'Besides, I'll be out for quite a while when I go to meet Ethan's family. That's going to be nerve-racking enough. I don't think I could face going out twice.'

'What are you going to wear, Sal?'

It was a question Sally had spent much time pondering over in recent days. In an effort to find something suitable she had been looking in the various shops she passed whilst out delivering pies.

'I've seen a dress in a pawnshop in the high street that might do. It looks as though it should be a good fit and it isn't too expensive.'

'What's it made of?'

Sally frowned. 'I don't know. Cotton, I suppose.'

'You should have something better than cotton if you want to impress Ethan's ma. You could wear my silk dress – but it would be too small for you.'

Ruth struggled to move higher up in the bed, but when Sally tried to help her, she said, 'No, leave me. Just pass me my purse from the shelf.'

The request puzzled Sally. As far as she was aware, the purse contained no money. All the cash possessed by Ruth had been spent long ago, during their many lean times. Nevertheless, she crossed the room, took down the worn leather purse from a shelf, and handed it to her sister.

Clumsily, Ruth opened one of the many compartments of the purse and took out a key.

'That's the key to your trunk.'

Living in the one room, the girls had no possessions that were not familiar to the other – with a single exception.

In a corner of the room stood a small trunk that belonged to Ruth. It was always kept locked. What was more, it had never been opened in Sally's presence.

Holding out the key in a weak and shaking hand, Ruth said, 'Here, open it.'

'Are you sure?' Sally took the key uncertainly. It felt wrong. Almost as though Ruth was relinquishing an important part of herself.

'Of course I'm sure. Go on, open it.'

Crossing the creaking floor to the corner of the room, Sally kneeled beside the old bow-topped leather trunk. After a quick, confirmatory glance at Ruth, she inserted the key in the lock and turned it.

The lock was stiff, as she had expected it would be, but when the key eventually turned, the lid sprang up slightly and she lifted it open.

There was a pile of clothing in the trunk. Ruth had never been a particularly tidy person, but everything here was meticulously folded.

Turning back to her sister, Sally asked, 'What am I looking for?'

'Anything that takes your fancy. Much of it is far too old-fashioned, but I know there's a nice petticoat in there. I wore it myself once, for a special occasion. Just have a look through and see what you can find.'

Sally found the petticoat. Made of layered silk, it was far more expensive than anything she had ever seen before. Then she unfolded a beautiful, rich maroon velvet cloak with tiered lilac silk fringing. When she unfolded it she discovered it was also decorated with two heraldic crests, one on either side of the fastening at the neck.

'This is *beautiful*, Ruth. Where did you get it?'

'It belonged to our ma. Don't ask me how she got it. Probably from the big house where she worked. Take it if you like it. The slip as well.'

'Do you mean it, Ruth? You don't mind? The cloak would go beautifully with the dress I saw.'

'Of course I don't mind. She was your ma just as much as mine. She'd love you to wear it. I should have given it to you long before this.'

'No. This is just the right occasion. Oh, thank you, Ruth! I couldn't have wished for anything better.'

Hurrying to the bed, Sally gave her sister an affectionate hug, trying not to notice how thin Ruth had become.

'Go on with you,' said Ruth. 'Now, shut the chest and give me back the key.'

Sally was about to close the chest when she saw a bundle of letters, tied with ribbon. Lifting them out, she held them up for Ruth to see. 'What are these?'

'Put them back! Go on. I said you could have any of the clothes. Nothing else.'

Ruth spoke so sharply it took Sally aback. It also set Ruth coughing alarmingly.

Hurriedly dropping the letters in the chest, Sally turned the key to lock it. Then she went to the bed to lift her sister. She had to rub Ruth's back for a long time before she stopped coughing and could be laid back once more, still gasping for breath.

That night, as Sally lay in the darkness, listening to Ruth's weak and shallow breathing, she wondered what could have been in the letters to make her sister so upset. She thought they must be from a man who had once been a part of Ruth's life, although she had never spoken of anyone in particular.

As she lay there thinking her own, night-time thoughts, Sally's hand strayed beneath her pillow. She had placed the cloak there and she touched the velvet with its silk fringes lovingly.

It had once belonged to her mother. Had been worn by her. She suddenly felt warm inside.

The cloak was the best present Ruth could have given to her. The best present *anyone* could have given her.

28

Christmas Eve dawned crisp and clear. Sally walked to work filled with a sense of excitement, which she contained with great difficulty.

The excitement had been building up inside her for some days now and was not entirely due to the cloak she had been given by Ruth. It had much to do with Christmas itself.

Walking around the streets of Plymouth making her deliveries, she had seen Christmas decorations appear in many of the shops and houses of the town.

The grocers in the main shopping streets had an awesome variety of goods on display in their windows: Fancy cakes, biscuits, dried fruits; goods of every description. The list was endless.

Butchers too, not usually known for their decorative skills, offered chickens, ducks, geese, turkeys and colourful pheasants, hanging row upon feathered row outside their shops, while on white trays in the window, long strings of sausages spelled out the message 'Happy Christmas'.

In the residential streets, wreaths of holly and ivy were affixed to many doors. As she passed by, Sally could see chains of coloured paper and sprigs of holly brightening even the most drab rooms.

Today was special for another reason. With Ethan and his brother still helping with deliveries, and the demand for pies finally falling away, Grace had said Sally could take a couple of hours off, in order to buy Christmas presents. She would be spending the money she had been able to save from her pay. With the occasional tips she received, it amounted to more money than she had ever possessed before.

Rachel would be coming with her, to spend money given to her by the extremely generous Grace and Alfie.

Sally had already decided upon most of the presents she would be buying. She had chosen them from the shop windows she passed as her deliveries took her through the shopping areas.

'What are you going to buy for that young man of yours, Sally?' The question came from Grace as they worked to prepare the shop for the day and it sent a small cloud scudding across the horizon of Sally's happiness.

'I don't know yet.'

'You don't know?' echoed Grace. 'Here we are, the day before Christmas, and you don't know what you're going to buy for your young man? You've left things a bit late, girl!'

'I know,' Sally said unhappily. 'You see, I know what Ethan *wants*. He'd love to have another flute, to replace the one that was broken by the Skeleton Army.'

'That's a very expensive present to buy for any young man,' commented Grace.

'I know,' admitted Sally. 'But he's been very good to me and Ruth and I've seen a flute I know he'd love. It's in the pawnshop where I bought the dress I'm wearing to go to his house. It's beautiful – but that's just the trouble. It's *too* beautiful. The pawnbroker wants a lot of money for it. I've been in his shop five times to try to get him to sell it to me for less than he's asking, but he won't drop the price quite enough.'

'How much are you short of the asking price?' queried Grace.

'Twenty-five shillings,' Sally admitted gloomily. 'It was *thirty*-five. He's dropped the price by ten shillings, but he won't come down any more.'

Grace was fully aware that Alfie was giving her a stern warning stare. She chose not to look directly at him, and without a word, she walked from the kitchen to the shop.

Returning only a few minutes later, she took Sally's hand, put two banknotes in it and closed her fingers about them.

Opening her hand, Sally looked down and saw a pound note and a ten shilling note.

'Thirty shillings! What's this for?'

'Alfie and I have enjoyed the best year we've ever had in the shop. Far better than we expected. You've worked hard while you've been here, girl, contributing in no small measure to our success. We decided it should be a good year for you too.'

Grace used the 'we' freely, but she did not look at Alfie. He, in his turn, was trying unsuccessfully to appear as though he had been consulted on the generous gift.

'Now, off you go and buy that flute before someone else takes a liking to it,' said Grace. 'Take Rachel with you. I know she has one or two things she wants to buy.'

Hardly able to contain her delight, Sally flung her arms about Grace and gave her a warm hug. Then she repeated it with Alfie.

When the two happy girls had departed from the shop, chattering excitedly together, Alfie said huskily, 'You know, Grace, the last young girl to give me a hug like that was our Mary.'

'Then it was money well spent, Alfie. She's a fine young girl, that one. So too is Rachel. I'm glad they've become such firm friends. They're good for each other. They're good for us, too. I only hope young Ethan realises what a treasure he has in Sally. I'd hate for him to break her heart.'

Sally and Rachel's shopping expedition began on a high note. The two girls spent a long time in a haberdashery shop as Rachel chose ribbons for the other girls at the Refuge. Then she bought embroidered handkerchiefs for Grace and Captain Eva.

Sally purchased a couple of presents here too, including one of the embroidered handkerchiefs. She thought it would make a nice present for Ethan's mother.

In a nearby shop she bought a kaleidoscope. It formed a variety of colourful patterns when shaken and held to the eye. It would keep Ruth amused for many of her waking hours and bring a welcome splash of colour into her drab and pain-filled life.

But although Sally was enjoying this part of her shopping, she was anxious to get to the pawnbroker's and secure the flute she was buying for Ethan.

She breathed a sigh of relief when they reached the shop and she saw it still displayed in the window. It was surrounded by a wide selection of unclaimed pledges, set out haphazardly.

Shoes and satin slippers were piled upon silver-tipped walking-canes. A couple of cheap watches were half-hidden by a variety of baubles – and a quantity of assorted wedding rings were threaded on a piece of string stretched between two shelves. The mark of respectability they had once represented had, in most cases, been sacrificed to satisfy a family's hunger.

The knowledge that she possessed enough money to pay the pawnbroker's asking price for the flute made Sally feel so confident she decided she would make one more attempt to drive the price down still further.

When it became evident to Rachel that the negotiations were likely to be protracted, she said, 'I'm going to have a look in the window of the jewellers we just passed. I'll see you there when you've done here.'

Sally's haggling eventually paid off. The pawnbroker knew he was unlikely to have any more customers before Christmas. He was also aware that those who would come to his shop after the holiday would be pawning goods, not buying them.

When Sally produced money from her purse as proof she was seriously contemplating buying the flute, the pawnbroker agreed to reduce the price by a further two shillings.

Delighted with her purchase and the price she had paid for it, Sally waited for the pawnbroker to fit the musical instrument into a velvet-lined carrying case. The task had just been completed when Rachel ran in the shop and clutched Sally, her face drained of colour and her eyes wide with terror.

'What's the matter, Rachel? What's happened?' Sally put the concerned questions to the younger girl as she clung to her arm, momentarily struck dumb.

'I . . . I've just seen him,' gasped Rachel, finding her voice at last, but shaking in fear. 'He's out there – and I think he saw me!'

'Who's out there? What are you talking about?'

'*Him* . . . ! Sid Darling. He was standing on the pavement, just across the road. I'm sure he saw me . . .'

The pawnbroker had been as startled as Sally by the dramatic return of Rachel. He listened with growing concern to the conversation between the two girls.

Now he said, 'You've made an enemy of Sid Darling? How?'

'How doesn't matter,' said Sally. 'What *does* matter is that he'll kill both of us if he can lay his hands on us.'

In addition to his lawful business as a pawnbroker, the owner of the shop had a very lucrative sideline as a 'fence': a receiver and distributor of stolen goods. He was familiar with the town's criminals. Among them, Sid Darling's name was frequently to the fore; he was one of the most feared and disliked men in the criminal fraternity.

'Did he see you come in here?' he asked Rachel.

'No. A furniture van passed between us. That's when I ran in here.'

The pawnbroker peered over the board that separated the window display from the shop.

Sid Darling, appearing agitated, was still standing

on the opposite pavement. He was unable to cross the road because of heavy traffic, and was trying to see into a shop farther along the street, away from the pawnbroker's.

'Quick, through here.'

The pawnbroker led the way through a door at the rear of the shop. It led into his living quarters, from where a door opened into a side alleyway.

'Go that way,' he said to the two girls, pointing along the alleyway, away from Union Street. 'It will bring you out in East Street. If Sid Darling comes in here I'll deny having had any young girls in my shop today. But if ever he catches up with you, remember – you've never been here.'

A few minutes later, after fleeing in a state close to panic through the narrow alleyway, the two girls emerged in East Street. Here they stopped running, but did not dawdle, their shopping expedition at a premature end.

Neither girl felt safe until they tumbled inside Alfie and Grace Philpott's pie shop and blurted out the story of their narrow escape.

Despite the fright she had received, Sally felt the shopping expedition had been a success. She had bought Ethan the Christmas present he most wanted.

29

'Of course you're going, Sal. Ethan and his family are expecting you. Besides, you've been in all day, looking after me. That's no way to spend Christmas.'

Ruth spoke from the bed, propped up by both of the pillows belonging to the sisters. Her Christmas present from Sally lay on the quilt beside her.

The quilt itself had been donated to Ruth by the ever-generous Grace, as a result of a visit to the room in the Pin's Lane house by Rachel, a few days before. Rachel had returned to the shop and mentioned to Grace that the bed in the room was covered only by a rough blanket. The following day Grace had appeared in the shop with the quilt and asked Sally if she could make use of it. She had bought a new one, she said. If Sally did not want it she would throw it out as she had no room to store it.

'I like being at home with you,' Sally protested. 'We never seem to be able to spend enough time together now I'm working.'

'I like having you here with me,' said Ruth. 'But you

know how talking tires me. I shall go to sleep very happily, thinking of you enjoying a lovely time with Ethan and his family.'

Lifting the kaleidoscope, she added, 'If you leave the lamp turned up a little higher than usual I'll be able to look through this for a while. It's a truly lovely present, Sal. The best I've ever had. The colours in the patterns are just unbelievable.'

Ruth had spent most of her waking hours that day gazing into the kaleidoscope. It had proved to be a very successful gift.

In fact, the whole day had so far been a happy one. Nevertheless, Sally was viewing her visit to Ethan's home with very mixed feelings. Indeed, she could not remember ever feeling more nervous.

'Do you *really* think this dress is all right?' It was a question she had asked many times that evening.

'It's lovely, Sal – and so are you. Ethan's a very lucky young man. I hope he realises just *how* lucky.'

In truth, the dress was a trifle small for Sally. Accentuating the maturity of her body, it would not serve her for very long, but Ruth said nothing of this. She knew Sally was delighted with her purchase, despite the misgivings she was voicing now.

'That cloak will go beautifully with it too,' she added, as Sally placed it around her shoulders and fastened it at her neck.

Suddenly and without any warning, the happiness Sally had managed to hold inside her all day welled up and broke free.

'Oh, I'm *so* lucky to have a sister like you!' Sally flung herself at the frail, bed-ridden girl and gave her a fierce hug.

'Steady, Sal!' Ruth returned the hug with a warm but weak embrace. 'I love you too. Now, before we both get all silly, off you go and let the Shields family see what a lucky young man Ethan is.'

To Sally's great surprise, Ethan was waiting for her downstairs in the passageway of the Pin's Lane house, talking to his uncle.

'I thought I'd come and collect you, just in case you'd changed your mind,' explained Ethan, revealing an understanding of her that Sally found comforting, yet vaguely disturbing. 'I'm glad you haven't – and you look wonderful, Sally.'

His compliment pleased her more than he would ever know. Happily reassured, she slipped her arm through his. 'Come on then, before I *do* change my mind.'

'Are you going to be warm enough? It's a cold evening.'

'Of course I am. I've got a cloak that used to belong to my ma and we'll be at your house before I have time to get cold.'

She *would* be cold – it was a frosty evening – but her shivers were as likely to be the result of excitement as anything else.

Aware of Sally's nervousness, Ethan chatted happily along the way to help her feel at ease. He was curious to know what the parcels she carried contained – especially the long parcel wrapped in brightly coloured paper.

'I've just bought a couple of little things for your ma and pa, that's all,' she fibbed.

'That parcel doesn't look like a *little* thing to me,' he pointed out.

'Well, you'll find out what it is soon enough,' she said, squeezing his arm happily.

Ethan's home was only a few streets distant from Pin's Lane, and even though Sally was now beginning to feel the cold they reached it far more quickly than she would have liked. She was not really certain she was quite ready to meet the large Shields family.

But it was too late to turn back. Ethan pushed open the door of his house and they were immediately greeted by the sound of laughter and loud voices.

The sounds came from the ground-floor front room, but Ethan's mother was in the kitchen. She had been awaiting the young couple's arrival and hurried forward to greet her youngest son and his friend.

Sally liked her immediately. A plump, motherly woman, Doris Shields was instinctively aware of Sally's nervousness. Putting an arm about her shoulders, she squeezed her affectionately.

'So *you're* Sally? Well, everyone's been telling me what a plucky girl you are, but no one thought to tell me how pretty you are – and what a lovely cloak you're wearing! I don't think I've ever seen one quite like it.'

'It belonged to my ma,' Sally said proudly, speaking for the first time.

'Did it, indeed? Well, that makes it even more special. Let me take it from you and put it somewhere very safe.'

Undoing the fastening, Sally took the cloak from about her shoulders and proudly handed it to Doris Shields.

Aware of Sally's regard for the cloak, the motherly woman said, 'We'll put it safe on a hook in here.' As she spoke, she opened a door that hid a cupboard beneath the stairs and hung up the cloak with exaggerated care.

While this was being done, Ethan gave Sally a reassuring smile and whispered, 'See! I told you there was nothing to worry about.'

The cloak safely put away, Doris led the way to the room from which all the noise was emanating.

'Quiet everyone . . .' She needed to raise her voice and shout the request twice more before the noise subsided.

'That's better.' Putting a reassuring arm across Sally's shoulders, she said, 'This is Sally, Ethan's friend. She's come to spend a part of Christmas with us.'

As she was speaking, Sally glanced at the two other young women in the room. One of them, probably only a year or so older than herself was introduced as Phoebe. She was the girlfriend of Joe, with whom Sally had worked at the pie shop.

A dark, rather haughty-looking girl, she wore a dress that immediately made Sally feel uncomfortable about her own secondhand frock. It was in green, shot-silk and worn off the shoulder, displaying smooth skin that would have been the envy of any society woman.

She acknowledged the introduction in a manner that did nothing to dispel Sally's feeling that this girl had a very high opinion of herself.

The other woman was in her early twenties and was Albert's wife. In contrast to Phoebe, Sophie Shields was more plainly dressed and she gave Sally a warm and open smile.

'It's nice to meet you at last,' she said. 'I can see now why Ethan talks about you so much.'

'And so he should,' said Henry Shields. 'She saved his life over at Shepherd's Wharf, when all those girls were taken off the Belgian boat. I'm glad to see you again, Sally.'

Doris now introduced Sally to her other sons, rattling through their names so quickly Sally could not remember afterwards who was who.

The introductions over, there was a brief, uncertain silence. It was broken by Ethan. 'Now Sally's met everyone, I think she has a present for you, Ma. You too, Pa.'

'A present for me?' queried Doris. 'You shouldn't have spent your hard-earned money on such things, young lady.'

When the handkerchief was unwrapped, Doris shook it out and said, 'This is *lovely*, Sally. Just look at the embroidery! Have you ever seen such fine stitching?'

Henry Shields was equally effusive about the pipe Sally had bought for him, but Ethan's puzzled glance went to the long package Sally was still holding. He had believed it to be the present she had brought for his mother.

Holding it out to him, she said, 'This is for you.'

His surprise was genuine. 'What is it?'

'I'd say the way to find out would be to open it,' said his father, with a grin. 'You'll never know if you stand there looking as though you're afraid it's going to bite you.'

'Well, you never know,' Joe said cheekily. 'It could be a conger eel, like that one Bill Grady caught over by Eddystone. He gave it to his wife for her birthday. Not only was it still alive but when she hit him with it the conger bit half his ear off.'

While his brother was speaking, Ethan was taking off the wrapping paper. When he exposed the long, leather case, his other brothers made equally flippant suggestions about what it might contain.

Carefully opening the case, Ethan gasped, 'It's a flute!'

Everyone in the room crowded around to look as Ethan removed it from the case and held it up.

'It's beautiful, Sally! Absolutely *wonderful*!'

Ethan was quite overwhelmed to have received such a present. Looking accusingly at Sally, he said, 'You shouldn't have, Sally. It must have cost you the *earth*. I've never seen such a fine flute.'

Delighted by his reaction to the present, Sally said, 'I know how upset you were when your other one got broken. I saw this one and wanted to buy it for you. I got it for a lot less than the price that was being asked.'

'All the same . . .'

Ethan was worried, but his father broke in upon his concern.

'Instead of standing there saying the girl *shouldn't* have bought it, I think you should be saying a great big "thank you" to her – and I don't mean you should shake her hand, neither.'

'Thank you, Sally,' Ethan said awkwardly. 'It's the best present anyone's ever given me.'

'Then don't just stand there gawking,' said his mother. 'Give the girl a great big, grateful kiss. You've got me worrying about what sort of a son I've brought up.'

Ethan self-consciously kissed Sally and the cheer that rose from his brothers made both of them blush with deep embarrassment.

'Well, now that's done with, perhaps you can give us a tune,' said his father.

'All right, but first, I've got a present for Sally,' said Ethan. 'It's nowhere as grand as this,' he held up the flute, 'but I hope you like it, Sally.'

His present was an enamelled heart on a fine silver chain, which thrilled Sally. When he had fastened it about her neck, she gave him a kiss without anyone having to prompt her.

Afterwards, Ethan played his new flute while the others sang. The flute made a very pleasant sound and Ethan declared it not only looked good but sounded better than any other instrument he had ever heard.

The evening passed by very quickly and Sally enjoyed herself much more than she had believed possible. She found the Shields family very easy to get along with and she liked them much more than she had expected.

They ate, sang and drank, and when the clock on the mantelshelf struck the hour of eleven, it was with real reluctance that Sally said she would have to go home.

Her announcement was greeted with a chorus of protests, but Doris realised that Sally did not like to leave Ruth for longer than was absolutely necessary. She led Sally from the room after she had said a warm 'Goodnight' to everyone.

In the passageway, Doris handed Sally her cloak, then pressed something into her hand. When Sally looked down she saw that it was a silver brooch, set with a number of coloured stones.

'It's my Christmas present to you, Sally,' said Doris. 'It once belonged to my mother. She used to wear it on her cloak. I thought you might like to do the same.'

30

In the kitchen of the Shields' home, after Sally and Ethan had left, Phoebe and Sophie were washing up, while Doris was in the front room gathering dirty dishes.

'What do you think of the girl Ethan has found for himself?' asked Phoebe, with a sly glance at her companion.

'I think she's sweet, don't you?'

'She's all right, I suppose,' Phoebe agreed grudgingly. 'But that dress! I'm surprised it didn't burst at the seams during the evening. It's much too small for her across the shoulders and bosom, yet far too loose at the waist. It looked to me as though she'd bought it in a second-hand clothes shop.'

Carrying a pile of dirty plates, Doris returned to the kitchen in time to hear Phoebe's last remark.

'I've no doubt that's *exactly* where she bought the frock – and there's no shame on her for that. Where did the dress you're wearing come from, Phoebe?'

Phoebe had not intended that her criticism of Sally's clothes should be overheard by Doris. Naming one of the town's best-known stores, she replied, 'Dingles.'

'Did you pay for it with your own money?'

'No, my mother bought it for me.'

'Sally has no mother to buy clothes for her. No father, either. Not only does she have to work hard for every penny, but she has to take care of a bed-ridden sister, too. I think she's a little marvel – and generous too. Rather than spend money on herself, she bought Ethan the thing he wanted more than anything else in this world. I hope our Ethan realises how lucky he is and hangs on to young Sally. He's not likely to find another like her.'

'Well! Ethan's little waif certainly seems to have made an impression on his mother,' Phoebe said petulantly, when Doris had returned to the front room. 'I've never heard her praising me like that.'

Sophie smiled sweetly at her companion, who had been extremely parsimonious in her choice of a Christmas present for Ethan's brother Joe. 'Perhaps you should buy your clothes from the same shop as Sally.'

Walking through the narrow streets to Pin's Lane with Ethan, Sally felt happier than she could ever remember. Despite her earlier misgivings, she had thoroughly enjoyed her evening with the Shields. It was the first time in her life she had experienced what it was to be a member of a complete family, and Doris had told her she would be welcome at the Shields' home any time she cared to call.

She clung to Ethan's arm and it all added to the warm sense of belonging. She felt she was no longer a young girl buffeted this way and that by life. She had regular work and was bringing in a wage that, if not exactly high, was adequate. She also had a man who was kind, considerate and courageous – one who was beginning to play an increasingly important part in her life.

Sally was beginning to look to the future. *Her* future. A future that included Ethan and his family. Just thinking of it gave her a warm feeling deep inside and she squeezed his arm happily.

'Did you enjoy your evening after all?' Ethan asked her.

'It was the best time I've ever had. I think your ma is wonderful – and I like your brothers, they're fun. Sophie too. I could be very good friends with her.'

'How about Phoebe?' Ethan asked the question tongue in cheek.

'She's all right,' Sally said cautiously. 'But I think she might have been a little spoiled by her ma and pa.'

Ethan laughed merrily. 'Phoebe has been a *lot* spoiled, we all know that, but she's not all bad. She's quite kind, really. It's just that she hasn't had to face up to the realities of life. Joe's besotted with her, but I can't see her settling for being the wife of a fisherman.'

'Why not? I'd be proud to be the wife of a fisherman.'

They both realised the implications of her words and were silent for a couple of minutes. Then Sally said, 'Thank you for inviting me to your home, Ethan. I really did enjoy meeting your family.'

They turned a corner and were now in an alleyway where there were no gaslamps. Suddenly, without any warning, Ethan stopped, pulled Sally clumsily to him, and kissed her.

She made no attempt to stop him, but when he broke away, she said, shakily, 'Why did you do that?'

'Because . . . I wanted to. I'm sorry, I . . .'

'No, don't be sorry, Ethan. I wanted you to. I want you to kiss me again.'

She came to him this time and the kiss lasted much longer. They did not break away from each other until they heard footsteps and the sound of voices coming along the alleyway.

Now they walked along with an arm about each other, needing to say nothing. All too soon, it seemed, they reached Pin's Lane.

When they arrived at the house where Sally lived, they went inside and were talking softly in the downstairs passageway when the door of Charlie's room opened. He peered around the open door to see who was there.

'Hello, you two. What are you doing out here? Did you decide to go out again after you came home?'

Sally and Ethan looked at each other quizzically, and Ethan said, 'What do you mean, Uncle Charlie? Sally has been at our house with me and the family all evening. We've just left and come straight here.'

'Don't try pulling the wool over my eyes, you two. What you get up to is your business, but I heard you upstairs not much more than an hour ago. I should know, that creaking floor in Sally's room has been driving me mad for years. When she's home I can tell you exactly where she's standing because of the noise made by the loose boards. Ruth hasn't got out of bed in weeks, so it must have been Sally.'

'Wait here, Ethan. I'll go up and make sure everything's all right.'

Without waiting for a reply, Sally left Ethan and his uncle and ran up the stairs to the first floor.

Ethan was repeating his explanation when there was a scream that sent him bounding up the stairs to the room Sally shared with Ruth.

At the bedside, Sally was trying to raise the inert figure of her sister. When she saw Ethan enter the room, she cried, 'Help me. Help me to sit her up, Ethan. Quickly.'

Ethan was shocked by the pallor of Ruth's skin. He touched her and felt her coldness. 'Just a minute Sally . . .' He took Ruth's arm and felt for a pulse.

There was nothing.

Gently, he pulled Sally away and laid the thin body of Ruth back on the bed.

'It's no use, Sally. I'm afraid she's dead.'

'No . . . ! She can't be.'

Sally's wail of despair made him wince. 'She is. There's nothing you can do for her now.' He tried to draw her gently away from the bed, but she fought against him and broke free.

As huge sobs racked her body, Sally shook with hysterical shock. 'How? Why did it happen?'

'She's been very ill for a long time, Sally. This could have happened at any time.'

'But why tonight, Ethan? Why did it have to happen tonight . . . ?'

He tried to draw her to him, but she pulled away once again.

Trying desperately hard to regain a grip on her emotions, Sally cried, 'No, Ethan! She didn't just die because of her illness. I know she didn't. Someone has been here.'

'You don't know that, Sally. I know Uncle Charlie thought he heard something, but you can't rely on anything he says. He probably imagined it, and he's been drinking, probably for most of the day.'

'No. No! Someone *has* been here. Look!'

Bending down, Sally picked up something from the floor. As she lifted it, tiny, brightly coloured pieces of shiny paper fell to the floor.

It was the kaleidoscope she had bought for Ruth. Split open at the sides, it had been crushed almost flat.

'This is the present I bought Ruth for Christmas. Someone's trodden on it. It couldn't be Ruth, she wasn't able to get out of bed. Someone *has* been here, Ethan. I know it. Charlie was right.'

She looked at Ethan, her face contorted in agony. 'Ruth didn't just die, Ethan. She was *killed!* Someone murdered her.'

31

After he had gently covered Ruth's face with the quilt
donated by Grace Philpott, Ethan managed to persuade
Sally to go downstairs with him to Charlie's room.

She was still sobbing and at times became almost
hysterical. More than once Ethan had to prevent her
from hurrying upstairs again, as she struggled to accept
that Ruth *really* was dead.

'What shall I do, Ethan? What's going to happen to
me now?'

'We'll talk about that tomorrow. You'd better come
back home with me tonight. It'll be a bit crowded in the
house, but Ma will find room for you. Come on, let's go
right away. Ma will know what to do.' He put an arm
around her but she wriggled free.

'I can't just walk away and leave Ruth lying up there
on her own.'

'You must, Sally. She'll need to be examined by a
doctor, but it's still Christmas Day. We won't be able
to find anyone until tomorrow.'

'The police . . . ? They should be called.'

'They wouldn't do anything until a doctor has seen Ruth.'

Ethan doubted the police would wish to become involved in Ruth's death, anyway. They would be no more convinced than he was that her death was in any way suspicious. But he kept such views to himself.

'I don't want to go to your house, Ethan.' Sally spoke through her tears.

'Why not?' Her refusal took him by surprise.

'Because . . . because I had such a happy time there this evening. We all did. It wouldn't seem right. Not for me, nor for the others.' She began sobbing again and Ethan put his arms about her and held her to him.

He understood what she was saying, and gently he said, 'You can't stay here, Sally. Can you think of anywhere else you could go? To the Philpotts' home, perhaps?'

Sally shook her head and now the tears were as much for herself as for Ruth. She needed to face the stark reality that without Ruth she belonged nowhere. To no one. She had felt close to Ethan, especially today, but she could not expect him to assume responsibility for her – nor would she want him to. Not just yet.

'Look, why don't we go and speak to Captain Eva?' suggested Ethan. 'She'll have room for you there – and will know what ought to be done in the morning.'

After only a moment's hesitation, Sally nodded her head in assent. Captain Eva was just the person to turn to in an emergency.

Ethan had been concerned that Captain Eva might have already gone to bed and would be difficult to rouse, but there appeared to be lights on in most of the rooms in

the Refuge. In fact, there had been a disturbance at the
large house.

In recent days Captain Eva had given refuge to a
number of young prostitutes who had expressed a
desire to escape their way of life, which was her original
purpose in coming to Plymouth. Tonight, for one of
the girls the thought of all her former associates out
celebrating had been too much. She had slipped out of
the house, got violently drunk and then made a noisy
return, waking all her fellow residents.

In fact, she had only returned to gather up her few
belongings, intending to return to her former ways.
However, she caused such a fuss that she was arrested
by the police immediately after leaving the house, for
being 'drunk and disorderly'.

Captain Eva pleaded in vain with the police for the
girl to be released and allowed to return to the house.
The young woman struggled violently, calling the two
arresting constables every name she could think of from
her considerable and colourful vocabulary, as she was
dragged away to the police station.

This incident had only just been played out when
Ethan and Sally appeared.

Eva immediately took charge of the distraught young
girl and led her inside the house. Ethan wanted to remain
with Sally, but the Salvation Army officer declared firmly
she would take care of her and put her to bed when she
was less upset.

In the morning Eva would contact a doctor, and the
police, if necessary. Should Ethan care to return then,
as she was quite sure he would, she had no doubt Sally
would want to see him.

*   *   *

Ethan's route home took him past the end of Pin's Lane. Acting on an impulse he turned in to the lane and made his way to the house where Ruth lay dead.

He climbed the stairs and entered the room Ruth had shared with Sally. The lamp had been left burning, but turned down very low. It would burn until morning, giving a dim light that, in the circumstances, Ethan found eerie.

Trying not to look at the bed, where Ruth's body lay covered by the quilt, Ethan walked across the room and picked up the broken kaleidoscope. Examining it, he frowned. It certainly looked as though someone had stepped on it. If so, Sally could possibly be right. Ruth might not have met a natural death.

Of course, Sally might have trodden on it herself, in the panic of the moment when she found Ruth . . .

There was a sound from the hall outside the room. A moment later the door opened cautiously, and Charlie peered inside.

'Oh, it's you . . .' Breathing heavily as a result of his exertions climbing the stairs, Charlie appeared relieved. 'I couldn't sleep and heard the boards creaking up here. I was afraid that whoever had been here earlier might have come back. It makes a man uneasy when people wander about the house at all times of the night. Especially when there's a dead girl lying here.'

'So you're quite sure you *did* hear someone up here earlier?'

'Of course I'm sure. My chest might not be so good, but it doesn't affect my hearing. Whoever was here was a sight bigger than you, too. These boards have creaked for as long as I've been living in this house. I know every sound they make. I could tell if a cat walked across the floor.'

As they talked, they saw a lamp being lit in an upstairs room of a house backing on to the one they were in. A man and a woman were in the room. The woman stared from the window at Ethan and Charlie, before drawing the curtains.

The curtains were too small for the window. Even when drawn there was a gap of about the width of a man's hand. Through this Ethan could see the woman undressing. He turned his back on her quickly; Charlie did not.

'Who's that?' Ethan asked, embarrassed.

'"Devonport Lil". She's a tart – and a busy one. She must have picked up a shy man tonight. Half the time she doesn't even bother to pull the curtains. She'll undress and dress in front of the open window too, not caring who might be watching.'

'Do you think she might have seen whoever was in this room earlier tonight?'

'She might. She's been home more than usual, it being Christmas. But I wouldn't go over there alone to ask her. If word got back to your ma and pa that you'd been in that house they'd throw you out for sure.'

'Thanks for the warning, Uncle, but I don't think she'd appreciate me asking questions of her right now anyway. Come on, let's leave poor Ruth in peace.'

And with a final look at the still form lying hidden beneath the quilt, he followed Charlie from the room.

32

When Ethan arrived at the Salvation Army Refuge the following morning, the streets were quiet. Most people seemed to be taking full advantage of the holiday and sleeping off the effects of the previous day's celebrations.

But Captain Eva had been up for some hours. She was the ideal woman to handle a situation such as that now facing Sally.

Possessing an apparently limitless reserve of energy, Eva was an efficient organiser and, in addition, she felt a deep and honest compassion for all who were in need of help.

She had already called on Grace Philpott to inform her what had happened. Deeply concerned for Sally, that big-hearted woman, with Rachel in tow, had hurried to the house to express her sympathy. She was with Sally now, comforting her as best she could.

Eva had also called in a local doctor to certify Ruth's death and had spoken to an undertaker. She would later visit the room where Ruth lay.

For the majority of Pin's Lane's residents, their final resting place was destined to be an unmarked pauper's grave. However, the ever-generous Grace Philpott promised Sally that Ruth would be given 'as fine a burial as could be arranged'.

Such arrangements would need to wait. Sally's suspicions about the circumstances of Ruth's death had been passed on to the doctor.

The emaciated state of Ruth's body made the doctor highly sceptical that her death had been due to anything other than natural causes, but he was a cautious man. He had her body removed to the mortuary so that a post-mortem might be carried out.

Eva told Ethan of all that had been happening during his absence and he informed her of his late-night visit to Pin's Lane, and the conversation he had held with his uncle Charlie.

'When you leave, I'll come with you,' she said. 'I think you and I should call on your uncle and also make a few enquiries around Pin's Lane. But before we do that I'll take you up to see Sally. I'm afraid she's still extremely upset.'

Ethan found Sally both tired and very depressed. She had been far too distraught to sleep, and this morning she was suffering from a deep sense of guilt. She felt it had been wrong to be out enjoying herself while Ruth was dying – in whatever manner her death had occurred.

'You really mustn't think like that, Sally,' said Ethan. 'If someone else was responsible for Ruth's death, they'd have probably killed you too, had you been there.'

'What do you mean . . . "If"? Someone *had* been in

the room. I *know* it. I can guess who it was, too. It was Sid Darling and he was there looking for *me*. When he didn't find me, he killed Ruth instead. She was far too weak to do anything to defend herself. However you look at it, it *is* my fault she's dead.'

Sally had spoken vehemently, bringing herself close to tears once more and Grace, who was still in the room, tried to calm her.

'Now, Sally, such talk helps no one. If Sid Darling *is* involved in this then, from what I hear about him, he wouldn't have spared either of you. Or anyone else who got in his way, come to that. As it is, you're here, safe and sound. I don't doubt that's the way your poor sister would have wanted it to be.'

'Mrs Philpott is right, Sally,' said Ethan. He was deeply unhappy to have upset Sally, when all he had tried to do was comfort her. 'The thing Ruth would have wanted more than anything else would be to know you were safe.'

Sally shook her head, her face contorted in anguish. 'I should have been with her, instead of out enjoying myself. I could have saved her.' Suddenly, she began trembling violently and Grace immediately wrapped her arms about her.

'You must try not to upset yourself so, my love. None of this has been your fault, or Ethan's, either. You'll realise it yourself as soon as you've had time to get over the shock of all that's happened. Ethan will leave you now, but he'll be back to see you most days to find out how you are, I'm sure. You're not on your own, dear, just remember that. There are a whole lot of people about you who care. We all care very much.' As she held Sally close in a bid to stop her trembling, Grace made a faint movement of her head in Ethan's direction, indicating that he should leave the room.

Visibly upset, he did so, but not before murmuring a faint and unacknowledged 'Goodbye' to Sally. On a small table in the room he left behind a note from his mother, in which she expressed her deep sympathy. With the note was a bag of cakes she had made up for Sally.

Downstairs, Ethan found Eva battling to replace a high shelf, knocked down by one of the girls earlier that morning.

Taking over the task from her, he told her of Sally's reaction to his visit.

'You mustn't feel in any way to blame,' Eva said sympathetically. 'Sally doesn't really know what she's saying right now. She's hurt, shocked – yes, and frightened too. Sally's all alone in the world now, or believes she is.'

Ethan shook his head vigorously. 'She's not, and never will be if I have my way.'

Eva put out a hand and rested it gently upon his arm. 'I'm delighted to hear it, Ethan. She is going to need all the help she can get, from you in particular. My dearest wish is that you should both find your happiness within the Salvation Army but, whatever happens, I will pray that you find it together. Now, you seem to have fixed that shelf. Shall we go and see what we can learn at Pin's Lane?'

33

When Captain Eva and Ethan reached the Pin's Lane house, they first called on Charlie Shields. The Salvation Army captain questioned him closely to learn the exact time he had heard someone moving around in the upstairs room.

He admitted to having been drinking heavily to celebrate Christmas and, as Captain Eva later pointed out to Ethan, this would detract seriously from his value as a prosecution witness should Ruth's death result in a trial.

Nevertheless, by the dint of much patience – and a little bullying – it was ascertained that Charlie had heard someone in the upstairs room between nine and nine-thirty the previous evening.

'Who else lives in the house?' asked Captain Eva.

'No one, except me and the Harrups, although I suppose it's just Sally, now Ruth's dead. I have both rooms downstairs. There's another room opening off the landing upstairs, but the woman who rented it was arrested about two years ago for robbing one of the men she brought home with her. She got three years, but someone's been paying the rent for her. When she gets out again she'll no doubt move back, but there's no one up there right now.'

'Well, let's go upstairs to Sally's room, shall we?'

The three of them went up the stairs. As a result of the conversation they had just had, they were very aware of the creaking of the floorboards on the landing.

The sound was even louder when they entered the room rented out to Sally and her sister. Ethan's glance went automatically to the bed. The last time he had been in the room the body of Ruth was lying there. It had gone now, but the memory had not.

Eva picked up the broken kaleidoscope. Holding it in her hand, she stood at the window in silence for some time.

Abruptly turning to her companions, she said, 'Charlie, tell me what you know about the people who live in the houses that back on to here.'

At first, Charlie protested he knew nothing at all of them. He 'minded his own business' and hoped they did the same. However, after skilful and patient questioning, Eva established that he knew most of the occupants, together with their predominantly dubious occupations.

Among them was the prostitute Devonport Lil.

'I think we'll go and speak to her first,' declared Eva. 'From what you've already said, it's possible she might have seen something.'

Giving a meaningful glance at the clock on the mantelshelf in the room, Charlie said, 'She'll not thank you for waking her at this hour. She doesn't rise until the afternoon.'

'I'm not looking for her thanks,' retorted Eva. 'As for the hours she keeps . . . they're God-given and ought to be spent honouring His bountifulness, not in playing the Devil's game. Come, Ethan. Let's find out what this woman can tell us.'

The houses backing on to those in Pin's Lane were approached via an alleyway. Cluttered with filth that had accumulated over many months, it was being scavenged by dogs, cats and rats.

It was a scene Eva had encountered in the slums of many other towns and cities in England. However, familiarity did not make it any more palatable. She wrinkled her nose in disgust as she lifted her skirts and tried to avoid the more offensive rubbish.

The house they were seeking had a neglected look about it. Paint was peeling from the door and window frames, and a number of glass panes in the ground-floor windows were missing and had been replaced with sacking and folded newspapers.

The door was opened to Eva's persistent knocking by Clara Flood, the landlady of the house. A stooped and untidy grey-haired little woman, she took one look at Captain Eva's uniform and attempted to close the door again immediately.

The Salvationist had considerable experience of dealing with householders who had no wish to speak with her. The landlady found a foot effectively preventing the door from closing.

After a couple of half-hearted attempts to kick the foot clear of the doorway, Clara conceded defeat. Reluctantly, she opened the door wide once more.

'What d'yer want?' she demanded.

'I want to have a few words with the woman who lives in the back room upstairs. I believe she's known as Devonport Lil.'

'She won't want to see *you*,' Clara replied positively. 'Not at this time of day, she won't. Come back about five o'clock.'

'She'll speak to me now.' Unceremoniously pushing open the door as wide as it would go, Eva said over her shoulder, 'Come along, Ethan.' She headed for the stairs, situated half-way along a narrow, dark, musty-smelling passageway.

With a half-apologetic shrug at the scowling woman who stood holding the open door, Ethan stepped inside the passageway and followed the Salvation Army captain up the stairs.

There were two doors opening off the landing. Eva knocked heavily on the door of the room where she believed Devonport Lil to be.

After waiting for a few moments without receiving a reply, she knocked once more, at the same time trying the latch. The door appeared to be bolted on the inside.

'Who is it . . . ? What d'you want?' A sleepy and indignant voice came to them from inside the room.

'I want to talk to you.'

'Go away. Come back tonight.'

Eva knocked again. When she received no reply this time, she continued to knock, long and loud, before saying, 'I can keep this up all day if I need to. You might as well open the door and speak to me, then you can go back to sleep again.'

Ethan and Eva heard grumbling from inside the room before the door opened. A woman stood in the doorway.

Sleep-filled eyes looked Captain Eva up and down from beneath heavy, puffy lids. Then she asked irritably, 'What the bloody hell do you want at this time of the day?'

'I want to talk to you . . .' Raising her voice, Eva added, 'Out of hearing of others.' Stepping inside the room, she motioned for Ethan to follow.

The room was as untidy as the woman. An aroma of cheap scent hung on the air, used in an apparent attempt to override the general odours of the house.

As Devonport Lil closed the door, frowning disapprovingly, Eva strode to the window and drew back the curtains.

Blinking against the sudden unwelcome influx of light, the prostitute demanded, 'Here! Just who do you think you are, coming in here and doing as you like?'

Instead of answering her question, Eva pointed across the two tiny, back-to-back yards to the room where Ruth had died. 'What do you know of the people who live over there?'

The woman's attitude underwent an extraordinary change and fear replaced belligerence. 'I didn't see nothing – or no one.'

'In view of the fact that you've answered the question before I've even asked it, it's quite obvious you *did* see something last night. Who did you see over there, Lil?'

'I told you, I didn't see no one.' Devonport Lil gave the impression of being thoroughly frightened.

'It was Sid Darling, wasn't it? What was he doing?'

'I couldn't see what he was doing. Like I just said, I can't tell you nothing.'

'So it *was* him who was over there! Do you know a girl died in that room last night?'

'One'll die in *this* room if he knows I've said anything about him.'

'I'm not the police, Lil, but the girl who died wasn't the one he was after. He'll come back to kill her too if we aren't able to stop him.'

'What do you think *you* can do against the likes of Sid Darling?' Devonport Lil spoke contemptuously. 'He'd eat the whole of the Salvation Army for breakfast. Me too if he learns I've been talking to you. Anyway, I only saw him over there. I didn't see him do anything.'

'This was about half past nine last night, is that right?'

The prostitute nodded. 'Probably, although it might have been closer to nine o'clock. That's all I'm saying. If you bring the police into this I'll swear I saw nothing. Now, I'm not talking to you any more, so you might as well go.'

34

As Ethan and Captain Eva carefully picked their way once more through the rubbish-cluttered alleyway, he asked, 'What are we going to do now?'

'Somehow, we need to persuade the police to step up their efforts to have Sid Darling arrested. Until he's put out of the way Sally is never going to be safe.'

'But surely now we know what he's done to Ruth, the police will arrest him for murdering her?'

'What exactly do we *know* he's done, Ethan? We're fairly certain he was in the room yesterday evening – and we know that Ruth died. The woman we've just spoken to will never stand up in court and admit that she saw Sid Darling in Ruth's room. If the doctor who carries out the post-mortem confirms she was murdered, then we can tell the police all we know. When they eventually arrest Sid Darling they'll question him about it. However, we need to remember that he's already a wanted man – and the police haven't been very successful in arresting him, even though he's been seen by a number of people, including poor Rachel.

This latest incident has terrified her. She believes he'll come after her as well as Sally – and she could well be right.'

'What can we do? We can't allow him to put Sally and Rachel in terror and get away with killing Ruth – and I'm convinced that's what he did.'

'So am I, but without proof he'll never be convicted in a court.' She added bitterly, 'Perhaps we should provide him with a Salvation Army uniform. That would ensure his arrest, at least.'

They walked in silence for a while before Eva said, 'I'll go and speak to Percy Mallett. He'll at least listen to what I say, and he may be able to use his influence to have Sid Darling arrested.'

Percy Mallett listened to Eva courteously. He expressed concern that Sid Darling was still at large. At the same time, he confirmed what she already knew. Without firm evidence against him and witnesses prepared to testify to what they had seen, Sid Darling would never be charged with murder.

'Nevertheless, I will speak to the chief constable about the failure to arrest this man on the charges concerning those young girls. Perhaps the knowledge that I am taking a personal interest in the case will succeed where the due process of the law has failed.'

As Percy Mallett was walking Eva to the door of his house, he said, 'We have a new inspector in the Force, Captain. His name is Ian Lovat. He has been brought to Plymouth to form a detective section. There are those who feel he is too young to hold such a post, but he had a remarkable record of thief-taking in the London Force. He spent much of his service there working in plain-clothes. Inspector Lovat accepted the post only when we agreed to give him a completely free hand to carry out his duties. The chief constable had grave reservations about allowing him such independence, but he was overruled by my committee. I think Inspector Lovat might be able to help in the matter of Mr Darling. I'll ask him to call upon you.'

'Thank you very much, Mr Mallett. I regret I don't have your faith in policemen – wherever they are from – but none of the girls in my care can afford to rest easy until Sid Darling has been arrested and brought to justice.'

When Inspector Ian Lovat called at the Salvation Army Refuge in the Barbican, the door was opened by one of the girls. After showing him in to the front lounge, she went to find Eva.

The Salvation Army officer was busy in the small linen room, on the second floor of the house. Entering, the girl said coyly, 'There's a man come to the house looking for you, Captain Eva. A very handsome man.'

'Oh! Did he tell you his name and his business?'

'No. I did ask him, but he said his business was "personal" – with you.'

Eva frowned. 'Did he, now? Very well, Joan, I'll come down and speak to him.'

With another of the girls, she had been checking through a stack of sheets that had been donated to the home by a well-wisher. It was necessary to sort out those that were too badly worn and would need to be torn up for dusters, or perhaps made into pillow-cases. She now asked Joan to take her place.

As she started down the stairs she could hear the two

girls whispering together about the 'handsome man' who had come calling on her. She smiled to herself. She was aware the girls were concerned there was no man in her life. They were convinced that, at the age of twenty-three, she was well and truly 'on the shelf'.

All the same, she wondered who her visitor might be.

Ian Lovat was a tall, sandy-haired man, with a ready smile. When he spoke, it was with the soft accent of the west coast of Scotland.

'Good morning, Captain Cassington. I am Ian Lovat. Mr Mallett asked me to come along to see you to discuss the problems you are having with this man Sidney Darling.'

'Oh, you're *Inspector* Lovat? It's very kind of you to come and call on me so quickly.'

'Mr Mallett told me of your concern for the girls who are here with you. I've read the notices that have been put out about Darling, but perhaps you will tell me what you know of him?'

As they sat together in the lounge, Eva told the detective how girls had been lured to Plymouth by an advertisement offering posts in domestic service and what had happened to them on their arrival. The inspector made notes as she explained Sally's part in raising the alarm and told him of the fight at Shepherd's Wharf and the rescue of the girls.

Finally, she told him of the latest incident which had culminated in the death of Ruth in suspicious circumstances.

Ian Lovat was silent for a while, then he said, 'This girl, Sally Harrup, seems to be at the heart of all that's going on in this matter.'

'She's a bright girl, Inspector. She's nice too – in every sense of the word.'

He nodded. 'I'm sure she is. I look forward to meeting her in due course. I'll wait until she has made a full recovery from the sad death of her sister. It must have been a very nasty shock for her.'

Having a policeman express sympathy for someone even remotely associated with the Salvation Army was a new experience for Eva. However, she tried not to allow her surprise to show.

'Why did you not call in the police when you first had suspicions of what was going on?' He put the question to her as he was returning his notebook to a pocket.

'With all due respect to you, Inspector Lovat, my experience has been that it is a waste of everyone's time for a member of the Salvation Army to report *anything* to the police, no matter how serious. It serves only to bring that individual to their attention. As likely as not, it ultimately results in his, or her, own arrest.'

'I feel that's a rather unkind generalisation, but I can understand your attitude. There does seem to be a degree of resentment among certain policemen towards your organisation.'

'That resentment resulted in my being sentenced to prison shortly before Christmas, Inspector. My offence was nothing more serious than marching to a prayer meeting here in Plymouth. So my "attitude", as you describe it, is hardly surprising.'

'You have my sympathy, Captain. However, I assure you that I have nothing but admiration for the Salvation Army and its founder. I spent a while working among the people of Poplar, in London. I am aware of the wonderful work done by your organisation among the most unfortunate and under-privileged members of our society. I assure you of my whole-hearted support. I trust you will give me yours. Hopefully, we will then be able to bring Sidney Darling to justice and sound the death knoll to a vile trade that brings shame upon us all.'

Eva looked at Ian Lovat in silence for a few moments. Suddenly, she smiled. 'Inspector Lovat, I think you and I are going to work well together. Now, let me show you over the house. Along the way I will tell you what I intend to achieve here. Then I will introduce you to Rachel. She has suffered more than any of the girls because of Mr Darling. I am quite certain she will talk to you when I tell her you are the man who is going to arrest him.'

35

The inquest on Ruth Harrup was attended by Sally, Eva and Ethan. It was an unhappy and frustratingly perfunctory affair.

The surgeon who had carried out the post-mortem had been unable to discover any unnatural cause for her death. Indeed, he was unable to say with any degree of certainty exactly what *had* caused her to die.

However, he was able to inform the coroner that Ruth's lungs were in such an advanced stage of disease, it was really quite remarkable she had lived for so long.

Ian Lovat was also in court. During the surgeon's evidence, the coroner was startled to have a note passed to him from the inspector, via the coroner's officer.

Reading from the note, the coroner asked the surgeon, 'Is it possible the deceased woman might have died as a result of suffocation? By a pillow being placed over her face, for instance?'

The surgeon mulled over the question for a moment or two before delivering a somewhat cautious reply. 'It is not *impossible*, but in view of the advanced stage of her lung disease my opinion is that her death was brought about by natural causes.'

The coroner looked across the courtroom with a questioning glance at Inspector Lovat and the policeman nodded his head. A few minutes later the coroner delivered his verdict.

The recorded cause of the death of Ruth Harrup was 'Natural causes'.

Outside the courtroom, Sally was bewildered by the verdict. 'It just isn't true! Sid Darling killed her. We know he was in the room because someone trod on Ruth's Christmas present. That and the pillow from the bottom of the bed that I found on the floor. She wouldn't have moved that. She never had before.'

'Unfortunately, all that is no more than supposition, Sally,' said the inspector. 'It's hardly even circumstantial evidence.'

Sally was unsure of the meaning of both 'supposition' and 'circumstantial', but she *did* believe she knew how Ruth's death had occurred.

She continued her protest until Ian Lovat said, 'You believe Sid Darling did it – and so do I. Proving it is quite another matter. Nevertheless, I shall try, I can assure you of that.'

'No you won't,' Sally retorted bitterly. 'Because he's never going to be arrested.'

'Oh, he'll be arrested all right,' he assured her confidently. 'Even though I doubt it's imminent. I have reliable information that Sid Darling has left Plymouth for a while.'

'There you are then,' Sally said scornfully. 'He did it and now he's run off. He'll never be caught, you'll see.'

'He'll be back. Mother Darling is still living in Mary Street. He'll return to her one day. When he does, he'll be arrested.' Resting a hand on Sally's shoulder, he added sympathetically, 'I give you my word on that, Sally – and I always keep my word.'

With this promise, Ian Lovat left to return to the police station, leaving Sally with Eva and Ethan.

She had received a great deal of support in the coroner's court. Her two companions and the inspector had been with her for the whole of the proceedings. Grace had wanted to attend too, but Alfie successfully protested that, however much he sympathised with Sally, he simply could not run the pie shop with only Rachel to help him.

As a result, Grace had stayed to work in the shop. Sally would not be returning there until after Ruth's funeral. In the meantime, Grace, generous as ever, assured her she would be paid a wage equal to that she had been earning before the tragedy.

Sally had been living in the Salvation Army home ever since Ruth's death, but she knew she would need to think about her future now and decide whether or not to keep on the room in Pin's Lane.

Ruth's funeral took place on a day as bleak and cold as the occasion itself. The church was not crowded, but there were many more in the congregation than Sally had anticipated.

The whole of Ethan's family attended, including Sophie. Phoebe did not attend, but she sent an extravagant wreath.

Grace and Alfie were there, having closed the shop for a few hours. So too was Captain Eva, with all the girls from the home, together with Captain Wardle and a few members of the Salvation Army.

Some of the neighbours from Pin's Lane also attended. Among their number were a couple of the girls who had once solicited on the streets of Plymouth with Ruth.

The vicar, who had been expecting far fewer in the funeral congregation, mumbled a totally inaccurate eulogy, but it pleased Sally.

The interment in the churchyard took long enough to cause everyone present to shiver in the cold wind. Although Sally came very close to breaking down, the strong arm of Grace about her provided just enough strength and comfort to hold off her tears.

Afterwards, when the party moved towards the gate of the burial ground, slowed by all those who came up to offer their condolences to Sally, Grace asked her what she intended doing now and where she intended to live.

'Captain Eva has said I can stay in the house with her for as long as I wish. I'll probably stay for a while, at least.'

'Well, you need never be short of a place to live, dear,' said Grace. 'Alfie and me made room for Rachel. It would be no more trouble to take you in too. You could share with Rachel. It would be good company for her. We've already talked it over and she would like that.'

As Sally murmured her thanks, Ethan's mother said, 'I'm not able to offer you a home, Sally, much as I would like to. With five boys in the house and only three bedrooms between seven of us, it's more than a little crowded. I can't wait for some of them to get married and move to a home of their own. But there's always food in the house, so you need never go hungry. Come to us for as many meals as you like. We'll always be delighted to have you. I want you to remember that.'

'You are lucky in having so many good friends, Sally,' commented Eva. 'And you can add everyone at the home and Central headquarters to your list. But what are you going to do right now?'

'I think I'll go to Pin's Lane and tidy up Ruth's things. But I don't think I could sleep there on my own. Not yet, anyway. So I'd like to come back to the Refuge tonight. Tomorrow, I'll start work again and think seriously about the future.'

'Only come in if you feel like it, mind,' said Grace. 'Although we'll be delighted to have you back with us, won't we, Alfie?'

Alfie agreed with all honesty that he was looking forward to her return to work. Having no one reliable to deliver their wares had been adversely affecting the business. Rachel was a very willing young girl, but she did not yet know the Plymouth area and was still nervous about going out on her own.

'Thank you all. Thank you for helping me – and for what you've done for Ruth today. It was a lovely funeral. Ruth never ever believed she would have one like that . . .' Sally's voice broke, despite her determination to maintain tight control of herself. Recovering as best she could, she said abruptly, 'I'm going to Pin's Lane now.'

As she turned away and set off hurriedly, Ethan caught up with her. 'I'll come with you.' Aware that she was about to protest, he added quickly, 'I'll just see you to the house and stay with Uncle Charlie while you go up to your room. I know you'd rather be on your own up there for a while. Just remember I'm close at hand in case you feel you need me. Uncle Charlie isn't feeling too well at the moment. That's the reason he wasn't at the funeral today. I know he'd been hoping to make it to the church.'

Sally wanted a little time on her own while she did what needed to be done, but knowing Ethan was in the house too would be reassuring.

Without saying a word, she slipped her hand in his, thinking how lucky she was to have found him.

Behind them, at the gate to the burial ground, Doris Shields watched them walking off hand-in-hand. She wondered, somewhat wistfully, whether her youngest son would be the next to leave the family home.

Beside her, as he lit his pipe, Henry Shields had been watching the young couple too. Correctly interpreting his wife's expression, he took her arm and said gently, 'The lad could do a whole lot worse, Doris. That young girl has something about her. Reminds me a little of the girl I married . . .'

36

When Sally and Ethan reached the Pin's Lane house they found Charlie waiting for them at the door of his room. He had been seated at the window of his room watching out for them.

His first words showed he had been waiting for Sally. 'I hoped you might come back here,' he said. 'I wanted to be at the funeral, but this weather sets my chest off. I dared not leave the house. If I'd gone you wouldn't have heard nothing but my coughing in the church. All the same, I was thinking of Ruth.'

'I'm sure you were, Charlie. Thank you.'

'Will you be moving back here now?'

He sounded a little too eager and Sally remembered his habits before Ethan had appeared on the scene. 'Not for a while. I've just come back to sort out a few of Ruth's things.'

Shrugging off his disappointment, Charlie asked, 'What shall I tell the rent man when he comes this week? The last time he came he wanted to know whether he should find someone else to take your room.'

'You can tell him if I want to move out I'll tell him – and he'll get any rent that's owing him. I'm only a fortnight behind. There are many around here who owe him far more than that.' Sally spoke angrily, and Ethan said hurriedly, 'Would you like me to go upstairs first, Sally?'

'Would you, Ethan? I know it's silly, but I'll feel happier if you make sure there's no one there. Then I'd like to go through Ruth's things on my own.'

'Of course. I'll come back down here and wait with Uncle Charlie until you're finished.'

When Ethan had returned downstairs, Sally stood alone in the upstairs room for some minutes. It felt wrong without Ruth lying in the bed. Horribly wrong. She realised she needed to shake off such feelings.

Going to the window, she opened it wide. The cold air from outside made her shiver, but it drove out the smell of the damp and mustiness that pervaded the room.

Suddenly, she heard a bird singing from the branch of a solitary tree that grew in a backyard farther along the lane. The song was as beautiful as it was out of place amidst the squalor of the Barbican slum.

Listening to the song brought a lump to Sally's throat – but it did something else too. Something indefinable. The song of the lone, defiant bird held a message of optimism.

It was the frailest of threads on which to pin her hopes for the future, but it somehow gave her just a little of the strength she so desperately needed at this time.

Turning back into the room, she felt able to carry out the tasks for which she had come here.

There were very few of Ruth's clothes in the chest of drawers; just a few underclothes, a frock and two nightdresses. Ruth's outdoor clothes had been sold long before, when things were going badly for the two girls and it became clear that Ruth was never going to recover.

But there was still the trunk . . .

Sally reached up and located the purse, hidden at the rear of the high shelf. She took out the key and, turning it in the stiff lock, she lifted the lid of the trunk and began rummaging inside.

There were a few clothes and shoes that had mainly belonged to their mother. Taking them out one by one, she laid them on the bare floorboards.

Next came a few strands of cheap beads, a hat, two cheap gilded – and empty – jewellery boxes, and the bundle of letters she had seen once before, tied up with a pink ribbon.

Sally untied the ribbon with a sense of curiosity rather than excitement. Taking the first letter from its envelope, she began to read.

She was half-way through it before realisation of what she was reading hit her.

It was a letter from the man who was her father!

Trembling with excitement, Sally looked at the printed address at the top of the single sheet of paper. It was Lanhydrock House, in Cornwall.

She read through the remainder of the letter eagerly, only to find it tantalisingly brief and disappointingly formal. However, it revealed a great deal about the relationship between her parents.

In a bold, but untidy hand, the letter read:

Dear Molly,

I thank you for your letter. I must warn you yet again that your are not to write to me here and put my position at risk. If you do so again I will refuse to send you any more money and will leave you to fend for yourself in a manner to which you are undoubtedly familiar.

That I send you any money at all is because I have no wish to see the sins of the mother visited upon the child by reason of an immoral upbringing.

You ask if I might not plead with the family to take you back into their employ; you must realise this is not possible. You were dismissed because you became pregnant. The family is hardly likely to allow you to return now you have a bastard child. Besides, how would I explain to them that I am still in touch with you?

No, you must make a future for you and the child in Plymouth. Opportunities for gainful employment will exist there, even for a woman such as yourself.

I will continue to send small sums of money from time to time but, I repeat, do *not* write to me here again.

The letter was signed, 'Yours faithfully, Robert Sanderson'.

Sally looked once again at the top of the page. There was a date of 12 August 1858. She was disappointed. The date was before she was born. The 'child' referred to in the letter must have been Ruth.

Yet Ruth had always said their mother had been adamant that both girls shared the same father – and there were other letters.

More than an hour later, Sally was still reading. She now had a much clearer picture of her mother and the life she had led. She had learned something about her father too – and was quite convinced that the man who had written the letters *was* her father.

Despite his earlier demand that her mother cease writing to him, she had evidently ignored his wishes. It was apparent too that, over the years covered by the letters, his determination to have nothing to do with her mother had been eroded by her persistence.

Towards the end of the correspondence, he had written to say he had found work for her, helping a washerwoman in the Cornish town of Bodmin, not far from Lanhydrock House.

There was a gap in the letters then, for quite a while. It was broken by a single letter, filled with Robert Sanderson's anger.

Sally's mother was in Plymouth once again – and was expecting another baby. This final letter was sent in 1863, so the baby this time had to be Sally and Sanderson was again the father.

His anger was due to his belief that Sally's mother had become pregnant deliberately, in order that she might give up work. He also accused her of nursing a vain hope that he would keep her.

Apparently money *had* been sent to her, but it was accompanied by a warning. The writer warned her that if she tried to name him as the father, he would so blacken her character, she was likely to spend the rest of her life in prison.

His anger leapt out at Sally from the single page even after all these years. It was hardly surprising this was the last letter in the bundle.

Sally was still on her knees beside the trunk when Ethan returned to the room, concerned that she was still here.

'Are you all right, Sally? I was getting worried about you.'

'Yes, I'm all right.'

'What do you want to do now? Where do you want to go?'

Standing up, still clutching the letters, Sally said, 'I think I'll go to the pie shop. I want to tell Grace I won't be coming to work tomorrow after all. I'm going to see if my father is still at Lanhydrock House. In Cornwall.'

37

'Are you quite certain this is what you want to do, Sally?'

Eva expressed her concern as Sally boarded the train that would take her across the River Tamar to Cornwall and, hopefully, a meeting with the father she had never known.

Sally nodded a reply.

She was under no illusions about the reception she was likely to receive from the man she believed to be her father. The last letter he had sent to her mother had made his feelings perfectly clear.

However, she remembered the change in the tone of the letters over the years before that. Sally hoped that time might have mellowed him once more. That he would at least acknowledge her and perhaps show regret at Ruth's death.

She wondered whether he was aware her mother had died all those years ago. He might even have tried to find her. The address on the few envelopes that had been kept with the letters no longer existed, so he would have had great difficulty locating her.

Of course, there was a strong possibility he was no longer at Lanhydrock House. If this proved to be so, she might at least learn where he had gone.

Captain Eva, Ethan and Grace had all tried to dissuade Sally from making this journey – at least until enquiries had been made concerning Robert Sanderson. Whether he was still at Lanhydrock House and, if he was, his position there and his present family circumstances.

This latter consideration far from worrying Sally actually excited her. She might have other brothers and sisters – or *half*-brothers and -sisters. They would never be able to take the place of Ruth, of course, but it would be wonderful to discover a whole new family.

She had discussed this aspect of her quest with Ethan. He too had warned her against undue optimism. He had wanted to accompany her, even though it was good fishing weather, but she had declined his offer. She felt this was something she needed to do by herself. It was almost as though she owed it to Ruth.

Sitting on the train, Sally thought about her late sister. She wondered why Ruth had never said anything about the letters to her. Why *she* had never tried to contact their father . . . ?

Watching from the platform of Plymouth railway station as the train disappeared from view, Eva tried to tell herself there was probably no justification for the concern she felt about Sally's self-imposed mission to Lanhydrock House. Yet she felt decidedly uneasy about the whole business.

For all the worldliness Sally displayed here in Plymouth, she had never before travelled beyond the town's boundaries. Eva knew just how vulnerable she was at the moment, having so recently lost her sister.

At least the Salvation Army officer had been able to provide her with a stout pair of elastic-sided boots. They had come from the stock donated to the organisation by well-wishers, for distribution to the poor.

Had she not done so, Sally would have set off wearing entirely unsuitable light town shoes. Although satisfactorily shod, Sally was, Eva felt, not dressed for travelling so far. True, she was wearing the warm cloak that had once been her mother's, but beneath it she had on only the thin frock she had bought to wear to Ethan's house.

Sally knew nothing of Captain Eva's thoughts. She felt very grown-up and sophisticated. At least she believed this was what she was showing to the world.

Inside, she felt less so.

She was no stranger to trains. They were part of everyday life in Plymouth. There were few places in and about the town where they could not be heard or seen. Yet this was the first time she had travelled in one and it was very exciting.

The first part of the journey involved a crossing of the River Tamar on the high suspension bridge that linked Devon with Cornwall. Sally held her breath as she looked down to the waters of the River Tamar far below the train. Downriver, a great many warships were anchored in long lines extending beyond the Hamoaze and the naval dockyard of Devonport.

After skirting numerous creeks, each with a wide variety of small boats scattered about on mud, water and dry land, the railway line curved inland. Smoke from the engine now spread across hills and valleys.

After less than an hour, the train was steaming noisily along the side of a wooded slope, which rose from a valley road. Suddenly the train driver pulled the whistle cord and sent a long, raucous signal echoing across the valley, and the train began to slow as it approached Bodmin Road station. Sally had been told she would need to alight here for Lanhydrock House.

Now, for the first time, she wished she had accepted Ethan's offer to accompany her.

A few minutes later, standing alone on the platform as the train steamed westwards on its journey, she felt even more uncertain of herself.

'Can I help you, Miss?'

The question came from a young railway porter, scarcely older than herself. He had appeared, unnoticed, on the platform behind her.

'I want to go to Lanhydrock House – but I don't know the way,' she said, relieved to have found someone from whom to ask directions.

The young porter looked her up and down, deciding on the form his reply would take. She wore an expensive cloak, but the dress visible beneath it and the cheap bonnet reassured him he was not addressing 'gentry'.

'It's easy enough to get there, but you'll find the paths a bit muddy. You'll need to hoist your dress well clear of your ankles if you don't want to get it dirty. Come outside the station and I'll show you the way.'

Sally followed him to a carriage park and he pointed westward, in the direction taken by the train.

'Go along there, following the path beside the railway until it turns off to the right. You'll see a bridge then. Cross it, over the river, and go through the iron gate on the left. You're then on the drive that leads up to the big house.'

'How far is it?' she asked anxiously, seeing the railway line disappearing into the distance.

'About a mile and a half. I walk up there quite often. My ma is a lady's maid at the house. Are you going up there for work?'

'No. I'm looking for someone, but . . . I don't even know if he's still there.'

'If he is I'll know him. I know everyone up at the house. What's his name?'

'Robert Sanderson.'

'The butler! I'll say he's there – but you'd better watch your step with him. He's an absolute Tartar. He's got an eye for the ladies, too. Especially young ones, like you. I wouldn't like to tell you how many young girls I've seen weeping on this station because of him. They'd been dismissed, all of 'em. Some because they "wouldn't", the others because they "did" and ended up in trouble. What d'you want him for?'

'It's personal,' said Sally, trying not to show the dismay she felt at his words.

'Oh, personal, is it? Well, don't say I haven't warned you about him – and don't let him lead you off somewhere so he can "take down your particulars". Five minutes alone with him and it'll be more than your particulars he'll have down. I can tell you *that*!'

38

Walking from the railway station, Sally thought about the porter's words. She wondered how much of what he had said was the truth and how much mere malicious gossip.

Whatever the truth of it, she had learned two things. The man she believed to be her father was the butler at Lanhydrock House – and he was still there!

Sally was not entirely certain what a butler did, but it was evident from what the young porter had said that it was something very important.

The thought that such a man might very soon acknowledge her as his daughter excited her, but once again she wished Ethan was here with her. Sally felt certain *he* would know what a butler did.

She soon realised the porter had been accurate about one thing. The path beside the railway line *was* very muddy. She was forced to walk with the hem of her skirt held up almost to her knees until she left the path and turned in at the entrance to the Lanhydrock Estate.

Here, she spent many minutes cleaning mud from her boots with grass torn from the verge at the side of the roadway.

Passing through the gate into the drive she found herself on a long gravelled avenue, flanked by rows of tall, mature trees.

Even though it was winter and the trees were denuded of leaves, they were still impressive.

Even more impressive was her first sight of the house, which did not come into view until she had walked quite a way along the tree-lined driveway.

Built in a U-shape, with the open end facing her, the house was battlemented, with an immaculate garden to the front and sides and a detached gatehouse some distance in front of the house itself.

But it was the sheer size of the house that Sally found awesome. It was *huge*. Even the gatehouse was larger than three of the houses in Pin's Lane!

Stopping in front of the gatehouse, Sally looked through the archway at the house itself. She knew she would never be able to summon up enough courage to pass through and knock on the front door.

She also realised that house servants would not be allowed to use the main entrance, so there had to be another door. While she was looking around for it, an aged gardener put his head above the low wall surrounding the garden.

'Hello! You here looking for work?'

'No. I'm here to speak with Mr Sanderson – he's the butler.'

'I know very well who he is, missie. There's no one worked here longer than me. I'd been here nigh on half a lifetime before ever he came here. I've seen enough young girls like you come and go in that time, too, I can tell you. Full of their cheek they are when they arrive. Laughing at me and saying I ought to be put out to grass – I've heard 'em all right. But I've still been working here when they've gone off crying, with a bundle of belongings on their shoulder and a bundle of trouble under their girdle. Make certain it don't happen to you too, girl.'

Sally thought of telling him once again that she had not come to Lanhydrock House seeking work, but decided it would be a waste of time. He was probably deaf. However, she thought she would ask him if he remembered her mother.

'Molly Harrup?' he repeated. 'Can't say I do. What was she working as? Kitchen maid? Housemaid?'

Sally had to confess she did not know.

'Don't know? I knew what my mother did – yes, and my grandmother and great grandmother, too. They were all housemaids right here at the house. Didn't you ever ask her?'

'She died when I was very small.'

'Ah! Well, you can't be blamed for not knowing about her then, I suppose. But couldn't your father have told you?'

'I never knew him.'

'I see,' the old gardener said knowingly. 'Well, you're not the first who never knew her father, and you won't be the last. But I can't stand here talking to you. I've got work to do. I hope they take you on up at the house, but I wouldn't count on it, if I was you. They've not needed to take on anyone new for a while now. You'll find the servants' door around the corner, through the coachyard. That's where you want to go – but you'd better be quick about it. The family don't like to see servants standing about in front of the house.'

The servants' door at the rear of the great house was opened by a red-faced kitchen maid, who had a lock of untidy hair hanging down over one eye. She appeared harassed.

Wasting no time on pleasantries, she asked, 'What do you want? If you're selling something – we ain't buying. If you're looking for work, we don't need anyone.'

'I'm not selling anything and I don't need work. I've come to speak to Mr Sanderson.'

The kitchen maid's manner underwent a subtle change. Less aggressively, she asked, 'You want the butler?' Her gaze took in Sally from her bonnet to the elastic-sided boots, visible beneath the hem of her too-small dress. Clearly puzzled, she asked, 'What do you want him for?'

'I'll tell that to *him*, if you don't mind.'

'*I* don't mind, but *he* will if it's someone wasting his time, and I don't want him telling me off. Who shall I say is calling on him?'

'Tell him . . . Tell him it's the daughter of Molly Harrup.'

'Is that all?'

'That's all.'

More uncertain than ever, the kitchen maid said, 'I'll tell him, but don't be surprised if he won't see you. He's not a great one for unexpected visitors, especially when his Lordship has a shooting party staying in the house.'

When the maid had gone, Sally was left waiting outside the servants' door. She had a moment of sheer panic. The maid had mentioned 'his Lordship'! Sally knew nothing at all about the peerage. Had she been questioned about them she would have said that all lords and ladies were related to the Queen.

Now here she was, standing outside the house of a lord, waiting for a man whose daily life was tied up with such people.

And that man was her father.

39

When the door opened once more, Sally had her back to it. She was watching the Lanhydrock House grooms. They had rolled a light landau from the coach house and were busily engaged in preparing the two horses that were to draw it.

Hearing the door open behind her, Sally turned. She was taken aback by the man standing before her. He was more than six feet tall and stoutly built, with greying hair, and, dressed in white tie and tailcoat, he made a very impressive sight.

Even in her present, highly emotional state, Sally found it easy to see why young servant girls would fall for him in droves. However, his expression was not intended to charm her and when he spoke his voice was brusque.

'What nonsense is this, girl? You're not Molly Harrup's daughter. What's your game, eh?'

His greeting was not the one she had foolishly hoped he might give to her.

'I *am* her daughter. That's why I've come to see you—'

'Don't lie to me, girl. Her daughter came here some five or six years ago, begging money from me. If she's sent you to do the same, you're out of luck. It didn't work then and it won't work now. In fact, I've a good mind to call the police . . .'

'Nobody has sent me, and I don't want anything from you. I . . . I didn't know Ruth had already been to see you. She never said anything to me about it. It's just . . . when she died I found some letters you'd written to our ma.'

'Ruth Harrup's dead?' For a moment the butler dropped his belligerence, but only for a moment. 'What's this about letters? She never said anything about them to me.'

'She never said anything about them to *me*, either,' Sally replied. 'But when I found them, I realised . . . I realised . . .'

She found it difficult to say what she wanted to this large, aggressive and unfriendly man who overawed her. He was a stranger. A *cold* stranger. But the words had to be said.

'I realised . . . you are my father.'

'That is a load of nonsense, girl, as well you know.'

The butler spoke the words angrily. When he immediately closed the door behind him, Sally realised the words had been intended for any of the servants who might be listening in to the conversation.

'Now, what is all this about? Why have you come here? If it's money—'

'It's got nothing to do with money. I don't want *anything* from you.'

Sally found herself ridiculously close to tears – and she realised it *was* ridiculous. She had known when she decided to come to Lanhydrock House that she could not expect instant acknowledgement and affection from the man she still believed to be her father. Yet she had nursed a forlorn hope . . .

She was not even certain what it was she *had* hoped for. Perhaps, having lost Ruth, she wanted to feel she was not entirely alone in the world. That she belonged to someone.

'These letters . . . Do you have them with you? I'd like to see them.'

'No, I left them at home.'

Sally realised he was worried about the existence of the letters; far more concerned about them than he was about her.

She accepted now that she should not have come here. She should have listened to Captain Eva and to Ethan. Suddenly, Ethan was the one she wanted to be with more than anyone else she knew. Certainly more than with this man to whom she would never mean anything.

'You don't need to worry about the letters. You'll never hear about them again – or me, either.'

Turning, Sally began to walk away swiftly from the door.

'Just a minute, young lady. Come back here. There are a few more things I want to know . . .'

Instead of obeying his call, Sally took to her heels and ran. Her one thought was to get away from Lanhydrock House and Robert Sanderson as quickly as she could. To return to Plymouth and to Ethan.

As she fled from the coach-house yard, she ran headlong into a group of about seven or eight men, members of Lord Robartes' shooting party.

She would have carried on past them, but one of the younger men grabbed and held her.

'Not so fast, young lady. Where do you think you're going?'

'More to the point,' said an older man, 'where has she *been*? Do you see the coat of arms on the cloak she's wearing?'

The younger man who was holding her turned her around without releasing his grip and peered at the woven shields to which the cloak's clasp was attached.

'Good Lord! It's the Robartes coat of arms. *Our* coat of arms. I do believe we've caught ourselves a little thief, Uncle.'

'Where did you get the cloak from, young lady? Have you been inside the house?'

'No – and I haven't pinched anything, either. This cloak belonged to my ma. Let me go, I want to go back to Plymouth.'

'I've no doubt you do,' said the older man. 'But you aren't going anywhere just yet, young lady. In fact, I doubt if you'll be going anywhere for quite some time. Take her to the house and have her locked away, Donald. Then call the police and tell them to come and collect her. We won't let the little baggage interfere with our shooting . . .'

40

Held in the grip of two members of Lord Robartes' shooting party, Sally struggled and fought vigorously. Rather than run the risk of losing her on their way to the house, they decided to lock her in a harness room, inside the coach house.

The room possessed only a single, small window, at a height she could not reach, even when she tried jumping up at it – and she tried many times. She also spent a great deal of time and energy beating on the door and shouting to be released.

Sally was in a furious temper. Being wrongly accused of theft was bad enough but, before shutting her in the harness room, her captors had taken away her cloak. The loss of this precious piece of clothing upset her even more than the fact that she now had only a thin dress to protect her from the cold.

As it became increasingly apparent that raging against her arrest and imprisonment was futile, she calmed down. Only now did she begin to feel the cold. Fortunately, she spotted some horse blankets folded on a rack. Taking down two, she unfolded them and wrapped them about her.

Now for the first time she began to think about her predicament. She wondered what would happen to her when the police arrived. Sally realised she would find it difficult to prove she had *not* stolen the cloak, especially as it was embroidered with the coat of arms of the family who had arrested her. The police were hardly likely to accept her word against that of the owner of such a grand house.

Sally remained locked in the harness room for almost four hours before she heard voices in the coach house beyond the door. A bolt was withdrawn, and when the door was opened a groom entered the harness room. He was followed by two policemen, one wearing the stripes of a sergeant.

Both uniformed men looked at her sternly and the sergeant said, 'So you're the young thief, eh? You've landed yourself in a whole lot of trouble, young lady. Stealing from a house is a very serious offence.'

'I didn't steal nothing,' Sally declared hotly. 'That cloak belonged to my ma.'

'Oh? Are you saying it was her who stole it? Or perhaps you're trying to tell us she belonged to Lord Robartes' family?'

The sergeant's sarcastic suggestion brought smiles to the faces of the constable and the groom.

'Put the handcuffs on her, Constable,' the sergeant instructed. 'We'll take her to Bodmin and lock her in a cell while all this is sorted out.'

Turning his back on Sally, he asked the groom, 'What time will his Lordship be returning to the house?'

'Not until well after dark,' replied the groom. 'They're

shooting in the lower woods. When they've done they're all going to Glynn House, down in the valley, for a drink or two before coming back here.'

'No matter,' said the sergeant. 'This young lady won't be going anywhere. I'll leave a message for his Lordship to say I'll call on him tomorrow morning. We can sort this out then.'

'He won't have much time to spare for you then, either,' said the groom. 'It's an even busier shooting day tomorrow. The Lord Lieutenant and his guests are coming across to join the shooting party. Rumour has it among the servants that the Prince of Wales might be in the party too.'

Duly impressed, the sergeant said, 'No doubt the inspector will call on his Lordship and arrange a time that's convenient to everyone. Come along, Constable. Bring this young thief out and we'll get her back to Bodmin.'

When the police inspector came to Sally's cell that evening, she repeated her story. She also explained for the first time why she had come to the house from Plymouth.

It was apparent to her that the inspector was not convinced by her story.

'Are you asking me to believe you've waited seventeen years before coming to find the man you claim is your father?' the inspector asked in disbelief.

'I had no idea who my father was until I read my mother's letters yesterday,' Sally replied bitterly. 'I wish now she'd burned them years ago.'

'No doubt you do,' the inspector said wryly. 'If the letters ever existed in the first place. I don't suppose you happen to have brought them with you?'

'No, they're in my room in Pin's Lane. In Plymouth.'

'Of course.' Once again there was scepticism in the inspector's voice. 'It might interest you to know we have already spoken to Mr Sanderson, the butler at Lanhydrock. He says you came to the back door with some cock-and-bull story that made no sense to him whatsoever. He realised afterwards it was some sort of subterfuge, so that you, or an accomplice, could somehow sneak into the house and steal whatever you could lay your hands on. It was unlucky that you chose something embroidered with Lord Robartes' coat of arms. That was a very foolish mistake. But most criminals slip up in some way or another.'

'I didn't steal the cloak,' Sally repeated. 'And I want it back again. It belonged to my mother.'

'Well, even if your story is true – and I will tell you now, I don't believe you – but, even if it *were* true, she must have stolen it from Lanhydrock House in the first place, so you are in possession of stolen property. I tell you, your situation is not a happy one, my girl.'

When the inspector had left her, Sally sat on the wooden platform that served as a bed and felt hot tears burning her eyes. She *was* telling the truth, yet no one would believe her.

She wished yet again that she had brought Ethan along with her. He would know what to do.

41

When Ethan arrived at the Refuge, he found Inspector Ian Lovat already there, although it was not yet nine o'clock in the morning.

'Has Sally arrived back from Cornwall?' Ethan asked the question anxiously.

He had been at the house ten hours before, asking the same question. The answer from Eva was the same as it had been then.

'No.' Aware that Ethan was genuinely concerned, she added, 'Perhaps she was late getting back and didn't want to disturb us. She might have gone to Pin's Lane.'

Ethan shook his head. 'I went there before coming here. I've called on Grace Philpott too. Sally's not been to either place. I'm worried about her, Captain Eva. We were supposed to meet up last night, so she could tell me all about the man she was going to see – her father.'

Trying to reassure him, Eva said, 'You never know, she and her father might have got on very well together.

If that were the case he might have persuaded her to stay overnight.'

'I don't think so. If he'd felt anything at all for her, he'd have tried to find her long before this. Besides, I read a couple of the letters he'd sent to Sally's ma. They weren't the letters of a man likely to welcome Sally as his long-lost daughter.'

They were holding their conversation in the kitchen, where Ian Lovat was seated with a cup of tea in his hand. He had called at the Refuge to interview one of the girls, who was certain that, on the previous day, she had seen the second man who had been at Mother Darling's when the girls had been held captive and Rachel assaulted.

'Where exactly was Sally going?' he asked.

'To a big house near Bodmin, in Cornwall,' replied Eva. 'I don't know what it is called, but I was with her when she bought her railway ticket. She was leaving the train at Bodmin Road.'

'The house is called Lan . . . something,' Ethan said thoughtfully. 'I remember – it's called Lanhydrock. That's it, Lanhydrock House.'

Writing down the name in his notebook, Ian Lovat said, 'One of my men arrested a man during the night who is wanted by the police in Bodmin. I need to send a telegraph message to arrange for them to collect him. If you like, I'll ask the inspector in charge to make a few enquiries at this house.'

'That could prove embarrassing if this man is trying to keep his indiscretions from his employers,' Eva said doubtfully.

'I shouldn't think so,' said Ethan. 'We don't even know who he is, or what he does there – but I *am* very worried about Sally. Yes, please see if you can find out anything, Inspector. If the police at Bodmin aren't able to help, I'll go to Lanhydrock myself.'

'I'll send the telegraph as soon as I return to the station. Where will I find you if I have any information?'

'Well, I should have gone fishing today, but my pa said I could take the day off to make sure Sally is all right.'

'Then you can stay here and help me shift furniture around while you wait to hear from Inspector Lovat,' said Eva, never one to miss an opportunity. Turning to Ian Lovat, she asked, 'Can you get the information to him here, if need be?'

Smiling at her opportunism, the inspector replied, 'I'll come along myself, if nothing else needing my attention crops up in the meantime.'

'Splendid! Then it's all settled. I'll make certain we have a kettle boiling for when you arrive.'

She explained to Ethan, 'I've never known such a man for his tea. If it wasn't for the fact he gets it free wherever he goes, he would no doubt spend all his earnings on it . . .'

Ethan hardly had time to shift more than a few pieces of furniture before Ian Lovat returned to the house in the Barbican. One look at the detective inspector's face and Ethan immediately stopped what he was doing.

'You've heard something about Sally? What is it? Where is she?'

'It's not good news, I'm afraid. She's been arrested for stealing from Lanhydrock House. It's the home of Lord Robartes and it was he who caught her. There was a telegraph message at the station asking if we knew anything about her.'

Ethan was so astounded by the news that he reached behind him for the table he had been moving and sat down on the edge of it.

'Sally caught stealing . . . ? I just don't believe it. She's not a thief. There must be some mistake. What is she supposed to have stolen?'

'A cloak. I'm afraid there can be no mistake. It has Lord Robartes' coat of arms embroidered on it and she was wearing it when he caught her.'

'I know that cloak,' said Ethan. 'It had belonged to her mother and was kept in a chest in her room. She was given it by her sister. She wore it when she came to our house on Christmas Day. My ma can vouch for that. She said what a splendid cloak it was. Why, it must have been in the trunk for almost twenty years before it was given to Sally.'

'That's perfectly true,' agreed Eva. 'She was wearing the same cloak when I saw her off at the railway station. I remember the coat-of-arms embroidery too. There were two of them, one on either side of the neck where the chain and clasp were attached.'

'You're quite certain of this? Certain enough to stand up in court and give evidence on Sally's behalf?'

'Absolutely.'

'Quite certain.'

Eva and Ethan spoke in unison.

'In that case, I'll telegraph to Bodmin police station again and arrange for them to collect their wanted man at Bodmin Road railway station this afternoon. I'll take him down myself. You can both travel on the same train. After I've handed over the prisoner, we'll all pay a call on Lord Robartes at Lanhydrock House.'

42

When the train came to a steam-escaping halt at Bodmin Road station, three policemen were waiting on the platform. One was the inspector who had refused to believe Sally's story.

The inspector shook Ethan's hand amiably enough, but greeted Captain Eva with a certain reserve. The Bodmin police had not yet met up with any member of the Salvation Army, but he had read of the problems encountered by colleagues in other places.

'I thought I would come to meet you. We can go up to Lanhydrock House together, while my constable takes the prisoner to town. I didn't realise you would be bringing others with you.'

'Captain Cassington and Ethan are both witnesses to the fact that Sally Harrup was in possession of the cloak before she went to Lanhydrock House,' Ian Lovat explained. 'Not only that, Ethan saw the letters Sally believed to be from her father, who works at the house. I thought that if it could all be explained to the Robartes family, the girl might be released. It's quite clear that

with these witnesses – and others who would be called
– a prosecution for theft would fail.'

'If all you say is true, I must agree with you,' said
the inspector. 'But there are one or two things that
need to be cleared up before I can release the girl and
a number of matters need clarifying. I have a pony and
trap outside the station. We can all squeeze into that
to travel to the house. The constables can walk back to
town with the prisoner.'

Ethan was visibly impressed with his first glimpse of
the house, as the pony pulling the trap trotted up the
long drive between the trees. It was even grander than
Edgcumbe House, the big house he would see across
Plymouth Sound whenever the family's fishing boat left
Plymouth harbour. This house, with its own church nes-
tling among the trees behind it, had a feeling of warmth
and timelessness. As though it really *belonged* here.

There was a moment's debate between the two inspectors as to whether they should go to the main door or
first make their presence known at the servants' door.

Ian Lovat was adamant. Their business was with the
master of the house. It was he who had been responsible
for arresting Sally. Therefore, they should go to the main
entrance.

The door was opened by a maid, who seemed as
uncertain as the Bodmin police inspector as to whether
she should invite them to wait in the front hall or send
them to the kitchen door. The dilemma was solved for
her by the older of two ladies who came into the hall
while she was making up her mind.

'Good afternoon, Inspector Rowe. We don't often see
you at Lanhydrock. What can we do for you?' Rather
less cordially, she added, 'And who are these people?'

'Good afternoon, Lady Robartes. I came here to see if I might have a word with his Lordship. This is Inspector Lovat, head of the Criminal Investigation Department in Plymouth. The others are Miss Cassington, of the Salvation Army, and a Mr Shields. They are here on behalf of the young lady who was apprehended by his Lordship yesterday.'

'Oh yes, the girl who managed to get into the house and steal some clothing.'

'Sally didn't steal anything,' Ethan declared, indignantly. 'She's not a thief!'

'Ahem!' The Bodmin police inspector coughed hastily before Lady Robartes could react to Ethan's outburst. 'I fear there might have been some mistake, my Lady. It would seem the young lady was telling the truth when she said she did not steal the cloak.'

'But my husband said it was embroidered with our coat of arms. It must have come from the house.'

'That is quite true, my Lady. It undoubtedly *did* come from the house – but certainly not yesterday.'

Lady Robartes looked puzzled, then she said, 'I think we had all better go to my study and sort this out.'

To her companion, she said, 'Nancy, I wonder if you would tell the others I will be with them as soon as possible.' And to the visitors she said, 'Would you all like to follow me?'

Lady Robartes led the way along a passageway, to a small, cosily furnished room, which had a welcoming log fire burning in the fireplace.

When everyone was seated, Lady Robartes said, 'Now, who is going to tell me what this is all about?'

Her visitors all looked at each other and Captain Eva said, 'I think perhaps Ethan would be the best person to tell you something about Sally, of her background and the events that led up to her coming here yesterday. Ethan?'

Hesitantly at first, but with growing assurance, Ethan told of Sally's life, of her home in Pin's Lane, the story of the cloak, and of the recent death of her sister and the discovery of the letters.

When he ended, Lady Robartes, genuinely moved, said, 'What a dreadfully tragic story!' Shifting her attention to Captain Eva, she asked, 'Do you mind telling me how you came to be acquainted with the girl?'

Captain Eva related the story of how Sally had heard Rachel's cries for help, and told of all that had happened as a result.

'No doubt this is why you are involved?' she said to Ian Lovat.

'That's right, m'Lady – and from all I have seen of young Sally, I would back up everything that has been said. I believe her to be an honest, hard-working girl. In view of her background, I would say that in itself does very great credit to her. Perhaps we could speak to your butler, to see what he has to say about all this. After all, it was in his power to have prevented Sally's arrest had he wanted to.'

'I am afraid Sanderson is not in the house. He asked if he might take the remainder of the day off after ensuring all arrangements had been made for lunch today. He said he had urgent personal business in Plymouth.'

The two police inspectors exchanged quizzical glances and the Bodmin inspector said, almost apologetically, 'Mr Sanderson called in at the police station this morning. He told the constable on duty he was trying to remember whether he might have sent letters to anyone in Plymouth that might have found their way into Miss Harrup's hands. He thought that might have prompted her – and possibly her accomplices too – to plan to rob this house. He asked where she was living in Plymouth.'

'Did the constable tell him?' Ian Lovat asked sharply.

'I'm afraid so. There was no reason why he should not. Sanderson holds an important and responsible position in Lord Robartes' household.'

'Lady Robartes, may I make use of one of your servants – a groom, perhaps? I would like him to take a message to the telegraph office in Bodmin.' The request was made by Ian Lovat.

'Of course – but you surely do not think Sanderson has gone to this girl's address in Plymouth?'

'Although he's no doubt firmly convinced that Sally will be convicted of theft, he dare not risk having his letters fall into anyone else's hands. He has a great deal to lose.'

'So you really *do* believe Sanderson is the girl's father?' Lady Robartes was aghast. 'Yet he is willing to have her sent to prison unjustly rather than acknowledge her? It is absolutely monstrous!'

'Nevertheless, that's what I believe, m'Lady.'

'Then please write your message, Inspector. I will call for a maid to fetch a groom.'

While Ian Lovat was writing, the Bodmin police inspector spoke to Lady Robartes. 'Of course, there are still one or two matters that need to be cleared up before we bring this matter to a conclusion. The mystery of the cloak the girl was wearing, for instance. If she didn't steal it, then how had it come into her mother's hands?'

'How old was this young girl's sister? The one who has so recently died?' Lady Robartes put the questions to Ethan.

'It's difficult to say. She was so ill . . . but she couldn't have been more than twenty-two or -three.'

'I see.' Lady Robartes looked thoughtful. 'We've had a great many changes in the domestic staff since then, but Cook has been with us for thirty or more years. I'll send for her.'

There was a tapestry bell-pull beside the fireplace. Lady Robartes gave it a vigorous tug before asking, 'Tell me again, what is the name of this unfortunate young girl?'

'Sally Harrup.' Captain Eva supplied the answer.

The maid who answered the summons was promptly sent off to fetch the cook. A few minutes later a plump, rosy-cheeked woman arrived, drying newly washed hands on her white apron.

'You sent for me, m'Lady?'

'That's right, Esther. You've been with the family for a very long time. I want you to try to remember a servant who was here about twenty or more years ago. A young woman named Harrup.'

'Molly Harrup? Miss Lydia's maid? Yes, m'Lady, I remember her very well. A very pretty girl, she was. Far too pretty for her own good. That was her trouble. She had all the men hereabouts chasing after her – and she didn't run from them quite as fast as she should have. She landed herself in trouble, that's why she had to leave.'

'I see.' Glancing at the others, Lady Robartes said, 'Well, that part of the girl's story is accurate, at least.'

Returning her attention to the cook, she said, 'Now,

Esther, can you recall whether suspicion for her condition fell upon any particular man? A member of the domestic staff, perhaps?'

'Nothing that came from Molly herself, m'Lady. She never breathed a word to anyone of the man responsible for her state. Mind you, I always had my suspicions, and nothing's happened since to make me change 'em. Indeed, I'm more convinced now than I was then.'

'Who do you believe was responsible, Esther?'

The cook glanced at the others in the room before saying, 'Begging your pardon, m'Lady, I'd rather not say. I have no proof, you understand. If I was to be wrong I'd be doing him an unforgivable disservice. No, after all these years it's better left unsaid.'

'Esther,' Lady Robartes spoke sharply, 'after all these years it's time a very serious and cruel wrong is put right. If the man you suspect of fathering Molly Harrup's child, or children, is not the man we have in mind, it will go no farther than this room. On the other hand, if it *is* the man we suspect it to be, you will be helping to prevent a dreadful miscarriage of justice. Now, who is this man?'

When the cook still remained silent, Lady Robartes said, 'Esther, I *demand* that you tell us THIS INSTANT!'

With exaggerated reluctance, the Lanhydrock cook broke her silence. 'Like I said, m'Lady, nobody knew for certain, but there was a couple of us was convinced it was Mr Sanderson, the butler. Him whose voice was raised loudest in saying the family ought to have her sent as far away from Lanhydrock as was possible.'

43

Once the Lanhydrock House cook had unburdened herself of her long-held suspicions about the butler, events moved swiftly.

It transpired that 'Miss Lydia', for whom Molly Harrup had once worked, had married into one of the old-established Cornish families. She was now Mrs Treffry. Her husband was a member of Lord Robartes' shooting party and they were both guests in the house that had been her home for so many years of her early life.

Called to the room where the others were gathered, she remembered Molly Harrup immediately. She was, said Lydia Treffry, a bright and happy young girl who went about her work cheerfully and efficiently. She had been very sorry to lose her services when Molly disclosed her pregnancy and was ordered to leave the house.

Lydia Treffry was intrigued by the events of the day and, as the party drank tea, she was able to solve the mystery of the cloak bearing the Robartes coat of arms.

'Yes I remember it well,' she mused. 'I had it for some years. Molly thought it was one of the most beautiful articles of clothing she had ever seen. She was so fond of it that, when she left, I gave it to her as a present.'

When told of the trouble it had caused Sally, Lydia Treffry was extremely upset. 'The poor child!' she repeated for the third time. 'You must have her released *immediately*, Inspector.'

The Bodmin policeman said he would return to the police station right away and arrange for her to be set free.

'Would it not be quicker to send a groom with a message to have her freed?' asked Lady Robartes.

The inspector explained that, as the senior officer for the area, he would need to sign the papers necessary to authorise her release.

Lydia Treffry was a lady who was used to having things done when she asked for them. 'The moment you've completed all your official nonsense, send the girl to me here. I want to see what she looks like and tell her something of her mother. Molly was a lovely girl. Why she ever became involved with that scoundrel Sanderson, I'll never know. He was always far too ingratiating for my liking. No doubt he used his position to take advantage of impressionable young servant girls.'

'I feel we must try to make amends to the girl too,' said Lady Robartes. 'I know my husband would say the same, were he here. Had he not acted so hastily she would have been spared a great deal of grief. As for that scoundrel Sanderson . . . His attitude towards her would have been sufficient to upset the most insensitive of girls, and I am given the impression she is certainly not that!'

Inspector Rowe said, 'I will leave now, m'lady, but I should be back within the hour with Miss Harrup. She will no doubt be greatly relieved to put all this behind her.'

'I believe she is more likely to be very upset by the actions of the man who is her father,' declared Captain Eva. 'The loss of her sister has left her feeling very much alone in the world. No number of friends can take the place of a family.'

'Can I come with you to bring Sally back?' Ethan asked the Bodmin police inspector.

'If you wish.' Inspector Rowe was secretly relieved. Having Ethan present when the girl was released, to explain what was happening, would obviate a need to explain the mistakes that had led to her arrest at Lanhydrock House.

'I'll come with you too,' Ian Lovat stood up to leave with them, but Lady Robartes had other ideas.

'No you won't,' she said firmly. 'You and the Salvation Army captain can remain here and tell me more about this girl, before she is brought to the house.'

Returning her attention to the Bodmin inspector, she said, 'You can send one of your men here from Bodmin, too, in case that rogue Sanderson returns. I will have his personal belongings packed and taken to the gatehouse. He shall collect them from there, together with any salary that may be owing to him. I have no wish to see him again and he will not be allowed back in the house.'

'If my guess of what he is doing right now is correct, I think it highly probable that he'll be having a spell in prison,' said Ian Lovat. 'I doubt whether it will be as long as he deserves, but it will give him a salutary lesson.'

'It is no more than he deserves,' Lydia Treffry said angrily. 'When I think of the life poor Molly was forced to lead because of him . . .'

44

When she was first arrested, Sally's initial reaction was one of indignation. It was not entirely because her freedom had been taken from her, or because she had been accused of a crime she had not committed. She was angry most of all because her cloak had been taken away from her. The cloak that had once been worn by her mother.

Conveyed to Bodmin police station and left alone in a cell for many hours, she gradually began to calm down. As she did so, realisation of the seriousness of her predicament dawned on her. All due, in no small measure, to the attitude of the Lanhydrock butler towards her.

He *was* her father. After seeing him she had no doubts at all. He possessed many facial features that reminded her strongly of Ruth. She must resemble him, too. People had always commented upon how alike she and Ruth were.

Thinking about her father now made her even more unhappy.

She had realised when she set out from Plymouth that it would be foolish to set her hopes too high. Yet there had been a forlorn hope, buried deep inside her, that if only she could have an opportunity to speak to him, everything would miraculously become all right. The empty years would fall away, he would be sorry for the way he had treated her mother and would suddenly become the father she had always secretly craved.

She now realised just how stupid she had been. It had been no more than a desperate bid to have someone to whom she belonged.

The man she had spoken too had been a stranger. An indifferent and selfish stranger. He cared for the children he had fathered no more than a stray dog would for a litter of pups it had sired.

She wondered what was going to happen to her now. Would Ethan come looking for her when she failed to return to Plymouth? She was fairly certain he would – but when?

Once she had been taken before a magistrate it would be too late. She never doubted she would be found guilty, despite her innocence. If Lord Robartes, or a member of his household, came to court and told the magistrates she had stolen the cloak, they were hardly likely to take her word against his!

Sally had plenty of time to ponder her situation. Except for a policeman who spoke no more than a few grumpy words when he brought her a meal that evening, no one came to see her.

By nightfall, she was feeling despondent and found it difficult to sleep. When she did doze off for a while she was awakened by the sound of a noisy man, apparently the worse for drink, being placed in a nearby cell.

A short while after this there was mayhem in the police station. Sally could hear the voices of a great many men – and women too – raised in excited protest. It was difficult to know what it was all about. Only an occasional word was in English.

Soon, she heard cell doors along the corridor in which her own cell was situated being opened and slammed shut. Then her own cell door was opened. Two women were roughly pushed inside and the door slammed behind them.

Now Sally understood why she had not been able to understand what was going on. The two women were gypsies. It was probable the men who had been making so much noise were gypsies too.

The women looked as though they had been involved in a fight; one had a badly scratched face and the clothes of both were torn.

One of them spoke to her, but when she failed to understand what was being said, the women said something contemptuously to her companion. The only word Sally was able to make out was *'Gorgio!'*

Soon the two women were shouting to attract the attention of those in the cells about them. When others began replying, Sally realised there would be no more sleep for her that night.

The morning after her arrest was just as busy in the police station. All available policemen based in the market town had been called in to help convey the gypsies to the courtroom.

Many of the arrested men and women had been drunk the night before. Sally had thought this was the reason they had made so much fuss. But when most of them had sobered up in the morning, they were, if anything, even louder.

By the time the gypsies had been removed from the cells, Sally's head was aching. She also realised she was hungry, but she needed to wait for another hour before breakfast was brought to her.

The meal had been cooked by the wife of a constable who lived in a house adjacent to the police station. As a result, it was of a much higher standard than she might otherwise have received.

The woman brought it herself. A middle-aged, stoutly built woman, hers was the first sympathetic voice Sally had heard since her arrest. The woman was also more informative than a constable might have been.

'Here you are, love. I'm sorry it's so late, but you must have heard all the noise going on. A whole lot of gypsies set up a camp just outside town last night. After they'd been drinking for a few hours they decided they'd come in and take back one of their girls who was planning to marry a *didekei*. As far as I could make out that's someone who travels around like they do but who isn't a true gypsy. They're very particular about that sort of thing, or so I'm told. From what I hear, they began fighting among themselves even before they found the girl.'

As Sally sat on the edge of the wooden bed and tucked in to her breakfast, the woman showed no inclination to leave the cell.

'Those of 'em who haven't ended up in hospital are being taken before the magistrate this morning and I hope he puts the whole rowdy lot of 'em away for a very long time.'

'Will I be going to court when the gypsies have been dealt with?'

'Well, my husband thought that's what was going to happen to you, but Inspector Rowe has had a message from someone in Plymouth. Another inspector. I don't know what it was all about, but it seems you won't be going to court before he gets here.'

Puzzled, and with her mouth half-full of fried bread, Sally asked, 'What's the name of this inspector in Plymouth – and what's he got to do with me?' She could think of no Plymouth policeman who would be sufficiently interested in her to travel to Bodmin in order to speak to her.

'Are you sure it's a policeman? It couldn't have been a Salvation Army captain, perhaps?'

'I don't think anyone would have confused a Salvation Army captain with a police inspector. No, it was an inspector all right. It's got everyone wondering just what's going on. Have you been up to anything in Plymouth that might make the police there interested in you?'

Sally could not think of anything. However, Ruth had always said that once the police had you in their clutches they were likely to accuse you of all sorts of things you knew nothing about.

Later that morning a constable brought a mop and bucket of water and ordered her to clean out the cell. He could throw no light upon what was happening.

'Your guess is as good as mine,' he said. 'One thing's certain though, you won't be going to court today, so you'd better make a good job of cleaning up this cell. You're likely to be here for another twenty-four hours, at least.'

Sally ate an indifferent midday meal. It was brought to

her by a constable, who seemed determined to say as little as possible. She then decided to stretch out on the uncomfortable plank bed, in the hope of catching up on some of the sleep she had lost the night before.

She was just dozing off when she was awakened by the sound of metal grating against metal as a key was turned in the lock of the cell door.

She sat up on the bed as the cell door was swung open. The uncommunicative constable who had brought her midday meal was standing there.

With him was a tall, uniformed policeman wearing the insignia of an inspector.

Behind them was – Ethan!

45

When Sally saw Ethan, she experienced a feeling she had never known before. In that moment all her despondency lifted and she knew all was going to be well. Ignoring the others, she ran to him and flung her arms about him.

'I knew you'd come looking for me. I *knew* it.'

When her arms dropped away from him, she took hold of his hand, reluctant to release her hold on him. When the door of the cell was slammed shut behind her, she looked around in surprise.

'What's happening?'

'You're free to leave the police station,' the Bodmin inspector explained. 'All the charges against you have been dropped.'

'You mean . . . you've found out I really have been telling you the truth?'

'That's right, Sally,' said Ethan. 'Lady Robartes found the person who gave the cloak to your mother. She's a niece of Lord Robartes and once lived at Lanhydrock. She's actually staying at the house right now. It seems your mother was her maid before becoming pregnant.'

'She really knew my ma?! Where's the cloak now? I want it back.'

'You'll be given it when you get to Lanhydrock House,' Inspector Rowe replied. 'Lady Robartes wants to meet you. One of my constables will drive you there now.'

'Will I be able to meet the lady my ma worked for too?'

The inspector nodded. 'The last thing she said when we left was that we were to be sure to take you back there. She wants to meet you.'

Sally smiled happily at Ethan, but her mood changed abruptly and she turned back to Inspector Rowe. 'What's happening about my . . . about the butler at the house?'

'He's been arrested in Plymouth. A message has just arrived. He was caught after breaking into your room. It seems he was looking for the letters he sent to your mother.'

'Oh!' Sally's expression showed her unhappiness. 'What will happen to him now?'

'You'll need to ask Inspector Lovat that question. He's at Lanhydrock House too, with Miss Cassington, of the Salvation Army. Now, there are a few formalities to complete, then you can be on your way . . .'

Ten minutes later Sally left the Bodmin police station. She was holding Ethan's hand once more, as though afraid he might disappear at any moment.

Inspector Rowe did not return to Lanhydrock House with Sally and Ethan. They were conveyed by pony and trap, driven by a constable. Although he seemed in a great hurry, he was more cheerful and talkative than any of the policemen Sally had met during her time in the Bodmin police station cell.

He told them that the gypsies had refused to testify against one another, even though some had sustained painful injuries during the fighting between the two gypsy factions. As a consequence, they were all warned about their future conduct and fined the maximum amount possible for disturbing the peace, with the alternative of a month's imprisonment in default.

The fines were totted up and paid in gold sovereigns by a gypsy who appeared to be their leader, but who had not been involved in the fracas.

It was quite evident that the constable did not like gypsies. Thus it came as no surprise to Sally when he explained why he was in such a hurry to get them to Lanhydrock House. It was planned to move the gypsies from their encampment that afternoon – and he did not want to miss the 'fun'.

When they reached the big house, the constable was uncertain to which entrance he should take them. The problem was solved by Lydia Treffry, who, passing by a window in the main hall, had witnessed their arrival. Opening the door, she beckoned for them to come in.

Lydia Treffry was a tall, distinguished-looking woman who possessed an elegant beauty. Sally felt tongue-tied in her presence and it was left to the other woman to speak first.

'So you are Sally! You know, I really believe I would have recognised you had we met elsewhere. You are so like your mother. My poor dear, what we have put you through – and all because I made a present of a cloak to your mother so many years ago. We are so dreadfully sorry – but come along and meet Lady

Robartes. We have been having a most interesting chat to Miss Cassington – or *Captain* Cassington, as I believe she prefers to be known.'

Walking in front of them down the hall, she continued, 'That handsome young police inspector is with her too. You have made some very good friends, Sally. They have been telling Lady Robartes and myself how your keen sense of duty saved those poor unfortunate girls who would otherwise have been taken to Belgium. Your mother would have been very proud of you, Sally. She too was a girl with high principles. At least, she was before she fell under the influence of that scoundrel Sanderson.'

Opening a door, Lydia Treffry preceded them into the room where the others were seated.

Eva immediately sprang to her feet to greet Sally. Holding out her arms, she embraced Sally warmly, exclaiming, 'You poor girl! Thank the Lord we were able to get here before you were committed to prison. I shudder every time I think that had we not arrived when we did you might have been sent to that awful place.'

Before Sally could be formally introduced to Lady Robartes, the older woman said, 'I am terribly sorry that we were responsible for your arrest, child. What can we possibly do to make amends for such a ghastly mistake?'

Sally replied by asking a question that took everyone by surprise. 'What is going to happen to Mr Sanderson?'

Ian Lovat had been reading the telegram received by Inspector Rowe at Bodmin police station and it was he who replied. 'Sanderson's been arrested and has been taken to Plymouth police station and lodged in the cells there. He'll be charged with breaking into your room with intent to steal. He will no doubt be sent to prison.'

'I don't want that to happen,' Sally said unexpectedly. 'I don't think he's a very nice person and he treated my ma badly, but she never made trouble for him and I don't want to, neither.'

'He would have let *you* go to prison without raising a finger to help,' Lydia Treffry spoke gently and sympathetically.

'That doesn't matter now,' Sally replied stubbornly. 'I don't want him to be put away.'

Lydia Treffry looked at Ian Lovat questioningly. He shrugged. 'We can't proceed against him without Sally's co-operation.'

'I think I can understand Sally's feelings,' said Lydia Treffry. 'But it is galling to think that Sanderson will walk away from this mess scot-free.'

'Not quite,' Lady Robartes said in a firm voice. 'He will be dismissed from Lanhydrock House and I doubt he'll ever again find gainful employment.'

'That wasn't meant to happen, either.' Sally was unhappy at the way things had turned out. 'I came here because I just wanted to see him. I hoped he might have been just a little bit happy to see me. I didn't want anything from him – nor did I want to see him punished.'

'If I'm perfectly honest, my dear, he should have been dismissed years ago,' said Lady Robartes. 'There have been a great many rumours about him. I ignored them because butlers are very hard to find these days. Unfortunately, I allowed him rather too much authority. He was allowed to dismiss any servants he felt were unsatisfactory. Looking back over the years, I realise now that some went in rather puzzling circumstances. It is quite clear to me now that he took advantage of the authority vested in him.'

Sally was still unhappy, but the subject was changed by Lydia Treffry.

'I have something here I feel you might like to have, Sally.'

She passed over an attractive silver frame, which held a photograph of a pretty young girl of about twenty years of age, dressed in a maid's uniform. She looked very much like Ruth. Sally realised immediately who it must be.

'It's my ma!'

'That's right. When I was living here a photographer was brought to Lanhydrock. Everyone in the household had their photograph taken. This was hanging in the servants' hall with the others. Lady Robartes found a frame for it and we thought you might like to take it with you, as a present.'

'It's a wonderful present . . . I've always wondered what she looked like . . . ! I only wish Ruth could have seen this.' Tears sprang to Sally's eyes and she could only manage an emotional, 'Thank you.'

Eva had told Lady Robartes and Lydia Treffry of the tragic death of Ruth on Christmas Day. The latter now said, 'My dear child, it is a very small gesture of contrition on our part. I believe my aunt wishes to give you a small sum of money, by way of compensation for your suffering and I have an offer I would beg you to consider. I have an invalid daughter at my home, in Fowey. I would be most happy if you would consider entering domestic service in my house and helping to take care of her. No, you do not have to give me your answer right away. Please think about it and call to see me if you would like to take the post. It is a very happy household. I have no doubt you would enjoy it there.'

An hour later, Sally was being driven to the railway station in the Robartes' coach, accompanied by Ethan, Captain Eva and Ian Lovat.

She had Ethan by her side, was carrying the silver-framed photograph of her mother, had twenty guineas jangling dully in a pocket of her dress, and had been offered a secure post in domestic service with Lydia Treffry.

Wistfully, she wished Ruth was still alive so she might have been able to share such good fortune with her.

But Ruth was dead. The only relative Sally now had was Sanderson, Lanhydrock House's disgraced ex-butler.

46

To all who looked for the signs, the countryside in and around Plymouth was hinting that spring was not far away. Snowdrops had come and gone, primroses were in abundance, and yellow daffodils danced to the tune of a boisterous wind.

Sally was still living at the Salvation Army Refuge, but she continued to pay the rent for the room in Pin's Lane and had been returning there more often just recently.

On occasions, if she felt particularly nervous about the possibility of meeting up with the still-elusive Sid Darling and Ethan was not able to accompany her, she would take Zulu Joe along for company.

The giant African was now employed at the Refuge as a handyman-cum-night watchman – and was a friend to everybody who lived there.

Always proudly dressed in his Salvation Army uniform, Zulu Joe was perfectly happy with his simple and silent way of life.

Although unable to talk, he could often be heard

humming a tune as he worked about the large house. Whenever he went out, his large uniformed figure did much to draw attention and he was an impressive advertisement for the Salvation Army.

Sally was still working for Alfie and Grace Philpott – and seeing Ethan as often as she could.

She was concerned for him at the present time. The weather had been consistently bad for weeks and Plymouth fishermen were able to put to sea for only the occasional day. The profit made by the Shields family before Christmas was now no more than a wistful memory.

There was no work for Ethan or his brother at the pie shop either. The residents of Plymouth seemed to have been practising prolonged thrift after the excesses of Christmastide.

Not that Ethan was wasting his time. One of the Salvation Army bandsmen had been teaching him to read music. Unfortunately for Sally, this meant that he was not always able to meet her as often as both of them would have liked.

Sally was thinking of all these things as she walked along Union Street with an empty basket. She had just made a couple of deliveries to shopkeepers unable to leave their premises for a lunch break. Now she was on her way back to the pie shop to collect more orders.

As she approached one of the many public houses in the street, she saw a man lurch drunkenly from the premises to the pavement outside. Once there, he began walking as though the pavement was a flight of stairs he was having difficulty negotiating.

Sally stepped into the gutter to avoid him. As she passed by, she thought there was something familiar about him. Looking back, she stopped suddenly.

She watched him for a few moments with increasing disbelief. Not until he looked directly at her did she know for certain. It was Robert Sanderson, ex-butler to Lord and Lady Robartes of Lanhydrock House.

Her father!

But this was not the imposing, smart man feared by the other servants. A man who had set standards for the household of a peer of the realm.

He must have had almost two weeks' growth of stubble on his cheeks. His clothes were stained and creased and looked as though they had not been taken off since he last applied a razor to his face.

Obviously intoxicated, he was able to stand – but only just.

As Sally watched, he staggered to the edge of the pavement. She held her breath in alarm as it seemed he might fall into the busy road, in the path of passing traffic.

At the last minute, he recovered and lurched in the opposite direction. Colliding with the wall of a shop, he stood with his back to it, for support.

Retracing her footsteps, Sally stood looking at him uncertainly.

Peering at her, Sanderson made a visible effort to concentrate. 'Molly . . . ?' He shook his head in confusion. 'No, it can't be.'

Suddenly, he seemed to partially sober up. 'I know you! You're the one who had me thrown out of Lanhydrock. Molly's daughter. No wonder I thought you were her. You said you were *my* daughter, too.' He shook his head again, this time so vigorously it caused him to momentarily lose his balance.

Recovering with difficulty, he said, 'No daughter of mine would have had me dismissed after thirty years of service. Thirty years . . . and they threw me out. Wouldn't even let me go to the house to collect my things. They had them heaped up in the gatehouse. Thirty years. Thirty wasted years . . .' His voice tailed away and his chin dropped on his chest.

Sally thought with alarm that he was about to cry. 'We ought to get you home. Where are you living?'

'Living? You call this *living*? No, girl, I stopped living when they threw me out of Lanhydrock House. After thirty years. Can you believe it!'

Pushing himself away from the wall, he stood swaying before her dangerously. 'Of course, *you* can believe it. You're the one who caused it to happen.'

'Where are you staying in Plymouth?' Sally persisted, 'I'll help you get there.'

'Where am I staying?' he repeated. 'This doorway. That doorway, what does it matter? I'm a vagrant, that's what the constables call me. A vagrant. After thirty years of living in one of the finest houses in the land . . .'

Sally knew she should leave him where he was. Robert Sanderson was trouble. He had been the downfall of her mother and she doubted very much whether his present adversity had done anything to change his selfish and uncaring nature.

Nevertheless, he *was* her father. Nothing could change that.

She would take him to the room in Pin's Lane.

47

When Sally finished work that evening she did not return immediately to the Refuge. Instead, she went to Pin's Lane. With her, she carried one of Alfie's pies. It was to have been for her own supper, but she believed the man who was her father had far more need of it.

Much to her surprise, she found Ethan at the house. He had been on his way to see her, but called in on his uncle first, to deliver a meal his mother had cooked for him.

Charlie had not been well for a week or so. The cold and wet weather had aggravated his chest complaint, preventing him from maintaining his usual vigil on the steps in front of the house.

However, there was nothing wrong with his hearing, as his first words to Sally proved.

Spitefully, he said, 'Taking up your sister's old habits now, are we?'

Frowning, she said, 'I don't have the faintest idea what you're talking about. What habits am I supposed to be taking up?'

'You know very well what I'm talking about. Does our Ethan know you've been taking men up to your room?'

As Ethan protested to his uncle, Sally said, 'You're a wicked, trouble-making old man, Charlie. I thought you'd changed for the better, but you haven't. The "men" you're talking about is one man. I took him up there this afternoon and, no, I haven't had time to tell Ethan about him yet.'

Ethan was looking bewildered and Sally explained, 'It's my father. I found him in Union Street today. He . . . he wasn't well, so I brought him here.'

'Not well?! Drunk, you mean,' Charlie said scornfully. 'I can tell the sounds of a drunken man – and anyone who's sober doesn't pee out of the window – not in daylight, anyway.'

Ethan was looking to Sally for a further explanation and she gave it to him. 'He was in danger of falling in front of a horse and cart, so I brought him here. I hardly recognised him, Ethan, he's let himself go so much – and it's me who's responsible for that.'

'You're not responsible for anything he does, Sally. He has no one to blame but himself. He deserves everything that's happened to him – and more.'

'That's all very well for you to say, Ethan Shields. You've got a father – yes, and a mother and brothers too. He's all I've got in the world.'

'You have me.'

'When I see you. You're usually off doing something else these days.'

It was a most unfair observation and Sally recognised it as such, but she felt angry with both Ethan and herself.

She felt hurt too. This was the first quarrel she and Ethan had ever had.

'Anyway, I'm not standing here arguing with you. I've got his supper here. I'm taking it up to him before it gets cold.'

She swept up the stairs from the passageway outside Charlie's room. Although he had not been asked to accompany her, Ethan followed Sally up the stairs.

The lamp in the room was burning although the curtains had not been drawn, and Robert Sanderson was lying on the bed. He was not asleep.

He turned his head when Sally and Ethan entered the room. Glaring at Ethan, he demanded irritably, 'Who's this?'

'Ethan.' She did not feel it necessary to explain their relationship. 'He's been visiting his uncle who lives downstairs. I've brought supper for you. I thought you could probably do with something to eat.'

'You're right there, girl. I feel as though I haven't eaten for a week or more.'

Sally put the pie on a plate and passed it to him, together with a knife and fork. He began eating it immediately.

'What are you going to do with yourself now?' asked Sally. 'Do you have any plans for finding work?'

'Looking like this?' The hand holding the knife made a gesture indicating the clothes he was wearing. 'Who's going to employ a butler with no references and dressed like this?'

'There's other work you could do apart from being a butler,' Ethan said unsympathetically. 'Half the fishermen in Plymouth need to find other work in winter when the weather's the way it is now. You don't find

them staggering around Union Street looking for someone to feel sorry for them.'

'Ethan! That's not fair.' Sally rounded on him.

'Isn't it? I didn't notice him running to help *you*
when you were arrested at Lanhydrock for something
he could have put right with just a word to someone.'

Ethan glared at Sanderson, before saying to Sally, 'I'll
be downstairs with Uncle Charlie for a while. Then I'll
get on off home. You know where to find me – if you
want to.'

When he had left the room, Robert Sanderson said,
'What's that young man to you?'

'He's a friend. A very good friend.'

Sally was extremely upset by the manner of Ethan's
leaving, but she would not allow her father to see that
it mattered to her.

'I'm sorry to have come between you and your friend,'
Sanderson said, with an uncharacteristic display of
humility. 'If you think I should leave I can always
find myself somewhere else to stay. I managed before
you found me.'

'There's no need for that.'

Sally was in a dilemma. She wanted to go downstairs,
find Ethan and put things right between them. But she
felt she could not just walk out on her father. 'What *do*
you intend to do with yourself?'

'I need to find work but I don't have experience of
anything except being a butler. Anyway, I have no hope
of finding work while I'm like this. Will you let me stay
here for a while so I can get myself cleaned up and in
a fit state to work?' He made an exaggerated gesture of
helplessness. 'I know I have no right to ask any favours
of you at all. I'll quite understand if you turn me out to

fend for myself – but I would be extremely grateful if I could stay for a while. Who knows, we might be able to find what's been absent from both our lives all these years. You, a father, and me – a daughter.'

Sally hesitated. She did not fully trust this man – and yet . . .

'All right, you can stay for a while – but not for ever. I have to pay rent for this room so I'll expect you to help towards it.'

'Of course. I have no money right now, but as soon as I find work I'll be able to pay a share of the rent.'

'When you find work, you'll need to get a place of your own, too,' Sally pointed out.

'I realise that. Now, my being here will pose certain problems. What do you suggest we do for the sleeping arrangements?'

'That's no problem,' declared Sally. 'I won't be sleeping here. I'm staying at a house owned by the Salvation Army. I'll call in most days, to see how you're getting on.'

Sally thought he seemed disappointed and she was pleased. If he wanted her around there was hope that he might turn out to be the father for whom she had always longed.

'I must go downstairs now and see if I can catch Ethan before he leaves.'

'Before you do, will you explain to me where everything is. The toilet, water . . . that sort of thing. And how far away are the nearest shops? I don't know Plymouth very well.'

He kept her talking for far longer than she had intended remaining with him. By the time she went downstairs Ethan had left.

Sally walked to the Refuge with very mixed feelings
that night. The gap between herself and her father had
been bridged to a certain extent, but she had fallen out
with Ethan and this made her deeply unhappy.

48

'What's the matter with Sally? Whenever I talk to her I might as well be standing in the next room for all the response I get.'

'She's all right,' replied Rachel. 'She's got a lot to think about at the moment, that's all.'

She and Grace were talking as they worked together in the kitchen of the shop. Sally had just left with a basket of deliveries for the staff at the railway station. On two occasions Grace had spoken to her and had had to repeat her words twice because Sally did not hear her the first time.

'How do you know? Is something going on with that young man of hers that I should know about as her employer? She's not going to tell me she'll have to give up work because she's pregnant, or anything like that?'

'No. In fact, I think she and Ethan have had a little quarrel, that's all. She's not happy because she feels she's to blame.'

'Oh! What was the quarrel about?'

'I don't know.'

Rachel did not like lying to Grace, but Sally had told her in confidence about her father after the two girls met up with him when they were out making a delivery together.

Rachel had taken an immediate dislike to Sanderson, but she would not betray the confidence Sally had placed in her. Rachel was also an orphan. She knew what Sally must be feeling to have the father she had never known suddenly come into her life.

'If you learn anything more, be sure to let me know. We can't have her moping about as though she's in a different world to the rest of us. She and Ethan need to sort things out quickly. He's a nice young man. The two of them are meant for each other.'

Sally's preoccupation stemmed from two causes. The first was her father. He showed no indication of either attempting to obtain work or moving away from Pin's Lane. Indeed, he was trying to persuade her to move back there, to take care of him and in order that they might 'get to know each other a little better'.

Her other concern was the one Rachel had given to Grace: Ethan. There had been no opportunity for her to put things right between them. The morning after her father moved in to Pin's Lane, the Plymouth fishing fleet had put to sea.

Rumour around the quayside was that it had been forced to go far beyond its traditional fishing grounds in search of its quarry. Competition was particularly fierce this year. In addition to the Cornish boats, the traditional rivals of the Plymouth men, there was a huge fleet of steam-powered east coast drifters in the west countrymen's traditional fishing area. Foreign boats were also moving in.

The Plymouth boats had been at sea for three days and there was still no sign of their return, although some of the east coast boats had put in to Plymouth to sell their own harvest of the sea.

The east coast boats had been at sea for some time and their particular fishing methods had brought them good catches. As a result, the Barbican quay was a hive of industry. Fish was being brought ashore, prepared, then boxed for despatch to markets throughout the country.

Such activity meant that the publicans in the harbour area were also having a busy time. Fishermen and their many helpers drank heavily as they worked. They also needed to eat and the publicans ordered a great many of Alfie Philpott's pies.

Most sent their pot boys to collect them, but there were not always enough cooked and ready, so Sally spent a great deal of time going back and forth to the quay.

It was on one such visit that she unexpectedly met with her father. He was going towards a public house called The Jolly Waterman, in company with a man who looked as though he might well be a chimney sweep.

Marching up to him, a basket over her arm, Sally said, 'I thought you were going out to find work today?' Pointing in the direction of the public house, she added, 'You're not going to find it in there.'

Angrily, her father said, 'Don't you *dare* tell me what I should or shouldn't be doing, girl. Not unless you want to have your ears well and truly boxed. Now, clear off. I'll talk to you later.'

'No you won't!' Sally was equally angry. 'And when

you get back to Pin's Lane you'll find what few belongings you've got outside, on the pavement. You'd better not be too long getting back there. They won't stay very long before someone runs off with them.'

Sally turned and walked away. Before she reached the next corner, her father caught up with her. Grasping her arm and pulling her to a halt, he said, 'I'm sorry, Sally. I shouldn't have spoken to you like that, but I'm not used to being told what I should be doing by a young girl. Any young girl. The man I'm with is . . . is a business associate. We're discussing something of importance.'

'You're discussing business with *him*,' Sally said scornfully. 'Don't tell me you're thinking of becoming a chimney sweep. I won't believe you.'

'I'm not thinking of doing it myself, but I'm hoping to be able to put something his way. Something that might prove lucrative for all of us.'

'What do you mean?' Sally eyed him uncertainly. 'Is it something dishonest?'

'I can't say any more about it right now, girl. I tell you what, though. You be waiting for me in the room later this evening and I might be able to tell you more then. Right now I've got to go back and speak to this man – and he won't wait for ever. Will you be at Pin's Lane when I get there?'

'Are you telling me the truth? You really are going to talk business with this bloke? You're not just saying it because I've threatened to throw your things out in the street?'

'Be back at the room when I get there and you'll find out.'

'All right – but don't be too late. I'm not going to wait up half the night for you.'

'Good girl! I'll see you later.'

Her father hurried away, leaving Sally wondering whether she had done the right thing. She did not entirely trust him, but it would be a great step forward in their relationship if he decided to take her into his confidence.

Moving on, she wished Ethan was not at sea with his father and brothers. He was the only one she could have talked to about what was going on.

She was missing him far more than she had believed she ever would. She determined that when he returned she would apologise for the cross words that had passed between them and they would make up.

This thought made her even happier than the belief that her father was about to confide in her.

49

When she finished work that evening, Sally went directly to Pin's Lane. She met Charlie in the passageway outside his room. He was carrying a mug of tea from his small kitchen to the room at the front of the house, where he now spent much of his time sitting at the window, as the weather was too cold for him to sit outside on the step.

'Well, well! What are you doing here? Moving back in, are we? I hope so. You're a lot quieter than him you've got staying up there – and *you* were always home before the rest of the street had gone to sleep. He isn't. It wouldn't be so bad if he came in sober. He's usually so drunk I'm surprised he hasn't fallen back down the stairs and injured himself before now.'

Charlie coughed and then cleared his throat noisily before continuing. 'He's no quieter when he gets upstairs. It sounds as though he's falling against every bit of furniture in the room, knocking over just about everything that can fall down. I'll be surprised if you've got anything left in one piece up there.'

'Well, he should be back earlier tonight. He's coming to tell me about some business he's been discussing.' Sally spoke defensively, but Charlie was not impressed.

'Him, discussing business? The only business he knows is *funny* business. You ask Devonport Lil. He was over there with her only yesterday.'

'You're lying, Charlie Shields. He wouldn't go with her – even if he knew about her.'

'Oh, he knows, all right. I was out in the backyard when she had someone up in her room – the curtains only half-drawn, as usual. He was watching her too, from the window up in your room. Oh, he realised what she was doing all right and he wasted no time getting over there. I saw him there myself. You should have listened to our Ethan and had nothing to do with him. You've got along without him for all these years. You could have managed well enough without him now.'

Leaving Charlie still grumbling, Sally made her way up the stairs. She thought Charlie was probably making up the story about her father and Devonport Lil. He had never allowed the truth to stand in the way of his imagination.

Entering the upstairs room, it was immediately evident that despite the position he had held at Lanhydrock House, Robert Sanderson was not a naturally tidy person. It was doubtful whether he had made any attempt to clean the room since he had been there. Even the bedclothes were strewn on the floor beside the bed.

The room was also cold and unwelcoming.

There was kindling wood and coal in the cupboard in a corner of the room. Lighting a fire, Sally put the kettle on.

Before it boiled, she made the bed and began tidying

up. It still gave her an uneasy feeling to be in the room without Ruth being here too, lying in the bed she had occupied for so long.

It had been hard to take care of Ruth and at the same time go out to work, bringing in enough money to pay the rent and keep them both. Yet, looking back on it, Sally remembered only the loving companionship there had been between them. How she had looked forward to coming home to her sister each day, knowing that Ruth would be equally pleased to see her.

That was the way families should be. The way the Shields family felt about one another. It was how she had hoped things would be between herself and her father.

Perhaps they might still be like that one day.

However, it soon became clear that her hopes he might return early would not be realised.

When the clock on the mantelshelf chimed the quarter hour at ten forty-five, she decided to return to the Refuge. Zulu Joe occupied the room closest to the front door of the Salvation Army home – he would hear her, however lightly she knocked on the door. But if Captain Eva was still awake she would want to know where Sally had been and she was not yet ready to tell her the truth.

The tidying of the room had been completed long before and Sally now moved the slowly steaming kettle to one side of the hob. She was about to leave when she heard someone ponderously climbing the stairs.

She knew it had to be her father. From the noise he was making she realised Charlie had not been exaggerating about that, at least. Robert Sanderson had returned to Pin's Lane, but he was not a fully sober man.

Sally had turned down the wick of the lamp in the room. Now she turned it up once more and replaced the kettle on the glowing coals. It sounded as though he had need of a strong coffee. She had already checked the food cupboard. There was just enough left in a tin to make a couple of cups.

The door opened and her father entered the room. It was immediately apparent that he had drunk far more than was good for him.

Blinking in the light given out by the lamp, he seemed puzzled by the fact that it was lit. Then he saw Sally.

'Molly! What are you doing here?'

'It's not Molly,' she retorted. 'It's Sally, your daughter. I'm here because you promised that if I waited for you here you'd be home early.'

'Did I? I can't remember.'

'Well, you did. You said it just before you went inside The Jolly Waterman with someone you needed to talk business with – or so you told me. You promised to come home early and tell me about it.'

'Ah yes! I remember now. You told me off, didn't you?' He wagged a finger unsteadily in her general direction. 'You always were a spirited girl, Molly. It's one of the things I particularly liked about you – but it wasn't the only thing, mind.'

'It's *Sally*, not Molly,' she repeated. 'Anyway, what was this business you were going to tell me about?'

'Ah! You're not the only one who would like to know that, my girl. No doubt Lord and Lady Robartes would like to know, too. In fact, m'Lord and Lady would like to know more than anyone else, but they're not going to. Not just yet, anyway.'

'What do you mean? What have they got to do with any business of yours?'

'Never you mind, Molly,' her father said drunkenly. 'It's nothing you ought to know about. But they'll be sorry.'

'This is a stupid conversation,' said Sally. 'I might just as well have gone back to the Refuge when I finished work and left you in the mess I found this room in. I'm going now. I'll come back when you're sober – if you ever are. Perhaps you'll make more sense then.'

'No, don't go. You don't want to go yet, do you?'

'Yes, I do.'

Sally moved towards the door, but he lurched to one side and stood in front of it.

'Do you mind standing out of the way? It's getting late.'

'Late? We've got the whole night in front of us. It'll be just like old times, do you remember them, Molly? Yes, of course you do. Come on, show me you haven't forgotten . . .'

He reached out for her but she slipped under his arm and grabbed for the door latch. She had hold of it and pulled hard, but the door opened no more than a hand's breadth. Robert Sanderson's foot prevented it from opening any further.

He took a rough grip on her arm and yanked her hard away from the door. Caught off balance, she crashed against the bed and fell back on to it – and he fell with her.

He still had hold of her arm and she attempted to throw him off with violent movements of her body, but it seemed only to excite him.

As they struggled, he drove a knee into a muscle on

the inside of one of her thighs. The sudden pain caused her to open her legs involuntarily. His body covered hers completely and he was pushing against her.

'Stop it. STOP IT! You're my father. Stop it, I say—'

'Who says I'm your father? Is that what she told you?' He did not sound quite so drunk now. Sally realised he was fully aware of who she was – and of what he was trying to do.

'Your father could have been any one of half a dozen men, but I was the one she decided had more to offer her than any of the others. Come on, now. Don't tell me you haven't done this before . . .' As he spoke, he pushed his arm between their bodies and forced his hand down between her legs. As he fumbled, clumsily, he hurt her and she screamed.

'Shut up, you stupid little bitch!'

His face was close to hers. Forcing her head up from the bed, she caught his nose between her teeth and bit him – hard.

He shouted in agony and as his grip on her relaxed, she was able to push him away and wriggle free, falling to the floor beside the bed.

Unfortunately, she fell on the side of the bed farthest from the door. By the time she reached it, he had recovered sufficiently to grab her once more.

This time, he hit her with his free hand and she was knocked back into the room. Coming after her, he struck out again – and yet again. When she fell to the floor he dragged her to her feet and struck her once more, thoroughly enraged.

'I'll make you suffer before I do it, believe me. You'll never bite me again, even if I need to knock out all your teeth to make certain of it.'

She could taste blood in her mouth now and she was terrified that he was going to kill her. His next blow knocked her back to the fireplace. As she fell against it, her flailing arm struck the kettle standing on the hob.

It was hot. Normally she would have taken a cloth with which to pick it up, but not now.

Snatching hold of the handle, she swung the kettle in an arc and threw it, striking Sanderson on the side of his neck. The lid flew off and boiling water cascaded over him.

Now it was his turn to scream. It was an agonised sound that seemed to go on for ever.

He was still screaming when Sally reached the foot of the stairs and ran past a startled Charlie.

'What's happening? What's going on up there?'

Sally did not answer. Pushing past him, she fled out to Pin's Lane and carried on running through the rain-washed streets of the Barbican.

50

Sally ran all the way to the Salvation Army Refuge but saw nothing of the streets or the people she passed along the way. Blinded by tears for much of the time, she was guided more by instinct than sight.

When she reached her destination she hesitated for a moment before knocking at the door. It was a blustery night and her hair was wet and in disarray. Her face ached so much she knew it must be badly bruised as a result of the beating she had taken from her father. Her wrist was painful, scalded by water from the kettle and her frock had been torn during the struggle.

Aware of the state she was in, she contemplated not knocking at the door – but there was nowhere else she could go tonight.

She rapped on the door quietly, hoping she might be able to slip past Zulu Joe and hurry to her room without him noticing her injuries.

Her hopes were not realised. The door was opened not by Zulu Joe but by Captain Eva.

'Ah, there you are. I knew you weren't in and had come down to see if . . . Sally! What have you been up to? What's happened to you?

She gripped Sally's arm, causing her to wince. The arm had been bruised by Sanderson when he threw her back from the door.

Eva drew Sally to the gas-light in the hall. Here she inspected her bruised face and torn frock.

Looking grim, she said, 'You'd better come with me to the bathroom . . . Joe, do you think you could go to the kitchen and brew up some tea for us?'

In the bathroom, Eva inspected Sally's bruised face and scalded hand and demanded once more that Sally tell her what had happened.

Hesitantly and still very close to tears, Sally told the Salvationist of the meeting with her father in Union Street, which resulted in her taking him to the room in Pin's Lane. Then she outlined much of what had occurred that evening.

The Salvation Army captain's first reaction was one of anger and she scolded Sally. 'You were a very silly girl for not telling anyone what was going on. Tonight might well have ended in tragedy for you . . .'

Standing back to hold Sally at arm's length, Eva gazed at her bruised face and distraught expression. Suddenly her expression softened. Wrapping Sally in her arms, she pulled her close.

'You poor girl! You've been treated abominably. Any man in his right mind would be absolutely delighted to discover he had a daughter like you. In spite of the way he behaved to you at Lanhydrock House, you took pity on him and let him stay in your room – only to end up being treated like this. He may, or may not, be your father, Sally. He certainly doesn't deserve a daughter like you.'

'I think I must have scalded him badly . . .' Sally choked on her words. 'What will happen to me if he dies?'

'He probably wasn't hurt as badly as you think.' Eva tried to allay Sally's fears. 'After I've put some opium ointment on those bruises I'll send Zulu Joe to Pin's Lane to find out how he is. We'll also wrap something about your wrist. The scald is already blistering. We don't want anything infecting it. Ah! Here's Joe with the tea now . . .'

When Zulu Joe returned to the Refuge from Pin's Lane, he wrote a single word on the piece of paper Captain Eva gave to him.

'Gone.'

'Gone where?' asked Sally.

Zulu Joe shrugged and wrote, 'Man in downstairs room said he went soon after you ran from house. Took all things with him.'

'There you are,' said Eva, much relieved in spite of her earlier proclaimed confidence. 'He couldn't have been hurt as badly as you thought.'

She smiled comfortingly at Sally. 'I know it's not what you were hoping for from him, Sally, but the best thing that could happen now would be for him to get out of your life forever. However, there's nothing to prevent you praying for him. I will do the same. Now, I think it's time you went to bed. If you wish, I'll tell Grace Philpott in the morning that you aren't well enough to go in to work.'

'No,' Sally said firmly. 'I'll be all right to work.

Besides, when I was at the fish quay today they seemed to think the fishing fleet would probably return to harbour tomorrow. I've got a large delivery to take there and hope I might see Ethan. I'll tell him that he was right all along and say I'm sorry for quarrelling with him.'

'Good girl!' Eva put an arm about Sally's shoulders and hugged her once more. 'My mother always used to say that next to a good square meal, there's nothing appeals to a man quite as much as having a woman apologise to him.'

Later, lying in bed, thinking about the events of the day, Sally realised she had forgotten to tell Captain Eva what her father had said about Lord and Lady Robartes. That they would be sorry for dismissing him.

She decided she would tell her in the morning.

The boiling water from the kettle saturated Robert Sanderson's upper body and sobered him far more rapidly than any known beverage.

The agony from his burns brought previously dulled nerves to life, cutting incisively through the alcoholic fog that enveloped his brain.

When his screaming died away, it left him gasping for breath – but he was thinking now.

He realised he must get away from Pin's Lane as quickly as he could and find someone to help him.

Robert Sanderson knew very few people in Plymouth. It would not be easy to find medical aid at this time of night, especially someone who would help without asking too many questions.

The only person he could think of immediately was

the woman who lived in the house backing on to Pin's Lane. Devonport Lil.

Gathering up any belongings that came immediately to hand, he stuffed them in a battered suitcase. The exertion caused him to whimper in pain. Then, slowly and painfully, he picked up the suitcase and made his way down the stairs.

From the doorway of his room, Charlie Shields watched the other man making his way cautiously down the stairs, carrying his suitcase. There was insufficient light to allow him to see the scalds on the other man's neck.

'Leaving are we?' snapped Charlie, unable to disguise his delight. 'It's not before time. I don't know what you've been up to tonight, mister, but if it's what I think it is, you'd better go a long, long way from here. Sally's young man has five brothers and they're all fishermen. Come tomorrow they'll be looking for you – and they'll find you if you're still in Plymouth. You'll have no reason to go looking for girls once they've finished with you.'

Charlie was still standing in the doorway of the house, chuckling, when Robert Sanderson left Pin's Lane behind and passed out of hearing around the corner.

51

The door to the house where Devonport Lil had her room was kept locked. Clara Flood took a fee from her lodger for every man she brought back, and by not allowing the prostitute to have her own key, the mercenary old landlady ensured she was not cheated of any of her dues.

When Clara Flood opened the door and saw only Robert Sanderson standing there, she said, 'Devonport Lil's not in. She's been spending nights on one of the ships lately. It's so as she don't have to pay me anything extra, I expect.'

Robert Sanderson was in great pain. It had been an effort to get this far. Only the thought that he might find someone here to help had kept him going.

His shoulders sagged in acknowledgement of defeat.

There was a strong smell of gin on Clara Flood's breath, but she was not drunk. Peering at the suitcase he was carrying, she said, 'Are you looking for a room? If you are, I've got one I can rent to you. It'll be a week's money in advance – no matter how long you're staying.'

Sanderson grasped at the unexpected lifeline eagerly. 'Paying in advance is no problem, but I need to see a doctor urgently. Do you know one who'll see me – now?'

Clara Flood had been opening the door to him, but now she stopped. 'What's wrong with you?' she demanded. 'Is it catching? Something you've caught from one of the girls?'

'I've been badly scalded – in an accident. I need treatment right away.'

'You certain that's all it is?'

'Quite certain. Now . . . can I come in?'

'I'll treat it for you, if you like – but it'll cost you extra.'

'You? What do you know about medicine?'

'As much as most of your so-called "doctors". I followed the army in India with my husband for twenty years before he died in my arms. I've treated every kind of wound you could think of. Yes, and helped surgeons amputate enough limbs to serve a whole regiment. There's nothing you could have that I haven't seen before. Where are you scalded?'

'My neck's particularly bad, but the boiling water went through my shirt to my chest, back and shoulder.'

'Come on inside and I'll take a look at it. Once I've decided what needs to be done I'll want payment before I treat you.'

'Just do whatever needs to be done. You'll get your money.'

'Right, your room is upstairs, at the front of the house. Go up there and take your coat and shirt off. I'll be with you in a minute or two.'

Clara Flood worked for more than an hour cleaning

and dressing Sanderson's scalds. When her ministrations were finished, she told him that although the scalds were extremely painful, all except a wound on the side of his neck would heal fairly quickly.

She then gave him something to help him to sleep and left him alone in the dingy and not-too-clean room.

The injuries inflicted by Sally upset Sanderson's plans to settle his score with Lord and Lady Robartes. He had expected that in the process he would acquire enough money to set himself up in a small business.

The man who was to help him in this ambitious and criminal venture was Harry Maggs, a chimney sweep Sanderson had met recently in a Plymouth public house. As a small boy Maggs had swept the chimneys at Lanhydrock and claimed to know the house intimately.

He was well aware of the many items of value kept in the house. He was an apprentice when his master had been caught pilfering from Lanhydrock during one of his professional visits and had been transported. It was a fate Maggs had avoided only because transportation had now been abolished. He had, however, served many terms of imprisonment.

Maggs had always nursed a grudge against the Robartes, holding the family accountable for all that had happened to him; in his view, they had been responsible for having his master imprisoned, leaving him to 'fall into bad company'.

The meeting with Sanderson allowed both men to share their grievances on the Robartes, and Maggs had eagerly agreed to the ex-butler's plan, which would make them rich and the Robartes somewhat poorer.

The planned robbery had been carefully thought through. Sanderson had kept a duplicate key to the servants' door at the side of Lanhydrock House. The door was locked and bolted from the inside at night, but Sanderson was aware that some of the house servants were in the habit of sneaking out for romantic liaisons, leaving the door unbolted.

The ex-butler had lost none of his womanising traits with the passing of the years. Before the abrupt termination of his employment, he had been carrying on an affair with one of the housemaids. He suspected that she had fallen pregnant. If so, she would be deeply concerned about her future and he could use this to his advantage. He had written to her expressing a wish to meet her one night. She was to creep out of the house when the family and servants were asleep. He would send her another letter giving details of the time and place.

It was Sanderson's intention that, when a meeting with the housemaid had been arranged, he would give his key to the sweep. While the girl was absent, the sweep would enter the house, armed with a list, drawn up by the ex-butler, directing him what to take and where he would find it.

There were some extremely valuable items in Lanhydrock and the two men would be able to sell them on for a very good price.

But stealing was not all that Sanderson had planned. Thanks to Sanderson's knowledge of the household routine, Maggs would have already spent two days inside the house sweeping chimneys and reacquainting himself with the layout. During this time he would stuff a number of paraffin-soaked sacks up the kitchen chimney in a strategic spot, using his expert knowledge.

The next time a fire was lit in the kitchen, the sacking would catch light, causing considerable damage to the ancient house. In this way, Sanderson felt, he would have gained revenge for his dismissal.

His injuries had caused an unexpected setback, but the plan had been delayed by only a few weeks. That time would be spent ensuring the sweep knew exactly what he had to do and became thoroughly conversant with the current layout of Lanhydrock House, thus ensuring the full success of their venture.

52

'Are you quite sure you're feeling well enough to make the deliveries today, dear?' Grace's concern was clear on her face as she put the question to Sally. 'You don't look too good this morning.'

'I'll be far better working than moping around feeling sorry for myself.'

Unable to hide her bruises, Sally had told Grace and Alfie about allowing her father to use her room in Pin's Lane and had relayed the events of the previous evening. Grace had been particularly incensed, uttering blood-thirsty threats of what she would do to Sanderson if ever their paths crossed.

'Well, as long as you're feeling up to it – but I'll not rest easy until that young man of yours is back to look after you.'

'He may already be back,' said Alfie. 'I spoke to one of the fishmongers from town when I was opening up the shop. He said many of the Plymouth boats came in overnight. It seems they've not had much luck and have returned with poor catches. The weather was bad and they had to shelter in the Scillies for much of the time.'

The thought of seeing Ethan again thrilled Sally. She really missed him and after the events of recent weeks she *needed* him – although she wished her face was not so badly bruised.

She was confident that once she had apologised for her behaviour when they last met, they would be able to put their foolish quarrel behind them.

When she took a delivery to the quay later that morning she looked around eagerly for the *Mermaid*. It was nowhere to be seen and she was deeply disappointed.

When she questioned one of the fish buyers, he seemed surprised but not concerned that the Shields' boat was not in harbour.

'A dozen or so boats are still out,' he said. 'Don't worry, they'll all be in by tonight – and I hope they'll bring in more fish than the others.'

Sally made two more deliveries to the fish quay that day, and on each occasion she enquired after the *Mermaid*, but it had still not returned to harbour.

By the time Sally's working day came to an end it was dark, but she went to the quay one last time.

The fish sales had finished for the day now, but a number of fishermen were still working on their boats. From one of them she learned that the *Mermaid* was now the only boat belonging to the Plymouth fishing fleet that had not returned to harbour.

When she expressed her concern, the fisherman shrugged, 'Henry Shields is a man who likes to go his own way. The fish didn't seem to be running, so he probably went somewhere else to find them. I only hope he caught more than the rest of us did.'

As she walked away from the fish quay, Sally thought of what the fisherman had said. She should have been reassured by his words, but she was not.

She was walking slowly in the direction of the Salvation Army Refuge, but acting upon a sudden impulse, she turned and retraced her steps. She had decided to pay a call on Doris Shields.

When Sally arrived at the house, she discovered she was not the only person worried about the *Mermaid* and its crew. The door was opened by Sophie, and when Sally entered the kitchen she saw Phoebe seated there, drinking tea with Doris Shields.

When Doris saw Sally, she exclaimed, 'My dear child! What have you been up to? Your poor face . . . !'

Sally had been so preoccupied with thoughts of Ethan, she had temporarily forgotten the bruising on her face. Now, inhibited somewhat by the presence of Phoebe, whose attitude exuded disapproval, she gave Ethan's mother a brief version of the previous night's events.

'Ethan warned me against having anything to do with my father,' she concluded. 'I should have listened to him.'

'He wasn't happy about leaving you in the house with him,' Doris agreed. 'He spoke to me and his pa about it. He even thought of returning to Pin's Lane. I'm sorry to say it was me who talked him out of it. The hour was getting late and I knew he and the others would be making an early start next morning. I should have listened to him, he's always been a good judge of people.'

'I don't suppose I would have taken any notice of him,' Sally said unhappily. 'Not then, anyway. All I could think of was having my father with me at last.

Me and Ethan came very close to quarrelling about it.'

'I don't think Ethan saw it as a quarrel,' Doris said reassuringly. 'He understood how you felt. He was reluctant to say anything against your pa – but he *was* worried for you.'

'I know – and I've come here because I'm worried about *him*. I thought the *Mermaid* would have returned with the other boats. Do you know what might be happening?'

'We're all worried about them,' said Sophie. 'We expected them back today, whatever the other boats did.'

'Tomorrow is my birthday,' Doris explained. 'My fiftieth birthday. For weeks all the family have been making a big thing about it. Ethan's pa has always brought me flowers for my birthday. He wouldn't want to miss this one. Besides, the boys were planning to give me a party – that's another thing Ethan was going to talk to you about on the night before they sailed. He wanted to invite you and ask your opinion about one or two things.'

'You . . . you don't think anything could have happened to them?' Sally put the question hesitantly.

Doris shook her head emphatically. 'There's not a finer fisherman along the whole of this coast than my husband. In all probability he's found the fish the others were looking for and is staying out until he's taken as many as he can. There's no doubting we can do with the money. They'll be back tomorrow absolutely full of themselves, just you wait and see.'

53

Inspector Ian Lovat had become a regular visitor to the Salvation Army Refuge. Although his visits did not always have a purely professional purpose, he justified them by the fact that he occasionally picked up a snippet of useful information from one or other of the girls who were resident there.

However, today he had called at Eva's request, to discuss an advertisement placed in a provincial news-paper, which had been sent to her by a colleague. The advertisement was identical to the one that had brought Rachel and her companions to Plymouth. The only difference was that this one gave an answering address in Falmouth in nearby Cornwall. However, it was close enough to arouse suspicion.

'Of course, it might be a perfectly legitimate and respectable organisation,' Eva said now to Ian Lovat, 'but the wording is almost identical to the last adver-tisement. I'm also suspicious because the address is not too many miles from here. I believe the same people as before are involved.'

'We can't be certain of that,' Ian Lovat replied cautiously. 'The problem is that the address to which these girls are asked to write is a box number. I could have inquiries made, but my jurisdiction doesn't extend beyond Plymouth.'

'Does that mean you can't do anything to help?' Eva was indignant.

'No, it merely means I mustn't be seen to be doing anything that might possibly be construed as exceeding my duty. I can certainly ask the Falmouth police to make a few inquiries about the people behind this – but I've no doubt the group will have covered their tracks well.'

'Wouldn't they be likely to be scared off and move elsewhere, away from the West Country, if the police start making inquiries?'

'Probably,' the inspector agreed, 'but it will at least save those poor unsuspecting girls who reply to this particular advertisement.'

'That's merely a short-term solution. I want to stamp out this trade once and for all – even if it means breaking the law to do it.'

'You shouldn't be saying that to me,' Ian Lovat pointed out, but it was only the gentlest of reprimands. He knew the strength of Eva's views on this subject and respected them. He also enjoyed her company.

Eva looked forward to his visits too. She found she was able to converse with him more freely than with anyone she had ever known, male or female, in or outside the Salvation Army.

Nevertheless, she was passionate in her opposition to this particular aspect of vice. 'I am prepared to go to any lengths to bring this vile trade to an end. No price would be too high to pay. If I were younger and could enlist the aid of a reputable newspaper to publish my findings, I'd answer one of these advertisements myself and expose these people for what they are.'

'Finding a newspaper would pose no problem,' said Ian Lovat, not really believing Eva was entirely serious. 'A friend I made during my days in London is Carl Milton, editor of the *Mayfair Gazette*. He feels almost as strongly as you do about organised vice. As a matter of fact, he has run numerous campaigns against it in his newspaper. However, for you – or any other woman, for that matter – to play such a part would be far too dangerous. The people involved in this business – and that's exactly what it is, *big* business – have far too much to lose to allow a woman to stand in their way. You would simply disappear.'

'That wouldn't happen if someone was monitoring each move as it was made,' Eva persisted. 'Besides, just think of the magnificent victory if it were to succeed!'

'And if it didn't?' countered the policeman.

'What is one life, willingly given, when weighed against the hundreds, thousands, even, who might be spared a lifetime of shame and degradation?'

'You're really serious about this!' Ian Lovat was suddenly genuinely alarmed. 'It's madness. You couldn't rely upon the police to co-operate in such an unorthodox scheme. Quite apart from any other consideration, the route taken by these people crosses far too many boundaries – both national and international. There would be no continuity in police action. You could disappear forever anywhere along the route. Even worse, you might end up as just another victim of the vice trade.'

'"Just another victim", Ian? Each of the victims is a decent, ordinary young girl, like Rachel. Every one of them possesses thoughts and feelings and standards of decency that match my own. Yet they will be degraded and brutalised in a manner that beggars description. How would I feel – how would *you* feel if we knew I was about to suffer such a fate and no one was prepared to lift a finger to help? Would you use these "boundaries" of which you speak as an excuse for doing nothing? It is because those in authority can find such excuses that this trade flourishes. Such thinking ensures that the brothels of Europe will be supplied with innocent young English girls for as long as they want them.'

'Your feelings about this are both understandable and commendable. I can assure you that, as a policeman, I'll take all possible measures to stamp out this trade in Plymouth, but I can do very little beyond the boundaries of this borough. However, if you want to ensure it's brought to the attention of those in a position to really do something about it, I'll write a letter to my editor friend. I'll suggest he gets in touch with you with a view to running the story of what happened to Rachel. It won't please my chief constable, or the members of the borough council, but, as you rightly say, there is no place for such a degrading trade in a civilised country like ours.'

'Thank you, Ian, you're a very good friend.'

Eva occasionally wondered whether it might be possible for Ian Lovat to become more than a friend, but it could not be. She had dedicated her life to the cause of the Salvation Army.

Ian Lovat was still at the Refuge when Sally returned there later that evening.

'We were beginning to worry about you,' said Eva.

'I've told Inspector Lovat what happened to you last night. He would like to speak to you about it.'

'I've already told you everything that needs telling,' Sally said guardedly. 'There's nothing more to say.'

'The bruising on your face makes explanations unnecessary,' Ian Lovat said, tight-lipped. 'It must have been a vicious attack.'

'Have you been to Pin's Lane this evening, Sally?' asked Eva.

'No.'

Almost afraid to ask the question, Sally asked Ian Lovat hesitantly, 'Have you?'

'I went there this afternoon. Your room was empty. The man on the ground floor said Sanderson left soon after you ran from the house. He was carrying a suitcase.'

'Charlie doesn't miss much that goes on around him,' Sally mused.

'Captain Eva has told me you met up with your father in Union Street. Was anyone with him?'

'No.' Sally wondered why he had asked such a question.

'You're quite certain?'

'He was on his own – and very drunk.'

The inspector seemed disappointed with her reply and Sally added, 'I didn't see anyone with him then – but I did yesterday. They were going into The Jolly Waterman together.'

'Was it a man? Can you describe him to me?'

'He was too dirty to tell what he really looked like. I think he was a chimney sweep.'

'Ah! That's the man,' Ian Lovat said enigmatically. 'You've no idea who he is?'

'None at all. Why do you ask?'

'Someone overheard Sanderson and this man talking. It sounded as though they were planning a burglary, but my informant heard no more than that. If I knew who this man was I'd have him followed.'

Sally hesitated, wondering whether she should repeat the threats her father had made against the owners of Lanhydrock House. She decided against it.

One reason was the natural suspicion all residents of the Barbican had of the police – even this man, who had done so much to help her. Another was that, despite all he had done, Robert Sanderson was still her father.

Ian Lovat was disappointed. He believed Sally knew more than she was telling him, but he did not press her on the matter.

Sensing Sally's conflict of loyalties, Eva changed the subject by asking her where she had been since leaving work. She suggested Sally should keep away from Pin's Lane unless she had Ethan with her.

'Ethan was the reason I didn't come here straight from work,' Sally explained. 'His boat hasn't returned to harbour with the others today. Nobody seems to know where it is, so I went to see his mother to see if she knew anything.'

Eva immediately put thoughts of Robert Sanderson to one side. 'The whole of the Shields family are on that boat! Is there reason to believe something might have happened to them?'

'Ethan's ma doesn't think so, and one of the fishermen said that Ethan's pa tends to go his own way, but I can tell that everyone's worried. Tomorrow is Mrs Shields's birthday – her fiftieth. Ethan's pa has never failed to spend a birthday with her. If the *Mermaid* doesn't return tomorrow I think she'll really be worried. We all will.'

Eva looked at Sally, standing before her wearing second-hand clothes and with a badly beaten face. Her heart went out to the young girl, yet again. She would pray particularly hard tonight that another tragedy was not about to strike Sally's young life.

54

The Shieldses' boat did not return to Plymouth on Doris's fiftieth birthday. Nor did it enter the small harbour the day after.

The absence of the small boat from its home port was now causing great concern among the Shieldses' fellow fishermen. Nevertheless, Doris still insisted her family would bring the *Mermaid* safely into harbour, riding low in the water with the fish they had caught.

Her faith no longer convinced anyone. Sophie confessed her deep concern to Sally late on the second day after Doris's birthday.

The two young women were together on the fish quay. They had come here because a number of east coast boats had arrived with their catches, netted off the Isles of Scilly. Both young women hoped there might news of the *Mermaid*.

Their hopes were all too quickly dashed. All the fishermen told the same story. The Plymouth fishing boat had not been seen.

'I'm becoming really worried now, Sally.' Sophie was

close to tears. 'I don't know what I'll do if Albert's lost. I just don't.'

'Don't even think about it,' Sally replied, with far more optimism than she felt. 'You've heard everyone say that Henry Shields is the best fisherman along the whole of this coast. He wouldn't do anything to put his boat and all his sons at risk. Albert and the others will come back and we'll both feel silly for having worried about them.' In a bid to change the subject, she said, 'I've not seen Phoebe lately. Has she been to the house?'

'No, and I doubt if we'll see her again,' Sophie said bitterly. She only came around the other day because she sensed a drama. She wanted to be at the centre of it and have everyone feel sorry for her. It's been dragging on too long for her now. There's no drama in a *missing* boat. Besides, I believe she's seeing someone else and has been for quite some time. It will please her parents. They would never have accepted a fisherman in the family.'

The two girls parted temporarily, to pass either side of baskets of fish being unloaded on to the quayside from the east coast boats.

'Mind you, there are others who care, even though they don't know us very well. That Salvation Army woman, Captain Eva, for one. She came around to the house today, to speak to Ma Shields and me. She said the whole of the Plymouth corps of the Salvation Army are praying for Ethan and the others.'

'We should all take heart from that,' Sally said attempting to cheer up the other woman. 'Captain Eva doesn't do things by halves. You can bet that when she prays, God listens. Ethan, Albert and the others couldn't wish for anyone better on their side and praying for them.'

Sophie gave Sally a weak smile. It disappeared again very quickly as she asked, 'What do you *really* think, Sally? Do you honestly believe they'll return safely?'

It was a question Sally had tried not to ask herself. She had avoided facing up to the probable reason behind the *Mermaid*'s failure to return to Plymouth.

Nevertheless, she knew what Sophie wanted to hear and phrased her reply accordingly. 'I'm certainly not willing to believe that Ethan and the others *aren't* coming back. Neither are you – and Ma Shields certainly isn't.'

Unseen by Sophie, she crossed her fingers firmly as she added, 'They'll come back safely, you'll see . . .'

Sally's confidence was desperately shaken two days later when another steam-trawler from Lowestoft put in to Plymouth. It had been working fishing grounds to the south of the Scilly Isles, and pieces of splintered wood, painted bright blue, had been hauled on board in the trawler's nets.

The crew had made enquiries from fishermen on a boat they met up with just off Plymouth and learned of the missing boat.

The broken wood was taken to the Shieldses' house and when Sally arrived at the house that evening, she saw it piled in the passageway, just inside the door. Immediately she remembered Ethan telling her that the boat was being painted. He had even told her the colour . . . it was bright blue!

Suddenly, she felt unable to stay and face Doris and Sophie Shields. Sally turned around and ran blindly through the streets of the Barbican.

Unwilling to share her emotions with anyone, she could not return to the Refuge. She did not want to speak to anyone, anywhere. All she wanted was to be alone with her sorrow.

The only place she could think of was the room in Pin's Lane. Blundering through the front door, she ran upstairs.

It was dark here, but she did not want a light. She felt a need to hide from the whole world. Everything in her life was going wrong. Desperately wrong.

Giving way to an uncharacteristic bout of self-pity, she believed she must be the unluckiest person in the whole world.

Like a small, hurt animal, she crouched in a corner of the room, her head against the wall.

55

Captain Eva was visiting Rachel at the flat above the pie shop when Alfie came in. He brought news of the Lowestoft trawler that had come into Sutton harbour with wreckage, almost certainly from the *Mermaid*.

The Salvationist felt the pain of the news as acutely as though someone had dealt her a physical blow.

'I must go to the Shieldses' house and speak to Ethan's mother,' she said, rising to her feet immediately. 'Doris Shields has six sons and a husband on that boat. This is enough to derange her.'

'See if Sally is there too,' said Grace. 'That poor girl has had more to contend with than should come into any young girl's life.'

'I'll come with you,' Rachel said to Eva. 'I'd like to help Sally if I can, just as she helped me when I needed it.'

'You really shouldn't be going out at all, dear,' said Grace. 'You haven't been very well these last few days. You're still looking very pale.'

'I'll be all right. I'll just go and get my coat.'

When Rachel had left the room, Grace spoke to Eva in an exaggerated whisper. 'She's not been her usual cheerful self just lately. Tired and moping around the house. She's as likely as not to burst into tears at the slightest provocation.' Nodding conspiratorially, she added, 'I think it must be her age.'

As Eva and Rachel made their way to the home of the Shields family, Eva broached the subject of Grace's anxiety.

'Grace is very concerned about you, Rachel. I know she's not used to having a young girl about the house, but is there anything wrong that I can help with?'

Rachel looked up at her companion. 'I'm all right. Grace worries too much about me – but she's very kind.' It was too dark for Eva to be able to read the girl's expression.

'You're lucky to have found her, Rachel. She thinks the world of you.'

'I know, but she sometimes speaks to me as if I was the little girl she lost all those years ago. I'm not, though. It's a great responsibility.'

Eva smiled. Rachel was growing up. She had no doubt that Grace was right in her assessment of what was wrong with her.

Eva and Rachel did not stay very long at Doris Shields's house. The wreckage was still piled in the passageway and Sophie was obviously very close to tears. But not Doris Shields.

She was refusing to accept that her family and their boat had been lost. Despite the evidence of the splintered timbers, she was adamant that her husband and sons would soon return safely to Plymouth.

Faced with such unshakeable faith, Eva realised that sympathy would be out of place. She expressed her thoughts aloud to Sophie as Albert's young wife escorted the two visitors from the kitchen to the street.

The expression on Sophie's face told Eva that she did not share the convictions of her mother-in-law. The strain of maintaining the pretence was beginning to show.

'I'm afraid of what she'll do when all hope has finally disappeared and she realises just how great her loss is,' she said. Close to tears, she added, 'I'm not sure I'll be able to cope with it, either.'

'I'll come visiting as often as I can,' Eva offered. 'In the meantime, if you need anything, don't hesitate to call for my help. You know where you can find me.'

She was about to walk away when she remembered the other reason she and Rachel had come to the house. 'By the way, do you know where we might find Sally?'

'She was here earlier this evening. She came inside the house, took one look at the wreckage in the passage, then turned and fled. I never had a chance to say a word to her. Like me, she doesn't share Mrs Shields's optimism. I didn't worry too much about her when she left because I thought she would go straight back to you, at the Refuge. Are you certain she isn't there?'

'She might be there now,' replied Eva. 'We'll look in at Pin's Lane on the way back, just in case she decided to go there so she could be on her own.'

She hoped her reply would satisfy Sophie. She had no wish to add to her worries. If Doris Shields had indeed lost her entire family in one cruel stroke, Albert's wife would be taking on a great burden.

When Eva and Rachel reached Pin's Lane and entered the house, Charlie came to the door of his room.

'What's going on tonight? I've never known so many people to be coming in and out.'

'Why, who else has been here?' Eva asked sharply, suddenly fearful that Sid Darling might have been one of the 'many' visitors to the house.

It immediately became apparent that Charlie had been exaggerating.

'Well, apart from you two, someone came running through the passageway and up the stairs about an hour ago. It sounded like young Sally, but I wasn't going upstairs on my own, in case it was someone else.' Sniffing noisily, Charlie added, 'Whoever it is, they're very quiet up there now. They haven't made a single sound since they came in, but I know they haven't come back down again. What's going on?'

'Haven't you heard about Henry Shields's boat? I felt certain the family would have told you . . .'

'Told me *what*?' Charlie demanded impatiently. 'Whatever it is, I'm obviously the last to know. That's the trouble with not being well enough to get out and about. You have to rely on others to let you know what's going on in the world.'

'Go back in your room and sit down and I'll come in and tell you.' Eva was aware she was dealing with a sick man who might take the news badly.

At the same time she gave an uncertain glance up the unlighted stairs. Aware of her concern, Rachel said, 'It's all right, while you're speaking to Charlie, I'll go upstairs and see if Sally is there.' Hesitating for a moment, she added, 'But I would like a candle to light the way. It looks dark.'

'Take that one,' said Charlie, pointing to the stub of a candle burning in a chipped enamel candleholder. 'But don't forget to bring it back down again. I keep it burning there to show me the way to my kitchen.'

56

Holding the candle at head height in front of her, Rachel made her way cautiously up the creaking stairs. In truth, she was not as brave as she had tried to appear to Captain Eva. Charlie had been fairly certain the footsteps he had heard going upstairs were Sally's, but the knowledge that he had heard nothing since was unnerving.

What if someone had been waiting in the room for her? What if . . . ?

When the candle and holder began shaking in her hand, Rachel made a determined effort to pull herself together. She told herself she was being foolish. Had anyone been waiting for Sally in the upstairs room there would have been *more* noise, not less.

Despite her determination to be brave, her heart was beating faster than normal as she gently pushed open the door to Sally's room.

She held the candle high in front of her, as she peered into the room, so as to shed its light as far as possible. Unable to see anything at first, she grew puzzled. Taking a first step inside the room, she held the candle even higher.

A slight movement in a corner of the room was so unexpected and sudden that Rachel almost dropped the candle in fright.

'Is that you, Sally?'

'Yes.' Her voice sounded thick and slurred, as though she had been drinking. 'What are you doing here?'

'Captain Eva and me went looking for you at Ethan's house. The wife of one of his brothers said you'd been there but had run off again. Captain Eva thought you might have come here. She's downstairs now, talking to Charlie.'

When Sally made no immediate reply, Rachel asked, 'Do you want me to light the lamp for you?'

'No! And I didn't need anyone to come looking for me. All I wanted was to be on my own for a while, in the dark.'

'That's the way I felt for a few days after I'd been taken off the boat. I was glad afterwards that you, Captain Eva and Grace were there to help me though.'

When Sally remained silent once more, Rachel asked uncertainly, 'Do you want me to go?'

Sally shook her head. 'It's all right.' She still sat in the corner of the room, her arms locked around her drawn-up knees.

Rachel set the candle down on the table, then walked across the room to stand by the bed.

'I . . . I'm sorry about Ethan.'

'Nobody knows for sure yet what's happened to him and the others,' Sally snapped fiercely.

'No, of course not,' Rachel agreed hastily.

There was silence between the two for a while, before

Rachel said hesitantly, 'Sally, I know this isn't the right time to talk about such things, but . . . could you tell me something? Something important?'

'What?'

'How can you tell if you're having a baby?'

Sally was startled out of her deep unhappiness. 'How do you . . . ? Why, there are a whole lot of ways, I suppose. Your body changes. You—' Belatedly, the import of the question penetrated Sally's dulled brain. 'Rachel! You don't think . . . ? Oh no, it couldn't happen to you.' Her own deep misery momentarily pushed to one side, she looked aghast at her companion. 'But . . . you *can't*. You're too young!'

'I was twelve a few weeks ago,' Rachel replied wretchedly, '. . . and I think I *am*. What can I do, Sally?'

'There's nothing you can do. At least, nothing that's really safe.'

'I don't care about *safe*. I'll kill myself before I have Sid Darling's baby – or the baby of any of the others who did this to me. But I think it must be his.'

'Have you spoken to anyone else about this? Captain Eva . . . ?'

'I don't want anyone else to know – ever! I've only told you because I trust you – and because I need your help. You must promise never to tell Grace, Sally. If you do I'll run off and kill myself. I promise you I will.'

'You mustn't talk like that, Rachel. Whatever happens, no one will even blame *you*. This certainly isn't your fault.'

The loss of the *Mermaid* was still a heavy, black load that weighed Sally down, but Rachel's revelation had made it lose its immediacy.

'I don't care about any of that. I'm just *not* going to have it . . .'

At that moment, both girls heard the stairs creaking loudly as someone made their way up them. A few seconds later Captain Eva entered the room.

'Hello, Sally,' she said sympathetically. 'I'm desperately sorry to hear the tragic news about Ethan's fishing boat.'

The hurt returned, but Sally said defiantly, 'They've only found a bit of old wreckage. It doesn't mean Ethan and the others have been lost.'

'That's quite true,' admitted Eva. 'And you're absolutely right. We must cling to hope for as long as is reasonable.'

Although she was convinced there *was* no hope, Eva believed the impact of the loss of Ethan would lessen for Sally with the passing of time. She was not as certain the same would apply to Doris Shields, faced with her far greater tragedy.

'Do you want to stay here tonight, Sally, or will you return to the Refuge with me?'

'I'll come to the Refuge a little later. Perhaps Rachel will stay with me for a while?'

'I'm sure she will.'

Unaware of the true reason for Sally's suggestion, Eva was delighted the two girls had become such firm friends that each could be a comfort to the other at a time of such deep trouble.

'I'll go downstairs and make certain Charlie is all right before I go. He knew nothing about his brother's boat being lost. It's hit him very hard. Afterwards, I'll go and tell Grace what Rachel is doing. I'll see you later at the Refuge. May I say I'm very impressed with your courage and fortitude, Sally – but I'm not really surprised.'

When Eva had gone, Sally said, 'Now, what are we going to do about you, Rachel? I still think it would be best to tell Captain Eva, or Grace.'

Rachel shook her head vigorously. 'If I can get rid of the baby there's no reason why anyone apart from you should ever know.'

'I don't think getting rid of it is quite that easy,' said Sally. She was standing up, close to the window now. As both girls looked out a lamp was lit in the kitchen beneath the room occupied by Devonport Lil.

A few moments later, Clara Flood could be seen moving about, busying herself in the kitchen.

Pointing to her, Sally said, 'If you're not sensible, you could end up in the hands of someone like her. Ruth used to say she's got rid of more babies than King Herod, but I wouldn't want to have her doing anything to me. She's a horrible old woman.'

Turning away from the window, she continued. 'I believe there are one or two things you can take to try to get rid of a baby, but they don't always work. I'll ask some of the girls who are staying at the Refuge if they know of anything. I don't doubt some of them will have had to deal with a similar problem.'

'Beg them to help, Sally. I'm sorry to have troubled you at a time like this, but I've been worrying myself sick about it. I couldn't think of anyone else I could turn to.'

As the girls left the house in Pin's Lane a little later, Sally realised that having Rachel's very real problem to think about had somehow made her own sorrow easier to cope with.

57

Questioning the girls in the Refuge about getting rid of an unwanted baby was much easier than Sally had anticipated – but it also proved embarrassing.

Without exception they thought she must be pregnant by Ethan, who had now been lost at sea and so could not marry her.

Each of the girls had her own recipe for procuring a miscarriage. Most involved mixing a potion, the main ingredient of which was alcohol.

Sally explained this to Rachel as they walked around the streets of Plymouth together the next day, making deliveries for Grace and Alfie.

'Do you think I'll be able to take it without Grace knowing?' asked Rachel.

'Are you used to strong drink?' Sally countered.

'No, I don't like it.'

'Then you'll never be able to keep it from her. You'll be drunk long before you've taken enough for it to do what you want it to.'

'What can I do then?'

Sally shrugged. She felt dreadfully tired. She had not slept the previous night. Every time she dozed off, Ethan's face haunted her dreams and she woke herself, and Rachel once, by calling his name aloud. 'I don't know. Have the baby and decide what you're going to do about it then, I suppose.'

'I'm *not* going to have it, Sally. I'm *not*!'

Rachel spoke so vehemently that a woman passing by looked at her disapprovingly and stepped from the pavement to avoid her.

The girls walked on in silence for a while before Rachel said, 'Would I be able to take this stuff in the Refuge without anyone knowing?'

Sally was about to give her a negative reply. Then she remembered that only a few nights before she had been invited to join some of the girls at the Refuge, who had consumed the contents of a bottle of gin before going to bed.

'You might,' she admitted.

'Then that's what I'll do. I'll stay there with you for a while. Until I've got rid of it.'

'What will you tell Grace? She'll be very unhappy if you move out from her place.'

'She'll be even more unhappy if I inflict an unwanted baby on her. I'll tell her I'm staying there to be near you while you're so upset about Ethan.'

'Thank you very much!' Sally spoke indignantly. 'Don't you think I've got enough to worry about as it is?'

'Yes, you have,' admitted Rachel. 'But I'm desperate for help, Sally. Any help I can get.'

'All right,' Sally relented. She had grown very fond of Rachel and did not like to see her so unhappy.

'You make your excuses to Grace and I'll arrange with
Captain Eva for a bed to be put in my room for you.
I don't like lying to her, and she certainly wouldn't
approve of what we're doing, but I feel she'd at least
understand.'

Both Grace and Captain Eva agreed to the temporary
arrangement so readily that it made Sally feel even
more guilty. However, she told herself she was doing
the right thing for Rachel.

It also gave her something to think about other than
Ethan . . . yet she managed to feel deeply guilty about
this too.

That evening, Sally heated gin in a saucepan balancing on the fire in her room. On the table, folded in a
small paper bag, was a brown, spicy-smelling powder
that had been purchased for Sally by one of the recently
'saved' prostitutes. It was to be poured in the gin when
it was sufficiently heated.

'Is it going to work?' Rachel asked anxiously.

'I don't know,' Sally replied honestly. 'Annie gave me
the stuff to put in the gin. She said sometimes it works,
sometimes it doesn't.'

'How much of it do I have to drink?'

'As much as you can. All of it, if possible.'

Rachel looked aghast. 'But . . . won't it make me
ill?'

'Probably – but I think that's the idea. If you make
yourself really ill you might lose the baby.'

As she was speaking, Sally moved the saucepan from
the fire, using a cloth to hold the handle. She half filled
a mug with hot gin, then spooned a quantity of powder
from the paper bag into it.

After she had stirred it vigorously, Sally passed the mug to Rachel without comment.

Taking a sip, the younger girl recoiled in disgust.

'Ugh! It's *horrible*!'

Despite the seriousness of what they were doing, Sally gave her friend a weak smile. 'You're not drinking to enjoy it, Rachel. If it does what you want it to do it'll be the best drink you've ever had, won't it? Now, get it down, there's lots more left.'

Rachel downed the concoction in a series of great gulps. Occasionally gagging, she did her best to control the urge to be sick. When the mug was empty, she stood in the middle of the room fighting for breath, her cheeks flushed and red.

Expressionless, Sally took the mug from Rachel's hands, mixed more powder and hot gin and held the mug out to the younger girl once more.

'I'm not sure I can take any more, Sally. I feel funny. All light-headed.'

'You'll need to take a whole lot more than you have if it's to do anything. Annie told me she's known some girls who've had to drink two whole bottles of gin before it's had any effect. You've had no more than half a mugful. Look . . .' She held up the half-full bottle. 'There's a lot to go yet.'

Rachel groaned. Feeling increasingly light-headed, she took the mug from Sally and lifted it to her lips.

58

That night, Rachel was so violently ill that Sally feared Eva would hear her and come upstairs to find out what was happening.

Fortunately, the Salvation Army officer was at a meeting and did not return to the Refuge until late. She did call out a soft 'Good night' outside the door but, receiving no reply, took herself off to bed, believing the two girls to be asleep.

Sally wondered what Eva's reaction would have been had she known Sally was inside the room, holding a towel to Rachel's mouth as a gag to prevent her groans from being heard.

The following morning, Rachel felt twice as ill as Sally told her she looked. Although she was convinced she was dying, Rachel had not aborted the baby she was carrying.

As the two girls walked to work at the shop, Rachel asked, 'Will I have to go through all that again, Sally?'

'You tell me. You're the one who wants to get rid of a baby.'

'Then I'll do it . . . but isn't there something else I can take? Something that doesn't taste quite so horrible.'

'All the girls have different ideas on what should be taken. We'll try another one tonight – but I doubt if you'll enjoy it any more. It involves hot gin again – they all do. It's only the stuff that goes in it that's different.'

Rachel groaned. 'People who drink for pleasure must be mad! Once this is over I'll never touch another drop for as long as I live – but I *am* going to get rid of this baby.'

When they arrived at the shop, Grace threw up her hands in horror when she saw the state Rachel was in.

'My dear soul, look at you! Anyone would think you hadn't slept for a week! You're not much better, Sally. I'd better not give either of you very much to do today.'

'Why don't you give them each a pie and put 'em to bed?' Alfie asked sarcastically. 'I sometimes wonder how we manage to make any money at all, Grace. It wouldn't surprise me if you were to tell me one day you wanted to turn the whole business over to the Salvation Army!'

'We could do a whole lot worse than that, Alfie Philpott, and it would stand us in good stead when we are brought before our maker.'

Alfie realised his attempt at sarcasm had gone seriously wrong. Alarmed that he might have put a radical idea into the mind of his unpredictable wife, he said hurriedly, 'I've no intention of going to meet my maker just yet. When I do, I doubt if he'll frown on the fact that

I've worked hard and made a success of the life he gave to me.'

'He'll look more kindly upon you if you can show you've been generous to those less fortunate than yourself during your lifetime,' Grace retorted. 'Anyway, we won't lose any customers today. I'll make the deliveries myself, if I have to.'

'You won't need to do that,' Sally assured her. 'Rachel and me are tired, but we're not invalids. We can make all the deliveries.'

'Well . . . all right, if you're quite sure,' said an unconvinced Grace. 'But you make certain you both come back here for a proper meal when the midday deliveries have been made.'

The last thing Rachel wanted to think about right now was food, but she said nothing. She sincerely hoped Sally had been telling the truth when she said she would feel better as the day went along.

That evening's attempt to bring about a miscarriage was no more successful than the previous evening's. If anything, Rachel was more ill than she had been the night before and was once more quite convinced she was going to die.

But Sally soon had something more to worry about. The next afternoon, as she was making her deliveries, she called in to see Doris Shields and found Sophie deeply concerned about the mental state of her mother-in-law.

'She refuses to face the facts,' Sophie said unhappily. 'I'm quite certain she lies awake for most of the night grieving for Henry and the boys, but she won't discuss it with me, or with anyone else. My fear is that if she carries on like this she'll go out of her mind. I'm finding it very hard to cope with, Sally.' Hesitantly, she asked, 'Do you think you could move in and stay with me for a night or two? I'd really appreciate having your company.'

Sally thought of Rachel and her problem. The younger girl had already hinted that she doubted if she could take any more of the alcoholic treatment. Besides, it did not seem to be succeeding in its aim.

'Let me go back to the Refuge to collect a few things, then I'll return.'

'Thanks, Sally,' Sophie said gratefully. 'It will help just having you here to talk to, even if neither of us are able to do anything to help Mrs Shields.'

At the Refuge, Rachel seemed as relieved as Sally had hoped she might be. She admitted she did not feel she could cope with deliberately making herself violently ill for a third night.

'But what else can I try, Sally?' she pleaded. 'I *must* get rid of it, somehow.'

'Let me think about it.'

In fact, Sally had already given the matter some thought. She would be staying in the Shieldses' home with Sophie. Albert's wife had worked on the quay with the Scots fisherwomen who came down to help their men-folk when they were fishing the Channel waters at certain times of the year.

The Scots women had a vocabulary that was the equal of Cornish fishermen. They also brought with them a reputation for immorality that had grown to near-legendary proportions over the years.

Sophie might have heard them discussing the best means of procuring a miscarriage. However, Sally did not want her jumping to the same conclusions as the girls in the Refuge. She decided she would let Sophie into Rachel's secret. She had absolute trust in the wife of Ethan's brother, and felt certain she would prove to be a useful ally.

59

Sophie was utterly appalled to hear of Rachel's condition. She believed, as did Sally, that the unfortunate young girl had already suffered quite enough.

'She's so *young*, Sally. To have gone through all that's happened to her – and now to have to face this . . . It seems all wrong. Yet the man who is the cause of all this is still out there somewhere. Why haven't the police caught up with him?'

'No one can find him. He's certainly gone from Plymouth. Inspector Lovat believes he's probably left England. Wanted notices have been sent to every police force in the country. If he was around he would have been caught by now.'

'Where does this inspector believe he's gone?'

'Most probably to Belgium. That's where the girls were being sent. He knows people there.'

'It's appalling to think there are such men in the world.' Although Sophie had her own problems with which to come to terms, she asked, 'Is there anything I can do to help?'

'Not unless you know of a foolproof means of getting rid of the baby she's carrying.'

Sophie shook her head sadly. 'There's no such thing, Sally. I've listened to the Scots women down the quay talking about it – other women too. If you're lucky – very lucky – something you try *might* work. Most times it doesn't. She'll have to get used to the idea of having the baby. Once it's been born she might be able to have it adopted, or something. Mind you, that won't be easy, either. It seems there are far more babies being born than there are women who want 'em.'

'I've already told her she should wait until the baby's born, but she's determined to get rid of it now.'

'It seems everyone has more than their share of problems. Right now, Albert's ma is mine. I keep hoping she'll break down and cry, or become hysterical, or something. I'd find it a lot easier to take than this quiet, unshakeable faith that the *Mermaid* is going to come riding in on the next tide.'

Sophie's statement sounded harsh, but even as she spoke tears began rolling unchecked down her cheeks.

Putting an arm about her, Sally said, 'I'll do what I can to help, Sophie. I know these last few days can't have been easy for you.'

Seated at the kitchen table, sharing a meal with Sophie and Doris Shields, Sally soon realised what Albert's wife was finding so difficult.

Doris Shields's self-control was unnerving. There were no tears and she showed little emotion. She seemed to have complete control of herself.

Half-way through the meal, Doris looked at the clock and said, 'I wonder if Henry and the boys will bring the

Mermaid in on tonight's tide? They'd better not leave it too late if they are. The tide will be turning in another half an hour or so. When they do arrive they'll no doubt be hungry. Is there plenty of food in the house, Sophie?'

Sophie had been gazing down at her plate while Doris was talking.

When she looked up, she said, 'There'll be more than enough for everyone.'

'Good. There's nothing like fishing to give a man an appetite.' Shifting her attention to Sally, she said, 'They'll certainly eat more than you, young lady. You've been prodding and picking at that food as though you might have lost something in it.'

'I'm sorry, Mrs Shields. I don't seem to be very hungry this evening.'

'That's the result of working in a pie shop, with the smell of cooking in your nostrils all day. It's bound to take the edge off your appetite. Why don't you two girls finish your meal and go on down to the harbour? See if there's any sign of Henry and the boys. I'll clear the table and wash up while you're gone.'

'I'll stay and give you a hand,' said Sophie. 'It's a bit cold out there for me.' Humouring her mother-in-law, she added, 'Albert doesn't always walk home the same way from the harbour. It depends where they're able to berth the boat. It won't be easy today, with so many east coast boats in. I wouldn't want to miss him if he came home one way and I went to the harbour the other.'

Aware that Sally was worried about Rachel, Sophie gave her an understanding smile. 'There's no need for you to stay in. I'll be all right.'

'Thanks. I'll just pop out and have a few words with

Rachel, then I'll come back and keep you company for
the remainder of the evening.'

Sally expected to find Rachel at the Refuge. She had said
she intended staying on there for a few more days. But
there were only three girls in the house and Rachel was
not one of them. The others had gone to a meeting at
Central Hall with Captain Eva, and Sally thought Rachel
must have gone with them.

In two minds about whether to return to the Shieldses'
house immediately or to go to Central Hall first, Sally
chose the latter option.

The prayer meeting was already in progress in the hall
and was well attended – but there was an opposition
meeting taking place outside.

About forty men, some of them holding aloft Skeleton
Army banners, were singing bawdy, music-hall songs at
the top of their voices in an attempt to drown the sound
of those inside, but Sally had no difficulty slipping past
them and into the hall.

Inside, the worshippers were doing their best to ignore
the competition from the street outside. Standing at the
back of the hall, Sally tried to locate Rachel in the
crowd.

Opposition to the Salvation Army had escalated in
recent weeks. The large number of broken windows
in the hall bore testimony to the violence of the Skeleton Army.

It made the hall colder than it might have been,
particularly for those of the congregation who were
inadequately clothed.

Sally thought it would probably not have displeased
the founder of the Salvation Army. Captain Eva had

once told her that General William Booth had decreed his 'soldiers' should take a cold bath daily. He believed it to be both hygienic and strengthening for the forces of the Lord.

He would no doubt have been well pleased with the congregation too. What it lacked in physical comfort was more than compensated by its spiritual enthusiasm and religious fervour.

Captain Wardle was conducting the meeting, with Captain Eva on the platform beside him. A tall, distinguished man, his oratory was attracting men and women to the front of the hall to pledge themselves to the Lord's cause.

Sally was not seeking salvation, but Rachel, and this was not easy. Then, to her surprise, she picked out Grace Philpott in the crowd, close to the front of the hall.

The congregation was standing and Sally was unable to see whether Rachel was with her, but she felt she probably was. If so, she would be unable to discuss Rachel's problems with her this evening.

There was little point in staying. Sally turned to leave when there was a sudden commotion at one of the broken windows.

The next moment, a great many pigeons flew into the hall, released from a large basket held up to one of the windows.

The sudden influx of the confused and frightened birds should have provided a sufficient diversion in itself, but someone had hit upon the idea of attaching loose paper packets of fine-ground red pepper to each of the birds.

As the panic-stricken pigeons flew around the hall,

the packets broke open and clouds of choking red pepper floated down upon the congregation.

Coughing and sneezing and with their eyes smarting, members of the congregation stampeded for the door. Those who made it to the street first were greeted by the jeers and blows of the Skeleton Army.

Evading most of the waiting rowdies, Sally did not wait to see how the others fared. She ran for the Shieldses' home, leaving the mayhem of Central Hall behind her.

She hoped Rachel and Grace would escape safely, but was not unduly concerned for them. Salvation Army officers were used to such happenings at their meetings. Once the pepper had settled they would keep the majority of their congregation in the hall. Their opponents would soon tire of their 'fun' and return to the public houses from which most had set out earlier in the evening.

60

Doris Shields was quite rational the following morning. After expressing surprise that Sally had spent the night in her house, she cooked breakfast for herself and the two younger women.

While she cooked, Doris speculated on whether the *Mermaid* was likely to return to harbour that day.

When she added that she was beginning to feel anxious about her menfolk, Sophie and Sally looked at each other but said nothing. Both believed that the situation had passed way beyond the stage when she should be feeling anxious; Doris Shields should by now have been sharing the grief her daughter-in-law and Sally were experiencing.

Before setting off for the pie shop, Sally promised Sophie that she would return to the house that evening.

Her route to work took her past the fish quay, where boats were setting out for the day's fishing. Although the wreckage in the Shieldses' passageway should have provided irrefutable evidence of the fate of the men of the family, and despite her concern that Doris was not facing up to the facts, a part of Sally still held out hope for a miracle, and her eyes scoured the harbour.

As Sally made her way along the quayside, she was greeted sympathetically by those few fishermen who were aware of her association with the Shields family.

At the shop, Sally found Alfie already swabbing the floor. It was a task she usually performed.

'You're late, girl,' Alfie scowled at her.

'I'm sorry, Alfie. Mrs Shields put me all behind this morning.'

As they spoke she took off her coat. Tying an apron about her waist, she said, 'Give me the mop. I'll finish cleaning the floor.'

Instead of handing the mop to her, Alfie demanded, 'What do you mean, Mrs Shields put you all behind? Have you been to her house this morning? Was Rachel with you, or did you leave her at the Refuge?'

Sally looked at him in bewilderment. 'Isn't she here? I thought . . .'

Her thoughts were never voiced. Grace put her head out of the kitchen and said cheerfully, 'Hello, Sally. Is Rachel with you?'

Sally was confused. 'No. I thought she was with you. I . . . I didn't stay at the Refuge last night, I slept at Ethan's house. I was keeping Sophie company because she was so worried about Doris Shields.'

As she spoke, she was thinking of the true reason Rachel had stayed at the Refuge the previous couple of nights. Sally thought Rachel must have decided to spend a third night there after leaving Central Hall. She might have tried yet again to bring on a miscarriage, helped in her efforts this time by the reformed prostitutes at the Refuge. But she could not explain this to Grace or Alfie.

Thinking quickly, she said, 'No one at the Refuge must have thought to wake her up. Knowing I wasn't there, they must have forgotten her.'

Grace's expression was one of puzzlement. 'But . . . if you weren't staying there, why didn't she come back here for the night?'

'Perhaps I didn't make it clear to her that I would be spending the night at the Shieldses' house.' Stripping off her apron, Sally added hurriedly, 'I'll go and wake her. I won't be long. I'll run all the way.'

Before Grace could question her further, she ran from the shop, pretending not to hear Alfie's protests.

She did not stop running until she reached the Refuge, fearful that this time Rachel might have made herself seriously ill. And with no one on hand to help her, anything might have happened . . .

The front door of the Refuge was standing open. Zulu Joe was inside the entrance, cleaning panes of coloured glass set into an inner door.

He gave Sally a broad smile, but her response was to ask him if he had seen Rachel that morning.

When Zulu Joe shook his head, Sally pushed past him. 'I'd better go to my room and see if she's still asleep there.'

Zulu Joe followed Sally and was close behind her when she opened the door and discovered the room to be empty. 'Oh! She must have already gone out. We probably passed each other somewhere between here and the pie shop.'

There was a tap on her shoulder. Sally turned to see her companion writing in the small notebook he always carried in his pocket.

When he handed the notebook to her, she read, 'Not here last night.'

Sally's expression showed her concern. 'Are you quite sure, Joe? Isn't there a chance she came to the Refuge without you noticing?'

He shook his head and wrote on the pad, 'Trouble last night at Central Hall. Captain Eva checked all rooms in case anyone hurt. Looked in here before remembered you away for few nights. Expect Rachel with lady you both working for.'

'No, I've just come from there. Could I have a page from your notebook, Joe. I'd like to leave a message in the room for her, just in case she comes back here. I want to tell her to come straight to the shop. We're all worried about her.'

Sally had a sudden thought: Zulu Joe would have been at the meeting at Central Hall the previous night, for a time, at least.

'Was Rachel at the meeting last night?'

He shook his head.

Sally should have been relieved to know that Rachel's disappearance was not connected with the violence at the meeting, but she was not. She was fully aware of how determined Rachel was not to have the baby she was carrying and how upset she had been when everything the two girls had tried so far had failed. Sally tried to ignore the nagging suspicion that in her desperation the younger girl might have contemplated committing suicide.

She shuddered and tried to shake off such thoughts.

She needed to keep calm and think sensibly. It was going to be difficult enough breaking the news that Rachel had disappeared to Grace and Alfie.

61

'Why would Rachel just disappear like this without telling anyone? Without telling *me*? It just isn't like the girl.'

Explaining to Grace that she had been unable to discover the whereabouts of Rachel had been quite as difficult as Sally had anticipated.

The pie-shop owners were not only hurt but also concerned for Rachel. They had become extremely fond of the young orphan girl, and had even discussed adopting her.

It was Alfie who replied to his wife's questions now. 'Perhaps she's met up with a young man and gone off with him somewhere.'

'Nonsense!' replied Grace. 'She's much too young for that. Besides, Sally would have known about it if she had, wouldn't you?'

Sally nodded silently. She felt extremely unhappy about keeping the secret of Rachel's pregnancy from the couple who had been so good to them both. However, there might be a simple explanation for Rachel's disappearance. If there was and Rachel returned to find Sally had told the couple about her condition, relations between the two girls would be very difficult.

On the other hand, if Rachel had tried to do away with herself . . .

'Do you have any idea why she might have wanted to go away, Sally? She's had no messages from members of her family that she never told Alfie and me about?'

'Nothing I know of,' Sally replied miserably. 'While I'm delivering today, I'll ask around, just in case anyone's seen her. I've left a note for her at the Refuge – and Zulu Joe will let Captain Eva know that she's gone missing. Try not to worry, I'm sure she'll be found.'

'That's a whole lot easier to say than do, Sally. To tell you the truth, I'm worried sick. I really don't know how I'm going to get through the day. I'd report her missing to the police if I thought it would do any good . . .'

'We'll make the effort to carry on here as normal,' said her more practical husband. 'It will help no one if our business suffers. All our regulars know Rachel. We'll tell them she's gone missing. You never know, one of them might have seen her, or know where she is.'

'Well, you're going to have to manage without me for half an hour,' said Grace. 'I'm off to the railway station to ask if anyone there has seen her. Then I'll pop along to the Refuge just in case Captain Eva's learned anything.'

Grace's enquiries at both places drew a blank. When she returned, the pie shop was not a happy place to be. Sally was glad to escape and begin her deliveries. Nevertheless, she too was very concerned about the missing girl.

*   *   *

One of Sally's last deliveries that afternoon was to customs officers in a bonded warehouse close to the harbour.

The customs officer in charge insisted upon examining the half-dozen pies before he would pay for them. He pointed out that one had a broken crust. The damage was hardly worthy of note but the officer refused to pay for it. He suggested Sally might care to donate it free, as a sign of goodwill.

Sally retorted that she would take the pie away with her. She was not particularly perturbed that the customs officer had expressed dissatisfaction with her wares. It had happened before with customers and no doubt would again.

When she left the warehouse she decided to take the rejected pie to Pin's Lane for Charlie Shields; she knew Grace would not mind.

Charlie was depressed because of the absence of any news about the *Mermaid*, but he did his best to sound optimistic. 'The Lowestoft boat only brought in *pieces* of their boat. She could be badly damaged but still afloat. I've heard Henry say more than once that she was the best boat he ever sailed in – and he's sailed in a few.'

Taking the pie from her, he said, 'I'll just put this in a dish on the hob to keep hot while I set the table. It's a sight better than the chunk of cheese I was going to have with the bread left over from the weekend.'

As Charlie busied himself heating the pie, he continued talking. 'I'm pleased to see you looking so well too. I was a bit worried about you when I found the blood after you'd left. Where was it you cut yourself? I can't see no bandage.'

Sally looked at him as though he had taken leave of

his senses. 'What are you talking about? I haven't cut myself. Even if I had, how could you possibly know?'

Now it was Charlie's turn to appear puzzled. 'I'm talking about last night, when you came to the house. After you'd gone I found heavy spots of blood in the passage. On the stairs too. I thought you must have cut yourself and come here to bind it up before having it properly seen to – and don't try to tell me it wasn't you who came into the house. I know different.'

'Are you saying you thought you saw me come to my room yesterday?'

'I didn't exactly *see* you, but I recognised your footsteps on the stairs – and I know I wasn't mistaken. Them floorboards was creaking under the weight of a young girl. If it wasn't you, who else would it have been, eh? Tell me that.'

Sally thought she probably knew the answer to Charlie's question, but she asked, 'What time was this – and are you quite certain that you heard whoever it was go out again?'

Less positive now, Charlie replied, 'I couldn't be certain, but it must have been about an hour or so before I went to bed – I'm going earlier these nights. A sign of growing old, I suppose, but it saves burning oil. As for the time you, or whoever else it was, left, it couldn't have been more than ten or fifteen minutes later. I was in the kitchen when the front door slammed shut—' Suddenly breaking off, Charlie looked thoughtful before adding, 'Come to think of it, the door might have blown shut when I opened the back door to the yard. It's done it before and there was quite a strong wind blowing.' He looked at Sally, still not entirely convinced. 'But if it wasn't you, then who could it have been?'

'I've got a very good idea.' Thinking about the blood Charlie had found on the stairs and in the passageway, Sally added, 'But I hope I'm wrong.'

She hurried up the stairs, leaving Charlie looking after her, uncertainly.

At the entrance to her room, Sally paused, suddenly reluctant to confirm what she suspected.

Bracing herself, she pushed open the door – and her worst fears were realised immediately.

Lying on the bed, eyes closed, was Rachel. The lower half of her dress and the bedclothes about her were stained with blood and Sally knew immediately what must have happened.

Rachel had found someone to abort her baby – and it would seem it had gone hideously wrong.

62

Soon after Sally had told Rachel she would be spending the night at the Shieldses' and had left the Refuge, Rachel left the house too, telling no one where she was going, or how long she would be out.

She headed for the Barbican but was careful not to pass within sight of the pie shop belonging to Alfie and Grace Philpott.

In the maze of narrow streets, Rachel headed for Pin's Lane in order to get a sense of direction. Skirting the lane itself, she turned into an alleyway that ran parallel with it.

She had been here earlier in the day, to make certain she would be able to identify the house for which she was now making – should the need arise. But when Sally told her she would not be spending the night at the Refuge, it seemed to Rachel an opportunity that was not to be wasted, and now was the time to act.

Arriving at the door of the house she had pin-pointed earlier, she hesitated, remembering the warnings Sally had given her about the course she was about to take.

Then Rachel's resolution hardened. She was determined not to have Sid Darling's baby, whatever the cost to her might be.

The door was opened in response to her knock by Clara Flood, landlady of Devonport Lil and one-time Indian mutiny 'nurse'.

'What do you want?' Clara Flood demanded surlily. 'If it's a room you're looking for, they're all taken – unless you can do what you want in less than an hour.'

'I'm not looking for a room. If you're Clara Flood, I came looking for *you*. I . . . I'm in trouble. I was told you'd be able to help me.'

'*You*, in trouble? Why, you're hardly old enough to know what trouble is.'

'I know, right enough, and I was told you could help me.'

'I'm always ready to help any poor soul that's in need, but there's a limit to what a body can do. Especially a poor widow-woman with no one to support her.'

'I can pay for any help you give me.'

'Pay? How much?'

'I've got five pounds here,' Rachel said eagerly. She had saved most of the money given to her by Grace and Alfie over Christmas. This, together with the generous wage paid to her for helping around the shop, plus two pounds she had 'borrowed' from the money drawer behind the counter amounted to more than five pounds. But she was wise enough not to disclose to Clara Flood the full amount she possessed.

'Five pounds? Are you asking me to risk spending the rest of my life in gaol for a mere five pounds? I'm sorry, dearie, but you'll have to find someone else to do it for you.'

As Rachel turned away, disconsolately, Clara Flood added hurriedly, 'Mind you, if you was to offer me *ten* pounds, I might just do it as a special favour, seeing as how you're so young.'

'I haven't got ten pounds. I could give you six.'

'Make it eight and you can go off and start life afresh,' said Clara Flood. 'No one will ever know you did anything wrong.'

Rachel took out a tapestry purse that had been a present from Sally at Christmas. Carefully counting the coins, she said plaintively, 'All I have is six pounds, four and sevenpence.'

'If that's all you have, then I wouldn't see a young girl's life ruined for the sake of a few shillings. Give me the money and come on in.'

'Now?' Rachel was taken by surprise.

'You were expecting to make an appointment?' Clara Flood asked sarcastically. 'No, you come on in, dearie. The sooner it's done the better. How many months gone are you . . . ?'

As she followed the woman to a back upstairs room a man came down the stairs past them – and Rachel's heart missed a beat. It was Robert Sanderson. Sally's father!

She put her head down and hurried past him, hoping he had not recognised her on the dark staircase.

Had she looked back, she would have seen him standing at the foot of the stairs, looking up at her, his expression a mixture of dismay and disbelief. But Clara Flood was already ushering her into a small room, in which the only piece of furniture was a narrow bed. In place of bedclothes, the bed was covered with a red, india-rubber sheet.

'Take your underclothes off, dearie, then get up on the bed and pull all your clothes up above your waist.'

When Rachel hesitated, Clara Flood snapped irritably, 'Come on, it's too late to be shy now. The time for that was when you let your young man get you in this condition.'

'I didn't *let* anyone do anything to me,' Rachel retorted bitterly. 'I just couldn't do anything to stop them.'

Clara Flood rounded on her immediately. 'You were raped? Are the police involved in this? I'm not doing anything to help you if the police have got anything to do with you.'

'No one knows about it – and they won't,' Rachel lied. 'Anyway, the man who did it isn't around now.'

'Well, as long as you're quite certain. I've got too much to lose if anyone learns I go around doing favours for girls like you. If no one knows then it's all right – and we'll keep it that way. It'll be better for you and it's better for me. Now, are you ready?'

Lying back on the bed, Rachel pulled her clothes up about her waist, trying not to be embarrassed. The rubber sheet was cold on her bottom and she made an involuntary movement.

'Now, whatever I do, you must keep absolutely still, do you understand? This is an operation. A delicate operation.'

'Will it hurt?' Rachel asked fearfully, staring at the other woman, who was now holding a long knitting needle in her hand.

'Not half as much as having a baby would. Now just you look away. Better still, close your eyes. But, whatever I do, try not to move. Just leave me to get on with it.'

Rachel tried to do as the abortionist told her, but she did not find it easy. First of all she could feel the woman's broken nails digging into her flesh. It hurt, and she whimpered. Then, without warning, Rachel felt something sliding inside her and she realised with horror that it must be the knitting needle.

Suddenly, the woman pressed hard and Rachel felt a horrific pain, which seemed to fill her stomach and her groin before travelling down to her thighs.

Despite the instructions she had been given, Rachel cried out and writhed in agony.

'That's enough! Please stop – it hurts!'

'Damn you, girl! Keep still. I'm not finished yet. Keep still, do you hear?'

There was another wave of excruciating pain – then Clara Flood had finished. She stood holding the bloody knitting needle and Rachel saw perspiration running down the side of her face, from her temples.

'That's it. Now, off with you. Go back to wherever it is you live and lie down. You'll feel awful for a day or two, but then it will all be over. Come on, up you get and go.'

Rachel still felt pain, but it was not as bad now. She told herself that if it didn't get any worse and she really had lost the baby, she would be able to cope with it.

She had left the house and was walking along the alleyway towards Pin's Lane when the pain came flooding back. She realised too that she was bleeding quite severely.

The pain was like a severe cramp that became steadily worse until she found walking almost impossible. If it did not let up she realised there would be no way she would make it back to the Refuge – or even to the home of Grace and Alfie.

Holding her lower stomach, she was doubled up in agony, when she left the alleyway and found herself in Pin's Lane.

Further along the lane she could see the open door of Sally's house and she headed for it in a crouching run. Passing through the doorway she made her way along the passageway. As she climbed the stairs, it seemed to her she was tackling a mountain and she found herself praying that Sally's room would be unlocked.

It was. Moments later, moaning in agony, she was in the room. Not even bothering to kick off her shoes, she climbed on the bed and must have passed into unconsciousness within minutes.

She regained consciousness more than once during the next twenty-four hours, although by now time meant nothing to her. The pain had grown until it felt as though it was consuming the whole of the inside of her stomach.

She was delirious too, on occasions, seeing strange creatures lurking in the corners of the room. Once she felt quite certain her mother was beside her, holding her hand.

But nothing was quite real until she opened her eyes and saw Sally standing beside the bed looking down at her, an expression of horror on her face.

63

Sally's first thought was that Rachel was dead – and there was no doubt in her mind what had killed her.

When Rachel opened her eyes, Sally felt overwhelming relief. Taking the younger girl's hand, she said, 'Rachel! What have you been up to? Why didn't you come and find someone to help you?'

'I'm sorry, Sally. It . . . came on so sudden. I've made a mess of your bed . . .'

'That doesn't matter. What *does* is that I find someone to help you, as quickly as I can.'

'Don't tell Grace!' Rachel pleaded.

'This can't be kept a secret now, Rachel. I'm going to have to call on Grace to get you to a hospital. I don't know what you've done to yourself, but you need a doctor to see to you.'

Rachel closed her eyes and her face screwed up in agony. Sally was not certain whether it was physical pain or the knowledge that her condition could no longer remain a secret.

'I'll be as quick as I can. In the meantime I'll ask

Charlie to listen out for you. He can't climb the stairs, but if he hears you call out he'll go and fetch one of the neighbours.'

'Sally . . . fetch me a drink of water before you go. My mouth feels so dry.'

'I'll go and get some from Charlie's kitchen.'

Downstairs, as she took water from a bucket in the kitchen, Sally gave the bewildered man brief details of what was happening.

He agreed to listen for any sound from upstairs, but asked, 'How did she get herself in such a state?'

'I don't know and she's too sick to ask right now – but it's one more thing Sid Darling will have to answer for one day.'

It became apparent to Sally when she raised Rachel in the bed in order to drink that the young girl was in great pain. She was deeply concerned.

After making her as comfortable as she could, she hurried off to tell Grace.

The two pie-shop owners listened in growing dismay and disbelief as Sally told them how she had found Rachel and of the condition she was in.

'You mean . . . she's been carrying a baby all this time and never told me about it?'

'She never told me until a couple of days ago and made me swear not to tell anyone else.'

'It's not the sort of secret you should have kept to yourself,' Grace said with stern disapproval. 'She's far too young to have this hanging over her. Do you have any idea how she brought this miscarriage about?'

Sally shook her head. 'I think it might be more serious than a miscarriage.'

'You mean . . . you think she might have had an *abortion*?' Grace looked at Sally in disbelief. 'She wouldn't have known how to go about such a thing . . .' Looking at Sally suspiciously, she added, 'Would she?'

'I certainly never told her,' said Sally.

She had forgotten pointing out the house where Clara Flood lived and warning Rachel that if she was not careful she might end up in the hands of someone like the elderly abortionist.

'Right now she needs to get to a hospital urgently. She's lost a lot of blood and seems to be very weak.'

'Go and stay with her, Grace,' said Alfie. 'I'll fetch a doctor and a carriage to take her to the hospital. Meanwhile, you stay here and look after the shop, Sally. I won't be long.'

Left in the shop on her own, Sally did not have very many customers to serve. She had time to think of the new disaster the day had brought but hoped Rachel's condition would prove to be less serious than it appeared.

Somehow, after Rachel had been taken to hospital, Alfie and Sally got through the remainder of the day until it was time to shut up the shop. Grace had still not returned and Alfie said he would go to the hospital to learn what was happening.

Sally felt she could not face Grace again immediately. She told Alfie she would go to the Refuge and tell Captain Eva what had happened. Then she intended going to see how Ethan's mother was.

She would visit the hospital later that night to enquire after Rachel. She secretly hoped Grace might have gone home by then. Sally did not want to have to submit to more awkward questioning.

Nevertheless, she felt very guilty about not telling Grace about Rachel's pregnancy. It would also have passed responsibility to someone who might have been able to deal with the problem differently.

64

When Sally arrived at the Salvation Army Refuge, she found Eva drinking tea in the kitchen. Inspector Ian Lovat was with her.

One look at Sally's face was sufficient to bring Eva to her feet. 'What's the matter, Sally – is it something to do with Rachel?'

Zulu Joe had told her of Sally's visit and of the search being carried out for the young girl.

The guilt Sally had been feeling since finding Rachel suddenly overwhelmed her. She could only nod, numbly, wishing she had found Captain Eva alone.

'Here, come and sit down. I'll pour you a cup of sweet tea while you talk to Captain Eva.' Ian Lovat rose from his chair and pushed it towards Sally.

Sally sat on the chair with Eva's arm about her shoulders, as the policeman crossed the room to where the teapot sat on the gas stove.

'Can you tell me about it, Sally,' the Salvationist coaxed her.

After taking a few moments to compose herself, Sally

said, 'Rachel was expecting a baby. I think she's done something silly to get rid of it.'

'A baby? Surely not? Why, she's hardly old enough.' Eva's reaction echoed that of Grace Philpott.

'Rachel is quite sure she is . . . or *was*. I don't think she is any more.'

'Who is the father . . . ?' Even as Eva put the question, the answer came to her. She spoke his name out loud, 'Sid Darling!'

Sally nodded once more. 'Rachel thinks so. Him, or one of the Belgian fishermen. Whichever one it was, she's determined not to have the baby.'

'You must have known about this before today, Sally. When did she tell you?'

'A couple of days ago. She made me promise not to tell anyone.'

'That's one promise you shouldn't have kept. But it's too late for recriminations now. What has poor Rachel done – taken something?'

'It's worse than that. I believe she's found someone to do something to her. Either that, or she's done something to herself. I found her lying on the bed in my room at Pin's Lane. She'd been there since yesterday. There was blood everywhere.'

'Dear God!' exclaimed Eva. 'What an utterly stupid thing to do. Where is she now?'

'I ran to tell Grace. She and Alfie have got her to hospital. Grace has been there with her ever since. Alfie went there as soon as we closed the shop.' Scarcely able to hold her emotions in check, she added, 'I think she's very, very ill.'

'I'll go to the hospital right away. First I must tell Zulu Joe and the girls what I'm doing.'

Half-way to the door, Eva stopped and turned to ask Sally, 'Do you think any of the girls here had anything to do with the condition Rachel's in?'

'I don't know. I don't think so.'

'Good. All the same, I'll have a word with them later tonight.'

When Eva had left the kitchen, Sally sipped the tea Ian Lovat had placed on the table beside her, her hand shaking. Now the detective said, 'You do realise that abortion is a serious criminal offence, Sally?'

'So is what Sid Darling did to Rachel, but you haven't caught him yet, have you?'

'No,' he admitted. 'But I can assure you it's not for the want of trying and we'll continue to search for him until we find him. Right now we're talking about Rachel's abortion – if that's what it turns out to be. The law regards it as a very serious offence. If you know more than you've said, you had better tell someone everything you know. It would be far better for you if that someone were me. Do you have any idea who else might be involved?'

'No.' Remembering the two nights she had spent with Rachel trying to induce a miscarriage, Sally hoped she sounded more convincing than she felt. She added, 'I didn't think she'd do anything as stupid as this. I told her the best thing she could do was to have the baby, then see about having it adopted if she still didn't want it.'

Ian Lovat nodded his approval. 'I'll need to speak to you again sometime. Unfortunately, now I know about it I am going to have to make an official report. How ill do you think she is?'

'Very ill. I've never seen so much blood anywhere as there was on the bed.'

'I sincerely hope she's not as serious as it sounds, Sally. The trouble is that people who do this sort of thing usually end up killing someone. It's an operation that even a skilful surgeon is reluctant to perform.'

Sally was still trembling as a result of his words when Eva returned to the kitchen to say she was leaving for the hospital.

Ian Lovat said he would go with her. Before they left the house, Captain Eva asked Sally if she would like to accompany them.

'I don't think it would be wise to see Grace again just yet. She's angry with me for not telling her that Rachel was expecting a baby. She said I should have told her, but I couldn't say anything to her – or to you. Not after promising Rachel I wouldn't.'

'Don't worry, Sally. Grace is a very understanding woman. When she's had time to think about things she'll realise what a difficult situation you were in. She'll be very worried about Rachel right now, as we all are. I'll speak to her if the opportunity arises.'

In truth, there was another reason Sally did not want to accompany Captain Eva to the hospital. She needed to think about what Ian Lovat had said. She wondered whether she could get into trouble for what she had done in the earlier attempts to bring about a miscarriage for Rachel.

65

When Harry Maggs stopped outside the house of Clara Flood, force of habit caused him to look furtively around before knocking at the door.

It was opened by Clara Flood and Maggs was taken by surprise – he had not been expecting a woman.

Looking him up and down with increasing distaste, Clara Flood said, 'I don't need a chimney sweep. When I do I'll send for someone I know, not a sweep who's going to bring more soot into the house on his clothes than he takes from my chimney.'

Maggs was not a prepossessing man. Small and slightly built, his shoulders hunched forward unhealthily and every line of his gnarled face was heavily ingrained with soot. From the age of six he had spent his life cleaning chimneys and had deeply held convictions that bathing and sweeping chimneys were mutually exclusive.

'I'm not here to sweep chimneys. I came to see if Mr Sanderson was home.'

'And what would he be wanting with the likes of you?'

Harry Maggs decided that Clara Flood had dominated the conversation for long enough. 'Is Mr Sanderson here? It's him I want to be talking to, not you.'

'Is it now? Well, you just wait there and I'll see if he wants to speak to *you*.'

The door was slammed shut in Maggs's face and he was left standing uneasily in the narrow street.

Inside the house, Clara Flood wheezed her way up the stairs and banged on the door of her lodger. When it was opened by Robert Sanderson, she said, 'There's some chimney sweep outside. He says he wants to talk to you.'

'Maggs? What's he doing here?'

'You'll need to ask *him* that, not me, but if you have him inside the house make sure he does all his talking standing up. I'm not having a man wearing such clothes sitting on my furniture.

When Sanderson opened the door to Harry Maggs, he repeated the question he had asked Clara Flood, 'What are you doing here? How did you know where to find me?' Before Maggs could answer, the ex-Lanhydrock butler said, 'We can't talk out here. Come in.'

He led the way to his room, the two men standing to one side on the narrow stairway to allow Clara Flood to pass on her disapproving way back to her room on the ground floor.

When they were inside Sanderson's sparsely furnished room and the door firmly closed, Maggs said, 'I hadn't seen or heard anything of you for a few days. I went to the house in Pin's Lane where you'd been staying and a bloke by the name of Charlie said you'd gone. He said I should try here. That you used to spend as much time here with Devonport Lil as over in Pin's

Lane when you were living there. I thought I'd better come and see if you were here, to find out what's going on.'

Robert Sanderson looked with distaste at the man standing before him. Had he not needed him for the plans he had made, he would have scorned even to speak to him.

'You're a fool! If anyone sees us together we'll never be able to do as we've planned.'

'You've nothing to worry about,' Maggs said sulkily. 'There's nobody in Plymouth who knows who you are, or where you once worked.'

'That's where you're wrong,' retorted Sanderson. 'There's this Charlie – and there was a girl in this very house only yesterday who knew me. Now, if you've nothing else to say, I suggest you go.'

'You still haven't told me when we're going to do the job,' protested Maggs. 'I'm losing business waiting for you to make up your mind.'

'When we do what we've planned, you'll never need to worry yourself about going to work again. I can't tell you when it's going to be until I get a reply to the letter I've sent to the housemaid at Lanhydrock House. It should be any day now. When it arrives, I'll come and find you at The Jolly Watchman, so just be patient for a while longer. Now, it's time you went, before Clara Flood comes up here to make sure you're not sitting down on any of her furniture.'

When he had let Harry Maggs out of the house, Robert Sanderson turned around to find his landlady standing in the passageway.

'Who's that man you've just let out?'

'No one in particular. I met him in a public house a

while ago and took pity on him. It was a mistake. He called today trying to borrow money from me.'

'You can tell him I don't want to see him here again. He lowers the tone of the house. If you've got many friends like him I'll be asking you to leave, too.'

'He won't be coming here again, I promise you that. Talking of visitors, who was that charming young girl who was with you when we passed on the stairs yesterday? I suppose she's not a friend of Devonport Lil? If she is I'd like to be introduced to her.'

Clara Flood rounded on him so suddenly he took a pace backwards in surprise. 'You saw no girl here yesterday – you understand? Any more than I saw the man who was just visiting you. People in this house either mind their own business – or they go.'

'Of course. I understand. We neither of us saw anyone at all.'

Despite his assurance to Clara Flood, Robert Sanderson questioned Devonport Lil that evening about the girl he had seen with the landlady.

They were sharing a bottle of gin in the prostitute's room. Lil was having a lean time at the moment; a great many Plymouth-based naval vessels had been sent to South Africa because of troubles being experienced there with both the Zulu nation and the Boers.

Lil reiterated what Clara Flood had told him. 'Forget you've ever seen the girl. That way you can plead you know nothing of what goes on in this house. It'll be better for you in the long run.'

'But why? She was just a young girl. What harm could she possibly be up to?'

She looked at him pityingly. 'Where have you been

all your life? Don't you know why the girl was here? Clara's been carrying out abortions for years. She's not the best, by any means, but she's certainly well known by the girls who work Union Street.'

'You mean . . . that girl was here to have an abortion? But she was so young!'

'So what? If you're going on the game you've got to make a start while you're young enough to make good money. Some of us started earlier than others. Now, have you come here to do business with me, or just to drink all my gin . . . ?'

66

The subject of the conversation between Robert Sanderson and Devonport Lil died the following day. The cause of her death was septicaemia. According to the doctor who had been treating her since her admission to the hospital, it had been caused by the instrument used to bring about the abortion; it had been neither clean nor accurately wielded.

Sally learned of Rachel's death that evening from Eva. Afterwards, she spent many hours in her room, weeping for the death of the young girl who had known such unhappiness and brutality in her short lifetime.

The manner of Rachel's death meant that the Plymouth police now became actively involved. But Ian Lovat was not the investigating officer. Instead, a rather dour police inspector came to the Refuge to interview the girls living there.

Although Sally had been Rachel's close friend and had been the one to find her at Pin's Lane, she was interrogated at no greater length or in any more detail than the others.

Once the policeman had established a possible reason for Rachel taking refuge in Sally's room in the first place, he seemed to lose all interest in anything Sally might have been able to tell him.

His manner and apparent lack of enthusiasm angered Sally, who was already distressed by the death of her friend.

After the inspector had left the Refuge, Sally asked Eva why Ian Lovat had not been put in charge of the investigation.

'He isn't able to make a decision on what cases he will or will not take on,' she replied. 'Anyway, he's away for a few days. Before he left he hinted he might be leaving Plymouth altogether in the near future.'

'Why?' Sally voiced her dismay. 'He's not been in Plymouth for very long.'

Eva shrugged. 'No doubt he has his reasons. We may be friends, but he doesn't tell me everything.'

She sounded unhappy and Sally suddenly felt very sorry for her. It had been apparent to the occupants of the Refuge for some time now that Captain Eva was growing very fond of Ian Lovat. It was generally assumed that he felt the same way about her, and the girls had been waiting with some interest to see whether a romance would develop between the couple.

Later that evening, Sally attended a highly emotional prayer meeting in the Refuge to pray for the dead girl. Eva took the meeting, which was attended by all the other women and girls who lived in the house, and who had known Rachel.

* * *

An additional problem in Sally's life, one she found particularly upsetting, was the unforgiving and unbending attitude Grace now adopted towards her.

Grace had spent many hours in the hospital with Rachel and was with her when she died. Not unnaturally, she was deeply affected by all that had happened.

The morning after Rachel's death, although still distraught, Sally decided she should go into work. To her dismay, when she arrived at the shop Alfie told her it might be better if she did not show herself there for a while.

When Sally wanted to know why, he told her that Grace was particularly bitter that Sally had not told her of the young girl's condition. Had she done so, Grace was convinced they might have been able to prevent her tragic death.

'But Rachel made me promise,' said Sally, reduced to tears by Alfie's words. 'She felt so ashamed because she was expecting. Grace was the last person she wanted to know about it.'

'I realise that,' Alfie said sympathetically. 'Grace will too, in time. But if she sees you now she'll probably say things that won't be easily mended, even though she might regret them later. Stay away for a few days, Sally. I'll get word to you when I feel the time is right for you to come back to work again.'

Going to the cash drawer in the shop, he took out a couple of pounds and handed them to her. 'All that's happened is not your fault, I realise that. Take this to tide you over until you're back working with us once more.'

Sally was grateful for the money, but she left the pie shop with a very heavy heart, uncertain of what the future held for her now. She had become fond of Grace. Both she and Alfie had been very kind to her.

She realised she would probably never return to their employ again. Grace had really loved Rachel and would be reminded of what had happened every time she saw Sally. Working together would simply not be possible.

It seemed to Sally that her whole world was collapsing about her. She felt lower than at any time since Ruth's death.

She spent the remainder of that day sharing Sophie Shields's problems. Doris Shields had seemingly lost touch with reality, and was making life very difficult for her daughter-in-law.

Each and every day, she spoke as though she was expecting her husband and sons to walk through the door at any moment. Sally did not know how Sophie managed to cope with her. She was glad when it was evening and she could find an excuse to return to the Refuge to speak to Captain Eva.

Eva was sympathetic to Sally about her problems, but she said, 'I wish I could feel that Rachel was likely to be the last victim of the evil men who raped her, but the trade in girls is still going on. Look . . .' From her desk, she took a piece of paper torn from a newspaper and handed it to Sally.

It was a repeat of the advertisement she had been sent by her colleague, seeking girls for domestic service. It now suggested that suitable applicants might soon find themselves working for titled families. They were promised lucrative posts with some of the most important families in the land, together with the opportunity to travel with them on their European journeys.

It concluded with the suggestion that the posts advertised were ideally suited for young girls contemplating a full-time career in domestic service. Preference would be given to girls with no home ties, who could devote themselves to their career and be free to travel wherever their employers wished to take them.

'This sounds too good to be true,' commented Sally. 'It's just the kind of thing that brought Rachel to Plymouth. Where does it come from?'

'This one is from a Dorset newspaper,' replied Eva. 'One of my friends sent it to me, but I've seen others, right here in Devon.'

'Do you think Sid Darling is involved this time?'

Eva shook her head. 'I don't think so. Inspector Lovat says Darling is out of the country, and I believe him – but I do think this is a very suspect advertisement. The address to write to is in Falmouth. It's hardly a central base from which to place servants all over the country. My friend sent it to me because, if it *is* genuine, she has a girl she would like to send there.'

The Salvationist threw the cutting down upon her desk in a gesture of frustration. 'I *know* it isn't genuine. The trouble is proving it. Dear God! I would dearly love to be able to put a stop to this trade once and for all. I tell you, Sally, if I was younger I'd reply to the advertisement myself and show these people up for what they are.'

As Eva shook her head angrily, Sally was thinking hard. Now she said, 'Why not let me do it instead?'

'*You?* No, Sally, I couldn't ask you to do anything like this.'

'You're not asking, I'm suggesting it to you.'

'But . . . why? You of all people should realise just how dangerous it would be to get yourself involved in something like this.'

'I don't know. I feel I owe it to Rachel, somehow. Besides, I can't think of anyone better, can you? I know all the dangers involved and I'd be going into it with my eyes open. The only thing is . . . what would you be able to do to make certain I *wouldn't* end up in Belgium, or somewhere like that?'

'I could organise all that, Sally – and I'd let you know exactly what we are doing, every step of the way. If you're really serious about this I'll contact the editor of a London paper with whom I have already been in correspondence. That would mean maximum publicity. With the Salvation Army behind you, we would ensure, first and foremost, that you would never be in danger. That would be my prime consideration, I assure you.'

Eva was quivering with excitement at the thought of what they might achieve. Yet she wanted to be quite certain that Sally knew what she was letting herself in for.

'Would you really do this, Sally? I don't want to bring any sort of pressure on you, but putting a stop to this has been my life's ambition. Ever since this despicable trade was first brought to my notice. Are you absolutely certain?'

In truth, although she had volunteered herself, Sally had very real doubts about the venture, but she nodded. 'Yes, I'll do it.'

67

A few days later Eva took a train to London to seek the backing of the authorities at Salvation Army headquarters for her scheme to expose those who were luring girls into prostitution. Meanwhile, Ian Lovat returned to Plymouth.

Within hours, he paid a visit to the Refuge.

He was disappointed when Sally informed him that the Salvation Army officer was not there, but he accepted her offer of a cup of tea.

When they were both seated in the kitchen, Sally asked, 'Have you come to speak to Captain Eva about Rachel?'

'No, another officer is still dealing with that,' replied Ian Lovat. 'I can't interfere with his investigation right now, although I might well take over from him in the very near future. It's a very sad business. I hope this abortionist is soon caught and put away. I doubt very much whether Rachel was her first victim.'

'Poor Rachel didn't deserve to have something like that happen to her.'

Aware of her distress, Ian Lovat changed the subject. 'Do you know why Captain Eva has gone to London? I hope the Salvation Army is not considering moving her on.'

'You'll need to ask her about that, when she comes back.'

Ian Lovat smiled wryly. 'If it's something she feels I ought not to know, I doubt if she'll tell me.'

'Then you can't expect me to tell you anything that she wouldn't,' declared Sally.

'Oh! So there *is* something going on that I would like to know about?'

'I didn't say that,' retorted Sally. 'Besides, do you always tell her what *you're* doing? Where you've been for the last couple of days, for instance?'

'No,' confessed the policeman. 'But I will, in due course.'

'Good! I think Captain Eva was quite hurt that you went away without saying where you were going.'

'Did she tell you that?' There was eagerness in Ian Lovat's voice as he asked the question.

'She didn't have to.' Encouraged by his interest in Captain Eva's reaction to his absence, Sally asked, 'Are you in love with her?'

The detective inspector remained silent for so long that Sally thought she might have overstepped the bounds of familiarity with him. Then he said, quietly, 'Yes, Sally, I am.'

'Do you intend asking her to marry you?'

'You're asking some very personal questions, young lady. The answer is . . . I don't know. We are each of us very committed to the work we do. We're both doing something that's important, to us and to others, but it sometimes clashes. That poses a major problem. If I'm not prepared to give up my work, I could hardly ask Captain Eva to give up hers.'

Disappointed that there seemed to be no hope of the two getting married in the near future, Sally asked, 'Couldn't you tell her what you've just told me and see what she has to say about it?'

Putting his cup down on the table, Ian Lovat shook his head as he stood up to take his leave.

'No, Sally. If I were to mention marriage to her and she turned me down, nothing would ever be quite the same between us. I enjoy her company too much to want to risk losing it. We'll leave things as they are. For the time being, at least.'

'But . . . you could go on like that until you are both old!'

He smiled. 'That's very true, but I'd rather do that than risk losing her altogether. Now, if there's nothing else you feel I ought to know, I'll leave and come visiting again when Captain Eva has returned from London.'

When he had gone, Sally wondered how anyone in love could look at their relationship in such a calculated and matter-of-fact manner.

She knew that if there was any hope of Ethan returning to her, there would be no sacrifice too great to make in order to ensure nothing ever came between them again.

Thoughts of Ethan made her deeply despondent. It seemed that since he had gone missing, nothing in her life had gone right. She had lost her work; the girl who was possibly her closest friend; her father – and, of course, Ethan himself.

Now she was about to embark on a venture that was

both dangerous and fraught with difficulty. She consoled herself with the thought that if it was successful, it could prove to be a turning-point in her life – and it *had* to be successful.

It was a chance to achieve something positive, something that would help bring to an end the kidnapping of young girls for the brothels of Europe, saving thousands of girls from a life of brutality and degradation.

If she never did anything worthwhile in her life again, Sally felt she could always look back upon this one thing with great pride.

She hoped Captain Eva would receive the support she was seeking in London. Sally wanted things to begin moving as quickly as possible.

Until she took up her role in Captain Eva's crusade, her life would be in limbo. She could not seek work, neither could she discuss with anyone else what was being planned.

Sally decided she would spend the day at the Shieldses' house. There might be something she could do to help the hard-pressed Sophie to cope with the problem of her disturbed mother-in-law.

68

Robert Sanderson and Harry Maggs each journeyed in his own fashion from Plymouth to their common destination in Cornwall.

The ex-Lanhydrock House butler travelled in comparative comfort, by coach, taking a somewhat circuitous route. He had decided against using the train; he was well known at Bodmin Road railway station and did not wish to draw attention to himself and his changed circumstances.

Harry Maggs enjoyed none of the comforts enjoyed by Sanderson. He crossed the River Tamar on the ferry to Saltash and walked through the narrow lanes of Cornwall. He pushed before him a wheelbarrow on which were a quantity of sacks, a large flagon containing paraffin and the brushes that constituted the tools of his trade.

Heading for Lanhydrock House, he had been fully briefed by the ex-butler. If he carried out his crucial part of the plan, their foray into Cornwall would make them both rich and satisfy Sanderson's determination to make the owners of the great house suffer for his humiliation.

It was a simple but clever plan.

The itinerant chimney sweep who visited Lanhydrock House annually to carry out his work always arrived during the first week in May. It was now very early April.

Maggs would say he had been sent by the regular sweep, who had been forced into retirement by ill-health. Sanderson had given him sufficient details of the other sweep to ensure his story would sound genuine.

The timing of the plan was crucial and Maggs would state that the two days of this week was the only period available for him to carry out the work involved.

Fortunately, due to the passage of years no one in the household would possibly be able to identify Maggs as the boy who was apprenticed to the sweep transported for stealing from the house: he had changed a great deal since then.

Another factor in Maggs's favour was the appointment of a new butler only the week before. When Maggs put in his appearance at the servants' door, the butler referred the question of chimney sweeping to the Robartes' steward. That important official considered it to be so far beneath him to discuss such a matter that Harry Maggs was told to get on with whatever needed to be done.

This he proceeded to do, informing the steward that the previous sweep had described the layout of the chimneys in such detail that Maggs felt he was, 'as familiar with them as I am with the back of me own 'and'.

Repeating the conversation to the new butler, the

steward remarked that he doubted if the ingrained soot
to be found on Maggs had allowed him to view the back
of it for more years than he was able to count.

Once in the house, Maggs set about carrying out the
plan formulated by Robert Sanderson. Going from room
to room, ostensibly checking out the various fireplaces,
he pinpointed all the items the ex-butler had declared
to be worth stealing.

Maggs then began work on the chimneys. He made
an excellent job of them, and had cleaned more than half
by the end of the first day.

As a result of this day's work he was not watched
quite so closely when he returned the following morning. The kitchen fire was dowsed after lunch, enabling
him to climb up inside the huge chimney.

It was here the chimney sweep would set in motion
the plan that was designed to destroy all evidence of the
proposed burglary. At the very least, it would ensure
that the loss of items would not be discovered for some
time to come.

His instructions were to leave in place the majority
of the soot in the kitchen chimney. Before claiming to
have completed his work, he would place four paraffin-
soaked sacks on a chimney ledge, at the rear of which
was an exposed wooden beam that had been thoroughly
dried out by more than two hundred years of proximity
to the heat drawn up the chimney from the kitchen fire.
The fire that was bound to ensue would cause great
confusion among family and staff. No one would go
around checking whether valuable items remained in
their proper places – or whether they were there at all.

The robbery was planned for that night, after Maggs
had completed his second day's sweeping. Entry to the

house would be made by means of the key retained by Sanderson.

At the time of the robbery, the ex-butler would be 'entertaining' the enamoured housemaid in one of the outbuildings beside the house. The maid would have drawn the bolts on the inside of the servants' door in order to slip out, and, having locked the door behind her with a key kept in a cupboard in the servants' hall, in case of fire, she would feel the house was adequately secured.

During her absence, Maggs would slip inside the house, fill two sacks with silver and other valuables, and lower them out of the window of the dairy scullery. They would then be collected by himself and the ex-butler when the latter had parted company with the housemaid.

The whole operation was planned to last no longer than two hours, commencing at midnight.

Afterwards, the two men would load the stolen goods into the sweep's barrow and make their escape under cover of darkness.

Robert Sanderson's plan relied very heavily on the chimney-sweep carrying out his instructions to the letter.

However, as the ex-butler was fully aware, his accomplice was not the most reliable man to successfully carry off such a daring burglary.

69

Robert Sanderson's carefully thought-out plan began to go wrong long before the housemaid quietly drew back the bolts to the servants' door, opened it with the key from the hall cupboard and slipped into the night to meet her discredited lover.

When Harry Maggs completed his second day's work at Lanhydrock House, he did what he had been doing for very many years at the end of his working day with money in his pocket.

He went in search of a drink.

Sanderson had told him to keep clear of the well-policed town of Bodmin and Maggs kept to this part of the plan at least. After making enquiries of the servants, Maggs made his way to the hamlet of Sweetshouse, about a mile from Lanhydrock. The landlord of the small country public house earned only a meagre living from a small number of regular local drinkers, and so the thirsty chimney sweep was given a warm welcome.

Maggs had promised Sanderson he would enter Lanhydrock House soon after midnight, but at that time he was still in the Sweetshouse public house. It was more than an hour later before he turned the key in the lock of the servants' door and, somewhat unsteadily, entered the house.

He carried with him a small bull's-eye lantern, lit by a piece of candle. It was a lamp that he found useful when he was working inside some of the darker chimneys.

Leaving the servants' hall behind he carried the lantern beneath his coat, using it only occasionally. His drunken clumsiness would have left Sanderson aghast, but it seemed the household was not alert tonight.

All the finest household silver was kept locked in a safe in the butler's ground-floor pantry, with the bed of a young male servant beside it. Fortunately for Maggs, the young man was a very heavy sleeper and would hear nothing beyond the walls of his cell-like 'bedroom'.

The chimney sweep made his way from room to room, taking the pieces listed by Robert Sanderson. He also added a considerable number of additional items of lesser value, which had earlier taken his fancy.

He was still filling the first sack when the housemaid returned from her nocturnal liaison. By this time he was well behind schedule.

The plan had been that he should be well clear of the house by the time she returned and bolted the door once again.

Harry Maggs shrugged off the certain knowledge that Sanderson was going to be very angry with him. The ex-butler might be very clever at making plans and telling others how they should do things, but he was not the one who had to carry them out.

That had been left to Maggs. Now he would do it *his* way.

When the second sack had been filled, it was heavier than the first, but it followed its fellow out of the dairy scullery window.

With the window open, Maggs listened, expecting to hear some sound from Sanderson. All was silent.

He was not to know that the angry ex-butler was at that very moment carrying the first laden sack to the chimney-sweep's barrow, hidden in the woods behind the house.

The burglary should have been completed by now and the two men heading away from the house with two sacks bulging with stolen valuables. However, Maggs had still not collected all the items listed by his accomplice – or all the additional items he planned to steal.

He would not leave until he had filled a third sack – but his greed proved his undoing.

Finally collecting all the items he intended taking, he put them through the window, as before. Then he made his way to the side door, drew the bolts and felt in his pocket for Sanderson's key.

It was not there.

Searching feverishly through all his pockets, he found many holes, but no key.

Had Maggs only known, he was standing within an arm's length of his means of escape – the same key used by the housemaid. But he did not know.

Nevertheless, he considered that losing the key was more a nuisance than a disaster. He would return to the dairy scullery and exit the house by squeezing through the narrow window.

No sooner had he reached this decision than he was alarmed by the sound of voices at the top of the stairs that led to the women servants' quarters.

Hurrying along the passageway, he passed by the foot of the stairs before the women reached the ground floor. Farther along the passageway, he had almost reached the men's staircase when he heard someone coming down these too, and a light was casting a flickering shadow on the wall.

Caught between the two groups of servants, Maggs panicked. Opening the nearest door, he found himself in the kitchen. He realised the danger this posed only when the two groups met and began talking outside the door.

The handle turned but the door opened no more than a couple of inches before it stopped. The woman opening it paused to make a crude remark to one of the men approaching from the other staircase.

There was only one escape route left open now – and Maggs took it. His feet had just disappeared out of sight up the chimney when the first of the servants entered the kitchen, holding a candle aloft.

'What's this then?' Maggs heard one of the men say, 'Has no one brought in any kindling? It should have been done last thing by the scullery maid. She knew we were having to start cooking early today in readiness for the party.'

'No need to fret yourself about having no kindling,' a woman's voice replied. 'The chimney's only just been swept. Put the wood and coal in. We'll pour some paraffin over it. We'll have it going in no time at all.'

'You'd better not let Cook catch you using paraffin on a kitchen fire,' said another woman. 'She says you can taste it in the food.'

'Well Cook's not here, is she?' said the man who had spoken before. 'Come on, get the fire going and put the kettle on for a cup of tea. Then we can open all the windows. There won't be the faintest whiff of paraffin time Cook comes down.'

Harry Maggs climbed the chimney much faster than he would have moved had he been working. A paraffin-fed fire would send flames far up the chimney. He wanted to be well clear before that happened.

'What's that noise?' One of the women, helping to light the fire, had heard Maggs making his escape.

'Probably a jackdaw,' replied one of the men. 'There's been a pair of them around just lately. Get that fire going and they'll be away fast enough.'

Maggs reached a junction where another chimney joined that from the kitchen. Moving into the other chimney, Maggs breathed a sigh of relief. He was safe for the time being at least.

Trapped in the house, he would not be able to make good his escape until everyone had gone to bed. That was likely to be very late if they were having a party.

However, it was not a total disaster. If Sanderson had removed the three sacks, the night's contents would be safe enough hidden in the woods. Maggs would find the ex-butler when he left his refuge that night. They would divide the spoils then.

The chimney Maggs was now in led down to a bed-room fire that had been bricked in to make it smaller. He would not be able to escape that way, but he was not unduly concerned. There was a shelf here, wide enough for him to settle down and sleep the day around. He would think about making his escape when he awoke.

70

Harry Maggs awoke suddenly. For some moments he did not know where he was. When he reached out and his hand dropped from the ledge into the emptiness inside the chimney, he remembered.

But there was something else. Something that had nothing to do with chimneys. It was a strange noise and it puzzled him. The sound seemed to fill the air all about him. A frightening, unceasing crackling. It was the sound of wood being consumed by fire.

He could smell smoke too now and, with a spasm of fear, he realised it was not the comforting aroma of a fire burning in a household grate.

It was not even a cooking fire, burning in the huge kitchen fireplace of Lanhydrock House.

This was a greedy, all-consuming fire, fanned by a wind that had been building up the previous night when he had entered the house.

The extent of the fire could be measured by the fact that smoke was being sucked up through the chimney that led from the bedroom beneath. Yet, when he looked down, he could see no domestic fire burning in the grate.

It meant the fire had to be in the room itself. The house was on fire!

Still half stupified from sleep, Maggs was belatedly galvanised into action. He scrambled to his feet on the ledge that had provided him with a sleeping space.

There was no escape for him down the chimney where he was. The alterations to the fireplace in the room below meant it was much too small to squeeze through.

He would need to make his escape through the kitchen.

He climbed towards the junction of the chimneys. Reaching it, he was alarmed at the amount of smoke pouring up from the kitchen. It was so thick he began choking.

But, despite the discomfort, he had to escape – and he needed to move quickly. Nevertheless, he began his descent cautiously, coughing all the while.

He had not gone far when he became aware of an intense heat rising from the kitchen.

The chimney also was on fire and, suddenly, Maggs remembered the paraffin-soaked sacks he had placed alongside the exposed beam in this very chimney. That must have been what had started all this.

Retching and choking, he was forced to return up the chimney, climbing blindly in the thick smoke.

He had a moment of panic when he missed a foot-hold. For a few terrified moments he was convinced he would tumble back down the wide chimney, into the fire below.

Then, gasping for breath, he reached the junction

with the bedroom chimney once more. There was little respite for him here. The smoke from the bedroom was far more dense than before.

Maggs realised there was only one possible route to safety. He would need to climb to the top of the tall chimney and make his escape over the roof.

It would not be easy. The soot he had left inside the chimney was burning, giving off acrid, lung-searing smoke.

The heat from the kitchen fire was also increasing. He could feel it even at this great height. Most alarming of all, the very bricks of the chimney were hot to the touch. He was aware that the heat could only be coming from *outside*.

His eyes smarting and with agonisingly painful lungs, Harry Maggs somehow managed to claw his way up the inside of the chimney, heading for the lighter grey of the sky outside, glimpsed intermittently through the darker grey of the smoke from the burning house.

His lungs labouring for air, he was not yet aware of the roar that grew louder as he neared the top of the chimney. He thought there must be a fierce gale blowing outside the house.

Suddenly and virtually unseeing, his head emerged from the top of the chimney. There *was* a gale-force wind blowing away much of the smoke but, as he filled his lungs with life-giving air, he became aware that the sound he could hear was not that of the wind.

Rubbing his eyes in an effort to clear them, he took in the frightening scene about him.

Much of the roof on this wing of the house had already collapsed, the great beams burned away. The remainder might have been a scene from Dante's *Inferno*.

Flames, fanned by the wind, were being blown sideways, but they still climbed high into the sky, far beyond the height of the tall chimneys.

The roar he had heard was the sound of the great house being consumed by the voracious appetite of the conflagration that he, Harry Maggs, had begun.

There would be no escape for him by this – or any other – route.

Even as the realisation came to him, he was granted a mercifully swift release from his terror. From somewhere far below there was an explosion. It came from within the kitchen area.

The chimney beneath him shook alarmingly – then collapsed. Tons of masonry crashed down through the burning house, into the very heart of the inferno.

It was the dying spasm of a once-magnificent house. Harry Maggs died with it.

Waiting impatiently in the darkness, Robert Sanderson fumed at the incompetent recklessness of his accomplice. He had already taken two sacks of stolen items to the wheelbarrow hidden in the woods, but there was still no sign of Harry Maggs.

Returning to the rear of the house, he unexpectedly came across the third sack. He guessed immediately what the chimney sweep was doing.

Castigating the absent Maggs for a greedy fool, he picked up the third bag to take it to the woods and hide it with the others.

As he did so, he saw the light from lamps come on in the kitchen and heard voices. His first thought was that Maggs had been discovered. Then he heard a woman laugh as the kitchen window was flung open.

Sanderson guessed that there was to be some kind of function in the house that day. On such occasions it was usual for certain members of the numerous kitchen staff to rise very early. They would bring the ovens up to the correct heat and have everything in readiness for the appearance of the cook.

The most serious question for Sanderson right now was the whereabouts of Harry Maggs. Was he hiding somewhere in the house – or had he already made his way outside and they had missed each other in the darkness?

Sanderson cursed his accomplice. The man was an utter fool!

Had Maggs kept to the plan they had made, they would both have been many miles from Lanhydrock by now, with property worth hundreds of pounds. Thousands, even.

Now his plans were in ruins. The only thing that was certain was that it was unsafe for him to remain in the vicinity of the house.

He would make for Bodmin. When it was light and people were moving about the town, he would find a small inn to purchase breakfast and a cheap room.

It was still far too close to Lanhydrock for comfort but, with any luck, the beard he had grown and the cheap clothes he was wearing would stand him in good stead. He would not be recognised as the once-immaculate butler of Lanhydrock House.

71

Robert Sanderson had been awake for more than twenty-four hours and his activities during the night had left him physically and mentally exhausted. As a result, in spite of his concern for the fate of Harry Maggs and the plans they had made, he slept heavily.

He did not wake until mid-afternoon, and was immediately aware of a great deal of activity in the street outside the small inn. There seemed to be far more people and vehicles than were normal in the quiet country town. Rising from his bed he opened the window, and felt an indefinable sense of excitement in the air.

After splashing some cold water over his face, he made his way downstairs to the dining room and ordered a drink and a meal. As he ate, he could see through the windows that most of the people seemed to be heading out of Bodmin along the road to the south of the town.

When he commented upon the activity to the serving girl, she said, 'It's the fire, sir. Up at Lanhydrock House. They say the whole house is burning to the ground. All the policemen in town have gone there. They've sent soldiers from the barracks, too. No one in the county has ever seen a fire like it. Everyone who isn't doing anything else has gone there to watch what's going on. Frightening, they say it is. Poor old Lady Robartes has had to be rescued from an upstairs window and one of the servant girls hurt herself when she jumped from another one. 'Tis a terrible thing to happen to such a lovely place.'

'Does anyone have any idea how the fire was started?'

'Doesn't seem like it. I heard say that it probably started in the kitchen chimney. But my sister works in the kitchen at the house, and she was telling me only last night about them having the sweep in there. Shifty-looking man she said he was. Doesn't sound as though he was very good at his job, either, not if the fire really did start in a chimney. Now, shall I pour you another cup of tea?'

Despite his changed appearance, Robert Sanderson felt it wise not to risk being seen in the vicinity of Lanhydrock House in daylight. Not with all that was going on there. He was known to have a deep grudge against the family. If he were recognised, an astute policeman might start asking him awkward questions. He decided to wait until it was dark before going to look at the burning house.

When the sun had gone down, Sanderson set off for the great house. There were many people on the road, all travelling in the same direction.

Men, women and children, their day's work over, were hurrying to witness the greatest disaster to occur in the area in living memory.

One of the county's grandest and most beautiful residences, the house had been at the heart of all that happened in this part of Cornwall for hundreds of years. It had been a focal point in times of trouble.

When a bitterly fought Civil War was raging throughout the land, Lanhydrock House had changed hands on more than one occasion. Yet its importance was appreciated by both sides and it had survived, intact.

The head of the Robartes family had fought on behalf of the Parliamentary cause, yet he managed to retain ownership of the house and lands when the war ended. Then, with Charles II on the throne, the fortunes and influence of the family increased with passing years.

Now the focal point of the family's power was being carried on the wind to the farthest corners of the extensive estate.

Standing amidst the crowd, watching firemen, policemen and soldiers fighting a losing battle against the fire, Robert Sanderson should have felt a deep and malicious joy. He had struck a devastating blow against the family for whom he bore a deep and bitter grudge. But the knowledge gave him no satisfaction whatsoever.

As he watched, flames leapt three times higher than the remaining tall chimneys of the house, fanned by a lessening, but still strong wind.

An eerie red glow illuminated the huge crowd. It showed the Herculean – but futile – efforts of the many fire-fighters.

A huge pall of smoke billowed from the conflagration, sweeping across the Cornish countryside for very many miles, contaminating the air inside cottages far removed from the Lanhydrock Estate. Meanwhile, the glow in the night sky was visible to those as far away as the north and south coasts of Cornwall.

Standing silent in the crowd, Sanderson heard many and contradictory rumours about the fate of the Robartes family, whose home this had been.

One was that Lady Robartes, heartbroken by the devastation of the house she loved, suffered a breakdown and had been escorted to the home of the local vicar.

Viewing the fire that had been planned by himself as an act of revenge, Robert Sanderson suddenly felt very frightened. All he wanted now was to put many miles between himself and the scene of his Pyrrhic victory.

On his way here from Bodmin, he had intended making his way to the woods behind the house to ensure the property stolen by Maggs was still safely hidden.

He had nursed a faint hope that the chimney sweep had made a miraculous escape from the blazing house. But he now realised it was not very likely. Having seen the extent of the fire, he was convinced the body of Harry Maggs was somewhere inside the burning house and would probably never be found.

Sanderson did not have the will to carry out his intentions tonight. Besides, although the policemen in the area were fully occupied, there were far too many people wandering around the countryside, on their way to or from the blazing manor house.

Suddenly sick of everything about him, Robert Sanderson hurried from the scene of the fire. Throwing caution to the wind, he made his way to Bodmin Road railway station. Purchasing a ticket, he hid in the shadows until the arrival of the last train back to Plymouth.

He sat huddled in a seat in the corner of a carriage, lost in his thoughts. It was impossible not to dwell upon the enormity of all that had been brought about as a result of the plans he had made with the Plymouth chimney sweep.

72

During the two days she spent in London, Captain Eva had three meetings with Carl Milton, the influential editor of the *Mayfair Gazette*. Milton would provide any assistance she might need to carry out her plan and promised that all the resources of his newspaper would be placed at her disposal.

However, much to her dismay, the newspaper editor's enthusiasm for her crusade was not shared by senior officers of the Salvation Army.

It was, perhaps, unfortunate that William Booth and his second-in-command were both out of the country. Without his decisive leadership, no one at the Salvation Army's London headquarters was prepared to offer active support to such a daring scheme. They were aware that it was likely to have widespread repercussions, not only in England but in Europe too.

Eva was advised to delay carrying out her plan until she had been able to discuss it in detail with General Booth. The suggestion fell only marginally short of a command, but Captain Eva knew she could not wait.

If she did not take action immediately she would be abandoning an unknown number of girls to a life of enforced prostitution.

There was also the possibility that future advertisements of a similar nature might not be brought to her attention.

Eva was convinced it was of the utmost importance to act *now* and she had already set the wheels of her plan in motion.

Before leaving Plymouth she had replied, on Sally's behalf, to the address in the newspaper, giving the house of a Plymouth Salvation Army supporter, living in a country area of Devon, as the return address. The response from the advertiser would be brought to Eva at the Plymouth Refuge as soon as it was received.

By the time she returned from London, Eva had decided she would ignore the advice of her superiors.

Back in the Refuge once more, she discussed with Sally the implications of the reluctance of the Salvation Army headquarters' staff to become involved with the scheme she had planned.

'You don't have to go ahead with it if you'd rather not,' she said to Sally.

'Why should I want to back out?' Sally asked defiantly. 'Is what they say going to make any real difference to anything you want to do?'

'No, I can still count on the support of my members in the West Country, unless headquarters send out a direct order forbidding them to help me – and I don't think they will do that – but—'

Sally interrupted Eva. 'If we don't do something, there are likely to be a lot more girls who will end up like Rachel. As long as I know Zulu Joe is close enough to hear me if I scream for help, I'll be all right.'

'You're a brave girl, Sally. You have my word that I wouldn't allow you to do this if I wasn't convinced we would be able to help you if anything goes wrong.'

Despite her assurance, Captain Eva would have been much happier to have had the backing of William Booth and the staff at the Salvation Army headquarters.

The reply to Captain Eva's letter was brought to the Refuge two days later from the false address she had given at Okehampton in Devon.

The letter would have satisfied all but the most suspicious recipient. It declared that so many girls had replied to the advertisement, it had been decided to take on no more prospective domestic servants. However, Sally sounded as though she was just the type of girl they were looking for and, in view of this, they had decided to make an exception in her case.

She was to catch a train to Truro in Cornwall, where she would transfer to another train to Falmouth, arriving there at eight o'clock in the evening. Travelling with her would be all the other girls who were to enter domestic service.

They would be met at Falmouth railway station and taken to a house in the town. After a meal they would be allocated a room in order that they might have a good night's sleep before beginning their new life the following day.

It all sounded highly organised. However, reading the letter, Sally had a funny feeling in her stomach as she realised that it was no longer merely a vague plan. It was really going to happen.

*　　*　　*

The day before setting off for Falmouth, Sally attended Rachel's funeral with Captain Eva. It had been organised by Grace and Alfie and was a very moving service.

Both pie-shop owners were at the church and Alfie acknowledged Sally's presence with a nod of his head. His lips moved too, but he was too far away for Sally to hear what, if anything, he said.

Grace was standing beside him. She looked ill and strained and she never once glanced in Sally's direction.

Sally was very hurt by Grace's indifference. She wanted to go and speak to the woman who had been such a kind employer, but Eva dissuaded her. She suggested that in view of the anguish Grace was quite obviously suffering, she could not be expected to behave rationally. Eva felt quite certain that Grace would feel differently about everything when sufficient time had elapsed to allow her grief to subside.

In view of all that was going to happen in the next few days, Sally would have liked things between her and Grace settled before she went, but it was apparent it would need to await a more propitious moment.

73

Sally set off for Falmouth late on Saturday afternoon, travelling on a train from Plymouth. No uniformed Salvation Army officer was present at the station to see her off.

There was a strong possibility that other applicants were travelling on the same train, and a careless word dropped in the hearing of those who met them might well arouse suspicion.

Captain Eva was not in Plymouth. She was aware that if her plan were to succeed, it would be necessary for the officers of the Falmouth Salvation Army to become heavily involved. She had travelled there the day before, in order to make the necessary arrangements.

Nevertheless, Zulu Joe travelled on the same train as Sally. So too did a couple of the Plymouth Salvation Army 'soldiers'. More would be in the vicinity of the railway station when Sally arrived at her destination.

Eva was well aware that she was playing a very dangerous game and she was doing all within her power to ensure Sally's safety.

When Sally changed trains at Truro she was able to pick out other applicants. They all gathered somewhat self-consciously on the same platform, each carrying a pitifully small number of worldly possessions.

Most, although not all, appeared to be younger than Sally and she realised it had not been entirely necessary to give a false age.

Gradually, the girls drew together in a group, introducing themselves to each other.

There were fifteen altogether, including Sally. All were greatly excited at the thought of taking up a new way of life. It upset Sally to think of the disappointment in store for them.

Yet she was happy in the knowledge that she would be instrumental in saving them from a way of life that would bring them even more unhappiness than they had already known.

The girls talked of the life they thought lay ahead of them. There was laughter among the other girls when, in a moment of bravado, one of them said, 'I hope I go to a house with lots of men servants – *young* men servants.'

As the laughter died away, a young girl who reminded Sally painfully of Rachel sidled up to her. Small and quiet, Sally thought her a natural victim.

Shyly, she said, 'My name's Constance – although I'm always called Connie. What's yours?'

'Sally.' She smiled at her.

'That's a nicer name than mine. What sort of house do you hope to go to?'

Sally shrugged. Then, remembering she was acting a part, said, 'I don't really mind very much. How about you?'

'I don't care, either. Anything will be better than the workhouse I've just left.'

Connie's likeness to Rachel grew in Sally's mind and she asked, 'Don't you have any parents?'

'No. They both died when I was small. I was brought up by my grandma, but she died two years ago too. Since then I've lived in the workhouse – although I'd hardly call it *living*. Everyone just exists there, one day at a time, hoping the next day's going to be better. It never is.' With a wan smile, she shook off the image she had just created and asked Sally, 'Do you have any family?'

'I lived with my sister for almost as long as I can remember. She died on Christmas Day.'

'I'm sorry,' Connie's sympathy was genuine. 'That must have been awful for you.'

A train arriving noisily on a nearby platform brought all conversation to a halt for a few minutes.

When the sound died away, Connie asked, 'Do you know anything about being "in service"?'

'Not really.'

'Or me, but I don't care. The thought of learning something, of belonging somewhere, is exciting enough. Do you think some of us will go to the same houses? It would be nice to be with someone we knew, wouldn't it?'

As they talked, Sally glimpsed Zulu Joe standing farther along the platform. He did not appear to be watching her, but Sally knew he was keeping her in view. It made her feel considerably safer.

She had been concerned that he might be conspicuous, but Falmouth was a very busy and cosmopolitan port. In fact there was a party of Lascars on the station, as well as a group of West African seamen. All were on their way to join ships.

Glancing about her Sally wondered which of her fellow passengers were also members of the Salvation Army.

The plan was that they would follow the girls to the house to which they were being taken. When the girls' destination was established, one of the Salvation Army members would inform the officer commanding the local corps. Captain Eva would be with him.

Men and women would then be despatched to maintain a vigil, night and day if necessary, until the girls were moved from the house.

It was at this point that Eva's plans became somewhat vague. When Sally had left Plymouth it had still not been decided whether the rescue should take place at the house.

Eva favoured leaving it until the girls were at the dockside, before they were taken on board a boat. She was convinced there *would* be a boat at Falmouth, somewhere, waiting for them, but the rescuers would first need to locate it.

All who knew what was happening agreed that a rescue at the house would be far safer. However, the newspaper editor felt that a last-minute rescue – perhaps just as the girls were about to be carried off to a continental brothel – would have a much more dramatic impact upon his readers.

It should also impress those in authority, who, it was hoped, would tighten up the laws to prevent a similar occurrence in the future.

Connie carried on chattering to Sally, seeming not to

care whether or not she received replies from her companion. She was happy just to be free of the constraints of the workhouse, able to talk to someone close to her own age.

A few minutes later the train for Falmouth arrived and the girls all clambered on board, crowding into two compartments.

Connie made quite certain she was in the same compartment as Sally. The journey did not take very long and the younger girl grew increasingly excited as they neared their destination, especially when the crowded harbour came into view.

Indeed, the girls behaved more as though they were on a Sunday-school outing than travelling to take up menial tasks in someone else's home.

Connie remained close to Sally when they disembarked. She seemed glad to have found a companion who appeared to be both sensible and dependable.

A man and a woman were waiting for the girls. They introduced themselves as Victoria and Wallace Pearce.

As she remembered the men who had been involved in the attempt to kidnap Rachel and the other girls in Plymouth, Sally took an instant dislike to Wallace Pearce. He was not a prepossessing character, being both surly and shifty.

It was the woman who did most of the talking. So much so that few of the girls were able to put any of their excited questions to her. Those who succeeded were told that all their queries would be answered when they reached the house where they were to spend the night.

There was a closed van waiting outside in the station yard, in which Wallace would drive the girls to their destination.

It was crowded inside the van and there were no windows, only two ventilated grilles high up on the sides of the van, but the girls were too excited to care. Seats made of wooden slats were placed along either side of the van. There was room for all the girls on them – but only just.

However, the crowding and the jostling and falling about when the van got under way only added to the general feeling of adventure. The girls continued to squeal and giggle, even when Wallace called in through one of the grilles for them to be quiet because they were passing through a 'select residential area'.

Unable to see where they were going, Sally realised they were climbing a hill from the station. At one stage they jolted over a cobbled stretch of roadway that bounced the girls about and rattled their teeth, causing them to squeal even more.

Eventually, after perhaps twenty minutes, the van came to a halt and the rear door was opened.

'Here we are,' said Victoria, as they all stepped from the van. 'Inside the house, all of you. There's a nice meal waiting for you there. When you've eaten you'll meet the woman in charge of the agency. She's the one who'll allocate you to the families who will be employing you. There are very pleasant surprises for some of you, I can tell you. We've had applications for staff from some of the most influential families in the county. At least half of them have titles. Now, gather your things and follow me inside the house.'

Walking down a steep path to a large, fairly modern house, Sally found her heart beginning to beat much faster in anticipation of what lay ahead.

It was hard to resist the urge to turn around to see

if she could spot Zulu Joe or any Salvation Army men or women near. She would need to trust that they were not far away and would come to the rescue when they were needed.

Even had Sally noticed the twitching of the lace curtain at an upstairs window, she would probably not have been particularly concerned.

But had she recognised the woman who had disturbed the curtain in order to get a clearer look at the girls coming along the path, Sally in particular, she would have turned around and fled.

The woman at the window was Mother Darling.

74

Ian Lovat called at the Refuge to talk to Eva little more than an hour after Sally had left Plymouth bound for Falmouth. Due to his own pressures of work and Eva's absence in London, he had not seen her since her return. Now he learned she had gone off somewhere else.

The young Salvation Army lieutenant left in charge of the house during Eva's absence knew where her superior had gone, and why, but she had been sworn to secrecy. Newly arrived in Plymouth from London, she had learned to distrust policemen and she told Ian Lovat merely that Captain Eva was 'not here'.

'Then can you tell me when she'll be back? Better still, where she is now. I'll go and find her.'

'I don't know where she is.'

Despite the young Salvation Army officer's assertion, Ian Lovat felt she was being deliberately evasive. It served to increase the suspicions he had about Eva's whereabouts – and he was genuinely alarmed.

'Look, this is important. Very important! If you can help me at all, you must.'

'I've told you, I don't know.'

The young woman sensed the urgency in Ian Lovat's plea. For a moment she weakened and almost told him what he wanted to know. Then she remembered how adamant Captain Eva had been. She had been ordered to say nothing to *anyone*.

Ian Lovat made one last plea. 'I hope you're telling me the truth. Captain Eva might have placed herself in very great danger.'

Once again the lieutenant almost weakened. However, stories of the subterfuge used by members of the police Criminal Investigation Department in order to convict members of the Salvation Army had been rife among those with whom she worked. Determined not to be taken in, she said, 'I can't tell you what I don't know.'

Ian Lovat realised he was wasting time – and time could be of vital importance. He turned to go. Suddenly he stopped and swung around to face the young woman once more.

'I'd like to speak to Sally.'

Taken by surprise, the Salvation Army lieutenant replied, 'She's not here either.'

'Will she be back tonight?'

'I . . . I don't know. I don't think so.'

Now Ian Lovat was certain that his uneasiness was justified. The plan that Captain Eva had been wanting to put in motion for so long was taking place. He made one last desperate plea.

'I've no doubt you've been told to say nothing about what's going on, but I *do* have a very good idea what it is and I am not exaggerating when I say that Captain Eva and Sally are in grave danger. Is that something you and your conscience are going to be able to live with?'

The young lieutenant felt as though she was standing on the edge of a deep abyss. She wished she might have been able to turn to Captain Wardle for advice, but he was in London and besides he was not aware of what was happening. At this precise moment she was the senior Salvation Army officer in Plymouth.

She said doggedly, 'I have nothing more to say to you, Inspector Lovat.'

He decided he had wasted enough time. Besides, he had just thought of someone who might know exactly what was going on.

The telephone Ian Lovat used in order to call London was one of a very few in Plymouth. It was installed in the office of the admiral who was Flag Officer for the busy naval base.

Ian Lovat called Carl Milton, editor of the *Mayfair Gazette*.

At first, although the two men were long-standing friends, the London editor was as reluctant as the Salvation Army lieutenant had been to tell the detective inspector what was happening.

'I'm sorry, Ian. I'd like to tell you what is going on, but it would mean breaking a professional trust. I can't do that.'

'Damn your professional trust, Carl. The lives of two people, Captain Eva and, more particularly, Sally Harrup, are seriously at risk. You talk of professional trust. This matter is so serious that I'm willing to break *mine* – but if it ever gets into print I'll see that you lose your job and never again get to be so much as a teaboy on any newspaper in the land.'

Satisfied that the newspaper editor was fully aware of the seriousness of the situation, Ian Lovat continued, 'Now listen carefully. You've no doubt been told about Mother Darling's part in the business involving young girls being shipped to Belgian brothels? Well, she's disappeared. I believe she's gone to join her son. I don't know whether you're aware that he's wanted for questioning by police here in connection with the death of Sally's sister. I believe he and his mother are behind the latest advertisement offering posts in so-called "domestic service" for young and gullible girls. They both know Sally. Mother Darling has met Captain Eva too. If, as I believe, Sally has been sent to answer this advertisement then she'll be recognised. Once the Darling's realise a trap has been laid for them they'll be even more dangerous. If I can learn what's going on, I might be able to do something to save them. If I don't, this whole mad scheme that you and Captain Eva have cooked up is likely to have tragic results.'

Pausing only long enough to give the London editor time to digest what he had been told, Ian Lovat said, 'Now, are you going to tell me exactly what's going on?'

After a lengthy pause, Carl Milton said, 'Are you telling me the truth about this, Ian? You're not deliberately exaggerating the danger they're both in?'

'I've never been more serious in my life, Carl.'

The London editor took a deep breath before saying, 'Then I have no alternative, do I? You're right, Sally volunteered to help expose what's happening to the girls who apply for posts in domestic service. She answered the advertisement and is on her way to Falmouth at this very moment – a number of other girls will be doing

the same. Captain Eva went there herself last night.
There are a great many people keeping track of Sally
and the other girls. I doubt if anything can happen to
them – at least, not if the people who are behind this
don't realise we are on to them. If they do . . . ? Well,
you know the answer to that better than I do. We don't
have an address in Falmouth for the girls, but if you
need any more help, contact the senior Salvation Army
officer there. He knows what's happening and should
be able to tell you where the girls and Captain Eva are,
and what he and his people are doing to help. I have
a reporter and a photographer in Falmouth too. They'll
be with Captain Eva, wherever she is.'

'Thanks, Carl. I'll get on to it right away and I'll go
down to Falmouth myself, just as quickly as I can.'

'By the way, try to give me a story on this one, Ian. If it
comes off we should be able to blow this filthy business
sky-high.'

Grimly, Ian Lovat said, 'If everyone comes safely out
of this you'll get your story. If not . . . I'd say you're
likely to get ten years, instead.'

The Flag Officer's telephone had been installed in a
small room off the admiral's office, accessible to no one
but the senior naval officer and his private secretary.
Only the urgency of the detective inspector's need had
persuaded them that this was an emergency that could
not be resolved by any other means.

During Ian Lovat's telephone conversation with Carl
Milton, the door between the telephone room and the
admiral's office had been left ajar. As a consequence,
much of the conversation had been overheard by the
senior naval officer.

As Ian Lovat came out of the telephone room, the admiral commented, 'You have a problem on your hands, Inspector.'

'Yes, sir. A number of young ladies are in trouble in Falmouth. I need to get there very quickly and see what I can do to help.'

'Can you tell me about it?'

Ian Lovat hesitated. It was unethical to discuss police business with outsiders – however exalted their position. Furthermore, although he was grateful for the help given to him by the admiral, he was also anxious to get on his way.

'The problem is at Falmouth, I understand?' persisted the admiral. 'Am I right in thinking you need to go there as a matter of some urgency?'

'Yes. I'll catch the first available train.'

'I don't think there is one for a couple of hours,' the admiral said knowledgeably. 'When you do catch it you'll need to wait at Truro for a connection. However, if there really *is* great urgency I can probably get you there far more quickly. Tell me about it.'

The admiral's words cut through Ian Lovat's reluctance to divulge information. The naval officer had probably already overheard enough of the conversation with Carl Milton to have formed a good idea of what was happening.

He gave the admiral the background to Captain Eva's crusade against the luring of young girls to the brothels of Europe, outlining the action he believed she was taking. He then explained the developments he felt put her and Sally in grave danger.

'Is such a trade really going on in this country of ours, Inspector?' The admiral was more outraged than shocked. 'I know it goes on in north African countries. The navy has been involved on occasions in trying to put a stop to it there. But right here on our own doorstep, with young *English* girls . . . ? It's unthinkable.'

'It's nevertheless true, sir. In fact, unless I can get to Falmouth in time we can probably add murder to what will take place there.'

'Then the navy will need to come to the rescue,' the admiral said firmly. 'A steam packet is due to leave for Falmouth this evening. I'll have the sailing brought forward. You can go with it. I'll send orders to the captain right away. You can accompany the messenger and be in Falmouth within four hours. There are marines on board too. If you need them, they are at your disposal.'

75

Inside the Falmouth house, Mother Darling stayed well out of the way of the girls, remaining in the upstairs room from which she had seen Sally.

After about half an hour, 'Victoria Pearce' made her way to the room to find out why she had not come downstairs to meet the girls. Mother Darling alarmed her by saying she had recognised one of the girls.

'She's a pretty little thing. Slim, with fair hair, wearing a green coat and with a green ribbon in her hair.'

'That sounds like Sally,' said the other woman. 'She comes from Devon. Near Honiton, I believe.'

'Sally's her right name, but she doesn't come from Honiton. She's a Plymouth girl, from the Barbican, and she's mixed up with the Salvation Army. It's her who had the fishermen raid the Belgian boat and take off the girls the last time we did this.'

The woman was frightened and it showed. 'Do you think she's going to try to do the same again? What shall we do?'

'Carry on as planned – at least we will as far as the

other girls are concerned. I'll arrange something special for this little madam. There are a few old scores to be settled with her.'

'But what about the Salvation Army? You know how they feel about what we're doing. If they've taken a hand in this we could be in real trouble. I don't like it. I don't like it one little bit.'

'No one's asking you to like it. I'm not saying *I* like it, but I think we can teach this particular young lady a lesson she'll wish she never learned. I know someone who's going to be very happy to get his hands on her. She's caused my Sid more trouble than any man should have to put up with.' Rubbing her hands together in malicious glee, Mother Darling added, 'Oh yes, he'll be *very* pleased to teach her a lesson.'

'But what about her friends in the Salvation Army?' persisted the other woman. 'If this girl's up to something she won't be in this alone.'

'Of course she won't, but they're going to have to prove we've done something to break the law. Before they can do that they'll need to have her back with them. They'll find that's not going to be quite as easy as they think.'

'What if they've had her followed and are watching the house right now? They'll have seen her and the other girls arrive.'

Mother Darling looked at the other woman contemptuously. 'What if they *have* seen them arrive? We'll make quite sure they don't see them leave again. I had this house chosen with just this sort of problem in mind. There's a small gate from the back garden. It leads to a narrow footpath that comes out on a street way down the hill. Unless you'd been shown it you'd never know the gate, or the lane to it, existed. When we've dealt with this particular girl we'll get them all out that way. Her friends can watch the front of the house for as long as they like. By the time they realise they've been wasting their time, young Sally whatever-she's-calling-herself will have got her comeuppance.'

She sniffed disapprovingly. 'If we'd been using this place for the last lot we'd never have been rumbled and Sid wouldn't be a wanted man now. The trouble was, he got lazy and a bit too cocky. He thought it was easy and he wouldn't listen to me. He decided to bring everything closer to home. Look where it got him!'

Her companion was still uneasy. 'What do I do where this girl's concerned?'

'Go back downstairs and behave as though everything's perfectly normal. Treat this Sally exactly the same as you do everyone else – but watch her. See if she drinks any of the wine. She probably won't. When the others are too stupid to know what's going on send Wallace up here to fetch me. But whatever you do, don't leave the girl on her own. We don't want her getting up to any of her tricks. We'll deal with her when I come downstairs.'

The woman shook her head doubtfully. 'I still don't like it. Too many people seem to know what's going on. If something goes wrong . . .'

'Just do as you're told and leave me to do the thinking. We'll be out of here by midnight. Once the girls have gone no one will be able to prove anything, no matter what they might believe. If Sid had done that in the first place he wouldn't be in the mess he is now. Go on, off you go. Do as I've told you and think of the money you'll get when the girls are on board the boat.'

The woman went off, still shaking her head dubiously, leaving Mother Darling staring after her contemptuously.

Instead of being reassured by everything that should have marked the beginning of what she believed was going to be a new way of life, Connie was more uncertain than before. As a result, she stayed very close to Sally.

When the girls were seated around a huge kitchen table, wine was brought to them in two large jugs, as a special 'treat' to have with their meal.

Sally was tempted to suggest the younger girl leave the wine alone, but that would have meant making up an explanation for her suggestion. She decided against it.

The drugged wine – and Sally was certain it *was* drugged – would help to relax Connie. When the time came for Captain Eva and the other members of the Salvation Army to move in and rescue them, she would ensure nothing happened to the nervous young girl.

She wondered exactly when Captain Eva intended making her move. The most likely time would be as they were about to board the boat that was probably moored somewhere in Falmouth harbour. When it happened, Sally would be ready to take her part in the action . . .

'Aren't you drinking your wine, dear? Come along now, there's lots here. It was bought 'specially for you girls. We can't waste it now, can we?'

'I'm a slow drinker.' Sally smiled in what she hoped was a disarming fashion at the woman.

Some of the girls were already beginning to show signs that confirmed her suspicions. When the meal was begun there had been much excited conversation, accentuated for a while by the wine. That had now ceased altogether. Those who had drunk too freely were beginning to nod off to sleep. Others were having difficulty stringing words together in order to hold an intelligible conversation.

Sally was the only girl not affected by the wine and she realised the woman was looking at her suspiciously.

Then one of the girls slipped off her stool. The woman went to her aid and had great difficulty lifting her to a chair.

Sally took the opportunity to pour her doctored wine into the mugs of Connie and the girl seated on her other side.

She then tried to act as though she had drunk as much as the others in the room.

In another twenty minutes the room was silent. Unable to talk coherently, the girls had given up trying. It was doubtful if any of them would have been able to walk unaided.

When the woman left the room, Sally thought something must be about to happen. She felt excitement surge through her.

She was quite right. Things *were* about to happen, but they were not what she was expecting.

The door opened and the woman returned, but she was not alone. With her was the man she had introduced to the girls as her husband – and Mother Darling!

Sally was utterly dismayed. Her instinct was to flee, but she realised she would not have made it to the door. Dropping her head and resting her chin on her chest, she hoped Mother Darling would not see her face and recognise her.

Such subterfuge was a waste of time, although for a moment she felt a glimmer of hope. It seemed the man and two women might pass her by. Then a hand gripped her hair and pulled her head back viciously.

She looked up into the face of a vindictive Mother Darling.

'Hello, dearie. How nice of you to come calling on me. I've been hoping we would meet again.'

For a wild moment, Sally considered bluffing it out and pretending she was as drugged as the others. Then common-sense took over. She realised it would not work. There was no point in play-acting any more.

'Let go of my hair, you're hurting me.'

'Hurting you? You've not begun to feel pain yet, dearie – but you will when Sid gets hold of you.'

Sally went cold at the mention of the bullying procurer's name.

'Let me take her upstairs for a while,' Wallace said eagerly. 'I'll give her a taste of what she can expect when she gets to Belgium. I'd enjoy that.'

'You might,' agreed Mother Darling. 'But you're not going to. That's something Sid will want to do himself. Since you're itching to get your hands on her, why don't you hold her while we pour some of this lovely wine down her throat. It would be a pity to waste it. I don't think she's even tasted it yet.'

As she was speaking, Mother Darling pulled Sally to her feet by her hair.

Sally tried to turn upon her, but 'Wallace Pearce' stepped forward and wrapped his arms about her. He held her in a grip that defied the most determined attempts to fight against him.

While Sally was held with her arms pinioned to her sides, the woman who claimed to be Wallace's wife held her nose and Mother Darling began to pour drugged wine down her throat.

Sally choked, gagged and tried to spit out the wine, but it was in vain. By the time her three captors had completed their work she had drunk more than any of the other girls.

Her head began to swim. She was still able to think, but it was in a vague, abstract way.

Eventually, she realised she was losing control of her limbs. She could feel herself sinking in the arms of the man holding her, yet she could do nothing about it.

Sally tried hard to fight against the feeling of acute lethargy, but she heard Mother Darling say, 'I think we've done a good job there, Fred. We'll not have a peep out of her until she's on the boat. I've no doubt Sid will be able to bring some feeling back to her then. In the meantime, if her friends are waiting for her to give some signal to them, they're going to be disappointed.'

Her gloating ceased and she became briskly efficient. 'Right, the van's waiting at the bottom of the path behind the house. Take her first.'

It sounded to Sally as though Mother Darling was speaking from far away and what she was saying had nothing to do with her.

She was half carried, half led from the house, but it felt as though she was observing something that was happening to someone else.

Sally was placed in a van that might or might not

have been the one that had brought her and the other girls from the station.

She was hardly aware of the others being brought to the van. Then they set off and those girls who had been placed upon the wooden seats fell to the floor.

Moments later, Sally lost consciousness.

Her last thought was of Ethan and she tried to call out to him. She felt certain he would know what to do . . .

76

At the Shieldses' house, on the Barbican, Sophie was in the kitchen, peeling potatoes in readiness for the evening meal she would make for herself and Doris Shields.

Miserably, she thought how this used to be a happy time for her. Sophie and Albert had been married for only a year and with each homecoming came the thrills felt by a new wife very much in love with her husband. She enjoyed preparing a meal for Albert, having it ready for when he returned to their small house after a day's fishing.

Now, everything in her life had changed. Instead of welcoming home a lively and loving husband, she was merely going through the motions of producing edible food for herself and a woman who seemed to have lost all touch with normality.

It would be a dismal mealtime, as all meals had been since the men of the family had been lost at sea.

Doris would sit down and eat her meal in silence before suddenly saying, 'I wonder what Henry and the boys are doing now? They won't be eating as well as us, I'll be bound, but I hope they're taking care of themselves.'

The first few times it had been said, Sophie tried gently to convince Doris that the men and their boat had been lost. She no longer made the effort. Doris did not seem to hear a word that was said to her on the subject and firmly refused to face up to what must have happened.

It was almost as though God, or nature – Sophie's faith had been sorely tried just recently – had shut off the part of Doris's brain that was capable of accepting such facts.

In all other respects, Doris Shields behaved perfectly normally. In sharp contrast, Sophie increasingly felt her own life was taking on an air of unreality.

Doris was at this moment in the small back garden of the house, planting some flower seedlings given to her by a sympathetic neighbour.

While Sophie was working, thinking her own unhappy thoughts, she heard a knock at the door. It was a positive, imperious sound. One that *demanded* an immediate reply.

Frowning, Sophie picked up a small towel and dried her hands as she walked from the kitchen to the front door. She wondered who it could be. The only person who occasionally called in was Sally, if she was delivering in the area. But she would not knock at the door in such a fashion.

Opening the door, Sophie was surprised to see a uniformed naval petty officer standing there. In his hand he held a yellow envelope.

'Mrs Shields?'

When Sophie nodded, not considering which Mrs Shields he might be asking for, the sailor said, 'I've got a telegraph message here for you, ma'am. It arrived at the Flag Officer's headquarters this afternoon.'

Sophie went cold. It must be something to do with Albert and the others. Perhaps a naval vessel had found one of the bodies . . .

Raising a hand to his forehead, the sailor walked away, leaving Sophie with the sealed envelope.

Closing the door, Sophie walked along the passage to the kitchen, the envelope and the message it contained in her hand.

It was not until Doris Shields called from the garden to ask who had been at the door that Sophie ripped open the envelope, her hands trembling.

She read the first few lines and suddenly the room reeled around her. She reached out for the table to support herself, but the room would not stay still.

Suddenly, hot tears sprang to her eyes. She needed to brush them away before she could read on.

But these were tears of the sheerest joy.

At that moment Doris appeared at the kitchen door, her hands covered in earth.

'Who was that at the door—'

Her words were cut off as Sophie leapt forward and hugged her so tightly the older woman began to protest.

'It's Pa and the boys, Ma. THEY'RE SAFE! They're *alive!*' She continued to hug her mother-in-law, tears coursing down her face.

Suddenly, she became aware that Doris was trembling. Drawing back, she looked at the older woman in concern.

Her face bloodless and dark-eyed, Doris asked tremulously, 'Are you certain . . . ? How do you know?'

'It's true, Ma. We've just had a telegram delivered

from the naval Flag Officer at Mount Wise. He's had a telegram – from Gibraltar. Listen, this is what it says:

'"Regret fishing boat *Mermaid* was sunk by HMS *Roarer* south of Isles of Scilly. Happy to report that crew of seven, all members of Shields family from the Barbican, Plymouth, are safe, although Joseph Shields sustained broken arm. All transferred to steamship *Eastern Prince*, bound for Falmouth."

'It's signed, Flag Officer, Gibraltar.'

Tearfully jubilant, Sophie looked up from the telegram and was immediately concerned by what she saw. The older woman's face seemed to crumple before her eyes and Sophie needed to help her to a chair.

The next moment, Doris did what everyone had been waiting for her to do ever since her family had gone missing. She began to cry.

Dropping to her knees beside the chair, Sophie held her mother-in-law to her. Doris cried as Sophie had never heard anyone cry before and was inconsolable for a long, long time.

When the tears eventually ceased, Doris's body was racked by sobs for many more minutes. Then she pushed Sophie away.

'I'm all right now. The boys are safe, Pa's safe, and, God willing, they'll be home with us soon. I never thought we were going to see them again, Sophie. Never.'

Astounded by the unexpected admission, Sophie said, 'But you're the one who always said they *would* come back! You had the faith the rest of us lacked.'

'I had to believe that, Sophie. Had I thought otherwise I would have gone mad. I couldn't have lived – because there would have been nothing to live for.'

Looking at her in open admiration, Sophie said, 'Ma Shields, you're a remarkable woman.'

'No, Sophie, I'm a very ordinary woman – and I've been a very frightened one. Now I'm very, very happy, but I feel absolutely drained of energy. I'm sure I could sleep for a week or more.'

'I feel the same, Ma. I was peeling potatoes, but I can't even think of doing anything so ordinary right now. I . . . I just don't know what to do.'

'You can go and tell Sally. In her own way that girl's felt as deeply about the loss of Ethan as any of us. She ought to be told the good news right away.'

'I'll go straightaway, Ma – but are you going to be all right?'

'How could I be anything else at such a moment, Sophie. Go on, away you go.'

Sophie pulled off her apron and hurried from the kitchen. She had reached the front door when Doris called after her.

'Sophie?'

'Yes, Ma?'

'I want you to know that I think you've been absolutely marvellous through all this. I couldn't have wished for a better daughter and I realise it hasn't been an easy time for you, either.'

'It hasn't been easy for any of us – especially you.' Running back to the kitchen, Sophie kissed and hugged Doris.

Then, bubbling over with happiness, she said, 'I'll go and tell Sally now. I'll let the men on the fish quay know along the way. Then I'll bring Sally back with me and buy something so we can have a bit of a celebration. I feel so happy I could burst.'

77

Believing that Sophie already had enough to worry about, Sally had not told her of the strained relationship between herself and Grace Philpott. For the same reason, she had not mentioned that she was no longer working at the pie shop.

As a result, when Sophie sought out Sally, it was there she went first of all.

Alfie was working behind the counter. When Sophie introduced herself and asked after Sally, he said, with some embarrassment, 'She isn't here. In fact, she doesn't work here any more. Hasn't she told you?'

The news came as a shock to Sophie and she said so. 'Why not? How long is it since she left . . . ?'

'Alfie! Are you busy out there? I could do with some help in here . . .'

Grace's head appeared through the bamboo slats of the hanging curtain between shop and kitchen and Alfie said, 'This young lady's come asking for Sally.'

'Well, she's not going to find her here.' Emerging from the kitchen, Grace added, 'What do you want with her?'

Instead of resenting Grace's nosiness, Sophie was delighted to be able to share the good news she bore.

'I'm Sophie Shields, married to Ethan's brother. I'm looking for her to tell her some wonderful news. Ethan's safe. All the boys are safe. Their father too. The *Mermaid* was sunk by a warship but Albert and the others were all picked up and put on board a steamship. They'll be coming back and landed at Falmouth.'

'I'm absolutely delighted to hear the news about Ethan. He's a very nice young man. I'm just as pleased about the others too, of course. It's marvellous news for you – and for Ethan's mother in particular. It was unthinkable that a woman should lose her whole family in such a tragic fashion. But I can't pass on the news to Sally. She doesn't work here any more.' Grace's mouth clamped shut in an uncharacteristic expression.

'But . . . why has she left? She seemed so happy working for you.'

'I thought I could trust her,' Grace said bitterly. 'She let me down very badly over something involving a poor young girl who was living here. Someone Alfie and I had grown very fond of.'

'You're talking of Rachel,' said Sophie. 'So it must be the fact that Sally never told you Rachel was pregnant.'

'You knew about it too?! I must have been the only one around here who *didn't*!'

'The reason Sally kept it from you was because Rachel made her promise not to tell you. Sally isn't a girl who would break a promise. I'd have thought you would know how trustworthy she is; she was working for you for quite some time.'

'If it hadn't been for her, Rachel might still be alive today.'

'That's not true,' said Sophie. 'Rachel was desperate to get rid of the baby without you finding out. Sally didn't agree with her. She tried to persuade her to tell you. She felt you *ought* to know. As it was, when Rachel refused point blank, Sally tried to help her get rid of the baby by taking something. She even asked me to speak to the Scots fisherwomen down on the fish quay, to see if they knew of any way it could be done. When nothing worked, she warned Rachel that if she didn't forget all about trying to get rid of the baby, she'd end up in the hands of someone like the old abortionist who lives in one of the houses behind Pin's Lane.'

'An abortionist lives there? Who is she, do you know her name?'

'No, but I do know that Sally would have done anything to prevent what happened. She thought the world of Rachel. To punish her on top of all that happened is very unfair. She must have been very hurt. I'm going to Pin's Lane now, to see if she's there.'

When Sophie had left the shop, Alfie said to Grace, 'She's right you know, Grace. We've been very unfair to young Sally, in more ways than one. You treated her almost like a daughter before Rachel came along. Then you shifted your affection, although young Sally never changed. She never became jealous, as many other young girls might have done. In fact, she was delighted that Rachel had found someone to love and care for her. She cared and tried to protect her too, as best she could. The way we treated Sally must have been very hurtful to the girl.'

'I still think she should have told me what was going on,' Grace said defensively.

'Do you, Grace? Even though she'd given her word?

I think it shows just how fond of Rachel she was. It would have been an opportunity for her to ingratiate herself with you by breaking Rachel's trust. She didn't.' Aware that his words were having an effect on her, Alfie continued, 'You were always the one to tell me Sally deserved a chance – and you were right. Now it's you who are denying her that.'

Turning away from him, Grace went back into the kitchen without saying a word in reply.

For perhaps twenty minutes the sounds of pots and pans could be heard as she cooked, washed and cleared up. Then she appeared from behind the bamboo curtain once more.

Less belligerently than before, she asked, 'Do you really believe I behaved so badly towards Sally, Alfie? I was terribly hurt that she didn't tell me about poor Rachel's condition, you know.'

'No, Grace. You were hurt because you allowed yourself to grow very fond of Rachel and you lost her, just as we did our Mary. You wanted someone to blame and you turned on Sally, even though it wasn't her fault. She did the right thing by Rachel.'

'If you thought that, why didn't you say something to me at the time?'

'You weren't ready to listen to anything anyone said to you then, Grace. Besides, I knew you would come round to seeing things right, sooner or later.'

'Losing Rachel did hurt, Alfie. I haven't felt pain like that since . . . since we lost our Mary.'

'I know.' Alfie put a comforting arm about his wife's shoulders. 'It upset me too. More than you'll ever know. But I think you ought to do the right thing by Sally now. After all, we have each other. She's had no one she could turn to, has she? Not since she believed she'd lost young Ethan too.'

'Are you telling me I should go and find her and tell her I'm sorry?'

'I'm not *telling* you anything Grace. I don't think I need to. No one could ever take the place of our Mary. I'm not at all sure either of us really wants them to – but one thing I do know. In all the time she was working for us, young Sally did many a good turn for us – and never a bad one.'

Grace was silent for some minutes, then she said, 'You're quite right, of course, Alfie. There's no one knows me better than you.' Close to tears, she asked, 'What do you think I ought to do?'

'You don't really need me to tell you that either, Grace. Go and find Sally. Tell her you're sorry. You'll never have a better opportunity than today. If she's at the Salvation Army house with that woman captain you'll be able to tell her that Ethan's safe after all. For being the bearer of such news I don't doubt she'd forgive you anything.'

Dabbing at her eyes with a corner of her apron, Grace gave him a watery smile. 'Bless you, Alfie. I don't know what I ever did to deserve a man like you, I'm sure. Whatever it was, I'll always be grateful for it. You're quite right. I'll go and find Sally, tell her the wonderful news of her young man and say I'm sorry for what I said and did to her. I'll try to put things right between us.'

She started to untie her apron. Startled, Alfie said, 'You're going right this minute?'

'You know me, Alfie. I don't waste any time once I've made up my mind to do something. Besides, as you said yourself, I ought to put things right as soon as I can – and there's no time like the present.'

For a moment it seemed Alfie might argue with her, then he shrugged his shoulders. 'All right, Grace. You do whatever you feel is best. The sooner we have her back here working for us, the better it will be for everyone. It will make the loss of a few hours of business worthwhile.'

Arriving at the Refuge, Grace asked first after Sally, then for Captain Eva.

She received the same reply in respect of each of them, as had Ian Lovat, and from the same young woman.

The young Salvation Army lieutenant added, 'I don't know why the two of them are so popular today.'

'Why, who else has been asking for them?' Grace thought that perhaps Sophie Shields had called at the Refuge.

'It was a detective inspector. He seemed very agitated to find they had both gone.'

'Ian Lovat? What did he want with them?'

More cautiously, the young lieutenant said, 'I don't know and I couldn't tell him any more than I'm telling you now.'

Sensing a mystery, Grace asked, 'Are Captain Eve and Sally off somewhere together? When are you expecting them back?'

'They didn't leave together. More than that I can't tell you, Mrs Philpott. Although I do know they won't be back tonight.'

Grace was not satisfied with the Salvation Army officer's reply, but she was aware she would learn nothing more here. She would go and find Ian Lovat.

78

Once Grace Philpott took the bit between her teeth, she was not an easy woman to be diverted from any chosen course. Like Ian Lovat, she suspected something was going on that involved both Captain Eva and young Sally.

Believing, quite rightly, that she knew what it was all about, Grace was thoroughly alarmed.

She knew how passionately Captain Eva felt about the scandalous trade in providing English girls for prostitution on the Continent. She would not be above taking unjustified risks involving herself – and others. Determined to put a stop to the trade, she would count the cost later.

Grace already knew from various conversations with Captain Eva of the most recent advertisements placed in regional newspapers. Sally's place in Captain Eva's scheme was less clear, but she looked younger than her years and it did not take an intellectual to work out the part she was best suited to play.

The knowledge that her own actions might have

prompted Sally to take such an active and dangerous role did not make Grace feel any more comfortable about what she believed was going on.

Sally had gone through a thoroughly miserable time. First losing her sister, then believing Ethan had been lost at sea and finally being thrown out of work and blamed for the death of Rachel, the girl she had helped and befriended.

Grace was an explosive, emotional woman, but she was also fair-minded, and was honest enough with herself to accept she had unfairly laid the blame upon Sally for what had happened to Rachel.

She was determined that Sally would come to no harm as a result.

Detective Inspector Ian Lovat was, of course, not at the police headquarters. Despite Grace's insistence that she needed to speak to him as a matter of great urgency, she could learn nothing of his whereabouts.

Eventually, quietly fuming at the frustration of having to deal with unhelpful policemen, she left the building. Outside the main entrance, she was startled to see her uncle being escorted to his carriage by a tall, distinguished-looking man, who was wearing a uniform Grace did not immediately recognise as being that of Plymouth's Chief Constable.

'Uncle Percy!'

The chairman of the Police Authority turned to see Grace calling out his name as she hurried towards him.

'You're just the man I want to see.'

If Percy Mallett felt a momentary sinking feeling at her words, he did not allow it to show. 'Grace! You're the last person I expected to meet here. What are you doing at Police Headquarters?' Suddenly remembering his manners, he introduced her to the man who was seeing him off the premises. 'Grace, may I introduce Chief Constable Frost? Chief Constable, this is Grace Philpott, my neice.'

The two shook hands and Grace said, 'I came here looking for Ian Lovat, but he's nowhere to be found. No one in there . . .' she jerked her head contemptuously towards the building she had just left, 'seems to know where he is.'

The chief constable smiled. 'I think I can answer your question, Mrs Philpott. Detective Inspector has gone to Falmouth. He took passage on a naval vessel this afternoon.'

'Falmouth? Why Falmouth? Is that where Captain Eva and Sally are?'

Now it was the turn of the chief constable to appear startled. 'Captain Eva Cassington, of the Salvation Army? I know nothing of what she might be doing – and I doubt if Inspector Lovat does. He has gone there in the hope of arresting a man who is wanted on warrant in this city.'

Grace was disappointed. She had felt certain Ian Lovat would have learned what Captain Eva was up to and left the city in search of her.

Suddenly, she said, 'This wanted man . . . what's his name?'

For a moment it seemed the chief constable would refuse to give her an answer, but he saw that Percy Mallett was interested too.

'His name is Sidney Darling. He's wanted for questioning about a serious assault on a young girl.'

'Sid Darling's mixed up in far more than assaults on girls, I can tell you that for nothing,' Grace said vehemently. To her uncle, she said, 'I think Captain Eva might have used Sally to answer one of those advertisements, offering young girls attractive posts in domestic service and giving them a Falmouth address to reply to. But domestic service isn't where they're going to end up. What's more, if Sid Darling's there he must be mixed up in this. Sally will be in grave danger. Sid Darling knows her – and he has a score to settle. If Captain Eva had known Sid Darling was involved she'd never have gone ahead with this.'

'Are you certain of what you're saying, Grace . . . ?'

'I'm not certain of anything, but Sally and Captain Eva aren't at the Refuge – and Ian Lovat's gone to Falmouth because he believes Sid Darling's there. It all hangs together a little too well for my liking.'

Percy Mallett was thoughtful for a few moments, then he nodded his head. 'You're probably right, Grace. This could be extremely serious.'

Successfully hiding the irritation he felt, the chief constable said, 'Would you care to tell me exactly what is going on? Or, at least, what is *believed* to be going on?'

Grace was the first to answer him. 'Sid Darling is a very dangerous man who is heavily involved in shipping unsuspecting young girls to brothels on the Continent. You remember the scandalous case we had in Plymouth at the end of last year? It's the reason a warrant was sworn out for Sid Darling. The trade has being going on for a very long time. Captain Eva is absolutely determined to stamp it out. It's highly probable she's connived at having a young girl reply to the advertisement in order to expose the whole thing and put a stop to it.'

'If she has taken such a course of action then she is behaving in a highly irresponsible manner! Matters such as this are best left to the police to deal with.' Chief Constable Frost was indignant.

'Perhaps – but at least she's doing *something*. What are *you* doing to bring this trade to an end?' Grace issued the challenge to him.

'If someone can provide evidence that it really is going on here, in Plymouth, I will order that action be taken immediately,' replied the chief constable.

'Where it's happening doesn't matter a great deal if you're one of the girls being shipped to a brothel in France or Belgium. As for the evidence . . . no doubt that's what Captain Eva is gathering right now.'

Turning to her uncle, Grace asked, 'What can we do to help? Can we get to Falmouth tonight?'

'We won't be able to travel there today, Grace. Why not telegraph a warning about Sid Darling to the Salvation Army in Falmouth? They could probably warn Captain Eva.'

'We might already be too late,' declared a very worried Grace. 'I'd be much happier if I were there myself.'

'By the time a telegram reaches Falmouth, Inspector Lovat should already be there,' said the chief constable. 'He's a very capable and resourceful man. He'll sort things out, I have no doubt at all – but I will send a telegram to the chief constable of Cornwall, requesting that he gives Lovat every possible assistance.'

'Ian Lovat doesn't even know what Sid Darling looks like,' retorted Grace. 'I do. We'll send a telegram – and hope the man in charge of the Salvation Army at

Falmouth knows what's going on. But I can't leave it there. If we've heard nothing by morning I'm going too – and I know who'll help me get there. The fishermen down at Sutton Harbour were absolutely incensed at what was going on when Sally foiled Sid Darling and his gang before. One of them will take me, I'm certain of it. Uncle Percy, will you drive me to the telegraph office, then I'll go down to the harbour . . .'

'I will!' Percy Mallett was suddenly enthusiastic. 'What's more, if you make this journey tomorrow, I'll come with you.'

'I'll see that you are kept fully informed of developments, Mr Mallett. Hopefully, the matter will be fully resolved by morning and save you an unnecessary journey.'

'You'll do more than that, Chief Constable. If this matter puts an end to this vile trade, you'll add Inspector Lovat's name to the next promotion list – and I'll ensure that he is selected.'

79

It had been a confusing time for Ethan and the male members of his family. When the *Mermaid* collided with the warship events happened so speedily the fishermen had had no time for fear. No time for anything except survival.

The *Mermaid* had been fishing south of the Isles of Scilly on her own. Most of the other boats had given up all hope of a good catch. Bringing in their nets, they had set a course for Plymouth.

There was a heavy sea mist in the area. This not only prevented the lookout on HMS *Roarer* from seeing them, but also muffled the sound of the warship's engines. By the time the crew of the *Mermaid* realised a ship was bearing down on them it was too late to take action to avoid a collision.

The iron warship cut the fishing boat virtually in half and it sank within minutes. Ethan jumped over the side only moments before HMS *Roarer* ploughed into the smaller vessel. His father and two of his brothers did the same.

The other brothers made their escape from the stricken fishing boat moments later, but Joe was struck by a piece of broken mast and was floundering in the water with a broken arm.

Swimming to the aid of his brother, Ethan towed him to a piece of floating wreckage. This soon became a focal point for each member of the family.

Fortunately, the warship's lookout had spotted the fishing boat seconds before the collision. Although his shouted warning came too late to avoid disaster, it meant that HMS *Roarer* came to a halt almost immediately. A boat was quickly lowered to rescue the fishermen and take them on board.

While the ship's surgeon set Joe's arm, the others were lent dry clothing. Then they were given liberal tots of rum, which served to warm them and lessen the shock of losing their boat.

The Plymouth men were made to feel very welcome on board the warship. The commanding officer and Henry Shields were also able to agree on a joint report of the collision. It would be filed when the warship docked at Gibraltar for coaling.

Before this occurred, they met up with a passenger-carrying steamship. The *Eastern Prince* was bound for Falmouth, from the Far East. At the request of the warship's commanding officer, the other vessel's captain agreed to take the seven shipwrecked men on board.

The fishermen were transferred when both vessels were off the coast of Portugal, after the warship's captain promised that a telegraph message would be sent to Doris Shields when he reached Gibraltar.

Unfortunately, the warship was intercepted by a small naval sailing vessel when still some miles from its destination and sent to North Africa, to demand the release of a number of sailors shipwrecked and imprisoned there. As a result the telegram to Doris Shields was not sent until much later than was anticipated.

The fishermen's voyage home took quite a long time, too, the steamship making two ports of call before reaching Falmouth. As a result, Ethan and the others found themselves exploring the streets of Bilbao in Spain and, later, Brest in France, before reaching England.

They had little money in their pockets when the *Mermaid* went down, but the passengers on the ship that had taken them on board had made a collection. Enough money was donated to enable the shipwrecked fishermen to purchase a number of lace handkerchiefs in Brest as presents for Doris, Sophie and Sally.

It was with great excitement that the seven Plymouth men caught their first glimpse of the Cornish coast at The Lizard, on their return. They were not on the main deck with the other passengers, having been invited to the bridge.

They shared their privileged vantage point with the captain and a pilot, as the steamship nosed its way past Black Rock and turned to enter Falmouth's sheltered harbour.

Each of the men was occupied with his own thoughts. Believing that Doris had known for some time that he and the others were safe, Henry Shields was already thinking ahead to the type of fishing boat he would purchase with the money he expected to collect from the insurer of his boat.

With the additional compensation he had been told

he might expect from the Royal Navy, he hoped to be able to purchase a steam-trawler. His recent experiences had convinced him that this was where the future lay for all men who earned a living from the sea.

Ethan was looking forward to being with Sally once more. He hoped she had been worried about his absence – but not *too* much. Sally would have been relieved had she known that he had completely forgotten about the 'quarrel' that had so played upon her mind.

Suddenly, as the ship edged slowly towards its berth, Ethan frowned. Pointing to a large trawler moored alongside a small jetty, away from most of the other shipping, he said to the others, 'Look! Do any of you recognise that boat?'

There was some shaking of heads before Joe said, 'It looks like that Belgian fishing boat we had in Sutton harbour. The one that had young Rachel and the others on board. What was it called, can anyone remember?'

'It was the *Astique*,' Ethan replied. 'And it certainly looks like the same boat.'

'I can't say I know the name, but it's Belgian all right,' confirmed the pilot. 'They came in late yesterday. Didn't want a pilot and asked for a quiet berth. Said they had a few problems and wanted space to spread their gear out. I reckon they must have had a day off today, though, there's not been much sign of anyone doing any work.'

'I doubt if you'll see any work being done,' Ethan said, tight-faced. 'Not if it's the boat I think it is. I doubt if it'll be there come morning, either.'

The conversation with the pilot came to an end at this point. A large sailing vessel was leaving port and the pilot of the steamship soundly cursed the man at the helm of the other vessel as he was forced to stop engines and make a series of complicated manoeuvres in order to avoid the risk of a collision.

Minutes later the seven fishermen clattered down the ladder to the main deck as the steamship prepared to come alongside the quay.

The Shields family had been lent sufficient money to make their way to Plymouth by train. All were anxious to get home. Henry and Albert Shields, in particular, were eager to be reunited with their wives.

Ethan was anxious to see Sally again, but the boat moored alongside the Falmouth quay bothered him greatly. When he set foot on dry land, he looked across to where the Belgian vessel was moored and reached a sudden decision.

'I'm not happy seeing that boat there. If I don't do something about it, I'll forever wonder what it's up to. I'm going across to have a look at it. If is the *Astique* I'm going to the police.'

'Now don't get mixed up in anything,' cautioned his father. 'We've had enough excitement to last us a lifetime these past few weeks. Besides, I want to get home to your ma. She'll know we're safe, but that won't stop her worrying.'

'I don't suppose it will take me long,' said Ethan. 'I'm as anxious to be home as you are – but I wouldn't forgive myself if it's the *Astique* and its crew were up to their usual tricks and I did nothing about it. Hopefully I'll be proven wrong and be with you in time to catch the same train.'

'I'll come with you, Ethan,' Joe said unexpectedly. 'I can't do much with this broken arm, but I can keep you company – and if they're at all suspicious they wouldn't expect trouble from someone with his arm in plaster.'

80

The fishing boat was indeed the *Astique* and a couple of men dressed as fishermen were standing talking on deck. Ethan thought they had most probably been posted as lookouts.

Fortunately, as Joe had predicted, they saw nothing sinister in two young men, one with a broken arm encased in plaster of Paris, walking on the quayside. Once past the foreign boat, the two brothers pretended to gaze out to sea from the end of the quay, before strolling back towards the town again.

When trouble came, it was not from the men on the trawler. Ethan and Joe were clear of the jetty and out of sight of the trawler when they were stopped by two men who emerged from a nearby building they had thought to be empty.

'What were you doing along there on the quay?' One of the men put the unexpected question to them.

Uncertain who the men were, Ethan said, 'Nothing in particular. Just taking a walk.'

'I shouldn't have thought there was much to see,'

commented the second man. 'Nothing that couldn't be better seen from elsewhere – unless, of course, you have an interest in the Belgian boat?'

When neither of the Shields brothers made any reply, the first man said to his companion, 'Do you think Mr Lovat would be interested in them?'

Ethan seized upon the name immediately, 'Are you talking of Ian Lovat? Inspector Ian Lovat?'

'You know him?' The first man put the question to Ethan.

'Yes – and if he's interested in the *Astique* I'd like to get a message to him.'

Both men looked at each other and the older of the two nodded. 'All right, I'll take you to him.'

To his companion, he said, 'You stay here. I'll be back as soon as I can.'

They did not have very far to walk. Ian Lovat and a Cornwall Constabulary inspector had taken over a room in the main customs building, close to the harbour-side.

Ian Lovat was seated at a table talking when the three men entered the room and he got to his feet immediately, an expression of delight on his face.

'Ethan! What are you doing here? Everyone in Plymouth feared you and your family were lost at sea! It was even reported in the newspapers . . .'

'We were sunk by a warship and have just arrived back on a steamship – but explanations can wait. As we came in I saw a Belgian fishing boat. Joe and I have just been down to take a closer look. It's the one we took the girls off, in Sutton harbour.'

'I thought it was!' Ian Lovat glanced at the Falmouth policeman triumphantly. 'That's why we're having it watched.' Suddenly, his expression changed and he became serious. 'There was another advertisement in the newspapers, offering posts in domestic service to young girls. Captain Eva decided she would take the opportunity to show these people up for what they really are. She has the support of the editor of one of the London newspapers. We believe she's out there somewhere, probably watching a house where they've taken the girls.'

'Good for her,' declared Ethan. 'It's time someone acted to put a stop to what's going on . . . But you said she's *probably* watching a house. Don't you know for sure? Aren't you working with her?'

Ian Lovat shook his head. 'She didn't tell me of her plans because she knew I didn't approve of her getting mixed up in something like this. This is work for the police, not for an organisation like the Salvation Army.'

Ethan shrugged. 'The police don't seem to have put themselves out to do anything about it in the past. I'm with Captain Eva.'

'You might change your mind when you hear the full story – or as much of it as I know. It would appear she's sent someone along pretending to want to go into domestic service to learn what's going on. That someone is Sally.'

Ethan's mouth dropped open and his expression turned to one of horror. 'Sally? But why? Why should she want to do something like this?'

'That's a long story too, Ethan. Briefly, Sally thought she had lost you, then young Rachel discovered she was pregnant, found someone to abort her – and died as a result. Grace Philpott blamed Sally and dismissed her from the shop.'

'Oh my God! What a mess. Poor Sally.'

'I'm afraid it's not just *poor* Sally. I believe her life is in very real danger,' Ian Lovat said grimly. 'It's probable that Sid and Mother Darling are mixed up in this business – just as they were before – and, of course, they both know Sally.'

Ethan looked at Ian Lovat aghast. 'If Sid Darling gets his hands on Sally he'll kill her. What are you doing about it – and where's Sally now?'

'There's very little we can do right at this moment. We don't know where anyone is – although it's certain all the girls are somewhere in the Falmouth area. The Salvation Army officer in charge of this area is helping Captain Eva – but he seems to have disappeared too. Our only hope is the boat. I wasn't a hundred per cent certain it was the right one until you confirmed it. All we can do now is keep the boat under observation and move in when the moment is right. That means, when the girls are taken there.'

'But what about Sid Darling? He wouldn't think twice of killing Sally if he believed it might help to save him. Where is he?'

'I wish I could answer that, Ethan. I can't. We must hope he's on the boat with the fishermen.'

'But what if he isn't? What if he's ashore somewhere – in the same house as Sally? You know what he did to Rachel. He could be doing the same to Sally . . .' Ethan's voice broke as he thought of the unthinkable.

'We can do no more for now, Ethan. It won't be long until it's dark. As soon as it is we'll move off to the jetty where the Belgian boat's moored. If luck is with us we'll have this whole thing wrapped up within the next few hours and everyone will be where they ought to be. That includes Sid Darling.'

As he pulled up chairs for the two Plymouth fishermen, Ian Lovat tried not to think of what might happen if luck was *not* on their side.

81

Outside the house high on the hill above Falmouth harbour, where Sally and the other girls were being held, Captain Eva waited in hiding with the Falmouth Salvation Army officers and those who had accompanied her from Plymouth, as the sun sank over the distant horizon and gaslights illuminated the streets and houses of the town.

It was now that Eva expected the girls to be taken from the house to a waiting boat, while it was still early enough for a closed van being drawn through the streets not to excite attention.

As time passed and nothing happened, Eva began to feel uneasy. She shared her thoughts with the Falmouth commanding officer.

'I don't like this. It's too quiet. I would have expected things to be happening by now.'

'The girls must still be inside the house. Nothing has arrived to take them away.'

Eva entertained her own thoughts on the matter, but she did not want to say anything at the moment.

They continued to keep watch on the house until one

of the Plymouth Salvationists said, 'Look! The lights are going out on the ground floor. It seems the girls are about to be moved.'

'I don't think so,' Eva replied grimly. 'If you ask me, I'd say that whoever is in the house is preparing for bed.'

'You mean . . . they're going to keep the girls in the house overnight?' The question came from the Falmouth commanding officer.

'No. I believe we're wasting our time here. We've been tricked. I think the girls have already gone.' Eva made the statement with a sick feeling in the pit of her stomach. If the girls *had* been taken from the house it meant that her planned exposé had gone disastrously wrong. Not only would she have failed to prevent the unsuspecting girls from being abducted, but she had been responsible for sending Sally off with them.

'There must be something we can do to find out.' The voice of the Falmouth commanding officer broke into her tortured thoughts.

'Yes. We'll call on whoever is in the house right now and try to learn what's going on.'

'But if the girls are still in there all your plans will have come to nothing.'

'If we find the girls inside the house I'll fall on my knees and thank the Lord,' said Eva. 'But I fear He'll be hearing only a *plea* from me tonight.'

By the time Captain Eva, accompanied by a number of fellow Salvationists, reached the door of the house, the light in the front hall had been extinguished. Eva's repeated knocking brought a slow response. Eventually, she could hear the grumbling of a woman as she descended the stairs, holding a lighted candle.

When the woman reached the door, she called out, 'Who is it? What do you want at this time of the night?'

'It's the Salvation Army. I want to talk to you.'

'Can't it wait until morning? I was about to go to bed.'

'No, it can't wait. If you don't open the door now I'll call on the police and have them break it down.'

There was more grumbling from inside the house. Then there was the sound of a bolt being drawn. When the door opened, an elderly woman stood in the doorway, holding a candle aloft.

'*You!* What are you doing here?' Eva's worst fears were realised as she saw Mother Darling standing before her.

'I might ask the same of you, dearie. You seem to make a habit of disturbing folk late at night.'

Mother Darling's response appeared to be that of a reasonable woman indignant at being disturbed. The commanding officer of the Falmouth Salvation Army looked at Captain Eva uncertainly.

'I think you know why we're here, Mrs Darling. Where are the girls?'

'Girls? I don't know what you're talking about, dearie. I'm here for the sake of my health. It isn't what it used to be and I need to get away from Plymouth every so often. As for girls . . . I suppose you want to search the house, same as you did in Plymouth. Well, you're quite welcome, I'm sure – but you can be quite certain that I'll be lodging a complaint with the police tomorrow. I'm not having you following me around the country, forcing yourself into my house late at night whenever you've got nothing better to do. Well, are you coming in? I'm not standing out here all night, catching me death of cold just to talk to you.'

Captain Eva knew instinctively there would be nothing to find inside the house. At that moment, a hand tugged at her sleeve. It was Zulu Joe. He motioned for her to follow him.

She turned away and hurried after the African Salvationist without another word to Mother Darling.

As the door closed behind the evil old woman, those still standing outside could hear Mother Darling chuckling to herself as she drove home the bolt on the door. She was convinced she had once more outwitted the Salvation Army officer from Plymouth.

82

When Zulu Joe showed Captain Eva the hidden gate leading from the garden of the house, a sense of panic threatened to engulf her.

Not only had she and the other Salvation Army watchers been tricked, but – far more seriously – the Darlings were part of the operation and they knew Sally's true identity.

Sally was in grave danger. It took a very real effort on Eva's part to control her fear and to think effectively.

'What shall we do?' Less directly involved than his Plymouth colleague, the Falmouth commanding officer was nevertheless concerned. If things had gone seriously wrong, Captain Eva would face the full wrath of the Salvation Army's explosive leader, but he too would suffer censure.

'You must call on every man and woman you can muster. Tell them to go out on the waterfront. Speak to anyone who might know something. We're looking for a boat that isn't what it's purported to be. Most probably it will be a foreign one. I believe it will probably be Belgian. It will be moored alongside, probably somewhere quiet. It will certainly be well away from other boats and clear of busy areas.'

'What are you going to do?'

'I'm going to the police station to speak to the officer in charge. When I see him I'll confess to everything I've done and ask for his assistance.'

'What of all your plans – and your own future? This could put an end to everything to which you've devoted your whole life.'

'I knew what I was putting at risk when I took this action. What I foolishly didn't realise was the sacrifices others might need to make. It's become far too serious for concern about what happens to *me*. We have to try to save these girls – Sally especially. If anything has happened to her I will never be at peace with myself again.'

In the Falmouth house that served as a small police station, the constable on duty did not appear to take very seriously Captain Eva's request to see a senior police officer. There was little sense of urgency, until a man came in who introduced himself to her as the 'Superintendent of Police'.

It was now Eva realised why it had been so difficult to convince the constable that a serious crime was taking place in the town. The Superintendent told her the Falmouth police force comprised only himself and two constables. His own somewhat grandiose title meant nothing. Before being placed in charge of the borough police 'force', he had been the town's watchman!

Eva was dismayed. Sally and the other girls had

probably been taken to a boat crewed by tough Belgian seamen. It would take more than three policemen and a handful of Salvation Army officers to prevent them from setting sail.

However, the 'superintendent' persuaded her to tell him what was happening. She had hardly begun the story before he interrupted her.

'Ah! We heard something about such goings-on and realised it was too much for us to handle. As soon as I learned about it, I sent a telegraph message off to Cornwall's Chief Constable. He's sent men to help and more are following.'

'Thank heaven for that!' exclaimed Eva. Then, puzzled, she asked, 'But . . . how did you come to hear about what was happening?'

'I think the best person to answer all such questions would be that Inspector Lovat, from Plymouth.'

'Ian Lovat is here, in Falmouth?' Eva's bewilderment increased with each piece of information she received from the Falmouth policeman.

'That's right, he's at Customs House, down on the quay. I'll take you there.'

Outside, Eva gave the briefest explanation to Zulu Joe as they followed the policeman through the town, heading for the dockside area.

On the way they learned that only six or seven county policemen had so far arrived in the town. Eva said nothing, but she believed it would be far too small a force to prevent the Belgians from carrying off the girls.

The party had almost reached its destination when they became aware of a great commotion, somewhere along the sea front, to the south of the customs quay.

'That sounds as though it's coming from where the Belgian fishing boat is moored,' the Falmouth policeman commented. 'Inspector Lovat was very interested in that boat. I believe he sent two of the Bodmin men to watch it.'

'If it's a Belgian boat, that'll be where the girls will have been taken,' said Eva, alarmed by the disturbing sound that could be heard. 'Let's get down there quickly and see if we can help.'

She began to run, with Zulu Joe at her side. This in itself was hazardous. The quay was ill-lit and small boats, piles of rope and other obstructions were strewn all about them.

The Falmouth policeman paused to light a bull's-eye lantern he was carrying, before hurrying after the others.

Suddenly, as they neared the spot where the *Astique* was moored, they heard the sound of a shot – then another! Eva went cold. If the Belgians were carrying arms there was no chance at all of preventing them from carrying out their intentions.

It seemed others thought so too. The shouting ceased, although excited voices could still be heard.

Just then, someone came running towards them. The policeman shone his lamp ahead and the light picked out a rough-looking man dressed as a fisherman.

'Stop! Stop right where you are!' The policeman ran to obstruct the fleeing man, but the man, desperate to get away, struck and knocked the policeman to one side. The man continued running.

The policeman's lantern had fallen to the ground, but the darkness did not deter Zulu Joe. He succeeded where the police 'superintendent' had failed. The would-be escapist was wrestled to the ground. He fought furiously and although he could not escape from his silent captor, he succeeded in regaining his feet.

Zulu Joe grappled with him and both men staggered to the edge of the quay.

'Look out!'

Eva's cry of warning came too late. Both men fell from sight and there was a loud splash as they hit the water.

By now, the Falmouth policeman had regained his feet. Locating his lantern, he relit it. Standing at the water's edge, Eva called, 'Quick. Bring the lantern here.'

The policeman joined Captain Eva and, in the yellow light of the lantern, they were able to pick out Zulu Joe, treading water.

There was no sign of the other man.

'Over here.' The policeman shone the lamp towards a metal ladder, secured to the quay wall, and Zulu Joe swam in that direction.

When Zulu Joe was safely ashore, the policeman swept the water with the beam from his lamp, but there was no sign of the other man.

'Let's get along to the boat and see what's happening there,' said Eva. 'I'm concerned for the girls. Those gun shots . . .'

'Be careful,' warned the policeman. 'If someone is shooting, it will be dangerous for you.'

'Whoever it is, it can't be the Belgians,' Eva pointed out. 'Otherwise the man who fell in the water wouldn't have been so anxious to make his escape. Let's go and find out what's going on.'

At the boat's moorings there was a number of men carrying lanterns, which were shone in the direction of the newcomers as they approached. Among those about the boat was a group of red-jacketed Royal Marines – and these were the men who were carrying arms.

Captain Eva could not imagine how British Marines had become involved in what was going on. However, it was evident they had played an important part in turning the tables in favour of the policemen.

'So you've finally put in an appearance!' Ian Lovat's words were directed at Eva from the darkness behind one of the lanterns. 'It's a good job we were here, or your little plan was likely to have gone horribly wrong.'

Captain Eva ignored the implied criticism in his words. There were a great many questions she wanted to ask him, but for now she posed the one that was uppermost in her mind. 'Do you have the girls?'

'We have. They're all a bit dozey – from some form of drug, I suspect. A few are still only semi-conscious but as far as I can make out they haven't been harmed. We won't know for certain until they are able to speak sensibly to us.'

'Is Sally with them?'

'She is.'

'Thank God!' It came out as a mere whisper, but the two words could not have been more meaningful. 'Where is she now? Can I see her?'

'Of course.'

Despite his earlier implied criticism, Ian knew exactly how Eva was feeling. In fact, he knew far more about the real person who chose to hide behind the Salvation Army uniform than she realised.

'She's being taken care of by Ethan.'

'ETHAN?!' For just a moment, Captain Eva thought the

Plymouth detective had gone out of his mind. 'But . . .
he's been lost at sea.'

'Well, now he's been found. You've got a whole lot
of catching up to do, Eva.'

It was the first time he had used her Christian name
without preceding it with her Salvation Army rank, but
she hardly noticed.

'Is Sally aware that he's with her?'

'I don't think so. For some reason, she appears to be
far more heavily drugged than the others.'

'That would be Mother Darling's doing. She was at
the house where the girls were taken. She must have
recognised Sally. The poor girl.'

'It would have been far more serious than "poor girl"
had we not got on to this in time. You shouldn't have
tried to do this on you own, Eva. It could have had
disastrous results for everyone concerned.'

'I do realise that now,' she admitted, displaying an
uncharacteristic humility. 'But how did you learn about
it?'

'We've been keeping watch on Mother Darling for
some time. She was seen to take a train from Plymouth,
bound for Falmouth – and here we are. Unfortunately,
we don't appear to have captured Sid Darling, although
I'm convinced he was involved in this too. Unfortunately, one of the men from the boat managed to escape;
I have an uncomfortable feeling it might have been him.'

'I doubt if he's still alive – whoever he is.' Eva pointed
to Zulu Joe who was dripping water and shivering. She
told Ian Lovat of the fight.

'It's a great pity we didn't get him, if only to be certain
who he is. It might have been one of the Belgians for all
we know. All we'll ever know, perhaps.'

Zulu Joe touched Eva's arm. When she looked at him, he shook his head. Touching his lips, he pointed first to the Salvationist, then to the policeman.

'Zulu Joe is saying the man he fought with spoke English.'

'Then it probably *was* Sid Darling. I'll have boats put out to see if we can find him – or his body. If he's drowned it will save everyone a great deal of trouble.'

'At least we've recovered Sally safely. You shouldn't have let her take part in your scheme, Captain Eva. It was only the sheerest luck that she isn't on her way to Belgium right now – with Sid Darling.'

Ethan came out of the darkness to direct his fairly gentle criticism at Eva.

When she had hugged him tightly and said how happy she was that he was safe, Eva said, 'I'm sorry about what happened to Sally, Ethan – but, as you said, she is safe, although I still don't know what's going on right now. It seems to become more confusing by the minute.'

'It's becoming clearer,' said Ethan. 'One of the policemen speaks French. He's been questioning the Belgians. It seems Sid Darling *did* come here as a member of the crew of the Belgian fishing boat. When Inspector Lovat signalled for the Marines to come in and help arrest the crew of the fishing boat, he made a bolt for it. We'll talk about the rest later. I want to get back to Sally. I don't think she'll come round for another hour or more, but I mean to be with her when she does.'

83

Sally came to her senses slowly and painfully, in a darkened room. As she had never been intoxicated, she did not recognise her symptoms as those of a hangover, exacerbated by the drug that had been added to the wine.

She groaned. Her head felt as though knuckles were being kneaded into her temples and waves of nausea threatened to overwhelm her.

She was about to groan once more, consciously this time, when memories flooded back. She remembered the Falmouth house – and Mother Darling forcing drugged wine down her throat. There were less clear memories of a bumpy and uncomfortable ride in a van.

That had been her final memory. The knowledge that she and the others were being taken somewhere. Probably to a boat that would transport them to a brothel in Europe . . . But where was she now? Surely they had not arrived at their destination? She could not believe she had been unconscious for such a length of time.

Feeling about her, she ascertained she was lying on a bed. She could also hear voices somewhere in the distance. Sally could not understand what they were saying and for a few moments imagined they were talking in a foreign language. If so, she *must* have arrived at the European destination.

Then, as Sally focused on the voices, she realised she could not understand what they were saying because they were coming from some distance away. Probably from a downstairs room. It was distance, not another language, that made it impossible for her to understand the conversation.

Despite the throbbing pain in her head, Sally tried hard to concentrate on the voices. They were definitely speaking English.

That at least was something in her favour. If she could make good her escape she would not be in a strange country. She might be able to call for help from someone nearby.

There was a moment of panic as she imagined the voices to be those of Sid and Mother Darling and their accomplices.

The thought brought her sitting upright much faster than was wise in her present condition. The increased pain in her temples made her flinch, but her main thought now was of escape.

Although the room was in darkness, light was showing beneath the door. She would need to be cautious when she left the room.

She was summoning the will-power to swing her feet to the floor when she heard footsteps outside the room. They were followed by the sound of a hand on the door latch.

Flinging herself back on the bed, Sally closed her eyes and lay perfectly still.

Someone crossed the room towards her. Sally was aware that a light, probably from outside the room, was shining across her face. She tried to relax and breathe as though still unconscious.

She sensed it was a man standing beside the bed. He remained in the room for so long, she began to fear it would not be possible to keep up her pretence for very much longer. Then, to her great relief, he tiptoed away.

He had reached the door when a voice called from downstairs, 'Is there any sign of her coming round yet?'

The voice sounded familiar, but she was unable to identify it immediately.

The door closed before the man who had been in her room replied, 'She's still unconscious. I'm worried about her, Joe. I think I'll ask Captain Eva to call out the doctor again.'

The man who had called from the ground floor spoke once more. He did not think it necessary to call out the doctor, who would surely only repeat what he had said before – but Sally was not listening. She had recognised the voice of the man who had come to her room.

It was Ethan – and he was talking to his brother Joe.

For the briefest of moments, Sally wondered if she was hallucinating. Then, convinced she was not, she cried, 'Ethan! ETHAN!'

Scrambling from the bed, Sally headed towards the strip of light visible beneath the door. She was far more unsteady than she had realised. Veering seriously to one side of the door, she had great difficulty correcting her course.

'ETHAN!'

As she called to him once more, she crashed into a chair and stumbled to the floor. There was a moment of panic when she feared Ethan had not heard her and would go away from her again.

Then the door was flung open and Ethan stood in the doorway. It took a moment for him to locate her. Then he found her and was holding her close to him.

To her great distress, Sally suddenly began crying uncontrollably. As Ethan held her, she sobbed, 'I'm sorry, Ethan. Sorry we quarrelled before you went away.'

'Quarrelled? What quarrel? Anyway, it doesn't matter. Nothing matters now we're together again. Nothing at all.'

Sally clung to him, only vaguely aware people were crowding in the doorway of the bedroom. They were people she knew, but she could think of no explanation for them all being here together.

She recognised Ian Lovat, Captain Eva, the reporter from the London newspaper, whom she had met briefly in Plymouth, Joe Shields, Zulu Joe . . .

There were others too. Some in the uniform of the Salvation Army, others were policemen.

It was all too confusing. Sally clung to Ethan ever more tightly. There would need to be lengthy explanations later. For now it was enough to have Ethan with her. Safe and well – and *real*. Explanations could wait.

In the early hours of the morning, many of those who

had participated in the events of the night were crowded in the sitting room of the Falmouth Salvation Army chief, piecing together all that had happened.

Ethan's story had already been told. Ian Lovat's too. He had been aware of the pitifully small complement of the Falmouth police force, and had feared reinforcements from the County Police would not arrive in time. He had decided to take advantage of the admiral's offer to call on the services of the Royal Marines on board the vessel that had brought him to Falmouth, a decision that had decisively turned the tide of events in his favour. When the girls were seen to arrive on the jetty in the van, a signal had been flashed to the warship, moored offshore.

Minutes later, the Marines, who had been waiting in a steam launch, swarmed over the side of the Belgian steam-trawler. The fierce fight that ensued ended when the Sergeant of Marines ordered his men to fire two warning shots into the night air.

The girls, still suffering from the effects of the drugged wine, had been taken to the homes of various Salvation Army members.

Five of them, including Sally and Connie, were carried to the Salvation Army chief's home.

All had awakened frightened and bewildered. Recovering now, they sat with their rescuers and listened in wide-eyed silence to the story of how close they had come to being carried off to a life of degradation.

The girls felt great relief that the plans of Sid Darling and his colleagues had been foiled, but relief was accompanied by disappointment. They had left their homes in expectation of a new and more fulfilling life. Now their hopes had been dashed. For some, there could be no return to the life they had previously known.

One such girl was Connie.

The sharing of experiences came to an end when Eva told of her part in setting the wheels in motion in a bid to trap the would-be abductors. It was a plan that had been foiled by Mother Darling's appearance on the scene.

'What will happen to Mother Darling now?' asked Sally. 'Will she be put in prison for the part she's played?'

'Probably not,' admitted Ian Lovat. 'The men sent to arrest her say she's offered to turn Queen's Evidence and testify against her accomplices – including her son. I'd like to see her put away, but Sid Darling is my first priority. I have a dying declaration, given to me by Rachel. It will stand up in court, but we're going to need Mother Darling's evidence if we're to convict everyone of the charges that will be brought against them.'

Standing up, Ian Lovat stretched wearily. 'I think we all ought to go off and try to snatch some sleep now. There aren't many hours left in the night and we all have a busy day ahead of us tomorrow.' Smiling at Eva, he said, 'For a while I thought things were going to go wrong, but in the end everything happened just the way it should.'

'Thanks to you,' Eva admitted ruefully. 'If you hadn't become involved it would have been a total disaster. It's taught me a very serious lesson.'

'I'm glad it's all ended well for everyone,' the reporter from the London newspaper chipped in. 'As far as I'm concerned, I have the story of a lifetime. My editor is going to be delighted. We have a story that will be the envy of all the London newspapers. I have no doubt at all it will influence the men who make the laws of our country. The trade in young English girls may not come to an end immediately, but it will soon – thanks to all of you.'

'Talking of the law . . .' An inspector of the Cornwall Constabulary, who had been one of the last to arrive in Falmouth, now spoke to Ian Lovat. 'I have a man in custody in Bodmin who is asking to speak to you. He says he has some important information about a young Plymouth girl who died after an abortion.'

Aware of the glances that were exchanged between Ian Lovat, Captain Eva and Sally, the policeman continued, 'He obviously hopes you'll put in a good word for him, of course, but you might like to see him.'

'I most certainly would,' said Ian Lovat. 'What's his name?'

'Sanderson,' replied the Bodmin policeman. 'Robert Sanderson.'

84

Sally had been shaken by the news that her father was in custody, suspected of stealing from the home of his former employers, but it did not entirely surprise her.

She felt guilty that she had no wish to see him, but now that Ethan had been returned to her, she did not want to let him out of her sight. She was even reluctant to leave him when everyone snatched a couple of hours' sleep in the house of the Falmouth Salvation Army officer.

Once morning came and the young couple were reunited, Sally never left Ethan's side. With Captain Eva, Zulu Joe, Joe Shields and the Salvation Army 'soldiers', they caught a train first to Truro, then a connection to Plymouth.

Also with them was Connie.

Meanwhile, Ian Lovat was travelling in a carriage to Bodmin with the Cornwall Constabulary police inspector. Once there, he would learn exactly how much Robert Sanderson knew about the fatal abortion performed upon Rachel.

When the large party arrived in Plymouth, Ethan and Joe were anxious to be reunited with their mother. Sally had told them of Doris's refusal to accept that she had lost her entire family, despite the evidence of the wreckage found by the Lowestoft boat. Sally accompanied the brothers to their home.

Connie wanted to go with her new-found friend, but Eva took her instead to the Refuge. Here they encountered an anxious Grace, who was still desperately trying to learn what Sally and Captain Eva were up to, and was within an hour of making an arranged sea voyage to Falmouth in a fishing boat.

The Salvation Army captain gave Grace a résumé of the previous night's activities and introduced her to the young orphan who had accompanied her to the Refuge.

Looking sympathetically at the small and rather frail young girl who was standing forlornly in the centre of the Refuge kitchen, Grace said, 'It's lucky for you Captain Eva decided to take action when she did, young lady. If she hadn't set out to rescue you from the likes of Sid Darling, no one else would have. She's an angel in her own right, I'm telling you.'

Embarrassed by such fulsome praise, Eva said, 'Connie was befriended in the first place by Sally. It seems Sally looked after Connie as best she could, right up until the time Mother Darling recognised her and had drugged wine poured down her throat until she passed out.'

'Where's Sally now?' asked a concerned Grace. 'Why hasn't she come back here with you? Is she all right?'

When Eva told her of Ethan's return and of the part he had played in the rescue, Grace said emotionally, 'I'm so happy for her – happy for them both, of course, but especially for Sally. Perhaps life will be good to her now. For a while, at least. It's no more than she deserves, poor little soul. When you see her, tell her to come and see me. I've an apology to make.'

To Connie, she said, 'If Sally's taken you under her wing, you've found yourself a staunch friend, young lady. One who'll stand by you, come hell or high water.'

She looked at the vulnerable young girl and her heart went out to her. 'You look as though you could do with a bit of fattening up. I believe you were a workhouse girl?'

Connie nodded unhappily.

'Never mind, you'll soon put that behind you and we'll see what can be done to put a bit of meat on your bones.' Speaking to Eva, she said, 'Let her come home with me for now. I'll bring her back to the Refuge later on. Come along, young Connie. I'll introduce you to my husband. You can tell him all that Sally's been up to. Got a soft spot for her, has Alfie. Always has had, right from the first. He'll take to you too, I know he will . . .'

Watching the two go off together, Eva knew that Connie had already gone part of the way towards filling the place in Grace's heart left empty by the death of Rachel.

Thoughts of Rachel saddened Eva. She consoled herself with the thought that she – or, to be more truthful, Ian Lovat – had prevented the same thing happening to other innocent young girls. However, until the fate of Sid Darling had been established, there was always a strong possibility that such a thing would happen yet again, somewhere else in the country. This despite the countrywide publicity that would be given to recent events by editor Carl Milton and the *Mayfair Gazette*.

When Ethan and Joe walked through the door of their Barbican home, Doris Shields's happiness was complete. There were tears and excitement all round.

Eventually Henry Shields asked his sons about the Belgian fishing boat they had gone to investigate. Ethan and Joe filled their family in on all that had happened in Falmouth and of the part Sally had played.

Now it was Sally's turn to receive the attention of the whole family. The role of heroine was an embarrassing one for her, and she tried to pass it off by speaking of her happiness and disbelief when she came to her senses in the bedroom of the Falmouth house and realised Ethan was alive and in the room with her.

As she watched the looks that passed between the young couple, and their evident unwillingness to stray more than an arm's length from each other, Doris realised it would not be long before she would lose Ethan again. This time for good.

She thought he could not have found a girl she liked more.

Then Sophie insisted that Sally be shown the presents the men had bought on their way home in the *Eastern Prince*.

The remainder of the day was very happy for everyone in the house. It was a day Sally would always remember: the day when she truly felt she had been accepted as a full member of a large and close family.

85

Robert Sanderson was arrested when he returned to the woods beside Lanhydrock House. His intention had been to retrieve the stolen property hidden there on the night of the fire that had almost completely destroyed the great house.

The fire had also resulted in the death of Lady Robartes a few days afterwards. She had never recovered from the shock of seeing her precious home destroyed.

The hidden hoard had been discovered by one of the Lanhydrock Estate gamekeepers. He had promptly reported his find to the Bodmin police, who had kept watch on it, ever since.

Fortunately for Sanderson, the police believed the property to have been stolen by someone else, during the confusing aftermath of the fire.

Sanderson's, story was that when he heard news of the fire, he had returned to view the damage caused to the great house where he had been employed for so many years. Aware that he would not be welcomed by the family, he did not take the most public route. Instead, he made his way there through the woods.

As he neared Lanhydrock, he claimed to have heard someone approaching along the path towards him. Not wishing to be seen, he sought a hiding place off the path. In so doing, he stumbled across the cache of stolen property. Unsure of what to do about it, he had left it there.

It was only after giving the matter a great deal of thought that he had decided to return to the wood, collect the stolen property and take it to the police station. After all, he had worked for the family for a great many years. He still felt a certain duty towards them . . . !

The policeman interrogating Sanderson pointed out that when he was arrested he had been pushing the sweep's cart in the opposite direction to the nearest police station, which was in Bodmin.

Sanderson's response was that he was too embarrassed to take it to the county town, where the circumstances of his dismissal would be known. He was taking it instead to Lostwithiel, a small town to the south of Lanhydrock.

'Do you believe him?' Ian Lovat put the question to the Cornish inspector as they drove to Bodmin in a light carriage belonging to the Cornwall Constabulary.

'No,' the other man replied firmly. 'I believe the man to be a liar. Unfortunately, he is a plausible liar. I have no evidence against him of theft and I think he might convince a jury he is telling the truth.'

'He's certainly a very nasty piece of work,' commented Ian Lovat. 'He was seen with a chimney sweep in Plymouth some time before the fire. They were overheard planning something that might well have been a robbery at Lanhydrock – but that, of course, would have indicated prior knowledge of the fire!'

'Do you know where this chimney sweep is now?' asked the inspector.

Ian Lovat shook his head. 'He hasn't been seen for a week or two. But have a word with the Lanhydrock servants. Sanderson wasn't particularly liked by the household staff. They might be able to tell you something. Someone might have some useful information about either Sanderson or the sweep.'

'What about your own case? This young girl who died from the abortion? News of it reached us at the time. It was a very nasty business indeed. I don't want to put your inquiries in jeopardy by upsetting Sanderson at this stage.'

'We don't know yet whether he has any useful information to give me. If he has, I'll get it in writing to make certain he doesn't try to retract at some future date.'

Robert Sanderson was desperately unhappy at being locked up in the Bodmin police station. Ironically, he was in the same cell occupied by Sally during her stay there.

His first question to Ian Lovat was whether, by giving him information about the abortion, the Plymouth inspector could arrange for him to be given bail.

'No,' Ian Lovat replied without preamble. 'If you have information about a serious crime, it is your *duty* to tell me about it. If you do, I'll make certain you are given full credit for your help when you are brought before the court.'

He looked unsmilingly at Sanderson, remembering

the way this man had behaved towards Sally. 'On the other hand, if you know something about the abortion carried out on this unfortunate young girl and *don't* tell me, I will make it my business to ensure the judge is told about that too. He'll no doubt bear it in mind when he comes to sentence you.'

'That's not fair,' protested Sanderson. 'I'm not guilty of anything. All I was doing when I was stopped in the wood was trying to help the police—'

'I don't want to hear anything about the offence for which you've been arrested. That's between you and the Cornwall police. I'm here because I was told you have something to tell me. If you have, I'm ready to listen. If not, I'll go.'

Sanderson licked his lips uncertainly. 'Do I have your promise that you'll put in a good word for me if I tell you what I know?'

'I've already said so. But I don't deal in rumour or surmise. It will need to be something I can use – and I'll want it in writing. Now, what do you wish to tell me?'

Avoiding the eyes of the uncompromising detective, Sanderson said, 'The abortion was carried out by Clara Flood. She lives in Jed's Alley – that's at the back of Pin's Lane.'

'What number – and how do you know about it?'

'It's number three and it's where I'm living – or was living – before I was brought in here. I know about it because I saw the girl there with Clara. I'd seen her before with Sally – that's Sally Harrup. I know the room where the abortion was carried out, too. It's upstairs, next to mine. I had a peep inside once, when Clara was out of the house. There's not much in there except for a bed with a rubber sheet on it, a few bowls and some things that look like knitting needles.'

'I see.'

Ian Lovat had been watching the other man as he spoke. He was convinced Sanderson was telling the truth, but he still asked, 'Is there anyone else in the house who can corroborate what you've just told me?'

Sanderson hesitated, but for only a few moments. 'Yes, Devonport Lil. She has the other room upstairs, the one overlooking the backyard. She told me she'd seen the girl leaving. Doubled over in pain she was, according to her. She said she knew what had been happening to the poor kid and declared it wasn't the first girl she'd seen there, not by a long chalk. But she said that this one was the youngest she'd ever known Clara do it to.'

'All right, I'll have a word with this Devonport Lil. When we've got all this down in writing I'll tell Inspector Rowe you've been helpful. I suggest you are just as forthcoming with him. You'll find it the best policy in the long run.'

Later, when Ian Lovat had recorded Robert Sanderson's statement and left the Bodmin police station, the ex-Lanhydrock butler thought about the advice he had been given by the Plymouth detective inspector.

He knew he could tell the Bodmin superintendent nothing. If the Cornish police knew the truth of what had happened at Lanhydrock, he would never be a free man again.

86

On his return to Plymouth, Ian Lovat reported to his chief constable the results of his foray in Cornwall. Also present in the office was Percy Mallett, the chairman of the Police Authority.

Although the man Ian Lovat had travelled to Falmouth to arrest had succeeded in avoiding him, the circumstances of his escape left it doubtful he was still alive. Apart from this setback, the outcome of the detective inspector's actions was considered to be highly satisfactory.

An organisation that had shipped many hundreds of young English girls to the brothels of Europe had been broken up and its latest operation foiled. Many arrests had been made and a report praising the efficiency of the Plymouth detective force was to be published in a national newspaper.

The chief constable and Percy Mallett were both extremely pleased with the results, and Ian Lovat left the office with the praises of his chief constable ringing in his ears. He was accompanied by the chairman of the Police authority.

'What will happen to those unfortunate young women now?' Percy Mallett asked, as the two men walked along a corridor in the police headquarters.

'Some will stay with the Salvation Army in Falmouth until they decide what they want to do. Others came to Plymouth. No doubt those who have homes will want to return to them. One of them – the youngest – has no one at all. She returned to Plymouth with Captain Eva.'

'No doubt I'll hear all about her in due course, from my niece, Grace,' said Percy Mallett, smiling wryly.

'I'm quite certain you will, sir. She has a very similar background to Rachel and isn't dissimilar in appearance.'

'Oh dear! I do hope she won't bring similar sorrow with her. Grace is always seeking someone to take the place of her daughter Mary. She has never got over the tragic loss. But how about this other girl, the plucky young thing who went into the hornets' nest, purporting to be a candidate for domestic service?'

'Sally had a very lucky escape,' admitted Ian Lovat. 'One of the women involved in procuring the girls is Mother Darling – the mother of Sid Darling. She was at the house the girls were taken to in Falmouth and, unfortunately, she recognised Sally as the girl who had foiled their previous operation. Sally was forcibly plied with far more drink and drugs than the other girls and was deeply unconscious when we rescued her. I shudder to think what would have happened had we not got to her when we did. She'd have been at the mercy of Sid Darling. That's a fate I wouldn't wish upon man or beast.'

'Is there some way we can officially recognise this young girl's courage?' asked Percy Mallett. 'Perhaps award her a substantial sum of money? I understand she is an orphan and in somewhat straitened circumstances. Such an award would be a practical and popular gesture.'

Ian Lovat shook his head. 'It would indicate official approval of what was basically a most irregular adventure. I am very fond of Captain Eva and a great admirer of her dedication and determination, but I cannot officially condone a scheme that carried with it such a high degree of risk. I doubt if the Salvation Army itself will pat her on the head and tell her how well she's done once the full story is made public.'

Ian Lovat was correct in his assessment of the reaction of the Salvation Army towards Eva's actions.

When the detective inspector called at the Refuge, the day after his return to Plymouth, he learned that Eva had been summoned to the Salvation Army's London headquarters.

He had called at the Refuge to take a statement from Sally about the events leading up to Rachel's death. Once his official business was complete, Ian Lovat expressed disappointment that Eva was not at the Refuge. He had that morning received a very important letter and wanted to discuss its contents with her.

'Did she give you any indication of when she was likely to be back?' he asked Sally.

'I don't think she knew. I suppose it depends on how much of a ticking-off they decide to give her. Did you know they told her she wasn't to go ahead with her plan to catch Mother Darling and the others?'

'She didn't tell me in so many words, but I would have been very surprised had they agreed to go along with it. I think she organised it by having those she involved believe it had the sanction of their headquarters. It could be very serious for her. The Salvation Army shows a great deal of understanding towards the sinners with whom it works, but I'm afraid it doesn't extend to those within its own ranks who fail to toe the official line.'

'What do you think will happen to her?' Sally asked anxiously. 'Will they punish her in some way?'

'I'm afraid I can't give you an answer to that.'

As he gathered up the papers on the table in front of him, Ian Lovat smiled. 'However, I'm sure we'll be able to work something out for her.'

87

Eva was not having a happy time in London. She had caught the early-morning train from Plymouth, arriving at the headquarters of the Salvation Army soon after noon.

Unfortunately, Lieutenant Commissioner Bolt, the senior staff officer who would interview her, had just gone to lunch. Eva waited outside his office for more than two hours before finally being shown inside.

Seated on the far side of a large leather-topped desk, the senior officer wasted no time on niceties.

Frowning his disapproval, he pushed a newspaper across the desk towards her. 'I presume you have read this, Captain Cassington?'

Bold black headlines stared up at her. 'SALVATION ARMY LASSIE EXPOSES PROCURERS OF YOUNG GIRLS'. Beneath the banner headlines, somewhat smaller but still bold in typeface, it declared, 'Plymouth Salvation Army lass rescues young English girls, bound for the brothels of Europe'.

'I bought a paper at Paddington railway station and

read it while I was waiting for you to finish your lunch,' said Eva, refusing to be browbeaten by the very senior Salvation Army officer.

Lieutenant Commissioner Bolt flushed angrily. 'Do you remember standing before me only a few days ago and being told categorically that you were not to go ahead with this foolhardy idea of yours?'

'We discussed the matter, yes.'

'Yet you went ahead, even though you were aware it would most likely bring the reputation of the Salvation Army into disrepute. Why?'

'I disagree that it has brought us into disrepute. Indeed, I believe it has shown everyone the Salvation Army not only cares about such matters, but that we are prepared to take action to put things to rights.'

'It is not a part of your duty to assess public opinion, Captain Cassington. That is for officers of far more senior rank than yourself. Can you offer any other excuse for your blatant disregard of a direct order?'

'Yes. You are talking of orders, regulations and public opinion. My concern was with the lives of a number of young girls – real people – who would have ended up in brothels had something not been done to prevent it happening.'

'Did you not consider passing your information to the police, whose duty it is to deal with such matters?'

'When did the police last act on something *you* told them, Commissioner Bolt?'

The senior Salvation Army officer flushed again. He had recently been arrested by police after he had complained to them of missile throwers at an open-air meeting.

'You prevaricate, Captain. When you were last in

London you were told not to proceed with the plans you laid before me. Despite that, you went ahead with a scheme that was foolhardy, ill conceived – and in direct contravention of an order.'

Containing her anger, Eva said, 'With due respect, Commissioner Bolt, you *advised* me against the course of action I took. You did not *order* me to abandon it. Besides, had I done nothing, fifteen young girls would have been held prisoner in European brothels now. Instead, they have been given an opportunity to lead decent and useful lives – and reason to be everlastingly grateful to the Salvation Army.'

'Other means of rescuing these girls were open to you, Captain Cassington. Fifteen girls may be grateful, but many thousands, no, *tens* of thousands of decent people are shocked that the Salvation Army should ally itself with a newspaper in order to provide salacious reading for those who delight in such filth.'

'That was never my intention, Commissioner, nor that of the editor—'

Eva's protest was interrupted fiercely by the senior Salvation Army officer. 'The road to hell is paved with good intentions, Captain. I have no doubt your *intentions* were admirable. For that reason – and that reason alone – I will not dismiss you from the service. However, your blatant disregard of my order – or *advice*, call it what you will – has led to a great deal of criticism and adverse publicity for the Army. It comes at a time when it is least desirable – for reasons best known to those of us who are required to take such considerations into account when directing Army policy. It is because *we* and not *you* possess such knowledge that unquestioning obedience is required from all who serve as officers in the Salvation Army. You have fallen short of the standard expected of you, *Captain* Cassington. I regret this is the last occasion you will be addressed as such. I order that you be reduced to the rank of sergeant and transferred from Plymouth forthwith.'

Leaning back in his chair, Lieutenant Commissioner Bolt added, 'You may return to Plymouth now and settle your affairs. Details of your new appointment will reach you within a few days.'

Eva was shaken by the severity of her punishment. 'But . . . what of my work? The Refuge . . . and the girls there?'

'The work will be continued by an officer with suitable qualifications, *Sergeant* Cassington. It will perhaps provide you with another salutary lesson. Only the Lord Himself is indispensable.'

Eva left the office of the Salvation Army staff officer, her eyes burning with unshed tears. She felt she had been dealt with unfairly and with undue harshness.

The action taken to save the girls had been successful. True, it had come *close* to disaster, but that had been averted, thanks to Ian Lovat.

In the end, the Salvation Army had come out of it with considerable credit. Besides, the trade in young girls needed to be exposed in such a manner. It would not be brought to an end by ignoring it and pretending it did not exist. That was hypocritical.

She was very upset too that she was being ordered to abandon the Refuge in Plymouth that she had worked so hard to create.

For the first time since joining the Salvation Army, she wondered whether her own ideals were shared by those who held high office.

88

The girls and women living at the Salvation Army's Plymouth Refuge were distraught at the news that Eva Cassington was to be demoted and transferred, and someone else would take over the running of the hostel.

She had called them all together the morning after her late-night return from London and broken the news to them.

'Why should they want to *punish* you for what you've done?' One of the girls saved from Falmouth expressed the bewilderment of the others. 'What would have happened to us if you hadn't rescued us? Where would we be now? If the Salvation Army doesn't care about ordinary working girls like us, then who does it care about?'

'It does care, Rose. Perhaps Lieutenant Commissioner Bolt has things wrong about this, but he isn't representative of the Army as a whole.'

'He's representative enough to send you away because you've saved us. If that's how much the Salvation Army cares then I for one don't want to know about it. I'll go back to my village and put myself "on the parish" if I can't get any work.'

'I don't think I want to stay here, either,' said one of the recently reformed prostitutes. 'It's been all right having you in charge, but I wouldn't want to stay here if they put the likes of that young lieutenant in your place – I'm talking about the one who looked after the Refuge while you was away in Falmouth. She behaved as though she was afraid she might catch something if she came too close to any of us. She made me feel really uncomfortable.'

'Please don't do anything foolish just yet. We'll talk about it again when we've all had time to learn what is involved and who's likely to take over from me here.'

'Whoever it is will be coming to an empty house,' commented another of the girls. 'It's not just that they're making you leave – although that's bad enough. It's because no one has thought of *us*. What we might think – or even what's best for us. We came here because we thought the Salvation Army *really* cared. It seems it isn't them who cares, but you – and you're being sent away because of it.'

'That isn't so. It really isn't,' Eva said desperately. 'The Salvation Army *does* care for you, because God cares. But the members of the Salvation Army are only human. We don't always get it right. But things will work out. I *know* they will.'

The support and loyalty of the girls in the Refuge upset and alarmed Eva; she had no wish for all their hard work to be undone. But worse was to come.

Later that afternoon, Captain Wardle came to the Refuge with bad news.

Eva had called at his home the previous evening on her return from London. He and his wife had still been up, having conducted a late-night prayer meeting. Both had been deeply distressed by the actions of Lieutenant Commissioner Bolt. They and Eva had prayed together before she made her way back to the Refuge.

While Eva had been talking to the girls that morning, Wardle had received a visit from the owner of the house in which the Salvation Army Refuge had been established. He had become a frequent visitor to the Salvation Army's Plymouth headquarters and took a keen and generous interest in the work being done there.

When he was told of Captain Eva's demotion and the reason for it, he was incredulous. 'Demoted! For organising the rescue of those young girls? I've never heard of anything so preposterous! She should have been promoted. Indeed, if the views held by this lieutenant commissioner are those of the commanders of the Salvation Army, someone should put her in charge of the whole organisation.'

The generous Methodist's anger simmered during the whole of his visit. As he was leaving, he said to Captain Wardle, 'The more I think about the treatment meted out to Captain Eva, the angrier I become. You will inform your London headquarters that, in view of their actions, I intend to repossess my house as soon as they can find alternative accommodation for the present residents. I allowed my house to be used as a refuge because I was fired with the enthusiasm of the Salvation Army. I now realise the enthusiasm came from Captain Eva and is not shared by those who shape the Army's policies. It is most regrettable.'

When the wealthy philanthropist had left the head-quarters, Captain Wardle sat down and composed a telegraph message. When it was done, he sent it to Commissioner Hubble, the Salvation Army commissioner who had been visiting Plymouth when the house had been loaned to them as a refuge.

Then he went to call on his demoted colleague.

89

Ian Lovat had spent a very busy day investigating the movements of Robert Sanderson during the period leading up to his arrest. The inquiries were being made on behalf of the Cornwall Constabulary, but it gave him the opportunity to visit the house of Clara Flood without arousing her suspicions.

When the army widow left him alone upstairs in the house, so that he might search Sanderson's room, he took a look into the small room on the same floor.

All was exactly as had been described by Sanderson. The detective had no doubt at all that the room *was* used for carrying out abortions. All he needed now was a statement from Devonport Lil, confirming all that the ex-butler had disclosed.

He later discovered from one of his detectives, who had many informants working in the dock area, that he would need to wait a while before he could interview the dockyard prostitute. She was spending a couple of days and nights on board a Russian timber-carrying ship, currently unloading its cargo in the main Plymouth dock.

But for now, all Clara Flood would tell him was that her lodger was 'away from home on business'.

His day's work almost at an end, the detective returned to the police station and found Sally waiting for him.

Sally was feeling desperately sorry for her Salvation army friend and had gone to the Plymouth police station to tell Ian the result of Eva's visit to the Army's London headquarters.

'I think I might be able to cheer her up a little,' he said, when Sally ended her story with the statement that she had never seen Eva so unhappy.

On his way to the Barbican Refuge later that evening, Ian Lovat wondered whether the news he carried *would* be as well received as he hoped it might. He would soon know.

He was let into the house by a gloomy Zulu Joe, and was shown upstairs to the two rooms occupied by the Refuge's founder.

Eva was packing her things. She was pleased to see Ian and her expression showed it, but he thought she looked very tired and dispirited. She might even have been crying.

After listening to her account of her London interview with Lieutenant Commissioner Blunt, the sympathetic detective inspector said, 'I think the Salvation hierarchy is being very foolish. Most of the country's newspapers are carrying the story and are full of admiration for you and the Salvation Army. I even heard policemen in the station here in Plymouth praising what you did. It was indeed a superb achievement.'

Looking at the policeman to make quite certain he was not being sarcastic, Eva said, 'You know that isn't true,

Ian. The whole rescue attempt came closer to disaster than anyone but you and I will ever know. Had you not taken the action you did, the girls, including Sally, would have been in Belgium now, and I would have been forced to resign.'

'Had you not been so determined to stamp out this trade, the girls would have been in Belgium anyway.' He stoutly defended her actions.

Ian suddenly seemed less certain of himself. He watched Eva packing for a while, then, nervously, he asked, 'Eva, will you stop what you're doing for a while? I want to talk to you.'

She looked up at him in surprise. 'Is it something to do with what happened in Falmouth?'

'Not entirely – although if it hadn't happened, I wouldn't be speaking to you like this at all.'

His words made very little sense to her, but she obligingly put the rose-coloured glass vase she was wrapping down on a table and perched herself on the edge of a wooden chair.

The detective did not seem to find it easy to put the right words together. Eventually, he said, 'It's not only your life that is taking a new direction, Eva. Mine is too.'

'You don't mean that *you're* in trouble over what happened at Falmouth? That would be most unfair.'

An amused smile briefly crossed Ian's face. 'Not exactly. Do you remember that I was away from Plymouth for a few days a couple of weeks ago?'

Eva nodded. She had been hurt that Ian had not told her he would be away, or given her any explanation upon his return.

'I remember.'

'Well, I went out of the county – for an interview.'

'You mean you might be leaving Plymouth too?'

'That's right, but I didn't receive confirmation until yesterday.' Taking a deep breath, he said, 'I've been offered the post of Chief Constable of Brighton.' Ian Lovat tried to keep the pride he was feeling out of his voice, but he did not quite succeed.

'Ian! I'm delighted for you – but aren't you exceptionally young for such a responsible post?'

'Well, it's by no means the largest police force in existence, but they tell me I'll probably be the youngest chief constable in the country.' Pride crept back into his voice.

'Oh, I'm so happy for you, Ian. You are very, very clever – and you've kept it all so quiet! How could you?'

He shrugged, almost shyly. 'I couldn't say anything until it was confirmed. I thought I *might* be offered the post because the interview seemed to go so well, but I wanted to be absolutely certain before I told you.'

'And now you are! Well, we really should share such good news . . .'

She stood up, but Ian said, 'I haven't finished yet, Eva. Will you please sit down again?'

Surprised, Eva did as she was requested.

Nervously, he continued, 'If you could perhaps persuade your headquarters to send you to Brighton too, I'll ensure you have my full official backing to open a hostel for fallen women there. I'll also be in a position to ensure the Salvation Army has the support of the police – *my* police. It would be a considerable step forward for them, Eva.'

'It would indeed,' agreed Eva. She spoke thoughtfully, then added excitedly, 'It would also mean I could continue the work I really believe in—' Suddenly her enthusiasm died away. 'But I'm in disgrace at the moment and have been demoted. They wouldn't agree. Lieutenant Commissioner Bolt certainly wouldn't give such a project his support.'

She frowned, lost in her own thoughts. When she looked up, she saw his expression. 'Is there more, Ian?'

'Yes, there is a condition to my offer. A rather important one. If you agree to all I have just said, I would want you to marry me first. To come with me to Brighton – as my wife.'

Eva's mouth dropped open and she looked at Ian with an expression of utter and genuine disbelief.

'I . . . why? Why would you want me to marry you?'

'For the very obvious reason that I love you.'

'You *love* me?' she echoed. 'But . . . you've never said anything about it to me before today.' She was thoroughly confused.

'I'm saying it now. Will you marry me, Eva?'

'I . . . I can't answer you right away. It's come as a complete surprise. I'll need to think about it.'

'When you have, you'll realise it's the right thing to do, Eva. It's right for both of us.'

'I don't know about that, Ian. I really don't. I'll need to be convinced.'

Ian's deep disappointment showed. Standing up, he avoided her eyes as he said, 'I know it must have come as a shock . . . I'm sorry, but please think about it, I beg you.'

He had reached the door and had opened it before

she called out softly, 'You'll never be able to convince me if you're somewhere out there and I remain here. I *do* need convincing, Ian – and you're the only one who can do it . . .'

When Sally came up to Eva's room, to see if she could help her in any way, she was startled to find the door open and Eva and Ian inside the room, locked in a close embrace.

When Ian kissed Eva, Sally backed away and smiled happily. Everyone in the hostel had known for a very long time how the pair felt about each other.

It seemed that, at long last, they had found out too.

She wondered how it would affect the proposed transfer of the Salvation Army's ex-captain . . . ?

90

Early the next morning, Eva received a telegram. It had been sent from the London headquartes of the Salvation Army.

The source of the telegram came as a great surprise to Eva, but even before she opened the envelope she was startled to see it was addressed to 'Captain' Eva Cassington.

The contents were equally startling. The message read, 'Have read about your highly successful foray against those who have been carrying out the Devil's work. Well done! It is in the best traditions of the Salvation Army. Come to see me in London right away.'

The name at the bottom of the telegram was 'William Booth, General'.

It was a summons that could not be delayed. It was also highly exciting. Eva had been asked to meet with one of the greatest men in the country. The immense force of his personality was felt throughout the organisation he had founded, but this would be the first time Eva had met with him.

When she did, Eva believed she could put forward a convincing argument that would allow her to adapt the principles of the Plymouth Refuge to a similar establishment in Brighton.

What was more, Brighton was close enough to London for unfortunate women from the capital to be given sanctuary, free from the influences and temptations of a big city.

There was no time to inform Ian of this exciting new development. Instead, she scribbled a brief note to him and left it for Zulu Joe to deliver. If she hurried, she could catch a train and arrive at the Salvation Army headquarters by mid-afternoon. Then, if William Booth was able to see her right away, she could make the return journey and be back in Plymouth by midnight.

She also sent a telegram to London, telling the headquarters' staff that she was on her way but had no time to await a reply.

When Eva arrived breathlessly at Plymouth station, the train was about to leave. She barely had time to settle herself in a seat before the train pulled away with a series of bone-jerking movements.

She did not begin to compose herself until the train picked up speed. Soon the famous old town was far behind and smoke from the train was drifting over green fields and woodland.

Eva slept for much of the journey, but as the train drew slowly into Paddington station the excitement of London and her mission gripped Eva.

When the engineer closed off steam to the engine, the calls of the many vendors crowding the busy station could be heard more distinctly.

The station was as crowded as a busy market place.

There was food of every description and in many guises. Trinkets, too, flowers, lace, handkerchiefs . . . the variety of merchandise on offer was endless.

The vendors crowded around each arriving train, offering their wares to disembarking passengers. Eager to sell, the prices they asked fell as the passengers they were pestering drew farther away from the train.

Few of the vendors bothered the uniformed Captain Eva. Salvation Army members were known to carry very little money on their person.

She took a crowded horse-bus to the headquarters, marvelling along the way, as she always did, at the mass of people that filled the streets of the capital of England.

But Eva's excitement suffered a major setback when she walked into the Salvation Army building and announced that she was there to see General Booth, only to be told that the Salvation Army's founder had left the building not half an hour before. He had been called to Scotland for an emergency meeting with his commanders.

It was a great disappointment to Eva. The information that William Booth had arranged for her to see one of his most senior commissioners did nothing to cheer her.

She was to see Commissioner Hubble, whose friend was the Methodist benefactor who owned the building that housed the Refuge – the same man to whom Captain Wardle had sent his telegram.

He greeted Eva warmly. 'General Booth asked me to give you his deep apologies for not being able to greet you personally. He wanted to be here, I can assure you, but the emergency in Scotland had to take precedence. However, I can tell you he is well pleased with your actions. They have brought considerable credit to the Salvation Army. He would have told you that you have struck a bold and imaginative blow against evil men. The Lord will surely be smiling upon you.' The commissioner gave her a condescending smile that made her squirm.

'I don't think the lieutenant commissioner who interviewed me when I was last here would agree with you.'

'Lieutenant Commissioner Blunt was wrong,' was the commissioner's thin-lipped reply. 'The whole of the Army applauds you.'

'Then I think you should send a telegram of explanation to the benefactor who allowed his house to be used as a refuge,' said Eva. 'He has threatened to take it back because of Lieutenant Commissioner Blunt's actions.'

'Ah yes, the generous Mr Foote. Captain Wardle has already informed me of his views on the matter. I sent him a telegram only today. I assured him that we are all proud of you and the work you are doing on our behalf.'

Eva had the distinct impression that the Plymouth benefactor's threat had done more to determine her superiors' attitude towards her than her own actions had.

Although it was a matter she would have preferred to discuss with William Booth himself, she decided to bring up the subject of opening a refuge in Brighton.

The commissioner's initial reaction was one of enthusiasm, until he asked, 'This new chief constable . . . he is a Salvation Army member?'

'No, but he sympathises with our aims.'

The commissioner's expression changed. 'Oh! I am

afraid that poses a great many difficulties – for you, in particular.'

'If you're concerned about the relationship between Ian Lovat and myself, you needn't worry. He has asked me to marry him before we leave Plymouth. He wants me to be his wife when we arrive in Brighton.'

'I don't think you understand. Marriage to him is out of the question, Captain. An officer of your rank – or of any other rank, come to that – is not permitted to marry outside the Army. It is one of General Booth's basic requirements of his officers. You must have seen it in the regulations he has issued. Besides, why move when you are running the Plymouth Refuge so successfully?'

The commissioner's reaction to her proposal dismayed Eva, but she attempted to give him a reasoned reply. 'I want to move first of all because a very special man has asked me to marry him. Another reason is that opening a second refuge gives us an opportunity to build on the success of the Plymouth experiment. Finally, it is a chance for the Army to forge a link, however tenuous, with the police. That is something that's very badly needed, everywhere in the country.'

'Quite true, Captain, but you have done well with your work in Plymouth. I think it would be best if you were to remain there and consolidate your success.'

Eva left the Salvation Army headquarters as frustrated as she had been after her previous visit.

She felt Commissioner Hubble had patronised her. She was also deeply disturbed by the disclosure of General Booth's regulation about suitable marriages for Salvation Army officers.

Eva realised it was something she should have known

about. However, orders and regulations flowed from the pen of General William Booth on a daily basis, filling reams of notepaper. Those dealing with marriage had never been of any great interest to her – until now.

She realised she would have to reach a decision in the very near future about the course her life was to take. She would need to discuss it with Ian upon her return to Plymouth.

She thought deeply about the matter for much of the journey, as darkness overtook the train.

It was not until the train neared Plymouth that she stared out into the night and realised the answer had already been given to her.

It was the first time in her adult life that she had not turned to someone in the Salvation Army for the solution of a matter as important as this.

91

At about the time Captain Eva was being interviewed by the Salvation Army commissioner, Ian Lovat was arresting Clara Flood at her home.

He had finally succeeded in obtaining a witness statement from the elusive Devonport Lil. The prostitute had been arrested by a uniform policeman earlier that morning, on her way home from the docks. When she was approached by the policeman, she protested that she was singing because she was happy at having made a great deal of money during her sojourn on the Russian ship. As the explanation was accompanied by a great many unacceptable adjectives, the policeman declared she was 'drunk and disorderly' and arrested her.

It was not a particularly serious offence. When Ian Lovat explained to the station sergeant that Devonport Lil was a very important witness in the case against the abortionist who had killed young Rachel Green, it was agreed that a warning about her future conduct should suffice.

The prostitute had sobered considerably by the time

Ian Lovat interviewed her in the cells beneath the police station, and was at first reluctant to help the detective inspector.

However, when he assured her she would be free to go home once the interview was over, she became more co-operative and agreed with him that it was time Clara Flood was called to account for her illegal activities.

She confirmed what Robert Sanderson had already told him. Lil *had* seen Rachel leaving the house after her abortion. The girl was obviously in considerable pain; she had gone on her way doubled over and clutching her stomach.

Once the prostitute had made up her mind to tell Ian Lovat what she knew, there was no stopping her.

When Ian Lovat asked why she thought Rachel had been given an abortion by Clara Flood, Devonport Lil said it was well known among her fellow prostitutes that her landlady carried out such 'operations'. It was also accepted that she was not a particularly skilful abortionist.

When Ian Lovat said that rumour was not acceptable in a court of law, Lil retorted bitterly, 'Believe me, it's not just rumour. It's what she does.'

'You have personal experience?' Ian Lovat asked sharply. Evidence from someone who had actually been aborted would ensure that Clara Flood was convicted.

'I can't tell you that, can I? If I did, I'd be in dock alongside Clara.'

Ian Lovat shook his head. 'In most cases you would – but not with this one. It's far too serious. I'll ensure you are given immunity from prosecution in return for giving evidence against her. She's a very dangerous woman, Lil. Unless we can put her out of the way, many more young girls are going to suffer the same fate as poor Rachel.'

'Some already have,' declared the prostitute. 'I'll tell you something else she does, too. When Mother Darling is asked to provide a young girl for someone "special", she gets Clara Flood to examine her to make sure she's all she's supposed to be. Usually the girl is sent to London afterwards, although sometimes they're shipped abroad. It's happened far more often than you'd believe.'

'Are you certain of this?'

'Absolutely. She told me once. It was the anniversary of the death of her husband – the first one. She got so drunk she didn't know what she was telling me. She bragged that she had become so expert at what she did she could check whether a girl was a virgin with the girl hardly knowing what she was up to.'

Devonport Lil sniffed derisively. 'I could believe her if it was me she was talking about. Some of the men I get these days are finished before I know they've begun. But what she does ain't right – nor what Mother Darling's up to, neither.'

Looking at Ian Lovat as though she expected him to argue with her, she said bitterly, 'That Salvation Army captain did what was needed when she went down to Falmouth after them girls. I wish there'd been someone like her around when I was first put on the game. I might have had a husband, kids and a nice little home now. Instead of that, they'll find me dead in an alleyway one of these nights and no one will care any more than they would if it was some stray cat.'

Devonport Lil had become decidedly maudlin and Ian Lovat decided it was time he brought the interview to an end.

'You've been extremely helpful, Lil. Would you let me put all this in writing and then sign it for me?'

'Why not? Go on, you write it down. Mind you, I'd be a whole lot happier if you was able to put Sid Darling away before it came to court.'

'We're not even certain he's alive right now. There's a possibility he was drowned when the Belgian fishermen were arrested at Falmouth.'

'No such luck!' Lil declared vehemently. 'He's alive all right. Not only that, he's right here in Plymouth. You ask Florrie! She used to be one of his girls,' she added, as though that would explain everything.

Ian Lovat was alarmed. If Sid Darling was indeed alive and in Plymouth, then both Sally and Eva were at risk.

'Are you sure of this?' he asked.

'I saw Florrie only last night. She's got one of the finest black eyes you'll ever see – and she's left two of her teeth somewhere down on the dockside. Sid Darling found her and demanded that she give him her money. When she was a bit slow in coughing up, he laid into her. She'll need to carry out all her work in the dark for a week or two. No one's going to fancy her if they see her in the light.'

'Right, Lil. Let's get this statement down. Then I've got some urgent work to do.'

Ian Lovat knew that Sally had returned to work for Grace Philpott only that morning. He would warn her not to stray from the main thoroughfares until Sid Darling had been arrested.

Eva too would need to be on her guard. Sid Darling also had a score to settle with her. He would speak to Zulu Joe and tell him not to let her out of his sight while the hunt for Darling was on.

92

Life had taken a definite upturn for Sally. The day before Grace had sent a message to Sally at the Refuge, asking her if she would come back to work at the pie shop.

Grace made it clear that both she and Alfie missed her. She suggested she should bring Connie with her, if the young girl would come. They would find work for her in the kitchen. It would be an opportunity for her to earn some useful pocket money.

She added that if Connie proved suitable, they could no doubt offer her permanent work, with an opportunity to live in over the shop.

Sally had smiled when she read this. She felt she knew Grace very well. The shop owner would already have decided she wanted Connie to work at the shop and live on the premises.

Alfie would be aware of it too. He would no doubt accept it in the same uncomplaining way he had accepted Rachel.

Nevertheless, Sally felt it would be a very good thing from everyone's point of view. Particularly good for

Connie, and she deserved any good luck that might come her way.

Sally's own life was all she could want now that Ethan had returned to her. She wished the whole world could share her happiness.

The only cloud on her horizon was the knowledge that she would need to leave the Refuge when Captain Eva moved on from Plymouth. She was neither a fallen woman nor homeless. She would need to move back to Pin's Lane. Sally did not relish the thought of returning there just yet. There were still too many memories of Ruth – and the unresolved question of the whereabouts of Sid Darling.

Sally thought about this and about Captain Eva as she walked to work with Connie that morning. She still thought of the Salvationist as 'Captain'. The demotion seemed decidedly unfair to Sally. Captain Eva had worked exceptionally hard to make the Refuge a success. She wondered what effect the demotion and move would have upon her new-found relationship with Ian Lovat.

Sally also felt a twinge of sadness about all that was happening to the man who was her father. She could never forget the attack he had made on her, but, in time, she felt she might be able to forgive him. When he attacked her he had been drinking. In such a befuddled state he *might* have confused her with her mother, as she would have been when he knew her . . .

'Do you *really* think I'll be useful enough in the shop to earn a wage? I don't know very much about cooking. I don't know very much about *anything*, really. Although I suppose I'm quite good at cleaning – pots and pans, and things like that.' Connie's voice broke into her thoughts as they neared the shop. Sally realised the younger girl had problems too.

'I don't think you need worry about earning your money. Grace won't expect you to know all about pie making. If you're prepared to work at it, she'll teach you everything you need to know. Besides, she's already taken quite a shine to you. You'll be all right, believe me.'

'I hope so. I'd like to be able to move in with her and Alfie. I'd feel . . . I'd feel as though I *belonged* somewhere then. Not that it isn't nice at the Refuge,' she hastened to add, 'but it's a bit like the workhouse in a way . . . only better, of course.'

Sally smiled. She knew what the young girl was trying to say in her slightly confused manner. She would have felt the same had Ethan not been around.

When they reached the pie shop, Grace took one look at the two girls standing together, then suddenly opened her arms to Sally. She managed to get out the words 'I'm sorry!' before bursting into tears.

Alfie hurried from the kitchen at the sound of her crying. Looking highly embarrassed, he tried to comfort his wife, at the same time smiling sheepishly at each of the young girls in turn.

Regaining control of herself, Grace released Sally. Shaking herself free of Alfie's comforting arm, she blew her nose noisily before resuming her usual brisk and efficient manner.

'I never was one for hiding my emotions. They're better out than in, my mother used to say. Alfie and I are pleased to have you back with us, Sally. I should never have caused you to go away in the first place – but all that's in the past now. I don't think we need ever rake it up again. We've got a whole lot of deliveries to make this morning and there's plenty of work for us in the kitchen, Connie. Come with me. Have you ever done any cooking before . . . ?'

As Grace and Connie disappeared through the doorway to the kitchen, Alfie spoke quietly to Sally. 'I knew you'd be back with us again before too long, Sally. I'd just like to echo everything Grace said. It's nice to have you back.' As though embarrassed at voicing such emotions, Alfie added, 'Now I'd better get down to some work if you're going to have any pies to deliver. I doubt if anyone else is going to do very much today.'

Sally made a number of deliveries that day. The last one in particular took longer than expected. When she returned to the shop she found Ian Lovat there, plus Ethan, who was talking to an extremely agitated Grace.

'There you are, Sally! Thank the good Lord you're safe.'

Bewildered, Sally looked from one to the other. 'Safe? Why wouldn't I be?'

'We had reason to be concerned,' explained Ian Lovat. 'I've just been given information that Sid Darling is alive – and somewhere in Plymouth.'

Sally felt her stomach contract in sudden fear. 'You think he'll come looking for me?'

'I believe a number of people are at risk,' declared the detective, avoiding a direct answer. 'Particularly you and Captain Eva. She's gone to London today, so she's out of the way for the time being. I've told Zulu Joe to keep an eye on things at the Refuge. When I learned you were back at work, I came here to warn you and I met Ethan in the shop.'

'I called to invite you to our house tonight,' said Ethan, 'but if Sid Darling is around, I'd better come with you on your final deliveries.'

'Make certain you don't let her out of your sight,' warned Ian. 'If you have to go off somewhere – fishing, perhaps – then let me know. I'll arrange for a policeman to be somewhere near her all the time. Sid Darling is a very real threat.'

'Fortunately, I won't need to go fishing for a while,' said Ethan. 'Pa and Albert have gone to look at a steam-trawler today, but we won't be buying it until agreement has been reached between the insurance company and the navy. Pa reckons that will take a couple of weeks, at least.'

Although he was very concerned for Sally, Ethan thought that being in her company from dawn to dusk would not prove to be any hardship.

'Then that's all settled,' said Ian Lovat. 'I'm greatly relieved to know Sally will have you with her, Ethan. I'm almost as worried about Captain Eva. She sent me a note saying she hopes to return to Plymouth on the last train tonight. I'll make certain I'm there to meet her.'

93

When the train from London ended its journey at Plymouth railway station, shortly before midnight, Ian Lovat was one of about a dozen people waiting to meet the arriving passengers.

The manner in which Eva's face lit up when she saw him more than compensated for his half-hour wait on the draughty station.

Tucking her arm beneath his, she gave him a tired smile. 'This is an unexpected pleasure, Ian. I never expected you to be here to meet me this late at night.'

'I would have come anyway, to see how you got on in London, but there's a more sinister reason for my presence. Word is that Sid Darling is not only alive, but here, in Plymouth.'

Eva voiced her dismay. 'That's alarming news indeed. Has someone told Sally?'

Ian thought it typical of his companion that her first concern was not for herself. 'I've spoken to her and to Ethan. He's going to accompany her whenever she leaves the Refuge. I've also warned Zulu Joe to be especially vigilant – and to make certain you don't go out alone. I've got every policeman in Plymouth alerted to the fact that Sid Darling's here somewhere. I'm confident we'll catch him, but until we do we must all be on our guard.'

'I hope he's caught very soon – for everyone's sake.'

About to cross the road outside the station, they paused to allow a hackney carriage to pass by. When they were safely on the far pavement, Ian said, 'Now tell me all about your visit to London. Are you *Captain* or *Sergeant* Eva? Equally important, did they agree you can start up another refuge when you marry me and come to Brighton?'

'No. I was hoping to meet General Booth. I feel he would have been more understanding. I'm certain he would have appreciated the long-term advantage such a plan was likely to bring to the Salvation Army. Unfortunately, he had to go to Scotland. I saw Commissioner Hubble instead. He felt the best thing I could do was remain here and continue running the Refuge.'

'Oh! That poses a problem.' Ian experienced a sinking feeling. He knew how much the Plymouth Refuge meant to Eva. She had the chance to open a second refuge in Brighton, but he was not convinced it could take the place of the present one. 'Couldn't you appeal to General Booth?'

Captain Eva shook her head. 'He wouldn't override a decision made by such a senior officer. Besides, I believe the two men are close friends.'

She paused, but he said nothing, sensing she had more to say. She had.

'That wasn't all, Ian. Commissioner Hubble called my attention to a regulation made by General Booth some time ago. It prohibits any serving officer from marrying outside the service.'

Ian came to a halt and turned her to face him. 'Does this mean you're not going to marry me?'

When he had asked her to marry him, she had promised to give him an answer when she had given due thought to what it would mean to her career and all the things she hoped to achieve in life.

She countered his question with one of her own. 'How serious were you about helping me to set up a refuge in Brighton when you become chief constable there?'

'As serious as any man could be who is desperate enough to do anything if it will persuade the girl he loves to marry him.'

She smiled at him and he was able to see that she was very, very tired. The strain of her day was beginning to tell on her, both mentally and physically.

'Serious enough to help me start a refuge for women and girls from London – even if it doesn't have the backing of the Salvation Army?'

Ian looked at her with increasing excitement. 'Do you think you would be able to do that? Raise the money to get it off the ground – and meet all the expenses such a scheme would incur?'

'God doesn't only listen to the prayers of those who serve in the Salvation Army, Ian. He's answered my prayers before. I believe he will again. Besides, I would call on your friend, the editor of the *Mayfair Gazette*. It's a cause in which he takes a great interest. He would help me.'

'He wouldn't dare refuse – especially when I tell him what's at stake!' Ian could hardly contain his excitement. 'The answer to your question is an emphatic "yes"! I happen to believe in what you're doing. You would have my full backing to open a refuge in Brighton.'

'Then I will not only be following the path along which I believe the Lord has directed me – but also doing what my heart tells me I want to do. Yes, Ian, I'll marry you.'

'Even though it means you will have to leave the Salvation Army?'

She nodded. 'I wish it wasn't necessary, but I have thought long and hard about this on the journey from London. I believe Commissioner Hubble is wrong, but I can't change his decision. I will leave the Refuge here in Plymouth with regret, but I believe Captain Wardle's wife will be asked to take over the running of it. She can do it every bit as well as me. So, yes, I'll marry you. Just as soon as you can arrange it.'

A group of people walking along the pavement towards them were shocked to see a uniformed Salvation Army officer being taken in the arms of a man and kissed, in full public view.

Dividing in order to pass by, the happy couple heard one of the women whisper, 'It's disgusting. They must have been drinking – and her a Salvation Army officer, too!'

Grinning happily, Ian said, 'Do you know, I *do* feel as though I've been drinking. I feel happily intoxicated. I love you, Captain Eva. We'll be married just as soon as it can be arranged.'

'I would like that,' she said. 'Now, let's shock them some more . . . !'

94

News that the now famous Captain Eva was to leave the Salvation Army and the Refuge she had founded was widely reported in the national newspapers.

Many made much of the fact that she was being forced to leave in order to marry the man she loved.

The newspapers most opposed to the Salvation Army ridiculed William Booth's insistence that his officers could only marry within the organisation he had founded.

A telegram from the London headquarters of the Salvation Army, in response to Eva's resignation, failed to give even a grudging acknowledgement of her work at the Plymouth Refuge. It merely approved the appointment of Captain Wardle's wife, Helen, as the Refuge's new warden – with 'immediate effect'.

Fortunately, the two women had become firm friends during Eva's period of duty in the town. Helen told Eva she might remain at the Refuge until her marriage to Ian Lovat had taken place.

The wedding was planned for a little over three weeks' time, a week before Ian was due to leave Plymouth and take up his new post as Brighton's Chief Constable.

One of the first things Helen Wardle did on taking over the Refuge was to call all the residents together.

The women and girls were dismayed that Captain Eva was to leave and some wanted to leave straightaway. However, the more level-headed among them, aware that Eva would have left anyway in order to be with her husband-to-be, decided they would wait to see what life was going to be like under a new regime.

Helen informed them she planned no changes to the daily routine of the Refuge, or the manner in which it was run. The Refuge had proved itself to be an outstanding success under the management of Eva. She saw no reason to alter anything.

Her talk reassured most of the women and there was no more talk of a wholesale walk-out. Sally too was relieved. Helen Wardle had told her she should not think of moving from the Refuge until Sid Darling had been caught and put away.

Sid Darling's continued freedom remained a source of concern to Ian Lovat. In addition to his concern for those who were at risk, his failure to catch up with the elusive wanted man also dented his pride.

There was one further sighting of Darling. It occurred close to the Refuge, late one night.

When the constable detailed to keep watch on the building challenged the suspect, he ran away. The constable gave chase. He eventually caught up with the man some distance away, only to be knocked beneath the wheels of a passing carriage during the violent struggle that ensued.

The constable was fortunate to suffer no more than

a broken arm and badly bruised ribs. Sid Darling, for that is who it was, made good his escape.

Ethan and Sally were discussing the incident the day after it happened, soon after she had finished work.

They were on their way to Pin's Lane. Ethan's uncle was ill once more and Ethan was taking a few items of food to him. It also gave Sally an opportunity to check that all was well with her room and to dust off the furniture. It had not been touched for some time. Afterwards, she was to spend the remainder of the evening with Ethan, at the Shieldses' home.

'I wonder if it really was Sid Darling?' mused Ethan. 'No one seems absolutely certain.'

'*I'm* convinced it was him.' There was no doubt in Sally's mind. 'I bet he's been watching the Refuge. After what happened at Falmouth he'll be more determined than ever to get his hands on me. He'll also want to frighten the other girls before they're called to give evidence.'

'I hope they hurry up and catch him.' Ethan sounded concerned. 'Pa's heard from the insurance company more quickly than he expected. He's going ahead with buying this steam-trawler. Before we bring it back to Plymouth, he wants us all to go off to Brixham so the present owners can teach us how to handle her. The only one not going is Joe. He said he'll look after you while I'm away, but a man with a broken arm would be no match against Sid Darling.'

'You don't need to worry about me.' Sally spoke with more confidence than she felt. The constable's encounter with the man she was convinced to be Sid Darling had unnerved her. 'We can work as we are now, with me only making deliveries that keep me to the main roads and Joe delivering to other places. Then, when I finish work I'll go straight to the Refuge and stay there.'

'Well . . . Only if you're quite sure and promise you'll take no chances.'

Ethan was deeply concerned for Sally's safety, but he was also very excited at the thought of the family owning and working a steam-trawler. It was to be a major step forward for them.

'I can assure you I'll take no chances at all where Sid Darling is concerned!' Sally said emphatically. They were turning into Pin's Lane now and she added, 'Not even here. I'll let you go upstairs and check my room, while I call in to see how Charlie is.'

Charlie gave Sally a long homily on the state of his health while Ethan was upstairs. She thought he looked no worse than when she had shared the upstairs room with Ruth, but he became indignant when she told him so.

'That's easy enough for you to say, young lady. If I was as young as you, I've no doubt I could cope with many things a whole lot easier than I do now. You just wait until you get to my age. You'll find you have more sympathy for those in ill-health then. Not that it'll make any difference what I say to you. You youngsters have no thought for anyone except yourselves.'

As she had just brought him a couple of Grace's pies and Ethan was there to deliver some items from his mother, Sally thought his comments were particularly ill-timed, but she made no comment.

When Ethan came downstairs, Sally made her excuses to Charlie and left the room. She was half-way up the

stairs before Charlie came to the door of his room and
called after her.

'Here, this came for you yesterday.' In his hand he
held a letter. 'I was going to get someone to take it
around to the Philpotts' shop for you. Your coming
here has saved me the trouble.'

Sally was unused to receiving letters. She went back
down the stairs and took the letter from Charlie. Holding it in her hand, she gazed at it dubiously. Who would
have written to her?

Ethan had come into the passageway and she said to
him, 'I've got a letter! I wonder who it could be from?'

Ethan smiled. 'There's only one way to find out. Open
it and read what it says.'

Sally opened the envelope very carefully, as though
she might somehow damage its contents. Then she
unfolded the piece of paper it contained.

A great many conflicting expressions followed each
other across her face as she read. When she eventually
looked up and spoke, the reason for her uncertainty
became clear.

'It's from my father. He says he's had a great deal
of time to think about things while he's been in prison
awaiting trial and is sorry for all the unhappiness he's
caused me. He admits he *is* my father and has written
down all he can remember of our relatives and feels
certain they'll want to meet me. He wants to see me,
to give me their details and tell me about them. He's
also written a letter to Inspector Lovat that he'd like me
to collect and deliver personally.'

The emotion was too much for Sally. She was very
close to tears. Ethan moved towards her and hugged
her to him.

Despite his happiness for her, Ethan was not entirely convinced of the authenticity of Robert Sanderson's change of heart. He suspected it might be intended to gain sympathy with a jury when he came to trial.

In spite of such thoughts, Ethan said nothing. Happiness had been a rare commodity in Sally's life. He would not spoil this moment for her.

95

Since Eva had agreed to marry Ian, they had spent an increasing amount of time together. They discussed details of their forthcoming wedding and made plans for furnishing the home they would be setting up in Brighton.

If Eva felt any unhappiness about being forced to leave the Christian organisation to which she had devoted all her adult life, she did not allow it to show. To an onlooker, it would seem there was nothing on her mind but the forthcoming marriage.

Ian was with Eva when Sally brought the letter from her father to show to her. After reading it, Eva asked permission to pass it to Ian. When it was given, she handed it to him and said to Sally, 'What do you intend to do?'

'I shall go and see him,' Sally replied promptly.

'Are you quite sure you should? I mean, he didn't behave in a particularly fatherly fashion when you took pity on him before.'

'Things are different now. He's in prison – and won't

have been drinking. Besides, I really do think he's sorry for the way he behaved and wants to make it up to me.'

When Ian Lovat had read the letter, he frowned. 'If you'll pardon me for being painfully blunt, Sally, Robert Sanderson has never impressed me as being a man who is concerned for anyone other than himself.'

When Sally made no reply, the detective apologised. 'I shouldn't have said that, Sally. I'm sorry. Robert Sanderson is your father. The fact that he's now willing to acknowledge you might mean he's at last ready to face up to his responsibilities. When are you thinking of going to Bodmin gaol to see him?'

'I can't go until Sunday . . .' It was now Wednesday. '. . . I can't ask Grace for any more time off. Business is only just returning to normal, and Ethan won't be able to take a day off before then, either.'

'Then I'll tell you what I'll do. He says he has a letter for me too. As I need to speak to him before Clara Flood goes on trial we'll go and see him together.'

Sally looked disappointed. She had been looking forward to a rare opportunity of enjoying a day out with Ethan.

Correctly guessing the reason for her lack of enthusiasm, Ian explained, 'It would be a wise thing to do. You might have difficulty in obtaining permission to see him. Some governors are reluctant to allow remand prisoners to receive visitors. My presence should ensure that you succeed.'

It was enough to convince Sally. She agreed that Ian should accompany her and Ethan to Bodmin gaol the following Sunday.

Eva was invited to come along, but she declined.

Although no longer an officer of the Salvation Army, she would spend Sunday worshipping with her late colleagues.

Ian Lovat had told Sally he needed to speak to Robert Sanderson about the forthcoming trial of Clara Flood. This was true – but it was not the *whole* truth.

Inquiries had been made by his men about the chimney sweep seen with the ex-butler in the days before the fire and mysterious robbery at Lanhydrock House.

The chimney sweep's identity had now been established. When detectives went to Harry Maggs's lodgings they discovered he had not been home since a couple of days before the fire.

Searching through his belongings they found a detailed plan, which they later established was the plan of Lanhydrock House.

In the meantime, Bodmin police had questioned the house servants. They learned that a chimney sweep answering Harry Maggs's description had been sweeping chimneys at the great house only the day before the disastrous fire.

They further discovered that the story he had told, of the regular chimney sweep having retired, had been a lie. The man in question was, in fact, sweeping the chimneys of the Bodmin police headquarters while Robert Sanderson languished in the town's gaol, not very far away.

The whole thing pointed to a planned robbery rather than spur-of-the-moment opportunism. It also raised a number of grave questions about the cause of the fire and the present whereabouts of Maggs.

The Bodmin police had visited the town gaol and

questioned Robert Sanderson. But that had been before Ian Lovat's detectives had located and visited Harry Maggs's room in Plymouth.

A senior policeman travelled to Plymouth from Bodmin and had a lengthy meeting with Ian. It was decided that the Plymouth inspector should try to gain as much information as he could when he visited Sanderson to tie up a few loose ends in the case against Clara Flood.

Sally was blissfully unaware of what was in Ian Lovat's mind when he suggested they should both visit the gaol together.

She knew only that at last she had a father who was ready to acknowledge her as his own. She wished Ruth might have lived to witness this day.

96

Ian Lovat was the only one of the trio travelling from Plymouth to Bodmin who did not appear to be excited. Sally, in particular, found it difficult to remain still for more than a few moments at a time.

Her mood was infectious. Ethan was caught up in it – but he had other reasons to be happy. The boat bought by his father had exceeded all the family's expectations. It would be able to travel farther and faster and use larger nets to catch more fish than their last boat. It could put to sea in weather that would keep sail-powered boats in harbour.

Once the fish were caught, it would bring them back to harbour more swiftly than the other boats, scorning the direction of the wind.

There had been a lengthy family discussion about what the future would hold for them all as a result of buying the new boat. Samuel, the Shieldses' third son and the most financially attuned member of the family, had costed out the estimated expenses and profits of operating a coal-burning trawler.

He estimated that each of the sons would be earning a great deal more money than they had when the family fished with the *Mermaid*.

It would be possible to put enough money aside to enable them to purchase a second boat in another eighteen months' to two years' time.

Eventually, it might be possible for each member of the family to own his own boat, or, if they preferred, to have a family-owned fishing fleet.

With such prospects as these, Ethan decided he would ask Sally to marry him at the earliest opportunity. He knew such a marriage would have the approval of the entire Shields family.

He hoped it might be possible to ask her today, after their visit to the prison, if the opportunity arose.

Ian Lovat had already told them he would not be returning to Plymouth with them. He had arranged a meeting with some of the senior Bodmin policemen and would take a later train.

When they reached Bodmin Road railway station, the trio transferred to another train in which to complete their journey to Bodmin town and the gaol in which Robert Sanderson was being held.

Built at the lower end of the town, the prison was a dark and forbidding place. Sally shuddered as they walked through the gateway, beneath a fortress-like archway. Over it was incongruously etched the fifteen bezant shield of Cornwall, surmounted by three Prince of Wales feathers.

As this was a Sunday, the prison governor was not in the building. It was left to a senior warder to break some sensational news when Ian Lovat introduced himself and the others and stated their business.

'Robert Sanderson, you say?' said the warder. 'Well, I'm afraid you won't be able to interview him, Inspector.'

'Why not? Is he being kept in solitary or something? I can assure you, my business with him is of considerable importance – and this young lady is his daughter. He's asked her to visit him to collect some rather important information – together with a letter he has written to me.'

The senior warder appeared startled. 'His daughter, you say? We never knew anything about any daughter, or we'd have notified her right away. As far as we were aware he had no close relatives, anywhere.'

The senior warder's use of the past tense told its own story, but Ian needed to clarify the situation.

'I'm sorry . . . Notify her of *what*, exactly?'

'Of Sanderson's death. He hanged himself in his cell on Friday – the day before yesterday. Used his braces and a torn-up shirt to hang himself from the bars of his cell window. You'd have hardly believed it possible, would you . . . ?'

The senior warder's callous manner in breaking the news left Sally dismayed and in a state close to shock. Her knees felt suddenly weak. She might have collapsed had Ethan not put an arm about her in support.

They were in an office just inside the main prison entrance and Ethan lowered her to a chair, assisted by Ian.

It was the detective inspector who questioned the senior warder. 'Did the warder who discovered him find the letter in his cell that he said he had already written to me?'

'The body was discovered by his cell-mate, Ted

Harris, a prisoner awaiting trial for a violent assault. Almost killed a man after he'd been drinking and a thoroughly nasty piece of work. He woke up to find Sanderson hanging and already dead. He almost shouted the place down before we were able to get there and find out what had happened. But no letter from Sanderson was found in the cell.'

'That's very strange,' Ian said, perplexed. 'He wrote to Sally to say there was a letter.'

He frowned. 'Would you mind if I had a look in his cell and spoke to his cell-mate?'

The senior warder shrugged in a gesture of indifference. 'Please yourself, but I can assure you, you'll find nothing there – and I can only allow *you* inside the prison. I can't have a whole crowd of visitors wandering around.'

'I don't want to go to the cell,' Sally said, wretchedly.

Belatedly, the senior warder said, 'I'm sorry you had to hear the news about your father this way, miss. If I'd known he had a daughter . . .'

Looking at her more kindly, he added, 'You stay here while I take the inspector off to see Harris and the cell. Not that we'll find anything there. The remand cells may be better than those of the convicts, but there's still nowhere to hide anything.'

When the senior warder and Ian Lovat had gone, Ethan, concerned about Sally, said anxiously, 'Are you feeling all right? Is there anything I can get for you?'

She shook her head. 'I'll be all right in a while. It's my own fault, really. I should have known better than to get my hopes up in such a fashion. He didn't want to know about me in the first place. But he did say he'd made out a list of all his – *my* family. I'd have liked to have seen that.'

Feeling desperately sorry for her, Ethan took her hand and held it tightly. 'Perhaps Ian will find it. Let's hope so.'

97

By the time Ian Lovat returned to the small office inside the prison entrance, Sally had recovered much of her composure.

For her to suggest she had been heartbroken by news of the tragic death of the man who was her father would have been hypocritical. She had hardly known him. What little she had learned of him – much through unfortunate experience – had certainly not endeared him to her.

In fact, only Sid Darling had brought more unhappiness into her life. Yet, despite this, Robert Sanderson was still the man who had fathered her.

Furthermore, in his final letter he had acknowledged his paternity and promised to inform her of hitherto unknown relatives. She had been thrilled at the thought of meeting a family she had never known – and now would never know.

She found it difficult to believe he would deliberately have acted so cruelly in raising her hopes, knowing he intended to commit suicide before she arrived to speak to him.

'Did you find any letters?' Ethan put the question on behalf of Sally when Ian Lovat returned to the prison office.

The Plymouth detective inspector shook his head. 'No and his cell-mate claims that he isn't able to read, so would have no reason to steal letters, or even know who they might have been intended for, had there been any. But that doesn't mean the letters don't – or *didn't* – exist. I'm not convinced that the man who shared a cell with Sanderson is telling the truth about what happened.'

'You mean . . . he might have had something to do with the death of my father?' Sally looked at Ian with wide-eyed disbelief.

Ian shook his head. 'I'm not saying that, but there's something about this "Ted Harris" that bothers me. What's known of him?' Ian put the question to the senior warder.

'As far as I know, nothing at all. That's unusual in itself. Harris is such a violent man, even to the warders, that I would have expected him to have spent time in prison before. He claims to have no fixed address, no next-of-kin and he's not unlike Sanderson in that respect. The police at Bodmin may have more on him, but I doubt it, somehow. They usually tell us everything that's known about the men they bring to us here.'

'Could I speak to him?' Sally asked unexpectedly. 'If he does know anything about the letters he might be willing to tell me about them, where he wouldn't tell the police.'

'I'm sorry, I can't allow that,' the senior warder said firmly. 'Harris is due to appear before the court on charges involving violence – and that was against a woman.'

'I agree with all you've said,' agreed Ian Lovat, 'but it's a pity, all the same. I would like Sally to have seen Harris. There's something about him that troubles me, but I can't quite put a finger on it. Sally might just have been able to come up with something.'

'There's no reason at all why she shouldn't *see* him,' said the senior warder. 'I'll have Harris brought from his cell for exercise and take you to the governor's office. It overlooks the exercise yard.'

'Do you really think it will serve any useful purpose?' Ethan asked anxiously. Sally had largely recovered from the initial distress of learning of her father's death. He did not want her upset again.

It was Sally herself who decided the issue. 'I'd like to say I've seen him, at least,' she said. 'After all, he was the last one to see my father alive.'

Ethan shrugged. He had tried to save her further distress. He could do no more.

The prisoner had still not been brought into the exercise yard by the time the small party reached the governor's office and was gathered at the window.

There were no other prisoners in the yard and Ethan could sense the tension in Sally when she took hold of his arm.

Suddenly, there was a sound from immediately beneath the window, as the door from the prison building to the exercise yard was opened.

Moments later a warder and another man came into view. For a short while they could see only the top of the prisoner's head as he walked away from them.

Then, he reached a corner of the small enclosed space and changed direction. At the same time, he looked up at the sky.

Sally let out a short scream and clutched at Ethan's arm with both hands.

'It's him! It's HIM!' she gasped, close to hysteria.

'It's who?' demanded Ian.

Ethan, grim-faced, gave him the answer. 'That's not Ted Harris, or whatever he's calling himself, and it's hardly surprising that he's in for assaulting a woman. That's Sid Darling!'

98

'This puts an entirely new light on the matter of Sanderson's death,' Ian Lovat said to the senior warder. 'Although I doubt very much whether we'll ever be able to prove to a jury that Sid Darling is responsible for Sanderson's death.'

They had all returned to the office inside the main entrance of the prison.

The Plymouth detective inspector had been detailing the crimes for which Darling was being sought by the police forces of the two counties on either side of the River Tamar.

'What would you like me to do?' asked the senior warder, eager now to help in any way he could.

'I'd like you to have him thoroughly searched before you move him. Then make a search from top to bottom of the cell he shared with Sanderson. When I spoke to him earlier, Darling claimed to be unable to read. That isn't true.' Explaining, Ian continued, 'When we arrested Mother Darling and searched her house, we found letters from him. He had made written threats against Sally – threats I believe he had every intention of carrying out. If he had seen letters addressed to Sally and questioned Sanderson about them, he might have learned he was her rightful father and that the letters were an acknowledgement of the fact. Darling would have taken a malicious delight in destroying the letters. It would have given him a good reason to want to harm Sanderson too. We believe he carried out something similar against Sally's invalid sister when he went to the room they shared and found her there alone.'

Observing Sally's show of distress, he said, 'I'm sorry, Sally but I want to see Sid Darling receive his just deserts. Hopefully, Devonport Lil will be persuaded to admit she saw him in your room on the day in question. But before she gives evidence she'll want to know there's no chance of him ever being free to take his revenge upon her.'

'I'd like to see him pay for everything he's done,' Sally said fiercely. 'For Rachel's sake, as well as for everyone else who's ever suffered at his hands.'

'I'll see that he and the cell are searched thoroughly,' declared the senior warder. 'I personally don't believe the letters exist any more, but if they do you can be certain we'll find them.'

Outside the prison gate, Sally asked, in a lacklustre voice, 'What happens now?'

'I'm going to the police station for a meeting with the police inspector,' said Ian. 'We'll have rather more to talk about than was anticipated, but it should prove very interesting indeed. We'll no doubt pool all the evidence we have to ensure Darling is convicted. I shall do my best to see the conviction is for murder.

However, even if that fails, I doubt if he will ever see daylight as a free man again until he's too old to cause mischief to anyone. I'll see you two later.'

'What shall *we* do now?' asked Sally, as Ian Lovat walked briskly away in the direction of the police station. 'Our train doesn't leave for more than four hours and it's Sunday – there'll be no shops open.'

'Why don't we walk to Lanhydrock and see the damage caused by the fire?' suggested Ethan. 'We could head that way anyway, to catch the train from Bodmin Road.'

'All right,' agreed Sally. She sounded unenthusiastic, but she linked her arm through his and they made their way through the town to the road that would take them to Lanhydrock House.

Their destination was more than two miles away, but it was a fine day and they were in no hurry.

Sally had very little to say and responded in only a half-hearted way to Ethan's attempts to make conversation.

He knew she was thinking of all that had happened at the prison. He believed she had suffered great disappointment and unhappiness at the loss of her father and the opportunity to discover the identity of her relatives. He felt sorry for her. At the same time, he admired the brave front she was trying to put upon the events of the day.

Sally maintained her composure until the moment she saw the fire-stained shell that had once been the magnificent Lanhydrock House. Then, much to the surprise of Ethan and a number of other sightseers, she suddenly burst into tears.

Hurriedly, Ethan led her away, making for a nearby grassy bank. Here, an abundance of flowering plants escaped from a low-walled shrubbery and cascaded down the slope.

When Sally was seated on the grass, Ethan kneeled down beside her and held her until she ceased crying.

'I'm sorry, Ethan.' Her voice was muffled as she spoke into the shoulder of his coat. 'It's just . . . just seeing the house like this. It was so beautiful . . . and Lady Robartes loved it so much.'

Sally's views on Lady Robartes, who had been so kind to her, had been echoed around the county. Most of those who knew her were convinced she had died of a broken heart over the loss of her home.

'It was beautiful,' agreed Ethan, 'and it will be again – look, they've got scaffolding up and have started rebuilding already. They're leaving the disaster where it belongs. In the past.'

Pulling away from him, Sally looked up into his face. 'Is that what you think I should do, Ethan? Is that what you're trying to tell me?'

'Yes, I am.'

Sally was silent for some minutes. Then she said, 'You're right. I know you are, but it's easier for them. The family who lived here. When they're done they'll have a magnificent house again. They'll move back in and the lives of the whole family will revolve around the house once more, as it has done for hundreds of years. I don't have anything like that. First I lost Ruth; then the man who finally admitted he was my father and who was going to give me a new family; I'm losing Captain Eva too, because she's going off with Ian – and I've nothing to take their place.' Sally was trying to be brave, but she could not prevent her lower lip from trembling.

'You have me,' Ethan said quietly.

Managing a weak smile, Sally looked at him for a few moments before suddenly hugging him. 'Yes, you're right, Ethan. I have you – although for a while I was convinced I'd lost you too. I think that was the worst time of all.'

'Well, you haven't lost me – and you won't, unless you choose to, so why don't we put the past where it belongs. Behind us. Let's start building a new and wonderful future – just as they're doing with the house over there?'

Pulling back from him once more, Sally looked at Ethan uncertainly, wondering whether his words meant what she thought they did. What she *hoped* he was saying.

'What do you mean, Ethan?'

'I think you know what I mean, Sally. I'm asking you to marry me. To put all the unhappiness you've known behind you. Begin a new life, with me. With the new boat and all the plans we have for her, it should be a very good life. But only if you're part of it too. Will you marry me, Sally?'

Sally's emotions would not allow her to give him a spoken reply. Instead, she flung her arms about him and kissed him with all the passion she felt inside her.

As she clung to Ethan, all the unhappiness she had known in the past fell away.

When they eventually released their hold upon each other, they became aware of the bubbling song of a skylark, high above them.

Rising and falling on the still air, it filled the sky to overflowing. To the young couple, it seemed to proclaim to the world the joy they both felt in each other.

Author's Note

This novel is a work of fiction, conceived in the mind of the author, although many of the background incidents and the general picture of the times in which it is set are as accurate as research can make them.

The scandal of child prostitution and the procurement of young girls destined for the brothels of Europe continued until 1885, when a London newspaper editor decided on a course of action that shook the nation.

Acting in collaboration with the Salvation Army, he arranged to 'buy' a thirteen-year-old girl, have her certified a virgin, and taken to France in order to prove how easy it was.

Each stage of the proceedings was carefully supervised and reported in his newspaper. But the Victorian public was outraged by the disclosures, and the editor and those who had helped him were prosecuted and charged with a number of offences arising out of the staged incident.

Given the prudish morality of the day, the outcome was never in doubt. The editor was found guilty and served six months' imprisonment in Holloway gaol.

Nevertheless, by his sacrifice, he achieved much of what he and the Salvation Army had intended. The age of consent for girls was raised from thirteen to sixteen and laws passed to severely curtail the trade in providing young girls for the brothels of Europe.

The stature of the Salvation Army grew rapidly after this. It was, and is, respected throughout the world for its tireless efforts among the poor and needy, wherever they are to be found.

Much of the beautiful house of Lanhydrock, in Cornwall, *was* destroyed in a fierce fire in 1881. The fire originated in a kitchen chimney and was fanned by gale-force winds. It is true, too, that Lady Robartes died only days afterwards, broken-hearted at the loss of her magnificent home.

Lanhydrock House was faithfully rebuilt immediately after the fire and is now one of the loveliest gems in the crown of the National Trust.

Singing Spears

BOOK ONE

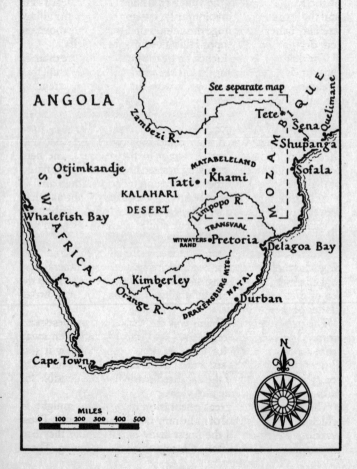

Southern Africa

in the 1880s

ANGOLA

Zambezi R.

MATABELELAND

S. W. AFRICA

Otjimkandje

Whalefish Bay

KALAHARI DESERT

Tati

Khami

Limpopo R.

TRANSVAAL

WITWATERS RAND

Pretoria

Kimberley

Orange R.

DRAKENSBURG MTS.

NATAL

Durban

Cape Town

MOZAMBIQUE

Quelimane

Tete

Sena

Shupanga

Sofala

See separate map

Delagoa Bay

MILES

0   100   200   300   400   500

N

CHAPTER ONE

An air of intense excitement enveloped the thatched mud huts of the King's kraal in the valley of Khami. Hearts beat faster and the mouth dried involuntarily. It was as though the village itself lay beneath the huge dust cloud that hung high above the red, dry-parched Matopos Hills like a giant umbrella.

The dust was being kicked up by the hooves of more than six thousand cattle. Pouring down the rounded slopes of a hill, they streamed towards the village, a wide, living ribbon extending for half-a-mile to the east.

The beasts were by no means prime cattle. They stumbled along with heads hanging low, red-rimmed eyes bulging from fear and exhaustion. A man could hide two fingers between their bony ribs. The cattle caught in the centre of the herd coughed and choked, swinging horned heads against the flanks of their neighbours as they breathed in more dust than air.

Yet, until a few weeks before, these scrawny animals had represented the proud wealth of a village of Manica tribesmen in their homeland around the foothills of the Inyanga mountains. Men had died for them.

Herding the cattle along their way were five hundred trotting Matabele warriors. Bedecked with ostrich feathers, they jogged along, hammering on taut hide war shields to keep the sea of cattle moving. Sunlight glinted on the gleaming, broad blades of their assegais.

The excitement in Khami was for the return of these warriors. The Matabele regiment – an 'impi' – had been away from its home kraal for three anxious months. Now it was almost home and the success of the foray was plain for all to see. The dust cloud of the captured cattle had been visible for hours before they came into view.

There would be a great celebration in the kraal tonight, in which all but a handful of mourning families would join. These warriors were part of the finest army in Africa and they had encountered little resistance during their campaigning. Those few tribes foolish enough to make a stand against them had been overwhelmed and slaughtered by the ruthless Matabele fighting-men.

Working in a back room of his stone-built store at the edge of the kraal, Daniel Retallick was aware of both the excitement and its cause. Twenty-six years of age now, he had been living in the royal kraal for almost five years. He had seen many victorious impis return. He knew that in addition to the cattle they would be bringing back prisoners. Captured children to be assimilated into the Matabele tribe, the girls as servants and chattels, the boys as warriors. There would be women prisoners too, to provide savage entertainment for the evening festivities.

Gritting his teeth against the images conjured up by the memories of previous 'entertainments', Daniel swung a wooden keg filled with gunpowder from the hard-packed dirt floor to the top of the three-tiered stack of barrels already against the stone wall.

Daniel loved the country of the Matabele, with its ancient hills and deep fertile valleys. Parched brown by the dry winter, it would erupt in a riot of flowering trees and shrubs in the rains of summer. He loved its people too and worked hard to protect them from the greed and exploitation of the English and the Boers who crowded Matabeleland's southern borders. But Daniel recognised the shortcomings of the tribe and its despotic ruler.

In his own quiet way, Daniel had tried to wean Mzilikazi, the Matabele King, away from many of the barbaric practices that more civilised nations found unacceptable. He was succeeding — but very slowly. He feared his efforts would be overtaken by the pressing needs of those men seeking entry to the riches they believed Matabeleland to hold.

Suddenly, the sound outside the store became a great roar that echoed from the surrounding hills. Leaping on the barrels of gunpowder, Daniel peered through a high, barred window. The returning warriors and the cattle were still more than a mile away. The object of the crowd's approbation was much closer.

Another roar, and the word 'BAYETE!' thundered to the sky from a thousand throats, setting a stack of tin plates

8

rattling on a shelf in the store. 'Bayete' was a greeting by the people to their Paramount Chief – their King.

Daniel eased the keg of gunpowder further on to the stack before jumping to the ground. Wiping perspiration from his face with the crumpled kerchief he wore about his neck, he made his way to the front door of the store.

To cries of 'He comes! The mountain walks among his people', Mzilikazi was going out to meet the returning warriors, accompanied by many of his three hundred wives. Daniel realised this raid must have been something out of the ordinary.

Absolute ruler of the Matabele nation and the suzerain of a dozen lesser tribes, forty-six years had passed since Mzilikazi's break from Shaka, the Zulu Chief. Heading northwards from Natal, Mzilikazi had taken his own people first to the Transvaal, then, later, across the Limpopo River. Here, in the hills and plains that would one day be known as Rhodesia, and later as Zimbabwe, he had welded them together as the powerful and much-feared Matabele nation.

In those days Mzilikazi had been a great chief and a warrior in the prime of life. Now, in 1868, he was almost eighty years of age and rarely left the royal enclosure. Monarch of a greatly expanded nation, heavy drinking and the cares of his warrior people had dulled his mind and taken a toll of his once-fine physique. Mzilikazi now weighed more than three hundred pounds and his gross body needed to be supported wherever he went by two of his strongest bodyguards.

But the eyes of Mzilikazi were still as keen as ever. He missed nothing. Surrounded though he was by hundreds of shouting and applauding subjects, Mzilikazi saw Daniel. Shaking himself free from his helpers, he held up a massive hand for silence. Immediately, all sound was cut off, leaving behind a stillness so unexpected that a startled flock of red-billed quelea birds took to the air in a whirring cloud from the trees in the King's royal enclosure.

'The day is too warm for work, trader,' called Mzilikazi to Daniel. 'Come! I go to meet my son, Kanje. He returns from his first raid against the Manicas.'

He waved an overweight arm in the direction of the hills, where the tail end of the cattle herd had just come into sight,

'See? The cattle he has brought to me move across the land like locusts. He has done well.'

At Mzilikazi's side one of his favourite younger wives beamed her pleasure at his words. She was the mother of Kanje and had worked hard for this moment. At night, in the sweaty darkness of Mzilikazi's hut, with no one near to remind the King of her lowly status as a junior wife, she had used every wile known to woman to further the career of her only son. Sired by Mzilikazi when she was hardly thirteen years old, Kanje was but one of many hundred such royal 'princes'. Less respectful subjects declared they were as numerous as ticks on the great royal herds. Few would even rise high enough to command one of the King's impis. Kanje's mother was determined that *her* son should profit from his royal heritage – and one day take the throne from his father.

'Are you coming with me, trader? Would you look upon the faces of the Manica women and their spawn? My runner tells me there are many.'

Over the King's head, Daniel could see the blood-red leaves of the royal msasa trees. He shuddered, then shook his head. 'This is a day for your warriors and their families, Mzilikazi. I have much work to do in my store.'

The mother of Kanje glared malevolently at Daniel, incensed by what she considered to be a slight to her son.

'You are not pleased that my warriors have won a great victory . . . ?' Mzilikazi's narrowed angrily and Daniel's heart sank. He was probably one of the King's most trusted friends and, in return, had a great affection for the despotic old ruler, but in recent months drink and senility had combined to make Mzilikazi dangerously unpredictable.

'I'm happy at the success of your army, Mzilikazi,' Daniel chose his words carefully. 'I congratulate you on having such a brave warrior for a son – but I am a white man. Looking upon the faces of those who are soon to die gives me no pleasure.'

To Daniel's relief, the frown lifted from Mzilikazi's face. Daniel's dislike of the Matabele's more violent ways was no secret to anyone. With an expression of amusement on his face, Mzilikazi looked at Daniel speculatively.

'Very well, trader. Stay and continue your work – but I insist that you attend the celebrations tonight. You understand me?'

The King's eyes held Daniel's and, sick to his stomach, Daniel could only nod his head in agreement. He knew he should have swallowed his pride and accompanied Mzilikazi to meet his son and the victorious Matabele warriors. True, there would have been isolated acts of cruelty perpetrated against the unfortunate Manica prisoners by the jeering villagers but it would be nothing compared to what he would be forced to witness at the evening's victory celebrations. After consuming gallons of thick, kraal-brewed beer, the Matabele had no inhibitions. They would lay the dust about the celebration fires with the blood of their prisoners.

Daniel looked wearily along the valley. The first cattle of the stolen herd were now passing the low wooden shacks of the mission station that occupied an isolated position beside the main track to the kraal. There was no sign of the missionaries, but Daniel knew they would not be missing a single incident happening outside. The quill pens would be scratching the pages of their journals in a fury tonight.

There were two missionaries resident at the mission station. One was a single man, the other accompanied by his wife. Theirs was a lonely and frustrated existence. The station had been established as the result of an unguarded promise made by Mzilikazi to the veteran missionary, Robert Moffat, some years before. But giving his word to allow a mission station to be built was one thing – permitting it to function successfully was something quite different. Mzilikazi was adamant that the missionaries must not preach to his people. Summary execution was speedily imposed on any subject who appeared ready for conversion to the white man's faith.

Daniel did not like the missionaries. Both were quarrelsome and bigotted men. Their ambition of converting the Matabele to Christianity involved sweeping away all tribal traditions and pride. Covering the people's nakedness with western-style clothing and modelling the Matabele along the lines of Sunday-school children. In pursuit of this aim the missionaries schemed and connived to bring Europeans to the country, ignoring the dangers of such a policy. They argued that there was nothing wrong in using powder and shot to blast the benefits of The Word into the lives of Mzilikazi's reluctant savages.

Nevertheless, in spite of his dislike for them, Daniel sympathised with the missionaries in their well-nigh impossible task. He felt a grudging admiration for their tenacity in remaining in this land, where they were so patently unwanted. Mzilikazi would not go back on the promise he had made to Moffat, but he made no secret of the fact that he would be happy if the two men abandoned the mission station and left the Matabele to the Devil – and Mzilikazi. In an attempt to achieve this aim, he insisted they perform various menial tasks for him that were beneath the dignity of his own warriors. In addition, he demanded that they grow produce for the royal household and gather wood for his fires.

The missionaries took up these additional burdens without complaint, but both men kept carefully detailed diaries of their humiliations. They hoped that future publication, together with information of the happenings in Matabeleland might arouse the passions of the British public and force the government to send an army against the Matabele and their despotic ruler. At the very least, the diaries should ensure appropriate recognition for their devotion to the Christian cause.

Thinking of the ordeal he would have to undergo that evening, Daniel wished the missionaries were men he could talk to. It would be even better if Sam Speke were in Khami . . . Sam and his daughter Victoria.

Sam Speke had come to Khami many years before, with Daniel. Married to a girl of the Herero tribe from South West Africa, Sam was currently on a visit with his family to his wife's village, almost a thousand miles away.

A solid, reliable man, Sam Speke had been with Daniel's parents when they were shipwrecked on the treacherous Skeleton Coast of South West Africa. Only three years old at the time, Daniel, with his family, had been given sanctuary by the Hereros and lived in their village for many years. Daniel's parents had returned to England when he moved to Matabeleland, but Sam Speke came with him. He helped run the Matabele end of a remarkable trade route extending more than half the breadth of the African continent. From Mzilikazi's capital to Whalefish Bay, on the Atlantic coast. The South West African end of the operation was looked after by Aaron Copping, Daniel's partner. Aaron had been trading in

Africa for most of his life and knew more about South West Africa than any other man alive.

Theirs was a unique trading venture. Initially, it had begun as a trading link between Whalefish Bay and the Herero heartland. Daniel had extended the route first to the Bechuanas at Lake Ngami, in the Kalahari Desert, and then to the land of the Matabele. It was a hazardous life, at best – but Daniel was the envy of a great many white adventurers. These were the men who were gradually edging the frontiers of exploration and commerce closer to Matabeleland. Only Mzilikazi's impis, jealously guarding the rich lands over which their King claimed jurisdiction, kept them at bay.

Mzilikazi did not trust white men. He occasionally befriended certain individuals, but their numbers could be counted on the fingers of one hand and their friendship did not change his opinion of their fellows. What he learned from these select few convinced Mzilikazi beyond all doubt that if ever his country were thrown open to them the way of life of the Matabele would end forever. Mzilikazi was determined it would not come to pass in his lifetime.

As the sun sank below the summit of the range of hills to the west of Khami, the taut monkey-skin drums began to beat out from the great square in the centre of the capital. Others took up the rhythm eagerly. Soon the sound of a hundred drums echoed back and forth between the rocky crags about the town. In the centre of the square many fires sprang up and impromptu dancing began. As the dancers shuffled and swayed together in the flickering light the rapidly growing crowds about them sang and clapped in time to the music.

Daniel had hoped to arrive late at the festivities and slip away at the earliest moment without being noticed. His plans were dashed when Jandu, another of Mzilikazi's many sons, arrived at the store with orders to escort him to the square.

'You are to be honoured tonight, trader,' Jandu called from the store-room as he weighed a new percussion rifle in his hands while Daniel dressed.

Daniel entered the store fastening the long sleeves of his shirt at the wrists. The mosquitoes were always worse at night and it paid to leave as little skin exposed as possible.

'Honoured . . . ?' he frowned at Jandu. 'I'm damned if I see it that way. There's no honour in watching unarmed women being hacked to death by young boys!'

Jandu looked very much like his father when he was amused, 'Those young boys will one day be men – and men must be warriors. They need to know the feel of a spear entering the body of an enemy . . . to know which thrusts kill and which only maim. Such knowledge can make the difference between life and death to a warrior in his first battle . . .'

Jandu held the gun in his hands close to the spluttering animal-oil lamp and peered down the barrel. 'Why should you care what happens to Manica women? Are they more to you than Matabele women?'

Mzilikazi's son voiced the curiosity felt by many of the Matabele at Daniel's apparent celibacy while living among them. It was in marked contrast to the behaviour of the few other white men who had visited Khami, seeking permission to hunt, or search for precious metals – or simply explore the land of the Matabele. Their eagerness to have a 'slave girl' was the subject of many ribald tribal jokes. It was rumoured that this was the real reason why so many white men wished to enter Mzilikazi's kingdom. Indeed, before the arrival of the missionary's wife it was believed by the Matabele that there could be no white women in Africa.

'They are no more, and no less, than any other women,' Daniel retorted, but Jandu had already dismissed the matter of Daniel's taste in women from his mind. He held the rifle out towards him.

'This is a good gun?'

'The best. A man's family would never go hungry if he hunted for food with one of those – but it will cost you more elephant tusks than you could collect in a full year.'

Jandu lowered the gun. With a snort of derision he tossed it carelessly aside on a pile of colourful blankets. 'My family has never been hungry – and I hunt only with a spear. Such guns are for white men – and my father's son, Kanje.'

Daniel looked at Jandu sharply. 'Kanje has one of these? I've traded only one since they arrived – to Mzilikazi.'

'Are such guns made only for you, trader? Kanje's raid took

him far from our home. He met with the bearded men who come on horses from the south.'

Daniel knew Jandu was talking about the Boers. Their mounted commandos often rode to the borders of Matabeleland in the hope of surprising a small group of tribesmen and stealing their cattle.

'Kanje captured rifles from the Boers? I don't believe it!'

Jandu allowed himself a quick smile. 'Had Kanje *captured* guns from the bearded ones the Matabele would have a future King who even I would follow without question. No, trader. Kanje and twenty of his men were *given* the guns when the bearded ones learned he was a son of Mzilikazi.'

'If Kanje's accepted gifts from the Boers he's a fool!'

Jandu nodded. 'I see you understand the situation. Kanje does not. As you say, he is a fool – a young fool. He would rule our people, yet does not realise he has already put himself in debt to the bearded ones. If ever he becomes King they will be here, demanding the right to trade.'

Daniel remembered the look Kanje's mother had given him earlier in the day. She was a strong-willed woman who would always influence her son. If Kanje ever ruled in his father's place Daniel's trading days with the Matabele would be over. The Boers would move in to take his place. Daniel knew this. So did Jandu.

'You and I should be of one mind, trader. We both have much to lose should my brother be chosen to lead our people. You, your trade. I . . . my life. While I and my other brothers live we would always pose a threat to him. Unfortunately, there is little I can do to prevent Kanje having his way. I am just one of Mzilikazi's many troublesome sons. But you have my father's ear. You are a trusted friend. He will listen to you.'

Daniel looked at Jandu suspiciously. About thirty years of age, the Matabele was tall, even when judged by the standards of his own tribe, and he had the massive chest of his father. He also had remarkably large eyes that at first glance appeared docile, but when given a direct glance, a man felt they were burning into his very soul. Jandu had only recently returned to Khami, after serving as an Induna, or commander, of one of the King's impis in a far-off border district.

A man of exceptional intelligence and presence, Jandu

15

would pose a threat to the ambitions of any of Mzilikazi's sons. Daniel hoped, for Jandu's sake, that he had not yet attracted too much attention. But, although he was impressed by what he had seen of the other man, Daniel was reluctant to be drawn into their accession feuds.

'You would like me to put in a good word for you, of course?'

To Daniel's surprise, Jandu shrugged his shoulders nonchalantly, 'There are many of my brothers who would rule better than I – but Kanje is not one of them. Under his leadership Matabeleland would become a skeleton, picked clean by the jackals who squat about our borders. I have no wish to see this happen.'

Daniel stared thoughtfully at Jandu, wondering whether all this was no more than a devious ploy by Mzilikazi himself to draw him into the intrigues of the King's court, and so declare himself. He dismissed the idea immediately. Mzilikazi knew him better. He had always been very careful to remain aloof from the constant scheming of those who surrounded the King.

'You need make no reply now, but do not take too long to think about what has been said here today. Mzilikazi is an old man.'

'True – but he is still King of the Matabele, and tonight I've been ordered to witness Kanje's triumph. Let's go and get it over with.'

CHAPTER TWO

When Daniel arrived in the great square the victory celebrations were well under way, huge wood fires blazing furiously. The area surrounding the kraal had long since been denuded of trees and the wood had been brought from the river valley, more than two miles distant from Khami. No effort was being spared to make this a night the King's subjects would long remember.

Around the fires beer gourds were passing from hand to hand, and mouth to mouth, the drinking accompanied by shouted bawdy jokes and loud, uninhibited laughter. Many of the men, particularly those with sons in the returning impi, had been celebrating from the moment the first warrior had been sighted on the hills beyond the capital.

In the cleared space between the fires the women danced in long, linked lines, stamping their feet, bodies newly anointed with animal fat, swaying in time to the music of the drummers.

The women of the royal harem, dressed in their finest beads and feathers were performing their own exclusive dance in the very centre of the square, watched by their happy and relaxed husband. Mzilikazi sat on a pile of cattle hides, drinking vast quantities of beer. He was far too close to the nearest fire for comfort, but seemed not to mind the glistening rivulets of perspiration that formed salt pools in the deep creases of his body.

Seeing Daniel, Mzilikazi roared for him to come and sit at his side. Daniel would have preferred to sit further away from the heat of the fire, but he dared not refuse. A gesture from the King dismissed Jandu, and Daniel chose a place on the heaped cow hides, accepting the gourd of beer that was quickly passed to him by one of Mzilikazi's wives.

The beer, brewed and drunk by the Matabele, had the consistency of a well-watered porridge. It smelled sour but the taste was not unpleasant. Under the watchful eyes of Mzilikazi, Daniel took a deep draught before setting the gourd down on the ground beside him.

Resting a heavy hand briefly on Daniel's shoulder, the Matabele King beamed at him benignly. 'I am pleased to see you are still one of us, trader,' he boomed. 'Now you will hear of my son's first raid.'

Clapping his hands, Mzilikazi ordered the dancers from the square.

As the women hurried to find space on the ground behind their menfolk, the crowd's excitement increased in volume, drowning the complaining lowing of the captured cattle, penned within the royal cattle kraal, just beyond the village.

Another signal from Mzilikazi, then he sprawled back on his hide throne to enjoy a re-enactment of the raid on the Manicas.

First to take the stage was the King's 'Inganga' – his 'witch-doctor'. Accompanied by two assistants, he wore a hideous mask and a tall headdress of fur and feathers and made a frightening giant figure in the capricious light from the fire. After performing a series of incredible leaps and contortions that had the appreciative crowd gasping in awe, the Inganga stood in front of Mzilikazi and scattered a variety of powdered potions to the four winds. Then he began extolling the virtues of the King, reminding his subjects of past victories. As each one was mentioned the great crowd let out a sigh of appreciation.

When he felt enough had been said to satisfy the King's vanity, the Inganga began telling his listeners of the success of Kanje's raid in the unknown lands of the Manica tribes. He reminded King and the subjects that it was he, the Inganga, who had sent the raiding-party on its way protected by some of his most powerful 'medicine'.

'Powerful it may have been,' interrupted the King. 'But some faces were missing from the returning impi. How many of my warriors died?'

The Inganga turned to the Induna of the impi, who fell to his knees in front of his King.

'Seven, Kumalo.' Kumalo meant literally 'Majesty'.

'Name them.'

The Induna called out seven names. As each rolled off his tongue there was a groan from the listening crowd, and a wail from the women of the dead warrior's family.

'How did they die?' asked the King, when the names were known.

'They died bravely, Kumalo. They were truly Matabele warriors.'

Mzilikazi nodded his satisfaction, 'Each elder son, or father of the dead men is to be given ten captured cattle.'

There was a sigh of approval from the crowd. It was a generous gesture.

Next, the Inganga gave details of the number of their enemies killed, cattle gained for the Matabele, and the number of prisoners secured.

As the Inganga spoke, evidence of his statistics were produced for the benefit of his audience. A dozen cattle, terrified by the din about them, were dragged into the square and Mzilikazi immediately ordered them to be killed and roasted over the fires for his people. Next came the unfortunate prisoners, women and boys, herded into the firelight to the derisive jeers of the spectators. Many of the captured women fell to their knees in front of Mzilikazi, begging him to spare their lives. The children who were to be assimilated into the tribe clung to their mothers, too bewildered to understand what was about to happen. After no more than a brief glance in their direction, Mzilikazi dismissed them from his presence.

Next, the Inganga's assistants ran towards Mzilikazi carrying two bulging hide bags. As the bags were upturned before the King a dozen dust-smeared heads thudded to the ground and a great roar of approval went up from the crowd.

Daniel had been prepared for this display of barbarism. He had witnessed such incidents before – but he was not expecting Mzilikazi's next move.

The Inganga peered at each head in turn, finally selecting one topped with short, curly grey hair. Carrying it to the King, he handed over the gruesome object, declaring it to be the head of the Chief of the Manica tribe.

Mzilikazi took the head and held it up before him, studying the features. Suddenly, he tossed the head through the air towards Daniel who caught it in an involuntary action.

'There, trader. Does he look as noble as a Matabele?'

Aware of the laughter of the watching Matabele, Daniel shrugged, carefully concealing the revulsion he felt. 'He looks like any other man. No doubt he was proud of his tribe, and honoured his ancestors.'

Daniel placed the gruesome trophy next to the King. Mzilikazi hurriedly pushed it to the ground and ordered the main event of the evening to begin.

Daniel had played upon the King's own superstitious beliefs. The Matabele were taught that if a man honoured his ancestors throughout his own life, his own spirit would be welcomed by them after death. These ancestral spirits would not be pleased with any mortal who made their task more difficult by separating head from body.

The Inganga's two assistants removed the heads of the dead Manica warriors and now the victorious Matabele impi marched proudly to the firelit square, applauded loudly by relatives and friends. Dressed in their warrior feathers and carrying tall, hide shields and broad-bladed assegais, they spread across the square, assuming the extended-horn battle formation of an attacking Matabele impi. This was the Zulu manoeuvre that had struck terror in the hearts of enemies from Natal to the Zambezi River.

Chanting slogans and thudding their feet heavily to the ground with each step, the impi advanced across the square until it was within a few paces of Mzilikazi. Then, with a great shout of 'Bayete!' it broke ranks and the warriors moved off to one side.

Their Induna stepped forward and began giving Mzilikazi a lurid account of the raid. He was a good narrator and the crowd remained absolutely silent, straining to hear the Induna's every word. As each man was mentioned, he stepped forward and re-enacted the incident that had provoked such an honour, each stroke of his assegai signifying the death of an enemy at his hands.

Finally it was the turn of Kanje to step forward and impress the King with a display of his prowess. Glistening muscles rippling, the junior son sprang from the ranks of his fellow warriors, scornfully discarding his shield. Brandishing an assegai in his right hand and a rifle in his left, he performed well. To the accompaniment of the Induna's recital, he vividly relived the highlights of his great adventure. The watching subjects held their breath as Kanje crept from the broken rocks of a Manica hillside towards an unsuspecting sentry. They gasped as he fought with three enemy warriors in desperate hand-to-hand combat and shouted an urgent warning when, hard-pressed by the Manica warriors, he was attacked from behind.

When the last of the Manicas had been overwhelmed by the ferocity of his lone attack, Kanje stood facing the King, his father. Head thrown back proudly, he awaited the praise that was his due. Behind him, the crowd exploded in a frenzy of applause. Kanje was the hero of the moment. This was assuredly the greatest day of his young life.

Kanje's moment of glory might have lasted longer had not the Induna been so carried away by the enthusiasm of the crowd that he forgot the suspicious and jealous nature of the Matabele King. Enthusiastically, he concluded his contribution to Kanje's realistic performance by declaring to Mzilikazi, 'Truly, Great One, all who saw Kanje in battle said that he fought as bravely as his father once did. You can be proud of him, Great King.'

'Proud? Proud of a warrior who has hardly left boyhood behind, yet returns from his first raid convinced he is as brave as Mzilikazi?'

The King struggled to his feet, throwing off the bodyguard who rushed to his aid. Standing unsteadily, glaring from the Induna to Kanje, he boomed, 'I have defeated warriors who were said to be unbeatable. Yes . . . and the bearded white men from the south too. You would liken a first-blooded boy to me? Induna – I spit upon you!'

Mzilikazi matched words with the deed as the terrified Induna stood before him, not daring to move a muscle.

'Guards! Bring the prisoners to me.' Mzilikazi roared the words and there was hurried movement from his bodyguard.

The spectators had maintained a frightened silence during the King's angry outburst, fearful lest the slightest sound be interpreted as criticism and so attract the ever-vigilant court executioners. Now they relaxed, eager for what they believed was to follow.

The Manica women and children were herded forward, but now they had been divided into two wailing groups, women in one, children in the other. The paths of their lives would divide sharply now. Life for the young boys would take an upward surge. Given to families among the Matabele people, they would be set to work as herd-boys until they were of an age to join one of Mzilikazi's impis.

There was no such future for the women. They would take only a few steps more along their particular path. It was Matabele tradition that they should be turned loose in the square and there hunted down and slaughtered by the older herd-boys, many themselves sons of earlier victims. Those boys who showed a particular aptitude for killing would be drafted to an impi to begin their training as Matabele warriors.

This was the moment Daniel had been dreading. He had witnessed a similar 'spear washing' ceremony in his first year with the tribe. The memory of the savagery had haunted him for many months.

The prisoners were brought before Mzilikazi and the herd-boys raised their assegais and waited in quivering anticipation. The moments of waiting grew longer, but still the order to release the Manica women did not come. Daniel had dropped his gaze when the women were pushed forward, now he looked up, to see the King studying him.

'You do not wish to see the women killed, trader? If you were King of the Matabele what would you do with them?'

'Let them join their sons and brothers and become useful members of the tribe,' declared Daniel, unhesitantly.

Mzilikazi shifted his gaze to the face of Kanje, still standing proudly before him. But when he spoke it was to Daniel once more. 'You have never given me bad advice – and your honesty is greater than that of my son. So be it.' To the Induna of his personal bodyguard, he called, 'Release the Manica women. They will become servants to the Matabele. Take them away now.'

As a howl of disappointment rose from the throats of those villagers close enough to hear Mzilikazi's words, one of the Manica women who had been following the conversation closely, broke away from the others and flung herself at Daniel's feet.

A guard seized her arm to drag her away, but Mzilikazi waved him off.

'Leave her!' Grinning broadly, he said to Daniel. 'You have saved their lives, the least you can do is contribute in some way to their keep. This girl shall be yours.' To the guard he said, 'Have her taken to the trader's store.'

Mzilikazi's good humour was short-lived. Before Daniel could reply, Kanje took an angry pace forward. 'The prisoners are mine. It has always been the custom for the herd-boys to kill captive women. Since when have the Matabele looked to a white man for orders?'

Mzilikazi was a huge man, yet at Kanje's words it seemed to his awestruck people that he swelled to twice his normal size, so great was his wrath. Lunging forward, he snatched the rifle from the hands of his recalcitrant younger son.

'The Matabele put themselves in the power of the white man from the day warriors accept gifts such as this from his hands. Do you think it was given to you because a white man wants you for a brother? Fool! Black men and white can never be brothers. He gives you guns because he knows it will make you put aside your spears and rely upon this alone.'

Mzilikazi shook the rifle above his head for everyone to see. 'One day you will find you have an enemy to fight – but no bullets for your gun. Then you will need to turn to the white man and plead with him for more. In exchange he will demand that you allow traders, hunters and gold-diggers in the lands of the Matabele. Once they are here they will multiply like weeds in a field tended by a lazy woman. Where one white man places his foot you will soon find a hundred. For every hundred there will one day be a thousand. When that happens it will be the white man and not the Matabele who rules this land and we will be as the Mashona – men of no account.'

Mzilikazi waved the rifle in Kanje's face and gave him a look of withering scorn. 'I taught the Matabele to fight like men. To look in the face of an enemy and be close enough to smell the fear ooze from him. A brave warrior draws strength from the terror he sees in the eyes of an enemy. A gun is for a coward, a man who knows he is less than his enemy.'

Gripping the rifle as though it were a throwing spear, Mzilikazi hurled it from him, into the fire. It landed at the heart of the blaze, scattering sparks high into the night air.

Turning his back on Kanje and ignoring the wife whose earlier pride had given way to tearful dismay, Mzilikazi tottered from the square on the arms of his two attendants.

Just as he was about to enter the royal enclosure, there was a sudden sharp explosion from the fire. Fragments of burning wood were hurled over the assembled impi and the nearby spectators. They fled in momentary panic.

One man was left behind, lying face downwards in the dirt. It was the Induna who had led Kanje's raid.

Daniel leaped from his seat of skins and kneeled beside the still form. Turning the Induna over he saw an ugly blue-edged wound, just beneath the man's ribs. He was dead, killed by the single bullet in Kanje's gun.

The bullet had merely saved the Induna from a far more unpleasant fate. After praising the younger son in such glowing terms, Mzilikazi could not have allowed him to live. Only Induna's who were unswervingly loyal to Mzilikazi led his regiments. Indunas who favoured younger sons were particularly dangerous to an aged king. After all, Mzilikazi had himself broken away from the Zulu nation and founded the Matabele empire with only a single impi.

But the incident with the rifle meant that Mzilikazi would not need to worry about a challenge to his authority for a very long time. His subjects regarded the Induna's death as an awesome example of their King's power. He had used his son's gun to kill one who had offended him, without any man's finger being on the trigger.

But if the King had consolidated his own position, Daniel had made a dangerous enemy. He saw the look that Kanje cast in his direction before hurrying off to choke on his humiliation. Not only had Daniel deprived the Matabele of their anticipated 'spear washing' spectacle, he had robbed Kanje of the adulation of the herd-boys who might have proved themselves tonight. They would have made the name 'Kanje' ring around the square, committing it to the memories of those elders who one day soon would meet to appoint Mzilikazi's successor.

Back in his store, Daniel found that Jandu was the warrior who had brought the Manica girl to his living quarters and he was waiting with her.

The girl told Daniel her name was Suliyana. She was younger than she had appeared during the brief glimpse he had of her in the square. Looking at her slim body, naked from the waist up, Daniel thought she was probably an under-nourished sixteen-year-old.

It seemed that Jandu's thoughts were moving along similar lines. 'You will need to feed her before you send her out to till your fields. She would be blown away by the first breeze that came along.'

'I can work as hard as any Matabele woman,' retorted Suliyana, scornfully. She had a soft, pleasant voice together with a disconcerting and challenging way of looking directly at the person to whom she was talking. 'And I will eat less than the women I saw in Mzilikazi's household.'

Jandu frowned and Daniel said hurriedly, 'I doubt if you'll be here long enough to impress me with your work – or lack of appetite. There's little enough room for one to live in this store.'

Jandu's frown became a smile. 'She'll have to stay here tonight. Mzilikazi will be very angry if you turn her out – and one night should be long enough to cause you much trouble, as Mzilikazi knows well. Just before you saved the lives of the Manica women a runner arrived with a message. Your friend Speke has returned to Matabeleland with his Herero wife and their daughter. They should reach Khami in the morning.'

CHAPTER THREE

Victoria Speke galloped her horse up to the door of the store a bare two hours after dawn. The manner of her arrival raised a cloud of choking dust in her wake and scattered bleary-eyed Matabele women, dogs and chickens.

She rode like a man and, with her short black hair and boy's clothing, an onlooker might have been excused for thinking she was an excited and boisterous youth, and not a lively young woman of twenty.

Sawing her horse to a slithering, foam-blowing halt, Victoria swung a leg across the pommel of the saddle. Kicking her other foot free of the stirrup, she slid to the ground with an agile, easy movement.

Running inside the store, she collided heavily with Daniel. Before he was able to recover his balance, her arms went about him and, while he pressed back against an uncomfortable stack of iron kettles and small cauldrons, Victoria kissed him with an ardour that would have raised eyebrows in even the most advanced-thinking European community.

'Daniel! It's good to be back. I've missed you . . . I feel I've been away from you for years! Have you missed me too? What's been happening?'

At that moment, Victoria caught sight of Suliyana.

The Manica girl was wearing no more, and no less, than she had on the day she was first captured. A string of beads about her waist, from which hung a brief leather apron, no more than eight inches square, at front and rear. She was standing by the store-blanket bed Daniel had provided for her in a corner of the store.

Victoria's hands dropped away from Daniel and went up to her thick, black hair in an automatic gesture. Stepping back from him, she looked from the girl to Daniel, her face registering incredulous disbelief, 'Who . . . who is this?'

Daniel had hoped to have Suliyana out of the store by the time Victoria and the others reached Khami. Victoria's early arrival had taken him by surprise. His embarrassed explanation was garbled and disjointed and did nothing to lessen Victoria's growing dismay.

'. . . at least she and the others are alive,' he ended, lamely.

'Others? You have more of them here?' Victoria cast a hurried glance about the store.

'No, of course not. Mzilikazi ordered Suliyana to be brought here. The others will be put to work in Khami.'

'And she's only been here since last night?'

'Of course. I was hoping to be rid of her by the time you arrived. You took me by surprise.'

'I can see *that*,' Victoria smiled again and Daniel relaxed. Fortunately, Victoria would never learn how difficult it had been to convince the Manica girl that she would not be sharing his bed.

Victoria took Daniel's hand and squeezed it so tightly she hurt his fingers. 'All right, I'll forgive you – but she can't stay here. She can come and work for us. We'll need some help in the house after all these months away.'

Sam Speke had built a large wooden cabin for his family. It was about fifty yards away from the store.

'Get your horse and I'll take you back along the trail to meet Dad and Aaron. On the way you can bring me up to date on all that's happened while I've been away.'

'Aaron is with you? Why? What's happening to our stores in South West Africa?'

'The fighting is bad, Daniel. While we were at home in Otjimkandje the village was raided three times, and most of the while the warriors are out raiding someone else. On the way we've passed through villages that have been razed to the ground. The stench of death is everywhere. Nobody is trading. Whatever one tribe needs it takes from another. It's dangerous for a man to have anything worth stealing. Even so, it took Dad a long time to persuade Aaron to leave with us . . . but there'll be time enough to talk about things like that when we meet up with the others. Let's just talk about you and me for a while.'

Since arriving in Khami, five years before, theirs had been a warm and easy relationship. Even then the fifteen-year-old Victoria had adored the twenty-one-year-old Daniel, already

27

experienced in trading and the harsh ways of nineteenth-century Africa. Nothing had ever been said, but it was assumed by those about them that one day they would marry and set up home together among the Matabele.

Suliyana watched as they walked away, hand-in-hand, Victoria leaning her slight body against Daniel. The Manica girl was filled with an emotion she had never before experienced. She did not recognise it as the pangs of jealousy.

Daniel was not the first European Suliyana had met. She came from a village which was frequently visited by Portuguese traders. Occasionally she would also see a Portuguese official who had reluctantly forsaken the comforts of coastal life in order to undertake a tour of inspection through the interior of Manicaland. It was an area to which Portugal laid a vague and somewhat indifferent claim.

But none of the Portuguese men Suliyana had met were like Daniel. The Portuguese would sit with the village elders, sipping the brandy they had brought with them, their bloodshot eyes following the swaying bodies of village girls as they passed by. As soon as night fell the officials disappeared into their huts. Giggling children would creep to the low doorways and listen to the Portuguese grunting like wart hogs as they made sweaty love to the women the village headman was obliged to provide.

Daniel was different. He was an altogether gentler man. Suliyana would have given herself to him willingly, but he had not taken her. She had been both hurt and confused at the time. Now she thought she knew the reason. He had been saving himself for the girl who touched his hand now.

Suliyana had also met those with skins the colour of Victoria – but never before a woman. There were many half-caste renegades roaming the hills and forests of the land that lay between her country and the sea. The Manica's called them 'Pombeiros'. They were bastards and descendants of bastards. The result of four centuries of haphazard colonisation by the men who had introduced God and the sword to the tribes of Mozambique.

The Pombeiros were the scourge of the land. They resented the fathers who had sired them so carelessly and scorned the tribes to which they did not – and would not – belong.

Outcasts from both societies, their numbers grew rapidly and they joined together to form formidable rebel forces. They traded in ivory and slaves and sold their military skill to warring chiefs. Between wars they terrorised the countryside far and wide.

Yes, Suliyana had met Pombeiros before. It was only because her own tribe was strong that she did not remember such meetings with shame. Suliyana believed that Daniel was worthy of more than a Pombeiro girl.

Daniel and Victoria met up with Sam Speke, Mary and Aaron with their half-dozen ox-wagons in a narrow, dust-dry valley, five miles west of Khami. About the valley towered rounded granite hills, worn smooth by the wind and rain of twenty-five million African years. Here and there, giant rocks balanced one upon the other in defiance of the elements, recording the incredible depth of the aeons of erosion.

The men exchanged boisterous greetings before Daniel asked Aaron about the South West African end of their trade route.

Much of the humour left the aged Jew's lined face and he spread his arms wide in a characteristic gesture. 'How can you set a few shillings profit against a man's life, Daniel? The country is in turmoil. Not only is tribe fighting against tribe, but village against village. I've spent days negotiating a safe passage through the territory of a chief, only to be attacked by one of his own kraal heads who has changed sides. I stayed as long as I could – longer than any other trader, but I had to make the decision to get out while we still had some trade goods left. There will be no more business in South West until the wars are over.'

The finality of Aaron's statement left Daniel stunned. The whole of the Matabele trading operation depended upon being able to carry ivory, ostrich feathers and animal skins to the South West African port of Whalefish Bay.

'Don't let it worry you, Daniel,' the bearded Jewish trader tried to make light of their problems. 'I hear the Boers are trekking all the way from the Cape to the borders of Matabeleland. If they can do it, so can we. We'll carry our goods to Natal, use Durban . . . or Delagoa Bay.'

Daniel shook his head. 'We'd be crossing the country of both the Boers and the Zulus. Neither would think twice about killing us. If we escaped them our oxen would be eaten alive by Tsetse fly.'

'So, what do we do? Are you suggesting we throw away all our years of hard work? Become shopkeepers in Cape Town, maybe?'

Daniel said nothing for a few minutes. He had ruled out Aaron's proposed route to the Indian Ocean, but there *was* an alternative. . . .

Thoughtfully, he said, 'A few months ago Mzilikazi sent me to warn off an expedition trying to enter Matabeleland from the Kalahari. With the party was an artist. During a conversation I had with him he told me he'd travelled up the Zambezi River from the Indian Ocean in company with a missionary. On that occasion they only got as far as some rapids at Cabora Bassa, three hundred miles upriver. Later, the missionary followed the river on his own and reached the Makololo tribe. Their country is well to the north east, so a trading route along the Zambeze River is feasible. Not only that, the artist had heard of a route inland from Sofala, well to the south of the Zambezi. That would suit us even better.'

'There! Didn't I say you'd think of something? But how do we find this route?'

'I suppose I'll have to go and search for it. The main problem will be the tribes along the way. The first will be the Mashona. I don't anticipate any trouble with them. I've traded with them before and they owe allegiance to Mzilikazi – but I'm more worried about the Manicas. Their lands are beyond the Mashona and one of Mzilikazi's impis has just returned from a raid against them. They're hardly likely to welcome us with open arms.'

'Oh, I don't know,' interjected Victoria, mischievously. 'I saw the look your little Manica girl gave you before we left. I wouldn't say they seem *un*friendly people.'

Victoria had made the remark sarcastically, peeved because she had been back for no more than an hour and Daniel was already talking of going away. But, much to her dismay, Daniel seized upon her words, the sarcasm ignored.

'I think you've come up with the answer.' Seeing the puzzled expressions on the faces of the others, Daniel explained quickly about Kanje's raid and its consequence. 'It means that not only have we someone who knows Manicaland, but her family should be grateful enough to have her back to be ready to help us.'

'Wasn't I right to leave South West?' Aaron lifted his hands to the sky in gratitude. 'Lord, I should have known you wouldn't slam a door in my face without opening another.'

Daniel grinned ruefully. 'Save your thanks until we reach the Indian Ocean, Aaron. A lot can happen between here and there.'

Victoria also had misgivings, but for very different reasons. Daniel would be taking a Manica girl – a *grateful* Manica girl, on a long journey through unknown country. Together they would share dangers and new, exciting experiences. Victoria had no doubt the Manica girl would use her big, expressive brown eyes to good purpose along the way. Tears of frustration stung her eyes like grains of fine sand. Angrily she blinked them back. Pulling the reins of her startled horse towards her, she leaped upon its back and rode away along the track.

Sam Speke watched her go, a troubled frown on his face. He understood what was upsetting her. If only Daniel would say something to her about their future together . . . . Victoria was of an age for marriage – and Daniel was the man she had chosen. Sam Speke had always given his daughter everything she wanted. He would not allow the one thing she desired more than any other to escape from her now.

With a sigh, he cracked the long, rawhide whip over the flanks of his oxen. As the patient beasts leaned into their yokes, Sam Speke spoke to his wife, Mary, who clung to the seat beside him. 'I reckon I'll need to go with young Daniel on this trip of his to the coast. Our Victoria would never recover if he got lost somewhere along the way.'

Riding ahead of the others, Daniel caught up with Victoria where the rough path from the west joined the main track into the valley from the south. The mission station was only a few hundred yards distant and Victoria was talking to the two missionaries.

This was not the moment to ask Victoria why she had ridden

off so hastily, and one of the missionaries was beckoning to him. 'I've been waiting to have a word with you, Retallick. You know, of course, that Mzilikazi's impis have been on the rampage again? One returned only yesterday with thousands of stolen cattle and at least a hundred women prisoners. It sickened me to see them. The good Lord alone knows how many more were slaughtered. Can't you put a stop to such ghastly happenings? I know you live in the kraal with these savages, but you're a white man, after all. You *must* do something.'

The Reverend Farewell Loveday had been born in the Cape Colony thirty years before. At the age of seven he had accompanied his missionary parents on a recklessly misguided evangelistic voyage to the Natal coast, almost a thousand miles beyond the protection of the nearest British garrison. Only two days after they landed, the infant Farewell Loveday saw his parents hacked to pieces by the broad-bladed assegais of Shaka's Zulus. The experience rendered him totally unsuited for missionary work but, brought up by missionary colleagues of his late father, Farewell Loveday's future role in life was never in doubt. Now he was labouring amidst the Matabele, an off-shoot of the Zulu tribe he both hated and feared.

Leaning forward in his saddle, Daniel said cryptically, 'Plead with the Lord, Farewell. He's the only one who can influence Mzilikazi. I certainly can't – and I didn't see you outside registering a protest when the impi passed by the mission station.'

'You know as well as I do, they'd have overrun me with their stolen cattle.'

Swinging his horse's head away from the Reverend Farewell Loveday, Daniel spoke to the second missionary who stood nervously dabbing his unnaturally pale face with a damp handkerchief. 'How about you, Reverend Pugh-Williams? Didn't you think of pointing out the error of their ways to the warriors of the impi?'

'I . . . I was sick. Too sick to leave my bed. I should be there now . . . I'm not a well man.' The Reverend Pugh-Williams stammered the words unhappily in his sing-song Welsh voice.

Daniel's scornful look was tinged with pity. Arnold Pugh-Williams was a weak man. His failings would have been apparent in whatever calling he chose, in any country. Here, in the heart of Africa where a man needed to be strong to survive, he was an object of derision. His only defence against the harsh world about him lay in his illnesses, some real, but most imagined. When things became too much for him he took to his bed, tended in a somewhat desultory manner by his wife. He would have left Khami within weeks of his arrival had it not been for her. Helena Pugh-Williams insisted that The Lord's will had brought them to Khami – so here they must stay. The daughter of an English Anglican Bishop, Helena Pugh-Williams was an attractive and strong-willed young woman. Malicious Cape Town gossip had it that *she* had persuaded her timid husband to go to Khami – in order to be near the more ebullient Farewell Loveday.

'This heathen country is in sore need of red-blooded white men,' Farewell Loveday complained bitterly. 'I have a great many Boer friends who wouldn't stand by and stick their heads in the sand while Mzilikazi's warriors hacked innocent women to death. I trust their screams didn't keep *you* awake last night, Retallick?'

'They didn't,' replied Daniel, truthfully. 'And I hope you didn't report their deaths in your diary because they are still alive! Oh, and so that you might keep your journal accurate, there were only forty prisoners brought in, not a hundred.'

Jerking the reins of his horse, Daniel rode on to the store, Victoria falling silently in place behind him.

A basic difference of opinion separated Daniel and the two missionaries. Farewell Loveday, in particular, was working to have Matabeleland thrown open to white settlers, many of whom had already tried to obtain land grants from Mzilikazi. By far the most persistent were the Boers. Chafing at the petty restrictions imposed upon them by the rapidly expanding authority of the British administration in the Cape Colony, the Boers had set up their own Republic of Transvaal, extending to the southernmost limits of Mzilikazi's lands.

Only the ferocity and weight of numbers of Mzilikazi's warriors kept the Boers to the south of the Limpopo River. Missionaries of all denominations constantly fired their hopes of a northward trek, believing the Boers to be the only hope of forcing Christian standards on the Matabele and their vassals.

Daniel's experiences in South West Africa made him rather more sceptical of the outcome of such a white invasion. In that unfortunate territory traders had set one tribe against another, selling arms to each of the combatants in turn and making huge profits. In Matabeleland a confrontation between Boer and native would be bound to result in bitter and bloody fighting. The Boers wanted to carve out farms and homesteads to pass on to their sons and grandchildren. Those of them who had seen Matabeleland enthused about its lush, rolling hills and bountiful rivers and streams. Here a man could raise two crops every year.

Mzilikazi knew the worth of his lands. In order to keep them he and his warriors would fight to the death. However, his policy of maintaining a huge, well-trained army, coupled with the firm exclusion of whites from Matabeleland had succeeded in giving his people peace – so far. Many years before, a Boer adventurer *had* brought a large party to Matabeleland. Mounted and well-armed, they were confident of their superiority. They had stolen a great many Matabele cattle – but never got them back to Transvaal. Mzilikazi ambushed the raiders among the hills of the Matopos. Wounding many Boers, he slew all their retainers and recovered his cattle.

Since that day no European had entered Matabeleland without first obtaining Mzilikazi's permission. If relations between Matabele and white man were cool, at least they were not spilling each other's blood.

Daniel tackled Suliyana later that evening in Sam Speke's house, to which she had reluctantly moved. Victoria brought her to the room where Daniel, Aaron and Sam Speke were enjoying the brandy carried from the coast of South West Africa. Suliyana stood before them without any show of self-consciousness, and her eyes went instinctively to Daniel.

He smiled at her with more friendliness than he had dared display the previous evening. 'Suliyana, we've been talking here about setting up a new route to the coast for our trade goods. If it went through the country of your people do you think they would welcome us?'

Suliyana was an intelligent girl and she realised immediately how important she might be to the white man who had saved her life, but she contained her excitement as she answered.

'My people have never fought the white man. You will be welcome in our villages.'

Daniel's interest quickened at her words and he removed the pipe from his mouth. 'Other white men have been to your land?'

'Many come there, but they do not speak your language. They are the Mapunga – the rice eaters.'

'The Portuguese! Do these men bring trade goods from the sea?'

'Some do. I too have seen the sea upon which the white man floats his great wooden houses.'

'You've been to the sea and seen ships?' Daniel's excitement was shared by the others. 'What was the name of this place – and how far is it from your village?'

'The Mapunga call it "Sofala". It is ten days walk through the hills from my village.'

'Suliyana, if I return you to your people will you guide me to Sofala?'

'You are going to take me back to my village?' Now Suliyana's delight could not be hidden.

'Yes . . . that's if there's anyone left alive after Kanje's raid.'

Suliyana looked disdainful. 'The Matabele killed only old men and boys. They raided the working kraal of one of the headmen responsible for the chief's cattle. The headman was my uncle. I was visiting him from my own kraal, two days walk away. The Matabele would not dare attack such a place.'

- She smiled happily at Daniel. 'Yes, I will guide you to the coast. I, or some of my people. But do not tell them you are Mzilikazi's friend, only that you trade with his tribe. My people have heard much of Mzilikazi from our neighbours, the tribes you call the Mashona. They have suffered much from the Matabele.'

The Mashonas occupied the high plateau to the north west of Matabeleland, forming an uncomfortable buffer between the Matabele and the Manica.

'Will you travel alone to Manicaland, Daniel?' Victoria asked the question very quietly.

'I haven't given it any thought yet. I'll probably take a few Mashonas with me to look after the pack animals.'

35

The Mashonas and their allied tribes did most of the work about the Matabele capital. Their situation was scarcely better than that of slaves, but for most of them it was enough that they lived. The means used by Mzilikazi to subjugate them came very close to genocide and the whole tribe lived in constant fear of Matabele raids.

Daniel looked to where Aaron sat back in an armchair, contentedly puffing at his pipe. 'Would you like to come with me to Sofala, Aaron?'

'Me . . . . ? Go gallivanting about the country searching for the Indian Ocean? No, my boy, to me one stretch of water is the same as another. You go off and find your ocean, you are the young pioneer. I have spent many months journeying from the Atlantic and have had enough of travelling. I'm just a poor old man who should have retired many years ago.'

Daniel smiled. Aaron had spent all his adult life travelling through the trackless wastes of southern Africa, trading as he went. He could not change his way of life now, even if he were so inclined. But he *had* just completed a very exhausting journey. He had earned a rest.

'You know, I've got a hankering to see the Indian Ocean, Daniel.'

Sam Speke's words came as a complete surprise to everyone except his wife. No adventurous traveller, Sam was usually quite content to remain at the kraal, manufacturing furniture for the store and the mission church, and building wagons for Mzilikazi. They were wagons that would never be used because Mzilikazi refused to allow any of his oxen to haul them. The oxen, in common with his cattle, were as children to him. To set them to work would be 'cruel'.

Before Daniel could reply to Sam Speke, Victoria spoke to her father. 'If you go, then I can come too.'

Anticipating Daniel's objections, she said quickly to Suliyana, 'Would *I* be safe in your country too?'

It was a difficult question for the Manica girl to answer. Suliyana had her own plans for the journey. After struggling without success for the right reply, she shrugged and said noncommitally, 'My people do not attack women.'

Victoria turned triumphantly to Daniel. 'There! Now there's no reason at all why I shouldn't come with you. I'll be safe in Manicaland and we'll be under Mzilikazi's protection until we get there.'

Victoria knew she would eventually get her own way with her father, she always did. But she expected Daniel to object. To her surprise, he did no more than raise a nominal protest. Then he too accepted that she would go with him to the east coast.

Daniel knew full well that Victoria had over-simplified the difficulties they would encounter, but he would be happy to have her along. Not only was she an attractive girl, but she could outshoot and outride most men. All were welcome qualities in a companion for a long journey in Africa.

Before leaving Matabeleland it was necessary for all would-be travellers to be 'given the road' – permission to leave the country – from Mzilikazi. The Matabele King was far from enthusiastic about Daniel's proposed new trade route to the sea.

'You will find many Tsetse flies that way, trader. You will lose your horses and oxen.'

'Tsetse flies shouldn't bother me at this time of the year and I'll be back before the rains begin.'

The rainy season would begin in November or December and last no longer than three months. It was now June, the coolest month of the year. Daniel felt he had allowed himself ample time to reach the coast and return safely to Khami.

'You will meet with tribes who are enemies of the Matabele. I cannot spare warriors to protect you from them.'

'I have no wish to take any of your warriors, Mzilikazi. I'm setting out to establish a trade route to the coast. In order to do that I need to make friends. I'd find that difficult if I were travelling with one of your impis. Your warriors would attack anything that moved.'

Mzilikazi was suspicious of Daniel's motives, but he accepted that a new trade route had to be found. The Matabele king received half the profit on all the ivory Daniel shipped out and he needed the money to keep his wives supplied with the beads and baubles Daniel brought in for them. Mzilikazi's motive in not wanting Daniel to leave was not entirely mercenary. He was genuinely fond of the young trader who had made his home among the Matabele. Daniel was honest and forthright, and cared for Mzilikazi's people. The King had come to rely on his advice. Mzilikazi feared that Daniel might find another tribe that suited him better and not return to the Matabele.

'Oh, very well, go if you must. But you will take my son Jandu with you. One Matabele warrior will not provoke a war, but his presence will mean that an attack upon you is an attack upon Mzilikazi. Go, trader, but return quickly. I am an old man and will not live forever.'

Daniel smiled, Mzilikazi had been saying the same thing to him for years.

CHAPTER FOUR

Daniel set off for Manicaland at the end of June 1868. He planned to return to Khami by the end of October. It gave him four months to make a round trip of a thousand miles through unknown country. After giving the matter some consideration he had ruled out ox-wagons. Ponderous and slow, oxen could only make fifteen miles a day given the best of conditions. Across country it would have been necessary to select longer routes for them, or cut a track for them. Instead, Daniel took riding horses for himself, Victoria and Sam Speke and a dozen pack mules.

Jandu scorned the horses. He and Suliyana chose to travel on foot with the fifty Mashona tribesmen Daniel was taking along to look after the mules and the trekkers. The Mashonas would also act as an escort without exciting the animosity of those tribes who feared and hated the Matabele.

Most of Khami turned out to see the party off. Mzilikazi himself braved the chill morning air to bid a safe journey to his trader, and to his junior son. Only the two missionaries remained in their cabins, behind closed doors, but Daniel placed no significance on their churlishness.

Daniel felt he had remained in Khami for far too long. There had been many times when he wanted to make expeditions about the country, or travel to the unknown lands of the Mashona. Mzilikazi had always found a reason to refuse permission for Daniel to leave the royal kraal for more than a day or two.

Now Mzilikazi seemed to have run out of reasonable excuses to prevent Daniel from leaving. It was a sign of the King's advancing years. There had been a time when he would not have needed to find an excuse. A curt refusal would have been sufficient. Taking a last look back at Khami before he passed out of sight, Daniel wondered how many years Mzilikazi had left to him, and what changes his death would bring about. It was certain there would be a fierce dispute among his many sons before the leadership issue was decided.

Daniel looked to where Jandu strode along behind the riders and speculated on his chances of becoming the King of the Matabele. Daniel wished he knew more of the enigmatic younger son, but was satisfied he would get to know him better on the long journey that lay ahead.

For five days the party toiled through high veldt country that presented them with a wide variety of landscapes. There were thickly wooded valleys, wide rolling plains where the dry, coarse brown grass was higher than a man's head, and endless folds of broken-granite hills.

Up to this point the country had been familiar to Jandu, but on the sixth day they began to descend a rock-strewn slope to where a river could be seen winding its way through well-treed country below them. This was the furthest Jandu had ever been from his home village in this direction. Suliyana would be guilding them from here.

Although the river was no more than fifty yards wide, the muddy brown water was deeper than Daniel had expected. It was also well-stocked with crocodiles. Looking for a place to cross, Daniel walked his horse carefully along the bank of the river and stopped opposite a series of low mud-flats, lying cracked and summer dry in mid-stream.

On the mud-flats a great number of crocodiles lay belly down, like so many harmless, rough-barked logs. Then, no more than six feet from the bank where Daniel stood, the eyes and nostrils of a crocodile rose above the surface of the sluggish river without making a ripple. The eyes, black slits in an orange marble setting stared malevolently in Daniel's direction.

Beside him, Victoria reined in her horse and shuddered. 'I hate crocodiles. There's something evil about them.'

'I agree, but we have to get across the river and this looks the likeliest spot.'

Daniel slid his heavy double-barrelled elephant gun from the scabbard hanging in front of his saddle. Raising it to his shoulder and lining it on the almost submerged crocodile, he eased back the pin-firing hammers with his thumb. He fired both barrels in quick succession and the result was immediate and spectacular. The crocodile turned a cartwheel in the water before dropping back to thrash about in a dying frenzy that churned the water to blood tinged froth. Then the great reptile rolled over to expose a bright yellow stomach and disappeared beneath the surface of the river.

As the sound of the shots rolled away, the crocodiles on the mud flats raised themselves on short, stocky legs and flung themselves at the river with surprising speed, sliding beneath the surface with a protest of expelled breath.

Reloading his rifle, Daniel snapped off two more shots at crocodiles not sufficiently startled to swim well clear of the area of the proposed river crossing.

Calling for Victoria to cover him against any unexpected attack, Daniel coaxed his horse into the river. Snorting with fear, the animal eased forward gingerly and twice slipped out of its depth before emerging safely on the far side of the river.

Sam Speke took over the task of guarding the other bank of the river and Victoria crossed with the first of the pack-horses. Some horses were more reluctant to enter the river than others, yet all went well until the last animal was almost across. Then a piece of dead wood drifted slowly between the animal and the bank. Mistaking it for a crocodile, the horse reared and fought against the Mashona who struggled desperately to hold it.

Sliding his rifle into its scabbard, Daniel kneed his own horse into the water to go to the rescue of the hard-pressed African. Reaching from the saddle, he grasped the bridle and was turning to lead the terrified animal to safety when it reared up again, catching Daniel off-balance. Pulled from his saddle, he was unceremoniously dumped in the river.

Victoria sat on the muddy bank, rifle across her knees, and surveyed the scene with great amusement. As Daniel floundered ashore, followed by the belatedly subdued pack-horse, she leaned back on her elbows and laughed at his bedraggled appearance.

Suddenly, something moved beneath Victoria's right arm and her expression changed to one of horror. She leaped to her feet, a snake, fangs sunk deep into the flesh just above her elbow, dangling from the bare arm.

The snake dropped to the ground and Jandu darted forward and cut off its head with a single stroke of his razor-sharp assegai. But the damage had been done. Victoria stood clutching her arm, grimacing at the pain.

Daniel splashed through the last few feet of water and scrambled up the river bank to Victoria's side. Glancing at the decapitated snake, still squirming on the ground, his mouth set in a grim line. Putting an arm about Victoria, he led her to a nearby grass-covered hillock and lowered her gently to the ground.

'Lie back and stay as still as you possibly can.'

Calling the Mashona tribesman in charge of the pack-horses to him, Daniel took his whip and cut off a few feet of its length. Making it into a loose loop, he put it about Victoria's upper arm and drew it tight, making an effective tourniquet.

Victoria was in great pain now and Sam Speke, last man to cross the river, leaped from his horse and dropped to his knees beside his daughter. He had not seen the incident and looked to Daniel for an explanation.

Daniel nodded to where two of the Mashonas were examining the snake. 'Boomslang. We need to work fast. Hold her, Sam. Get Jandu to help you.'

A boomslang was one of Africa's deadliest snakes. A member of the cobra family, its bite was invariably fatal.

'You won't need to hold me, Daniel. You're going to cut?'

'Yes.' Daniel avoided her eyes, nodding his readiness to Sam Speke.

Daniel looked down at the back of Victoria's arm. It was no more than a couple of minutes since the snake had bitten her, but already the area about the twin punctures were ugly and puffy. He would have liked time to sterilise his skinning knife over a flame, but every second was precious now. Sam Speke held his daughter to him and Jandu took her arm in his strong hands, holding the elbow joint immobile.

Daniel sucked in a great gulp of air, steadied his hand, then made a deep slash diagonally across the puncture marks left by the hollow, poison-filled fangs of the boomslang.

Victoria twitched as blood welled out, but Daniel was not satisfied. He made another cut, half-an-inch above the first. This time Victoria cried out in pain, but Daniel already had his mouth to the incisions he had made. He sucked at the wound in a bid to draw out the poison, spitting blood on the ground. He repeated the treatment eight or nine times, then removed the tourniquet. He allowed the blood to flow freely from the knife-inflicted wounds for some minutes before applying ammonia from his medical bag and binding up the wound.

Standing up, Daniel discovered he was perspiring heavily, despite his recent ducking, and his knees felt weak and shaky. Smiling down at Victoria, he said, 'That should fix it. You'll be as fit as a grasshopper by morning.'

Daniel spoke with a cheerfulness he did not feel. Victoria made no reply and as Sam Speke turned her over in his arms, her head fell back loosely.

'She's fainted.' Sam Speke turned a worried face up to Daniel. 'Do you really believe she's going to be all right?'

'Of course.' Daniel did his best to sound convincing. He did not want Sam Speke to share his misgivings. The burly ex-sailor adored his daughter and Daniel was reluctant to add to his concern. 'We'll stop here for a while and let her rest. You make her comfortable, Sam. I'll get a camp organised.'

Daniel gave the orders to the Mashonas, but Suliyana already had a fire going. She had pushed a pot to the crackling heart of the fire and was carefully 'milking' the remains of the venom from the boomslang's fangs.

'What are you doing?'

Suliyana raised her head briefly. 'I'm making a soup from the poison of the snake. It will help Victoria – if we are in time.' Adding water to the pot from a gourd, she asked, 'Victoria means much much to you?'

'Yes.'

Suliyana looked at Daniel sympathetically. 'You need not worry about her. She will live. I know . . . .'

Suliyana's confident prediction was no more reassuring than her snake-poison soup had been when morning came. Victoria was still unconscious and her breathing had become shallow and laboured.

Sam Speke was beside himself with worry. He had remained at his daughter's side all night, keeping her warm with blankets, applying more ammonia to the snake bite when he could endure his own helplessness no longer.

When Daniel examined Victoria's arm he shared Sam Speke's concern. The arm was swollen to more than twice its normal size, the skin dark and mottled. The arm was hot to his touch and a trickle of yellow oozed from the wound.

'We've got to get help. She needs more treatment than we can give her here.'

Sam Speke looked at Daniel in desperation. 'But where can we take her? There isn't a doctor within five hundred miles . . . and not a missionary closer than Khami.'

While the two men were talking, Suliyana stood beside the still form of Victoria. When she turned to them it was evident that she had arrived at an important decision.

'We must take her to the White Mondoro.'

'The . . . who?'

'The Mondoro is the voice of Chiminuka – the great spirit worshipped by the Mashona and Manica people.'

The explanation came from Jandu, but for once he did not use the scornful tone that was usual when he spoke of the despised Mashonas. 'Chiminuka speaks only through the White Mondoro. He is said to be a great man.'

Daniel and Sam Speke exchanged glances. Both had lived in Africa far too long to scoff at the thought of a medium speaking with the voice of a god, and able to heal sickness. Besides, where there was an important medium there would also be a native doctor, skilled in the use of herbs and with some experience in treating snake bites.

'Where is this Mondoro?' Daniel asked Suliyana.

She indicated a direction about forty-five degrees south of the course they were on. 'That way. He lives in the Great House of the Chiefs. It is no more than half a day's walk.'

'We'll do it in less than that,' declared Daniel. 'Get a sling rigged up for Victoria, Sam. I'd prefer to be taking her to a European doctor, but anything's better than sitting here and watching her die. I'll set the Mashonas breaking up camp.'

The Mashonas seemed unusually reluctant to move. Not until Jandu stepped in did they make any real effort to prepare for the day's march.

'They are afraid that Chiminuka will be angry if they go uninvited to the Great House of the Chiefs,' explained Jandu. 'I had to convince them that the anger of Mzilikazi would be equally great and the consequences even more certain.'

Once on the move they found the going easier than before, the countryside being much flatter than the hills of Matabeleland. A mountain range loomed high in the distance, but only the occasional hill rose from the dusty, wooded plain on which they now travelled.

They had been on the move for three hours when Daniel first saw a group of tribesmen watching them silently from the slopes of one of the isolated hills. A mile further on, he looked back to see that the tribesmen had left the hill and were following at a distance of a couple of hundred yards. Leaning forward, Daniel released the strap securing his rifle.

'You will not need your gun,' Suliyana said quietly. 'Those men are Rozwis, the guardians of the Great House of the Chiefs. They do not harm those who come to them in peace.'

She pointed to where a solitary figure could be seen running ahead of them. 'See? They send a runner to say we are coming. It is their duty to keep the White Mondoro informed of all strangers. If we were a raiding party his guards would take him and hide him until it was safe once more.'

'You seem to know a great deal about this place,' commented Daniel. 'I thought your lands were still many miles from here?'

'They are, but the White Mondoro is known to my people.'

'This Mondoro. Why is he called "white"?'

'Because that is the colour of his skin . . . but he is not like you.' Suliyana gave Daniel a gentle smile. 'Be patient. You will soon see him for yourself. We are very close now.'

They entered a more thickly wooded area, and through the trees Daniel could see that their escort had increased in size. The silent warriors now moved on either side of them and fear oozed from every pore of the Mashona porters' bodies.

Suddenly they broke clear of the trees and Daniel reined in his horse, his mouth dropping open in sheer astonishment. In front of them was an incredible stone-built, fort-like building. Circular in shape, it was at least two hundred feet in diameter and had walls thirty feet high. Daniel had never seen anything like it before. Beyond the stone structure was a rocky, steep-sided hill on which similar stonework had been used to reinforce natural borders, creating a second, almost inviolable fortress.

Daniel had time for no more than a glance at these remarkable building achievements. Advancing towards him was a grizzle-haired old man flanked by an escort of warriors. Other spear-carrying warriors emerged from the trees about the new arrivals and took position beside the old man.

Daniel was nervous, but the man held up his hands, palms forward, in a gesture of peace. Then, to Daniel's surprise, he spoke to Suliyana first.

'Greetings, Suliyana, daughter of uTshwebe, Queen of the House of Rozwi. Our home is your home, as always. You and your friends have been expected and are welcome.'

At the old man's words, Jandu started violently and a look of awe crossed his face. In answer to Daniel's question, Jandu whispered, 'She is the daughter of uTshwebe . . . and a Rozwi!'

Before he could say more, Suliyana walked towards the old man, arms held out in greeting. But this was a Suliyana Daniel had not seen before. A new, confident girl who accepted the old man's deference as her due.

'Thank you, Pamire, Keeper of the Great House of the Chiefs. We have one with us who is very sick. She has been bitten by a snake – a boomslang.'

'When?'

'Yesterday. She has been bled and I gave her soup made from the poison of the same snake, but still she does not wake.'

Pamire nodded. 'You have done enough. She will not die. Bring her to my hut.'

Turning away, the old man walked off without a word of greeting to Daniel or the others. While they waited uncertainly, Suliyana called for the Mashonas to bring Victoria, then she followed Pamire. The Mashonas had also heard Pamire's respectful greeting and hurried to do Suliyana's bidding.

'Who is this uTshwebe?'

Daniel asked Jandu the question and the Matabele licked his dry lips anxiously before replying.

'uTshwebe is a chieftainess . . . but she is more than that too. Many men swear she is a goddess. They say she can walk upon water – like the bird after which she is named. She also has two hearts, and my people know this to be true. Many years ago a tribe of Zulus came far from the south to the lands of the Manica, who for hundreds of years had been ruled by the

46

Rozwi tribe, a people favoured by the gods. uTshwebe was captured by the Zulus and taken before their Chief. She refused to marry him and he became angry. He ordered one of his strongest warriors to plunge a spear through her heart. This he did and uTshwebe fell to the ground. A moment later she rose to her feet once more. Although bleeding from the wound which should have killed her, she spat in the face of the Chief. He immediately fell to the ground and died. His warriors fled. I have heard no one talk of seeing her since that day.'

Jandu gave Daniel a wide-eyed look of apprehension, 'What manner of people have we fallen in with? A woman who is the daughter of uTshwebe, a people who live in a great stone house . . . and a White Mondoro!'

Daniel remembered the night Suliyana had spent in his store at Khami. He wondered what would be happening to him now had he shared his bed with the daughter of a 'Goddess'.

Before Daniel could pursue this line of thought further, a warrior came to lead them to more modest accommodation than the Great House of the Chiefs. They were taken to huts in the valley, a hundred yards away. Here Daniel was given a hut of his own, Sam Speke being led away with the promise that he was being taken to Victoria. Food and milk were brought for Daniel, but when he tried to leave the hut to discuss what was happening with the others, he found his way barred by a spear, wielded by one of Pamire's warriors.

Daniel remained alone in the hut until darkness fell and the drums in the sprawling village about the great stone fortress began pounding out their rhythm, setting the night air throbbing.

Without warning, the blanket hanging over the open doorway was brushed aside and a warrior entered. Curtly ordering Daniel to follow him, he turned on his heel and ducked out of the hut.

Daniel stepped into the night and hurried after the uncommunicative warrior. Skirting the village, he was taken to the river. Here, in the light of half-a-dozen flickering torches, he saw Sam Speke and Jandu bathing under the watchful eyes of Pamire.

'I am sorry you have been left alone all day,' Pamire apologised. 'Chiminuka had to be told of your arrival and the woman made well. Now you will be taken to the Mondoro.'

'Victoria is all right? But . . . her arm?'

'She will always remember that she was bitten by a boom-slang, but I have healed worse cases. Now, join your friends in the river. You must wash the dirt of other places from your body before you enter the house of the Mondoro.'

The water of the river was cold, but Sam Speke delightedly splashed water at Daniel, behaving as though he were a young boy. When Daniel remonstrated, Sam Speke retorted, 'Daniel, I'd have plunged into iced water, aye, and fire too, for Victoria. If this god of theirs wants us to be clean when we meet his Mondoro, then that's the way we're going to be. I tell you, it was a miracle. They first forced a mixture of herbs down her throat, bled her from the arm a little, then tied this black stone over the wound. Twice they took it off and washed it in some evil-smelling potion. The third time they did it, Victoria came to. She complained that her arm hurt, and she had a headache, but you'd hardly think she'd had more than a heavy sleep. It's a miracle, right enough. I'll tell the world that.'

'I see Pamire has impressed you with his healing skill.' Suliyana had approached quietly. She walked into the river until the water rose above her knees. Then, quite unself-consciously, she removed the belt of beads about her waist, together with its attendant brief apron. Plunging deeper into the river, she swam away from them. The only man to show any embarrassment was Jandu.

When Suliyana turned and swam back to them, Sam Speke said, 'You've just left Victoria . . . she's still all right?'

Suliyana shook water from her short, tightly curled hair. 'I have washed her with water brought from the river. She will need help, but she is eager to visit the White Mondoro. Come now, before Chiminuka sends his lightning to move us.'

Before coming to the river, Sam Speke had fetched clean clothes for himself and Daniel from their saddlebags. As they dressed, he continued his eulogy of these people who had cured Victoria so rapidly.

Victoria was waiting in the village, borne between two of Pamire's warriors on the makeshift litter on which she had been brought to the Great House of the Chiefs. She held out a hand to Daniel and he gave it a reassuring squeeze before the procession got under way, accompanied by a great many torch-bearing warriors.

Once clear of the village the procession began to climb steps cut in the side of the huge rocky hill overlooking the great stone building. Behind them, voices joined the drums in a strange haunting chant unlike anything Daniel had ever heard in Africa. Its deep notes reminded him of an ancient Hebrew song that Aaron sometimes hummed as he worked in the Khami store.

When the first of the torch-bearers reached the top of the steep steps, Daniel was able to take a closer look at the walls, cleverly built to lock into the giant boulders strewn about the crest of the hill. As the party passed in through a low doorway and began twisting and turning along a narrow passageway, sometimes no wider than a man's shoulders, Daniel wondered even more about the origins of the two fortresses.

Ducking under a final low overhang of rock, Daniel found himself in an enclosure that was almost completely surrounded by giant, rounded boulders. Here was a flimsy shelter, no more than a flat roof of hides, backing on a low wall.

Beneath the shelter squatted a frail-looking man, a brightly patterned blanket wrapped about his shoulders to protect him from the chill of the night. He was younger than he appeared at first sight, but he was much lighter skinned than any African Daniel had ever met. It was not until the man raised his head and the torchlight fell upon his face, showing his opaque, pink eyes, that the truth was revealed. The White Mondoro was an albino. He was also totally blind.

Beside Daniel, Jandu recoiled in horror. An albino was abhorrent to the Matabele people. They were unnatural, imperfect beings. Any born to Matabele women were either killed at birth, or cast out of the tribe at the earliest opportunity. Now here was one who, it was claimed, was the medium through whom the spirit of the great god Chiminuka spoke to his people.

The White Mondoro's first words shook not only Jandu, but startled the whole party. As if his sightless eyes had been able to read Jandu's mind, he said; 'One of the strangers draws back from me. Is it because he is a slayer of our people and fears a blind man's revenge? O perhaps it is because he does not wish to hear the words of Chiminuka?'

The Mondoro's chuckle was that of an infirm man who spent his days and nights huddled too close to the lung-searing smoke of an ox-dung fire. 'Trouble not, son of Mzilikazi, I have neither the teeth, claws . . . nor yet the roar of a lion. I have only words. You will one day be a great man among your people. As a child you were once known as "The Scatterer". You will have that name again, but it will not be your enemies you cast to the winds. It will be your own people, the Matabele. They will be scattered and lost because of your deeds. You will not live to see it happen, Scatterer, and neither will I, but one day it will be the Mashona who rule all the peoples who now bow before Mzilikazi. The sons of your sons, and those of others here will witness the fulfilment of my words . . . and they will remember.'

The Mondoro had appeared to grow in stature as he spoke. His voice, loud and strong, carried to every corner of the enclosure. When he stopped speaking there was a long silence during the course of which he once again became a slight, sick man, chin sagging on the blanket about his chest and the breath in his throat heavy with spittle.

'Go!' the Mondoro croaked at last. 'Chiminuka will not speak again in your presence. It will take more than water to wash away the blood that will stain your hands.'

Pamire gave a peremptory nod of his head and four Mashona warriors closed in upon Jandu. Daniel started forward, but Suliyana put out a restraining hand to stop him. 'They will not harm him. We are all under Chiminuka's protection here.'

The Mondoro said nothing until Jandu had been led from the enclosure, then he once more raised his head. 'Chiminuka would speak to the white trader. Come, sit before me.'

Feeling extremely uneasy, Daniel walked to the shelter and squatted on the ground. The Mondoro reached out a hand and when he felt nothing, beckoned to Daniel. 'Come closer, I wish to touch you.'

Daniel moved forward until his knees almost touched those of the African medium. There was something eerie about sitting here in the ruins of what Daniel realised must be a very ancient building, with a blind albino who claimed to speak with the voice of a spirit god. Daniel did his best to remain completely rational, but knew he was not quite succeeding.

The Mondoro put out a hand and his fingers ran rapidly over every inch of Daniel's face. Then the fingers felt the material of Daniel's cloth shirt, and finally took hold of his hand.

'You do not understand, trader. You are afraid?'

'We came to you because we were in trouble. You and your people have saved the life of my friend's daughter. Why should I fear you? I am among friends.'

In spite of his words, Daniel had difficulty in maintaining an outward impression of calmness. In surroundings such as these a man could be tricked into believing anything. Daniel did not want to accept that he was in the presence of anything more sinister than a clever albino who had somehow survived native prejudice and achieved a position of importance among his people.

The grip on Daniel's hand tightened until it became painful. When the Mondoro spoke again it was with the voice that had foretold a grim future for Jandu.

'You have made your home among the Matabele. I see you going through life touching hands with many of them and they bow their heads respectfully to you. It is good, but it will not always be so. I see another hand stretching towards you – and it holds a spear. It is a day of much wind . . . there are many spears pointing at your people. The spears and the wind sing together. You hear the song and your heart weeps . . . but the tears are not for yourself—'

The voice broke and dropped to a whisper. 'As your heart weeps, so you will remember the words of Chiminuka's Mondoro.'

The Mondoro's hand slipped from Daniel's grasp and Daniel rose to his feet. He was perturbed at the other man's words, but he was still not certain.

'Trader,' Daniel had to lean forward to catch the words. 'Chiminuka spoke of what must be. Do not try to run from your destiny.'

'I will live my life as I think it should be lived . . . Madala.' Daniel added the courtesy title used when addressing tribal elders.

Sam Speke did not share Daniel's casual acceptance of the

Mondoro's words. 'Don't let anything he's said upset you, Daniel,' he hissed when Daniel returned to his place. 'There's half-a-dozen of these Mondoros scattered about Mashonaland. They all claim to speak for Chiminuka – Mwari, or some other such god—'

He broke off as the Mondoro said loudly, 'Where is the girl who was bitten by the snake? Bring her to me.'

Sam Speke had scornfully dismissed the Mondoro as a fraud, yet he was unhappy at the thought of him talking to Victoria. But before he could prevent it, Victoria had been carried forward by two warriors and set on the ground before the albino.

Daniel saw her recoil in revulsion as the Mondoro's hand explored her face then traced the lines of her slender neck down to her shoulders. Next the Mondoro took the arm that had been bitten by the snake and smoothed the wound with his finger, nodding in apparent satisfaction. 'It is good, the wound will heal well.'

Releasing her arm, he asked, 'What is your name?'

'Victoria . . . Victoria Speke.'

'We are much alike, you and I, Victoria.' The White Mondoro spoke with his own voice and it contained much sadness. 'I am of my people – yet am not one of them. You are born of two peoples – but are not of either. It is hard, child . . . but now Chiminuka would speak.'

The Mondoro's voice gained in power once again, 'For you there are bad times to come. You are a thread that joins white with black, yet you are not strong enough to pull them together, so you must break. One day, perhaps, there will be many such as you. The threads must join together to make a strong rope . . . but such a time is far, far away. Do not look for happiness, child, happiness is not within you – but you will seek it among your own kind—'

'What nonsense is he trying to feed her?' Sam Speke rose to his feet angrily, but one of Pamire's warriors barred his way with a spear. Only Daniel saw Victoria's stricken look as she turned at the commotion.

Victoria was carried back to her companions and Sam Speke put a comforting arm about her, grumbling all the while about 'stupid men who frighten young girls.'

Pamire asked the Mondoro whether Chiminuka would speak to Victoria's father.

'No. Chiminuka speaks only of the future. There is none for the father of the girl.' Daniel was glad that Sam Speke was too busy reassuring Victoria to hear what had been said.

Pamire signalled to his warriors and, one by one, Daniel and his companions were led away through the narrow passageway that led to the steps outside the hilltop fortress.

At the low, overhanging rock, Daniel paused to look back. Suliyana sat cross-legged before the Mondoro, both her hands held in his, her head bowed low as she listened intently to his words.

CHAPTER FIVE

Daniel and his party set off from the Great House of the Chiefs the next day. Daniel suggested it might be better if Victoria were allowed to rest in the Rozwi village for a while longer, but Sam Speke would not hear of it. The Mondoro's words to Victoria the previous evening had greatly upset her. He was determined she would not spend another night among his people.

Victoria was a very different girl to the one who had set off from Khami with such high hopes. She was strong enough to ride a horse today and showed no physical after-effects of her close encounter with death, but she was withdrawn and morose. Nothing Daniel said could jolt her out of her mood of apathy and, eventually, he left her alone and rode off to look for game.

Victoria improved slowly over the course of the next few days, but the warmth she and Daniel had always shared had somehow gone from their relationship. Daniel put her strange mood down to the pain she must still feel in her arm, even though Victoria insisted it no longer troubled her.

After spending a pleasant night camped by a hot spring, they began to ascend the mountains that had dominated the skyline for so many days, and now they caught glimpses of an ever higher range far to the east.

There were people here in the mountains, but they never came close. Daniel thought it unusual that they did not possess sufficient curiosity to come and meet the newcomers to their land.

When he mentioned it to Suliyana, she replied, 'They have learned their wisdom through the years. Men with horses have been to these mountains before – to take slaves. They still come, but see few Manicas, and fewer Mashonas. They have learned how to hide.'

Soon after noon, Suliyana directed them through a series of

deep valleys, tucked between well-wooded hills. Eventually they came out into another valley that must have been three miles wide, extending into the distance for as far as they could see. Ahead, no more than five miles away, was a very large kraal. The smoke from cooking fires hung over it like a hazy, blue cloud.

'That is Chena, my home . . . the village of uTshwebe, my mother.' She gave Jandu a sidelong glance. 'Does the thought of meeting uTshwebe fill you with fear, Matabele?'

Since setting out from Khami, a very easy relationship had developed between Jandu and Suliyana. He gave her a somewhat sheepish smile. 'Not unless she too speaks with the voice of Chiminuka.'

Suliyana's smile vanished. 'My mother hears many voices that are not heard by others, but when Chiminuka speaks all men should listen.'

'Talking of Chiminuka – you never did tell us what the Mondoro said to you after we had left,' Daniel said.

'It was a message for my mother,' Suliyana replied evasively. 'It will be known to you in due course. For now, you have other things to think about. There is a river between us and my village. The crossing-place is narrow, no wider than a man's shoulders. You must be careful.'

They reached the river soon afterwards – and suffered the first fatality of the long trek.

It came with a suddenness that took Daniel by surprise. The first few Mashona porters had reached the far bank and the remainder were strung out in a loose file across the river. As Daniel led his horse into the water there was a sudden commotion in mid-river and the glistening dark grey bulk of a three-ton hippopotamus emerged from the water.

The great animal had been making its way down the river, below the surface. Reaching the ford it surfaced, intending to cross the bar and continue on its peaceful way. Its sudden appearance caused consternation among the Mashonas. Deserting the pack-horses they beat the water to a frenzy in an attempt to escape. The hippopotamus was as surprised and frightened as they were and tried to leap over the bar to deeper water. Unfortunately, one of the Mashonas was in its path. The great jaws opened and closed upon the unfortunate man, the great yellow teeth almost cutting him in half.

Daniel's rifle cleared its scabbard while the tribesman's scream still lingered on the air. Both barrels were discharged into the hippopotamus's body just before it reached safety, the dead Mashona dangling from its cavernous mouth.

The bullets struck the animal just behind the left shoulder, narrowly missing its heart.

As Daniel hurriedly reloaded, standing waist-deep in the river, the Mashonas already ashore shouted that the hippopotamus had turned and was coming back towards the ford. Their observations were based on the bloody bubbles racing to the surface of the churned-up water as horses and men fought their way up the muddy river bank.

The hippopotamus erupted from the water not three yards from Daniel with a speed that belied its bulk. It was looking for someone to pay the price for the pain burning deep inside the huge body. Fortunately for Daniel its attention was diverted to the Mashonas shouting on the far bank and it charged at them in a series of ungainly leaps that threw water back over Daniel as he fired off another two shots. He placed them in almost the same spot as before, the shots echoed by the rifles of Victoria and Sam Speke.

The hippopotamus was dead before it hit the river bank, but its speed sent it skidding for twelve feet through mud and earth, bowling over three of the Mashonas along the way.

With the danger past, the Mashonas screeched their noisy relief, rejoicing at the vast supply of meat that lay before them. All concern for their more unfortunate companion was forgotten.

Grabbing the reins of his own horse and driving a couple of pack-horses before him, Daniel gained the bank where the others stood.

'That could have been much worse,' commented Sam Speke as he extended a hand to help Daniel ashore.

'Tell that to the man who died,' replied Daniel, grimly. 'But it looks as though our shots have stirred up the villagers. I hope they're as friendly as Suliyana promised they would be.'

Warriors could be seen pouring from the entrance to the Manica kraal. From this distance they reminded Daniel of bees leaving a smoked-out hive.

As the warriors drew nearer, sunlight glinted on the many spears and when the men formed a long battle line Daniel looked anxiously to where Suliyana stood.

Smiling reassuringly, Suliyana went out to meet her country-men – the effect was dramatic. When the Manica warriors moved close enough to recognise her they stopped in their tracks. Those behind continued to advance, then they too recognised her. Moments later the line of warriors became a series of disjointed groups and Jandu clicked his tongue against his teeth in noisy disapproval. Then, as Suliyana continued to walk towards the army of her people they began to back away from her, muttering anxiously among themselves.

It needed only one man to break and run and the whole of uTshwebe's army would have turned tail and fled. Then Suliyana called, 'Do the warriors of uTshwebe run from women now? Or have the memories of her people grown so short that even Chibisa fails to recognise his own sister?'

One of the warriors stepped from the ranks of the army hesitantly. 'My sister Suliyana was killed by the Matabele.'

Suliyana snorted derisively. 'I was taken prisoner to the village of Mzilikazi, the Matabele. Now I return to show white men the way to the sea. I also bear a message from Chiminuka for uTshwebe, my mother.'

Chibisa advanced slowly and cautiously, still not certain. Then, when he was closer, Suliyana grinned at him and suddenly all his fears disappeared. He ran forward and embraced her, shouting excitedly. The remainder of the war-riors surged forward, most of their attention directed at Suliyana – but a few were equally excited at the sight of the dead hippopotamus.

'It is the first hippopotamus seen in this river for longer than anyone can remember,' explained Suliyana when she brought her brother to meet Daniel. 'It is a good omen for your arrival at Chena.'

Daniel thought it was a strange mischance that the lost Mashona should have been in the path of the only hippo-potamus seen in the river for so long – but his fellow tribesmen already seemed to have forgotten him. They were cutting up the dead animal, reluctantly apportioning a share to the

Manicas. Leaving them to their bloody task, Daniel rounded up the pack-horses and, with the others, followed Suliyana and her brother to the village.

Messengers had run ahead to tell of the return of Suliyana. Queen uTshwebe, ruler of the tribes of the Manica valley came from the kraal to meet them. Tall and regal, she wore a cloak of civet skins about her shoulders and Daniel thought she was an artist's dream of an African queen. One of the last survivors of the once powerful Rozwi people, she was a benevolent ruler to her Manica people – but today she was a mother greeting the daughter she had thought dead.

When the emotional reunion had run its course, Suliyana introduced Daniel and his party. The Queen welcomed them all warmly – until Suliyana called Jandu forward.

Queen uTshwebe rounded on Daniel. 'You dare to bring a Matabele into my land?'

'King Mzilikazi has sent his own son with us to ensure that we pass safely through the lands of those chiefs who pay him homage.' Daniel hoped fervently he was choosing the right words. If he failed to satisfy Queen uTshwebe his journey to the Indian Ocean would end right here. 'He comes in peace, as do we.'

'Peace? No Matabele knows the meaning of the word. Mzilikazi least of all.'

Returning her attention to Jandu, uTshwebe said, 'You stare at me, Matabele. Is it because of the stories your people tell of me? You think they lie, perhaps? Then look here.'

Unfastening the neck of her cape, uTshwebe let it fall to the ground and stood naked to the waist. Cutting through her left breast was an ugly scar, the width of a man's hand – or an assegai blade.

'Look well – and remember, Jandu, son of Mzilikazi. When you return to your father tell him you have seen the scar borne by uTshwebe. Remind him that when the spear struck home it was the chief who ordered the blow who died, not me. I want no more Matabele raids upon my villages.'

'There will be no more raids,' promised Jandu, looking away from the mark of the spear that should have killed the Rozwi Queen.

'Good. Now you will be shown to your huts. Suliyana, you

have a message from Chiminuka. Come, I would hear his words.'

That night a celebration was held to mark Suliyana's return to her tribe. Cattle and goats were roasted and the Manica men and women took full advantage of the occasion, singing, dancing and eating their fill at the expense of their ruler.

Squatting on the ground close to a roaring fire, Daniel was filled with a sense of well-being. He enjoyed watching tribal dancing, especially when there were no undertones of war or violence to detract from his enjoyment. Unlike the Matabele, these were settled people who had lived in these same mountains and valleys for hundreds of years. Their lives had been untroubled by others until the breakaway elements of the Zulu nation began their journeys northward from Natal.

At the height of the celebrations, Daniel was summoned to sit beside uTshwebe. As he took his place the Queen handed him a gourd of beer, having first taken a polite swig to assure her guest it was not poisoned.

'You saved the lives of Suliyana and the other Manica women. I am pleased. You will always be welcome in my land.'

It was the opening for which Daniel had been waiting.

'Your words make me happy, uTshwebe. I make this journey to establish a trade route between Matabeleland and the sea. It is good to know your people will look on me as a friend.'

'You will need guides to take you through the Portuguese country – and porters. You will take Manicas. We are known to the tribes you will meet. Your Mashonas can stay here until your return.'

'Will Suliyana come with us?'

uTshwebe shook her head. 'No, there are slave-traders in the Portuguese lands. My daughter has escaped from captivity once. She might not be so fortunate again.'

uTshwebe nodded to where Victoria sat with her father, 'It will be better for the Mambari girl to remain here too. She would fetch a good price. I can send only a few warriors through the lands of others. Such a small party travelling with a valuable Mambari girl . . . ?' The Rozwi Queen left the remainder of the sentence to Daniel's imagination.

Daniel looked to where Victoria sat staring morosely into

the fire, seemingly oblivious to the noise and laughter about her. Her mood worried Daniel and he was pleased that uTshwebe's words gave him an excuse to leave her behind in Chena. A few weeks spent resting in a peaceful and secure village might restore her to full health. But how should he tell her? Daniel decided it was a problem that would wait until the right opportunity arose.

An hour after her conversation with Daniel, Queen uTshwebe retired to her hut. Daniel and the others followed suit soon afterwards. It had been a busy and eventful day.

After a while, only Jandu and Suliyana remained seated beside the dying fire. A few dancers were still performing in a small group on the far side of the kraal, but the majority had followed the example of their Queen. Soon the light from a liberal sprinkling of stars in the night sky took over the task of illumination from the many fires that now burned low in the kraal.

'Are you still frightened of uTshwebe, Jandu?' There was a glint of white teeth from Suliyana as she asked the question, but Jandu took it seriously and carefully weighed his reply.

'I have heard the stories of my people and with my own eyes have seen the scar she bears. But I have also talked to her and watched her when she is with her family and her people. I believe uTshwebe is a woman ... but one who has the protection of the gods.'

'And me, Jandu? Am I a woman?'

'You are truly a woman, Suliyana.' Jandu felt the stirrings of his body. He had heard such half-teasing questions before, put to him by hot, eager young girls around the fires of Matabele villages. But Jandu was unprepared for Suliyana's directness.

'You would like to share my blanket tonight?'

Jandu wanted her. Yet even as his desire became a fever, innate caution held him in check. One did not form a casual liaison with the daughter of a Queen – especially one such as uTshwebe.

'I would take you as a wife, Suliyana.'

The words came from his mouth as though uttered by someone else. Of course, Jandu had toyed with the idea of marriage with the Rozwi girl, from the moment he had learned she was the daughter of uTshwebe. It would be a good marriage. Certain to meet with the approval of Mzilikazi. It would also enhance Jandu's prestige in his own tribe . . . but Jandu had not intended putting his thoughts into words quite so soon.

Suliyana rose to her feet and extended a hand to Jandu.

'There will be time for marriage talk tomorrow. Come.'

Much later that night, when the drums had stilled and only the muffled sounds of the surrounding bush-veldt disturbed the night, Suliyana sighed contentedly and eased the weight of Jandu from her. His hands reached for her again, but she wriggled from his grasp.

'Wait, Jandu! You spoke earlier of marriage. Is such a thought still with you . . . now you have known me?'

'More than ever,' Jandu replied eagerly. He had never before enjoyed such a woman as the daughter of uTshwebe.

'I am not a village girl who can be bought for six cows. uTshwebe will ask a high bride-price for me.'

'I will pay whatever is asked. You will be able to hold your head high among the women of my people.'

'There is one other thing. I must always be your "great wife" – no matter how many women you marry.'

Jandu propped himself up on one elbow. 'You will always be the head of my household – but only a King has a "great wife".'

'One day you will be King, Jandu. It was told to me by the White Mondoro. I want my son to rule the Matabele. Only the first son of a "great wife" can be undisputed King. I must be sure, Jandu.'

'You have my promise, daughter of uTshwebe. You will become my "great wife", and you must give me many sons.'

Jandu reached for her again and this time she came to him eagerly. Chiminuka's prediction would be fulfilled.

The silence maintained by Victoria after her meeting with the Mondoro ended abruptly when Daniel told her she was to be left behind in Chena while he pushed on to the coast.

Angrily, she shouted, 'Had I wanted to sit around in some native village I could have stayed in Khami – among friends. Why must I stay here? I can keep up with the rest of you – and it's not my fault I was bitten by a snake. No, I'm not going to be left behind. The going is much easier now and we're only a few days from the sea.'

When Daniel tried to explain the reasons put forward by uTshwebe, Victoria brushed them aside with a petulance that he remembered from her childhood days, but which she had been careful to hide from him in more recent years.

'Don't try to fob me off with excuses, Daniel Retallick. You want me out of the way so that you can be alone with Suliyana. I should have realised that at the very beginning . . . after you'd spent the night together in your precious store.'

As soon as he was able to halt her angry flow of words, Daniel told Victoria that Suliyana would also be staying behind in the village.

Only slightly mollified, Victoria continued her tirade until she realised that Daniel would not be moved. She then lapsed once more into a sulky silence. After trying unsuccessfully to talk her out of it, Daniel went in search of her father.

Sam Speke was as reluctant as Victoria to remain behind in the Manica village, and for similar reasons. Sam Speke had known Daniel since he was a three-year-old child and Daniel was as a son to him. It was Sam Speke's dearest wish that one day Daniel and Victoria should be married. It was to help Victoria to achieve this end that he had set out on the journey that had almost cost Victoria her life. He was determined that her suffering would not prove in vain. She *would* get the man she loved – no matter what an albino witch-doctor might say to the contrary, but romance could not pursue its course if Daniel and Victoria were hundreds of miles apart.

However, common-sense eventually prevailed. Sam Speke reluctantly agreed to remain behind at uTshwebe's village while Daniel and Jandu pushed on for the coast.

For the remainder of that morning Daniel was busy organising the onward trek, with little opportunity to worry himself about Victoria's moods. He was aware of Jandu's presence as he loaded the packs, but it was not until Sam Speke went off in search of Victoria and Daniel was alone that Jandu told him of the decision to make Suliyana his wife. In the absence of his father, Mzilikazi, Jandu asked Daniel to negotiate the 'lobola' – the bride price, on his behalf.

The request took Daniel completely by surprise. He had been so wrapped up in his own problems he had not noticed how much attention Jandu and Suliyana were paying to each other.

'Are you quite certain of this, Jandu? Have you discussed marriage with Suliyana?'

Jandu nodded. 'It will be a good marriage. Suliyana thinks so too. She says it is the will of Chiminuka.'

'Then I'll be pleased to negotiate for you – and congratulations, Jandu. You're a lucky man. But before I go to see uTshwebe we'd better decide how many cows you're prepared to give for her.'

'As many as it takes. Agree to whatever uTshwebe asks. The important thing is to convince her that I will be a good husband for her daughter.'

Daniel was impatient to be on his way to the coast, but for such a reason as this he was happy to postpone his departure for a few days. The negotiations for a marriage between a son of Mzilikazi, and the only daughter of uTshwebe could not be hurried. It would provide the foundation of a powerful alliance between two great tribes – and ensure continuing friendship from them both for Daniel and his trading company.

uTshwebe received Daniel in the private enclosure that surrounded the royal household. As he sat opposite her he thought once again that she was a very handsome woman. Suliyana had told her mother that Jandu wished to marry her and uTshwebe was fully aware of the purpose of Daniel's visit, but she opened the conversation by making polite conversation. The Queen asked him about his family and the people of South West Africa where he had lived for so long, his trade, the state of his business.

In return, Daniel praised the kindness of uTshwebe's tribe and the beautiful country in which they lived and promised he would bring the Manicas and their Queen many gifts from the coast.

Finally, when he judged the time was right, Daniel broached the subject of the proposed marriage. Following the traditional pattern of such negotiations, Daniel began by praising Jandu, his father and his family. In view of the recent raid by the

Matabele into Manicaland Daniel was obliged to choose his words very carefully. He succeeded in a manner that brought a smile of delight to uTshwebe's face.

'Truly, trader, you are a man who thinks well before he speaks. I wish you were one of my own advisers – but you are here to speak for Jandu. Will he make a good husband for Suliyana? Would she be happy in the land of the Matabele, far from the hills of Manicaland?'

'She will be the envy of every Matabele woman. Jandu is one of Mzilikazi's favourite sons, and a brave warrior. He will be a good husband.'

'I have known many brave warriors . . . but few to whom I would entrust the future of my daughter.'

uTshwebe gave Daniel a sudden warm smile that broke the tension that had crept into the discussion. 'Suliyana told me of the night she spent in your store. Perhaps I should demand lobola from you and make her *your* bride.'

'It would be a great honour,' Daniel replied, adding hastily, 'but I am not yet ready for the responsibility of a wife and family.'

uTshwebe gave Daniel a shrewd look. 'Do not repeat those words to the Mambari girl. She is used to having the things she wants . . . and my eyes tell me she wants you.'

'She's a young girl and has met few men of her father's people,' explained Daniel. 'One day we'll probably marry, but not just yet.'

uTshwebe had her own thoughts on the matter, but she made no comment. Instead, she brought the talk back to the proposed marriage of her daughter with Jandu.

The bride-price was eventually agreed at one hundred prime cattle. It was extremely high, but if Suliyana wished to command the respect of the Matabele women among whom she would live it could not be less.

When Daniel returned to tell Jandu of the success of his mission, the Matabele was overjoyed – but the high bride-price created a problem. Protecting a herd of one hundred head of cattle on a journey from Khami to Manicaland would require a large escort of Matabele warriors who would spread fear and alarm along the route. There was also the possibility that the herd would include a number of cattle recently stolen from the

Manicas. It would be an inauspicious beginning for future relations between the two tribes.

Daniel suggested that he leave behind enough trade goods to purchase a hundred head of cattle. Sam Speke could conduct this aspect of the negotiations. It would give him something to occupy him while he awaited Daniel's return.

CHAPTER SIX

Daniel and Jandu set off from Chena with an escort of fifty Manica warriors. Jandu looked upon the light shields and throwing spears of the Manicas with barely concealed scorn. These were not warriors of the calibre of the Matabele. In battle the Manicas would throw their spears away, lea·ing themselves defenceless, then run for their lives. The short handle and wide blade of the Matabele assegai ensured that it could not be thrown. The warrior who held it had to stand his ground and engage an enemy in hand-to-hand combat. Developed by Mzilikazi himself, this was the tactic that made the Matabele warriors the most feared of all African tribes.

Wisely, Jandu said nothing of his thoughts, but he found it difficult to hide his contempt.

The first day's march was a gruelling slog over mountains higher than any Daniel had ever seen. He thought they must have been at least eight thousand feet high – but the view from the summit gave promise of better things to come. The land dropped away sharply to a green plain covered in lush vegetation. Unfortunately, as they descended so the temperature rose. By the second day they were in a steamy, unhealthy area that abounded in flies and biting insects.

Among the flies there must have been the feared tsetse. On the third day one of the pack-horses began to hang its head and stumble along so unsteadily that Daniel was obliged to remove the pack from its back and redistribute the contents among the other animals. That same night the horse lay down and died.

This was only a beginning. The next day Daniel's riding horse and two more of the pack animals collapsed. By the sixth day all the horses were dead and the disgruntled Manicas were complaining bitterly about having to carry the loads formerly borne by horses.

It was Jandu who eventually shamed the reluctant porters into silence. Shouldering the pack of one of the warriors who was protesting particularly loudly, Jandu set off at a cracking pace and kept it up all day. When they stopped to make camp he dropped the bundle at the feet of the Manica warrior without saying a word. That night the other Manicas berated their companion for giving Jandu the opportunity to dictate the pace of the day's march. The following morning the disgruntled warrior was the first to take up his load – and that same day they reached the sea.

Their sudden arrival at the coast came as a complete surprise to them all. They were following a faint, overgrown path through dense bush when the undergrowth ended abruptly and they were on a ridge of grass-tufted sand. On the far side of the ridge was the beach, sloping gently down to the sea not more than three hundred yards away. The sea was extremely shallow here, extending towards the far horizon for almost a mile before a change of colour indicated deeper water.

It was a moment of great excitement and the Manicas threw down their loads and dashed into the water, whooping in joy when they discovered a number of large spider crabs. Gathering them up in great scratching armfuls they carried them up the beach in anticipation of a feast.

Jandu had never before seen crabs. They had the appearance of large, hairy-legged spiders and he watched the antics of the Manicas with disbelief.

More to Jandu's liking was the rhinoceros which appeared unexpectedly from the thick undergrowth not fifty yards from the impromptu camp and stood sniffing the air suspiciously. The short-sighted animal was aware of unusual activity on the beach, but was unable to locate the cause. As it turned broadside on to the suddenly silent men to investigate a new and imagined sound, Daniel took careful aim and fired.

The front legs of the rhinoceros collapsed and the powerful animal's foremost horn dug into the sand, supporting the one-and-a-half-ton weight for a few seconds. A dying shudder upset the precarious balance and the rhinoceros crashed sideways to the ground.

With both fresh meat and sea food so plentiful, Daniel knew there would be no shifting the Manicas now. A camp was set up close enough to the rhinoceros for the men to stagger to the cooking fire with their loads of meat – yet far enough away to ensure they would not be bothered during the night with the quarrels of the scavengers.

It was one of the most pleasant camps Daniel could remember. Occasionally he woke to look up at the stars, listen to the whispering of the sea upon the beach and think of life. He hoped Victoria was making a good recovery and wished he could share this night with her.

Daniel's only concern was the fact that he had contracted a mild fever. It was no doubt a recurrence of the malaria from which he had suffered for many years. It returned intermittently, but had never been serious enough to really trouble him.

Daniel's happy frame of mind was rudely shattered soon after dawn. The Manicas were busy cooking as much meat as they could pile on the fires before the heat of the day became unbearable, when a shot rang out from the undergrowth. It was quickly followed by two more and one of the Manica warriors stumbled forward a few paces before pitching face downward on the sand.

'Get down – quickly!' Daniel called the warning as he himself dropped to the sand behind the scant shelter of a small, wind-shaped sand dune. Jandu and the Manica warriors followed his example more slowly, uncertain what was happening and another of their number fell to the ground with a musket ball lodged in the flesh of his thigh.

A thick cloud of black smoke seeped through the bushes from whence the shots had come and Daniel triggered the contents of one barrel of his rifle low into the undergrowth. He was rewarded with a cry of pain, but it did not fell the attacker and he could be heard crashing away through the bushes.

Daniel could not think who might want to attack him and his party in such a manner, but one of the Manica warriors muttered to his companion about 'Pombeiros', and Daniel knew they were being attacked by the half-caste Portuguese rebel traders.

More shots were fired at their vulnerable position on the beach, but the attackers had now moved further back to the shelter of some trees and the musket balls pattered harmlessly on the sand in front of Daniel and the Manicas.

The situation was a stalemate – but the advantage would be

held by the Pombeiros when the hot sun rose above the beach.

Aware of the danger of being pinned down on the beach in the full heat of the day, Jandu picked up his short assegai. Calling on the Manicas to follow him, he leaped over the low dune and sprinted towards the undergrowth.

After only a moment's hesitation, about twenty Manicas sprang to their feet and followed him. They may not have been willing porters, but they were enthusiastic warriors. The remainder of the Manicas would have charged after their companions had Daniel not shouted for them to remain with him. He would need them to protect the trade goods should the unseen attackers break from the cover of the undergrowth.

For a few minutes after the last of the Manicas had disappeared from sight there was a nerve-racking silence. Then a single shot was followed by the excited cries of the Manicas. Suddenly, a man dressed in dirty and ragged European clothing ran from the bushes clutching a musket. A flurry of spears followed him and Daniel saw two of them strike home. As the man fell, Daniel could see a red stain spreading wide over the man's shirt from an ugly wound in his left side. Jandu had already been in action with his broad-bladed assegai. The Pombeiro had been mortally wounded before the spears of the Manicas struck home.

There were no more shots now, but the unseen Manicas still called excitedly to each other from different parts of the dense undergrowth.

It was another half hour before Jandu returned to the beach with some of the Manicas. The antipathy between them had disappeared. For a while they would share the excitement and cameraderie of a battle in which men had died.

One Manica warrior lay dead and two had been shot. Neither of the wounded men were seriously hurt, although both would always bear scars that would be the envy of their companions. Two of the Pombeiros had also been killed, the second body being dragged from the undergrowth by the returning Manicas. He had been hit in the leg by one of Daniel's shots and, unable to keep up with the retreating bandits, he had been abandoned by them and hacked to death by uTshwebe's warriors.

Dressed in the ragged style adopted by natives in the habit of hanging around European towns, Daniel saw with a sense of shock that his features were as finely chiselled as his own. His skin much lighter than any African's.

'He's Portuguese.'

One of the Manicas shook his head. 'No, he is a Pombeiro. There are many in this country. They steal and kill as a way of life.'

'Then we'll do well to keep to the beach. They'll probably attack us again.'

'They have gone,' declared Jandu. 'They had horses not far away. We will not see them again. Unless the tsetse fly kills their horses too.'

Although Jandu was probably right, Daniel took his party northwards along the firm sand close to the sea's edge. Not only was it safer, but they would make faster time. The Manicas were not certain where they were but Daniel believed the Portuguese port of Sofala lay not many miles from where they were.

That night they camped on a narrow headland, setting a guard against a surprise attack by any enterprising Pombeiros. The night passed peacefully enough, but Daniel's fever flared up alarmingly. He woke with an illusion that the whole landscape was advancing upon him, then as rapidly retreating.

Dosing himself with quinine, Daniel kept going until noon, aided by a concerned Jandu. Then one of the Manicas who had been foraging ahead called excitedly from a small hill that he could see a big kraal with stone huts.

Daniel staggered his way to the top of the hill. When the world swirled less wildly about him, he caught a glimpse of an indifferent village at the water's edge, about a mile away. There was a church, a tumbledown fort, a couple of stone houses and an empty quay.

It was the last thing Daniel was to remember for a long time. As he watched, the village distorted grotesquely, the whole merging in an ever-growing cloud that rose to envelop Daniel and he pitched unconscious to the ground.

The dilapidated state of Sofala had been brought about by a series of raids made on the once great seaport by Pombeiros and migrating tribesmen during the past few decades.

For this same reason, the sight of fifty armed warriors

descending upon the village sent the remaining residents into a paroxysm of fear. Most ran to collect their valuables, in preparation for flight to the surrounding heavily wooded terrain. A few primed their guns, prepared to defend their ramshackle village against the approaching enemy.

Much to the relief of everyone, not least the would-be defenders, the bulk of the advancing warriors halted outside the town and laid down their arms. Only three men came on. One was a white man, being carried by the other two.

Most Portuguese spoke the language of the Manicas and they listened to their story with quickening interest, especially when the newcomers spoke of inflicting a defeat upon the Pombeiros. Only a few days before, Sofala had been treated to a rare visit by a troop of Portuguese soldiers. They had ridden all the way from Quelimane, on the trail of the Pombeiros who had attacked Daniel's party. A villager was immediately despatched to ride after the soldiers and inform them of this latest sighting. In the meantime, Daniel was carried to the stone-built house owned by an important official who was in the village on a visit from his estate in the interior of the country.

The next few days were an unreal nightmare for Daniel. During this time he was unable to distinguish waking moments from the dreams that appeared to haunt his sleep. Perspiration escaped from every pore of his body as he tossed and turned in a frantic effort to escape from the animals and unknown creatures that lurked in every corner of the room. There were blood-lettings and foul medicines, and faces ... many faces. One in particular kept recurring. Light-skinned, with dark eyes, and a frame of long, black hair, this face alone brought him peace.

Then, one morning, Daniel opened his eyes and became aware of the world once more. He found he was in a bed in an unfamiliar room. A room with furniture, and the feel of silk beneath his fingers. He turned his head to where a welcome breeze ruffled the curtains at the window. Puzzled, he tried to sit up, but he was too weak. The slight effort involved left him like a newly landed fish, gasping for breath.

Daniel tried to remember what had happened. What he was doing here, but his mind was no more functional than his body. At that moment, the door opened and a girl came in. She had the face of the one who had come to him in his fever.

Seeing his eyes open, she smiled in delight. The smile transformed her moderately attractive features into a face of great beauty. 'Ah! Louvar a Deus, Senhor.'

Observing Daniel's blank expression, the girl smiled, 'Pardon, Senhor. I forget. You are not Portuguese. I thanked God for your recovery. I am very happy that your fever has passed. You are fome . . . you are *hungry*, perhaps?'

Daniel nodded. He was gathering his thoughts now. He remembered who he was. What he had been doing before he became ill.

'Where am I? How long have I been here? Where are the others?'

'So many questions for a man who has just stepped back from the grave!' Placing a soft hand on his forehead, she said, 'You must not tax your mind too much yet. You are in Sofala. In the house of Senhor Pedro Carlos e Costa Farrao, Captain General of the North West District and Commandant of Sena. You have been here almost a whole week. The tribesmen who were with you have returned to their village – all except the Matabele. He alone refused to believe you would die.'

'Jandu! Where is he now?'

'You will see him soon enough. He comes every day . . . but no more questions. You must save your strength if you are to get well soon. I will bring soup.'

The girl turned to go. but when she reached the door, Daniel called, 'Wait! What's your name?'

She smiled. 'Elvira e Costa Farrao. This is my father's house.'

As the door closed quietly behind her, Daniel lay staring up at the plank ceiling of the bedroom for a long time. When the Manica warriors reached their village they would say that he was already dead. They could not risk incurring the Queen's wrath by admitting they had deserted him when he was desperately ill. He wondered how Victoria would take the news? He would have to send word that he was alive, before she and Sam Speke decided to return to Khami. But who could he ask to make such a journey? He would have to return himself. But he was not fit enough yet. How long would it be? A week? Perhaps two . . . .

His thoughts were interrupted by the return of Elvira. Her father was with her. Senhor Farrao helped his daughter to prop Daniel up on the pillows, then he beamed genially down at him, 'You are looking better, my young friend. It is good. For a while I and "O Medico" thought you would die. He told us so. Elvira . . . ? She said you would live. She has worked very hard to prove she knew best. Day and night she has been here with you. I told her to rest, we have other women to sit by your bedside. But no, she stayed.'

Senhor Farrao shrugged in an exaggerated manner. 'What daughter obeys her father when a handsome young man demands her attentions?'

Elvira chose to ignore her father, but Senhor Farrao put an arm about her shoulders affectionately. 'You did well, Elvira. I am proud of you. Now, feed your young invalid while I sit here and bore him with my talk.'

Daniel protested that he was able to spoon the soup to his mouth without assistance. He learned better when Elvira allowed him to try. His hand shook so much he dared not raise the spoon from the bowl.

'There,' declared Elvira decisively. 'No more argument, if you please. I will feed you.'

The soup tasted better than any food Daniel had ever taken. He felt the first spoonful travel all the way down to his contracted stomach. The mere thought of it was enough to put new strength in his body.

He was so engrossed in eating that it was a moment or two before he became aware that Senhor Farrao was talking to him.

'. . . our soldiers found the place where you had fought the Pombeiros – and discovered what remained of their bodies. You and your Manicas did better than the Portuguese army. Our soldiers galloped this way and that for days. They lost half their horses to tsetse fly and two soldiers were bitten by snakes, but they saw nothing of Pombeiros. In spite of this they claim to have chased them inland for twenty miles. They also say it was Mariano and his men. If they are right then no soldier could have caught him. Mariano knows Mozambique from end to end. He will be inland now, taking slaves. It is not so dangerous as trying to rob young English traders, eh?'

Senhor Farrao chuckled to himself for a few moments. Then he leaned closer to the bed. 'I have been talking to your Matabele . . . a most interesting native. Fascinating. The first of his tribe I have ever met. He is most concerned for you. He tells me you are here to seek a route to the sea for the goods you trade with his people. I know little of the lands beyond the Manica mountains, but I am surprised you chose to come across country to Sofala. It is very unhealthy between here and the mountains.'

Daniel gulped down the last spoonful of soup and leaned back into his pillows gratefully as Senhor Farrao continued.

'Forgive me, but I have inspected your goods. Indeed, I have them safely locked away in my own store. You have some excellent ivory – and those ostrich feathers! They are beautiful. What price are you expecting for them?'

'Forty pounds sterling for a pound of feathers.' Daniel felt drowsy now and he kept his reply brief.

'Forty pounds? Um . . . .' Senhor Farrao made some rapid mental calculations. 'That would be two hundred dollars . . . a good price. I will buy them all. If the price you ask for the rest of your goods is equally fair I will buy everything. But if you wish to have a regular trade with me you must bring your goods to Sena. It will be better for you, I think. The route will be healthier.'

'I don't know of Sena. I've been taking my goods to Whalefish Bay, in South West Africa, but the tribes are warring there.'

'South West Africa? You have actually crossed the African continent? From coast to coast?'

'I lived in South West. Then Mzilikazi invited me to his kraal,' Daniel yawned wearily; he felt very tired. 'It's a long story—'

'And one that will wait,' interjected Elvira firmly. 'You will sleep now. Father, it is time for you to leave.'

With her father's assistance, Elvira settled Daniel down in the bed and left him to sleep. Outside the room she chided her father. 'You wearied him with your talk. He must rest, he has been very ill.'

'Yes . . . yes, of course,' Senhor Farrao replied, abstractedly. 'But you heard what he said. This young man has journeyed from west to east across Africa. He knows the tribes of the interior – and he is here with us. He could help to realise the dream that every Portuguese man of vision has had for centuries. A colony extending from Angola in the west to Mozambique in the east. Such a belt across Africa would prevent England from expanding beyond her present territories. It could herald a new greatness for Portugal.'

'You forget that *he* is English. Why should he help *you*?'

Senhor Farrao put an arm about his daughter's shoulders and kissed her on the forehead. 'My dear, when he is fully recovered he will be filled with gratitude towards us for saving his life. You must nurse this adventurous young man well. I wish to take him to Sena with us.'

When Daniel awoke again it was evening. Through the window the sky over the sea was already darkening. Daniel was aware of someone else in the room and he thought it was Elvira. But then he saw the figure of Jandu standing motionless beside the door.

'Jandu! It's good to see you. Are you being looked after well?'

The big Matabele crossed the room and his relief was evident as he looked down at Daniel. 'They treat me well, my friend, and all the men are anxious to talk to me.' Jandu smiled. 'Indeed, it seems these people do little else but talk. When their soldiers returned from their unsuccessful search for the Pombeiros they boasted as though they had fought and won a great battle. In truth, the only enemies they saw were the bodies of the men we killed. They claim to have pursued the Pombeiros for twenty miles. I do not believe they left the beach. I look around this place and see houses in ruins after a raid. When I ask I learn that the raid took place ten years ago! The Portuguese do not move with any speed. I have seen only the woman of this house busy. She has taken good care of you. But for her you would not be alive now.'

'There are those at uTshwebe's village who will have been told that I died many days ago.'

Jandu snorted. 'Hah! The Manicas are not warriors but women. They talked of crops, and ground that needed to be tilled. Once out of sight of their village they begin looking over their shoulders ... but is it for the Mambari girl you are concerned? The daughter of your friend and his Herero woman?'

Daniel nodded. 'Yes, she'll be upset.'

'Perhaps – but she is less of a woman than the daughter of this house.'

Daniel bit back the retort that he did not want to hear Jandu's opinion of Victoria. Jandu was by nature a close-mouthed man, not in the habit of expressing opinions of others.

'Your friend Speke is very proud of his daughter and she knows this well. Anything she wants – he will give to her. She is accustomed to taking without giving in return. Because of this she has learned to think only of herself.'

'I hadn't realised that you'd studied her so closely, Jandu? Certainly not enough to have taken a dislike to her.'

'I neither like nor dislike her. I tell you only what I see. Others would tell you the same.'

'Oh? And do you have an opinion about Elvira Farrao?'

'The daughter of this house? *She* cares for others. It would have been easy for her to become as selfish as the Mambari girl, had she not had to look after her father. Now she puts others before herself. Her father, you – even I. She works hard and there is a fire inside her. *This* is a woman indeed, my friend.'

Daniel smiled. 'Thanks for your advice, Jandu ... and I realise I owe her my life. I must think of some way to repay her. But for now it's very important that I get word to Sam Speke. If I don't he's likely to return to Khami and give Mzilikazi news of my "death". After finally reaching the Indian Ocean I don't want to get back to Khami to find my trading company has folded up.'

The two men discussed the problem of sending news to uTshwebe's village. They were no closer to an answer when Elvira came into the room to light a lamp and order Jandu out.

'Jandu is very impressed with the way you've worked to nurse me back to health,' said Daniel when the lamp had been lit and placed on a table close to the bed. 'I owe you my life, I know. Saying "Thank you" just doesn't seem enough, but I'm saying it anyway. I am very grateful to you.'

Elvira was ridiculously pleased at his words, but she shrugged them off. 'I have had to nurse many people. My father, grandmother . . . and many of the servants at Sena.'

'What of your mother?'

'She died when I was very young. I never knew her.'

'I'm sorry. Tell me about your home and Sena. Is it very far from here?'

'Far enough. A day's voyage by sea to the mouth of the Zambezi River. Then perhaps five days travelling upriver – it depends on the time of the year. Sometimes, if there has been much rain, the current flows stronger than at others. You will see it for yourself. The ship has arrived to take us to the Zambezi. There will not be another for some months. We must leave in a day or two. You are not well enough to remain here. You will come with us.'

'That's impossible! I haven't yet said I *will* trade with Sena. Besides, I need to get back to u Tshwebe's village. My friends are there and believe me dead.'

'If you attempt to go to them before you are fully recovered they will be right . . . and it will not be safe for you to remain here after we have gone. There is much bad feeling in Mozambique towards the English. It has been that way since your country took over Natal and began pushing its borders northward from the Cape Colony. It is said you are trying to take over the whole of southern Africa – including those places where the Portuguese flag was first seen more than three hundred years ago. Some men say you want even Mozambique itself.'

'I know nothing of the ambitions of Great Britain,' replied Daniel. 'But I doubt whether any of it is true. Mzilikazi and the Matabele nation hold the country between Mozambique and South West Africa. South of Matabeleland are the Bechuanas and the Boers of Transvaal. The only Englishmen I know who are trying to come north are lone hunters and prospectors – and Mzilikazi will not even allow them to enter his country.'

Elvira shrugged. 'I tell you only what is said and believed by my countrymen. You will not be safe here.'

She looked at him from beneath long, dark lashes. 'Does the thought of travelling with me to my home distress you so much?'

'Of course not. But I must get word to my friends that I am still alive. They will be very upset.'

'One of these friends . . . is a girl?'

'Yes. She and her father came with me to Manicaland.'

Elvira's manner became suddenly brisk. 'I think it is better for this girl . . . and her father, to remain upset without cause. Try to go to them before you are well and you will throw away your life. But you must do as you wish. It is nothing to me. Now I have other things to do. I cannot stay here talking to you.'

Elvira swept from the room without a backward glance and Daniel wondered what he had said to make her so angry.

CHAPTER SEVEN

The following day, Daniel's fever returned. It lasted for only twenty-four hours, but at the end of that time he received tragic news that was to change all his plans.

The luggage and goods that Senhor Farrao and Elvira were taking home to Sena were loaded on the Portuguese merchant-man. Now, while the captain fumed at the delay, father and daughter were doing their best to persuade the weak but determined Daniel to take passage with them.

Daniel wanted to remain in the Farrao house until he regained his strength and then return to uTshwebe's village with Jandu. He argued that it might take a week – certainly no more than two.

There appeared to be little chance of the Farraos overcoming Daniel's stubbornness when from outside came the boom of the signal cannon in the village square. As the sound rolled away men began shouting excitedly while women's voices were raised in near-hysteria.

'Wait here,' Senhor Farrao gave the order to his daughter before running from the room. Ten minutes later he returned with two heavily perspiring Portuguese.

'A large war party of natives is advancing towards Sofala. There are at least five hundred warriors. It must be another rebellion. We cannot hope to fight such a number off. Including the ship's crew we can muster no more than forty men and perhaps a hundred native militia. It is chaotic in the streets already. Every native for miles around is in Sofala, seeking the protection we cannot give them.'

Senhor Farrao rapped an order to the two men. Drawing back the sheet covering Daniel, they lifted him clumsily from the bed.

'What are you going to do? Where are you taking me?'

'To the ship,' replied Senhor Farrao. 'It is our only hope of escape. Elvira, you go on ahead . . . quickly now.'

'Wait!' Daniel struggled feebly against the two men holding

him. 'It might be warriors of uTshwebe's tribe, come to take my "body" back with them.'

The idea sounded stupid as soon as he had made it. uTshwebe would not send a veritable army to recover the body of an almost unknown white man. Senhor Farrao too knew it was most improbable, but he gave new instructions to Daniel's hot and unhappy bearers.

'You can see the road into Sofala from the window of my bedroom,' he explained. 'But we must be quick. The ship's captain is nervous. If we delay too long he will leave without us.'

Daniel was hurried to the spacious bedroom of the owner of the house and the men held up Daniel so that he could look out from a window.

For a few minutes the glare of the afternoon sun blinded him. Then, as his vision improved, he saw the advancing warriors and knew immediately who they were. With their high, plumed head-dresses of ostrich feathers, and shields as tall as the men who held them, there could be no doubt. The sight of Jandu hurrying from the village to meet them was ample confirmation. A full Matabele regiment was advancing upon Sofala.

Daniel passed on the astonishing information to his companions and Senhor Farrao listened to the news in disbelief. 'A Matabele raiding party here in Mozambique? No, you must be mistaken. Perhaps it is another migration of Zulu tribes from the south—'

'They are Matabele,' insisted Daniel. 'See?'

The Induna leading the impi had seen Jundu and recognised him instantly. Halting his regiment, he advanced alone and saluted Jandu with assegai raised high in one hand, shield in the other.

Jandu acknowledged the salute and as both men met and embraced, Senhor Farrao's astonishment grew.

'This Jandu . . . who is he that his tribe should send an army hundreds of miles to find him?'

'He is a son of Mzilikazi.'

The expression of incredulity on the faces of Senhor Farrao and his daughter told Daniel that the reputation of the Matabele King was well known, even here.

'Something must have happened. Take me outside.'

'That will not be necessary,' said Elvira. 'Jandu is returning.'

Through the window, Daniel saw that Jandu was hurrying back towards Sofala. Meanwhile, the Induna returned to his men and they lowered their shields to the ground and squatted wearily beside them. It was apparent to the most nervous occupant of Sofala that this was no raiding party, intent upon murder and pillage.

'I think Daniel can go back to his bed and await the news from there,' said Elvira, firmly.

Ignoring Daniel's protests, the two men carried him to his sick room and dumped him unceremoniously on the bed as Elvira clucked in disapproval at the rough handling he was receiving from the nervous bearers.

Jandu entered Daniel's room a few minutes later and his expression was grave. 'I have sad news, trader. My own impi awaits me outside the village. They have come to tell me that the great mountain of Matabeleland has fallen. Mzilikazi, my father, is dead.'

Daniel was shocked. 'I'm sorry, Jandu . . . deeply sorry. I've lost a wise and great friend. But my grief is as nothing compared to that of you and your people.'

'Every man, woman and child of my people has lost their father,' declared Jandu. 'Before Mzilikazi there was no Matabele nation. I fear that unless a successor is found very quickly there will once again be no Matabele nation. I must return home immediately.'

'Of course. I wish I could come with you, but . . . .' Daniel shrugged helplessly. 'My thoughts go with you, Jandu.'

Jandu nodded. 'I will inform the spirit of my father that I carry with me the respects of his friend. He would understand. He was fond of you, trader.'

'And I of him . . . .' Daniel choked on his words. The illness that had laid him low had left him totally unable to cope with such an emotional crisis.

Jandu turned to leave, but Daniel called, 'Wait! You will call at uTshwebe's village?'

'Of course. I have a wife to take to Khami and share my sorrow. I will tell your friends where they might find you.'

* * *

At the wide, featureless estuary of the Zambezi River, the Portuguese sailors transferred their three passengers to Senhor Farrao's own river paddle-steamer, *Bartolomeo Dias*. Overland trekking with all its accompanying discomforts was not for the Captain General of Mozambique's North West District. His cabin on the river boat was fitted out with all the luxury that was possible in nineteenth-century Africa.

Daniel had a comfortable bunk in a deck house, but during the day, when the churning paddles of the shallow-draught vessel were driving *Bartolomeo Dias* further inland through green and evil-smelling swamp, he spent his time on deck. Relaxing beneath an awning that was stretched over two-thirds of the deck area, he enjoyed what little breeze there was.

For the first two days the paddle-steamer chugged between low mud banks choked with mangrove trees, the grotesque, tangled roots of which reared high above the water line at low tide. There was lush green grass here too, and rushes high enough to conceal a standing man.

Gradually, the estuary became a river. Still more than a mile wide, it was laced with ever-narrowing channels that could only be negotiated in daylight. At night, the silence was broken by the shrieks of animals and night-birds, and the sound of crocodiles and hippopotami slipping into the water all about the travellers.

This was an unhealthy area, notorious for striking men down with malaria. At Elvira's insistence they all took a dose of quinine three times a day until the boat left the swampland behind and steamed noisily up to the quay of the small, fortified village of Shupanga. News of their approach had travelled ahead of them and the small garrison was drawn up on a riverside lawn to salute the Captain General.

That night was spent ashore, in the stone house of the garrison commander. Daniel was welcomed courteously enough by the Portuguese officer and his half-caste family, but their greeting lacked warmth. The Zambezi had served as the highway to the interior of the province throughout its long history. The Portuguese hereabouts had seen many Englishmen pass along its braided waterways. They had come in pursuit of knowledge, converts to the gospel, or self-glorification. Few had bothered to hide their contempt for the half-hearted manner in which the Portuguese had developed the African colony. Those who survived to make the return journey hurried off to send despatches to the British government of the day, urging it to ignore the territorial claims of their recent hosts and send an army to occupy the rich and fertile region. Such conduct, coupled with Great Britain's alarming rate of expansion in southern Africa had soured traditional Portuguese hospitality towards their ancient allies.

As the evening wore on and it was ascertained that Daniel spoke no Portuguese, wine freed tongues usually tied by the rules of hospitality. The hosts questioned Senhor Farrao's wisdom in bringing Daniel so far up the Zambezi and making him welcome, instead of ordering him from the country.

When the arguments became more heated, Daniel realised from the furtive and occasionally hostile glances cast in his direction that the conversation was about him. He excused himself from the company, pleading his recent illness as an excuse to make his way slowly towards his sleeping quarters.

It was a cool night and, once outside on the wide balcony that stretched the whole length of the single-storey house, he paused to admire the full moon, riding high in the night sky. He decided he would sit here and enjoy a pipe of tobacco before turning in for the night. He filled his pipe and lit it, shielding the light with cupped hands against the light breeze, blowing inland along the river valley.

'You should be in bed, Daniel. The night air is too chill for an invalid.'

Elvira's voice from the shadows on the verandah startled Daniel. He had not seen her seated on the bench seat.

'Come, sit beside me. The smoke from your pipe will chase away the mosquitoes.'

Daniel accepted her offer and seated himself close to her. When the tobacco was well alight, he took the pipe from his mouth and said, 'Why are you out here all alone?'

'I have no wish to be in that room listening to the ill-mannered talk of my countrymen ... or in the kitchen with their African women.'

'I know nothing of their women, but the men don't seem to welcome strangers – or is it just Englishmen they don't like?'

'You understand what they say?' Elvira put the question sharply.

'I don't speak your language, but it isn't difficult to follow what they are saying. They don't want me here and are going to no great lengths to hide their sentiments.'

'They are concerned for their estates, and the way of life they have enjoyed for so many years. During the past few years we have seen more Englishmen than Portuguese this far up the Zambezi. They come here with such arrogance that the prazeros – the owners of the river estates – feel sure your country must be planning to take Mozambique from them.'

'You keep speaking of Britain as my country. I have told you before that I've lived in Africa since I was three years old.'

'I know. No doubt my father will tell this to the prazeros, but they are simple men. In Portugal they tended the land for a master, owning nothing. They came here because they were promised land of their own. It is a hard life for them, but they now have more than they can ever hope for anywhere else in the world.'

'You and your father are not simple people, Elvira. What are you doing here . . . and where did you learn to speak English so well?'

'Are you seeking mysteries, Daniel? If so, I am afraid you will be disappointed. My father is the youngest son of one of Portugal's greatest families. He loves Portugal and was often outspoken against the excesses of the ruling family, the Braganzas. After publicly challenging one of them to a duel, it was thought best that he be sent to an overseas colony. He chose to come here, with my mother. Publicly, of course, it was an "official appointment". He was given a grant of land and the post of Captain General of North West Mozambique.

'My father accepted that any future he had must lie here, in Mozambique. He settled down to the life of a prazero. I was born here . . . and my mother is buried on the river bank at Sena. I do not think we will leave now. As for my English . . . when my mother died there was a serious rebellion and I was sent to school in your Cape Colony. I remained there for a number of years, until I was able to persuade my father to let me return.'

Having reduced her life and that of her father to a few

minutes of conversation, Elvira began questioning Daniel in an attempt to fill in the details of his own life. Daniel was unused to talking about himself and she found it hard going. But, gradually, she learned of the foundering of the ship on which he and his parents were travelling when Daniel was three years of age. He told her of their desperate trek along the Skeleton Coast of South West Africa, of their unexpected rescue by Bushmen, and of the life that followed in a Herero village.

It took even more patience on Elvira's part to prise from Daniel the story of his love for Hannah, daughter of his trading partner, Aaron Copping. It was a story he had never before put into words for anyone. Elvira's hand found his when he told her in a hoarse voice of Hannah's suicide after she had been raped by a Boer trader. It was this tragedy that had brought him eastwards to Matabeleland, away from the painful memories of South West Africa.

'What of the other girl? The one you left behind in the Manica village?'

'Victoria? Her father was one of the seamen who survived the shipwreck with my parents. He married a Herero woman. They came to Matabeleland with me. Sam helps me to manage my trading store.'

'She is beautiful, this . . . Victoria?'

'Yes, I suppose she is,' Daniel replied. He had never really thought about it a great deal. Victoria had always been . . . well, just 'there'.

'You and she are to be married?' Suddenly his hand was empty once more.

'Nothing has ever been said in so many words,' said Daniel, choosing his words carefully. 'We have both assumed that one day we will marry, I suppose. Victoria is . . . well, she's a nice girl.'

'Ah! But she is not a *wonderful* girl? A girl who takes your breath away whenever you think of her? She is just a "nice" girl?'

'Yes.' Daniel felt he was being disloyal to Victoria and went on the defensive. 'She's a *very* nice girl. Is there anything wrong with that?'

'No, Daniel. There is nothing wrong with that at all. Come now, you have had a very tiring day. You must rest.'

* * *

The remainder of the voyage to Sena passed uneventfully. Once, a group of Pombeiro rebels came to the water's edge as the paddle-steamer passed, but they did no more than brandish empty muskets and shout equally empty threats. They were as ragged and careless of their dress as the Mashona tribesmen of the far interior, and hardly less black. A single shot above their heads from Senor Farrao's musket was sufficient to send them fleeing for the cover of the nearby tropical forest.

The paddle-steamer made hard work of the final thirty miles of river before Sena, but eventually it wheezed its way alongside the wooden jetty, steam escaping from a dozen loose joints as the engineer closed the steam valve and the boat came to a halt with a near-human sigh of relief.

Sena was hardly more imposing than Shupanga had been, but considerable effort had been put into making it secure against attacks from rebel tribesmen and marauding Pombeiros. The village had been built along the river bank and was surrounded on the land side by a double wooden stockade more than a mile in length. Inside was a fort, several stone houses, and a noisy native kraal. The finest house belonged to Senhor Farrao and had close-cropped lawns slipping away to the water's edge. From here there was a fine view to the north, where distant hills began crowding in upon the river.

Their arrival created even more of a stir than it had at Shupanga. The garrison, a motley collection of half-a-dozen Portuguese soldiers, a handful of half-castes and about a hundred Africans, were all well armed. They were also drilled better than their comrades down river.

As the Captain General stepped into the sunlight from his cabin, a couple of ancient 12-pounder cannons fired a welcoming salute.

The effect of this harmless cannonade was extremely gratifying to the gunners. The noise struck terror into every living creature within a mile of the landing stage. Animals fled in panic and birds took to the air with a noisy clatter of wings. In the native kraal, naked babies who a moment before had been playing happily in the dust, fled screaming to their mothers.

Senhor Farrao stepped ashore, acknowledging the salute of his garrison, then waited politely for Elvira and Daniel to step from the boat.

Elvira was assisted ashore by a young Portuguese officer dressed in a clean, white, linen uniform. His black hair glistened with a perfumed hair-dressing that assailed Daniel's nostrils when he was still six paces away. When Elvira stood safely on the bank, the dapper young officer raised her hand to his lips, holding it there as he bowed low. When Elvira smiled at the officer, Daniel frowned in sudden, unreasonable jealousy.

The young officer was introduced to Daniel by Senhor Farrao as Lieutenant Francisco St Anna of the Portuguese army, 'sent here to make soldiers of my farmers and their natives', explained the Captain General. 'And to tell me where I have been making mistakes in running my own militia for so many years.'

Lieutenant St Anna's bow to Daniel was no more than a perfunctory nod of the head. 'Senhor Farrao is too modest. He has built excellent defences here. If he has a fault at all it is that he is over generous . . . both to his friends and to strangers.'

Once again Daniel realised he was faced with the thinly veiled hostility he had encountered at Shupanga.

'There must be many who take advantage of such generosity,' he agreed amiably, before turning away to follow Senhor Farrao and Elvira along the path to the house.

That night Daniel sat down to eat in a style he had never before experienced. The table was set with fine silver and porcelain from the most renowned potteries of Europe. The food, excellently cooked and served, was accompanied by wine of a quality to delight the most critical connoisseur.

As the evening wore on, the talk turned to Mzilikazi's death and the impact it would have upon the Matabele. Daniel was surprised at the lack of knowledge the Portuguese possessed of the interior. Both Senhor Farrao and the young lieutenant appeared to believe that the Matabele lands were adjacent to Manicaland, the tribal area that spread along the Mozambique border.

They looked sceptical when Daniel told them that Matabeleland was five hundred miles from Sena, situated on the far side of the lands of the Mashonas. Lieutenant St Anna went so far as to accuse Daniel of deliberately misleading them, adding that such talk was calculated to fool the Portuguese and allow Britain to drive a wedge between their colonies of Angola and Mozambique.

Daniel patiently told the young officer that Mzilikazi kept *all* Europeans south of the Limpopo River, thus effectively preventing such a 'wedge'. Lieutenant St Anna refused to accept his explanation, dismissing the idea of a tribal leader who could successfully dictate to Europeans.

'Not that it matters in the least. All the lands of the interior belong to Portugal,' he declared sweepingly. 'It was given to us by the Monomatapa, almost three hundred years ago.'

The Monomatapa was an ancient African ruler of the lands now called Matabeleland, Manicaland and Mashonaland.

'It was later taken back again by one of his successors,' corrected Daniel, grateful to the missionaries at Khami, who in a rare moment of friendly generosity had loaned him a number of books on the history of southern Africa. 'There was not a Portuguese left alive away from the coastal areas by the beginning of the eighteenth century. The Matabele have never seen a Portuguese – and I doubt very much whether the Mashona have met more than one or two. No, Lieutenant, I don't know where you set your borders, but Central Africa – from the Zambezi south to the Transvaal – belongs to the Matabele. Neither your army, nor ours, will ever take it from them.'

Lieutenant St Anna stood up a trifle unsteadily and said, 'I cannot speak for the army of Britain . . . we have seen nothing of it here, in Africa, but I can assure you, sir, that a Portuguese soldier will fight to the death for what is his.'

Ostensibly, Lieutenant Francisco St Anna was talking about the fighting ability of the Portuguese army, but Daniel was left in no doubt that he was being warned off Elvira.

Bowing stiffly to his host and to Elvira, Lieutenant St Anna left the room on legs that behaved as though they were carrying the Portuguese officer up a steep hill.

Senhor Farrao smiled benignly. 'Francisco is a passionate young man, Daniel. I beg you to forgive his bad manners. He is honest, and a first-class soldier. We all sleep more safely in our beds since he came to Sena to take charge of our garrison.'

'Perhaps,' said Elvira. 'But "poor Francisco" must be quite certain where his responsibilities begin – and where they end.

Like Portugal, if Francisco tries to claim what is not his he might receive an unpleasant surprise. Now I too will retire to bed. Good night, Daniel. Good night, father.'

Elvira swept from the room, leaving Senhor Pedro Carlos e Costa Farrao with a worried frown on his face. He had hoped that bringing Daniel to Sena might help Portugal to gain a rich empire in Africa. He had never considered that he might lose a daughter in the process.

CHAPTER EIGHT

After his arrival at Sena, Daniel made steady progress towards good health. By mid-August he was out riding with Elvira and beginning to make plans to return overland to Matabeleland.

Senhor Farrao had generously told Daniel he could take half-a-dozen of his best horses with him to Khami. These were the mounts that were usually sent to a farm near Quelimane, clear of all danger from the tsetse fly for the hot, wet months of summer. Inland, the threat faded as the coastal plains gave way to the healthier uplands.

One day Daniel and Elvira rode to the top of a hill, about six miles from the Sena stockade. Here, Elvira set out a picnic for them while a bored Portuguese soldier and twelve militiamen maintained a guard from a discreet distance.

For more than an hour they sat on the hilltop, admiring the lush country on all sides while Elvira pointed out places of particular interest. Daniel commented that it was a great pity no determined effort had been made to cultivate such a fertile and well-watered area.

'A determined effort *was* made,' replied Elvira. She pointed out a number of large clearings where there were no trees, only lush, green vegetation. 'My father persuaded the government in Portugal to send out a number of peasants, offering them good land along the river. They became prazeros. All they could cultivate became theirs. It was a great opportunity for them – but the scheme failed. The peasants had been used to having their lives organised for them by a *patron*. Here they not only had to work for themselves, but also to *think* for themselves. It was necessary to plan crops and manage native labour. It was too much for them. They were peasants, not prazeros. They grew dissatisfied and lazy. Some left Mozambique for Brazil. Others returned to Portugal. When the Pombeiros struck in this area it was the final blow to my father's great experiment. Those "prazeros" who were not killed moved into our kraal. Now they work for my father and are once more content. He has become their *patron*.'

'I sometimes wish I had someone to do my thinking for me,' said Daniel. 'I might have avoided a great many of the mistakes I've made in the past. But I've grown too used to working things out in my own way. I couldn't change now.'

'You have thought out for yourself that you must leave us soon?'

'I have a company to run.'

As they talked they had begun to walk slowly along the bush-covered crest of the hill, leaving their escort lounging in the ground behind them.

'Have you decided where you will bring the goods you trade from Matabeleland?'

'No. I don't know what the country is like between here and Khami – and the distance is more than to Sofala.'

It was a lie. Daniel had already made up his mind to trade with Senhor Farrao at Sena – but he wanted to know how Elvira would react if there was the chance she would not see him again. It had become very important to him.

Elvira lapsed into an unhappy silence and Daniel said, quietly, 'Unless the route is quite impossible I'll be bringing my goods to your father, here at Sena.'

'Even though it is further than to Sofala?'

'Even if I find it's twice the distance,' he admitted.

The next moment Elvira was in his arms, her face against his chest and she was trembling violently. Lifting her chin gently, he brought his mouth down hard upon hers. She responded to him immediately, then suddenly she pushed him away.

Looking up at him, she pleaded, 'Please, Daniel . . . don't kiss me unless it means something to you too.'

It took him a moment to realise the full implication of her words. Saying nothing, he pulled her to him. Her eyes were still searching his face, but as he kissed her once more they closed. Her arms went about his neck and her body moulded to his.

They were interrupted by the sound of the Portuguese guard clearing his throat noisily nearby. Elvira broke free and Daniel turned to see the soldier leering at Elvira.

'What do you want?' snapped Daniel, angrily. It was doubtful whether the soldier understood, but he stopped leering and rattled something off in Portuguese to Elvira, at the same time gesticulating towards the distant river.

'A boat is coming,' explained Elvira.

Scanning the winding course of the Zambezi, Daniel finally made out a faint plume of smoke rising above the trees that hid much of the river from view.

'Our boat is not due back here for at least another two weeks,' said Elvira. 'Something must have happened.'

Minutes later they were cantering the horses down the hillside towards Sena. The Portuguese soldier was not a good horseman and he bounced awkwardly in his saddle far behind them. Further back, the militiamen ran as fast as they could in a vain attempt to keep up with the riders.

They arrived at the landing-stage to find that the whole village had turned out to meet the unexpected steamer, brought from their huts and houses by the vessel's hoarse steam whistle. It had been sounding continuously from the moment it had come within view of Sena.

It was not the *Bartolomeo Dias*. This was a stern-wheel paddle-steamer never before seen on the Zambezi. As the craft hugged the bank nearest the jetty, it could be seen that the deck was crowded with blue-uniformed Portuguese soldiers.

Shouted questions and answers began as soon as the vessel came within hailing distance, but as the shouted conversations were in Portuguese, Daniel did not understand a word. With everyone shouting at the same time it was doubtful whether those on the bank were any the wiser.

As the steamer bumped against the wooden jetty a man in civilian clothes pushed his way through the noisy, gesticulating soldiers. With a sudden shock, Daniel recognised Sam Speke. But this was not the cheerful, one-time sailor Daniel had left at uTshwebe's village. Sam Speke looked ill and tired, his eyes dark-circled and his normally chubby face gaunt and un-shaven.

Daniel pushed his way through the crowd on the river bank and reached the boat as Sam Speke jumped ashore.

Clasping his friend's hand in both his own, Daniel asked, 'Sam! What's happening? Did you get my message from Jandu?' Daniel searched the faces on the boat. 'Where's Victoria?'

The grip of Sam Speke's hand tightened involuntarily, 'That's why I'm here, Daniel. She's gone . . . run off with a Pombeiro. A murdering, thieving scoundrel named "Mariano".'

When Daniel left uTshwebe's village, Victoria was very unhappy, and unsettled. True, much of her unhappiness stemmed from the prophecies of the White Mondoro, but Victoria was honest enough with herself to admit that it went back further. To her return from South West Africa, in fact. She had been away from Daniel for many months, living in a country ravaged by war. During the long days there she had hugged to herself a dream of Daniel. Gradually, she had weaved her hopes of a future with Daniel into a tangled fantasy that helped to keep the tragedy of day-to-day life among the warring Hereros at bay. By the time she left South West Africa the fantasy had become as real to her as life itself and she fed it on the long homeward journey with thoughts of a dramatic and romantic reunion.

When the reunion finally took place it came as a bitter disappointment. Daniel was not the besotted lover of her imagination. He was the man he had always been, rather reserved, his mind filled with the problems of running a trading company in the heart of a primitive continent.

The disappointment had remained with her until the snake bite resulted in her being given a bleak vision of the future by the Mondoro.

But there was something else. Something that hurt even more than the Mondoro's foreboding. It was the grotesque albino's declaration that she too was an outcast — set apart from those she loved.

Victoria had never before thought seriously about her mixed parentage. She accompanied her father everywhere, accepted by Daniel and the few other white people she met, and made welcome in their homes, or about their camp-fires. She had always regarded herself as one of them without question — until the Mondoro spoke to her.

Victoria was both hurt and confused. She needed to talk to someone . . . to Daniel. Unfortunately, before an opportunity arose, Daniel went away.

Suliyana could see how unhappy Victoria was and she did her best to be kind, but Victoria could not bare her heart to the

Manica girl. Suliyana had absolute faith in Chiminuka's spokesman. She would not say the words Victoria wanted to hear. Neither could she tell her father what was troubling her. He would have taken the blame for her hurt upon himself. There was no alternative for Victoria but to keep the problem bottled inside her. It was a heavy burden.

Not until the returning Manica warriors told a stunned Victoria and her father of Daniel's death from fever did grief drive away all other emotions. At first she refused to believe the news, but the men all had the same story to tell. The expedition to the coast had gone through 'bad' country. The horses had died. Daniel had contracted fever and they had been attacked by Portuguese dissidents. uTshwebe's men swore they had fulfilled their mission faithfully. They had, they said, carried the dying Daniel to the white man's kraal by the sea, so that he might die among his own people.

Reluctantly, Victoria had to accept that they were telling the truth. The only discrepancy in the warriors' stories concerned the whereabouts of Jandu. Most of the Manicas insisted he had stayed at Sofala. Others said he had returned to his home without bothering to come with them to Chena. When questioned further, the returning warriors merely shrugged their shoulders and looked surly. What did it matter? Jandu was a Matabele, not one of them. What he did was his own business.

When Sam Speke pointed out that Jandu had paid the full lobola for Suliyana and would hardly return home without his bride, they became even more evasive. Jandu had made it quite clear he had a low opinion of the Manicas as men, why should he have more regard for one of their women? The bride-price had been paid with Daniel's goods. Now Daniel was dead. What had the Matabele lost?

Sam Speke was of the opinion that the Manica warriors had killed Jandu somewhere on the return journey from the coast, but Suliyana was confident he would return to her. It was Chiminuka's will. It was probable that Jandu had tired of the company of the Manicas — or believed they meant him harm, and slipped away from them.

Before the village had time to recover from the excitement of the return of their warriors, it received another visit, one that caused a great stir. The newcomers were men of the Matabele impi carrying news of Mzilikazi's death – and they sought Jandu.

The quaking Manica warriors were brought before the Induna of the impi, and this time they did not lie. Jandu had been left behind at Sofala. He was, they assured the Induna, alive and well.

The Matabele impi was in a huge Manica kraal containing more than three thousand warriors, all of whom hated the Matabele and envied them their reputation as great fighting men. uTshwebe could have called on ten times that number from the surrounding mountains, yet the Induna was as contemptuous of the Manica warriors as Jandu had been.

'I hope your tongues have fed on the truth,' he told Jandu's late travelling companions. 'If you have lied I will return and cut them out before I raze this village to the ground. Even that will not be the end. If Jandu has died by your hands the spears of the Matabele nation will point at you. Our armies will come and we will not return home until the name of Manica is no more.'

There were angry shouts from those warriors who had not been on the journey to the coast until uTshwebe stepped forward and demanded silence.

To the Induna, the Rozwi Queen said, 'If my warriors have lied they will answer to me. Jandu has paid the bride-price for Suliyana, my daughter. He is my son. There will be no more talk of war between us.'

The Matabele Induna refused the offer of huts in which his warriors might rest. Since leaving Khami they had averaged fifty miles a day through difficult and unknown country, sending out small advance parties to capture elusive local tribesmen and so learn the route taken by Jandu and the others. The impi would not be allowed to rest until it had accomplished its mission. The Induna asked uTshwebe only that he and his men be given a hot meal and reliable directions to Sofala. He refused the offer of a Manica guide, declaring that the man would not be able to keep up with the impi.

As the warriors ate, Sam Speke talked with the Induna. He asked whether Jandu was being sought because he was to become the next King of the Matabele.

The Induna shook his head. It was dangerous to be drawn

into speculation on such a subject. If he intimated support for the wrong man he would not survive the coronation.

'I seek Jandu because he is the King's son, and we are Jandu's impi. Mzilikazi has many sons eager to take his place. Kanje is favoured by many. Others say that only Kulumani, the son of Mzilikazi by his chief wife, must become King. But no one has seen Kulumani for very many years. Some say he lives in a white man's house in the Cape Colony. Others whisper that he was killed by Mzilikazi because he tried to take the King's place too soon, when our tribe first came to Matabeleland. The selection of a King is not in my hands. I am concerned only that if Jandu does not return to Khami quickly his enemies will say he thought ill of his father and is afraid to greet his spirit. Once such talk begins even his friends will be afraid to support him against his brothers.'

'Will you be returning this way?'

The Induna nodded, 'Jandu has married uTshwebe's daughter. It is a good marriage, one to please the Council of Elders. They will name the new King. Jandu will want to take her to Khami with him. If Jandu is dead . . . but we will not think of that. It will be better for you to remain here and come to Khami with us. When the news of Mzilikazi's death reaches the tribes of the amaHoli they will suddenly become brave. The land will not be safe for travellers.'

The Induna used the all-embracing derisory word 'amaHoli', meaning 'men of no account'. He was referring to the vassal tribes who dwelled about the borders of Matabeleland, but the term was used to describe anyone who was not a Matabele.

When the Induna set off on his journey to Sofala, Sam Speke travelled with him for half a day. He left filled with admiration for the men of the impi who maintained a mile-consuming trot for hour after tireless hour.

It was dusk by the time Sam Speke got back to uTshwebe's village and he was surprised to see a number of unfamiliar tribesmen camped outside the kraal. Dressed in ragged European clothing, they were all armed with ancient muskets. Nearby, four thin and bony horses grazed on the sparse grass.

Entering the village, Sam Speke saw more strangers seated about his own camp fire. But these were not natives – they were

Pombeiros. Six of them, they had travelled through tsetse fly country, losing all their mounts but the four Sam Speke had seen. These men too were well armed, but in common with their followers, the guns were a motley collection of aged muzzle-loaders.

Victoria was seated at the fireside with the men. Her cheeks flushed, she was having an animated conversation with the man who appeared to lead the Pombeiros. Sam Speke took an instant dislike to the half-caste Portuguese. The lightest-skinned man of the group, he sported a moustache and scrubby beard and his long, dark hair was tied behind his head in a style that had been fashionable in Europe more than half a century before.

When Sam Speke reached the fireside the Pombeiro stood up and gave him a shallow bow. He snapped an order at his companions and they too rose to their feet, with varying degrees of reluctance.

'Happy to meet you.' The Pombeiro extended a hand to Sam Speke. 'My name is Mariano. I am a trader – as you are too, I believe?' Unused to speaking the language, Mariano's English was thick with accent.

'I trade in merchandise. What's your speciality – slaves?'

Mariano's ingratiating smile left his face for only a fleeting moment. 'I trade in whatever gives me a living. If white men want ivory, I get ivory. If they cannot get black women for themselves, then I take slaves. We Pombeiros have to earn our place in the white man's world.' Mariano gave Victoria a sidelong glance. 'It's not a thing you white men boast about, but we make lovely bastardos, don't we?'

Sam Speke's anger flared and the rifle he was holding arced through the air, the butt striking Mariano just below his cheekbone, knocking him to the ground. As the Pombeiro scrambled to a sitting position and snatched at the knife tucked in his belt he found himself looking into the barrel of Sam Speke's rifle. The click of the hammer being drawn back sounded ominously loud.

'Choose your words more carefully when you speak of my daughter. You may be a bastard . . . she's not.'

Mariano's hand dropped away from the knife. With the rifle barrel following him, he rose slowly to his feet. Behind him his

97

companions fingered their muskets nervously, unable to interfere while Sam Speke kept his finger on the trigger. All about
the campfire uTshwebe's tribesmen edged quickly away,
anticipating trouble.

Mariano dusted himself down carefully and when he spoke
only his eyes betrayed the anger he felt. 'Your daughter is
fortunate to know her father. That is to your credit – but if you
ever strike me again I'll kill you.'

Turning away, Mariano signalled to his companions and
they followed him silently from the camp fire.

Sam Speke eased down the hammer on his rifle with relief.
He knew he had come very close to death. His relief was
short-lived. Victoria, fists tightly clenched at her sides and with
tears starting from her eyes, sprang to her feet and glared at
him furiously.

'What did you do that for? Why did you hit him?'

Sam Speke was taken aback by the vehemence of his daughter's words. 'You heard what he said? I'm not having some
Portuguese half-caste talk about you like that—'

'*I'm* a half-caste – or had you forgotten? Would you have hit
a white man for saying what Mariano did?'

'I'd hit anyone who spoke about you in such a manner . . .
but why are we quarrelling? You're not the same as that . . .
that – trash.'

'I'm *exactly* like him. Don't you remember what the Mondoro said? He told me that my future lies with my own kind.'

Half-blinded by her tears, Victoria turned and fled towards
her hut, ignoring her father's calls for her to return.

'Damn! damn! damn!' Sam Speke cursed the Mondoro,
Mariano, and the whole disastrous expedition that had
brought them to uTshwebe's village.

Sam Speke would have liked to devote the whole of the next
day to restoring good relations with his daughter, but he had
promised uTshwebe he would hunt down a leopard which was
playing havoc with the goat herds of a village some miles away.
Before he left, he went to Victoria's hut to say goodbye to her.
She was quieter than usual, but to his great relief she no longer
seemed angry with him. Sam Speke left her with a promise that
he would return with a leopard skin as a gift.

It was a promise that proved easier to make than to fulfil.

For three days Sam Speke and the Manica hunters stalked the leopard without having a single sighting. Each night it proved it was still in the area by forcing a way inside a goat pen and slaughtering the helpless creatures as they ran about in close-packed, bleating terror.

Sam Speke decided a change of tactics was called for. He built a platform six feet high in the largest goat pen and on this precarious perch kept watch for the killer cat.

His first night's vigil was an utter waste of time. He heard the deep, throaty cough of the leopard as it circled the thorn barrier about the pen, but the animal made no attempt to come inside to where Sam Speke waited.

Nevertheless, the following night Sam Speke resumed his vigil. There was a bright, three-quarter moon and the goats settled down to sleep, reassured by the presence of a human in their midst.

Sam Speke waited and watched for hours without incident and began to think this night's watch too was doomed to failure. He dozed off, but suddenly jerked fully awake, aware of a disturbance among the goats in the pen beneath him. Sam Speke listened intently, hoping to hear the leopard's cough from somewhere outside the pen. He could hear only the terror-stricken bleating of the goats.

He contemplated dropping from the platform and patrolling the inside perimeter of the pen, when suddenly he saw a movement in the shadows, not more than fifteen feet away. It was on the *inside* of the pen!

At that moment the nerve of one of the more timid goats snapped and it fled from beneath the shelter. The sudden movement stampeded the remainder and they poured out from beneath the flimsy platform, the fleeter animals attempting to leap over the backs of their slower companions.

The platform jerked and shuddered alarmingly as the panic-stricken goats pushed and jostled against the supporting posts. One goat, brought face-to-face with a post, turned. It was immediately jammed against the wooden pole while those behind, anxious not to be left by the others, charged on.

Their weight proved too much for the temporary structure. The platform gave a mighty lurch and tilted alarmingly. Sam Speke clutched at the side — and missed. Before he could save himself he was thrown to the ground, falling beneath the sharp little hooves of the last few goats.

Choking in the pall of dust kicked up by the goats, Sam Speke rose to his hands and knees, bruised and scratched. During a momentary lull in his own coughing, he realised with a sudden thrill of horror that the sound was being echoed from somewhere close at hand – but thorn fences did not throw back echoes!

During the fall Sam Speke had lost his gun and for a few moments he came close to panic. The hooves of the frightened goats might have kicked it yards away from him. Still on hands and knees, he began groping about him frantically. The coughing of the leopard became a growl and the terrified goats set off for another corner of the pen, bleating pitiably.

Sam Speke was hardly aware of the goats now. He had detected a movement in the shadows nearby. The moonlight caught a green reflection in the leopard's eyes as it slunk into the light, belly low, tail twitching spasmodically.

At that moment Sam Speke's fingers touched the butt of his rifle. Even as the leopard sprang he threw himself to one side in a desperate dive. His finger found the trigger of his gun and he rolled over, using the rifle to ward off the leopard's attack. The great cat tried to cuff the muzzle aside, but Sam Speke's finger squeezed the trigger and the gun fired with a muffled 'Crack!'

Sam Speke smelled burning fur. A fraction of a second later two hundred pounds of screaming, spitting leopard fell upon him.

Instinctively, Sam Speke covered his head with his arms and rolled away, oblivious of the claws that etched two bloody lines down his back. Suddenly he was clear, although the screaming of the leopard continued. Scrambling gratefully to his feet, Sam Speke watched the death throes of the beautiful animal as it threshed about in the moonlight. Shot through both lungs, the leopard snarled in pain and anger, tearing at the place where the bullet had entered its body. After only a few minutes of torment, the leopard collapsed on its side, blood bubbling from its mouth and nostrils as it lay panting its life away.

When Sam Speke recovered his gun, he found the butt had

been broken in two. He levered a cartridge into the breech and the leopard raised its head to look at him.

Hunter and prey gazed at each other for half a minute before a bullet from the shattered rifle ended the animal's misery.

The shots had roused the village and soon men came running to the pen. When the light from their spluttering torches fell upon the dead leopard they crowded around Sam Speke, pointing in awe to his dishevelled condition and the broken rifle. The village headman expressed the heartfelt gratitude of the Manicas and tried to persuade Sam Speke to adjourn to his hut and celebrate the success of his night's vigil. But Sam Speke had enjoyed enough excitement for one night. There was a bright moon high in the sky, and uTshwebe's village was no more than a few hours ride away.

He had promised the leopard skin to Victoria. Asking the headman to have it skinned right away, he limped off to prepare his horse for the night's ride. As he went he became aware that he was aching in every limb.

Sam Speke reached uTshwebe's village just before dawn. A few women were already abroad, sleepily building up cooking fires for the first meal of the day. His arrival did much to awaken the remainder of the village as the dogs got scent of the bloody leopard skin he carried on the saddle before him.

The cooking fire before his own hut was no more than a low heap of faintly smoking ashes. Sam Speke paused to throw on some twigs and poke it into life before going on to Victoria's hut and presenting his daughter with the hard-won trophy.

As he straightened up from the fire he thought he saw someone slip from the doorway of Victoria's hut and disappear into the shadows.

'Victoria . . . is that you?'

There was no reply. Frowning, Sam Speke strode to the hut. He could see no one, but he distinctly heard the sound of footsteps running away in the darkness.

Quickly, Sam Speke returned to his fire and thrust a dry piece of wood into the low flames. It took only seconds to burst into flame and, carrying the crackling torch to Victoria's hut, he ducked inside.

'Victoria, are you all right?'

Naked, Victoria grabbed for her clothes. She was far too

alert to have been woken up by his call. As Sam Speke put a light to a candle and doused the rough torch, Victoria looked at him with wide-eyed apprehension. She shrugged her way into a shirt, but not before he saw the bite, as big as a man's thumb-print, on her neck just beneath the collar bone.

Sam Speke stared at his daughter in horrified disbelief. He knew now he had not been mistaken. He *had* seen someone leaving Victoria's hut. He knew who it must be, yet he was not willing to believe the overwhelming evidence of his own eyes.

'Victoria . . . not with Mariano? Please God . . . not with him?'

She could not meet his eyes and he knew the worst.

'Why? Why? So soon after Daniel—'

'Daniel's *dead* and I'm alive – although you don't seem to realise that. I'm a *woman* now, not your little girl. Where will I ever find a man in Khami? Or do you want me to marry a Matabele? Yes, I slept with Mariano – and I'll do it again and again, because he's the only chance I'll ever have of getting a man.'

Sam Speke struck Victoria across the face with the back of his hand and sent her reeling across the hut, 'Then you'll need to learn to live without one . . . because I'm going to kill him.' Beside himself with anger, Sam Speke stumbled outside.

In his own hut he found a spare musket. It was an old, muzzle-loading percussion gun, but it would serve until he had repaired the stock of his own Wilson breech-loader. It would kill a man. Impatiently, Sam Speke searched for his powder-horn and ready-made musket balls. Loading and priming the gun carefully, he slung the powder-horn and shot pouch across his shoulders and ducked out through the doorway of his hut.

Greeted by the restless lowing of the Manica cattle, the dawn was streaking the eastern sky with thin layers of light as Sam Speke headed for the Pombeiro camping area. His earlier rage had now been replaced by a cold determination. He was setting out to kill Mariano. He should have warned him off in no uncertain terms when he first came to the Manica village. He would, had he believed that his daughter was foolish enough to become infatuated with a thieving Pombeiro slaver.

Sam Speke winced at the memory of striking Victoria. He should not have done that. But she would understand why when things were back to normal again. When the memory of Daniel's death no longer clouded her judgement. They would return to Khami as soon as possible. Today. Along the way they would discuss the future. They would move on from Khami. He would take her to Whalefish Bay . . . or somewhere else where Victoria could meet respectable young men.

At the edge of the village, Sam Speke brought his gun to the ready. The camp fires of the Pombeiros were burning low, but there was enough daylight now to make out the forms of the sleeping men who lay nearby. He picked his way carefully between them, searching for Mariano. The Pombeiro would not be asleep, but he might be shamming.

There was no sign of the half-caste Portuguese – or the other Pombeiros. The men about the camp fires were the armed slaves Mariano had brought to Manicaland with him. Sam Speke kicked one of them awake and asked where Mariano was sleeping. His question was greeted with a blank stare. Most of these slaves came from well to the north of the Zambezi River, speaking a different dialect to the southern tribes. A few of them spoke Portuguese, but Sam Speke understood neither language. Eventually, by constantly repeating the name of Mariano, he made himself understood.

Shivering in the chill morning air, one of the slaves led Sam Speke towards a camp fire set apart from the others. When he reached the spot, the slave stopped in surprise. Running to one of his companions he shook him into wakefulness and pointed towards the Pombeiro's fire, gesticulating and shouting in his own language.

The words needed no translation. Mariano and his companions had gone – but they had not left empty-handed. Dawn came rapidly in the Manica mountains and it was now light enough to see that the gate of the pen where horses were kept stood wide open. Not only were the Pombeiro horses gone but Daniel's pack-horses, Victoria's riding horse and the one just set loose by Sam Speke.

Angrily Sam Speke strode back to the village. Victoria must have warned Mariano. By her foolishness she had lost their horses.

He burst into her hut, determined that on this occasion he would not be easily placated by his wilful, spoiled daughter.

The hut was empty. Victoria's gun and a few hastily gathered items of clothing had gone too.

In that moment, on a chill Manica morning, Sam Speke's world collapsed about him. Sinking to his knees, he put his face in his hands and wept for Victoria.

CHAPTER NINE

When Sam Speke arrived at Sena, he had been searching for Victoria for six weeks. At first he was accompanied by a large party of Manica warriors, sent out by uTshwebe. When it became clear that Mariano and his party were heading for the unknown country of northern Mozambique, the warriors insisted upon returning to their home village. Here Sam Speke received the first good news that had come his way for weeks. Jandu had passed through the village to claim his bride, leaving word that Daniel was alive and had been taken to Sena by Senhor Farrao.

With only two Manica guides, Sam Speke followed Daniel's route to Sofala, then travelled in a small fishing boat along the coast to Quelimane. Rumour was rife here of a rebel band led by Mariano terrorising the populace of the interior. An army was being assembled to set off after the Pombeiro. When the general commanding the Portuguese army in Mozambique heard Sam Speke's story, he sent him upriver in the army's stern-wheeled paddle-steamer, newly arrived from Portugal. With him went a full company of regular Portuguese soldiers.

That evening, Sam Speke related the full story of events at uTshwebe's village. He told it to Daniel and Elvira as they stood on the balcony of Senhor Farrao's house, looking down the sloping grass lawns to the river, its muddy water dull, unpolished gold in the moonlight. In the house behind them there was the sound of ribald laughter from the newly arrived Portuguese officers as one of their number shared a joke with his host.

'I'll find her, Daniel. I'll find her if it means staying here in Mozambique for the rest of my days. All I ask is that you tell Mary what I'm doing . . . and look after her for me.'

'We'll go back to Khami together,' declared Daniel, firmly. 'When we've found Victoria.'

'You are not a fit man,' said Elvira gently. 'Please, leave this to our soldiers.'

'The army will be out to kill Mariano,' replied Daniel. 'They'll not concern themselves with a . . . a girl who has gone off with Mariano willingly.'

He had almost referred to Victoria as a 'half-caste'. The realisation both shocked and dismayed him. It was as though by joining Mariano she had stepped over a barrier he had never before realised was there.

One of the Portuguese officers – and there were a great many of them with the small force – came on the verandah with a glass in his hand and put an arm across Sam Speke's shoulders.

'Hello, my friend. Don't worry, Mariano will soon stand in front of a firing squad, and your daughter will be home where she belongs.'

As other Portuguese officers left the heat of the house, bringing the noise and laughter to the verandah, Elvira stepped down to the path and made her way towards the river. Daniel caught up with her as she passed through the shadows cast by a clump of bauhinia trees.

'Why did you rush away so suddenly?'

Elvira countered with a question of her own. 'Why are you going off with the soldiers? Why not stay here and wait for their return?'

'Sam Speke is my friend. He needs my help.'

'Mariano is his daughter's man. When the choice had to be made between him and her father she chose Mariano. Do you think she will have changed her mind, already? Or is it that you believe she will return for you?'

'I don't know,' said Daniel honestly. 'I only know I must try to get her away from Mariano. He's a murderer and a thief. She deserves better.'

Elvira turned on him fiercely. 'Your Victoria slept with her man because that was the only way she knew to keep him. Is that what I must do to keep you, Daniel? Is that the way things are done among the Matabele – and all those other tribes you have lived with?'

'You don't have to do anything to keep me. If you are sure you want me, I'll be back.'

'I want you, Daniel. More than anything in my life I want you.' Elvira spoke with all the desperate passion of an eighteen-year-old, in love for the first time.

From the verandah of Senhor Farrao's house, Sam Speke saw the two shadows beside the trees merge into one. He realised that, although Daniel was alive, his own hopes for Victoria and Daniel had died at Sofala.

A week later, the Portuguese army was still at Sena. One delay had followed another. The senior officers continually made detailed plans for the campaign, only to cancel them within hours. It seemed to Daniel and Sam Speke that the whole expedition was doomed to end here at Sena in utter chaos. Then refugees began streaming into Senhor Farrao's stockade from upriver, fleeing from Mariano and his Pombeiro rebels.

When villagers arrived from Chemba, no more than twenty miles away, such panic erupted inside the Sena stockade it was as though the Portuguese soldiers had heard of Mariano's attacks for the first time. Now, finally, the Portuguese commander made a determined attempt to bring some organisation to his small expeditionary force. Calling all his men together, he told them they would be leaving the stockade to fight for the glory of Portugal. Upon their return to Quelimane, he promised that they would be hailed as heroes. History would record their names on its pages as the soldiers who had rid Mozambique of the scourge of Mariano and his Pombeiro rebels.

The cheers that greeted the Colonel's stirring speech were all that a commanding officer could wish for. With 120 men such as these, he felt confident of carving a path across Africa, if need be.

The majority of the soldiers and all the officers travelled upriver on board their stern-wheeled paddle-steamer. The under-powered vessel could make no more than two knots against the sluggish Zambezi current, but its low speed and frequent grounding on hidden mud banks suited those soldiers who marched along the river bank, grumbling at the comparative comfort of their more fortunate comrades.

Marching with the regular soldiers were Lieutenant St Anna and his native militia. The young Portuguese officer had pleaded with the Colonel to give his militiamen the opportunity to put their months of hard training to the test. Airily, the Colonel had agreed, stipulating that Lieutenant St Anna must keep his natives out of the way of the professional soldiers when the actual fighting began.

To Daniel, used to the workmanlike preparations of the Matabele army, there was something farcical about this expedition. Only Lieutenant St Anna's militia displayed any degree of discipline. The regular soldiers marching with them straggled along a mile of river bank, while their officers sat on the deck of the paddle-steamer, swigging red wine and deploring the heat of the day.

Daniel and Sam Speke travelled on the boat for the first day and night, but then they asked to be put ashore, unable to endure the noise on board any longer. There was a constant clank and splash of the great paddle, the rumble and hiss of steam – but above all, the babble of voices raised in never-ending complaint or argument.

Once ashore, Sam Speke stayed with the main body of the army while Daniel, impatient of their slow progress, forged a mile or two ahead with a small scouting party of St Anna's militia.

There was little fear of ambush here. The grass, trampled down by the hooves and feet of an abundance of game animals, lay brown and lifeless all about the gaunt, leafless trees. The whole Zambezi valley waited for the rains that would transform the parched landscape.

At first there was little to be seen to account for the mass evacuation of the local populace to the safety of the Sena stockade. The mystery deepened when Daniel and the scouting party entered Chemba. The village was exactly as the inhabitants had left it. Evidence of their hasty departure was everywhere. Cooking pots stood on the cold, grey ashes of dead fires. Chickens strutted about the village, pecking at imaginary seeds, or breaking into a high-stepping run in pursuit of any insect careless enough to alight within their view.

There was even a bewildered, bleating, young goat who ran towards the new arrivals, pitifully pleased to discover that the human race had not vanished entirely from the face of the earth. The young animal would have been wiser to remain in hiding. One slash of a militiaman's knife ensured that the advance party, at least, would not go to sleep hungry that night.

When the main body of the Portuguese expeditionary force arrived, it was decided to spend that night at Chemba, with the steamer tied alongside the bank. The Colonel called a conference to discuss the little army's next move. He was of the opinion that the villagers of the area had been frightened by nothing more serious than unsubstantiated rumour and was in favour of returning to Sena until proof of Mariano's presence in the area was forthcoming.

Most of the Portuguese officers were against such a swift return. They argued that the force should continue upriver for another few days, at least. The Portuguese Colonel eventually agreed, but with a bad grace. He had anticipated a swift and not too serious engagement with the rebels, followed by a triumphant return to the comfort of his villa and mistress at Quelimane. He had even composed the self-congratulatory report that would be sent on to Lisbon. Senior promotions were made from such reports – they were not the result of weeks spent perspiring in discomfort on some filthy river that few officials in Portugal had ever heard of. After all, he had attained the rank of colonel without ever setting foot on a battlefield. Now was not the time to change the habits of a lifetime.

The next morning, Daniel once again set out ahead of the main army, in company with St Anna's scouts. There were a number of small kraals along the bank and, shortly before noon, the leader of the scouts halted Daniel with a gentle touch on his arm. He could not speak English, but his attitude, nose in the air, told Daniel as clearly as words why he had stopped. Daniel too could smell something new. It was the faint scent of wood-smoke hanging on the air.

The small party moved forward cautiously and now another, less palatable smell reached their nostrils. Not more than a hundred paces ahead, around a bend in the riverside path, they arrived at the edge of a village . . . or what had once been a village. Now not a hut remained standing. Charred circles on the ground indicated where they had once stood, with here and there a tumbled frame skeleton of charred wood.

That was not all. This village had not been evacuated and the occupants had been slaughtered where they were caught. It was difficult to say how many victims the Pombeiros had claimed because the scavengers had moved in when the renegades left. Hyaena, wild dog and jackal had all taken advantage of the Pombeiros' ferocity.

Sickened, Daniel turned away from the scene of carnage and destruction, but the leader of the scouts was picking through the wreckage, examining the bodies of his unfortunate countrymen. When he was satisfied, he held up two fingers to Daniel, 'Anteontem' – 'The day before yesterday'.

Daniel accepted that the mutilated bodies had lain in the razed village for two days, but his concern now was for a Senhor Alvara. According to Senhor Farrao, Alvara, with his brother and their families, farmed some miles beyond Chemba. The farm could not be far from here.

Daniel mentioned the name to the leader of the scouting party. The African pointed ahead, to where the track followed the river bank. He said something in Portuguese to Daniel and shook his head, but when Daniel set off along the track, the militiaman shrugged and set off after him.

Daniel and the scouts passed through two more tiny settlements, both put to the torch. Then, in the distance, he saw a long, low, stone house surrounded by a stout wooden stockade. The house was built in a good defensive position on a small hill and for a few moments Daniel's hopes soared. Then he saw that the stockade gate stood open.

The two Alvara brothers lay dead in the first room Daniel entered. Both had been stripped of their clothing. Beyond them, in the bedrooms, lay the bodies of the Alvara women, their two African wives and three daughters. Two of the girls lay spread-eagled on the bed, their throats cut. The others lay naked on the floor, shot dead by the men who had raped them there.

Daniel felt ill. Going outside the house, he leaned against the stone wall and sucked in great gulps of air. At this moment he felt he hated the Pombeiro, Mariano, more than any man he knew. Standing there, he remembered that Senhor Farrao had told him the two brothers operated a ferry service across the river – but Daniel could see no sign of a boat.

Not until he hurried to the river bank did he see what he was seeking. The ferry lay half-submerged on the far side of the river. The Pombeiros must have crossed the river and sunk the ferry to prevent any pursuit.

Daniel was still standing on the river bank when he heard the roar of a cannon. It sounded as though it had been fired about a mile downriver. As the men of the scouting party ran from the Alvara house, where Daniel suspected they had been looting, there was another cannon shot. This time it was accompanied by the distant crackle of musket fire.

Daniel set off along the path at a trot, the scouts on his heels. By the time they reached the scene of the massacre at the first kraal they had found, they could see what was happening. Mariano had set a clever ambush for the paddle-steamer carrying the Portuguese officers and men. Just beyond the village, the main channel of the quarter-of-a-mile-wide river took a wide sweep to pass within fifty yards of the opposite bank. When the asthmatic little steamer arrived at this spot it had been fired upon by a well-concealed small cannon. The ancient gun, brought upriver from the ancient fort at Quelimane had stood outside the door of the Alvara brothers' house until twenty-four hours ago. Now it was being used against the army of the nation it had served for more than two hundred years.

The range at this spot was so short that even the inexperienced Pombeiro gunners could not miss their target. To make things even easier for them, The Portuguese pilot on board the steamer had run his craft aground on a mud bank when the first six-pound cannon ball struck home. The boat and its occupants were sitting targets for the Pombeiros who raked the vessel with musket fire between cannon shots.

By the time of Daniel's arrival the deck was littered with dead and dying soldiers. A few had abandoned the helpless vessel and screamed for mercy as they floundered waist-deep in mud, caught in the musket fire of the Pombeiros. The only mercy they were given was a swift end to their terror. A few soldiers made a determined attempt to reach the safety of the south bank, where their companions yelled useless encouragement to them, but the mud held them fast until they too were picked off by the gleeful Pombeiro marksmen.

Lieutenant St Anna's militiamen, terrified by the booming of the cannon, milled about adding to the confusion, ignoring St

Anna's shrill orders to form up and return the Pombeiros' fire. Only a few of those regular Portuguese soldiers who had been marching with them were kneeling down and returning the fire of the rebels hidden across the river.

'Aim for the cannon when you next see it fire,' called Daniel, and commenced to set an example. His gun was far superior to those used by the Portuguese soldiers and, when Sam Speke joined him, they were able to place their bullets in the thicket from whence smoke poured after every cannon shot.

Their firing brought quick results. After some initial commotion in the bushes across the river, the cannonade ceased. It resumed again some minutes later from a spot further along the river bank, but the accurate shooting of Daniel and Sam Speke had unsettled the aim of the gunners. The cannon balls now fell harmlessly in the mud of the river.

When Daniel, Sam Speke and the Portuguese soldiers began firing at the new position, the rebel gunners decided they had seen enough action for one day and abandoned their stolen cannon. Nevertheless, the success of the ambush had exceeded all Mariano's expectations. The Portuguese army's newly acquired stern-wheeler was settling to the bottom of the Zambezi River – carrying with it the bodies of some of Mozambique's most senior army officers. Only five soldiers succeeded in floundering through the glutinous mud to the safety of the river bank.

Lieutenant St Anna's militiamen located two dug-out canoes at the edge of the nearby village and launched them in the main channel of the river. They managed to get on board the steamer before it slid off the mud bank and sank, but only eleven men, all wounded, were found alive.

Using the same canoes, the militiamen and the remnant of the expeditionary force were ferried across the river to search the surrounding undergrowth for Mariano's men.

They found the abandoned cannon and two dead rebels, but Mariano and his men had left the scene of their remarkable victory. Not until late that evening, when the last of the militiamen had been ferried across the river did one of the scouts who had accompanied Daniel, discover a live rebel. He was one of Mariano's slave-warriors. Wounded and abandoned by his companions, the unfortunate Bemba tribesman had hidden himself beneath branches and dried grass, hoping to crawl away when night fell. Abducted from his village north of the Zambezi when no more than a boy, he was an unwilling rebel, but that made no difference to his captors. When Daniel arrived on the scene he was being pounded insensible by the butts of the militiamen's muskets.

Knocking the guns aside, Daniel threatened to shoot anyone else who touched the wounded man. His action was not taken through any sense of compassion. He wanted information, and the Bemba might be able to provide some answers.

With Lieutenant St Anna acting as interpreter, Daniel asked whether Victoria was with Mariano. The reply was in Portuguese, but Daniel feared the worst when the tribesman shook his head.

'She was taken ill with fever,' explained St Anna, to Daniel's relief. 'Mariano left her at Chief Vumba's kraal.'

'Where's that?'

Lieutenant St Anna put the question to the Bemba, who inclined his head in a vague, westerly direction.

'He knows only that it is inland, many days' march away.'

'Is that where Mariano has gone now?'

The Bemba's reply caused consternation among the militiamen, who had been following the questioning with a surly lack of interest until now. Lieutenant St Anna snapped a question back at the rebel, but this time the reply came as no more than a faint nod.

Lieutenant St Anna stood up abruptly, his face pale, 'He says that Mariano is on his way to attack Sena.'

It was impossible to set off immediately. Dusk was already falling, and this side of the river was unfamiliar country to everyone.

After a sleepless night, Daniel, Sam Speke and Lieutenant St Anna set off just before dawn with the few able-bodied Portuguese survivors and the bulk of the militia. The remainder would return to Sena at a slower pace, bringing the wounded.

First, they had the frustratingly slow task of recrossing the river, being uncertain of crossing places further downstream. Once across, they set off at a pace that would have done credit to a Matabele impi, making much better time than when the slow-moving steamer had dictated their pace. Even so, when they found the shallow river crossing used by Mariano and his men they learned from the signs that they were a full day behind the rebels.

At nightfall there was a brief discussion among the men. The Portuguese regular soldiers were in favour of camping for the night. They had spent a gruelling couple of days and were exhausted – but the militiamen had families at the fort and they had seen what Mariano and his Pombeiros could do. It was agreed that they should march through the night.

They travelled much more slowly than before, caution being very necessary along the bank of the river. Every wild animal for miles around came here to drink during the night. At about midnight the moon rose over the horizon like a great pumpkin lantern. Now the militiamen were in country they knew well and the pace increased once more.

Sena was reached about half an hour before dawn. The stockaded village was so quiet that Lieutenant St Anna whispered hopefully that they might have passed the rebels during the night without seeing each other.

Daniel would have given much to believe him, but Mariano must have known the survivors of the ambush would follow his trail and eventually guess at his destination. He would have wasted no time in falling upon the almost defenceless village.

One of the militiamen was detailed to scale the palissade and learn what the position was inside. He returned as the first traces of dawn lightened the sky above the flat lands to the east. The militiaman brought the grim news that Mariano had attacked shortly after dusk and was in possession of most of the stockade – including Senhor Farrao's house. Senhor Farrao himself was in the stone-built fort which served as the arsenal for the militia, where he and a few men were still holding out against the rebels.

'Is Elvira in the fort with him?' Daniel asked anxiously.

'I don't know,' came Lieutenant St Anna's whispered reply. 'My man got his information from an old woman. She could not tell him much – but come, we must get inside the stockade before it is light if we are to surprise Mariano.'

Half a dozen militiamen were sent over the pallisade, with

orders to open the gate. They did their work well and silently, using knife and spear to silence the dozing guards. With the gates standing open to them, a plan was hastily agreed upon. About a third of the militiamen would move on their own village while Daniel and Sam Speke led a handful of militiamen against Senhor Farrao's house. Meanwhile, Lieutenant St Anna and the remainder of his men would take on the Pombeiros and their followers who were besieging the fort.

The plan was a simple but sound one and might well have spelled the end for Mariano and all his men had not one of the militiamen seen something move on his way to the village and fired before the others were in position. The shot was a good one and killed an early rising pig. It also woke everyone within the stockade.

Cursing the stupidity of the militiaman, Daniel made for the stone house at the run, Sam Speke lumbering along behind him.

Two Pombeiros broke from the house when Daniel was still some distance away. He fired both barrels of his rifle at them and had the satisfaction of seeing one fall to the ground. But the other paused to return the fire and a musket ball passed uncomfortably close to Daniel's ear. Afterwards, Daniel was to swear it had been Mariano himself, but at the time he was less certain. Shouting for one of the militiamen to pursue the fleeing man, Daniel continued his run towards the house, sliding new cartridges in his rifle as he went.

Hurling himself through the doorway, he fell over a body. It was one of Senhor Farrao's servants. Another lay a few feet inside the room. It was dark in here and when a white shadow appeared in a doorway leading off the room, Daniel called out a challenge, hesitating to shoot lest it was one of the household. The reply came in the form of a musket flash and a militiaman to one side of Daniel grunted in sudden pain.

Daniel's first shot dropped the man in the doorway and Sam Speke shot the man who took his place. Then they heard a crash of splintering wood and glass from the rear of the house as another Pombeiro dived through a window and made his escape.

Stepping over the bodies in the doorway, Daniel entered the

first bedroom cautiously, his rifle held before him. His eyes were becoming accustomed to the gloom now and he saw it was empty. Militiamen were in the second bedroom and he left them to search there. In the third bedroom there was the aroma of a perfume he had smelled before. This was Elvira's room. It was also the room from which the Pombeiro had jumped through the window. Daniel was relieved to find the room apparently empty.

Then he heard a faint sound and thumbed back the hammers on his rifle quickly. He waited for the sound to be repeated. When it came it sounded as though a small puppy was whimpering for attention. Something stirred in a corner of the room and Daniel moved towards it cautiously.

When he was no more than two paces away, a light breeze wafted a curtain free of the shattered window and Daniel saw the figure in the corner of the room was that of a crouching woman – a naked woman. His throat suddenly went dry.

'Elvira . . . ?' He hoped – he *prayed* it would not be her. When she turned her face up to him it was battered and misshapen from a severe beating.

'Oh my God!' Daniel dropped to his knees beside her, but she squirmed away, trying to burrow further into the corner.

'Go away . . . Please . . . ! Please!'

Daniel breathed again. It was not Elvira, but her maid. Gently, Daniel put his arms beneath the sobbing girl. Lifting her, he carried her from the room.

Daniel found Senhor Farrao in the fort where Elvira lay wounded. She had been hit in the stomach by a long-distance shot from a Pombeiro musket when they first stormed the stockade. Lying in bed in Lieutenant St Anna's room in the fort, she looked close to death.

Wringing his hands in anguish, Senhor Farrao looked down at his daughter and called on the Blessed Mother to be merciful to her. It was doubtful whether Elvira even knew he was there and taking the stricken man's arm, Daniel led him from the room.

'Elvira needs medical attention,' he said. 'Is there a doctor nearby?'

For a moment it seemed Senhor Farrao's grief would prove

too much for rational thought, but he made a great effort and gained control of himself. 'I . . . . I'll send for Senhora Lopes, if she still lives. She is not a doctor, but she always treats our wounded.'

Senhora Lopes was indeed alive. The daughter of a Portuguese father and a Manica woman, she was now married to a Portuguese – and she was a very capable and resourceful woman. During the brief occupation of the stockade by the Pombeiros, she had hidden herself and her daughter in the hayrack of a small building occupied by an evil-tempered pedigree bull, owned by Senhor Farrao. It was the only place outside the stone fort to escape the attentions of Mariano's men.

Brought to the bedroom, she made sympathetic noises over the still form of Elvira, then promptly ushered Daniel and Senhor Farrao from the room.

There was nothing Daniel could do here and he did not feel inclined to listen to any more of Senhor Farrao's lamentations. Desultory fighting was still in progress as the militia flushed the last of Mariano's men from the makeshift huts of the refugees from the river valley villages. Snatching up his rifle, Daniel went to assist St Anna's men.

By the time Daniel reached the scene, the brief but fierce battle was over. Lieutenant St Anna's militiamen had finally proved their worth and Daniel found the young Portuguese officer flushed and happy, proud of his men. But one look at Daniel's haggard face told him this was not the moment to solicit praise.

'I have heard about Elvira,' he said. 'Is she very bad? She will live?'

'She's alive, but unconscious . . . there's nothing we can do at the moment. Let's see if we've got Mariano.' Daniel desperately wanted to be doing something . . . anything. If he stopped he would think of Elvira . . . .

The bodies of the Pombeiros and their followers were brought to the ground in front of the fort and laid out for all to see, but Sam Speke confirmed that Mariano was not among them. Nevertheless, it was the end of the legend of invincibility that Mariano had built about himself. For ten years he and his men had terrorised the country without suffering a single defeat. It had even begun to be whispered that the Gods were fighting with him. Now, with thirty Pombeiros and two hundred rebel tribesmen lying dead, word of Mariano's great defeat would spread faster than he could ride – and Mariano was riding hard. He had left horses in a thorn corral outside the stockade for just such an emergency as this and at this very moment he and two of his lieutenants were riding away from Sena as fast as they could go.

Back at his house, as servants cleared up about them, Senhor Farrao explained what had happened when Mariano launched his night attack. The Pombeiros had been heard approaching, but it was thought they were men of the Portuguese army returning. No one imagined that Mariano would have the audacity to attack Sena while he was being hunted by the largest expeditionary force ever seen in this part of the country. Instead of manning the walls of the stockade to fight him off, the Pombeiro had found the gates thrown wide to welcome him! Called from his dinner table, Senhor Farrao had himself gone to the jetty with lamps, to guide in the expected steamer.

The ghastly mistake that had been made was realised when the Pombeiros charged through the gates, shooting those who had turned out to welcome them. Senhor Farrao had run to the house to fetch Elvira and she was shot as they came out through the door. Assisted by one of the servants they had barely made the safety of the fort ahead of Mariano and from here had conducted a successful defence against the Pombeiros' surprise attack.

Now it was the turn of Lieutenant Francisco St Anna to tell the Captain General the story of the Portuguese army's disastrous defeat at the hands of the Pombeiros.

Although it was not voiced aloud, everyone in the room knew that, had the rebels not been so decisively defeated at Sena, the débâcle on the river would have resulted in Senhor Farrao being stripped of all his offices. The Portuguese government was notorious for selecting scapegoats to take responsibility for its overseas failures.

When Daniel told of the capture of the Bemba rebel and his news of Victoria's whereabouts, Senhor Farrao surprised everyone by exclaiming, 'Vumba's kraal? I know it well. I went there many years ago on an official visit. Vumba is a chief of the northern Manicas. I negotiated a treaty of friendship with him.'

'This treaty is still in force?'

'Of course . . . but you are not going there?'

'I am, if you'll tell me where it is. I can do nothing for Elvira by remaining here. I'd rather be doing something positive to capture Mariano – and I'm certain Mariano will go to Vumba to lick his wounds. There's nothing left for him here. Will you give me a translation of your treaty – and have as many impressive-looking seals attached to it as you can find.'

'It will be ready by morning. Take the best of my horses . . . take all my horses. Kill Mariano and everything I own is yours.'

'You will need my militiamen with you,' declared Lieutenant St Anna. 'A treaty decorated with many seals is very impressive, but you will find a hundred well-armed men far more comforting if Chief Vumba wishes to forget his promise of friendship and side with Mariano. No doubt the chief has many reasons to fear Mariano, but he has seen no Portuguese soldiers in his lifetime – who do you think he should fear most?'

Daniel could see the wisdom of Lieutenant St Anna's argument, but he also remembered how reluctant the Portuguese expeditionary force had been to move off on the journey upriver.

'It's a kind offer,' he said diplomatically. 'But speed is more important than a show of force. I intend leaving tomorrow. If your men are ready, they can come along. If not, Sam and I will take our chances.'

Lieutenant St Anna was taken aback by Daniel's ultimatum, but going inland to Chief Vumba's kraal had become a matter of honour, 'We will be ready.' He bowed to Senhor Farrao. 'If you will excuse me. I have much to do.'

When Daniel looked in upon Elvira that night, Senhora Lopes was sitting with her. Putting a finger to her lips, Senhora Lopes ushered him from the room and followed him outside. Closing the door carefully behind her she reached for Daniel's hand and dropped something into it. When he looked down he saw it was a musket ball.

'You took this out? You operated on Elvira? Does Senhor Farrao know?'

'Would he have said "yes", had I asked his permission?' Senhora Lopes smiled. 'It was better this way, Senhor. Do not worry, she will live.' The smile left the woman's face. 'I cannot say whether she will ever have children, but she *will* live.'

Daniel looked from the lead ball in his hand to Senhora Lopes and she smiled again. 'I have taken musket balls from a great many wounded men. I am not a doctor, but few of my patients have died. Go now, Elvira sleeps and must not be disturbed. You can see her in the morning.'

Daniel returned to the fort the next morning, shortly before he and Sam Speke were due to set off with Lieutenant St Anna's militiamen.

The curtains in Elvira's room were closed, but there was enough sunlight seeping through for Daniel to see Elvira's face on the pillows and, as he looked down at her, she opened her eyes. The pain in them tore him apart, especially when she tried to smile at him.

Daniel stooped over her and kissed her cheek. 'I'm glad I am able to speak to you before I go.' He saw the dismay on her face and added quickly, 'I'll be back, I promise you. I want you to remember that, whatever happens.'

'Must you go?' It came out as a whisper.

'Yes, but I'll be thinking of you every minute I'm away. I love you, Elvira.'

'You're not just saying that because I'm ill. To make me feel better?'

'I'm saying it because it happens to be true. I didn't want to leave Sena without telling you.'

'I love you too, Daniel.'

Daniel took her hand and gripped it as tightly as he dared. 'Then you can be absolutely *certain* I'll come back to you.'

Bending over the bed again, he kissed her on her lips. As he straightened up and tried to pull his hand from hers, her fingers tightened and she held him fast.

'You . . . you're not going after Mariano again?'

'I must. We think we know where to find him. Victoria is ill with fever at a Manica kraal. Mariano will be on his way there now.'

'Is it for Mariano, or for Victoria you go, Daniel? I can understand Senhor Speke's eagerness to find his daughter . . . but you?'

'I want them both. Victoria because she is my friend's daughter — and Mariano because I'm going to kill him for what he's done here.'

CHAPTER TEN

Lieutenant Francisco St Anna's militiamen marched off from Sena with a jauntiness that was in marked contrast to the army that had set off upriver a week earlier. They had won a notable victory against the Pombeiros and their spirits were high. Lieutenant St Anna was convinced he now commanded a formidable fighting force. Hopefully, his faith in the militia would not be put to the test on this occasion, but no one could be certain. They were venturing into little-known territory.

There was another reason for the brisk pace maintained by the part-time native soldiers. Far away, above the sea to the east of Mozambique, the brilliant hue of the dawn sky had lately been dulled by wispy cloud. It quickly dispersed as the sun rose higher, but each day would persist for a little longer until great banks of storm cloud formed to dominate the whole sky.

Each morning the eyes of every tribesman and woman turned to the east to check on the progress of the build-up. It was almost time for the most crucial few months in the African calendar – the rainy season. This was the season when the Gods decided whether they would grant life or death to their peoples. If the rains came, it was life. If not, then death would stalk a drought-ridden continent.

Either way, it was a time for a man to be at home. The militiamen would follow Lieutenant Francisco St Anna and complete the annihilation of Mariano and his Pombeiros – but only because he had promised to bring them safely home to Sena before the first drop of rain fell.

The journey proved to be much easier than Daniel had anticipated. A day away from Sena they began climbing gently in a country of wide wooded valleys and great sweeping hills, topped with granite outcrops. By keeping to the slopes of the hills they made excellent progress. Daniel, with a good trader's eye, realised it was first-class trekking country. Oxen and wagons could negotiate these hills with little difficulty.

On the fourth day from Sena, the hills suddenly reared up and became mountains, but there was nothing here that Senhor Farrao had not described in detail. A short detour brought them to a pass that wound its way between crags towering to a height of eight thousand feet on either side.

On the fifth day they left the mountains behind and entered a huge valley with spectacular views that faded only with the mauve haze of distance. Here they found Vumba's kraal.

A couple of miles short of the Manica kraal, Lieutenant St Anna had his men form themselves into a passable marching formation. Then, with the Portuguese flag fluttering at the head of the column, they set off on the last leg of their journey to visit Chief Vumba, declared 'friend' of the Portuguese.

The force of a hundred men had seemed large when they set off from Sena, but so vast was the canvas of nature spread out here, that they were no more than a mere speck of movement on the valley floor.

They were expected. Indeed, there was no way for strangers to approach Vumba's village without being seen. Many Manica warriors were in evidence about the kraal, but Daniel noticed that they were careful not to bunch together in large enough groups to cause the Portuguese any concern. Before the militiamen entered the village, Daniel and Sam Speke took a ride around its perimeter to check on possible escape routes that might be taken by the Pombeiros. They returned just as Chief Vumba came out to the Portuguese officer and his small militia army.

The Manica chief was not pleased to see them. Through his interpreter, he asked St Anna why he had brought armed men to the lands of the Manicas. Had he come to fight?

Lieutenant St Anna expressed surprise that the Chief should entertain such bad thoughts about his friends. Why, he had even brought gifts to the Chief of the northern Manicas. A percussion musket, shot and powder and two rolls of calico were produced and laid on the ground before Vumba. Then St Anna produced the copy of the document of friendship, liberally adorned with the very impressive seals of the Captain General of the North West District of Mozambique. He read it first in Portuguese, then had it translated by one of his militiamen who spoke the Manica language fluently.

Chief Vumba looked uncomfortable, then said something to St Anna through the interpreter, at the same time pointing across the valley.

'He says no Portuguese have been to see him for so many years that he has found a new friend. A white man who came to him from the west. A man who stays with him and even now is working in the rocks, just a little way along the valley.'

Lieutenant St Anna began to ask Vumba about this new-found friend, but Daniel interrupted him impatiently. 'Save the diplomatic wrangling for some other time. Tell him we've come for the girl who has been recovering from fever in his village . . . and ask whether Mariano is here with her.'

Chief Vumba looked even more unhappy when the questions were put to him and his reply was accompanied by a great many gesticulations.

'He knows nothing of any girl, and there are no Pombeiros here.'

'He lies,' said Daniel. He nodded towards the cattle pen, about a hundred yards from where they stood. 'There's a small pen just the other side of the cattle with half-a-dozen horses inside – most of them stolen from me.'

Lieutenant St Anna nodded, but when he spoke he was careful not to show his feelings. 'It is regrettable, but I fear that Chief Vumba of the Manicas is not a man to be trusted. He needs to be taught a sharp lesson.'

Calling forward one of the militiamen, St Anna spoke to him at some length in a low voice. The militiaman looked frightened at first, but finally nodded his agreement and St Anna explained his intention to Daniel.

'I have told my man to shoot one of the cattle in the large pen . . . the chief's pen. I want to impress upon Vumba the destruction that one *hundred* men might do if he continues to lie to us.'

Daniel frowned anxiously. A chief's cattle meant more to him than any living creature. More than any member of his family with the exception of his eldest son. Lieutenant St Anna was taking a great gamble. Chief Vumba *might* decide it was time to tell the truth. On the other hand, he could order his warriors to fall upon the arrogant Portuguese officer and his men. If that happened they would be quickly overwhelmed by the sheer weight of numbers. There were at least a thousand spear-carrying Manicas in the crowd at Chief Vumba's back.

Lieutenant St Anna barked an order at his marksman. The man dropped to one knee, took quick aim — and fired.

A hundred yards away, one of Chief Vumba's cows collapsed at the knees and dropped to the ground without so much as a twitch, a well-aimed musket ball in her heart.

Chief Vumba's howl of protest brought angry mutterings from the assembled Manicas, but all sound ceased as St Anna's militia took up firing positions with well-practised precision.

'Tell Chief Vumba the choice is his,' said Lieutenant St Anna to his interpreter. 'We'll see if his love for a marauding, thieving Pombeiro is greater than his love for his own cattle.'

There was a confused babble of sound from the Manicas when St Anna's words were translated, but Chief Vumba's answer came hastily enough.

'Do not shoot any more cattle. He will give you the Pombeiro — and the girl.'

Before any more could be said, a heavily bearded man galloped up to the village from the direction of an area of broken rocks not far from the village. At first glance Daniel thought he was a Pombeiro, but Pombeiros did not sport heavy black beards, and the skin beneath the new arrival's unbuttoned shirt was as white as Daniel's own.

'What the 'ell's going on here, man? Who's doing the shooting — and what's the idea of this Portuguese flag, eh? Portugal has no jurisdiction here, it's too far inland.'

It was an accent Daniel had heard many times before. The thick, throaty intonation of a man who was more used to speaking Dutch than English. The newcomer was Andreus Van Niekerk, a Boer, descendant of the Dutch settlers who had colonised the Cape of Good Hope two hundred years before.

'We'll argue about who owns the country later. Right now we're after a Pombeiro named Mariano.'

'The half-caste Portuguese?' The Boer spat in the dust at his feet. 'Don't tell me you're risking a war over him? You'll find him drunk in his shack, with his woman. That's his place over there.'

He nodded towards a hut that was in need of new thatch, not thirty paces from where they were standing.

Lieutenant St Anna responded to the information swiftly. Ignoring Chief Vumba, he sent his militiamen to surround the hut, ensuring that no one could escape. To make doubly certain, he sent four of his men to guard the pen where Daniel had seen the horses, just in case Mariano had already left his hut.

Next, Lieutenant St Anna advanced to within a few feet of the low, blanket-covered doorway of the hut and called upon Mariano to come out and give himself up. The reply was a musket shot that left a smouldering hole in the blanket, the lead ball singing through the air only inches from St Anna's head.

The Portuguese officer ducked away quickly and called out an order to his men. The dozen or so militiamen stationed before the entrance to the hut put their guns to their shoulders. Before they could fire in through the doorway, Daniel called, 'Wait!'

Before St Anna could argue with him, Daniel ran forward to take up a crouching position beside the hut doorway.

'Victoria . . . are you inside?'

Daniel received a similar reply to the one given to Lieutenant St Anna, but this time the musket ball punched a fist-sized hole through the mud and wattle wall of the hut and shattered a hard-clay milk gourd standing in the shade of a hut twenty yards away.

Through the thin wall Daniel could hear the sound of a hoarse, whispered argument. Then Victoria called, 'Who . . . who is it?'

'It's Daniel.' Daniel crouched low, anticipating another shot, but it never came.

'Daniel! But I . . . we, were told you were dead!'

'You were told wrong – but come outside and let's talk.'

There was a quick movement inside the hut, then a man's voice called, 'No. She's staying here. If you attack she dies with us.'

'Victoria.' Sam Speke had run to Daniel's side and now he shouted to his daughter. 'Try to persuade them to give themselves up. The hut's surrounded by the Portuguese army. There's no escape.'

'Either we are *all* allowed to leave together, or we die

together,' shouted Mariano. 'Tell the soldiers to go back to Mozambique. This is not Portuguese territory.'

'Mariano, let my girl go, for God's sake! You do that and I'll do what I can to persuade the Lieutenant to allow you to go free.'

Mariano gave a short derisive laugh. 'Do you really expect him to listen to you after what we did to his army on the Zambezi River? Of course he won't – but he's going to have to come in after us, and Victoria will die with her own. There will be no more talk now. Go, or I shoot again – this time to kill.'

Sam Speke would have stayed to argue with the Pombeiro, but Daniel pulled him away and half-dragged him to where Lieutenant St Anna crouched beside another hut with a few of his troops.

He listened to Daniel's report of the conversation with Mariano impatiently. 'I expected nothing else. Mariano knows he will not leave Vumba's kraal alive.'

St Anna snapped an order to his men and two of them hurried away.

'What are you going to do?' Sam Speke watched the two men until they went out of sight between the huts. 'You can't attack, my daughter is in that hut.'

'So are the Pombeiros,' stated St Anna briskly. 'None of them are there against their will. However, I will not order my men to shoot into the hut until I have tried to drive them out by other means. Get back now, things will happen very quickly.'

At that moment, Daniel realised what Lieutenant St Anna had planned. The two men he had sent away suddenly appeared behind Mariano's hut and each of them carried a lighted torch. Creeping close to the hut they tossed the torches high in the air to land on the thatched roof. One torch rolled off to splutter harmlessly in the dust, but the other clung to the thatch and seconds later the tinder-dry roofing ignited with a mighty roar.

Sam Speke started forward, his daughter's name on his lips, but Daniel held him back. 'Wait, Sam. St Anna's idea might work.'

As they watched, thick choking smoke began to pour from the hut, around the sides of the blanket hanging at the door and the militiamen moved forward cautiously. A full minute passed and Daniel thought that he and St Anna might have underestimated the determination of Mariano and his men. Then the blanket was wrenched from the doorway and Victoria staggered from the hut, coughing and retching.

Sam Speke broke from Daniel's grasp and reached his daughter's side just as five Pombeiros burst from the hut. Their eyes streaming from the acrid black smoke, none of them could see where he was going, but each of them had a gun in his hand and they ran out firing wildly.

Sam Speke staggered and, as Victoria screamed, he fell to the ground in front of her. One of the militiamen was also hit and he sat on the ground clutching his stomach, screaming in agony and fear.

Daniel reached Sam Speke just as the militiamen, obeying Lieutenant St Anna's order not to shoot, began clubbing the Pombeiros to the ground with their rifle butts.

The Pombeiro bullet had struck Sam Speke in his side and it was immediately apparent to Daniel that it was a mortal wound. The ex-seaman knew it too. With Daniel supporting him in his arms and Victoria kneeling by his side, he tried desperately to speak to his daughter but the sound was choked off in his throat as blood welled up and dribbled from both corners of his mouth.

Three times Sam Speke tried to say something to Victoria before he finally accepted that the words were not going to come. Reaching out, he took her hand in his and died, looking up at her face.

Daniel was stunned at the sudden death of the man who had been his friend for as long as he could remember, sharing dangers and troubles across the breadth of Africa.

But his death was an even greater tragedy for Victoria. It had happened so quickly that, at first, she was quite unable to comprehend what had happened. When realisation finally came that her father was dead, she looked up at Daniel in horror.

'This is my fault, Daniel . . . . *I* killed him!' Suddenly she scrambled to her feet and turned as though she was going to hurl herself into the blazing hut.

Daniel grabbed her and held on as she struggled to get away.

'Let me go – Daniel, please let me go!'

'Get a grip on yourself. We came here to take you home. Do you want me to tell your mother that Sam died for nothing?'

Still struggling in his arms, Victoria began to scream. She did not stop until Daniel released one of his arms and slapped her sharply across the face. The sharp blow had an immediate effect. Victoria collapsed against him and began sobbing uncontrollably. Meanwhile, all about them, excited Manica tribesmen were working frantically to prevent the flying sparks from igniting the whole of the village.

At the insistence of Lieutenant St Anna, Daniel led Victoria away from the Manica village, leaving two of the militiamen to carry off Sam Speke's body. Pushing the badly beaten Pombeiros along before them, the remainder of St Anna's force retreated from the village and set up a defensive camp at the foot of a nearby hill, close to a spectacular waterfall that tumbled in a series of cataracts a hundred and fifty feet down the steep face.

For a couple of hours there was feverish activity in the Manica village and the anger of Chief Vumba and his tribe at the actions of the Portuguese militia was an almost tangible thing.

Just before dusk fell, Andreus Van Niekerk came to the camp leading a riding horse and two pack animals.

'You've stirred up a hornets' nest down there,' he declared angrily. 'Vumba's village is no place for a white man tonight – and you'd better keep a good guard posted. Vumba's warriors are just wild enough to want to give you a damn good fight.'

'If he allows his warriors to attack us Chief Vumba will learn the penalty for breaking a treaty of friendship.'

'Good. You teach a good, hard lesson, General. It will save me trouble if he learns it from you. I have a treaty with Chief Vumba too – and it's one he's not going to wriggle out of in a hurry.'

'*You* have a treaty?' Lieutenant St Anna looked at the Boer suspiciously. 'Vumba is a tribal chief in Portuguese territory. You have no right to come here and make a treaty with anyone.'

'More right than you, I'd say. I came here at Chief Vumba's invitation . . . I'd hardly say the same for you. Chief Vumba swears he *isn't* in Portuguese territory. I agree with him. So does the Government of Transvaal – and the British Government at Cape Town too, I reckon. You *might* have some jurisdiction along the Zambezi River – although from what I hear that's no more than a matter of opinion. You certainly have none here.'

'The Portuguese flag was planted here before the first Dutchman – or Englishman, had ever sighted the coast of South Africa.'

'You might as well have planted potatoes,' retorted Van Niekerk insultingly. 'This is free territory and that's just the way it's going to stay . . . for a while, at any rate.'

'What sort of a treaty have you made with Vumba?' Daniel asked Van Niekerk the question in a bid to head off an even more serious argument between the two men.

'I've got the sole mining rights for the whole of Manicaland on behalf of the Cape Mining Company,' replied Andreus Van Niekerk, proudly. 'Here, look at this.' He thrust his hand into a pocket and pulled out two irregular shaped objects that gleamed dully in the faint light that remained. 'They're gold nuggets. I picked them up in a stream not a mile from here. By this time next year there will be fifty miners working in these mountains.'

'How will you get that many men here?' asked Daniel sharply. 'They'll need to come through Matabeleland. Mzilikazi's policy has always been to keep white men out—'

'Mzilikazi's dead,' interrupted Andreus Van Niekerk. 'And the Matabele can't make up their mind who's going to take his place . . . not that I care, mind you. I've already got all the permission I need.'

Van Niekerk opened a pouch at his belt. Taking out a many-folded piece of paper, he handed it to Daniel.

Walking to the fireside, Daniel read the document in the light of the flames. Short and to the point, the note gave permission for Andreus Van Niekerk and employees of the Cape Mining Company to pass through the lands of the Matabele, and those of their vassals. It was signed, 'The Reverend Farewell Loveday, acting on behalf of Umnombati, Regent of the Matabele Nation.'

Daniel finished reading the permit and handed it back to Van Niekerk, shaking his head in disbelief. 'Farewell Loveday must be mad!' he exclaimed. 'How many of these has he issued?'

The Boer replaced the document in his pouch and shrugged his shoulders. 'I don't know . . . about fifty, or sixty, I suppose. What does it matter? The sooner this country is opened up, the better.'

'The better for whom?' retorted Daniel. 'Certainly not for the Matabele. To allow Europeans to enter Matabeleland right now is dangerous folly. Mzilikazi must have at least thirty sons who have a good claim to the throne. Each of them has his own impi, ready to back him. The whole country could erupt in bloodshed at any moment. Any white men in the country would be caught right in the middle of the fighting.'

'I'll look after myself, they'll need to do the same,' said Andreus Van Niekerk indifferently. 'Besides, the deaths of a few Englishmen might be all the excuse the British Government needs to send an army to Matabeleland and take over the country. That should suit you. If they're not up to it I'm quite sure the Government of Transvaal will be happy to do the job for them.'

'Such a move will unite the Matabele as nothing else could,' declared Daniel. 'Anyone who tries to move in can expect to be opposed by a well-disciplined army of at least thirty thousand men. It will be a blood bath.'

Andreus Van Niekerk looked slyly at Lieutenant St Anna, who frowned as he listened to both men discussing territory to which Portugal also laid claim. 'We could always call on the General's kaffirs to come and rescue us.'

Daniel ignored the Boer's sarcasm. 'With all that's happening in Matabeleland, the sooner I get back to Khami the better.'

'You're travelling to Khami? So am I.' Van Niekerk looked to where Victoria sat huddled in a blanket by the camp fire. 'Is she coming too?'

'Her mother is there. She's all the family she's got left now.'

Andreus Van Niekerk looked at Victoria speculatively. 'Um! I'd have preferred the company of another man. One who could handle a gun, but she'll help time to pass more quickly. It will take us ten days to reach Khami. By the time we get there I might have forgotton she's got a kaffir mother and has opened her legs to that son of a kaffir whore, Mariano.'

Andreus Van Niekerk rose to his feet and went off to unload his horses. Daniel watched him go, swallowing his anger. He would have preferred not to have the Boer's company to Khami, but he knew it would save him a great deal of time. Van Niekerk knew the route. All the same, Daniel thought the Boer was one of the most obnoxious men he had ever met.

That night a strong guard was placed about the camp. Lieutenant St Anna feared a surprise attack from Chief Vumba's Manicas, but when trouble arrived it came from *inside* the camp.

Daniel woke with a start as shots were fired from some-where nearby. The shots were followed by excited shouting and Daniel snatched up his rifle. By the time he reached the scene of the disturbance the excitement was over. When torches were lighted from a low-burning camp fire, it became apparent that Mariano and his Pombeiros had made a deter-mined bid for freedom. One Pombeiro and a militiaman lay dead on the ground. The other Pombeiros were being handled roughly and tied by their angry guards.

'How did they get free?' Daniel asked St Anna. When he had seen the Pombeiros shortly before he lay down to sleep, they were trussed so tightly he was concerned that the ropes would cut off the blood supply to their limbs.

'I thought of putting that question to *you*. They used this.'

Lieutenant St Anna tossed a razor-sharp skinning-knife through the air. Catching it by the handle, Daniel recognised it as his own. Kept in a sheath at the back of his belt, it had been on the ground beside him as he slept.

'Victoria!' he said quietly. She had been sleeping only a few feet from him.

'Who else? I should have anticipated such a rescue attempt. However, the death of another of my soldiers makes the decision I have to take easier than before. Go back to sleep now. There will be nothing more to disturb you tonight.'

Back at his own fire, Daniel threw on more wood, hoping Victoria would sit up and say something. But she lay still and gave no indication that she could hear him when he spoke softly to her. Tucking the knife and belt beneath the boots he was utilising as a pillow, Daniel lay down to sleep once more.

He was still awake when the first rays of the sun stirred the camp into life.

Lieutenant Francisco St Anna convened a court for the purpose of trying Mariano and his fellow Pombeiros on charges of insurrection and murder. The proceedings were both simple and brief. St Anna was prosecutor, the only witness – and the judge. He did not deem it necessary for the Pombeiros to have the benefit of a defence counsel. After listing the crimes of which the accused were charged, he pronounced sentence of death upon them – and wasted no time in ordering the sentence to be carried out.

Victoria knew nothing of what was happening. Crouching dejectedly at Daniel's camp fire, she waited for the coffee pot to come to the boil. When a great cheer rose from the assembled militia, she looked up to see her lover and his three companions twitching their lives away at the end of ropes hanging from two nearby trees.

Victoria started to her feet and began to scream, but Daniel was quick enough to intercept her as she tried to run to the scene of the executions.

'No . . . Victoria . . . . There's nothing you can do now.' He held her until the struggles gave way to a grief that was worse than she had shown for the death of her father.

Victoria had managed to gain control of herself by the time Andreus Van Niekerk strode angrily across the camp to Daniel. He had been remonstrating with Lieutenant St Anna. His anger was not because of the irregular and arbitrary nature of the Pombeiros' trial and execution, but because Mariano had managed to steal the Boer's horse during the escape attempt and it had been shot dead from beneath him.

After making a rough cross to mark Sam Speke's grave beside the waterfall, Daniel, Victoria and Van Niekerk were ready to depart for Khami. The Boer was still grumbling about having to ride one of his pack-horses. His mood was not improved when Daniel went to Vumba's village to reclaim his own horses and gave the best of them to Victoria to ride.

Chief Vumba was also unhappy. He had hoped to make the horses his own property, but the sight of the four bodies dangling from the trees made him disinclined to argue. When

Daniel presented two of the horses to him in return for the right to bring trade wagons through his territory, his humour improved.

Lieutenant Francisco St Anna's farewell to Daniel had a warmth about it that Daniel would not have thought possible when they had first met, only a few weeks before.

The Portuguese officer smiled when Daniel voiced his thoughts. 'Much has happened since then, Daniel. We have stood together in battle. At such times one learns the worth of a man very quickly. We will meet again, you and I, at Sena. I will convey your affection to Senhorita Farrao and will guard her with my life until you return for her. You look surprised. Did you think, perhaps, your feelings for her were a well-kept secret? Oh no! When you first arrived at Sena I realised I had lost any chance of gaining Elvira for myself. For that reason we could not be friends then. Now I know you better I am happy for her . . . and for you.' Shaking Daniel's hand warmly, Francisco St Anna strode away to attend to the breaking-up of his own camp.

Andreus Van Niekerk had not finished repacking his saddle-bags. Leaving him to catch up with them, Daniel and Victoria rode off slowly, alone for the first time since their unhappy reunion. As they rode past the dead Pombeiros, Victoria averted her eyes, biting her lower lip fiercely as she struggled to keep a firm grip on her emotions.

'Had it not happened here, the end would have been just as certain somewhere else,' said Daniel, as gently as his own feelings would allow. 'Mariano was no good. For what he and his men did at Sena I would have tracked him down and killed him myself.'

'Because of the girl the Portuguese officer was talking about . . . Elvira.'

'Partly . . . but there were other girls there who suffered more than gunshot wounds.'

'Who is this girl, Daniel?' Victoria chose to ignore what Mariano had done at Sena.

Daniel gave Victoria an outline of the way he and Elvira had met, telling of their journey together to Sena and the weeks he had spent there.

'Are you going to marry her?'

Daniel knew that Victoria wanted him to lie to her, but he could not. 'Yes, if she'll have me when I return to Sena.'

They rode in silence for a long while. Then, in a voice choked with emotion, Victoria asked, 'What will happen to me now? I . . . I feel as though I'm caught up in some unbelievable nightmare. When uTshwebe's warriors returned and said you were dead I didn't know what to do. I couldn't think straight. Every night I cried myself to sleep. For a while I . . . I thought I'd die too. It would have been better if I had,' she added bitterly. 'Instead . . . Mariano came along.'

Victoria gripped the pommel of her saddle so tightly her knuckles gleamed white against the worn, brown leather, 'I've made a complete mess of my life. Dad is dead because of me. He warned me against Mariano, at uTshwebe's village. Oh God! Why didn't I listen to him? How am I going to face ma . . . ?'

Daniel wanted to comfort her. He felt deeply sorry for what had happened to her, but there were some things he could not forget. 'Blaming yourself isn't going to bring Sam back. You've got to forget what's happened. It won't be easy, but for your own sake – and your mother's, you've got to pick up the threads of your life again.'

Victoria suddenly raised her head and looked directly at Daniel. 'If things had been different . . . . If you hadn't fallen ill and met Elvira, and I hadn't got mixed up with Mariano – would you ever have married me?'

'It's a question I've asked myself many times during these past couple of weeks. The honest answer is – I don't know.'

Victoria gave him a wan little smile that made him suddenly remember her as she had been when she was a small girl. 'That can only mean "No", Daniel. You made your mind up quickly enough once you'd met Elvira. It makes things easier for me, really. It means that I haven't lost you because of my stupidity. You were never mine to lose.'

'There'll be other men, Victoria. Some day the right one is going to ride in, take one look at you and carry you off to the nearest preacher.'

It was a half-hearted attempt to bridge the wide gap that had opened up between him and Victoria, but it failed miserably.

Victoria looked away from him before she spoke again, 'He'll need to be a very understanding man, Daniel. I'm carrying Mariano's child.'

CHAPTER ELEVEN

Andreus Van Niekerk soon proved himself to be quite as objectionable as Daniel had anticipated. After inquiring in the crudest manner into the relationship that existed between Daniel and Victoria, the Boer used every means short of actual physical force to persuade Victoria to share his blanket at night. He became so persistent that Daniel threatened to knock the Afrikaaner down if he did not leave her alone. Andreus Van Niekerk grumbled that it was none of Daniel's business. He uttered vague threats, but saved his advances for the occasions when Daniel went hunting, or rode off to find a detour more suitable for an ox-wagon laden with trade goods.

Eventually, Victoria put a stop to the Boer's amorous hopes in a way that made a deep and lasting impression upon him. With the Manica mountains three days behind them they were now on the edge of the Mashonaland plateau, close to the headwaters of the Sabi River. When Daniel sighted a herd of buffalo grazing in open bushland under the watchful eyes of a muscular young bull, it was agreed that buffalo meat would make a wonderful evening meal for the three travellers.

'The Lord could almost have laid the table for us,' said Daniel, sliding from his horse and pulling his rifle free from the saddle holster.

'From this range?' Van Niekerk was sceptical. 'That herd's four hundred yards away. Fire a shot from here and all you'll have for supper is a mouthful of dust.'

Daniel was about to prove Van Niekerk wrong when Victoria reined her horse in front of him, spoiling his aim. She carried the rifle that had belonged to her father. Without dismounting, she raised the weapon to her shoulder, took careful aim – and fired. To Daniel's delight and Andreus Van Niekerk's astonishment a fat buffalo cow on the edge of the herd took an involuntary step forward, then pitched on her side in the red dust.

The crack of the rifle-shot startled the herd, but they had

never before encountered gun-carrying hunters and did not associate the horses and their riders with the death of the buffalow cow. While they milled about, snorting their bewilderment, the herd-leader raised his great head and tested the air to the north, east, south and west. He was utterly confused. Advancing to where the dead cow lay stretched on the ground, his nose caught the scent of blood. He backed off in alarm, but the fear passed quickly. Death was as much a part of the bush veldt as the aged, balancing rocks, the gnarled thorn trees and tall dried grass. Three minutes after the echoes of the shot died away, the buffalo herd was grazing as though nothing had happened.

It took Andreus longer to recover. He had not believed such a shot possible – and had said so. To be forced to eat his words was bad enough, but to be proved wrong by a coloured *woman . . . .*!

'If you think that was a lucky shot I'll down another,' said Victoria, mockingly. Behind her, Daniel grinned at Van Niekerk's discomfiture.

'It was a good shot,' Van Niekerk conceded grudgingly. 'But it's easy to look clever when you've got a better gun than anyone else. Now I'll show you what hunting is really about.'

Van Niekerk pulled his own gun free from the saddle holster. It was a large-bore muzzle loader. Capable of punching a hole right through an elephant, it was notoriously inaccurate and far too heavy and clumsy for professional hunters. Swinging down from his horse, Andreus Van Niekerk set off at a crouching run through the long dry grass towards the buffalo herd.

Daniel's smile changed to a frown as he watched the Boer move closer to the herd. 'We'd better go and help him. The damn fool's so eager to prove he can shoot a buffalo he's likely to kill himself in the attempt.'

Mounting his horse, Daniel kneed it forward, rifle in his hand. Flicking the reins of her own horse, Victoria fell in beside him.

Meanwhile, so determined was Andreus Van Niekerk to down a buffalo that he had thrown off all reasonable caution. Closing in upon the herd he ignored the wind that blew from him towards the animals. His scent was caught first by a scarred old bull, the recently deposed herd-leader. He moved instinctively to put himself between the cows and the calves he had sired – only to be stopped by the young bull. The well-muscled younger animal had caught Van Niekerk's scent too and his grunt of alarm swiftly alerted the cows. They began calling their offspring as the bull turned to face the unseen threat.

At that moment, Andreus Van Niekerk rose to take up a shooting stance and he and the young herd-leader stared at each other, separated by no more than fifty yards of rough-grassed veldt.

The Boer brought the heavy rifle slowly and carefully up to his shoulder, but made no attempt to fire off a shot until the young bull turned to drive his herd away from the offensive smell of man. For a moment he stood broadside on to the Boer hunter – and Van Niekerk squeezed the trigger.

The big-bore gun threw high. Instead of penetrating the big bull's heart, the musket ball struck it just above the shoulder. With a bellow of pain, the wounded bull rounded on Van Niekerk as he desperately poured black powder down the barrel of his gun from the leather powder-horn hanging at his belt.

As the old bull took over the familiar task of ushering the herd clear of trouble, his wounded successor lowered his head and charged – and a three feet spread of curved horns bore down on the Boer hunter.

While Van Niekerk was still frantically ramming home the heavy lead musket ball, he realised the buffalo would reach him before he was ready to fire again. He looked about him desperately for somewhere to take refuge, but there was no tree within a reasonable distance that might take his weight. By the time this realisation came to him it was too late to run. He jumped to one side as the buffalo bull reached him, but a side swipe of the horns sent him tumbling heavily to the ground.

The bull slithered to a halt in a cloud of red dust and wheeled about, hot-eyed and angry. Andreus Van Niekerk's rifle, ramrod protruding from the barrel, lay where it had fallen, ten feet away. The Boer raised himself on one knee, aware that he was at the mercy of the enraged animal and could do nothing to help himself. The bull lowered its head once more, but before it could charge two rifles fired in unison. The buffalo's legs buckled and it fell dead to the ground.

When Daniel and Victoria rode up, the dust was beginning to settle. It had been Andreus Van Niekerk's intention to deny he was ever in danger, but as he slapped the dust from his clothing, his shaking hand betrayed him and the lie died on his lips.

'That was a damn fool thing to do!' Daniel exclaimed. 'You'd have got away with shooting a cow . . . any cow. But to go for a young bull . . . the herd leader at that! It was madness.'

'Yes, I know. I should have known better. I . . . I'm not the world's best shot either. You saved my life . . . both of you. I'm grateful. Very grateful.'

The Boer spoke the words looking at Victoria and Daniel's anger left him. Andreus Van Niekerk had swallowed a great deal of pride in acknowledging that he owed his life to a girl – and one with African blood in her veins.

To Daniel's surprise, Victoria suddenly threw her rifle to Van Niekerk, who caught it before it hit the ground. 'Here, take this. Learn how to use it properly and you'll have no need to poke a gun into a buffalo's ear before pulling the trigger. It's all right,' she added, as Van Niekerk opened his mouth to protest. 'That was my dad's gun. I've got one of my own.'

Abruptly, Victoria tugged at her horse's reins and the animal trotted briskly to where the other ponies stood with drooping reins, cropping at the coarse, dry grass.

Perplexed, Andreus Van Niekerk looked from the modern rifle in his hands to the departing girl. He turned to Daniel for an explanation, but Daniel shook his head. He was as baffled by Victoria's quixotic gesture as was the Boer. Van Niekerk had certainly not behaved in a manner to deserve such generosity . . . but Daniel accepted that Victoria was wiser in the ways of men than he was.

'She's quite a woman,' said Andreus Van Niekerk, grudgingly. 'She shoots better than a man.' He gazed admiringly after Victoria and Daniel knew she would have no more trouble from the Boer.

'You'll be needing cartridges for that gun. I have plenty, but you'll pay for them at trade rates. Now, give me some help with these buffalo we've killed, or there'll be no supper for anyone.'

During the night a fierce storm raged over the high hills to the north and although they enjoyed a dry camp where they were, they suffered from the effect of the distant rain the following day. They reached a river and found it swollen. It meant they would need to make a wide detour, following the swift-flowing river towards its source until they found a shallower crossing-place.

It was only a beginning. The next night the storm returned again. This time the rain fell over a far wider area and washed out their camp.

For days the travellers zig-zagged their way across the high plateau on which they now were, the storms adding many miles to their journey. Then, one bright, crisp morning, after they had suffered the nightly downpour, Daniel saw something that made all the additional hardship well worthwhile.

They had made camp the night before enveloped in thick grey rain cloud that laid an amorphous blanket over the whole land reducing visibility to a few yards.

Now it seemed the whole world was laid out before them in a panorama of breathtaking beauty. Only a few hundred yards from their camp the ground dropped away steeply to a valley that must have been ten miles wide and about twenty long. The valley ended, not in another range of hills, but with a further drop to lowland that extended to the southernmost borders of Mozambique, four hundred miles beyond the horizon.

A small river wound through the valley, fed by a dozen mountain streams cascading via moss-hung steps from the surrounding hills. The valley floor was not flat, but undulated gently, with here and there a small, round-topped hill and thick clumps of trees. Among them Daniel recognised the attractive Bauhinia, and the purple-flowering Citamusi.

The blue sky, lush green of the grass and the purple-flowering trees painted a picture on Daniel's memory that he would always remember. He had never seen a more beautiful place.

Daniel would have liked to spend time exploring the valley,

but Van Niekerk was impatient to reach Khami and send his report to the mining company for whom he worked. Daniel had to be content with entering the valley upon the map he was compiling, circling the area for future attention.

That afternoon, the travellers had an encounter that drove all thoughts of the valley from Daniel's mind for a while. They met up with a Matabele impi, heading eastwards to teach a sharp lesson to a Mashona village Headman. The vassal headman had sought to take advantage of Mzilikazi's death by withholding the annual payment of cattle, made to the Matabele to ensure immunity from their raids.

Heading the impi was Kanje, Mzilikazi's younger son. It was immediately apparent that Kanje had not forgiven Daniel for spoiling his homecoming celebrations. Ignoring Daniel, he put his questions to Van Niekerk, asking him for details of their journey. While the two men talked, the Matabele warriors of the impi began examining the loads carried by Daniel's pack-horses. It was mostly foodstuff, although there were also a certain amount of trade goods, as much as Senhor Farrao had been able to gather together at short notice.

The Matabele were a naturally inquisitive people and it was not unusual for a traveller to have every one of his possessions taken from the wagons and pack horses and held up for general inspection. Daniel was fully aware of this. He also knew that under Mzilikazi's rule every single item would be accounted for when Matabele curiosity had been satisfied. Such was not the case today.

Warriors began to move away, arms laden with the contents of the saddle-packs. Daniel unsheathed his gun and thumbed back the hammers, the double click sounding ominously loud.

'Tell your men to put back my trade goods, Kanje. I've not brought them this far only to be robbed by my friends.'

Kanje glared angrily at the gun pointing at his middle, not certain how far Daniel was prepared to go in defence of his property. They were anxious moments. A number of Kanje's men were armed with new muskets and were no doubt eager to use them. It appeared that someone believed Kanje would be the next Matabele King and was staking a claim to future trade concessions.

'Have the Matabele been reduced to stealing since they lost

their King – or is it only your regiment that has turned to scavenging?'

Kanje barked an order to his impi. Their expressions surly, the men about the horses moved away, those who had taken goods dumping them to the ground.

'You are carrying trade goods, yet you have no permission to trade.'

'My permission came from Mzilikazi. Is his memory already so dim that his word means nothing now?'

Kanje scowled. He did not enjoy bandying words with Daniel in front of his own men. 'You have no permit to be in our country. You must leave.'

'My home is at Khami. Come there with me and tell me in front of Mzilikazi's Council of Indunas that I am not welcome in your country. I'll get a permit, if one is necessary – *when* I reach Khami.'

Kanje's scowl grew deeper. At any other time he would have killed Daniel and his companions on the spot, taking a chance on being found out. But with the Matabele throne almost within his grasp there was too much to lose. He had laid his plans well – but he relied heavily on European backing. He would not alienate them now by killing Daniel. There would be time enough for that later.

'Go to Khami, trader . . . but you would be unwise to remain in our land. When there is a new King you will not be welcome among my people.'

'I'm aware there'll be no place for me if *you* become King, Kanje – but you are not the ruler of your people yet.'

Daniel threw the last few words after Kanje as he turned his back and walked away.

'You've made a bad enemy,' said Victoria, beside him. 'Kanje is very popular with the Mahaja – the young Matabele warriors.'

'Fortunately, the *Elders* will decide who is to become King. Kanje would tear the Matabele nation apart.'

Andreus Van Niekerk had been listening to their conversation with some surprise. Now he said, 'You mean there's some doubt about who'll become King? Kanje is already promising concessions. I've committed my own company pretty heavily as a result.'

143

'Then you'd better do something to cut your losses quickly,' suggested Daniel, unsympathetically. 'I'd give a dozen of Mzilikazi's sons a better chance than Kanje – and it's the senior Indunas who'll decide. You upset them and your company won't have a hope in hell of gaining a foothold in Matabeleland.'

Andreus Van Niekerk pressed Daniel to tell him more about the possible succession to the Matabele throne, but Daniel was in no mood to be helpful. Van Niekerk's declared aim was to bring a great many white miners into the country. Daniel held the conviction that an influx of white men would result in a conflict between the two races and have a disastrous ending for the people with whom he had made his home.

That night Daniel made camp in an ancient stone fortress that was a miniature version of The Great Home of the Chiefs, where Chiminuka spoke through his albino medium. Daniel could see that Victoria was affected by the similarity, but neither of them spoke of it. For his part, Daniel was relieved that they had been able to find a secure place in which to spend the night. He feared that Kanje might change his mind and return with his warriors to attack them.

Kanje did not return, and although Daniel was awakened in the night by what he at first thought to be gunfire, it turned out to be nothing more serious than thunder. He lay awake for an hour watching lightning scribbling on the sky far to the east. As the thunder rolled from hilltop to hilltop and grumbled against the stout stone walls of the ancient fortress, Daniel wondered what the future held for himself and the Matabele nation. Probably it was his surroundings that caused him to remember the predictions of the Mondoro and what he had said about Sam Speke having 'no future' to see. That prediction had proved to be tragically true. Daniel pondered upon the remainder of his words, but fell asleep before he had arrived at any conclusion.

The next day they had been travelling for less than an hour when they were intercepted by yet another Matabele impi – but this one was led by Jandu, and it was no chance meeting.

After he had greeted Daniel warmly, and answered questions about the health of Suliyana, Jandu explained the reason for his presence.

'I heard you were on your way to Khami and knew my brother, Kanje, would be in this area. He has taken on many of the airs of a King, but none of the responsibilities. I feared he and his impi might find you and do you harm.'

Jandu's words and manner were in marked contrast to those of his half-brother. Jandu spoke with a natural authority that was totally lacking in Kanje. Daniel hoped it had been duly noted by the elders of the Matabele tribe.

'I am pleased to see you have rescued the daughter of your friend Speke . . . but where is he?'

Daniel told Jandu of Sam Speke's death, without going into detail and the Matabele expressed his sympathy to Victoria, '. . . he was a good friend to my people. He will be greatly missed.'

Victoria's eyes immediately brimmed with tears and, in a bid to change the subject, Daniel asked whether the Matabele Council of Indunas had met to discuss the question of a successor to Mzilikazi.

Jandu made a gesture of frustration. 'They have met many times, yet my people are still without a King. Many Indunas insist that my father's true heir is Kulumani.'

'What does Umnombati say?'

Umnombati, the present Regent, was the oldest of the tribe's Indunas – and the most powerful. He alone of Mzilikazi's contemporaries had survived to enjoy old age and had been the Matabele King's friend and confidant to the very end. If any one man could influence the choice of the future Matabele King, it would be Umnombati.

Jandu gave a short laugh. 'When they talk of Kulumani, Umnombati holds his tongue – and with good reason. Many years ago word was given to the tribe that Kulumani had been sent to a small Zulu tribe many hundreds of miles to the south. It was a not uncommon custom to protect the King's heir from his enemies. Umnombati knew the truth. Acting upon my father's orders, he had taken Kulumani only as far as the river. There he strangled him and threw his body to the crocodiles.'

Daniel looked at Jandu in disbelief, 'Why? Why should Mzilikazi kill his own son – your brother?'

'To find the answer to this you need to know the story of my people, trader. Mzilikazi's father – my grandfather – once led

145

the Kumala clan, in the land your people now call Natal. He was falsely accused of treachery and executed by Zwide, paramount chief of the Kumala and many other tribes. Mzilikazi never recovered from the shock of his father's death. He eventually became chief of the Kumala clan himself and a great warrior in Zwide's army. Zwide was so pleased with him that he gave him two of his own daughters to be his chief wives. One of them bore him a son – Kulumani. But Mzilikazi had never forgiven Zwide for killing his father.

'When the opportunity arose, he joined with Shaka, Zwide's enemy and together they killed him. Yet still that was not enough. Mzilikazi was determined that no grandson of Zwide would ever rule the Matabele. Besides, Kulumani posed a very real threat as long as he lived because his mother also had her father's death to avenge! Kulumani was killed and Mzilikazi was able to rule his people without looking over his shoulder to see who waited at his back with a knife. So, you see, Umnombati is forced to sit and listen to the other Indunas calling for Kulumani to be found – and he can say nothing. He is old but he still values his own life.'

It was a horrific story, but Daniel had long ago ceased to be shocked by the ruthlessness of Mzilikazi. 'Umnombati is not too old to sell permits to anyone who wishes to enter Matabeleland, either.'

Jandu shrugged. 'Umnombati does no more than make two lines that cross each on a piece of white man's paper. Who is to say that these lines are his – and those are not? The Council of Indunas decided that the missionary, Farewell Loveday should write the permits for those men to whom Umnombati grants permission to enter Matabeleland. I am not an Induna of the Council. If I were I would want to know why for every permit signed by Umnombati, five men enter Matabeleland.'

'Are you certain of this?'

'As certain as I am of trouble when a new King is named. The impis are unhappy that the Council is doing nothing to prevent white men from trampling our land, shooting all the elephant and digging holes in the ground for gold. They will expect the new King to turn the white man out of our country. If he does not the impis will rebel against him. If he does, the white men will be angry.'

Jandu smiled ruefully. 'Your missionaries say they have come here to teach my people a wonderful new way of life, trader. If it is so wonderful, why do so many white men turn their back upon this way of life in their own lands and come to Matabeleland?'

As Daniel struggled to think of a convincing reply, Jandu said, 'But you have had many problems of your own. We will have time to talk of other things when we reach Khami. For now you must tell me of the things that have happened to you since we parted at Sofala. How is the daughter of Senhor Farrao? I am surprised you did not discover her worth for yourself and bring her back as your wife . . . .'

CHAPTER TWELVE

In Khami, Daniel could smell uncertainty in the air. It showed on the faces of the people and in the dejected demeanour of the normally proud Matabele warriors. Without a King they lacked a focal point for their fierce loyalty. In a desperate bid to keep the army together, their Indunas led them on an ever-increasing number of raids against surrounding tribes. But such diversions were not sufficient to prevent a number of bloody clashes between impis led by rival royal sons. One solution would have been to send each impi to a different region of the country until a King had been chosen, but the sons were reluctant to leave the capital for anything other than a morale-boosting raid against the Mashonas.

Daniel was quick to perceive the problems of the Matabele, but his first unhappy task was to return Victoria to her mother and inform the Herero tribeswoman that her husband was dead.

It was a difficult duty. Mary Speke had never felt at home among the Matabele. Now, with her husband gone, she felt her isolation more keenly than ever before. Daniel promised to guarantee her future, whether she decided to remain in Khami, or return to her native village in South West Africa, but it was doubtful whether the distraught widow listened to his words.

Her howls of grief quickly drove him from the house and he left Victoria to comfort her mother and tell her as much, or as little, as she wished of the events leading to Sam Speke's death.

Daniel found his partner in the store. Aaron had heard from Andreus Van Niekerk of Sam Speke's death and the news cast a pall over the success of Daniel's trip to the east coast. Eventually, the conversation turned to other matters and Aaron told Daniel of the difficulties he had been facing since the death of Mzilikazi.

'Difficulties, I say? Daniel, you wouldn't believe me if I told you the half of them. Things have changed here – and nothing for the better. The Matabele are edgy. Their concern is understandable. Some of the Europeans in this land have spent years behind bars. They'll be in prison again if the British or Transvaal authorities ever catch up with them. I'm not sure we did the right thing when we moved here, Daniel. Oh yes! I know we've made money from trading – good money too. But if things go on the way they are we'll lose the lot – our lives too. The country is fast becoming an unofficial penal colony.'

In spite of Aaron's pessimism, Daniel quickly learned that the shrewd old Jew had still succeeded in making a handsome profit on all their trading transactions during Daniel's absence. There was competition now, where there had been none before, but the new traders usually arrived with no more than a wagonload of goods to sell. Permits were being issued to whoever was able to pay the standing fee of fifteen pounds sterling, a bag of black gunpowder and a box of percussion caps, but the Indunas were adamant that the newcomers must not build houses, or even huts for themselves. All their business was being conducted from wagons.

Trading was bearable in the warm, dry, winter months, but with the rainy season at hand, all but the hardiest traders had called it a day and returned to more civilised parts. Aaron had bought up the stock of four such fair-weather traders, purchasing their wagons at bargain prices. These would be sold to ivory hunters next season – at a handsome profit, of course.

Later that night, as they enjoyed a drink together in the store and the rain beat a vigorous tattoo on the roof, Daniel told Aaron of Elvira. It was not easy. As he spoke, it seemed that the smiling ghost of Hannah, Aaron's daughter crept into the room to haunt them both, as she had haunted Daniel for so many years.

When Daniel told Aaron that he intended marrying the Portuguese Captain General's daughter, the old trader rose to his feet and hugged Daniel. There were tears in his eyes as he said, 'What can I say, Daniel? I am as happy for you as though you were my own son. She sounds just the girl for you. It's not good for a man to be alone for so long. A few more years and you'd grow to be like me. My Hannah would never have wanted that for you. I must meet this Elvira of yours. If we can find someone trustworthy to leave in charge of the store I'll come with you when you return to Sena.'

Talking about Elvira brought her closer to Daniel, but he knew it would be many months before he was able to return to Sena. Until the rains ended, the rivers would be swollen and impassable, while the short, dry grass of winter would soon be as tall as a man, its razor-edged stems sharp enough to lay open a man's arm, or a horse's leg. Until the dry season returned it was doubtful whether a messenger would get through with news of Elvira's recovery from her bullet wound.

The next day Daniel was summoned to the mission station outside the kraal by the Reverend Farewell Loveday.

When he walked into the little room used by the missionary as an office, Farewell Loveday was seated behind an elegant rosewood desk. Incongruous in its present setting, the desk had once enhanced the study of an East Anglian Bishop's palace. The missionary had been waiting for Daniel and he came straight to the point. 'It's been brought to my notice that you don't have a permit to be in Matabeleland.'

'No . . . and I don't intend applying for one. When I came to Matabeleland the only permission a man needed was the King's word and every man knew it had been given. If you were found in the country without it you were killed. That's the way things were when you came to Matabeleland too, remember? You asked me to use my influence with Mzilikazi on your behalf.'

The Reverend Farewell Loveday had the grace to look embarrassed, but it was a fleeting emotion.

'There was a despot on the throne then, Retallick. Now he's dead. We have a golden opportunity to bring some order to this land. To teach these poor people the advantages of progress and religion.'

'Perhaps you'll teach me at the same time,' Daniel retorted. 'From what I hear, all you've done is to put the Matabele at the mercy of the sweepings of the world's prisons.'

Farewell Loveday flushed angrily. 'I doubt if such an opinion was expressed by a Christian. Come to the mission church any Sunday and you'll meet the "sweepings of the world's prisons", as you call them. With their more enlightened Matabele brethren they will be praising the Lord's name – and it's only a beginning. Now that Kulumani's been found . . . .'

'Kulumani found? I thought he was dead.'

'So did a great many people. I'm pleased to say he's alive and well. Kulumani has been working for Theophilus Shepstone, Secretary for Native Affairs in Natal. What's more, he's had the benefit of Christian teaching.'

Armed with the information Jandu had given to him, Daniel was inclined to greet Farewell Loveday's news with some scepticism. However, Umnombati was an old man. He might well have been romanticising about his part in an event that would have been on the tongue of every tribal rumour-monger when he was a young man.

'Kulumani will need more than Christian teaching if he's to rule the Matabele and survive. He'll need the strength of his father and will have to become skilled in the politics of both the Boer and British governments, as well as those of his tribe. At least he'll have the advantage of speaking English. What's his job with Shepstone, interpreter?'

Farewell Loveday looked suddenly ill-at-ease, 'No . . . . he's a garden boy.' Aware of Daniel's expression of astonishment, he added quickly. 'But he *is* Kulumani. Shepstone is quite certain . . . .'

'Of course he is!' Daniel laughed out loud. 'By God, Loveday, I've got to admire your nerve . . . yours *and* Shepstone's. What could be more convenient than to have a Matabele King who's used to taking orders from his European masters? Surely you and Shepstone could have given him some semblance of dignity? A garden boy . . . . ?'

Daniel's laughter ceased and he leaned across the desk to look down at Farewell Loveday. 'Do you take the Matabele for fools? Or are you deliberately setting out to cause trouble? You try to put your garden boy on Mzilikazi's throne and you'll start a war that will spill the blood of both Christian and heathen, and set back your "progress" fifty years. Is this what you want?'

'He *is* Kulumani,' insisted Farewell Loveday, doggedly. 'You'll see for yourself before many more days have passed. The Reverend Pugh-Williams went to Natal to bring Kulumani home to his tribe. He should be here soon.'

Daniel looked surprised. 'But I saw Mrs Pugh-Williams outside.'

'She didn't go with her husband. She hasn't been well.'

Farewell Loveday made the statement sound so aggressive that Daniel was immediately reminded of the Matabele rumours concerning Loveday and Helena Pugh-Williams. It helped to convince him that Farewell Loveday's plans for Matabeleland were not entirely theocratic. The missionary had ambitions that extended beyond the narrow confines of his church.

'We still haven't settled the matter of your permit. If you intend to remain in Matabeleland you'll need to have one—'

'You can give me one when your garden boy is crowned King of the Matabele,' said Daniel. 'Until then I'll go about my business as I've always done.'

On his way back to the store from the mission station, Daniel pondered on his next move. It was evident from the advanced stage of Farewell Loveday's plans that they had been carefully thought out. No hint that their long-lost 'Prince' was on his way to Khami had been given to the Matabele. The missionary must have been confident of Kulumani's imminent arrival, or he would not have broken the news to Daniel now.

Timing was important for the success of such an audacious scheme. The news of the coming of the new King had to be leaked so that the excitement of his 'subjects' would reach its height when he arrived. Riding the wave of popular acclaim, his coronation could be rushed through and the Natal garden boy proclaimed King before doubts could be aired about the authenticity of 'Kulumani's' claim to the throne of Matabeleland.

Daniel was particularly concerned about the British Government's involvement in the plot. He did not believe Theophilus Shepstone would have submitted his garden boy's claim without their approval. It could mean that the British were prepared to send troops to assist the garden-boy King if his authority were seriously challenged. No doubt such an eventuality had been considered – based, of course, on Farewell Loveday's derisive assessment of the Matabele as a fighting nation.

If such assistance were forthcoming, Daniel believed the British army would suffer their greatest defeat in African history. He shuddered at the thought. Somehow, the claimant to the Matabele throne had to be prevented from entering the country until his dubious credentials were thoroughly checked.

There was only one man who could do this.

Daniel reached Umnombati's kraal late that afternoon, after a difficult ride through the worst storm of the rainy season. Hilltop was joined to hilltop by jagged lightning, and the crashing echoes of thunder had Daniel's mount dancing with fear, it's ears twitching as peal followed noisy peal. For the whole of the journey rain fell in torrents that turned the countryside into a slippery quagmire.

Daniel was shown into Umnombati's hut immediately upon his arrival, the old Induna commenting that a man who rode through such a storm must be on a very urgent mission.

Daniel was wearing a cape, but so heavy was the rain that it had found its way inside, soaking every item of clothing he wore. The old Induna clicked his tongue in distress at Daniel's condition and called two of his wives to the hut to dry the visitor. One wife was almost as old as Umnombati himself. The other was a recent acquisition, and very young. Ignoring Daniel's protests, the aged Induna ordered the women to strip off his wet clothes and rub him dry before wrapping him in a blanket by the fire, with a giant-sized gourd of beer beside him.

As the two women carried out their task, the senior wife, aware that her age put her beyond any scandal, kept up a constant stream of ribald remarks. The younger woman allowed herself only an occasional giggle, but more than once she gave Daniel a bold glance that went further than the senior wife's bawdiness.

Umnombati was aware of both glances and remarks, but his only response was an occasional amused chuckle. When Daniel was seated comfortably close to the fire that glowed cheerily in the centre of the circular hut, Umnombati waved his womenfolk out.

Once they had gone, Daniel repeated what Farewell Loveday had told him, and Umnombati listened in silence. When Daniel had ended, the Induna gazed into the fire for so long that Daniel feared the old man's mind had wandered elsewhere. Then Umnombati turned expressionless eyes upon Daniel.

'Did the missionary tell you what this ... "Kulumani" looked like?'

'No. Do you think he lies?'

'I *know* he lies.'

Through the smoke from the fire, Umnombati looked at Daniel but he was seeing another time. Another place.

'I knew Mzilikazi for more years than any other man. In all that time I never once failed him. That is why I lived when all others close to the King died.' Umnombati held out two bony hands, palms upward. They shook like corn in a wind. 'These two hands killed Kulumani. It was Mzilikazi's order. Afterwards I threw the body in the river and watched the crocodiles fight over it. If anyone says Kulumani lives he is a liar.'

'But what can you do? You can't tell the Tribal Council that you killed Kulumani. Too many Indunas are jealous of your power. They would have you executed.'

'Death is a young man's enemy, trader. I have walked beside him for too many years to have any fear left. If a man is coming here claiming to be Kulumani, I *must* tell the Council what I know ... but it has not come to that yet.'

Umnombati looked at Daniel speculatively. 'Why have you come here to warn me of this? If the man who calls himself Kulumani is made King he will owe a great debt to the white man. Have you spent so long with the Matabele that you have become one of us?'

'Perhaps. It's a question I've asked myself many times. I think the answer is that when I first came to Matabeleland Mzilikazi gave me his hand in friendship. In return I have given my heart to his people.'

Umnombati nodded his head approvingly. 'I know this to be true, trader. Mzilikazi told me many times that you are the only white man whose word he never doubted. Because you are also a man whose thoughts go deep you will know that a false King would bring great trouble to our country – for both Matabele and the white man.'

'I know this, Umnombati. If there's anything I can do to help—'

'There is. I need to meet this man who says he is Kulumani, but I am too old to walk and I cannot sit a horse. You have a wagon?'

'Of course, but it will be slow going.'

Umnombati snorted. 'Time is not important. You have ridden here through the rain. If the false Kulumani is on the other side of the Shashi River he will not be able to cross for days. If he crossed before the rains then he would already be in Khami. I will send a messenger to have your wagon sent here. You shall come with me.'

Theophilus Shepstone's ex-garden boy had not crossed the Shashi River. When Daniel's wagon swayed down the slope to the river bank, 'Kulumani' and the Reverend Arnold Pugh-Williams were huddled in a damp camp on the far bank of the swollen river, together with a retinue of disgruntled Bechuana porters. The porters had been reluctant to undertake a trip to the land of the warlike Matabele in the first place. The sight of Umnombati's fifteen-hundred-strong impi – the largest in the Matabele army – setting up camp on the opposite bank of the river proved too much for them. Most of the Bechuanas stole away in the night, forfeiting their pay and stealing only what they could carry off.

It was two more days before the river dropped sufficiently to allow Umnombati to cross the river, borne on the shoulders of one of his strongest warriors. Daniel went with him.

Arnold Pugh-Williams was, for once, genuinely sick. He had a fever and stood on the river bank in his damp and crumpled clothes, shivering uncontrollably. Only the realisation that he had almost accomplished an historic mission kept him on his feet. He believed that Umnombati, as the senior Induna of the Matabele nation, had come to welcome the new King, bringing an impressive impi to escort him to the capital.

'Kulumani' was not so certain. He hung back, staying close to the fire. He had no fever, but he was shaking almost as much as the missionary. 'Kulumani' was not an impressive man, certainly not cast in the mould of the man whose son he claimed to be. Not more than five feet six inches in height, he had only one eye. The real Kulumani was known to be blind in one eye, too, but Umnombati declared that it was an affliction the Royal Prince had suffered from birth and that both his eyes had been intact at the time of his murder.

Set down on the river bank, Umnombati appeared frail and

vulnerable. He stood and looked at the pretender to the Matabele throne for long minutes, which did nothing to put 'Kulumani' at his ease. Then the aged Induna said he wished to speak to 'Kulumani' alone.

For the first time, Arnold Pugh-Williams realised that this was not the welcoming party he had thought it to be. He looked from his protégé to Umnombati in sudden dismay.

'Umnombati wants to be certain it *is* Kulumani,' lied Daniel, feeling sorry for the inept missionary. He was certain Pugh-Williams had been unwittingly drawn into the conspiracy to put Shepstone's garden boy on the Matabele throne. 'If he's satisfied, your man will be allowed to go on – and he'll have an impressive escort.'

'*If* he's satisfied? Theophilus Shepstone has said he's Kulumani. Are you doubting his word?'

Daniel shrugged. 'Shepstone is nothing to the Matabele. They are the ones who have to be convinced. I suggest you and I leave Umnombati alone with Kulumani. You look as though you could do with a strong dose of quinine and a dry bed.'

Arnold Pugh-Williams was in the habit of taking daily doses of quinine, in the belief that it was a preventative as well as a cure for fever. Unfortunately, his return journey to Natal had taken him a month longer than estimated and he had used up his supply. He was pathetically grateful when Daniel swam his horse across the river to return with quinine and a dry set of clothes.

His pleasure was short-lived. Even as he emerged from his tent wearing the borrowed clothing, the meeting between Umnombati and 'Kulumani' came to an end. Ignoring the missionary, Umnombati said to Daniel, 'We need remain here no longer. I wish to return to Khami and speak to the Council of Chiefs.'

Daniel glanced over the Induna's head, to where Pugh-Williams' protégé sat staring dejectedly into the cooking-fire. 'What of "Kulumani"?'

Umnombati spat on the ground at his feet. 'Kulumani, indeed!' He raised a hand to point towards the imposter. 'He is no King. He is not even a Matabele – although before he learned to dig in the ground for a white man, he was a child prisoner of the Zulus for many years. Ask him, he is eager to tell the truth now.'

Daniel looked for the missionary's reaction to the blunt statement – and leaped forward in time to catch Pugh-Williams as he slumped senseless to the ground.

Umnombati looked down at the unconscious figure. Dryly, he said, 'I don't doubt that the white man's God is as all-powerful as is claimed, trader – but I will never understand why he chooses men like this to fight his battles.'

'I'm afraid Pugh-Williams is a born loser,' agreed Daniel, as he laid the missionary on the ground and called for one of Umnombati's warriors to fetch a blanket from the mission-ary's tent. 'But how did you persuade "Kulumani" to change his story?'

Umnombati chuckled wickedly. 'I said I would take him to the river where I had thrown Kulumani's body to the croco-diles and tell my warriors to throw him in too. When he walked from the river unharmed I would kneel at his feet and swear that he was the true King. After all, can a crocodile eat a man twice? It was then he remembered his name is Charlie and that he should be in Natal, digging the ground of his white master.'

Umnombati arrived in Khami to scenes of great excitement. Believing the arrival of the new 'King' to be only days away, Farewell Loveday had released the news of his coming.

The inhabitants of Khami, eager to get a first glimpse of their new ruler swarmed from the town to meet the old Regent's wagon. They quickly learned the truth from the men of Umnombati's impi. Their first reaction was one of anger. But as the full story of the pretender's background emerged, the mood of the crowd changed to one of amusement that the missionaries could have believed such a man to be the missing Kulumani. In their naïvety they believed the missionaries had been duped. Umnombati was happy for them to accept such a story. Had they suspected it was part of a European plot to foist an imposter on them, not a white man would have been safe in the land.

On the way to Khami, the wagon halted to allow Arnold Pugh-Williams to be carried inside his mission house and placed in the bed where he had spent so much of his mission service. While Helena Pugh-Williams put on a great show of anxious concern, Farewell Loveday tackled Daniel. His anger was hardly in keeping with the humility attributed to those who spread the Lord's word among those in need of example.

'This is your doing, Retallick,' Farewell Loveday spat the words out, his face pale with subdued rage. 'You put Umnombati up to warning Kulumani off.'

'Umnombati makes up his own mind about such matters,' commented Daniel, amiably. 'I think he knows enough about the real Kulumani to realise that your man was an imposter.'

'You'll pay for this, one day. I'll make certain there isn't a European in the country who doesn't know that you've deliberately thrown away the best chance there will ever be to give them a secure future in this land.'

'You can say what you like ... but I'd look to your own future. Arnold Pugh-Williams may be a poor specimen of a man but he's not a complete fool. He was delirious for much of the way here and seems to have it on his mind that there's something between you and his wife. I gather he's voiced his suspicions to the Bishop in Natal. I suggest you forget about Matabele politics and try a bit of praying.'

Daniel's warning alarmed Farewell Loveday. It was doubtful whether the mission authorities could prove anything against him, but they might withdraw him from the Khami mission station – and Farewell Loveday had too much at stake to leave Matabeleland now. He was convinced that the country would soon come under the protection of the British government. When that day arrived an Administrator would be needed who was familiar with the country and acceptable to its people. Farewell Loveday was determined to be that man.

His ambitions suffered a setback the following day. Umnombati called a meeting of all Indunas, both political and military. When Farewell Loveday put in an appearance, complete with bound notebook and pencil, there was a rumble of resentment from the military Indunas, always more ready to voice their opinions than their political counterparts.

Farewell Loveday explained that he was taking notes for the Queen of his own country, the 'Great White Mother', in order that she might better understand Matabele law and customs.

Umnombati declared that the Indunas had nothing to hide from any man – or any Queen. The missionary was welcome to remain and make his notes.

The Indunas sat in a great, loosely packed circle and listened as Umnombati told how he had spoken to the man who called himself Kulumani. He had satisfied himself beyond all doubt that the man was an imposter. He then spoke of the danger of allowing the Matabele nation to drift along without a King. As things stood at present, the nation had no sense of purpose, or direction, it's impis being free to raid and plunder at will. The old Induna declared that the Matabele must forget Kulumani. He was assuredly dead. They must elect a King from among Mzilikazi's many sons who had remained with the tribe, and whose ways they knew well.

There were those who disagreed with him. They stubbornly insisted that it must be Kulumani, or no one. However, the vast majority of the Indunas agreed with Umnombati. They realised that the Matabele were a young nation with few tribal traditions to fall back on. They needed a King to give the people guidance and put the heart back in the Matabele people.

The arguments raged back and forth for hours, until it began to emerge that the vast majority were swinging to Umnombati's side.

Finally, a satisfactory compromise was reached. A King should be chosen now. If Kulumani were not found within one year from the end of the rains, the new King would be confirmed in office.

Umnombati looked around the circle from man to man, his gaze not moving on until he had received a nod of agreement.

'Good!' Umnombati was well pleased. He had expected much stronger opposition to his idea. 'Now it only remains to choose which of Mzilikazi's sons shall take his father's place.'

A ripple of amusement ran through the gathering of Indunas at Umnombati's words. With so many sons eager to become King, this would undoubtedly be the hardest task of all.

First there came the process of elimination. This one would not suit because he had not yet proven himself in battle. That one because he favoured his mother's tribe. One of the first son's to be nominated was Mangwane, one of the elder Princes. Umnombati disclosed that Mangwane was at that moment being sought for execution, having been caught sleeping with one of the late Mzilikazi's young wives. According to Matabele law this was a crime akin to incest, the vilest of tribal crimes. The unfortunate widow, together with every one of her family, had already suffered the fate that awaited Mangwane.

As the merits and demerits of each candidate were discussed, two names recurred time and time again. It soon became apparent that the Matabele crown would pass to one of them. The names were Kanje – and Jandu.

This was the moment of truth. Both men were present and were fully aware that before the meeting broke up one of them would inherit the most powerful nation in Central Africa. The disappointed son could either pledge allegiance to his half-brother, or get as far away from Khami as he could in the shortest possible time. With the final choice of the tribe so finely balanced, the loser would pose a threat to the other for as long as he lived. The King-elect could not afford to rest until he was dead.

The issue was still not decided when Umnombati rose to his feet and began to relate the history of the Matabele nation. He began with Mzilikazi's break with Shaka, his Zulu overlord, forty years before. He described how Mzilikazi had led the Matabele to the land between the Shashi and Zambezi rivers, and reminded his listeners that in those earlier days victory was assured in battle for the leader with the most powerful army. North of the Orange River a man with a strong army was free to roam the face of Africa at will, harassing and conquering weaker tribes and settling wherever the land suited him. Since then the African way of life has changed dramatically. It was now the gun and not the spear that decided battles. Personal bravery and iron discipline were not enough. The new King must arm his armies to take their place in the changing world. He himself needed to be able to get along with the white man and gain his trust and friendship. Whether the Matabele liked it or not, the white man was moving in strength ever closer to Matabeleland's borders and would play an increasingly important part in the country's future . . . .

As Umnombati spoke, the sun sank beneath the rim of the

western hills. The flickering light from the fire illuminated faces that epitomised the vanishing Africa of which Umnombati was talking. This was a great indaba – a meeting of tribal Elders. A meeting at which they, and they alone, would decide the future of their own people. The power to make such decisions had already been taken away from many of the tribes to the south.

Only one man was insensitive to the poignancy of the historical moment . . . Farewell Loveday. He listened in increasing annoyance as Umnombati declared that the Matabele people needed a ruler who was aware of the changing pattern of Africa. A man so experienced with life that his head would control his heart. A man who had travelled beyond the borders of Matabeleland and seen the white man in his own home.

It soon became apparent that Umnombati was talking of Jandu. Farewell Loveday became dismayed at the increasing number of Indunas who nodded their agreement. Jandu was Daniel Retallick's friend. The missionary had pinned his hopes on Kanje being made King of the Matabele. Finally, he could keep silent no longer.

'Before you make up your minds you must consider that Jandu is an older man, already set in his ways. Kanje is young. Aware of the needs of his people. He knows many of the white men in your country now . . . . British and Afrikaans. He's respected by them.'

The icy silence with which his interruption was received finally registered with Farewell Loveday. He realised he had committed a grave breach of protocol. 'It's a personal point of view . . . a white man's opinion. I thought you would like to know.'

Umnombati turned his head first one way, and then another before he spoke.

'Has a dog come to play in our kraal and disturb a meeting of men? Surely not. It must have been the yapping of a jackal.'

Farewell Loveday burned with anger at the old Induna's insults.

'I should have asked permission before I spoke—'

'There it is again,' said Umnombati. 'My old ears caught the sound that time. It is nothing. No more than a white man's mule breaking wind. He has not the stomach for Matabele fare. But a mule cannot be taught good manners. Move closer to the fire and it will probably go away.'

Chuckling at Umnombati's insults, the Indunas moved to form a more tightly knit circle about the fire, leaving Farewell Loveday outside. Red-faced and angry he rose to his feet and stalked away, the bound ledger clutched tightly beneath his arm.

Kanje left the circle of Indunas at the same time. He was equally angry, but he concealed his feelings more successfully than Farewell Loveday. Only a few Indunas noticed him leave the fireside. One of them was Jandu. The King-elect had hoped that his half-brother would accept him as King. Now he knew he would one day have to fight and kill him.

CHAPTER THIRTEEN

Daniel heard the news of the Indunas' choice of Mzilikazi's successor the next morning and hurried off to congratulate Jandu. He found the King-elect inside the enclosure of his house. Shielded from prying eyes by a high, reed fence, Jandu was having his early morning bath, aided by Suliyana. About them relays of female slaves brought wooden buckets filled with water which they poured over the head of their master.

'I'm happy for you and the Matabele people,' said Daniel. 'The Indunas have made a wise choice. Now they have the leader the nation has been waiting for.'

He meant every word. It would be more than a year before the ceremony that would officially make Jandu King, but he would begin guiding the nation's destiny long before then. His advice would be sought by the Council of Indunas and no important decisions would be taken without his express approval.

'I suppose that now I am to be a King you will expect me to honour my debts, trader? I owe you a hundred head of cattle for Suliyana. She can hardly become my chief wife until I have paid the bride-price.'

Jandu was in a jovial mood and Daniel responded in similar vein. 'Perhaps you should wait until you're certain you'll keep her.' There was little fear of the remark causing offence. It was evident to everyone that Jandu and Suliyana were very happy together. She would become Chief Wife, and, as such, hold a powerful position in the land. Ruler of the King's household, she would organise the busy daily routine, maintaining a firm control over the other wives and be at the heart of all affairs of state. Daniel had no doubt at all that the daughter of uTshwebe would perform her duties well.

'Jandu will keep me,' said Suliyana, confidently. 'I will give him many sons. The Matabele will never be in any doubt about their next King.'

His ablutions completed, Jandu said, 'Come with me and

choose your cattle, trader. You will need herd boys – and grazing land. Do you have any place in mind?'

Daniel remembered the valley he had seen on his return journey from Sena. It was no more than two days ride from Khami. He told Jandu about the valley, adding that it was the most beautiful place he had ever seen.

Jandu nodded his understanding. 'My country is full of such places. I have seen many of them and never fail to marvel at such beauty.' He made a snap decision. 'Come, we will choose your cattle now and I will find you some Matabele herd boys. Then you and I will take the cattle to this valley you have found. No – it is not a matter for argument. When I am King I will rarely go beyond the bounds of my royal enclosure. I must make the most of the time I have left to me.'

When Daniel told Aaron he would be away from Khami for a few days, Aaron muttered that he might as well be trading on his own again. There was some justification for his complaint. A surprising amount of trade was coming in for the time of year. Many hunters had been taking full advantage of the present easy-to-come-by pass system in the belief that it would come to an end when a new King took the throne. Unable to ship their ivory and ostrich feathers out of the country because of high rivers and impassable roads, they were happy to sell them to Retallick and Copping.

'Look at these tusks,' said Aaron, pointing to a pile of first-class ivory. 'Each of them weighs at least eighty pounds. Should I have to move them by myself? Better I should have a sleeping partner. At least I could wake him when things get busy – but don't you worry about me. You go off and play with cattle in your valley. I'll wear myself out to see that we still have a trading company when you return.'

In spite of his grumbling, Aaron enjoyed haggling with the hunters. He also appreciated the good fortune the company would enjoy now that Jandu had succeeded his father. Had it been Kanje, Retallick and Copping would have been loading the contents of their store upon wagons, bidding farewell to Matabeleland for ever, leaving Boer traders to fight over their business.

Daniel selected a hundred prime cattle from Jandu's herds and purchased a fine, deep-chested bull to run with them. The

Matabele herd boys had been personally selected by Jandu and were aware of the honour accorded them. Twenty in number, they were accompanied by thirty captured Mashona boys. This small force would be expected to guard Daniel's cattle against thieves and predators – sacrificing their own lives if the need arose.

To his consternation, Daniel learned that the whole of Jandu's impi would accompany them to the valley, although he was quick to appreciate the necessity for such a large escort. Kanje and his supporters would dearly love to put Jandu out of the way. Only a large escort would deter them. As Jandu explained rather sadly to Daniel, his days of travelling alone, or with only a close friend, were over. He was now the most important person in the land, his every word and deed observed and commented upon by the Matabele people.

When they arrived at the valley Daniel had chosen for his cattle, Jandu was able to relax somewhat. After posting look-outs on the surrounding hills, he and Daniel set out to explore the valley. Jandu agreed immediately that it was a most attractive spot. 'This is a garden of the Gods, trader – an "Insimo" indeed.'

Daniel liked the name. It exactly summed up the feeling he had for the valley – the Insimo Valley.

That night they set up camp close to a waterfall. The water tumbled down a near vertical cliff-face to a clear, rock pool, surrounded by flowering trees and shrubs, the scent of which filled the evening air. It was a beautifully sheltered spot, yet from here one had a view that encompassed the whole of the valley and the panorama of the low-veldt beyond.

Daniel lit his pipe and stood watching the colours of the landscape darken and merge one into another as night advanced over the continent of Africa.

'You think deep thoughts, trader?' Jandu spoke the words softly as he stood beside Daniel.

'Not so deep. I was wondering what more a man could want if he had a house here and could gaze out upon this view every night?'

'He would find something more to seek . . . but such a man would indeed have much to envy. Tell me, when do you marry your Portuguese girl?'

'I hope to return to Sena as soon as the rains cease. If she is well enough and her father agrees, I will marry her then.'

'Her father will accept you as a son.' Jandu placed a reassuring hand on Daniel's shoulder. 'But it will be many months before you bring a wife to Matabeleland. Use that time well, my friend. Build a house for her . . . here, on this very spot. You have fallen in love with the valley – I give it to you. From hill-top to hill-top. It is yours for as long as I am welcome in your house. You will rule this valley, just as I rule the remainder of Matabeleland.'

Daniel found it difficult to grasp that he had just been given two hundred square miles of land, 'But . . . but I'm a trader, not a farmer.'

Jandu pointed to where the hundred cattle were being driven inside a hastily erected thorn-bush pen. 'By this time next year you will have twice as many cattle and you will be as concerned for them as though they were your own children. Tell me then that you are only a trader. You have a partner who can run your store. Where would you rather bring a young wife? To Khami, or to this valley? No, you have no need to answer. Build a splendid house, give her many women-servants to keep her company while you are away from home and she will stay happy.'

Daniel was overwhelmed by Jandu's great generosity, but when he tried to stammer his thanks, Jandu said simply, 'Friends do not need to express gratitude as do other men. Giving is all part of friendship.'

Before Daniel could think of an adequate reply, Jandu turned and walked off into the night.

On the return journey to Khami, Daniel's mind was full of thoughts and plans for the valley Jandu had given to him, but he found an unexpected matter awaiting his attention when he arrived at the store.

Andreus Van Niekerk was in the back room with Aaron. Both men were drinking, but the Boer was not drunk. When he spoke he was surprisingly subdued and polite.

'I'm sorry to trouble, you, Daniel. There's a little matter I'd like to discuss with you. It's . . . rather personal.'

Aaron took the broad hint. Downing his drink he stood up, a trifle unsteadily, Daniel thought.

'All right. All right. I'm just going. Oi! What sort of partnership is this? He goes . . . I have to stay in the store. He sets foot in the store again and has hardly bid me "Good day" before I'm told I'm not wanted – and that by a brandy-swilling Boer who's sat here for two days emptying bottles without paying me a penny piece. Perhaps one day my partner will sit down with me and we'll talk about business together.'

Daniel stood to one side as Aaron made his way to the door with exaggerated care. Aaron was no drinker . . . neither was he used to spending time trading over a store counter, his evenings taken up with compiling ledgers and making laborious lists of shortages and future trading requirements. Most of Aaron's life had been spent in an ox-wagon. It had been his home, his shop, and his passport to wherever trade and the whim took him. Aaron was a true descendant of his biblical namesake. He was a wanderer who would never find his promised land. His pleasure was in the seeking. He had remained at Khami for many months during Daniel's journey to the east coast and he was restless to be on the move.

It was the first time Daniel had seen his partner even slightly drunk and he spoke to Van Niekerk more abruptly than he intended. 'What is it you want? Couldn't it have waited until I had time to come home and sort out my own business?'

'I'm sorry. I know I'm being a damned nuisance, man, but it really can't wait. I should have left here two days ago, but I've stayed to see you first. You see, I've had a letter from the manager of my company. He's told me to forget the gold mines in Manicaland. It seems the Portuguese are raising a fuss. They claim it's their territory and my company aren't prepared to argue. Instead I'm to go straightaway to Tati. Gold has been found there and some prospectors have already struck it very rich. I'm to prospect and peg claims on behalf of my company.'

Tati was a few miles on the Matabele side of the Shashi River. Although claimed by both the Matabele and Bechuana, the area was not considered to be worth fighting over. As a result, it had become a 'no-man's land'. The discovery of gold might well change all that.

'I wish you luck,' said Daniel. 'But what does this have to do with me? I don't care where you prospect.'

'I'll be taking Victoria with me,' Van Niekerk said. 'I hoped you might speak to her mother for me. See if there's anything she wants ... I mean, I know she's only a kaffir, but I understand she was properly married to Victoria's father. With his death and Victoria going off with me I thought things might be hard for her. I'd like to help, if I can.'

Andreus Van Niekerk's news and his confusing mixture of emotions took Daniel by surprise. It had been no secret on the journey from Manicaland that Van Niekerk fancied Victoria, but she had shown only contempt for the Boer – or had she? Daniel remembered how she had given him her father's gun at the very moment when she might have thoroughly humiliated him. Daniel thought, not for the first time, that he would never understand women. As for Van Niekerk's concern for Mary Speke—! It was so out of keeping with Daniel's assessment of the Boer's character that he could only believe this meeting was one of Victoria's conditions for going off with Van Niekerk.

'What do you want me to tell Mary Speke? That you're taking her daughter to live in a camp full of prospectors, every one of whom will look on her as easy meat – just as you did on the way from Manicaland? Or perhaps you're going to marry her?'

'I can't marry her, you know that. I'm a Boer, my home is in Transvaal – and she's a baster. But I won't have any jaapies hanging round her. I'll look after her well, man. That's a promise.'

Daniel knew that Van Niekerk's promises would fade with every mile he put between himself and Khami. He was not happy at the thought of Victoria going off with the Boer to the goldfields of Tati. He could abandon her whenever he wished. But anything Daniel said to either Van Niekerk, or Victoria, would be wasted. If they had both made up their minds he could exert no pressure on them.

'I'll speak to Mary,' he said. 'But she's in no need of anything. Sam was a careful man. He's left enough behind to keep his family for the rest of their lives. When are you and Victoria setting out?'

'In the morning. I've been all packed ready to move for two days.'

'I'll see you before then, but don't expect me to bring you Mary Speke's blessing. Victoria is her only daughter.'

Daniel met Victoria coming out of the Speke house. She was red-eyed, as though she had been crying, but she looked at Daniel defiantly. 'If you're here to try to talk me out of going with Andreus to Tati, you can save your breath.'

'I realise that. I'm here to talk to Mary. To see if there's anything she wants. It's Van Niekerk's idea – but his concern doesn't extend to wanting her for a mother-in-law.'

'If it did she'd be asking him for lobola . . . .' Victoria fought against tears as she struggled to regain her composure. 'It's no good talking to her, Daniel. She's in there sitting on the floor in a corner of the room, singing a Herero mourning song. She's been like it ever since I came back from Manicaland. I can't stand it any more. It's as though she's never been married to a white man. I think she really *has* forgotten what chairs and tables and beds are for. I've asked her a hundred times a day what she wants and I get the same answer every time. She wants to go back to Hereroland. Once there she'll be able to forget Dad, forget she's ever had me and live like a tribeswoman until the day she dies.'

'I'll see she gets home,' Daniel spoke more gently to Victoria 'But do you think it's right to leave her now? When she's like this?'

'What would you like me to do? Go back with her and live like a Herero woman myself? Marry some old man and dig his fields and clean his pots with nothing to look forward to but the night when it's my turn to have him in my bed? Is that what you want for me, Daniel? If it is then you should have thought about it years ago – you and Dad. Instead of letting me come with you both wherever you went. Letting me ride horses and shoot guns. Allowing me to believe I belonged to your world. Treating me as though I were a white girl—'

Victoria choked on her words and now she could no longer control her tears. She turned to run but Daniel caught her arm and pulled her to him. With his arms about her, she clung to him fiercely, sobbing as though her heart would break, for many minutes.

When he thought she could hear him, Daniel said softly, 'You don't have to go to Hereroland – or to Tati with Van Niekerk. I'm building a place in a valley only two days ride from here. Come and live there. You'll be able to lead the life you've always known, with as much riding and hunting as you want. It's a wonderful place, Victoria . . . we saw it on the way to Khami, remember? You'll have a good life.'

Victoria pushed herself away from Daniel reluctantly. 'Your Portuguese bride will be there too, won't she? Do you think I could ever be happy watching you together? No – and I doubt whether she'll want to be tripping over me and my bastard all day.'

'Elvira will welcome your company. It's a beautiful place, but lonely. Think about it, Victoria . . . please.'

Victoria shook her head sadly. 'You really *don't* understand, do you? Only a few months ago I would have gone with you anywhere in the world. Things are different now – we both know that. I'm going with Andreus to Tati. Be sure to call on us if ever you're that way.'

'What does Van Niekerk say about the baby?'

The tears had been wiped away now, and Victoria looked at Daniel defiantly. 'He doesn't know. When it comes I'll tell him it's his.'

'You'll do that? He'll never believe you.'

'He'll believe me. I made certain of that on the way back from Manicaland . . . while you were off hunting.'

The admission shocked Daniel. For a few moments, while she was crying in his arms, he might have been holding the girl he had known since childhood. But this was not the girl he thought he knew as well as any sister. Victoria had changed.

'You couldn't have known anything about Van Niekerk going to Tati, not before we reached Khami.'

Victoria shrugged. 'No. I was hoping he'd take me to Cape Town with him. Oh, I know Andreus Van Niekerk isn't the greatest catch in the world and I'm not going to keep him for ever, but he maintains *some* of the standards I'm used to. He'll do for now.'

Daniel opened his mouth to speak, but Victoria cut him short. 'There's nothing more to be said . . . and I have a lot to do.'

She suddenly stood on tiptoe and kissed him briefly on the mouth. 'Goodbye, Daniel.' She gave him a thin, controlled smile. 'Forget what I've just said. Remember me as I was before I met Mariano – and before you met your Elvira.'

Victoria turned away abruptly and hurried to the enclosure where the horses were kept, leaving Daniel staring after her.

His thoughts were no clearer when he left Mary Speke. As Victoria had said, it was as though Sam Speke had never come into her life and talking of Victoria meant nothing to her. It was as though her daughter had never been born. Her mind had blotted out the happiness she had known for half a lifetime. Unable to cope with the tragic loss of her husband, Mary had turned instinctively to the familiar pattern of Herero life. She wanted to go back to Otjimkandje, the Herero village in South West Africa, where she would be among family and friends. Daniel promised her she would be taken home as soon as was possible.

Daniel and Aaron were discussing the matter that evening when Andreus Van Niekerk came back to the store. Aaron looked at him questioningly. 'I thought you were in a hurry to rush off to your goldfield? What do you want of me now? I should go for a walk – or pour you a brandy?'

Andreus Van Niekerk had not been blessed with a sense of humour. 'You can stay . . . but I'd like a drink.'

Van Niekerk appeared agitated and, when he had downed half the glass of brandy handed to him by Aaron, he blurted out his reason for coming to the store. 'You've been good to me, so I've come to warn you. You'd better get out of Khami, while you have the chance. There's going to be trouble.'

'What sort of trouble?' Daniel frowned, wondering whether Van Niekerk had been drinking before coming to the store.

'Big trouble, man! There's going to be a war. Kanje is going to kill Jandu and take over the Matabele tribe. A Boer commando of about fifty men and some Griquas have come up from Transvaal to help him. You'd better get out with whatever you can carry, while there's still time.'

Daniel eyed Andreus Van Niekerk suspiciously. 'How do you know about this?'

'Jan Potgieter is leading the commando. He's a cousin of mine. He's sent someone to warn me and to ask how many Boers are in Matabeleland. He wants them to join him. The messenger left Khami not half an hour ago.'

Now Daniel believed the Boer. 'What did you tell him?'

'I told him not to be a fool. That most white men in Matabeleland are English, like yourself. He'll get no help from anyone here.'

Andreus Van Niekerk downed the second half of his drink. 'Jan won't listen. He's from my mother's side of the family. Once they get an idea in their heads it takes the kick of a horse to shake it loose.'

'Where's Potgieter now?'

'Somewhere in the Matopos Hills, that's all I know.'

The Matopos was an area of massive, granite hills and deep valleys, a few miles south of Khami. There were also huge caves and forests where an army might hide without fear of detection. It was a good place from which to launch a surprise attack on Khami. It was also ideal country in which to set an ambush.

Leaving Aaron to replenish Van Niekerk's glass, Daniel hurried away in search of Jandu.

CHAPTER FOURTEEN

When Daniel rode into the valley camp of Jan Potgieter soon after daybreak two days later, there was consternation among the newly awakened Boer adventurers. They had chosen their camp-site well. In the very heart of the Matopos, the valley was steep-sided and had only one narrow entrance, easily guarded from the heights on either side.

'Who are you? What are you doing here?' The questions were in Afrikaans and a squat, thick-set man stalked to where Daniel slid easily from his horse. 'I should have known better than to leave two Griquas on guard together. They'd go to sleep if you fired a musket three feet away from them.'

Daniel doubted whether the Griqua sentries would hear a cannon fired alongside them now. They had been silenced by Jandu's men before daybreak.

'I heard you were on your way to help Kanje against his brother. I've come here to suggest you change your mind.'

'You've come? Who are you?'

'Daniel Retallick. I live in Khami.'

Jan Potgieter spat his contempt on the ground at Daniel's feet. 'I've heard of you. You're a kaffir-boetje.'

The term was a Boer insult, intimating that Daniel loved natives more than his own people. It had been levelled at Daniel on more than one occasion by disgruntled Boers.

'You've worked to keep us out of Matabeleland for years and now you've thrown in with Kanje's brother, eh? Well, you're out of luck, Retallick. Kanje is going to take over the Matabele tribe and he'll be helped by Transvaalers. You English have moved as far north as you're going.'

'All you'll succeed in doing is stir up a war that will spill over into the Transvaal. Jandu has been elected King of the Matabele by the full Council of Indunas. He's backed by an army of more than thirty thousand men.'

The gasp of incredulity from the listening Boers told Daniel that they had not been given a true picture of the situation in Matabeleland before they left Transvaal.

Jan Potgieter scowled. 'You're lying. Farewell Loveday agrees with Kanje. The army will come over to his side when they see that we're backing him.'

The mention of the Reverend Farewell Loveday made it clear that this was more than a desperate attempt by Kanje to seize the leadership of the Matabele nation. It was a plot that went much deeper than the personal jealousy of half-brothers. No doubt, before Farewell Loveday had put forward the idea, he had ensured that it was backed, unofficially or otherwise, by the unsophisticated Boer government of the Transvaal.

Jan Potgieter cleared his throat and spat at the ground again. 'Agh! What does it matter. There's going to be a fight between two kaffirs. One is friendly to me, so I help him. Who's going to complain about that, eh?'

Instead of replying, Daniel drew his rifle from the saddle holster and fired a single shot in the air. At the sudden noise, the Boer horses, tethered nearby, whinnied in fright, tugging on the long slip-rope to which they were all attached.

'What do you think you doing, man? If that's some form of signal—!'

'It *is* a signal. I thought you'd like to see a small part of the army that will fight Kanje – and you, if you support him. Take a look up at the ridge.'

'Jesus Cristus!' The oath came from one of the Boers and there were gasps of disbelief from the others. The next moment there was a rush for the muskets scattered about the camp. On the hills all about the valley, Matabele warriors had appeared, carrying shields and weapons. At very short notice, Jandu had still been able to muster four impis, a total of about four thousand men. They now occupied every ridge about the valley, deliberately deployed to achieve the maximum dramatic effect.

At a raised-arm signal from Jandu, the impis began beating their shields with the knobkerries each man carried. The sound bounced off the steep valley walls, echoing and re-echoing in a rising crescendo.

'These are only a few of Jandu's warriors,' Daniel was grim-faced. 'The rest are on their way here to fight you . . . and they're backed by every white hunter in the country.'

'Hell, Jan, we didn't come here to take on the whole

Matabele nation by ourselves,' one of Jan Potgieter's men voiced the opinion of his companions.

'Shut up!' Potgieter rounded on the man, but he too had been shaken by the sheer numbers of the Matabele on the hill-tops. He had only fifty Boers and about eighty Griquas. The secure valley in which he was camped had suddenly become an indefensible death-trap. If the Matabele attacked down the steep valley slopes their very momentum would carry them through the Boers. But they had no need to risk their own lives. They could sit up on the ridge and pick his men off as though they were rats in a bran tub.

Turning to Daniel, Potgieter said, 'All right. You're calling the tune. What do you want us to do?'

'Pile your guns in the middle of the valley, then ride out of here and don't return. If you do, the Matabele army will chase you all the way back to Transvaal – and beyond. You've got homes and womenfolk there, think of them.'

'You're sending us out through the Matabele without guns? Man, they'll slaughter us.'

'They'll slaughter you if you stay. Do as I say. I'm giving you Jandu's promise of safe conduct to the border. You'll live to tell your grandchildren how a "kaffir" keeps his word.'

Reluctantly, Jan Potgieter ordered his men to throw down their guns. When Jandu saw what was happening, he held his shield high in the air. Immediately, the drumming ceased and the silence that followed was more awesome than the earlier din.

Without their weapons, the tough Boers felt denuded. They lost no time in forming up and following Potgieter out of the valley. Only the Griquas looked fearfully over their shoulders as they went.

Daniel watched them ride off with a sense of great relief. Jandu had won the first battle in the Matabele war of succession without a shot being fired. Of even more importance, the immediate danger of Boer involvement had receded. But something would have to be done about the Reverend Farewell Loveday, before he plunged the whole country into a war that would have repercussions far beyond the borders of Matabeleland.

To Daniel's surprise, when he suggested to Jandu that he

should close the mission station, the Matabele King-elect shook his head. 'I cannot do this. My father permitted your people to build a mission in my country. He gave his word to Loveday that he might stay in Matabeleland as long as he wishes. Can I break the word of Mzilikazi?'

'No, but you can follow Mzilikazi's example. He allowed the missionaries in, but refused to allow them to preach to the Matabele people. You could make life so difficult for Farewell Loveday that he would have to pack up and go.'

Jandu smiled. 'You are my friend, trader. I too have thought of this. When I am King my first order will be to move my kraal many miles from here. The mission, of course, was given permission only to come to Khami. I will not order them to go, but they will see no Matabele. Only empty hills and the scavenging animals who take over deserted kraals.'

'That's an astute move, Jandu. Worthy of Mzilikazi himself. But first we have to keep you alive until you are proclaimed King.'

For a while, it seemed that Kanje's challenge to Jandu had ended with the ignominious retreat of Jan Potgieter's commando from Matabeleland. Kanje took his dissident impi off to the unhealthy swampland about the upper reaches of the Zambezi river, on Matabeleland's northern border. From here he harassed the Makololo tribes across the great river, and occasionally led his men against the northern villages of the Mashona.

The problem of Farewell Loveday also came to a temporary halt. The politically ambitious missionary was recalled to Cape Town to answer to the charges brought against him by Arnold Pugh-Williams. Incongruously, accuser and accused, together with Helena Pugh-Williams, the subject of the inquiry, all travelled southwards together in two ox-wagons. Arnold Pugh-Williams had not recovered from the bout of malaria that had laid him low, and had to be carried to his wagon to begin the twelve-hundred-mile, bone-jarring journey to the Cape.

With immediate problems out of the way, Daniel was impatient for the end of the rainy season. He wanted to return to Sena. In the meantime he supervised the building of a substantial stone house in the Insimo valley, and also bought in a record amount of ivory and ostrich feathers.

Aaron took a great interest in Daniel's valley home. At his suggestion, Daniel incorporated a store behind the house. Aaron would not be at Khami to see the project reach completion. He had volunteered to make the long journey to South West Africa with Mary Speke, taking half the trade goods with him. He set off many weeks before the rainy season came to an end. Travelling westwards, across the arid Kalahari Desert, any rain he encountered would be a blessing, not a disaster.

With Aaron gone, Daniel became more impatient than ever to leave for Sena. The house was well on the way to completion. The roof was on and only the fitting out of the interior remained.

At the end of February one of the herd boys came to Daniel and reported that a lion had attacked his cattle, killing a cow that was heavy in calf and dragging her body away to the long grass close to one of the small rivers that flowed off the hillside.

When Daniel asked why the herd boy and his companions had not driven the animal away before it was able to charge in among the cattle and make its kill, the herd boy turned around with some pride. Three deep, bloody furrows were gouged in his back, extending from shoulder to waist.

The young herd boy, no more than eleven years of age, had been with an older boy guarding the cattle when a lioness rose from her hiding place and made a bold charge into the midst of the cattle.

The older boy turned and ran, but the younger boy was made of sterner stuff. Armed with only a lightweight spear he struck at the lioness as she tore at the cow's windpipe.

The spear glanced off a bone in the great cat's rear leg, but it diverted her from her gory task for a moment. Turning on her young attacker, she dabbed a paw at him in reproach and, much as a cat gathers in a doomed mouse, pulled him to her.

Fortunately, at that moment the badly injured cow made a desperate attempt to struggle to her feet. The lioness turned on her once more, leaving the dazed herd boy to crawl away with the memory of a lion's hot breath on his face, and three scars on his back to proclaim his bravery.

After the young herd boy had shown him the place where the

attack had taken place, Daniel sent him back to Khami with a note for Jandu. The note would be read and translated by one of the Europeans staying there. In it Daniel detailed the bravery of the boy and suggested he should be rewarded by being taken into one of the Matabele training regiments, an ambition the boy might not otherwise achieve for another three years.

When the boy had left him, Daniel followed the spoor of the lioness through the lush grass. The trail was not hard to see, the cow had bled profusely. A few hundred yards from the scene of the attack, the trail led to a thick clump of undergrowth in the shadow of a tower of balancing rocks.

Daniel scouted all sides of the rock tower without picking up the trail of the lioness again and he knew the animal was still in the undergrowth – probably watching him at this very moment! The thought of it sent tingles up the back of his neck, but he could not allow the lioness to escape now. She had learned how easy it was to kill cattle. She would feed on nothing else until his hundred cows were gone. She had to be killed.

To go into the undergrowth was suicidal. Daniel decided that the only hope of seeing the lioness was to climb the rocks and look down on the area that was in shadow.

Climbing the rocks presented no problem. Carefully and silently, Daniel scaled them from the far side of the undergrowth. Once at the top he crawled out along a huge, flat rock until he was over the thick, tangled bushes. To his annoyance, he found that due to the overhang of one of the lower rocks he could see no more than half the area of undergrowth.

Daniel decided he must go lower. He climbed down until eventually he was no more than nine feet from the ground – no height at all to an attacking lioness!

Gingerly, he edged his way along the rock until he could see down into the undergrowth – and almost immediately below him he saw his dead cow. She had been ripped open and meat taken from the belly.

No sooner had he made this discovery than he became aware of a sound that had been present all along, but which he had erroneously dismissed as the drone of insect noises along the nearby river. It was a deep, regular, happy sound – the purring of a contented lioness!

Daniel froze. The lioness had to be close . . . very close, yet he could not see her. He scanned the undergrowth inch by inch until finally he came to a spot immediately below him that appeared to be a patch of dry grass in the deepest shadow. He was standing on a narrow ledge of rock, no more than twelve inches wide and was actually looking between his feet at the 'grass', when it moved and a pair of languid tawny eyes looked up at him.

With a grunt of disbelief the lioness scrambled to her feet and for a brief moment hesitated before springing. In that instant Daniel fired. Leaning forward in an attempt to make as accurate a shot as was possible. The kick of the rifle knocked Daniel sideways. He shifted his feet hurriedly in a bid to keep his balance, but the next moment he was treading air.

He crashed to the ground beside the quivering body of the lioness and took a rolling dive away from her, only to be brought up short by the body of the partly eaten cow. He expected to feel the jaws of the lioness close about his neck at any second, but no attack came and, looking over his shoulder fearfully, Daniel saw the lioness quivering from head to tail in her death throes. She would never kill another cow. His bullet had penetrated her brain. She was dead, but the taut nerves of her hunter's body had not yet accepted death.

Daniel put another bullet through her heart before ejecting the empty shell cases and reloading his gun.

As he took the bullets from his gun belt, he saw that his hands were covered with blood. It might have come from the lioness, or from the cow she had killed. He needed to wash his hands. Leaving the shadow of the balancing rocks, he made his way to the river.

The water was shallow and fast-running here and icy cold from a spring on the hill high above. The temperature meant there was no fear of crocodiles and, stripping off his shirt, Daniel plunged his head and arms in the river.

He came up blowing hard. Reaching for his shirt, Daniel dried his face on it. Suddenly he stopped short. Something beneath the surface of the water had caught his eye.

Reaching in elbow deep, he pulled out a round object the size of a musket ball that gleamed dully as he held it in the palm of his hand. Carrying it up to his mouth he tested it between his teeth. The give was just enough to tell Daniel he had found a nugget of pure, alluvial gold. A rapid search of the shallow river bed quickly provided three more – one of them larger than all the others put together.

Not only did Daniel own a beautiful valley – he also had a fortune in gold!

CHAPTER FIFTEEN

Victoria and Andreus Van Niekerk took a fortnight to reach Tati, a journey usually accomplished in four or five days. Van Niekerk's wagons had lain unattended in Khami during his expedition to Manicaland and sun and rain had taken their toll. Each broken axle cost them an extra day, and once a wheel collapsed and had to be rebuilt completely.

Victoria took full advantage of each delay to go off hunting by herself, keeping her and Andreus and their Kalanga porters in meat.

Because of the constant delays it was not a happy party that outspanned each evening. Victoria had quickly learned that Andreus Van Niekerk was not the strong, hard Boer he had appeared to be when she and Daniel had first met up with him. He complained about the laziness of the porters, but never gave them firm orders. If they did something he particularly disliked, he would bluster and berate them ineffectually. As a result, the mood of the Kalanga porters was one of surly truculence. When they had difficulties in crossing one swollen river, they were for abandoning the accident-prone Boer and returning to Khami. It was left to Victoria to bully and cajole them to heave the wagons through mud and wheel-high channels to the far bank. From that day, she took command of them, her knowledge of their language ensuring that there was no mistaking her orders.

On the fourteenth day after leaving Khami, the Van Niekerk wagons creaked through the mud of Tati's main 'street'. Africa's newest boom-town was an unprepossessing place. The majority of the buildings sprawled on either side of the muddy approach and most were constructed of mud and thatch. Beyond the town, the tents of the miners perched on and about the mountains of mine-waste. Here and there smaller mounds of gold-bearing quartz awaited crushing. The discovery of gold in this hitherto unknown corner of central Africa had attracted adventurers from many parts of the world. The accents of England, Transvaal, Ireland and Australia could all be heard on the streets here.

An option for much of the land where gold was to be found had been taken by a large British company, The London Goldfields Development Company. It was a grand-sounding name and the Tati operations were being directed by a personage of no less distinction – Sir William Ballard.

In a time and a place where men grew as rough and tough as their surroundings, Sir William Ballard stood out as a shining example of all that they had abandoned. Always formally dressed, he traversed the rough tracks between diggings riding in a neat, two-wheeled gig, drawn by a high-stepping horse of impeccable pedigree. When he was obliged to travel any distance from his Tati headquarters, Sir William was fortified by one or two crates of champagne, stored carefully beneath the high seat of his light gig. It was said that he could be tracked through virgin bushveldt by following the *Chocolat Menier* labels he scattered along the way. It was even rumoured that he bathed *every* day, although such an unlikely story was less widely believed.

Soon after his arrival, Sir William Ballard made a determined attempt to bring law and order to the isolated mining community. His first attack was upon the high incidence of drunkenness compounded by the local Bechuana tribesmen who made a good living from the sale of their home-brewed 'kaffir beer'. When it became apparent that this particular crusade was doomed to a far-from-dismal failure, Sir William displayed the business acumen that had put him at the head of his company's African ventures. He had two wagonloads of gin rushed up-country from Natal and opened the town's first gin shop, quickly taking back much of the salary his company paid to its hard-working miners.

Sir William also founded Tati's first Town Council, with himself as its chairman. The other serving members were the town's men of substance, storekeepers, transport owners, the gold assayer, and the manager of Sir William's gin shop. Together they formulated laws for their town, producing a penal code that listed crimes ranging from theft to murder. The punishments ranged from a whipping, for simple crimes, to shooting by firing-squad for murder.

In truth, Tati and its committee were in a unique situation. The area in which the town stood was claimed by no European power and remained the subject of a half-hearted dispute between Matabele and Bechuana tribes. In short, it was truly a 'no-man's land'. The only laws in force were those made by the men who lived there.

Early in 1869, only a couple of months before Victoria and Andreus Van Niekerk arrived, the first two European women reached the town. The wives of two shopkeepers, they formed the nucleus of Tati society. Under their influence the first permanent houses and a church were built.

This was the town to which Van Niekerk brought Victoria. The Boer represented a large mining concern which hoped to establish operations in the Tati area and it was made immediately apparent to him that he had committed an unpardonable blunder. He had brought a coloured girl to a white community. One in which there were white women and an embryo social structure. Van Niekerk had been prospecting for so long that he had almost forgotten the deep division between whites and non-whites – but he was given a swift reminder. Spurred on by the indignation of the town's ladies, Sir William Ballard sent for Andreus Van Niekerk.

The unfortunate Boer was informed bluntly that if he and his 'lady' stayed in Tati, Van Niekerk's company would lose every square inch of land in which it hoped to dig for gold. The displeasure of the two European ladies was no doubt heightened by Victoria's beauty, and the fact that she was an intelligent girl. They showed far less concern for the presence of the Bechuana girls who sat on the wooden sidewalk outside the gin shop selling their bodies in the bushes behind Sir William's house for beads and trinkets.

Andreus Van Niekerk set up his camp on the river bank, two miles outside Tati. It was only a temporary solution of his problems and no one was more aware of it than Van Niekerk himself. He spent much of his time in and about the town, prospecting, pegging claims and supervising the building of splendid offices for his company.

Victoria, the child inside her growing larger every day, found riding uncomfortable and rarely left the camp, spending her days with only a couple of surly Bechuana servants for company. Unused to talking to anyone during the day, she found it difficult to carry on enthusiastic conversation with Andreus when he returned full of his importance as the representative of the second largest mining company in Tati. The developing life inside her body made it equally difficult to respond to the bedtime demands of Andreus. Arguments between them became more frequent and soon he was spending less and less time at the camp with her, preferring the company of card-playing miners.

But Andreus Van Niekerk was no more successful at gambling than he was at any other pursuit. He began to lose more than he could afford. Food became short at the riverside camp. The Bechuana servants, fearing they would not be paid, disappeared one morning, carrying off Victoria's two best blankets with them.

That night Andreus Van Niekerk stumbled back to the camp at midnight – but he was not alone. Victoria heard the whispering outside her tent. When she called out to Andreus, the whispering ceased abruptly.

More curious than angry, Victoria rose from her bed. Scraping a light to a candle, she was about to go outside the tent when the flap was suddenly thrown open. Swaying alarmingly, Andreus Van Niekerk lurched inside. With him was a heavily bearded fellow Boer. Both men were red-eyed from drinking Sir William Ballard's cheap gin.

Blinking at her as she stood clutching the lighted candle, the newcomer rounded on Van Niekerk angrily. 'What sort of a crooked deal is this you've given me? You didn't tell me she was heavy with child.'

'Heavy . . . ? Heavy . . . ?' Andreus Van Niekerk mumbled drunkenly. 'She's not more than four or five months gone. She can't be.'

'What's all this about? Andreus, who is this?'

Both men ignored her.

'She's seven months if she's a day!' Andreus Van Niekerk could only blink stupidly as the words were roared at him. The newcomer peered more closely at Victoria in the candlelight, 'Um! She's good-looking, ja – but not worth the money you owe me. Agh! We'll argue about it in the morning.'

'You!' He jabbed a finger at Victoria. 'Put on some clothes and come with me.'

'I'll do no such thing! Who are you? Andreus! Will you tell me what this is all about?'

The heavily bearded Boer took her arm roughly. 'You can forget about Andreus. I'm Uiys du Toit. Andreus put you up against the money he owes me. You may not be worth much, but it seems you're all he has left.'

Victoria shook herself free. 'First of all, I'm not his to give away like some Bechuana girl. Get out of here – now!'

Uiys du Toit's eyes were dark and angry in the candlelight. 'You're forgetting your place, girl. It'll do you no good putting on airs and graces. You're mine, that's all there is to it. Hell! By the time I get you to my shack half the night will have been wasted. I'll have you here tonight and take you with me in the morning.'

Du Toit turned Andreus Van Niekerk about and propelled him outside. 'We won't need you. I'll have words with you in the morning. You'd better hope she's good to me, man.'

As Andreus Van Niekerk stumbled away from the tent mumbling drunkenly to himself, Uiys du Toit switched his attention back to Victoria. She pinched out the candle and attempted to slip past him in the darkness. He was too quick. His arms went about her and as she kicked and struggled, he wrestled her to the bed. When they fell to the ground together he was on top. His arms tightened about her and Victoria gasped noisily for breath. Still she kicked and struggled. Then, as his hairy face brushed against her lips, Victoria lunged forward and bit his cheek as hard as she could.

Uiys du Toit hooted in pain and released her. But before she could break free from him, his fist swung through the air and exploded against the side of her head. For a few moments she was dazed. It was time enough for him to pull her nightdress up about her waist.

Victoria's rifle was on the far side of the tent, but before she had gone to bed she had been doing some mending. The scissors were on the ground not far away. Feeling about her she located them and her fingers closed on the looped handles just as Uiys du Toit shifted his weight from her body to fumble with the top of his trousers.

Victoria stabbed him once . . . twice . . . three times. At the first blow his grunt was a mixture of surprise and disbelief. When the second blow was struck he shouted. As the scissors struck home in his side for the third time, he screamed in pain and rolled away from her.

The continuing screams of his countryman sobered Andreus Van Niekerk. Hurrying back to the tent, where Victoria had relit the candle, he leaned over Uiys du Toit and saw the blood spreading across the blankets beneath him. Du Toit's breathing was ragged and shallow and flecks of blood came up at Andreus Van Niekerk from the foam forming about the wounded man's lips.

Andreus Van Niekerk dragged du Toit from the tent by his ankles and somehow got him across the saddle of a horse. Then he led horse and burden away into the night, heading for Tati, but Uiys du Toit was dead long before the town doctor was wakened to tend him.

When Sir William Ballard led a party of grim-faced miners to the riverside camp to arrest Victoria at dawn the next morning, they found her writhing in labour. Her screams were more dreadful than any uttered by Uiys du Toit in his dying moments.

It was not one baby, but twins. A boy, spindly and sickly, and a girl. The desperate struggle put up by Victoria the previous night had done nothing to improve their chances. The boy child fought bravely for three hours and then died.

Victoria refused to relinquish her hold on the surviving baby and mother and child were carried to a wagon and taken to Tati. There they were locked in a windowless hut together.

Three days later, her baby still clutched tightly in her arms, Victoria went 'on trial' for the murder of Uiys du Toit. Sir William Ballard presided over the proceedings, determined to make an example of Victoria. She helped him by refusing to say anything in her own defence. However enough of the truth emerged to ensure an acquittal on the charge of murder. Indeed, there was a great deal of sympathy for her and the baby among the miners. A conviction would have resulted in wholesale rioting.

Sir William Ballard, well aware of popular feeling, gave

Victoria a long homily on the evils of loose-living. Then, ordering her from Tati, he released her.

In her weak state, with a baby to care for, the order to leave the mining town was a harsh and unchristian act, made as a sop to the outraged feelings of the town's European women.

Victoria left Tati with only the clothes she had worn in the town's mud-floored gaol. Yet, somehow, she and her baby survived the first night in the bushveldt.

The following day they were taken in by the wife of a leprous Bechuana tribesman. The unfortunate couple, themselves cast out by their people, had built a new life for themselves in a lonely part of the bushveldt, far from the eyes of their fellows.

With the simple family who had learned to cope with a tragedy far greater than her own, Victoria gradually learned to be a mother. She delighted in watching the baby she had named Therese grow stronger with the milk it took from her own body. But the respite and her new-found contentment were short-lived.

She had lived with the Bechuana couple for a month and was working in the small vegetable patch they had carved out of the virgin bush, when a European, Henry Swilley, came riding by. One of a group of three men who had a mining camp beside the river some distance from Tati, Swilley went to town only to bring back supplies of gin. Otherwise, he and his companions kept well clear of the town's social activities – and Sir William Ballard's administration.

The three men were referred to as Tati's 'Australian Miners' because they had spent many years working in the gold mines of New South Wales. In fact, the three were convicted English felons, carried in chains to Australia during the last years of Transportation. All had served their sentences in full. Swilley's crime had been one of highway robbery, for which his accomplice had been hanged. Swilley himself had been spared only because of his age. He was eleven years old at the time.

On the transport ship and during the long period spent in the Australian penal colony, Swilley had learned many things. First and foremost among these lessons was how to take the things he wanted from life . . . and still survive. The successful application of this knowledge had taken him from the goldfields of Australia, to the more remote gold-mining areas of

South Africa, and finally to Tati. Here, in their camp, beyond the limits of the town's jurisdiction, Swilley and his companions lived their lives untrammelled by the standards of behaviour set by other men.

When Henry Swilley saw Victoria, he wanted her. She had not heard his approach and was bending down to her tasks, the ends of her long skirt tied up about her waist, exposing her thighs as she worked. Swilley watched her for some minutes before making his presence known.

'Well, well! What have we got here?' Swilley urged his horse forward. 'That's no work for a pretty girl. Do you speak English?'

Victoria straightened up and looked at the miner, taking in at a glance his unkempt and disreputable appearance. 'I speak English better than you, by the sound of it. Now, go away. I have work to do.'

Henry Swilley was taken aback by both her command of English, and her disdainful manner, but he was quick to recover.

'You're bright, girl. Far too bright to be bending your back in some kaffir's garden. I've got two mates upriver. We're working a claim . . . a good claim. We need someone to do the cooking and manage the chores for us. How d'you fancy that for a job, eh?'

Swilley's offer appealed to her. Victoria was grateful to the Bechuana couple for giving her a home and taking care of her when she desperately needed help, but she longed for the company of Europeans. She did not particularly like the look of this man, but if there were three of them in the camp she should come to no harm. Victoria had only limited experience of white men and, despite her recent treatment at the hands of Andreus Van Niekerk she tended to judge them by the standards set by her father and Daniel. However, she did not want to appear too eager to accept Henry Swilley's offer. Turning her back on him, she said, 'I've got a job here, thanks. Besides. I've got a baby to think of.'

Frowning, Henry Swilley brought his horse closer, trampling the half-grown stalks of maize, around which Victoria had been weeding. The Bechuana woman had seen Swilley's arrival and watched apprehensively from the door of the hut as he talked to Victoria. Now, seeing her precious corn trampled into the ground by Swilley's horse, she emerged from her hut and began berating him in a shrill, angry voice.

The miner's answer was to yank at the rein of his horse, causing the animal to execute a tight turn. The horse's rump caught the Bechuana woman and sent her crashing heavily to the ground.

The woman's cry of pain brought her deformed husband limping from the hut, the stumps of his leprous fingers gripping the haft of a hunting spear.

Swilley saw him as he ducked through the doorway of the hut. Before the stricken tribesman could even straighten up, Swilley drew a heavy, Colt Dragoon revolver from his belt and put two .44 bullets through his head from point-blank range.

The Bechuana woman rose from the ground screaming hysterically at her husband's killer. Henry Swilley turned the gun on her and a heavy lead bullet tore a gaping hole through the fragile muscle wall of her heart.

Victoria snatched up her baby and looked at Swilley in speechless horror. He looked at her and shrugged matter-of-factly, 'I did them both a favour. He was dying a lingering death and she would never have been accepted back in her tribe. I reckon it's solved your problem about staying here, too. There's nothing to keep you now.'

Henry Swilley still held the revolver in his hand and Victoria knew that if she refused to go with him, or tried to escape, he would shoot her too. She protested that she wanted to bury the bodies of the two Bechuanas who had befriended her, but Swilley curtly ordered her to leave them where they were. Bodies buried in the ground could always be dug up and a cause of death established. Left where they were, the scavengers of the bush would get to work immediately night fell. By morning there would be nothing left in the small clearing but an empty hut and a deserted patch of kaffir corn.

Victoria's life with the three miners in their isolated camp was a continuous nightmare from the very beginning. Away from the eyes of their fellow men, the thin veneer of civilised behaviour had fallen away from the ex-convicts. Their camp was a squalid disgrace. They lived like animals — but abused

Victoria as no creature would have used one of its own kind.

For the first few days, Victoria suffered every kind of degradation in silence, fearing that her baby's life might be in danger if she remonstrated. Each night she prayed that she would awake in the morning and remember this only as a terrible nightmare that had been brushed away by the dawn's light. She would once more be the spoiled daughter of Sam Speke and would have only to walk a few yards from her home in Khami to be given a friendly smile from Daniel.

But the awakening never came. The nightmare went on and on. Victoria gave up her body to whatever demands the three miners made upon her, thankful that they ignored Therese, unless the baby cried too much. The good nights were the ones when they allowed her to drink with them and she could drink herself insensible, oblivious to whatever was happening to her.

Meanwhile, in the world that lay beyond the river-bank mining camp, word of the goldfields of Tati spread from coast to coast. The richness of the strike was much exaggerated. Rumour had it that gold was lying about in exposed reefs, just waiting for some fortunate miner to come along and collect enough to make him rich beyond his dreams.

The Matabele and Bechuana resurrected their respective claims to the area and their raiding parties met and fought within view of the terrified residents of Tati. The incident provoked an urgent plea from Sir William Ballard. He called for Great Britain to annexe the area in the name of the Crown – before another nation stepped in.

Sir William Ballard's warning was a valid one. The Boers of neighbouring Transvaal, in desperate need of funds with which to prop up their ailing, infant republic, were casting envious eyes upon the goldfield so tantalisingly close to their vaguely defined borders.

Although the Portuguese had no clear idea of Tati's geographical position, they too were determined not to be out-manoeuvred by the territorial ambitions of their newer colonial neighbours. The Governor of the Portuguese East African territory of Mozambique sent a strongly worded warning to the governments of both Great Britain and Transvaal. Buried beneath the wealth of flowery language was a reminder that all lands north of the Limpopo River were the sole property of His Most Faithful Majesty, King Luis I of Portugal.

It was a preposterous claim. Portuguese adventurers and conquistadors *had* passed through Mashonaland many centuries before. They had been followed by Jesuit missionaries who lived precariously in the northern part of what was now Matabeleland. But the tribes had soon tired of the stern-faced men who taught a joyless religion and promised only hellfire and damnation at the end of their unhappy lives. They turned on the Portuguese, massacring them in the shadows of their giant crosses. That had been during the last decade of the seventeenth century – and far to the north of the Tati goldfields. Two centuries of unrecorded history had passed since the language of Portugal had been heard on the high plateaus between the Zambezi and the Limpopo. Yet now the ghosts of the ancient conquistadors were being stirred into life by the gold finds at Tati.

Laughable though the Portuguese claim was, it brought death and violence to the area – in the shape of the Pombeiros. As was usual in the Portuguese province of Mozambique, any rumour that promised gold found its way to the ears of the half-caste rebels. Around more than one isolated campfire the discussion turned to the easy pickings to be won in a rich gold-mining area, unaccustomed to organised banditry.

One evening, the three miners in Henry Swilley's camp were beginning their evening meal, heaping abuse upon Victoria for keeping them waiting. As Swilley reached for the coffee pot, bubbling on the fire, he saw a movement along the riverside track leading to the camp. A moment later twenty mounted men rode slowly into view. Slumped untidily in their saddles, they presented a picture of apathy and indolence.

Henry Swilley spat contemptuously at the fire, 'Griquas. They won't trouble us.'

The Griquas were the misfits of Central Africa. A mixture of white and black blood in their veins, they had gathered together to form a loosely knit tribe. Quarrelling incessantly with their neighbours they were ever ready to serve the white men of any country, especially in time of war.

The mounted men followed the river-bank path, passing no more than fifty paces from the camp. As though suddenly seeing the three miners for the first time, the line of horsemen came to a ragged halt and the first three men urged their mounts in the direction of the camp fire.

'Those Griqua bastards are coming up here to beg some victuals from us,' grumbled one of the miners.

'Then they'll leave faster than they came,' declared Henry Swilley loudly.

As the three men rode casually up the slight slope from the river, they talked among themselves and Victoria's heart began to beat faster. The men were talking Portuguese. They were not Griquas – but Pombeiros.

The leader of the three Pombeiros stopped well short of the camp and nodded affably at the men who sipped their coffee about the fire.

'Good evening, Senhors. We are on our way to Tati. We have travelled far. I wonder if you might spare a cup of coffee?'

'You need wonder no more. You'll get no coffee here – nor anything else. Keep going upriver and you'll reach Tati. You might be lucky and scrounge a cup of coffee there . . . but I doubt it. You'll be no more welcome than you are here. Tati's a white man's town.'

There was something very familiar about the Pombeiro, but not until his eyes found hers did Victoria realise what it was. He bore a striking resemblance to Mariano!

'You're not so particular about the colour of a *girl*'s skin, eh?' The Pombeiro spoke to Swilley without taking his eyes from Victoria.

'We'll have less of your cheek,' said another of the ex-convicts. 'Get on your way before I kick your arse out of our camp.'

The Pombeiro's eyes glittered angrily, but he tugged on his horse's reins as though he would do as he was told.

'Wait!' The cry came from Victoria.

The Pombeiro pulled his horse to a halt.

'Take me with you . . . please!' Victoria had been with Mariano for only a few brief months and her Portuguese was far from perfect. She desperately hoped that the Pombeiro would understand her.

He did. Smiling in derision, he replied in the same language, What would I want with a white man's whore? The world is full of unbedded girls, just waiting for a Pombeiro to come along.'

The other Pombeiros smiled broadly at their leader's words. But Henry Swilley called, 'What the hell's going on? What language is that you're speaking, you coloured slut?'

Victoria snatched up her baby from the blanket on which she was lying. Holding her up to the Pombeiro, she said, 'This is the daughter of Mariano. Her twin brother is dead. Killed by white men such as these.'

The smiles disappeared from the faces of the three mounted men.

'You bore my brother's son? You must be . . . Victoria?'

Victoria nodded. 'And you are Philippe. He spoke of you often. Help me, please.'

'What do you want me to do?'

'Victoria, come here . . . right now, if you don't want the hiding of your life.'

Henry Swilley rose to his feet as though to carry out his threat there and then.

Victoria placed Therese on the ground quickly. 'Throw me your gun,' she hissed at Philippe.

Slipping his rifle from its holster beside the saddle, Philippe tossed it through the air to her.

Catching it clumsily, Victoria turned to face Henry Swilley. The ex-convict stopped and stared at her in disbelief. 'Don't be stupid, girl—'

They were the last words he ever uttered. The rifle was a large-bore, over-and-under hunting rifle and the bullet from the first barrel slammed into Swilley's chest, knocking him four feet backwards before he dropped to the ground.

One of Swilley's companions dived towards the tent where the guns were kept, but the bullet from the second barrel sent him face downwards in the stony earth.

The third miner died as he rose to his feet with arms raised in surrender, shot by one of Philippe's companions.

'Yes, you are Victoria.' Philippe's thin smile expressed his admiration. 'I heard you could shoot like a man. Now I believe it. Come, bring your child, we will leave this place.'

'Wait a moment.' Victoria ran to Henry Swilley's tent and returned dragging a heavy wooden box behind her. With no sign of emotion, she removed a bloody key from a string about Swilley's neck and returned to the box. Opening it, she took out twenty-five small, hard-packed bags and threw them to Philippe and his two companions.

'Swilley's been bragging that there were four hundred ounces of gold in here. There's little sense leaving it for someone else to steal.'

It was a sizeable fortune and represented the total output of Swilley's mine. Victoria had effectively bought her place in the Pombeiro band of Philippe, brother of Mariano.

Before the disappearance of the three 'Australians' came to the notice of their fellow miners, there were three more unsolved killings in the vicinity of Tati.

First to die was Andreus Van Niekerk, shot by a marksman's bullet as he staggered drunkenly through the ill-lit streets of the gold town in the early, dark hours of morning.

The others were Sir William Ballard and his unfortunate Bechuana driver, shot just outside Tati in broad daylight, as the director of the London Goldfields Development Company returned from an inspection of his company's outlying mines.

No assassin was ever apprehended for any of the killings. Not long afterwards, the failure of the mines in the Tati area left the town an empty shell, peopled by the ghosts of men who had once walked its streets, the town ordinances long-forgotten.

Meanwhile, three hundred miles away, Philippe, the Pombeiro was earning the appellation, 'The scourge of Mozambique'. It was a title that had been vacant since the death of his brother, Mariano.

CHAPTER SIXTEEN

Daniel was not able to set off for Mozambique until the end of March. The rains had ceased in Matabeleland, but in the uplands of Mashonaland, through which he would have to take his wagons, heavy cloud hung low over the hills and rain persisted for longer than in any other season the Matabeles could recall. For a month, while his trek oxen grew fat on the lush green grass of the Insimo valley, Daniel chafed at the unexpected delay. His wagons were loaded with a fortune in ivory – and he wanted to see Elvira again.

It was about three hundred and fifty miles from Insimo to the Portuguese settlement at Sena, but Daniel planned to make the long trek in a month. Much would depend on how well he remembered the route through Mashonaland and Manicaland, on the height of the rivers – and on the mood of the tribesmen he met along the way.

He would be travelling without a Matabele escort. A secure trade route was of great importance to Jandu too, but Kanje's men posed a constant threat to him. He needed all his warriors at home. The best Jandu could do was arm a hundred Kalanga tribesmen and send them to accompany the wagons. The Kalangas were vassals of the Matabele, used by them for menial tasks, and were scorned as warriors. However, their presence might make other tribes think twice about attacking Daniel.

At last, Daniel's patience ran out. Although dark clouds still brooded over the Mashona hills, he fancied they were lifting – and he was not prepared to wait any longer. He sent to Jandu to 'ask for the road'. It was an unnecessary courtesy, and the request was granted immediately.

On the day of departure, the Matabele King-elect rode into the Insimo valley, at the head of an impi. His horse was one Daniel had presented to him some months before, a highly valued 'salted' horse – one which had survived a bout of horse sickness and was now considered to be immune from further sickness. Jandu had become fond of riding and used the animal whenever possible.

Jandu and his impi travelled with Daniel until the sun was directly overhead and they reached the first river. The river was only a small one, but the rainwaters of the high Mashona plateau drained into it and it erupted from the hillside in a spectacular waterfall that cascaded down the rocky slope in a series of giant leaps, weaving rainbows into the lacework of spray that rose high in the air. Here Jandu announced he would have to return to Khami.

Clapping his hands together in the traditional gesture of friendship, he then clasped Daniel's hand in a spontaneous show of warmth. 'Goodbye, and take care, my friend. Be sure to bring your bride back in time to see me installed as King of the Matabele.'

'I'll be back long before then,' Daniel promised. Jandu's coronation was set for early 1870 – a year ahead. Daniel hoped to have established regular trade with Sena by then.

Daniel's trek to Sena went almost exactly to plan, although it was not without incident. The rains retreated eastward ahead of him, but the rivers were still dangerously swollen and he lost one wagon. It capsized in a strong river current and swept over a waterfall, disappearing in a deep chasm gouged in the Manica hills by the rushing waters of centuries of rainy seasons. Fortunately, the wagon had been only partly loaded, much of the ivory being portered across the river to lighten the wagons.

Three of the Kalanga tribesmen were also lost. One was taken by a crocodile, when drinking from a river. The other two were killed by the Mashonas in a daring attack on a foraging party.

This attack so enraged the remaining Kalangas that they forgot for a while they were a subject people, scorned and despised by their overlords. Led by their headman, they made a vengeful foray into the surrounding hills, firing every kraal they found and killing the Mashona occupants. When they returned to the wagons, the Kalangas had become warriors and it was in this mood that they continued the journey to Sena.

Not willing to put the new-found confidence of his escort to a further test, Daniel directed the wagons well to the north of Vumba's kraal. No doubt the Manica chief would think twice about incurring the displeasure of the Portuguese authorities once more but Daniel was taking no chances.

The long journey took only a few days longer than he had allowed and Daniel came within sight of the stockaded village on the first Sunday in May. It was usual for the Portuguese and their families to gather in the tiny mud and thatch church beside the fort on Sundays. Here, three or four times a year, a visiting priest would come from the coastal area to celebrate Mass for the isolated community. For the remainder of the year they had to make do with Bible reading and prayers conducted by Senhor Farrao.

On this Sunday the prayers remained securely locked in the hearts of the men and women of Sena. Days before, news had reached Senhor of the approach of armed men. Remembering the earlier raids of the Pombeiros, the populace of the surrounding countryside poured into Sena's stockade. The stout wooden walls were manned day and night by armed soldiers and militia, all nervously fingering the triggers of their ancient muskets. One evening, at dusk, an unsuspecting and short-sighted rhinoceros wandered absentmindedly from the cover of the thick bush, five hundred feet from the stockade. Immediately, a wild fusillade of shots rang out and musket balls pattered like hail among the leaves of the trees about the startled animal. Not one of them so much as grazed its tough hide but, confused by the soft sounds about him, and the crackle of exploding powder from the stockade that was too far away to see, the rhinoceros turned and trotted back to the safety of the bush.

Daniel knew nothing of this. Riding beside his lead-wagon as it lurched from the trees to open ground, he looked up to see the green and red flag of Portugal hanging limply above the fort of Sena and knew the long journey was over.

Flinging his hat high in the air, Daniel let out a yell that startled his horse and caused the Kalangas to rush to the head of the column, fearing something was amiss. The reaction from the stockade was far more dramatic. High on the wall of the fort there was a flash of igniting gunpowder and a large boom echoed along the river as a cannon was fired.

Brought up from Quelimane during the summer months and never before fired, the gun was badly layed. The cannon ball crashed harmlessly among the trees, well to one side of the wagons. Nevertheless, the shot terrified the Kalangas, who had never before heard cannon-fire. They promptly fled back to the safety of the bush. Daniel was alarmed. If a shot fell among the wagons the oxen would also bolt, overturning wagons and scattering his goods across miles of Portuguese territory.

Digging his spurs into the flanks of his horse, Daniel galloped towards the stockade, shouting for the Portuguese to hold their fire. He was too late to prevent a second shot but, fortunately, the gunners' aim was no better than before.

Daniel was recognised before a third shot could be fired. As he slid his horse to a halt before the stockade entrance, the heavy wooden bolts were slid back, the gates swung open and the slight, dark-haired figure of Elvira ran out.

Daniel leaped from his saddle and the next moment Elvira was in his arms. 'Daniel . . . Daniel!' Her voice was caught between tears and laughter. 'It's been more than half-a-year. I was beginning to believe you would not return—'

'You should have known better. I have a trading arrangement with your father.'

Daniel knew the joke had misfired when she turned a dismayed face up to his. 'That is the only reason you have returned to Sena? Because of your trading?'

When she saw his smile she shuddered violently and clung to him. 'Don't tease me about such things, Daniel. I have dreadful nightmares about you not wanting me.'

Pushing away from him she took his hand. After he satisfied himself that the Kalanga warriors had come out of hiding and were bringing on the wagons, they walked inside the stockade together. As they walked, she turned to him in a sudden gesture of sympathy. 'I am very sorry about your friend, Samuel. When Francisco returned and told us what had happened—' Her earlier uncertainty returned to her. 'Your friend's daughter . . . Victoria? You returned her safely to Khami?'

Some of Daniel's happiness left him and Elvira feared the worst.

'Yes, I returned her to Khami. But she didn't stay there long.'

He told Elvira about Andreus Van Niekerk. How the Boer

had taken Victoria to the Tati mines while Mary Speke had returned to South West Africa. '. . . So, you see, the Speke family has gone out of my life after being a part of it for as long as I can remember.'

'It must be very sad for you, Daniel. I am sorry.'

Elvira's expression belied her words, but by now they were at the fort and were quickly surrounded by Portuguese traders and soldiers who remembered Daniel from his earlier visit. Senhor Farrao was among them – and *Captain* Francisco St Anna, newly promoted as a direct result of his successful campaign in Manicaland. As Elvira explained, he was newly married too. When Daniel offered congratulations and asked about his wife, he was hastily informed that St Anna's wife was not well enough to leave Portugal just yet.

Sensing a mystery, Daniel said nothing. Later he learned that St Anna's marriage was the result of a scandal. The brilliant young army officer, fresh from battle, had succumbed to the charms of the passionate young daughter of a high government official. Her determination to hold nothing back from the young hero who was the toast of Portuguese society had brought the reward she sought. A hasty marriage had been arranged and she would come to Mozambique when their child was born.

The greeting given to Daniel by Senhor Farrao and Captain St Anna was courteous enough, but Daniel imagined it lacked warmth. He broached the subject that evening when he and Francisco St Anna were standing on the verandah, enjoying a drink and Elvira and Senhor Farrao were busy in the house.

'I've been looking forward to this particular drink throughout the whole of the trek, but I get the feeling I'm not particularly welcome in Sena.'

'No! No, that is not true, Daniel.' St Anna was full of concern. 'Senhor Farrao would be deeply hurt if he heard your words. His house is your house. It will always be so – he has said this to me many times. You must understand that Senhor Farrao finds himself in a difficult situation. He and Elvira both have a deep affection for you, but Senhor Farrao is an important official of the Portuguese Government. He is Captain General of the North West District of Mozambique, and very proud of the honour his country has bestowed upon him. He takes his duties very seriously. Unfortunately, the area of his jurisdiction has never been accurately defined. On one side it is bounded by the Quelimane district, but on the other . . . ?'

Francisco St Anna spread his arms wide in a gesture of helplessness. 'Our government in Portugal knows nothing of Mozambique. They insist that the lands taken by our conquistadors are still rightfully ours. They have received disturbing reports about the intentions of your country – and the Transvaal Republic, in the interior. Why, you can understand this. You are established in Matabeleland – and we both heard Van Niekerk's boast of bringing fifty miners to Manicaland. Orders have been received by all Captain Generals. They are to re-establish a Portuguese presence in the interior. Of course, it is quite impossible. We in Mozambique have neither the troops nor the resources to implement such an order.'

'You can forget about Van Niekerk and his fifty miners. His company has abandoned its plans for Manicaland and he's been sent to the goldfields, at Tati.'

'Ah yes . . . Tati! It is claimed that Tati is *also* Portuguese territory. A protest has been sent to your government, and that of Transvaal, demanding that the miners be withdrawn from Tati immediately.'

Daniel smiled, thinly. 'From what I hear, neither the British nor the Boers have any more jurisdiction over Tati than the Portuguese. The miners will tell them all to go to hell – and good luck to them.' He looked at St Anna quizzically. 'You can't seriously believe that Portugal has any claim on a place at least five hundred miles from the Indian Ocean? Why, apart from one or two villages like Sena, on the Zambezi, you've hardly colonised Mozambique to a depth of more than five miles from the coast!'

Captain St Anna grunted noncommittally. 'I keep my beliefs to myself, as all ambitious soldiers should. I am merely passing on the official attitude – as a friend.'

The discussion ended when Senhor Farrao came from the house to join them. Soon afterwards the three men and Elvira sat down to a dinner that would not have been out of place had the smoking tallow lamps and the humid, semi-tropical surroundings been exchanged for chandeliers and the paved steets of Lisbon.

Senhor Farrao managed to produce a mood to match the meal. Had Daniel not talked with Captain St Anna, he would have told himself he must have imagined Senhor Farrao's earlier reserve. Not until Daniel mentioned the valley given to him by Jandu did the guarded look appear again.

'This valley. It is many miles to the west of Sena?'

'Yes, a little over three hundred and fifty miles due south west – why?'

Senhor Farrao shook his head. 'Curiosity, no more.'

Inwardly, Senhor Farrao breathed a sigh of relief. He had recently paid a visit to the Governor of Mozambique, at Quelimane. After a long meeting the two men had agreed that they should urge their government to make a more realistic approach to the border question. The furthermost Portuguese settlement along the Zambezi River was Zumbo, four hundred and fifty miles inland. The Governor would suggest to his government that the border of Mozambique be set a few miles beyond Zumbo. Extending southwards, it would curve in to exclude the high Mashonaland plateau. Much of the land so claimed would undoubtedly be disputed by the British – and the Boers, but it should be possible to settle their differences without going to war. Senhor Farrao had just ascertained that Daniel's valley lay beyond the proposed border. There need be no quarrel between them.

Soon the conversation turned to trading. Senhor Farrao had inspected the goods brought by Daniel from Matabeleland, and was well pleased. He kept in close touch with the prices prevailing in Quelimane and knew he would make a handsome profit.

This knowledge, coupled with the excellence of the meal, mellowed the Captain General. He leaned back contentedly in his chair as brandy was poured in large, pot-bellied glasses, and blue tobacco smoke drifted upwards to hang in a flat, wispy cloud just beneath the ceiling.

'You will, of course, remain in Sena for a few months?'

'No. The truth is, I'd like to make one more trading trip before the next rainy season.'

Senhor Farrao raised his eyebrows, 'Indeed? Business is so good in the land of the Matabele?'

Daniel was not listening. He had seen the dismay on Elvira's face when he mentioned leaving again soon. He cleared his throat nervously. 'There's one other thing. I'd like to marry Elvira before I go – and take her with me.'

The words came out much faster than Daniel intended, tumbling over themselves in their hurry to be said.

There was a gasp of surprise from Elvira and Senhor Farrao stared thoughtfully at his glass as he lowered it slowly to the table. He was aware that Daniel and Elvira were very much in love and that the question of marriage had been discussed between them. But . . . so soon? However, Senhor Farrao was an observant man. He too had seen Elvira's dismay – and he had watched it become concealed joy when Daniel declared that he wanted them to be married quickly.

'This valley of yours – it is a safe place to have a home, a wife?'

Daniel nodded. 'I have already completed a stone house. It's a good house, Senhor Farrao. Elvira will not be ashamed of living there, and the valley is a present from Jandu. An attack on me there would be an attack on Jandu himself.' Even as he spoke the words, Daniel thought uncomfortably of Kanje, but now was not the time to entertain such doubts. 'Why not come and see the house for yourself?'

Why not indeed? Senhor Farrao's mind worked quickly. By claiming that one of their senior officials had travelled as far as Matabeleland, it might be possible to successfully push the border still further westwards .... Then Captain General Farrao looked again at the eagerness in his daughter's eyes. He remembered the time, many years before, when he had come to Mozambique with a young and starry-eyed bride. They had arrived with a dream. Together they were going to make a home in their own part of the Zambezi valley. Land that no man would take from them. It was to be a small private empire at the heart of the wilderness, just such a place as Daniel's own valley.

Senhor Farrao sighed. 'I would love to see this valley of yours, Daniel, but it is not possible. Perhaps one day things will be different and I will be able to come to visit my grandchildren, eh?'

'Then you'll let us marry? Before Daniel returns to Matabeleland?' Elvira's happiness was something Senhor Farrao had seen too little of in recent years. Such happiness was rare in Africa's harsh environment. Only the most unfeeling man would dare to shatter it – and Senhor Farrao was not such a man.

'If I say "no", I believe Daniel will carry you away with him anyway. Then I will have lost both my daughter and a valued trading partner. You have my blessing. I only wish your dear mother were here to share my joy for you both.'

Senhor Farrao had at first intended bringing the Bishop of Quelimane to Sena to perform the marriage ceremony, but when he put the idea to his future son-in-law, Daniel objected strongly.

Daniel remembered the total lack of organising ability shown by the senior officers of the Portuguese army. If the same incompetence extended to the church it would be many months before the marriage could take place.

But it was another argument put forward by Captain Francisco St Anna that eventually persuaded Senhor Farrao to abandon his plans for a grand wedding. The soldier suggested it might be better if the wedding of the Captain General of Mozambique's North West District to an *Englishman* were a more discreet affair.

Daniel and Elvira were married in July 1869 in Sena's tiny chapel. The ceremony was performed by a missionary priest from the garrison town of Tete, a hundred and fifty miles upriver. It may not have been a great occasion in the calendar of Mozambique's provincial society, but the day was declared a holiday in Sena and villagers, tribesmen, and Portuguese prazeros flocked to the stockaded village from the surrounding area. They brought presents for the young couple that ranged from bead purses and live chickens, to an antique, solid gold, christening cup.

After the ceremony, Senhor Farrao laid out a feast that was more than enough to fill the belly of every man, woman and child there. The wedding feast was followed by tribal dancing. Later still the nostalgic music of Portugal was sung and played by men and women, many of whom knew the home country only from the romanticised memoirs of fathers and grandfathers.

When it became clear that the celebrations would continue all night, Daniel and Elvira slipped away to the little honeymoon cottage especially prepared for them at the river's edge. Temporarily vacated by Captain St Anna's quartermaster and his small family, it had been newly decorated and furnished for the occasion by Senhor Farrao.

Daniel was about to slip into bed alongside Elvira, when the boom of the fort's signal cannon boomed forth, shaking the walls of the cottage. As its echoes died away, the voice of the look-out called out excitedly.

Elvira sat up quickly, drawing the sheet about her body.

'What is it? What's he saying?' Daniel asked.

'There's a fire, from either the de Souta or Nunes houses. Both are no more than two miles from here.'

At that moment the look-out called that he could see yet another fire, and among the cries of the crowd outside, Daniel heard a word that he recognised.

The word was . . . Pombeiros.

Daniel reached for his clothes, but Elvira stretched an arm from the bed and gripped his hand.

'Please, Daniel. Don't leave me. Not tonight.'

Daniel hesitated. Then he remembered another night, and a girl cowering in a corner of Elvira's room as Pombeiros fled to safety. His clothes dropped to the floor and a few moments later he was holding Elvira to him and her trembling had nothing to do with thoughts of Pombeiros.

Some hours later Daniel eased himself from Elvira's arms and slid quietly from the bed. Standing at the window he could see the flames of a fire licking skywards from yet another house. This one was on the slopes of a hill, many miles from the original fires. The Pombeiros were having a busy night.

There was a sound from the room behind him as Elvira slipped from the bed and joined him at the window, still naked. Putting an arm about his waist she rested her head against him and they gazed together through the window at the burning house. Suddenly, Elvira shuddered, and Daniel pulled her closer to him.

'I'm sorry Daniel. Looking at that fire, I remembered another night. I pray that no one is suffering as they were made to suffer then. Not tonight.'

The flames in the distant house reached the gunpowder store and it exploded with a flash that lit up the night sky, the sound of the explosion rattling the cottage windows seconds later.

Elvira moved from the window and as he followed her towards the bed she turned and clung to him fiercely. Their desire for each other grew stronger and Elvira whispered, 'Daniel . . . come back to bed now. I want you to love me. Ah! My marido, I want you . . . .'

CHAPTER SEVENTEEN

Daniel and Elvira left Sena with their wagons a week after the wedding. It was considered that the Pombeiros must be far away by now, but Senhor Farrao took no chances. Captain Francisco St Anna, with a large force of militia accompanied the newly-weds and their Kalanga tribesmen until they were well beyond the Manica mountains.

It was not far enough. Three days after the departure of St Anna and his troops, the Pombeiros struck.

Daniel was asleep in the living-wagon with Elvira when a faint sound woke him. It was not yet fully dawn, but a pale light seeped through the taut canvas above him. He listened and caught the soft jingle of metal upon metal. Such a sound as harness makes when a horse shakes its head. Daniel sat up hastily. The only horses accompanying the wagons were those belonging to Elvira and himself. They were tethered in a thorn-bush pen – without bridles.

He slipped quietly into his clothes, not wanting to waken Elvira at this stage. After checking his rifle, he unlaced the wagon flap and peeped outside.

What Daniel saw in the faint light filled him with dismay. There were many horsemen milling about the wagons. Some were herding the Kalanga tribesmen in one large group, the sleepy tribesmen behaving like docile, frightened sheep.

The horsemen were moving methodically from wagon to wagon and there must have been at least twenty of them, probably more. Dark though it was, Daniel instantly recognised them as Pombeiros.

'Elvira, wake up,' the words were whispered, but they were loud enough to waken her.

Startled, she opened her eyes and her lips parted to speak, but Daniel hurriedly clamped a hand over her mouth. 'Don't make a sound. Pombeiros – they're searching the wagons.'

Above his hand, Elvira's eyes widened in apprehension.

'Hurry and get dressed.' He put a loaded rifle on the wagon floor beside her. 'When you're ready I'm going to jump from the wagon and try to draw them away. As soon as you hear shooting pick up this gun and run for the thick bush beside the river. Hide there until the Pombeiros go – then head eastwards. Try to get back to Sena. It's a long way, but it's your only chance.'

He removed his hand from her mouth and snatched up a second rifle, easing a cartridge into the breech before laying the cartridge belt beside Elvira's gun.

'Wha . . . what will you do?' Still wide-eyed, Elvira asked the question in a hoarse, fear-tightened whisper as she shrugged a dress down over her body.

'I'll try to lose the Pombeiros in the bush. It shouldn't be hard in this light. They won't want to follow me far, the grass is too high.'

Daniel hoped she would not recognise the lie. He doubted whether he would reach the shelter of the nearest patch of long grass before the Pombeiros shot him down. His hope was that it would create sufficient diversion to enable Elvira to make good her own escape.

'I'll come with. We will live or die together—'

'There's no time to argue.' Daniel had heard a shot from one of the searching Pombeiros. They had found the crates of wine, a present from Senhor Farrao. They were stored in the wagon outspanned ahead of the living-wagon.

Throwing back the wagon-flap, Daniel vaulted to the ground – and found himself in the path of a Pombeiro who was riding towards the living-wagon. The Pombeiro shouted a warning and urged his horse forward. As Daniel scrambled to his feet, the rebel's horse bowled him over.

Daniel looked up to see the Pombeiro's rifle raised to gun him down. A shot rang out, but it left Daniel unscathed and it was the Pombeiro who slumped from his horse.

On the box-seat of the wagon, Elvira struggled to release the breech of her rifle, but it had jammed and as Daniel reached for his own gun, other Pombeiros fell on him and he was quickly pinned to the ground.

Another Pombeiro jumped from his horse to the wagon seat. Disarming Elvira, he threw her roughly to the ground. With a whoop of delight, two of the half-caste rebels leaped upon her. Shouting for them to leave her alone, Daniel struggled violently with the men who held him.

The two men manhandling Elvira had ripped her dress from throat to waist before the Pombeiro leader rode up and ordered them to release her.

One of the Pombeiros was reluctant to relinquish his prize. The leader spurred his horse forward, the short, rhinoceroshide whip in his hand cracked and the Pombeiro staggered back from Elvira, a bloody weal etched diagonally across his face from ear to mouth.

Shaking off the men who held him, Daniel went to Elvira, his own face bloodied and bruised. He pulled the torn dress up about her shoulders and she put up a hand to hold it in place. Her other hand found his and he squeezed her fingers in a futile bid to reassure her.

'What a very touching scene,' said the Pombeiro leader mockingly, as he looked down at them from his horse. He spoke in English, although his next words proved that he knew Elvira was Portuguese. 'We have captured a rich prize indeed. A fortune in trade goods *and* the daughter of a Provincial Captain General! You are far from home, Senhorita Farrao – ah! My apologies. Senhora Retallick. Your wedding was a day to remember – for all of us.'

'What do you intend doing with us?' asked Daniel.

'With *us*, trader? You are nothing to me. I have your wagons and your goods. I also have your wife . . . and Senhor Farrao will pay generously for her return, I think.'

'He will pay for my husband too,' said Elvira quickly.

The Pombeiro shook his head and smiled without humour. 'No, we will ask a *very* high price for you. He will not be able to afford more. Besides, it is a long ride to Sena and my men will need to guard you closely, day and night. Of course, they will expect you to reward them for taking such care of you.'

Spreading his hands in an apologetic gesture, the Pombeiro added, 'It would embarrass you to know that your husband was a witness to your "gratitude", would it not? It is better that you say goodbye to your husband now, Senhora, then you will forget him.'

He called an order in Portuguese and Daniel was seized by

two of the nearest Pombeiros. Elvira began screaming and jumped at the men, but she was quickly dragged away.

'Stop!' The cry, in a woman's voice went unheeded, but when a rifle shot rang out, much of the excitement about the two prisoners died away. Held fast by Pombeiros who had been securing his wrists with rope cut from one of his own wagons, Daniel looked on in disbelief as Victoria walked towards him, smoke trickling from the barrel of the rifle she held.

'Let them go,' she snapped.

When the Pombeiros were slow to respond Victoria raised the gun to her shoulder. Immediately, they leaped away from Daniel and those about Elvira stepped back hastily. They had been present when Victoria shot the two Australian miners. There had been others since. Victoria's ruthlessness was already a legend among the Pombeiros of Mozambique.

Victoria moved to release Daniel's wrists, but he slipped off the ropes without her aid and went to help Elvira. Shaken and dishevelled, Elvira held on to all the dignity she could muster. She knew who this Pombeiro girl must be and was determined that Victoria would not see her reduced to tears.

'What are you doing?' The demand came from Philippe as he confronted Victoria. 'What is this white man to you?'

'We were brought up together. His father and mine were friends.'

Philippe looked at Daniel with more interest than before. 'He does not seem eager to remember old friends now he moves among the Portuguese aristocracy. After all what is a poor Pombeiro girl compared to the daughter of a rich Portuguese Prazero?'

Daniel spoke to Victoria for the first time. 'Have you forgotten how your father died? Does his memory mean so little that you seek the company of these thieves and murderers?'

Daniel spoke quietly, but the words reached Philippe. The Pombeiro leaned forward in his saddle and he glared angrily at Daniel. 'You have married into a Portuguese family, yet you speak of *us* as thieves and murderers? When the Portuguese first came to this country they marched beneath a bloody cross. They massacred whole tribes in the sacred name of their "bountiful" God, and his "Mother of Mercy". Since then they have robbed the people of this land of everything they ever possessed – including pride. And you call Pombeiros murderers and robbers? Mother of God! The same words mean different things in each of our mouths, white man.'

Philippe jerked the reins of his horse savagely and the animal pranced in a full circle, snorting in pain as Philippe waited to hear Victoria's reply.

When she spoke, Victoria's voice was cold and controlled, 'These "thieves and murderers" are my people, Daniel. They always have been . . . but you and Dad forgot to tell me. There were many things you forgot to tell me. For instance, you led me to believe men treated women with chivalry. I had to find out for myself that chivalry is only for white women. I learned it in the goldfields of Tati, where a coloured girl is something to be won or lost in a game of cards. Or used like an animal by drunken miners. Oh yes, Dad's memory means something to me, Daniel! I have him to thank for bringing me into this world. For making me someone who belongs neither to Africa, nor to Europe. Can you imagine what it means not to belong anywhere? No, of course you can't – but the White Mondoro does. He told me to find my future among my own. Well, I have. I'm a Pombeiro. They are all the things you've called them – and more. But I don't wake up each morning filled with shame as I did in Tati.'

'Van Niekerk did this to you?'

'He and others – but forget them. They are all dead.'

Turning from Daniel, she spoke to the Pombeiro leader, 'I want you to set Daniel and his wife free, Philippe.'

Philippe opened his mouth to argue, but he could see by Victoria's strained expression just how important this was to her.

'All right.' He shrugged nonchalantly. 'I wasn't looking forward to a journey to Sena with the girl, anyway.'

Daniel's relief threatened to overwhelm him – but his business instincts came to the fore. 'What about my wagons?'

'Don't push me too far. I am a thief, remember? However, you are a friend of Victoria . . . and a trader, so you are almost one of us.' Philippe grinned. 'My men will take only what they can carry away. The rest, together with the wagons, are yours.'

'And the Kalangas?'

Philippe sighed. 'You ask for too much. Your Kalangas are young and strong. The French pay good money for such men. I will leave you enough to drive your wagons, no more.'

'I *have* to accept that. I'm not so sure the Matabele will. The Kalangas are their vassals.'

'I will discuss the matter with them, if ever the Matabele come to Mozambique,' Philippe retorted. Dismissing Daniel from his mind, he turned to Victoria, and his expression changed. 'Now I must explain my soft-heartedness to my men. It may be necessary to remind them I am still their leader. Bring your rifle and watch them closely while I am talking.'

Victoria nodded. She stood looking uncertainly at Daniel for a few moments. 'We've moved into different worlds, you and I, Daniel. For you it is better that I've gone from your life.' She inclined her head towards Elvira. 'You will never have to apologise to anyone for being married to her.'

'I have never apologised to anyone for you, and I never will,' declared Daniel quietly. 'Today you've saved our lives. There will always be a place for you in our home. You'll find it in the valley we saw, two days ride from Khami.'

Victoria nodded. 'I remember the place. Thank you for the offer, Daniel. I have a child. I may send her to you one day.' She looked to where the Pombeiros had one of the crates of wine on the ground and were inexpertly smashing off the necks of the bottles against nearby rocks. 'Inspan your wagon and leave quickly. I'll make sure your Kalangas follow with the remainder of the wagons as soon as the Pombeiros accept what's happening.'

Victoria joined Philippe as he rolled a cigarette and eyed the Pombeiros. 'Where's the baby?' He spoke without looking at her.

'With one of the men, in the bush.'

Philippe inclined his head. 'Why did you not want the white man to see your child?'

He looked at her quickly, catching her sudden confusion.

'I . . . I thought there might be shooting. Therese is safer where she is.'

'I see,' he saw only too well, but made no comment. 'Come. If my men drink too much they will leave nothing for your friend and his new wife to take home with them.'

Daniel and Elvira inspanned their oxen as quickly as they could. As the wagons creaked excruciatingly slowly from the camp, the voices of the Pombeiros rose in argument behind them.

'I hope Victoria knows what she's doing,' muttered Daniel, cracking the twenty-feet long bull whip as the oxen heaved the wagon through a patch of thick, coarse grass. 'If Philippe changes his mind we'll never make it to Insimo—'

'He won't change his mind,' replied Elvira confidently. 'Did you see the way he looked at Victoria? He is very much in love with her. He will do whatever she wants.'

'I hope you're right . . . and for her sake I pray it lasts.' Daniel spoke through his teeth as he sawed on the long reins to turn the lead oxen towards more even ground. 'There'll be little happiness for her with the Pombeiros if ever he tires of her.'

'I am right,' Elvira assured him.

She did not add that she was less certain of Victoria's feelings towards her Pombeiro lover. To do so would call for explanations. Only a fool would tell her husband that another woman was in love with him.

CHAPTER EIGHTEEN

Victoria kept her word to Daniel and, six days after the incident with the Pombeiros, Daniel brought his bride to the Insimo Valley. He had been away for three months. In his absence the Mashona servants had scoured the valley for unusual and attractive plants, setting their discoveries about the house in a profusion of colour. Insimo was more of a garden valley than ever before.

It was love at first sight for Elvira. The valley, the house and everything she saw filled her with delight.

Leaving Elvira to supervise the unpacking of the possessions brought from Sena, Daniel made a quick tour of inspection. Because of the plentiful supply of water the grass everywhere in the valley was lush green. It would never wither and die as it did in other parts of Matabeleland. The cattle too looked well and the first calves had been born. Healthy and long-legged, they were captured by eager Matabele herd-boys and brought to him for his approval.

Assured that all was well in his valley, Daniel returned to the house filled with an unaccustomed sense of well-being.

That evening, Daniel and Elvira stood on the wide verandah of their house and looked down the length of the Insimo valley. The sun had disappeared below the rim of the nearby hills, plunging the valley into cool shadow, but it still shone brightly upon the low-veldt to the south. To Elvira it seemed as though she were looking out from a darkened window at a bright, new world. She leaned against Daniel and he put an arm about her, understanding something of her emotions. Many evenings like this, when the house was being built, he had stood here alone, overcome by the sheer magnificence of Africa, and longing for the day when he would share it with Elvira. With his wife.

'It's so ... so very beautiful, Daniel. A truly enchanted place. This is going to be a marvellous home in which to bring up a family and teach them about life. I am so happy. So very, very happy.'

The next few weeks were idyllic. Daniel busied himself about the valley, building paddocks to hold the additional five hundred cattle he had decided to purchase. He also had the Mashona workers till a couple of acres of land. Here he planted maize, the ubiquitous corn of the Matabele. Used by them in a variety of ways with every meal, maize was also the basic ingredient of their thick, intoxicating beer, a drink consumed by Matabele men and women in vast quantities.

Daniel took Elvira to see the gold in the stream that flowed from the hillside into the valley. In only half an hour of searching they found enough nuggets to cover the palm of Daniel's hand. They discussed the significance of the gold at some length and Elvira agreed with the decision Daniel had reached soon after the find. It should remain a secret for as long as possible, in order that the character of the valley should not change.

So pleasant was life in the Insimo valley that when the time came for another trading journey to Sena, Daniel persuaded Aaron to take his place.

Aaron had returned to Matabeleland a month after Daniel. Mary had been delivered to her family in the Herero capital of Otjimkandje and Aaron remained in South West Africa long enough to see her settle back in tribal life as though she had never been away. His attempts to barter his goods were less successful. The wagon-loads of ivory and feathers were delivered to Whalefish Bay and sold at a very high price to the trade-hungry dealers, but few ships now called at the isolated port. Aaron could buy no goods to bring back to Matabeleland.

Many of the merchants of Whalefish Bay had closed their premises and returned to their countries of origin. One or two had been bought out by Germans. The Germans alone, of all the trading nations, were taking advantage of the tribal wars, supplying arms to any tribe rich enough to pay for them.

After such an unsatisfactory trading experience, Aaron was eager to make a trek to Sena. Little trouble was expected from the Pombeiros now, but with Kanje safely out of the way in the northern swamplands, Jandu sent half an impi to escort Aaron to his destination.

Only one cloud darkened the horizon of Daniel's life in that warm and pleasant winter of 1869. Farewell Loveday had returned to Khami.

When the two missionaries had set out for Cape Town earlier in the year, poor, weak Arnold Pugh-Williams was a sick man. Two weeks later, after a lifetime spent nursing imaginary illnesses, he died uncomplainingly of malaria in the heat of a Kalahari afternoon.

Arnold Pugh-Williams was buried in a sandy grave at the edge of the trail that cut through a corner of the wide desert. Within a week, all record of the feeble missionary's existence had disappeared. The shifting sands of the Kalahari quickly swallowed up his grave and the rough wooden cross was reduced to ashes on a Bushman's fire.

The death of Pugh-Williams caused the mission authorities acute embarrassment. There was now no one to press the charges for which they had brought Loveday to Cape Town. In addition, his arrival with Helena Pugh-Williams set tongues wagging furiously.

Anxious to avoid a full-blown scandal, the mission authorities granted Helena Pugh-Williams a small pension and booked her a passage on the first available ship to England. The Superintendent of the Mission Society gave Farewell Loveday a long lecture on the virtues of discretion – and then informed him of his transfer to a remote mission station in the heart of Natal.

The posting was humiliating to a man with the Reverend Loveday's ambitions. It was also likely to prove extremely uncomfortable. The initial complaint about his conduct had been made by Arnold Pugh-Williams to the Bishop of Natal.

After a lengthy discussion with Helena Pugh-Williams, Farewell Loveday resigned from the mission society. Marrying the widow of his late colleague in some haste, he set off with her to return to Khami as a freelance missionary/trader.

His actions caused the biggest scandal the British community in Cape Town had ever known, but Farewell Loveday was unrepentant. Indeed, he turned the furore to his own advantage. Returning to Khami via Transvaal, he stopped at Potchefstroom where he had two days of talks with President Pretorius and other officials of the Transvaal Assembly. Loveday told the Boers that he was prepared to help them to gain a foothold in Matabeleland – but he also made it clear that he was willing to sell his services to the highest bidder.

When Daniel came to Khami after Farewell Loveday's return and heard the news, he was incredulous and not a little hurt that Jandu should have allowed Farewell Loveday, of all people, to trade in direct competition with Retallick and Copping.

Jandu was apologetic. 'I am sorry, but I am not yet King. The full Council of Indunas agreed that Loveday should be allowed to stay in Matabeleland, to serve your God and to trade with our people.'

Daniel looked at Jandu suspiciously. 'The full Council of Indunas met to discuss whether a man should be allowed to trade with the Matabele? There's more to this than you're telling me, Jandu. What's Loveday offering to trade – guns?'

'Will *you* sell us guns?' Jandu countered.

'I would sell them to you willingly, but neither the British nor the Portuguese will let me have guns in the quantities you need. They've both learned from bitter experience that sooner or later the guns will be turned against them. Farewell Loveday must be getting them from the Boers. No doubt they're selling them to Kanje too, just as they were a year ago. But even the Boers are hesitant about selling guns to the tribes – unless the price is one they can't possibly refuse. What are you giving in return for these guns, Jandu?'

Jandu shrugged, 'Nothing . . . yet. When I am King they want me to sign a treaty of friendship with them. Is that so bad?'

'It depends what conditions they put into their "peace treaty".'

Jandu smiled. 'By then I will be King and able to appoint you as my adviser of treaties. But not so serious, trader. You own a beautiful piece of my country and come to buy five hundred cows from me. You are a rich man with a new bride. Why should you be concerned with trade at all? Remain at Insimo with your wife. Raise many cattle and fine children. Now, when can I bring Suliyana to visit you? She has spoken of nothing else since your return . . . .'

For a while Farewell Loveday's trading activities hit Retallick and Copping very hard. The Matabele tribesmen fortunate enough to kill an elephant or ostrich still came to Daniel. So too did the occasional English hunter on a brief visit to Matabeleland, but the majority of ivory and feathers went to Farewell Loveday.

Aaron returned as the rains broke in November and the partners spent many of the wet evenings on the verandah of the house at Insimo, discussing the future of trade in Matabeleland. As Jandu had said, they really had no need to trade any longer. Aaron had been trading for a lifetime and had accumulated enough money to enable him to live in modest comfort for what remained of his life. Even so, he swore he would die of boredom within a matter of weeks if he had to stop working.

Daniel too could cease trading without suffering hardship. He was building up a vast cattle herd in the Insimo valley and had asked Senhor Farrao to arrange to have a couple of high quality bulls shipped by sea from the Cape Colony during the 'cool' season. He hoped to produce superior cattle to those bred by the tribesmen. Such animals would command a very high price from the Matabele, to whom cattle were the ultimate status symbol.

Daniel had also proved that the Insimo valley was an ideal spot for growing maize. He had planted enough at the beginning of the season to meet the needs of the whole population of Khami. Of course, if all else failed there was always the gold! But Daniel refused to contemplate gold-mining for the time being – and he was not going to let Farewell Loveday drive him out of business without a fight. He and Aaron went ahead with their trading plans.

The rainy season of 1869/70 was a disastrously short one, lasting barely two months. It made little difference to Daniel, water was plentiful in the Insimo valley. But the rains meant life or death to many of the villagers in the tiny communities scattered throughout the surrounding hills. Their headmen consulted the uGangas – the tribal 'witch-doctors' and for once they were all in agreement. The rains had failed because the traditional ceremonies offering tribute to the Gods had not been performed – and these could not be held until there was a King to lead the celebrations. The Gods were offended. They needed to be appeased in time for the great ceremony of Nxwala – 'First Fruits', traditionally performed soon after the cessation of the rains. Last year this great ceremony had not taken place and now the Gods were showing their displeasure.

The Council of Indunas met and agreement was swiftly reached. A reasonable time had elapsed for the missing heir to put in an appearance. Kulumani was declared to be officially 'dead'. No man must ever utter his name again. The time had come for Jandu to take his place as King of the Matabele.

Jandu was told to prepare himself and orders went out for the headmen and Indunas of the impis, strategically scattered throughout Matabeleland, to return to Khami and salute their new King.

The celebrations began at the end of January 1870 and the entire populace turned their faces towards Khami to witness the coronation of the new Matabele King. For the first time since Mzilikazi's death, the impis came together as a great army – but not *every* impi obeyed the call of the Great Council. As coronation day drew near, five impis remained absent. Among them was the crack regiment of which Kanje was the Induna.

A message was sent out to the recalcitrant Indunas, carried by senior members of the Council, in order that there should be no mistaking the authority of the call. One regiment wavered and was welcomed back into the loyal army of the King-elect. The remaining four impis withdrew into the swamplands of the Makololo tribes – and the tribal Elders sent to change their hearts were never seen again.

This was not the time for the Matabele people to raise their voices in anger against Kanje and his adherents. It was an occasion for rejoicing and celebration. A time to laud the new King – and enjoy his generous hospitality.

The tribesmen and their families gathered in tens of thousands about the capital, their campfires lighting the bushveldt for many miles in every direction.

Daniel took Elvira to Khami in a horse-drawn wagon and they camped on a Kopje overlooking Khami, from which they would have a fine view of the whole coronation ceremonies. There were others here too, including all the Europeans who had gathered at the Matabele capital, hoping to gain concessions from a new and inexperienced King. Late arrivals on the kopje were Farewell Loveday and his wife. Helena Loveday was heavy with child and Elvira's heart went out to her as she struggled up the hill behind her husband. Elvira and Helena were the only two European women in the whole of Matabeleland, yet Helena Loveday acknowledged Elvira's presence with no more than a frigid inclination of her head, before turning away to talk with her husband.

As preparations for the coronation got under way, Jandu was taken to a small cluster of beehive-shaped huts, about two miles from Khami. Just before the actual ceremony began, he sent a message to Daniel, asking him to ride down to see him, bringing a spare horse. It seemed Jandu intended arriving for his coronation in some style.

Daniel reached the huts just as the Matabele army set forth from Khami to bring back their King. Dressed in ceremonial costume, each man's height was added to by a tall plume of feathers, rising eighteen inches from a band about his forehead. Across his shoulders, each warrior wore a cape of black skin, or feathers. A short skirt of skin hung from his waist, while arms and legs were decorated with bangles of beads.

In full battle array, the warriors were an awesome spectacle. Thirty-five thousand strong, they lined up twenty deep in the traditional 'head-and-horns' formation that their enemies had found invincible in the past.

In solid formation, a mile wide, the army advanced slowly across the space between Khami and the King's kraal until they were no more than a few hundred yards away. Then, at a given signal, their long shields decorated with two crossed spears were held in front of their bodies, forming blocks of different colours, each one representing a separate impi. Now the army moved more slowly, singing as they advanced and stamping their feet to the ground in unison, causing the earth to tremble before them.

Elvira thrilled as Jandu rode out from his kraal to meet his army, Daniel riding close behind him. A roar went up from the Matabele warriors as they swarmed about their King, enveloping the two horsemen in their midst. Moments later the ranks parted and Jandu and Daniel emerged, riding their horses at a slow walk. The great army fell in behind them, singing the praises of the King, who had himself served and fought in their ranks as a warrior.

Once he reached Khami, Jandu went forward with Daniel to meet the Great Council of Indunas, seated in the great cattle pen beneath the shade of the lone Indaba tree.

Jandu slipped to the ground to join the circle and as Daniel led the two horses away the coronation ceremony began. The senior Induna, Umnombati, related in a loud voice the reason why Jandu was undoubtedly the true heir to the Matabele throne, while lesser Indunas called out the praises of their new King. Meanwhile, hideously masked uGangas sprinkled specially prepared powders over their new ruler to cleanse him from all the impurities that might hamper him in his new role.

The first day's ceremonies came to an end when Umnombati pointed to Jandu and, in the loudest voice he could muster, cried, 'See him, warriors of the Matabele. Here is your King.'

That evening Daniel and Elvira went to Khami to spend the night in the store. The ceremonies and accompanying celebrations would continue for six days.

The next morning Suliyana came to the hut to take Elvira to the Royal enclosure to watch the proceedings in comfort, while Daniel was once again called upon to accompany Jandu.

This day's proceedings began with the ritual slaughter of black oxen, each one dedicated by Jandu to a named ancestor. Afterwards more cattle were killed, this time to feed the hungry warriors of the impis who pledged their loyalty to Jandu as they came forward to eat his meat.

So the daily ceremonies went on, often repetitious, but always colourful. On the final day Jandu was led away to a hill from which there was a panoramic view of much of Matabeleland. Here, his voice weak from six days of unaccustomed usage, the aged Umnombati made his final speech. Summing up all the dignity that his years had given to him, he slowly extended his arm and swept it in a wide arc to indicate much of the land about them.

'See, Jandu, there is the country of thy father. His cattle and his people are now yours. Take them and cherish them. Those who sin against your laws – punish. But those who obey – reward.'

Then the old man sank to his knees with some difficulty and banged his forehead on the ground at the younger man's feet. Jandu was now King of Matabeleland.

CHAPTER NINETEEN

After his coronation, it was expected that the new King would move to a new capital, as was the custom of his Zulu forefathers, and Indunas were sent out by the Council to choose a site. However, Jandu was in no immediate hurry to leave Khami. Suliyana was heavy with her first child and the present capital was pleasantly situated.

In the meantime, Jandu acquired sufficient muskets to arm two impis and he asked Daniel to train his warriors in the use of the unfamiliar weapons. The task was difficult, frustrating — and occasionally dangerous. The danger was due in no small measure to the poor quality of the guns supplied by Farewell Loveday. So bad were they that Daniel insisted that in future he be allowed to test every musket before it was accepted by the Matabele. The result was that two in three of the trade muskets were rejected as quite useless.

Alarmed by Daniel's actions, Farewell Loveday came to see him one day when Daniel was paying a visit to the Khami store. There had never been any pretence at friendship between them, but Loveday's manner was conciliatory — at first.

After admitting that rejection of two thirds of the muskets was playing havoc with his profits, Farewell Loveday indicated the goods piled up against the stone walls about the two men. 'You're a trader, Retallick. You know it's not possible to be too choosey about trade goods delivered this far from civilisation.'

'A good trader takes that into consideration when he sets his prices,' retorted Daniel. 'I'm testing guns as a friend of Jandu — not as a trader. Some of those I've sent back to you would have exploded in a man's face. As for the powder . . . !' He snorted derisively. 'It might have been brought to Africa by van Riebeeck!'

'The Matabele are given the same grade of powder as I sell to anyone else. I'm not an expert on gunpowder — and neither are you. Anyway, I have to take what I'm sent.'

'True. But Jandu doesn't. He'll take delivery of no second-rate goods while I'm around.'

'That may not be for much longer.' Farewell Loveday was stung into indiscretion. 'The Transvaalers have got your measure. They'll have you out of here so quick you'll be over the border before you have time to draw breath—'

Checking himself belatedly, Farewell Loveday gave Daniel a final glare before stomping from the store, slamming the door shut behind him. He left Daniel wondering what he had meant about the Transvaalers. They had no power here in Matabeleland and they would never dare to invade – or would they? Daniel decided he must pay more attention to the gossip of the few Europeans who came to his store. Someone had commented a few weeks earlier that there was a great deal of Boer activity in those regions of Transvaal closest to the Matabeleland border. Daniel had taken no notice of the remark then. Now he wished he had pressed the man to tell him more.

Before Daniel was able to look into the matter, Victoria entered his life once more. The end of the 1870 dry season was approaching and Daniel was at his Insimo home when one of the herd boys ran to the house to say that a rider was approaching along the valley.

Visitors to Insimo were so infrequent that Daniel and Elvira both hurried to the door. To their great surprise they saw Victoria nearing the house, riding a very weary horse. Slung in front of her was a young child, little more than a year old.

As Victoria pulled the horse to a halt she swayed in the saddle. Elvira ran past Daniel and accepted the child as Victoria swung it down to her. Victoria slipped from the saddle and Daniel stepped forward hurriedly to prevent her from falling.

'Daniel, I need help . . . Philippe is badly hurt.'

Victoria was obviously distressed, but Daniel found it difficult to summon up any sympathy for the Pombeiro.

'Troubles between the Portuguese army and Pombeiros are best left in Mozambique. Jandu can do without having them spill over into Matabeleland. What happened? Was there a fight?'

'It's nothing to do with the Portuguese.' Victoria clung to him as she pleaded. 'Daniel, I beg you to help him. There have been fights ... too many. Captain St Anna has militiamen in every town and village. Their orders are to shoot coloured men on sight – whether or not they are Pombeiros. Philippe decided we must leave Mozambique and begin a new life together. We are on our way to Otjimkandje.'

'To thieve – or to fight for the Herero?'

Victoria was very, very tired. Her eyes filled with tears of defeat and she dropped her hands from Daniel in despair. 'He hoped ... to trade. I said you might help him to make a new start. I should have known better. You have good reason to hate Pombeiros. You and your ... wife.'

She reached out and took Therese from Elvira. As her thin shirt tightened against her body, Daniel could see how thin she was. Standing beside her horse with Therese in her arms she managed to muster some of her old spirit.

'You are wrong about Philippe. He *has* stolen – and killed, but he grew up knowing no other way of life. He had two older brothers who were Pombeiros. Both are now dead. Philippe is a much gentler man than they. He has been kind to me and has a great love for Therese. He is my man, Daniel. A *good* man, whatever the world may say. I would die for him. I *will* die for him.'

Before Daniel could reply, Elvira put an arm about Victoria and began leading her towards the house. 'Daniel will bring your man to our home. You will both stay here with the baby.'

Victoria stopped and looked hopefully at Daniel. He capitulated, grateful to Elvira for taking the decision from him. 'I'll go and fetch Philippe. Where did this accident happen? How badly is he hurt?'

'It was no accident. We were attacked by a Matabele impi, no more than ten miles north of here. Philippe was shot in the leg. We had only one horse but managed to escape, leaving the impi our wagon and the oxen ... everything we owned.'

'A Matabele impi ten miles from here?' Daniel was startled. This was well off the beaten track for either a hunting party, or an impi raiding Mashona country.

'They were Kanje's men.'

'Are you certain? Quite certain?' Now Daniel was alarmed. Kanje's impi was supposed to be hiding in the Makololo swamps. They had been there since before Jandu's coronation.

'I lived with the Matabele for almost as many years as you, Daniel. The warriors carried shields bearing Kanje's colours. They were his men.'

'How long ago did all this happen. Are the impis heading this way?'

'I don't know. I don't think so. They seemed to be heading for Khami, but some of Kanje's men came after us. We were attacked just before dusk last night. We wandered around in circles in the darkness. By this morning Philippe was too weak to stay on the horse. I couldn't hold him and the baby. I left him in the shade of some overhanging rocks – about an hour's ride away.'

'You'd better come and show me the place. Elvira, give her food and drink while I organise some herd-boys to come with us.'

For a brief while Insimo was a scene of unusually hurried activity. Daniel issued muskets to some of his herd-boys and another was sent to ride to Khami to warn Jandu of Kanje's presence. Others were ordered to drive the herds of cattle to a high-walled side valley where they might be protected from Kanje's impi if the need arose. Most of the remaining herd boys were brought to the house and stationed with muskets behind heavily shuttered windows.

Daniel was grateful for the whim which had made him build the house so that it might be easily defended. The house could only be taken at the expense of massive loss of life on the part of the attackers – and Daniel believed Kanje had other plans for his warriors.

Daniel, Victoria and the mounted herd boys had travelled two miles from the house when, at the wide entrance to the valley, the youthful Matabele marksmen were called upon to put the training Daniel had given them to the test. Topping a small rise, they rode headlong into about fifty of Kanje's warriors, carrying guns in addition to their shields and spears.

With a cry of warning to the others, Daniel kneed his horse forward and charged through the ranks of the startled Matabele rebels, discharging both barrels of his rifle at the only warrior who retained sufficient wits to attempt to stop him.

Daniel's herd-boys and Victoria rode full tilt after him, firing as they came on and scattering Kanje's warriors.

When Daniel and his companions drew rein to reload, Kanje's men attempted an old-style Matabele charge. It became apparent immediately that the guns they carried were no more than morale-boosters. Four shots were fired at Daniel's party but the bullets went wide. The remaining warriors appeared to have little idea of firing a gun and one or two warriors threw them to the ground in disgust, trusting to their more familiar assegais.

The short, stabbing-spears were no match for the well-aimed muskets of Daniel's mounted party. When the first charge broke, seven men lay dead on the ground.

For fifteen minutes the one-sided battle followed the same pattern. Fire . . . and withdraw. Load, fire . . . and withdraw. It was so easy that long before the last few survivors threw down their arms and fled, Daniel was sickened by the slaughter he and the others had inflicted upon the foolishly courageous warriors of Kanje's impi.

Only the thought that they might go on to attack the house at Insimo kept him doggedly loading and raising the gun to his shoulder.

When all danger had passed, Daniel walked among the Matabele dead and picked up one of the rifles they had dropped. It was a brand-new Martini Henry breech loader, the moving parts still smeared with the grease put on by the manufacturers. It seemed that Kanje had access to a source of arms that was denied to his half-brother.

Mounting his horse again, he followed after Victoria and not long afterwards they reached the spot where she had left the badly wounded Philippe.

Delirious with pain and loss of blood, the Pombeiro tried to raise his gun and shoot Daniel as he leaned over him. He was so weak that Daniel simply plucked the gun from his hands and handed it to one of the herd-boys.

Daniel was horrified when Victoria changed the rough dressing she had left on Philippe's leg. One of Kanje's men must have been armed with a large-bore hunting rifle and been more skilled than his fellow-warriors. The heavy bullet had shattered the bone about four inches beneath Philippe's knee. He had lost so much blood it was a miracle he still lived. Victoria tied a fresh dressing about the leg, but they both

knew the wound needed urgent and expert attention – and that would be difficult to find.

It was a slow return journey to Insimo. Daniel held Philippe before him on his own horse and it was merciful that the wounded Pombeiro was unconscious for most of the way. They met with no more of Kanje's warriors and Daniel guessed that the survivors of the brief battle had fled after the main body of their impi.

At the house, Elvira was busy feeding Victoria's young daughter, but she handed Therese to her mother and helped Daniel to get Philippe to a bedroom. The dressing had slipped from his leg during the journey and Elvira threw up her hands in horror when she saw the wound. Wrinkling her nose, she said, 'It smells as though gangrene has already set in. Philippe needs more help than we can give him if he is to live.'

'I'll have to go to Farewell Loveday, at Khami, he has some medical knowledge. But I can't see him coming all this way . . . not for a Pombeiro.'

'You must persuade him, Daniel. Philippe is no longer a Pombeiro – and he is Victoria's man. We must do all we can.'

'All right, I'll leave now and take two of the herd boys with me. Keep the others in the house until I return – and maintain a watch around the clock. I'll be back as soon as I can.'

'Take care, Daniel. Victoria is not the only wife who is concerned for her husband.'

It was now almost noon. By taking spare horses with him and riding hard, Daniel hoped to arrive at Khami soon after nightfall – if he did not meet up with Kanje along the way.

Dusk found him still twenty miles short of his destination. Leaving the herd-boys at a Matabele kraal, Daniel took the best of the horses and rode on alone.

He reached Khami at a time when most families were settling down after the main evening meal. He went first to Jandu at the royal enclosure, to ensure he had been given the news of Kanje's return to Matabeleland.

Surprisingly, he found the new King in a relaxed and cheerful mood, accompanied by a very heavily pregnant Suliyana and surrounded by female slaves.

'Yes, trader. I received your message. Kanje and his men have now swung to the south, moving through the hills of the

Matapos. He hopes to take me by surprise – but I know his every move. Each hour one of the men following him returns to tell me of Kanje's progress. The longer he skulks in the hills the better. Already I have gathered an army that is large enough to defeat him in battle, but more impis arrive all the time, all eager to take part in the defeat of Kanje. Seat yourself, trader. I am glad you have come to be with me when I set off to meet my brother.'

'I am here to find Farewell Loveday.' Daniel told Jandu of Philippe, and how he had received his wound.

Jandu frowned. 'This is the same Mambari who took the Kalangas as slaves?'

'Yes.' It was futile to try to lie to Jandu. He would learn the truth in due course. 'He has given up the way of life he led then. He is Victoria's man. They have a young daughter and are on their way to South West Africa to begin a new life. If they hadn't run into Kanje, you might well have been taken by surprise.'

Jandu nodded his agreement. 'True. A few Kalangas must not be allowed to sour my gratitude. Victoria's man is very sick?'

'I've never seen a worse leg wound.'

'Then he is fortunate to have earned my gratitude. A white doctor is visiting Khami. Tonight he eats with Farewell Loveday. His name is Henkel and he has been waiting for many weeks to be given permission to "hunt" in Matabeleland. I do not believe he is a hunter. He is a man who walks with his eyes always searching the ground and he examines many stones. The Bechuanas who came with him say he digs holes in a search for gold. Find this doctor. Tell him he is to go to the Insimo valley. If he cures the Mambari he has my permission to "hunt". If the Mambari dies the doctor would do well to leave my country very quickly,' Jandu smiled. 'I would speak to this Mambari. A man who steals the servants of my people and then dares to return to my country is either a fool, or a brave man. I would know which of these he is.'

As Daniel turned to go, Jandu called, 'Wait! Send the doctor to Insimo with someone else. I want you with me when I fight Kanje.'

Daniel knew better than to argue. He walked from the royal

enclosure musing that Jandu was beginning to behave as a monarch ... but perhaps he always had. One thing was certain, in spite of his earlier doubts about taking the throne, Jandu had slipped easily into the role of ruler of the Matabele.

Daniel found Henkel, the German doctor, in Farewell Loveday's house. He and his host were coming to the end of a substantial meal. Daniel was shown to the dining-room by a servant and the sight of so much food made his stomach contract in a sharp reminder that he had not eaten since breakfast time.

When Daniel repeated Jandu's words, Henkel looked uncertainly at Farewell Loveday, seeking his advice.

'Who is the wounded man?'

'His name is Philippe. He's from Mozambique.'

'Philippe the Pombeiro?' Farewell Loveday hooted the words loudly. His flushed face was evidence that the wine had been as plentiful as the food that evening. 'I've heard of him. He's a thieving, lying, half-caste. Why should Jandu care whether he lives or dies, eh?'

'The King is grateful. Philippe was wounded by one of Kanje's men. Because of it I was able to warn Jandu that Kanje is in Matabeleland.'

'Kanje?' Farewell Loveday paled, 'He's not supposed . . . . He's . . . . What is he doing here?'

'He's come to fight Jandu, I should imagine. I hope you haven't been selling guns to him too, Loveday. If you have you'd better get packed and ready to leave in a hurry.'

Daniel had long suspected that Jandu's half-brother had left Matabeleland only in order to re-arm and await an opportunity to challenge Jandu for the throne of Matabeleland. Seeing Farewell Loveday's concern made many things fall into place. The missionary-trader had been playing a dangerous game. Supplying Jandu with old, worn-out muskets and at the same time arming Kanje's warriors with modern weapons.

With a whole country at stake, Farewell Loveday had apparently thought the risk was one that had to be taken. In the eyes of many, Kanje had as much right to the Matabele crown as Jandu. If he succeeded in defeating his half-brother in battle, Kanje would be recognised as King in his place. He could be expected to show favour to those who had supplied him with arms – perhaps by throwing his country open to the white man.

Suddenly, Daniel realised that this was more than one man's bid to make a fortune. Farewell Loveday could never have raised the money to buy such rifles as Daniel had seen. It would require a sum such as only a government might provide – and there was one government with more to gain than any other by securing Matabeleland – that of the Independent State of Transvaal. They had for long sought a means of expanding northwards. With a ruler of their choosing on the throne, Matabeleland would be theirs before its people realised what was happening.

Daniel made another calculated guess. With so much at stake, the Transvaalers would not leave Kanje to secure his throne backed by only a couple of dissident impis. Jandu had thought that Kanje was heading for the Matopos Hills hoping to attack Khami from there and take him by surprise. It was far more likely that Kanje was going there to link up with a Boer force for a combined attack! Jandu had to be warned.

To the German doctor, he said, 'Well, have you made up your mind? Are you coming?'

'I will come. What time will we leave in the morning?'

'There's a bright moon, you'll leave tonight. I'll send someone to accompany you and make sure you don't get lost. Pack only what will tie behind you on a horse. You'll find anything else you need at my place. I'll see you there in a few days.'

Before Kurt Henkel could argue, Daniel had gone. There were urgent matters to discuss with Jandu.

CHAPTER TWENTY

Jandu set off from Khami at dawn with four impis – a little more than five thousand men. It was the same number of warriors as Kanje had in his own army. Two more royal impis had been despatched to watch the river crossings far to the south. Daniel had convinced Jandu that the latest developments, coupled with persistent rumours of armed Boer commandoes just across the border, indicated a Transvaal involvement. Now Jandu was on his way to confront Kanje while runners were sending more impis to take up positions between Kanje and the Transvaal.

The latest reports put the position of the dissident Matabele warriors as no more than twenty miles from Khami but Jandu and his impis moved much faster than Kanje's men, who had brought their women and cattle with them from the lands of the Makololo.

Jandu's scouts had carried out their task well. By midmorning they were arriving from the shadowed valleys ahead of the advancing impis with increasing frequency, pinpointing the position of Kanje.

The opposing forces led by Mzilikazi's two sons met on a wide hillside overlooking a beautiful, fertile valley, when the sun stood high in the sky. It was a battleground chosen by Kanje once he realised he was being pursued.

Even at this late stage Jandu was reluctant to join battle with his half-brother. He sent an Induna to Kanje, urging him not to set brother against brother. To accept the decision of the Council of Indunas and return with his warriors to the Matabele people.

Jandu's plea was so uncharacteristic of the Matabele's warlike nature, that Kanje mistook forbearance for weakness. The King's army was no larger than his own, and Kanje's warriors were well armed with their modern rifles. Only two of Jandu's regiments carried guns and these were a laughable mixture of flintlock and percussion muskets, with no more than a handful of breech-loaders.

Kanje's response was a typical example of Matabele humour in its crudest form. The ranks of Kanje's warriors parted to allow a number of women through. When they were no more than a hundred yards from the royal army, they turned their backs on the King. Bending over, they raised the flaps of their short leather skirts high. The insult brought howls of anger from Jandu's men and it was as much as Jandu and Daniel could do to prevent the royal army breaking ranks and falling upon the dissidents.

Jandu's continued restraint was once more misconstrued by Kanje. His men bunched up in the traditional head-and-horns formation and, shouting insults, charged the ranks of the King's army.

It was a disastrous tactic. Those men in the 'head' of the battle formation were so tightly crowded together that only a few in the front rank could use their guns. Those on the strung-out 'horns' of the advance were too far away from their enemies to shoot with any accuracy – had they been trained in the use of their weapons.

As Kanje's impis swept forward, firing haphazardly and erratically, Jandu's own musketmen held their fire. Not until no more than forty yards separated the two armies did Daniel shout an order for the front rank to shoot.

The result was devastating. Musket balls and bullets poured into the closely packed ranks, many passing through the bodies of more than one man. As the leading rank fell to the ground, those coming behind stumbled over them. They rose to take the full force of a volley fired by the second rank of Jandu's warriors.

By the time the third rank opened fire Kanje's impis had been thrown into utter confusion and the attack lost its momentum. Then Jandu's voice roared forth above the din, calling upon his warriors to fall upon Kanje's impis using assegai and shield.

Thrusting and stabbing with their broad-bladed, short-handled assegais, the loyal warriors drove the dissidents before them until they finally broke and fled, seeking refuge among the broken rocks of the hillside. Behind them they left two thousand bodies strewn upon the bloody slope.

The battle now became a slaughter as Jandu's men swarmed up the hill and fell upon the women and children.

Daniel watched this cruel finale ashen-faced. He had seen warfare in South West Africa and been involved in tribal battles there, but he had never before witnessed bloodshed on this scale. The stench of death and the howls of the blood-hungry Matabele warriors terrified Daniel's snorting and protesting horse and Daniel rode him back along the slope to calm the animal down. It was now he saw Kanje. Daniel did not recognise him at first. He was one of three warriors who broke from a dense clump of Msasa trees, fleeing from the fury of Jandu's warriors.

Daniel had witnessed enough killing for one day. He reined his horse to one side, to allow them to pass. Then one of the warriors stopped and raised a rifle and Daniel recognised Kanje.

The hatred in Kanje's eyes bordered upon insanity. Daniel's revolver cleared the holster and he fired from the waist a split-second before Kanje's finger tightened on his own trigger. The rifle shot went wide as a heavy revolver bullet struck Kanje in the hip, the force of it knocking him to his knees. For a few moments the two men looked at each other. Then a dozen Matabele warriors, led by Jandu ran down the hill towards them. They had seen Kanje flee from the scene of the battle and come after him.

The warriors paused beside Kanje, spears raised and looked to their King. This was his half-brother, royal blood ran in Kanje's veins.

Before Jandu could give an order, Daniel said quickly, 'Spare him, Jandu. He's been discredited. His impi's defeated. He'll never pose a threat to you again.'

Jandu raised his eyes and Daniel saw in them the same frenzied excitement that was on the faces of the Matabele warriors.

'I *beg* you, Jandu, your father granted me the lives of Kanje's captives once, remember? One of them was Suliyana, your chief wife. Give me the life of your brother.'

The half-crazed look left Jandu's eyes, but the coldness that took its place was even more terrible.

'He is my brother, trader, but I am King. When I was made

King I swore to punish those who broke the laws of my people. There can be few who have broken more tribal laws than Kanje.' He pointed towards the unsighted battlefield. 'Thousands of my people are dead, more than any enemy has ever killed. They are dead because of the ambitions of Kanje, son of Mzilikazi – the father of the Matabele. Yet, had he beaten me he would have stood before the council of the Indunas and declared he so loved the Matabele that he would be their King. Yes, he is my brother, trader, but the Matabele are my children now. For their sake there can be no mercy for Kanje – kill him!'

The raised assegais came down again and again and Daniel turned his head away quickly. Minutes later Kanje was dead. The last threat to Jandu's throne had been removed.

It was a week before Daniel was permitted by Jandu to return to his home in the Insimo valley. During this time, at a crossing on the Shashi River, a minor clash occurred between Matabele impis and Boers and Daniel hurried to the scene. When he informed the Boer leader that Kanje was dead and his army destroyed, the commando leader decided that he and his men had no business to pursue in Matabeleland. Much to Daniel's relief they withdrew to the Transvaal.

One or two of Kanje's lesser Indunas had survived the battle and saw no reason to keep the secrets of the dead pretender. The Transvaal government *had* supported Kanje and they implicated Farewell Loveday in the intrigue.

Daniel felt certain the missionary-trader would be expelled from Matabeleland this time, but yet again the incredible power of Mzilikazi stretched beyond the grave and saved him. The dead King, father of the Matabele nation had made a promise to the ambitious missionary. No Matabele would dare break that promise. Besides, Jandu reasoned that Loveday would never again have the confidence of the Boers. He had urged them to annexe Matabeleland and his scheming had failed.

Another important factor now took away the immediate threat of Transvaal expansion into Matabeleland. Diamonds were discovered at Kimberley – and at the same time gold petered out in the mines of Tati. The eyes of Africa were turned to the south. Men temporarily abandoned their ambitions in the lands of the Matabele and headed for the more tangible fortunes to be found in the blue clay of Kimberley.

One man, however, thought he had discovered his Eldorado where others had failed. That man was Doctor Kurt Henkel.

Daniel returned from Khami armed with the knowledge that he was in a stronger position than ever before. Farewell Loveday was to remain in Matabeleland – but as a missionary only. The right to trade had been taken from him. Retallick and Copping was once more the only trading company operating in Matabeleland – and he had Insimo.

After the bloody battle between Jandu and Kanje, Daniel had sent a message of reassurance to Elvira, but as Jandu's impis scoured the countryside in search of Kanje supporters, the hills of Matabeleland echoed to rumour and counter-rumour. Elvira's relief at having Daniel home again threatened to overwhelm him.

In answer to Daniel's question about Philippe, Elvira told him that the wounded man had lost his leg. Doctor Henkel had been forced to amputate it just below the knee. Daniel winced at the thought of what such a loss would mean to a man like Philippe, who had spent such an active life in the saddle.

Daniel went to visit Philippe at the earliest opportunity and found Victoria in the room with him. Much to Daniel's surprise, Philippe did not share his misgivings about the loss of his limb.

'No one need feel sorry for me,' he insisted. 'Thanks to you and Victoria I am here. To give up now would mean that you both risked your own lives for nothing. No, I shall do all the things I did before.' He gave Daniel a pain-filled grin. 'Perhaps I'll be slower, but that is all. Once, at Quelimane, I saw a sailor with a wooden leg. He was the mate of a ship trading between India and Portugal. He boasted he could do anything any other man could do – and do most of them better. I'll be the same, I promise you.'

'I believe you,' said Daniel. 'But where will you go?'

Philippe looked to where Victoria stood at the foot of his bed, holding a thumb-sucking daughter. 'We'll find somewhere.'

'My only trading rival in Matabeleland has just gone out of

business,' said Daniel, as though thinking of the idea for the first time. 'I'm going to be busier than ever before. I'll need someone to run things in this valley while I'm away. Do you think you could take it on?'

Victoria looked at Daniel in delighted disbelief, then her expression underwent a change. 'You're forgetting ... Philippe carried off those Kalanga tribesmen. If Jandu learns Philippe is in Matabeleland he'll have him put to death.'

'Jandu knows. Philippe made amends when he ran across Kanje's men and I was able to warn Jandu. My offer stands if Philippe's up to it – and providing he can remember the Matabele are friends, not enemies.'

'I'll remember. You won't regret your kindness.' Philippe grimaced. In his excitement he had changed position and knocked the stump of his leg.

'When you're well and are learning to walk we'll talk about this again. Now, where's that German doctor? I want to have a word with him.'

One of the herd-boys told Daniel with a smile that Henkel had been seen heading along the valley to the east soon after breakfast. The Matabele thought the German doctor mad because he was in the habit of wandering along the valley and up the hillsides, tapping the rocks with a little hammer. Daniel was less amused. Before leaving Khami he had learned that Kurt Henkel was more than a doctor of medicine and a keen hunter. The German was a renowned geologist – and his African travels were being financed by a London mining company.

Daniel intended bringing Henkel back to the house and sending him on his way to Khami before he found what he was seeking – but Daniel was already too late. He found the doctor on the bank of the stream where Daniel knew there was gold. Kurt Henkel was on his knees, hammering a stake into the ground. In the stake were carved the German's initials.

'What do you think you're doing?' Daniel asked, angrily.

Henkel was taken by surprise by Daniel's sudden appearance, but he faced him defiantly. 'I am staking a claim for this area. You will find a stake with my initials at each corner of the area I am claiming . . . Stop! You cannot do this . . . .'

Henkel shouted in dismay as Daniel pulled the nearest stake

from the ground and tossed it into the stream, where it was quickly carried away by the tumbling water. Complaining bitterly, he trotted behind Daniel as he located three more stakes and treated them in a similar manner.

'. . . I have staked my claim in a manner that is internationally recognised. Certainly it is accepted by the government of Transvaal – and I hold a prospecting permit from them.'

Daniel rounded on Henkel. 'What has Transvaal to do with Matabeleland?'

Henkel looked genuinely surprised. 'They have jurisdiction here, no? Soon they will occupy the land and appoint an administrator. Herr Loveday told this to me. He is a man of God, he would not lie—'

Daniel snorted. 'The Reverend Loveday's God has little more influence in these parts than the Transvaal government. Jandu rules this land – all of it. He gave me this valley. As far as I'm concerned that includes mineral rights – and every other right. If you don't agree I'll take you along to Khami and you can argue points of law with Jandu. If you're lucky he'll do no more than send you packing. In the meantime you can empty your pockets and give me any gold you've already found.'

When it became clear to Henkel that his protests were in vain, he handed over two small nuggets. Then he tried to reason with Daniel, promising to make him a rich man if he would join forces with the London mining company and persuade Jandu to allow them into Matabeleland.

Daniel looked at the German pityingly. 'Look around you, Henkel. All the land you see belongs to me. I have cattle, maize – and a house in the most beautiful setting in Africa. What more do you think you can give to me?'

Picking up a small knapsack containing Henkel's geological tools, Daniel swung it through the air to the doctor. 'You're still free to wander as you wish in my valley – but in future one of my herd-boys will be with you. As soon as Victoria is able to cope with Philippe I'll have you escorted to the Transvaal border. If you've got any sense you'll forget everything you've found here. Jandu will never allow miners to enter his country. Any who do get past him will be shot the moment they set foot in my valley.'

In September 1870, it seemed the prospects for peace in Matabeleland had never been better. The territorial ambitions of the Transvaal Republic had been thwarted and they would never again be in a strong enough position to invade Matabeleland. Indeed, so chaotic did the situation become in the sparsely populated Boer Republic, that Transvaal was itself annexed by Great Britain in 1877.

Jandu, hailed by his people as 'the scatterer of his enemies' took the accolade as his royal name, thus fulfilling yet another of the prophesies of the White Mondoro. 'The Scatterer', or 'Lobengula' as he will hereafter be called, was so distressed by the wholesale slaughter of the flower of Matabele manhood, that he moved his capital to the place of the great battle and named it 'Bulawayo' – 'the place of the killing'. Those who came after thought the name had been given in pride. Only Daniel knew that his capital had been so-called because it was here that the heart of Jandu died and Lobengula, the scatterer of his own people, was born.

But even as the labour pains of the Matabele people gave birth to Lobengula and a new and hopeful reign began, the final chapter in the story of their nation had already begun. On the first day of September, in that same fateful year, a sickly youth of seventeen years stepped from the gangway of the sailing-ship *Endora* to the dockside at Durban, port for Natal. This was the homeland of the Zulus and birthplace of Mzilikazi, first King of the Matabele.

The delicate young man was the fifth child in an English vicar's family of eleven children. Because of his status, his pile of worldly possessions took up very little space on the stone paved dockside. Those who noticed him observed his unhealthy pallor and shook their heads, declaring he would never survive the rigours of African life.

Yet, in a few whirlwind years, this same youth would become a diamond millionaire, be elected Prime Minister of the Cape Colony and redraw the map of Africa. His grandiose dreams of empire would allow no room for a tribal kingdom – such an anachronism needed to be put where it belonged: within the pages of the history books.

This then was the man. His name – Cecil John Rhodes.

BOOK TWO

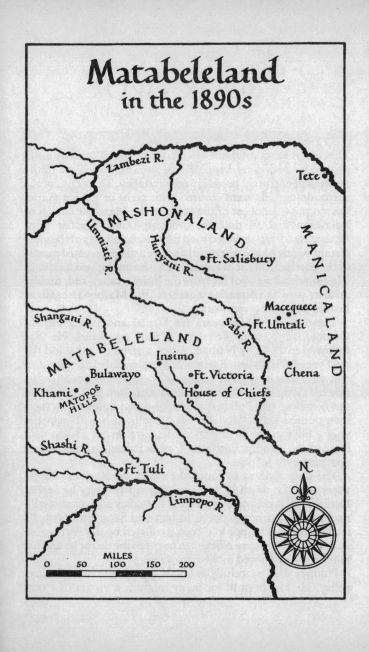

The early years of Lobengula's reign brought expansion, prosperity and great happiness to the Insimo valley. Cattle multiplied and great herds grazed the valley. The slopes of the surrounding hills were covered with acres of golden maize. Insimo provided most of the food for the Matabele capital of Bulawayo and, in times of drought, Daniel's maize went further afield. He provided food for the inhabitants of the most distant kraals of Matabeleland and even the persecuted people of the parched hills of Mashonaland. The unmapped border of Mashonaland was not far from the Insimo valley and, timidly at first, then in increasing numbers, the Mashonas came to Insimo and were given work.

These were fruitful years for Daniel and Elvira too. In October 1877, their first son, Wyatt, was born. He was followed in 1880 by Nathan. Adam arrived in 1883 and the next year a fourth son, Benjamin, completed their family.

It gave Daniel a great feeling of pride and achievement to ride off along the valley with young Benjamin perched on the saddle before him, while the other children followed on their own ponies. Daniel and the Matabele herd-boys taught the young brothers to hunt and track game. From Elvira, they learned the good manners that set a Portuguese gentleman apart from his fellows.

The only sadness to touch the valley during these happy years was the death of Philippe. For many years he served Daniel well, taking care of things in the valley and occasionally making the journey between Insimo and Sena with Daniel's trade wagons. Philippe had been pardoned by the Portuguese authorities, who were relieved to be rid of the threat he and his Pombeiros had posed to them for so long.

Philippe died peacefully in his sleep, at home in the Insimo valley. He had been ill for many months, a victim of a tiny parasite that infested the slower-running rivers of Matabeleland. His death came as a hard blow to Therese. Brought up in the belief that Philippe was her true father, she adored him.

Therese had grown into a girl as attractive and vivacious as Victoria had once been. Her mother guarded her jealously, determined that her daughter would not suffer as she once had.

Lobengula's early years were good for the Matabele nation too. With no one to dispute his leadership, and absolute power in his hands, Lobengula devoted himself to the betterment of his tribe.

He ruled with restraint and wisdom. If his people never moved forward in step with the world beyond the borders of Matabeleland, they still commanded the respect they had earned with Mzilikazi as King.

Lobengula gathered many wives about him during his reign, but none of them achieved the status accorded Suliyana. She bore two sons to ensure the succession of her children to the throne of Matabeleland. The eldest, Nyamatakah, was born in the year his father became King. The second, Lundi, arrived within a week of Wyatt Retallick. The two boys became firm friends from the moment they learned to toddle together. Both were happy to spend days in the home of the other and Lundi so impressed his father with talk of life in the Retallick household that Lobengula had a house built of stone for himself.

Farewell Loveday remained in Matabeleland and still lived with his wife and their many children in the neglected and seedy old mission of Khami. It had become the rendezvous of the gradually expanding group of hunters and concession seekers who found their way to Matabeleland. These seekers and hunters came from many countries. Some had ridden 'up-country' from the Cape Colony. A few had travelled from Britain and Australia. Many had merely waded across the muddy river that separated Matabeleland and Transvaal.

The concession seekers, ridden by greed and uncertainty, were a squabbling, suspicious, constantly changing community, but, unlike Mzilikazi, Lobengula at first seemed to enjoy having white men about him. He took their presents and accepted their flattery, giving very little in return.

In time, Lobengula also grew very fond of the white mens'

drink. Brandy, gin – even crates of champagne found their way to his stone-built house.

During his often prolonged bouts of drinking, Lobengula's benevolence occasionally exceeded caution. An increasing number of unscrupulous white men staggered from Lobengula's presence in a woefully drunken state – but happy in the knowledge that they had obtained mumbled permission to explore his lands.

Eventually, in spite of all that Daniel tried to do to prevent it happening, heavy drinking took its toll on Lobengula's health, just as it had with his father. The fit, athletic warrior that had been Jandu, gave way to the gross, overweight man who was King. Daniel's concern occasionally resulted in Lobengula giving up heavy drinking for days – sometimes weeks, but as soon as Daniel left Bulawayo, the King was persuaded to return to his habits.

As his mental and physical state deteriorated, so Lobengula emulated Mzilikazi by adopting more and more of his excesses. His impis extended the range of their raids and undertook expeditions against the warlike Barotse, across the Zambezi River. They also continued to raid the unfortunate Mashonas, pursuing both with great ferocity.

By the middle 1880s there were equally bloody happenings at home. The scheming Indunas frequently manoeuvred their King into situations which resulted in the deaths of many of his closest friends and advisers, leaving Lobengula a lonely and suspicious man.

Farewell Loveday had become reconciled with the mission authorities and reported all these happenings to the mission headquarters in London, his reports being seized upon and avidly repeated in the newspapers throughout Great Britain. Laymen, arrogant with the power of Britain's greatness, advocated sending an army to put an end to Lobengula's bloody reign. In cathedrals, churches and chapels, men of God prayed that the Lord might send someone to carry the candle of enlightenment to the Matabele.

Unknown to them all, such a redeemer was already on the scene. One who would make a great impact on Southern Africa and change history in a manner to leave even the empire-building Victorians breathless with admiration. A man whom Daniel's instincts recognised as more of a threat to the Matabele way of life than all the concession seekers and renegades who warmed their hands at Lobengula's fire.

Cecil Rhodes was no longer the sickly young man he had been in 1870. Working in the new diamond diggings at Kimberley and financing his efforts by making and selling home-made ice-cream, Rhodes' determination and hard work paid off when Luck threw in her elusive lot with him. The toiling miners of Kimberley struck hard, blue bed-rock. Convinced that their claims had 'bottomed-out', they were happy to sell them off for the price of their fares home. For sums ranging from fifty to one hundred and fifty pounds, they unloaded them on the foolish young man who was mortgaging his future to his own intuition.

When Rhodes owned almost the whole of the Kimberley claims, he brought in his own experts. They announced that the 'bed-rock' was in fact blue, diamond-bearing clay. Soon afterwards the rains arrived and confirmed their diagnosis. The 'rock' became a soft, squelching putty that yielded a fabulous crop of diamonds.

Rhodes reaped a vast fortune from Kimberley – then went on to accumulate another in the gold fields of Witwatersrand. Now a multi-millionaire, the youthful Rhodes used his money to buy a seat in the Cape parliament – and immediately embarked upon a remarkable plan to expand the British Empire.

Within a few years, in a successful bid to thwart similar expansion plans made by the Transvaal Republic, Rhodes had engineered the annexation of half of Bechuanaland to the Cape Colony, proclaiming the remainder a British Protectorate.

A few years later, this remarkable man had Transvaal itself annexed by the Crown. This proved too much for the undisciplined Boers. Temporarily putting aside their own differences, they united to inflict a humiliating defeat on the British army and, in 1881, took back their land.

The Boers had set back Rhodes' dream of Empire, but his eyes were already upon the vast lands extending for mile upon fertile mile to the north. Rhodes realised he was involved in a race against time. The territory over which Lobengula held sovereignty was being squeezed unmercifully by larger and more ambitious nations. Portugal, Transvaal and the Germans, newly-arrived in South West Africa, were poised to take advantage of a savage and unsophisticated ruler.

Cecil Rhodes knew the time had arrived to take the initiative. In so doing he would change the lives of hundreds of thousands of men. Among them would be Lobengula – and Daniel Retallick.

CHAPTER ONE

In 1887, Daniel still owned the only trading company of any note in Matabeleland, but maintaining his monopoly had become increasingly difficult. Trade through Mozambique had slowed to a trickle, due to the current hostility of the Portuguese government towards all things British.

Southern Africa became jittery as it became apparent to everyone that the stage was being set for a showdown between the countries jostling for colonial expansion north of the Limpopo River.

At the moment, Great Britain would appear to be the favourite to gain the rich prize. They had already pushed their influence to the Matabeleland border, standing shoulder to shoulder there with the more militant, but far less organised, Boer Republic of Transvaal.

Portugal, historically the country with the soundest claim to the coveted lands, could do little more than stand on the sidelines, complaining impotently, her government and army in disarray. Nevertheless, the Portuguese authorities in Mozambique were able to make it very difficult for a non-Portuguese trader to bring his goods through their country. Only the powerful influence of Senhor Farrao kept the door to the Indian Ocean ajar for Daniel.

Fortunately, Daniel was able to open up a route to the sea through Transvaal, thanks to the efforts of a Boer named Uiys Toblin. Quietly spoken and sincere, Toblin was a trader and part-time hunter who had been allowed by Lobengula to shoot lion in Matabeleland for many seasons. When Toblin offered to put his resources in Transvaal at their disposal, in return for a share of the Matabele market, Daniel and Aaron were quick to agree. The arrangement worked very well, but the government of Transvaal refused to allow the partners to trade in the one commodity that Lobengula desperately wanted. Guns.

Two years before, Lobengula's impis had suffered their first defeat since the early days of Mzilikazi's flight from Shaka. It happened in humiliating circumstances. On an annual raid in neighbouring Bechuanaland, they attacked an inferior number of Bechuana tribesmen, only to discover they were a part of the Bechuana King's army armed with modern rifles, supplied by the British. The defeat of the Matabele impi was decisive, very few warriors escaping to tell Lobengula of the debacle.

Lobengula realised, there and then, that his warriors had to have the white mens' weapons if his tribe were to survive. He asked Daniel for his help, but the numbers that Senhor Farrao was able to obtain were hardly enough to equip Lobengula's personal bodyguard, let alone the forty other impis stationed about his kingdom.

The problem had not been resolved when Toblin brought his family to the Insimo valley early in 1887, to spend some months with Daniel and Elvira. The visit provided a wonderful interlude for Elvira who was always grateful for female company – but the visit was not without its problems.

One evening, Daniel came in early from the valley where he had been supervising the breaking-in of a number of young colts from his own horse herd. Sitting on the verandah he was enjoying a drink with Uiys Toblin and Jaconus Van Eyck, a grizzled old hunter employed by Toblin. With Van Eyck's son Jannie, the men had been on a number of successful hunting trips in recent days. Suddenly, Daniel saw a grim-faced Victoria heading for the house, leading her tearful and reluctant daughter, Therese, by the hand.

The years had mellowed Victoria – but not much. On many occasions, especially when she was angry, she showed the spirit of the younger Victoria ... and she was angry now. Without a word of greeting, she strode on to the verandah and glared around her. Then, ignoring Daniel, she addressed her words to Jaconus Van Eyck.

'Where is he? It's no use trying to hide him from me. If I have to search for him I might have a gun in my hand when I catch up with him. If I do, I'll shoot him . . . .'

'Victoria, calm down! No one has the faintest idea what you're talking about. Where's who? Who are we supposed to be hiding?'

Victoria turned to Daniel and some of her anger died away. 'I'm sorry, Daniel. I had no right to come here like this.' She swung her attention back to Van Eyck. 'But he knows what I'm talking about. Ask him where his son is.'

Daniel began to understand. Therese was a very pretty eighteen-year-old with dark eyes and the vivacious ways of her mother. Van Eyck's son was of a similar age. A quiet, well-mannered boy. A good-looking boy . . . .

'I know where my Jannie is – but I'll not tell you while you're in your present mood. I suggest you control yourself, tell me what's happened. Then you and I will go and speak to him together.'

Almost as softly-spoken as Uiys Toblin, Jaconus Van Eyck's manner was mild, but his manner was deceptive. The hunter, now in his fifties, was a veteran of the Zulu wars in Natal. As a boy, he had survived an attack by Shaka's army on a Boer laager. He was a man whose courage needed bolstering by no bluster.

Victoria thrust Therese forward. 'Ask her what's happened. Perhaps she'll tell you more than she'll admit to me. What I do know is that she's been sneaking out of the house at night to see your son, when I thought she was in bed. I got the truth only today, after I overheard one of the Matabele herd-boys telling another that he'd seen Therese batheing in a pool up on the hill – with your son! I want to know what's going on. I know how the Boers treat coloured women – and I'm not having my daughter talked about by herd-boys. Neither do I intend being left with some Boer's bastard to look after, while he rides away scot-free.'

Jaconus Van Eyck looked seriously at the girl. 'Is there any likelihood that you're with child by Jannie?'

'No!' Therese's denial was emphatic and she looked at her mother in great distress. 'We've done nothing like that. I love Jannie, yes – and I think he loves me, but we've never done that together. Never—.' Suddenly she broke down and began sobbing. Daniel felt very sorry for the young girl having to endure such a humiliating ordeal.

'Love!' Victoria spat the word at her daughter. 'You're coloured. The daughter of a Pombeiro. A half-caste. Your precious Jannie is a Boer. Do you think it's *love* he feels for you? No, girl. You've led a sheltered life here. You've never been out of the valley . . . to the places where white men gather.

I have. *I'll* tell you about the 'love' you'll find with a Boer—'

Ignoring Victoria's outburst, Jaconus Van Eyck walked to
Therese. Putting a finger beneath her chin, he gently brought
her head up, forcing her to look at him.

'You say you think my Jannie loves you. Has he said so?'

As Van Eyck's finger dropped away from her chin, she
nodded vigorously. 'Yes.' It came out as a defiant whisper.

Jaconus Van Eyck smiled wistfully. 'Then you can be certain
you have the love of a very fine young man. Jannie doesn't lie.'
Turning to Daniel, he said. 'Perhaps you will give Victoria a
drink. I have a story I would like her to hear. It is something I
would like you all to hear.'

Daniel poured a drink and handed it to Victoria. When she
hesitated, Daniel said, 'Take it and sit down, for goodness sake
– and stop playing the angry mother. Therese, you sit down
too. I'll pour you a brandy. You look as though you have need
of it.'

Reluctantly, Victoria sat down and the tearful Therese took
the seat beside her.

Jaconus Van Eyck turned away from the others. As they
waited, he looked out at the magnificent view that had first
attracted Daniel to Insimo. For some minutes he stood with his
back to them. Then he turned round and sighed, 'You know,
this place reminds me of a valley I once found in the
Drakensberg mountains. I had hopes of building a home there,
one day. A home just like this . . . for Jannie's mother.'

A faraway look came into his eyes, but he shrugged it away
and addressed his story to Therese.

'What I am going to tell you now is a story that only a few
men know. Uiys is one, because he's more of a friend to me
than any other man has ever been. Many years ago – more than
twenty, I was riding northwards through the Transvaal, on
my way from Natal to Matabeleland. I'd been hunting and was
well away from any track or homestead. Riding through a
valley I suddenly came across a covered wagon, outspanned
beneath some trees. Nearby was a cow, a dog . . . and children.
Ja! There were many children. Naturally, I rode over to pay my
respects to whoever was living in this out-of-the-way place. I
was met by a musket, held in the hands of a very determined
woman. She told me in no uncertain terms that her husband

didn't welcome strangers. That I'd best be well clear of the valley before his return. I didn't believe her. The whole place had that look that a home . . . any home, gets when there's no man about to do all the odd-jobs a woman just can't tackle.'

Jaconus Van Eyck smiled, and there was a pensive look in his eyes as he paused to light his pipe. Blowing blue, aromatic smoke high in the air, he continued, 'I can picture the whole scene as though it all happened only yesterday. The valley, midsummer dry and parched. The tethered cow, with more ribs than meat on its body . . . and the woman. Holding out that flintlock musket, she was scared to hell-and-gone, but was determined not to show it. Behind her, peering around the edge of the wagon were wide-eyed kids . . . so many I couldn't be sure whether I'd counted six, or seven. There was a baby too, crawling in the dirt around a broken wagon wheel.'

Jaconus Van Eyck shrugged his shoulders and sucked noisily on his pipe. 'I wasn't going to stay where I wasn't wanted. Whether she had a man or not was none of my business. I rode off.'

Elvira and Mrs Toblin had come from the house in time to hear the beginning of Van Eyck's story. Elvira was standing by Daniel and her hand found his as the Boer hunter re-lived his memories.

'Yes, I rode off and left them. Didn't even look back until I was half-a-mile away. Then I saw them all lined up, watching me go. The woman, a babe in her arms, and six young 'uns – all girls, standing around her. It's hard to describe the way I felt then. I'd been ordered out of the valley at gunpoint . . . yet I couldn't get rid of the feeling I was letting them down. Running away. Try as I might, that little family group wouldn't leave my mind.

'That afternoon I shot an impala. It wasn't a huge one, no more than a hundred pounds, but I'd only eat a fraction of it. The rest would be wasted. I thought of that family yet again . . . .

'When I got back to the wagon the woman had put away her gun and the youngest of the girls waved. I knew that whatever might be said, they were happy to see me again. Man, it was almost like a homecoming.

'I said to the woman, "I know your husband doesn't like

strangers around, but I shot this impala and it's too big for me."

'She looked me straight in the eye and said, "I didn't fool you. You know there's no man about the place. He got himself trampled by a rhino six months ago. He's buried beneath that tree over there. I suppose that's the only reason we've stayed here – not that we've anywhere else to go."

'I could see that she'd had enough. What with the children, and no man. I've never known what to do when a woman is close to tears, so I just let the impala slide to the ground and turned my horse to leave. She called me back. Told me the least she could do was to cook me a meal.'

Jaconus Van Eyck took the pipe from his mouth and made a loud noise of appreciation with his tongue. 'Man, that was a meal! With all due respect to your own fine cooking, Mrs Retallick, it was a meal such as I'd never tasted before. I sat beside that fire, with the stars overhead, surrounded by six little girls who looked at me as though I were some kind of god, and the baby – it was a girl too – gurgling in its mother's arms. I swear I was as happy as though they were my own.'

Van Eyck's pipe had gone out. Sucking at it absent-mindedly, he pulled a wry face, spat over the side of the verandah and knocked the ashes from it. He began to refill the pipe slowly, completely engrossed in his memories.

'What happened then?' Elvira prompted. 'After you had finished your meal?'

Jaconus Van Eyck delayed the reply until his pipe was crackling comfortably again. 'I never left them. I stayed around and repaired everything that needed fixing. Then I went off and bought some trek-oxen and we headed north west, looking for a place where we could settle. We searched for nigh on three years. Then I remembered the valley I told you about earlier. The one in the Drakensbergs. I turned the wagon in that direction – but we never made it. Funny, really. Martha had produced seven strapping daughters for her first husband, all born with no trouble. Then she ups and dies giving birth to a scrawny little boy who couldn't have weighed no more than five pounds. That was my Jannie.'

'Oh Jaconus! I'm so sorry,' Elvira was close to tears. 'But . . . but what happened to the girls?'

'I brought 'em up myself. Just as Martha would have done. Got them all married off too, choosing husbands that Martha would have been proud of. They were no trouble, and they helped me as though I were their real father. They were good girls. It was Jannie who was the difficult one, in those early days. He would have died if I hadn't met up with a family of Bushmen. One of the women had milk and while I shot meat for the family she breast-fed Jannie. He survived to become a son that any man might be proud to have.'

The long silence that followed Jaconus Van Eyck's moving narrative was broken by Victoria. 'I'm sorry about your wife . . . but it has nothing to do with what's been going on between your boy and Therese.'

Jaconus Van Eyck removed the pipe from his mouth and jabbed it in Victoria's direction. 'It has *everything* to do with it. Martha was coloured. Her father was a Boer, but her mother was half-English, half-Bechuana. It never bothered me, and it never troubled her first husband. Neither did it cause any difficulty for any of Martha's seven daughters. Two of them married coloured men, the other five married Boers and made very good wives. So, now that's out of the way we can decide what we're going to do about our two children. If you still want to run Jannie out of the Insimo valley, I'll take him. Not because he's done anything wrong, but because I'm a guest here and I'll cause no trouble for Daniel and Mrs Retallick."

The pipe went back in Van Eyck's mouth and he spoke around it. 'On the other hand, if we're talking about your daughter's happiness and not your own pride we'd do better if I fetched Jannie and came to your house to discuss things there. Therese is a fine girl. I'd be proud to have her as my son's wife.'

Therese switched her gaze from Van Eyck to her mother and there was such pleading in her eyes that Elvira's heart went out to her.

Victoria stood up and, for a moment, Therese's hopes plummeted as she avoided looking at her. Then Victoria spoke to Jaconus Van Eyck in a strangely gruff voice. 'I'll be getting back to the house. We'll expect you and Jannie when you find him.'

The young couple wanted to marry immediately, but were

persuaded to wait for a few months. During this time Jannie was to remain at Insimo and build a cabin for his young bride-to-be. Once they were married, Daniel would employ Jannie to hunt game to feed the large numbers of Matabele and Mashona tribesmen who now worked in the valley.

Jaconus Van Eyck took his son to Bulawayo to discuss the wedding with the missionaries there and, much to Daniel's surprise, returned accompanied by Farewell Loveday.

Rumour about Lobengula's capital had it that Loveday was now a Rhodes man, but such a label meant nothing to the Matabele. Farewell Loveday, with his own almost eccentric blend of spiritual mysticism, coupled with sound business acumen, appealed to them. His acceptance by the tribe was matched only by Daniel's own.

It did not take Daniel long to learn that the rumours connecting the missionary with Rhodes were true. On the second evening of his visit, Farewell Loveday asked Daniel to ride with him to the brow of the hill at the back of the house. He claimed he wanted to witness a true, Insimo sunset.

Daniel took Loveday to one of the highest peaks for many miles around. From here there was a superb view along the valley to the lowlands, and over the broken hills to the north and west.

Farewell Loveday sat his horse, gazing about him with undisguised admiration. 'You are a fortunate man to live surrounded by so much God-given beauty, Daniel.'

'I think so,' Daniel agreed. He mistrusted Loveday – and believed this evening excursion was concerned with something more than the beauty of Insimo.

'Of course you do,' said Loveday, unctiously. 'But God created all this to be enjoyed by more than a mere handful of people.'

'The Matabele enjoy it. Lobengula himself agrees that it's one of the loveliest spots in his land.'

Daniel was being deliberately obtuse, waiting for Loveday to show his hand.

'The Matabele are heathens – and likely to remain so until we have enough good Christians in the country to teach them by example.'

Daniel snorted. 'They witness Christian example every day

in their own capital among the concession-seekers and jail-sweepings there. Their quarrelling, lying and whoring is notorious throughout southern Africa. I believe one of them recently brought the pox to Matabeleland and infected the women in Bulawayo. Is this the "example" you want to teach?'

Farewell Loveday flushed. 'All the more reason for civilisation to reach this country quickly and remind white men of their responsibilities. I talked to Mr Rhodes when I was in Kimberley, recently. He agrees with me.'

Daniel knew he was about to learn the real reason for Farewell Loveday's visit, and his willingness to come to Insimo to conduct the wedding ceremony for Jannie Van Eyck and Therese.

'I've heard a great deal about Mr Rhodes' plans,' he retorted. But Christian education for the natives has never been mentioned.'

'I don't know what you've heard, but I assure you that Mr Rhodes is a great man – and a great Christian. He is also an ambitious businessman.'

Farewell Loveday leaned closer to Daniel and lowered his voice as though someone might be listening in the vast emptiness about them. 'Rhodes wants to extend his influence north of the Limpopo. Not here, in Matabeleland – but in Mashonaland. He realises it would be most difficult for white men to live in peace under Lobengula's direct rule, so he's chosen Mashonaland. It's far enough from Lobengula's warriors to avoid trouble, but close enough for the Matabele to see for themselves the advantages of a well-run, Christian society.'

'Why Mashonaland? What's there for him?'

Behaving once more as though they might be overheard, Farewell Loveday said quickly. 'Gold. There's gold in Mashonaland.'

Daniel shrugged. 'Perhaps. But there's been little except rumour, so far.' He looked sharply at the other man. 'Why are you telling this to me?'

'Because between us you and I might change the course of Matabele history. The Indunas listen to me – but you are Lobengula's friend. He trusts you. If *you* suggest that Rhodes be given the sole concession to prospect and mine in Mashonaland I have no doubt it would be granted . . . . No, before you reject such a suggestion, hear me out. Rhodes isn't the only one after such a concession, as you must know. I'm not talking only of individuals who camp about Bulawayo. There is a great deal happening at international level. Transvaal trekkers are massing on the south bank of the Limpopo River. President Kruger is having difficulty preventing them from crossing and invading Lobengula's territory – if indeed Kruger *wants* to hold them back. The Portuguese have recently issued a map on which all of Mashonaland is shown as belonging to them . . . and much of Matabeleland too. In the north the Germans have pressed their claims as far as the border of Angola and are now disputing the Bechuana border with Great Britain. Very soon Lobengula will be forced to make a treaty with someone. His only choice will be . . . with whom? I suggest Rhodes is the obvious choice. I know him well and have always found him to be scrupulously fair. I would also point out that he has the might of Great Britain behind him.'

Daniel remained silent. Unpalatable though it was to him, much of what Farewell Loveday said made sense. He knew, as did Lobengula, that irresistible forces were building up about the borders of Matabeleland, squeezing the country ever tighter. Nevertheless, Daniel did not believe that Farewell Loveday had told him the whole truth about Rhodes' intentions.

'I'll give it some thought, but Lobengula doesn't like being forced into a corner any more than I do.'

'Nobody is *forcing* anyone anywhere,' purred Farewell Loveday, convinced his argument had won Daniel over to his side. 'I'm merely asking you to point out the facts to the King. You'll need money, perhaps, to win him over. With this in mind, Mr Rhodes has authorised me to put the sum of ten thousand pounds at your disposal, to do with as you will. I think you'll agree that he's being most generous . . . ?'

'Rhodes can keep his money,' retorted Daniel, angrily. 'I haven't said I'll help him – or anyone else, yet. You've given me something to think about, true – but that's all. When I reach a decision it will be in the best interest of the Matabele. Now, if you've had enough of the sunset, I suggest we return to the house and rejoin the others.'

Without waiting for a reply, Daniel reined his horse about and began the steep descent to the house.

CHAPTER TWO

Farewell Loveday returned to Khami without winning Daniel to his side, but after his departure Daniel thought long and hard about his words. He accepted that Lobengula might well be forced to give someone a concession, in order to safeguard the future of his country, but Daniel did not accept that Cecil Rhodes was the right man. True, Rhodes was one of the most influential men in southern Africa. He was also the richest. A member of the Cape parliament, it was hinted he would soon take over that country's premiership. But Cape Colony was a long way from Matabeleland. Other countries, Mozambique, Transvaal – and perhaps the Germans in South West Africa, were all within striking distance of Matabeleland.

Daniel felt Mozambique could be ruled out. The Pombeiros were active again. The Portuguese could not spare an army to occupy the interior. Daniel was less certain about the Germans in South West Africa, but from all he had heard they were fully occupied in their new colonial territory and were unlikely to risk losing all they had gained by taking on Lobengula and the Matabele nation.

This left only the Boer Republic of Transvaal – and Daniel admitted that it posed the greatest threat of all. Having recently regained their independence by defeating a British army at Majuba, the Boers would not hesitate to tackle the Matabele impis, no matter how awesome their reputation. Furthermore, the Boers suffered the same fears as Lobengula. That of being strangled out of existence by potentially hostile nations. For this reason alone they were unlikely to stand by and allow Lobengula to sign a treaty with any of the other parties.

Daniel gave the matter a great deal of thought before seeking Uiys Toblin and telling him of Farewell Loveday's proposition.

Toblin's initial reaction was cautious. 'Do you think Loveday really is Rhodes' emissary? Or is he trying to pull off a coup that he can sell to Rhodes, leaving the other concession hunters to go home and count their losses?'

'I believe he's Rhodes' man,' declared Daniel. 'To be charitable to him, I'm also convinced that Farewell Loveday believes the Church will gain by such a concession.'

Uiys Toblin snorted cynically. 'They might . . . but only if there's a long-term profit in it for Rhodes.' He looked at Daniel quizzically, from under lowered eyebrows. 'Why are you telling this to me? You must know that if I return to Transvaal and tell Paul Kruger what's in the wind he'll likely as not send his trekkers across the river – then send a Boer army to their aid if Lobengula attacks them. Kruger is a great believer in possession being nine-tenths of the law, Daniel. Even Rhodes would think twice about bringing an army this far up-country to dispossess him.'

'That's true, but it's a risk that has to be taken. I'm gambling on the fact that the Transvaal can ill afford a war at the moment. Kruger has as much land as can comfortably be administered and he's won a period of breathing space from the British. I'm certain he will forgo expansion for a treaty guaranteeing an independent but friendly country on his northern border – for a while, anyway.'

'If you can give him such a treaty I would agree with you – but why should you do this? You're English. Why should you throw in your lot with us Boers?'

'I have an English name, Uiys, but I've lived all my life in Africa and look upon the tribes as my people. I've carved out a good life for myself, here at Insimo. That life is secure only for as long as Lobengula and his heirs rule their own country. I don't trust Rhodes. I want things to remain exactly as they are. I believe this is the best way of ensuring they do.'

Uiys Toblin nodded. 'Perhaps. But will Lobengula agree to such a treaty?'

'After I've explained it to him, yes. The concession hunters have done their best to destroy him with drink, but Lobengula is still King of the Matabele. He knows instinctively what's best for his people. He'll sign.'

'Then I'll do the same on behalf of Paul Kruger and take the treaty to the Transvaal for his approval. When are you going to put this to Lobengula?'

258

'Right away, before Rhodes comes up with another plan that we'll know nothing about. We'll leave for Bulawayo in the morning.'

'Before we go I'll send Jaconus home to the Transvaal with my family. This treaty could stir up trouble with the concession hunters. I'd like my family well out of the way . . . just in case.'

Daniel agreed. As he had told Farewell Loveday, many of the so-called 'concession seekers' were, in reality, no more than fugitives from justice. They had found a safe and unexpected refuge from the law in Matabeleland. Few of them had any real interest in gaining entry to the interior of Matabeleland, or Mashonaland. They were quite content to remain at Lobengula's kraal, praising the King and enjoying the generosity of the unattached Matabele women. Any treaty concluded with one of the major powers would certainly contain a clause appertaining to the apprehension of fugitive criminals. For many it would amount to a death sentence. They would go to great lengths to prevent such a treaty being agreed.

As Daniel and Uiys Toblin approached Bulawayo it became increasingly apparent that all was not well. The Matabele capital was buzzing with excitement. Indunas hurried to and from the Royal Kraal, while armed impis trotted off in every direction.

With the two men were Wyatt, Daniel's ten-year-old son, and Lundi, second son of Lobengula and Suliyana. Lundi was returning home after having spent some months at Insimo.

As they entered the town, Lundi dug his heels into the ribs of his pony and galloped to head off a small impi led by a young and eager Induna. Moments later, Lundi rode back to the others, an expression of deep concern on his young face.

'What's happening? Are the impis out looking for someone?' It was a calculated guess on Daniel's part. Had there been danger from an invading army, the impis would be leaving Bulawayo in strength and all heading in the same direction.

'Yes,' Lundi answered Daniel's question, dark eyes wide. 'They are searching for Gamba. He and my sister, Hlomela,

259

were found lying together in the hills. The impis have been ordered to kill him.'

Daniel gasped. The Matabele did not usually take illicit relationships between unmarried men and young girls too seriously, even when one was the daughter of the King, and the other the best known and most respected Induna in the King's army. But Hlomela had been promised as a bride to Umzeila, the Shangaan chief whose tribe extended across the far side of the Limpopo River and provided a useful buffer between the Boers and Matabele. Such a promise was as binding as the marriage itself. The amorous young couple were guilty of an act that was tantamount to adultery – and the Matabele punishment for this was . . . death.

Such a punishment inflicted upon a man of Gamba's standing was likely to cause a deep and lasting division in the Matabele nation. Gamba belonged to the small, but influential band of Matabele aristocrats, the 'abeZanzi', or 'Men from the south'. Of pure Zulu descent, their ancestors had advised and supported Mzilikazi when he broke with the Zulu nation and headed north. They were, in fact, more truly Matabele than Lobengula himself – for the King's mother had been a Swazi! Gamba's death would anger the abeZanzi and might raise again the long-forgotten issue of Kulumani, Mzilikazi's missing son. The resentment aroused could plunge the land into bloody civil war once more.

Such a situation required cool and dispassionate evaluation. Usually Lobengula excelled in handling such matters – but only if he were sober.

Leaving Wyatt to open the trading store and make Uiys Toblin comfortable, Daniel rode with Lundi to the King's kraal. Lundi was particularly concerned about Hlomela's fate. She was actually his half-sister, her mother being herself a woman of the Shangaan tribe, but Hlomela had always been closer to Lundi than any of the other children of the King. Daniel did his best to reassure the boy, although he knew Hlomela's only hope of surviving lay in the fact that she was also the favourite of Lobengula himself.

Daniel found the King pacing the long living room of his stone-built hut, issuing rapid orders to an Induna who kneeled before him, eyes averted from the face of his angry ruler.

Lobengula's eldest son, Nyamatakah, a tall, rangey youth of seventeen, stood scowling near the window. Nearby, Hlomela's mother sat on the floor, wailing noisily. A number of lesser wives were also in the room, eyes rolling nervously, afraid of showing any sympathy towards their unfortunate fellow-wife.

'Ah! You have heard the news, trader? Have you come to share the sorrow of a father whose honour means nothing to an ungrateful daughter?'

Lobengula waved his hand in an impatient gesture of dismissal and the Induna rose to his feet and backed from the room, relieved that none of the King's anger had spilled over him.

Daniel had heard the last few instructions issued to the departing Induna and he said, 'You intend making Gamba's family suffer for his indiscretion?'

'Indiscretion? It is an act of betrayal. His family will die, everyone whose blood runs in Gamba's veins. I will make Hlomela watch their deaths and she will listen to them curse her with their dying breaths. You do not agree with this?'

Daniel assumed an air of indifference. He needed to tread warily. If he upset Lobengula now there would be little likelihood of a treaty with the Boers. On the other hand, he could not allow Lobengula to make a disastrous mistake.

'It's none of my business whether I agree or not – but it's not one of your wiser decisions.'

'Not one of my—? Are you mad? The girl is promised to Umzeila, yet I now learn she is carrying Gamba's child! Very well, given the same circumstances, what would you do?'

'I'd think very carefully before I killed off Gamba's family. That's not going to bring back Gamba. Only the Boers could do that for you. He'll be travelling through their territory right now, heading for his father's people in Natal. He's quite likely to be able to whip up enough feeling there to have an army sent to Matabeleland to fight a war of revenge against you.'

Lobengula looked as though he was about to speak, but Daniel said, 'Hear me out. Such an army would have to come through Transvaal. It would anger the Boers and upset a plan I wish to discuss with you . . . but we will talk of that later.'

Daniel had the King's attention, and he continued, 'What

will you do with Hlomela when Gamba's family are all dead, kill her too? You can hardly marry her off to anyone after this. All Bulawayo is aware of her shame. The most sensible solution would be to send one of Gamba's relatives after him and bring him back ·to marry Hlomela. Let him buy off Umzeila's injured pride and pay you lobola for your daughter. You'll be able to set the bride-price as high as you wish. His family is hardly likely to quibble.'

Lobengula's anger gave way to an expression of scowling concentration. Suddenly he smiled and flung an arm about Daniel's shoulders. 'Days spent working the land in your valley have not dulled the trader in you, my friend. Your words tell me this. Whatever befalls, be it good or bad, it must be made to yield a profit. Very well, I will take your advice.'

Lobengula turned to his eldest son who had heard all that had been said in the room. 'Tell the Indunas there are to be no killings. Then send orders for my impis to return – and take these women out with you.' Lobengula waved his wives away impatiently as Hlomela's mother crawled to his feet and began showering kisses upon them.

As they went, Lobengula smiled at Daniel. 'Gamba will need to call on the generosity of all his family if he is to meet the bride-price I shall ask for Hlomela.'

Nyamatakah left the room without a word, but his eyes betrayed the burning humiliation he felt. His father, King of the Matabele, had allowed a white man to alter an important decision that concerned tribal custom. Nyamatakah found it humiliating. He shared the views of the young warriors of the Matabele impis that all white men must be made to respect the authority of the King. If they did not they should be driven from the land. No one, not even an elder son, would question a decision made by the King. One day he, Nyamatakah, would rule the Matabele. He vowed that things would be different then.

Daniel had seen Nyamatakah's eyes as he turned away. 'Your son grows tall, Inkosi. One day soon he will command an impi.'

Lobengula snorted, but the derision was allied to a father's pride. 'Oh yes, he will be an Induna, but to be a King he must learn to see further than the tip of a spear. I hope he will have the wisdom to keep his brother, Lundi, close by him at all times. That boy is a thinker.'

'I came to Bulawayo today to return Lundi to his family . . . but there is another reason why I am here. I would like to talk to you of a treaty, Inkosi.' Daniel used the Matabele word for 'Great Chief', the closest word they had for 'King'.

'You too? I am surrounded by white men who want treaties . . . concessions, call them what you will. They are as persistent as flies about a sick cow. Everywhere I turn, they are there. Their clamour threatens to deafen me. Am I to hear it from you too now?'

'I'm not seeking a concession. My heart is with the Matabele. I believe the treaty I have in mind is in the best interests of your people. Let me tell you my thoughts.'

For a full hour Daniel sat with the King and told him why he thought a treaty between the Boers and the Matabele would be advantageous to Lobengula and his people. Lobengula asked a number of questions, but none that Daniel had not asked himself many times. He had the answers.

When Daniel ended, Lobengula sat for many minutes, his chin resting on his chest, saying nothing.

When he finally looked up, he said, 'You have echoed the fears I have kept locked in my heart for many years. To speak of them, even to my closest advisor, would be taken for weakness. A King must not doubt his own invincibility, or that of his army. To do so is to destroy the pride of his people. Yet you have put these thoughts into words – and offered me a solution. It may not be the right answer, my friend. I do not share your confidence in the Boers, but I accept that the Matabele have little choice. However, such a treaty cannot be made without the consent of the Council of Indunas. I will call them together and we will discuss this. Now, so much talking has made me thirsty. We will drink.'

It was dark when Daniel left Lobengula's house. As he made for the opening in the wooden stockade that surrounded the building, the slim figure of a girl slipped quietly from the shadows. Daniel halted uncertainly as she dropped to her knees and touched his feet with her forehead. Rising quickly, she whispered, 'I thank you for my life – and the lives of

Gamba and his unborn child. Your name will always be praised in our hut.'

It was Hlomela. Before Daniel could make a reply, she pushed something into his hand and ran off as quickly as she had appeared.

When he reached the store Daniel paused in the light shining from one of the windows and examined his unexpected gift. It was a pouch made from leopard skin and heavily decorated with white, green and black beads. Inside was a tightly wrapped package. Hlomela had presented Daniel with a good luck charm of the type that ingangas made up for young lovers, in order that their dreams might be fulfilled.

With a smile, Daniel tucked the pouch carefully inside a pocket. The charm appeared to have worked for the young couple. He hoped it might have retained some of its power for him.

What was probably of far more importance was the knowledge that he had gained some influential friends among Gamba's family.

CHAPTER THREE

The full Council of Indunas met two days after Daniel's talk with Lobengula. The discussions lasted for a week. Daniel would have preferred the meeting to have taken place in secret, but this was not the Matabele way. The Indunas sat around in a circle in the central cattle pen, surrounded by Matabele tribesmen and concession seekers. Daniel had no doubt that the decision of the Council would be immediately communicated to Rhodes.

The Indunas were almost equally divided on the question of a treaty with Transvaal. Only a final speech by Lobengula decided the issue. When a vote was taken, the decision was made to sign a treaty of friendship with the Transvaal Republic.

When the treaty was duly drawn-up, during the morning of the seventh day, Uiys Toblin signed on behalf of the Transvaal Republic. For the Matabele, Lobengula's 'X' was followed by the marks of half-a-dozen senior Indunas.

The celebrations to mark the signing of the treaty lasted for two days, then Uiys Toblin headed south with three ox wagons – and the treaty.

Daniel rose early the following day, to prepare for his return to Insimo, He had just finished washing when a young white man, in a state of exhaustion, staggered into Bulawayo, calling for Daniel. It was young Jannie Van Eyck. He carried alarming news. A strong force of Mashona warriors had made a surprise attack on the Insimo valley, killing a number of herd-boys and carrying off Nathan, Daniel's seven-year-old second son.

Jannie had been hunting some miles away when the incident happened. He heard of it only when he returned, many hours later. He had immediately set out to fetch Daniel. It was dusk by then, but he had ridden through the night, leading a spare horse. His first horse went lame before half the journey had been accomplished. The second collapsed and died twelve miles short of Bulawayo. Leaving the horse and saddle behind,

Jannie Van Eyck ran through lion-infested country during the two most dangerous hours, those that linked night and day.

Leaving the exhausted young hero to be put to bed, Daniel left Bulawayo accompanied by Wyatt, leading behind them all the horses they were able to borrow from the Europeans camped outside the Matabele capital.

By changing horses at frequent intervals, Daniel hoped to reach Insimo late that afternoon, twenty-four hours after the abduction of Nathan.

The two aching riders reached the valley when the sun was poised over the western hills. They found the house shuttered and barred as though to withstand a siege, but as Daniel slid from his horse, staggering as his tired legs took his weight, the door was thrown open. Elvira ran to him, their two younger children standing frightened and confused in the doorway.

Inside the house, Elvira explained in detail exactly what had happened. She confirmed what Daniel had already guessed. The dead Matabele herd-boys had put up a brave but futile fight against Nathan's kidnappers.

Later, Daniel questioned the other herd-boys who had witnessed the swift raid and they all agreed that there had been at least a hundred warriors in the raiding party.

It was an unheard-of number for the Mashonas to gather together. Unlike the Matabele, the Mashona did not regard themselves as belonging to a single nation, owing allegiance to a King, or paramount chief. The Mashonas lived in small villages, or family units, each independent of its neighbour. Their way of life had been dictated to them, to a large extent, by their Matabele overlords. Any hint of a Mashona federation would have brought the full weight of Lobengula's wrath down upon them. It was not an entirely satisfactory way of life, but a small group was easier to hide among the nearby hills when a Matabele raiding party was sighted. Not until one travelled beyond the accepted range of the annual Matabele raids were Mashona villages of any size sighted.

Daniel was questioning one of the herd boys about the raiders, when an aged Mashona said suddenly, 'These men were Mashona – but they were not warriors of the people.'

'What's that supposed to mean?' Daniel looked sharply at the speaker.

'They were the Mondoro's men. Guardians of the House of Chiefs.'

The unexpected news startled Daniel and brought back uneasy memories of many years before. 'Are you certain? Why would they come here to carry off my son?'

'They were the Mondoro's men,' repeated the old Mashona doggedly. 'I have been to the House of Chiefs many times. I recognised some of the warriors. As to why they took your son – who are we to question the warriors of a God?'

There was a murmur of agreement from the Mashona workers and one of the Matabele herd-boys spat on the ground contemptuously. 'The Mashona cringe in fright at the sound of wind in the trees. There is not a brave man among them.'

The comment brought a howl of protest from the Mashonas. The herd-boy who had spoken shifted his spear to his right hand and glared at them defiantly.

'There's been enough blood spilled,' Daniel snapped. 'It's a pity I didn't have this information at Bulawayo. I would have ridden directly to the House of Chiefs and saved a day. That day could make the difference between life and death. If you're going to remain in this valley you'll remember you *all* work for me – and it's to me you give your loyalty, not to a Mondoro.'

Daniel wished Jannie Van Eyck had been able to return to Insimo with him. The only other white man in the valley was Aaron, who was now a man of seventy years of age. He could not accompany Daniel on a wild rescue raid. Eventually, Daniel decided he would set off at dawn the next morning, accompanied by six of his longest serving Matabele herd-boys, each armed with a brand-new Winchester rifle. The guns were part of a consignment confiscated by Senhor Farrao from an American vessel caught trading with the Pombeiros, a hundred miles downriver from Sena. Each of the revolutionary rapid-firing rifles held fifteen shots, giving the small rescue party the fire power of a hundred men.

During the night, Jannie Van Eyck returned. He was tired but determined not to be left out of the rescue attempt. He brought news that Lobengula himself was on his way with his personal bodyguard – an impi of fifteen hundred seasoned warriors. Lobengula sent word that he would reach Insimo late the following day. He urged Daniel to wait for him before going in pursuit of the Mashona kidnappers.

Daniel was relieved to know he would have the backing of Lobengula's Matabele, but he had no intention of delaying his departure a moment later than was necessary. He set off with Jannie Van Eyck and the herd-boys before the sun put in an appearance above the horizon, riding into a beautiful, multi-coloured dawn that quickly pushed back the blanket of thin cloud draping the rocky hill-tops.

Gradually they left the high plateau behind and entered an area of broken hills and dense shrub. When the sun was at its height, they came in sight of the House of Chiefs, with Mondoro's rocky summit behind the circular stone building.

They had been expected. As the eight men slowed their horses to a walk and advanced in an open formation, a white clad figure came out to meet them. It was one of the Elders of the House of Chiefs.

The old man had no weapon visible, but Daniel was taking no chances. He kept his rifle trained on the approaching man until he stood before them and held his arms out wide, palms forward.

'I come alone – to take you to your son,' he said to Daniel.

'If he's been harmed in any way—' Daniel began, but the old man shook his head.

'He is well, although he will welcome the chance to return to his mother and father. He is but a child.'

Daniel looked suspiciously at the Elder, suspecting a trick. 'Why was he taken from his home and brought here in the first place?'

'It was an unfortunate mistake. It arose as a result of a visit to the White Mondoro by some Portuguese soldiers.'

Daniel was still not sure the Elder was telling the truth. The House of Chiefs was two hundred miles from the nearest settlement. He had never heard of them venturing this far inland.

' One of the Portuguese was an important man. He spoke of you, telling the Mondoro you now lived in a valley between this place and the great kraal of Lobengula. The White Mondoro expressed the wish that he might see you again – or one of your sons. Through him, the Mondoro said he would be able to foretell the future of our land for as long as the child had years to live. There were those who overheard the Mondoro's words. They were repeated many times until they reached the ears of the Chief of the Mondoro's army – but by now they had become a command. Anxious to please the Mondoro, the army was taken out to seek your child. The rest you know for yourself.'

The old man looked at Daniel's lathered horse, standing with drooping head, too tired to seek out the few blades of grass that had forced a way through the dry, hard-packed earth. 'Come. You have ridden far and must be tired. You and your men will need to rest before you take the boy.'

Daniel did not doubt the Elder's words, and his relief at knowing Nathan was safe was overwhelming, but he still exercised caution. 'I'll come inside – but alone.'

To Jannie Van Eyck, he said, 'If I'm not out by sunset, go back and tell Lobengula.'

If the old man was offended by Daniel's words, he did not allow such feelings to show. Bowing to Daniel, he said, 'As you wish. Follow me.'

Daniel led his horse through the opening in the massive walls of the House of Chiefs and almost immediately saw Nathan playing in the dust with a number of other children. When he saw his father, Nathan ran to him with a cry of delight. Then, the moment of reconciliation over, he was anxious to return to his young friends, giving Daniel a casual assurance that he was well, puzzled that such a question had been asked.

It was an embarrassing anti-climax to the 'rescue'. Leaving Nathan with his friends, Daniel was led away to a meal, prepared for him by women of the Mondoro's household.

After eating, Daniel was told the White Mondoro wished to speak to him. He agreed to the meeting, but only began to bathe after he had seen Nathan led out and handed over to Jannie Van Eyck.

The blind medium had grown older and frailer in the years since Daniel had last met him, but his memory was as sharp as ever. Running his sensitive fingers over Daniel's face, he nodded happily. 'The years treat you kindly, White Man.'

'I have a good life.'

'It is well. I am sorry it took an unfortunate misunderstanding to bring you back here.'

'It's a misunderstanding that may yet have tragic consequences, Mondoro. Lobengula is coming with a very large impi. Unless I can persuade him to turn back, your people must flee for their lives.'

'They will not leave without me and I am too old to run. Neither will you stop Lobengula, although I do not doubt you will try. I was aware when the Scatterer first came to the Great House of the Chiefs that he had been chosen by Chiminuka to end my life. Let Chiminuka's will be done. I die a happier death than will Lobengula.'

The White Mondoro raised his sightless eyes to Daniel. 'It matters little what the Matabele do to me now. I have given a long life to Chiminuka. I die happy in anticipation of receiving his reward. He will open my eyes to see the things that have been hidden from me in this life. But there is sorrow in my heart for those who must die with me and who enjoy no such wonderful hopes.'

The Mondoro's thin voice died away and there was a silence between the two men for perhaps three minutes. Then the medium of the Spirit God, Chiminuka, shivered violently. 'Go now, White Man. Take your son home. You can be proud of him. He will guard your heritage well, and increase it tenfold.'

The import of the Mondoro's words was not lost on Daniel. 'Nathan is my second son, not my heir.'

'I know this, White Man – and your first born will prove himself truly a man. But this is the child favoured by Chiminuka. It is he who will carry your line.'

Daniel and his party rode twenty miles before darkness overtook them. They made a dry camp among the tumbled granite rocks on the top of a low, kopje. The herd-boy sent ahead to find the camping site had surprised and shot a nice sized klipspringer on the hillside. As it roasted on a spit, a drowsy Nathan sat in the crook of Daniel's arm, leaning against his father and trying hard to stop his eyelids from closing. He was a contented and tired little boy. As Daniel held him he tried to be happy about the bright future predicted for his seven-year-old son – but he could not forget the Mondoro's prediction that Wyatt would not inherit Insimo.

The next morning they met up with the impressive impi led by Lobengula. Driven on by the urgings of their King, the impi moved fast. Lobengula, bedevilled by gout, the same ailment that had made a cripple of his father for so many years, was travelling in a wagon drawn by a team of salted horses. Inside the wagon, Lobengula reclined in a battered old armchair, presented to him by Daniel some years before.

Roaring at his driver whenever the wagon jolted his gouty leg, Lobengula's voice boomed out even louder when the wagon slowed on the ascent of a hill. Immediately, the warriors of the impi crowded around and, taking a grip on horse or wagon, ran it to the top of the rise.

It might have been a comic scene had Lobengula not been on his way to deal out death and torture to the warriors of the Mondoro.

Lobengula was overjoyed to see Nathan and Daniel reunited. After dangling the child on his knee for some while he gave him a small, boxed hand-gun that had been a present from one of the hopeful concession seekers.

In a bid to take advantage of Lobengula's jovial mood, Daniel explained about the mistake that had led to Nathan's abduction. He begged the King to turn around and return with his impi to Bulawayo. Daniel added that the Mondoro regretted the deaths of the herd-boys and would be willing to make generous compensation to their families. He went on to suggest that the King himself should choose cattle from Daniel's herds. He, in turn, would claim them from the Mondoro.

Lobengula's mood underwent an immediate change. 'No. The Elders of the House of Chiefs are men of the Rozwi tribe, the ancient leaders of the Mashona. If they go unpunished the Mashona will follow their example. No Matabele will be safe in his own country. I will have the heads of every warrior who raided the Insimo valley – and their families shall die with them. Come with us, trader. Bring your son and let him witness Lobengula punish those who carried him off from his home.'

Daniel argued with Lobengula, but only succeeded in angering him. Finally, he said, helplessly, 'The Mondoro was right. He told me you would not be turned aside.'

'The White Mondoro has always concerned himself over much with my future. He once told me I would scatter my own people. It was true . . . but I scatter only those who oppose me. Now it is my turn to play the soothsayer. I predict that the Mondoro and his people have only a few hours left upon this earth. I will remain at the House of Chiefs until I see my words come true.'

Lobengula rode away towards the House of Chiefs and Daniel watched him go, helpless to do anything to save the gentle old Mondoro. Daniel's six herd-boys rode with Lobengula, having begged for permission to go on the great raid with their King. On their return Daniel would have first-hand knowledge of the fate of the White Mondoro and his people.

CHAPTER FOUR

Lobengula's expedition against the House of Chiefs was proclaimed a great victory and celebrated as such in Bulawayo. For the first time in his reign, Lobengula bowed to custom and allowed the women prisoners to be used by senior herd-boys for the ceremonial 'washing of the spears'. To many of the younger warriors it seemed that the greatness of the Matabele had returned once again.

Daniel did not attend the celebrations, so sickened was he by the report on the raid, given to him by his herd-boys. The White Mondoro was dead. As predicted by Chiminuka, he was slain by 'the Scatterer'. But it was doubtful whether the far-seeing God had anticipated the manner of the medium's death. Lobengula had expressed curiosity about the whiteness of the albino's skin. Was he a white man through and through, or was there perhaps a black man like his fellows beneath the white skin?

In order to satisfy this passing curiosity, one of Lobengula's Indunas had the helpless old medium flayed alive. Relating the incident without a flicker of remorse, the excited herd-boy said, 'He was white all through – as white as you, but he screamed like a Mashona.'

The following day the herd-boys left Insimo for Bulawayo. Because of the prowess they had shown in slaughtering the inhabitants of the House of Chiefs, they had been accepted as warriors in Lobengula's impi.

Daniel did not go to Bulawayo again until November, when he received an urgent message that Lobengula wished to see him.

When Daniel arrived at the King's kraal he found a full meeting of the Council of Indunas in progress – and Farewell Loveday was with them. A murmur of anger arose from the Indunas when Daniel put in his appearance, but it was quickly silenced by Lobengula. Calling Daniel to him, the King placed in his hands a folded piece of paper, which showed evidence of having passed through many hands.

Without his customary greeting, Lobengula said seriously, 'When you were last in Bulawayo you used your friendship with me to obtain a treaty of peace between the Matabele and the people of your bearded friend. Read, trader. Is this the piece of paper we signed?'

Puzzled, Daniel read. His watchers, anxiously awaiting his reaction, saw astonishment and then anger register on his face.

'This is not the treaty that was signed here! That was a document professing friendship and co-operation. This makes it sound as though the Matabele have agreed to become the subjects of President Kruger. No, it most certainly is *not* the treaty.'

There was a gasp of anger from the assembled Indunas and, as the murmur of their voices gathered in strength, Daniel realised that the anger was no longer directed against him.

But Lobengula was still to be convinced. 'It is easy to put two strokes with a pen on a piece of paper and say "This mark was made by the King of the Matabele." But each white man makes a mark different to any other. Is this not the mark made by your bearded friend?'

Daniel examined the almost illegible signature at the foot of the page. 'It certainly *looks* like Uiys Toblin's signature, but only he would know for certain. Toblin is an honest man. He wouldn't try to cheat you in this way. I'll fetch him here to confirm what I've just told you. This is not the treaty that was signed here, in my presence.'

Now it was Lobengula's turn to look surprised, 'You have not heard? Your friend is dead. Killed by Bechuana tribesmen as he passed through their country after obtaining the treaty.'

The shock of the blunt statement rocked Daniel. 'The Bechuana are not in the habit of attacking white men who pass through their country.'

The easiest road from Bulawayo to the capital of Transvaal – or to anywhere south of Matabeleland – passed through Bechuanaland. Since the country had become a British Protectorate it was considered one of the safest routes in southern Africa. A number of ugly suspicions began to raise themselves in Daniel's mind. 'If he was killed by the Bechuana, what happened to the real treaty – and how did this worthless piece of paper find its way here?'

'Be careful how you handle that "worthless piece of paper", Mister Retallick. It's British Government property – and I understand your friends, the Boers, put great store by it.'

Farewell Loveday stepped forward and took the 'treaty' from Daniel's hand. 'This was sent to Sir Hercules Robinson, Governor of the Cape Colony, by the government of Transvaal. The accompanying letter claims the treaty was negotiated for them by Uiys Toblin. Sir Hercules asked me to bring it here and verify its authenticity. He'll be delighted to have the assurances of King Lobengula and yourself that the document is a forgery. However, it says very little for the morality of your friends, the Boers, that they should seek to tarnish the honour of a dead man by rewriting his hard-won treaty in such a way.'

'I'll know more about "tarnished honour" when I learn the truth about Toblin's death,' retorted Daniel. 'There are a great many people with good reasons for stopping a treaty of friendship between Transvaal and the Matabele from going through.'

'Perhaps. But *if* Toblin was killed by someone else it would appear the Transvaal government wasted no time in taking advantage of the fact and altering the document he had signed.'

Daniel refused to be drawn into an argument with Farewell Loveday. Turning to Lobengula, he said, 'I'm sorry this has happened, Inkosi. I'm convinced that whoever killed my friend is responsible for forging that treaty. I'll go to Bechuanaland and learn the truth.'

'I will give you an impi. They know how to get the truth from a Bechuana. It is time Chief Khama was taught that travellers to and from Matabeleland are under my protection. I will ensure they are not harmed in the future.'

'This isn't the time to go to war with the Bechuana,' said Daniel hastily. 'They're under the protection of the British now. Whatever you do, don't give Great Britain an excuse to send soldiers to Matabeleland. Repudiate the treaty you've just been shown and leave things at that for the time being. I'll return to Insimo now and collect my partner, Aaron. He was a friend of the Bechuanas in his early trading days.'

Farewell Loveday had listened to the exchange between Daniel and the King with barely concealed irritation. He was extremely jealous of the influence Daniel had with the Matabele ruler.

'I suggest you follow the advice you've just given the King,' he said to Daniel. 'Bechuanaland *is* now a British Protectorate and a full investigation into Toblin's death has already been carried out. You'd do well not to meddle in matters that don't concern you.'

'As it happens, this *does* concern me. Uiys Toblin had three wagonloads of trade goods with him when he left Bulawayo. They belonged to me. No one can question my right to find out what's happened to them. What else I learn in the process need worry only the men responsible for the death of Uiys Toblin.'

With this parting shot, Daniel took his leave of Lobengula and the Council of Indunas, and set out for Insimo.

Daniel and Aaron arrived at the border with Bechuanaland to find their way barred by a European officer of the Bechuanaland Border Police, backed by a large party of uniformed native police.

'I'm sorry, sir,' he replied, in answer to Daniel's indignant question. 'The border's closed. The tribes are fighting each other a little further on. It's not safe for travellers. If you're heading south, I suggest you follow the river on the Matabele side and go through Transvaal.'

'We're not passing *through*. We're on our way to see Chief Khama.'

'I'm sorry,' the policeman repeated. 'As your safety can't be guaranteed anywhere in the country, my orders are to allow no one to pass.'

'It's a pity someone didn't warn Uiys Toblin before he was murdered,' said Daniel angrily. 'I think this is a ploy to prevent us from learning the truth about his death.'

'Come, Daniel. We are doing no good here. The policeman has his orders.' Aaron turned his horse and walked it back the way they had come.

When Daniel caught up with him he was still furious. 'I'm not giving up. They're not going to keep me from seeing Khama.'

'Of course they aren't . . . but we couldn't discuss anything in front of him.' Aáron jerked his head in the direction of the policeman. 'He is called a "Border Policeman", I think he said. When I was trading with the Bechuanas there were no such things as borders – and I am too old to start recognising them now. Besides, we are simple men, Daniel. Can we be expected to look at the sand of the Kalahari Desert and say, "This piece here is Matabeleland – that piece a foot away is Bechuanaland"? Of course not. We'll ride back along the road until we're out of sight, then head westwards for a few miles.'

They crossed the border shortly before dusk, in an area of shallow, semi-sterile soil and stunted trees. Almost immediately they encountered another patrol of Bechuanaland Border Police. Fortunately, the men of the patrol were so busy talking and laughing among themselves that they passed over the fresh tracks made in the sandy soil by the horses of Daniel and Aaron, without noticing them. Barely concealed by a clump of thin shrub, the two anxious men pinched the nostrils of their mounts, acutely aware of the clear tracks leading to their unsubstantial hide-out.

When the patrol had passed out of sight, Daniel and Aaron headed into the desert to make their night-camp.

For the next few days they kept to the desert, staying well clear of the Bechuana villages and the tiny, desert-edge settlements. The going was hard but they kept on until their water ran out and they were forced to seek the people they had so carefully avoided until now.

They had wandered further into the Kalahari than they realised. Before long the thirsty horses began to stagger beneath the burden of their riders. To have continued riding would have killed them. But Aaron was an old man. He could not walk in the heat of the day.

They travelled for most of one night. When Aaron tired, Daniel helped him on his horse and they went on until the horse sank to its knees. Daniel coaxed it to its feet again and Aaron walked beside it for perhaps three or four miles, then he declared he was unable to take another step.

The two men lay down to rest. Before the extreme heat of the day became totally unbearable, Daniel pulled up as many bushes as he could, piling them into a heap. He made Aaron crawl beneath the meagre, makeshift shelter and both men rested until evening.

When the sun sank towards the horizon, the two men set off again, heading eastwards towards the sparsely populated region of Bechuanaland. Before they had been walking for an hour Aaron began staggering alarmingly. Daniel knew they could go no further without water. At dawn, leaving Aaron with the horses, Daniel set off, praying he would find a Bechuana village before the sun rose too high.

He had travelled for no more than two miles when he saw a diminutive figure jogging across the sand ahead of him. Crouching low, the man's eyes were studying the ground as he went. It was a Bushman.

Daniel shouted and the Bushman looked up from the faint tracks he was following. For a few moments he stood poised to run, uncertain of this strange man who staggered towards him, shouting and waving his arms. Panic gripped Daniel and his instinct was to shout louder, urging the Bushman to stay where he was. Fortunately, reason returned in time. Forcing himself to slow to a walk, Daniel raised his arm in greeting and croaked, 'I come in peace.'

It had been many years since Daniel had last spoken the Bushman language and the words came out with difficulty. But the Bushman understood – and stayed.

'I have a friend . . . and horses. Over there,' Daniel waved a hand vaguely. 'We are without water.'

The Bushman nodded. 'I have seen you.'

'You've seen us . . . but didn't come to offer help?'

'Many of my people have died because they offered help to the white man.' He put out a tentative hand to within an inch of Daniel's rifle. 'This is not a friend to the Bushman.'

Unslinging the rifle from his shoulder, Daniel held it out. 'Take it. It's yours in exchange for water.'

The Bushman shook his head. 'Such things are for the white man . . . and for the Bechuana. Not for a Bushman.'

From a small pouch slung about his neck, the Bushman took a small, wooden pipe. It was empty and he made the motions of filling it. Daniel reached inside a pocket and pulled out his tobacco pouch containing two large plugs of tobacco. He handed them to the Bushman who, after a moment's hesitation, handed one of them back.

'I will show you water,' he said. 'But first we will fetch the other white man.'

Instead of retracing Daniel's footsteps, the Bushman set off at an angle to them. Ten minutes later Daniel saw Aaron lying beside one of the horses on the hot sand. The other horse was attempting to graze the barren ground. Following the contours of the undulating land, Daniel had walked in a half-circle.

Aaron heard Daniel coming and raised his head eagerly. 'Daniel . . . that you? You've got water?' He croaked the words through cracked and dry lips.

'We're all right now. I've found a Bushman. He'll take us to water.'

With the Bushman's help, Daniel lifted Aaron to his feet and then tried to persuade the exhausted horses to come with them. Neither horse would move. Daniel tried again and again. Then the Bushman tugged at his sleeve.

'Leave them. Water is not far.'

To Daniel's astonishment, the Bushman led them no more than a hundred yards from the spot where Aaron had been lying. There was a slight depression in the ground here, no more. Certainly nothing that Daniel could see in the surrounding plant life to advertise the presence of water.

The Bushman knew better. Digging in the sand like a badger, he dug a hole as deep as his arm in the soft sand. Then, from nearby, he scraped away surface sand and produced a pointed hardwood stick, the tip hardened in some long-ago Bushman fire. With this stick he was able to dig still deeper, scooping the sand out behind him.

Soon the sand being excavated from the hole came out darkened with moisture. A few minutes more and the Bushman was satisfied. Squatting back on his heels, he waited, looking down into the hole.

After some minutes, he grunted in satisfaction. Rising to his feet, he said, 'There is water. Drink.'

When Daniel looked, he saw water oozing from the sand to form a clear puddle at the bottom of the hole. Unslinging his water bottle, he held it in the bottom of the Bushman's water-hole until it was half full. Then he carried it to where Aaron lay panting in the sun.

Aaron downed the half-bottle of water without once removing it from his lips, then croaked for more. But Daniel's next thoughts were for the horses. They had smelled the water. Half-crazed with thirst they would have trampled sand into the primitive water hole had Daniel not beaten them back. He satisfied their immediate thirst by pouring water in Aaron's cupped hands and allowing them each a single bottleful. They would all rest here tonight and drink their fill during the cool night hours, before moving off in the morning, before the sun rose.

So engrossed was Daniel with watering the horses that he did not see the Bushman leave. When he next thought of him, the Bushman was already a mile away, jogging along, head down, following the tracks he had left when Daniel called him. To the Bushman it mattered little that he had saved the lives of two Europeans. He would have been equally indifferent had they both died. They were not his people.

By morning Daniel and Aaron and their two horses were much improved after the well-watered rest and they were able to resume their journey.

That day they came across the first of a number of small, family communities and by evening reached the kraal of Khama, the Bechuana Chief. They received an unpleasant shock. The benevolent Chief Aaron had known during his trading days had died many years before. In his place was a very different man. Mission-educated, Chief Sekete Khama sported tattered European clothing, boasted of having only one wife – and had forced monogamy on his bewildered people. Had it not been for the support of the British government, Sekete would have been deposed and a more tractable Chief elected to rule the tribe. But Sekete was popular with the British government. He ruled as they wished him to rule. He was also important to the Mission authorities, being their most illustrious convert in the whole of Africa. Starved of success elsewhere, they magnified his importance out of all proportion. Each new attempt to emulate his European 'protectors' was flashed around the world as an example of positive missionary influence.

It seemed that forbearance was not one of the qualities instilled in Sekete by his training. When he heard that Daniel and Aaron came from Matabeleland, he accused them of being Matabele spies. Daniel tried repeatedly to tell the Bechuana Chief they were not interested in carrying tales back to Lobengula, but, when questioned about Uiys Toblin, Sekete Khama became furious. Storming from his hut, he called on the warriors of his bodyguard to arrest the white men and throw them into a nearby hut to await the arrival of the police.

The Bechuana police arrived the following day, a group of native policemen led by the same European who had turned them back on the border. He seemed more amused than angry at the manner in which they had disobeyed his instructions. He told them, almost apologetically, that he would have to arrest them and take them to Shoshung, the capital where the Bechuana Commissioner had his office. It was not an unpleasant journey. The trooper displayed a lively interest in the way of life in Matabeleland and was pleasant company.

When they reached the office of the Commissioner, the trooper gave Daniel a quiet but ominous warning about pursuing the manner of Uiys Toblin's death. 'It's a subject best forgotten,' he said. 'No good will come out of it – for you, or anyone else.'

Sir Sidney Shippard, Her Majesty's Commissioner for the British Protectorate of Bechuanaland, was a man who had been in Africa for most of his administrative life – and he was a man not used to having his actions questioned.

He informed Daniel that a full investigation had been carried out into the manner of Uiys Toblin's death. The matter was, he told Daniel, 'unfortunate'. But he went on to say that Toblin had brought his death upon himself. He was travelling with a party of Boer hunters who were known troublemakers. They had provoked an argument with a number of warriors, led by Sekete Khama's brother. During the brief ensuing battle Toblin had been fatally wounded.

When Daniel asked the names of the Boer 'troublemakers', Sir Sidney Shippard said he did not know them. To the question of where the Boer had been buried, he received the surprising reply that Toblin had been carried away by his companions.

Next, Daniel asked how many more men were killed or wounded on both sides, but at this juncture the administrator cut his questioning short.

'I have put everything I know in a report to Sir Hercules Robinson, the Governor of the Cape Colony. That report is confidential and I am not at liberty to discuss the matter. Of far more importance to me at the moment is the matter of your illegal entry into this Protectorate. I could have you fined, or imprisoned. Instead, you will be escorted back to Matabeleland as soon as possible.'

Sir Sidney Shippard smiled at Daniel. 'No doubt your family will be pleased to see you. Your wife must be concerned at being left alone with only Lobengula's savages for company.'

'She's as safe there as anywhere else in the world,' retorted Daniel. 'And she'll need to wait a while longer before she sees me. I'm going south. To Cape Town.'

It was a spur-of-the-moment decision that startled Aaron. Before he, or Sir Sidney Shippard could argue, Daniel added, 'If you won't show me your report I'll go to see someone who can . . . the Governor of the Cape. You *can* refuse me permission to pass through Bechuanaland, Sir Sidney, but I wouldn't advise it. The alternative route will take me through Transvaal. I feel that President Kruger would be very interested to hear that you'd refused me permission to go and see the Governor. It might lead to even more speculation on the circumstances surrounding Uiys Toblin's death.'

CHAPTER FIVE

Daniel and Aaron arrived in Cape Town on the first day of January, in the year 1888. It was a bright and crisp New Year's Day, with just a wisp of cloud adorning the flat-topped mountain behind the rapidly growing town. In the harbour, a wide miscellany of steam and sailing ships displayed flags representing half the sea-faring nations of the world.

It was many years since Aaron had last set foot in Cape Town, and for once the resourceful and capable old man seemed over-awed by his surroundings. Not until he and Daniel were comfortably ensconced in the house occupied by Jacob Jacobs, a trader only a few years his junior, did Aaron relax and become the confident Jewish trader once more.

As Jacobs busied himself preparing a meal for them, he kept up a constant barrage of small talk, giving them the latest colony gossip. Only when Daniel asked him whether he had heard anything concerning Uiys Toblin's death did the old trader's manner become serious.

Turning from the pot he had been vigorously stirring, he peered at Daniel over the top of his steamed-up spectacles.

'So you were a friend of Uiys Toblin, eh? What a man he must have been. When he lived I never heard of him. Now he's dead it seems the whole world is divided between those who were his friends – and his enemies. You want to know how he died! Shall I tell you how the Boers say he died? Or would you rather hear the story put about by Rhodes' men.'

'I'd prefer to hear the truth,' stated Daniel bluntly.

'Perhaps you would. There again, you might not,' said Jacob Jacobs, ambiguously. 'Either way, you're not going to get it. The most popular story at the moment is that Toblin's countrymen had him killed because he refused to put his signature to an altered version of the treaty.'

'All right,' Jacobs spread his hands wide in a gesture of apology. 'You don't like that story? Neither do I, so I'll tell you another version. The more scurrilous gossips suggest that he died because it wouldn't suit Rhodes' ambitions to have the Matabele sign a treaty with anyone but himself – but it's a rumour that men speak of in whispers. Rhodes has the money to buy off all criticism. Anyone he can't buy has a nasty habit of disappearing from the scene. Me, I don't believe anyone. I just repeat what the gossips say. It's certain that Toblin did himself no favour by making a treaty with Lobengula. An *honourable* treaty would suit no one in today's mood.'

'I persuaded Uiys Toblin to sign that treaty with Lobengula,' said Daniel. 'It *was* an honourable one.'

Jacob Jacobs gave Aaron a pleading look. 'You think I have no troubles of my own that you should bring an honest man to my house?'

Putting a plate of steaming meat, mashed mealies and pumpkin down on the table in front of Daniel, Jacobs said, 'Get that inside you. An honest man will have the stomach for little else but good food in Cape Town today.'

Turning back to Aaron, Jacob Jacobs suddenly gave his friend a brief, lop-sided grin. 'It's been a long time, Aaron. Far too long. Tell me, what brings you to Cape Town after so many years?'

'We've come because Daniel – my partner – wants to meet the Governor. I told him you are the man to fix it for him.'

'Well now, seeing him isn't going to be easy. Governors like people to believe they are very busy men. Sir Hercules Robinson is as good a governor as any we've had in the colony . . . but that's not saying a lot. The standard's not been high. I'll see what can be done, but you'll need to give me a few days.'

Putting a meal in front of Aaron, Jacob Jacobs bustled about the kitchen for a few minutes. Then, still wearing the holed slippers he wore about the house, he left the room without a word and Daniel heard him somewhere in the garden. It sounded as though he were talking to some chickens.

'Do you really think he'll be able to arrange a meeting with the Governor?' Daniel asked doubtfully.

Aaron chuckled, 'If *he* can't we've wasted a very long journey, Daniel. Don't let his appearance fool you. After Cecil Rhodes, Jacob is probably the richest man in the Cape. He has interests in a great many businesses, some he's taken from Rhodes. He even stood for Parliament against Rhodes once.

He lost, of course. Well, you've seen him. What chance could such a man have of defeating a living legend? Nevertheless, Jacob is not a man to be taken lightly. You'll have your meeting with Sir Hercules Robinson. I'll stake my share in our company on it.'

Exactly one week later, Daniel was shown into the Governor's office. The deference with which he was greeted was an indication of the standing of Jacob Jacobs in the Cape community – for Sir Hercules Robinson was a Rhodes' man. He listened, occasionally nodding sympathetically as Daniel explained his reasons for coming to Cape Town.

'Yes, yes, I can quite understand your concern,' the Governor said eventually. 'It was a most unfortunate business. Most unfortunate. I have seen Sir Sidney Shippard's report, of course, but I'm afraid its contents *are* confidential. They cannot be released without the express permission of the Foreign Secretary. However,' the Governor leaned towards Daniel in a gesture of implied familiarity, 'I don't mind telling you I am not satisfied. Not satisfied at all. I have asked Sir Sidney to come to Cape Town and explain certain aspects of his report. I would like you to remain in Cape Town until his arrival, Mr Retallick. I realise it will probably be inconvenient, but it will not be time wasted.'

Daniel was dismayed. 'Wait until Shippard gets here? If he comes in a wagon it might take three months, plus another month for your messenger to reach him!'

Sir Hercules Robinson smiled. 'This is not your uncivilised native kingdom, Mr Retallick. I will telegraph to Sir Sidney and he will ride to Kimberley and take a train from there. Did you not come that way?'

Daniel admitted that he and Isaac had not known of the railway, and had given the hurly-burly of Kimberley a wide berth.

'The railway journey takes a mere three days, Mr Retallick, although it will be a week or two before Sir Sidney reaches Kimberley. Stay here at the Cape for a while and enjoy a holiday. Before you know it Sir Sidney will be here and you will be able to take the train on your way home.'

The Governor stood up and extended a hand to Daniel, 'Now you must excuse me. I have a very busy afternoon . . .

new legislation, you know?' He walked Daniel to the door resting a friendly hand on his shoulder. 'We will be having a party at my residence next week. You must come and tell me about your Matabele Chief – or "King", I believe he calls himself. I am quite certain much of what we hear about him is sheer nonsense. Does he really practice cannibalism?'

Daniel fretted in Cape Town for six weeks after his meeting with the Governor. Sir Sidney Shippard did not arrive until the last week in February. During this time, Daniel learned that his long residence in Matabeleland and friendship with Lobengula were well-known facts in the Cape Colony. He was something of a celebrity. Because of this he was invited to a great many social functions. Daniel attended a few but felt so totally out of place that he declined all future invitations. The Cape colonials had only the vaguest knowledge of events in the interior. Their thinking was not far removed from that which prompted Sir Hercules Robinson to ask whether Lobengula practised cannibalism.

When Daniel was called to the Governor's office during the first week in March, he fully expected to meet Sir Sidney Shippard there. Much to his surprise, the Governor informed him that the Bechuanaland Commissioner had boarded a ship bound for England that very morning, 'to confer with the British Government on certain matters'.

'However, you will be pleased to hear that Sir Sidney Shippard has admitted to certain errors in his report.' Sir Hercules Robinson's manner was brisk. 'He agrees that Chief Sekete Khama was to blame for the regrettable incident in which Mr Toblin was killed, and your wagons stolen. If you care to submit a claim, full reparation will be made to you by Chief Sekete Khama. As this claim is being supported by the British Government, you will be paid in full.'

'My wagons and their contents are not important,' retorted Daniel. 'I didn't come all the way to Cape Town for the sake of three wagon-loads of trade goods. I came to learn the truth of Uiys Toblin's death.'

'Of course, of course,' soothed the British Governor. 'It seems the whole ghastly business was a most unfortunate misunderstanding. It was reported to Chief Sekete Khama that the Boers were massing on his borders and about to invade his country. He sent his brother and three hundred warriors to investigate. They met up with Toblin and his party and mistook them for part of the Boer invading force. There was a brief skirmish during the course of which Toblin was fatally wounded. That, very briefly, is what happened. Chief Sekete Khama is most upset at his brother's impetuousity and has forwarded a substantial sum of money to Transvaal, to provide a generous pension for Toblin's widow and dependants.'

'I'm sure that will make everyone happy,' commented Daniel sarcastically. 'I'll take the railway to Kimberley then head for Transvaal to tell Mrs Toblin the good news. But Sekete Khama didn't seem very upset about his brother's "mistake" when I spoke to him. Tell me, who carried word to him that the Boers were "massing on his borders"?'

Sir Hercules Robinson shuffled through the sheaf of papers lying on the desk before him. 'I am afraid I am unable to give you an answer to that question, Mr Retallick. It is not given in Sir Sidney's report.'

'And no one can ask him because he's on his way to England.' Daniel stood up. He did his best to control the anger he felt at having been so easily outwitted by the man seated on the other side of the large desk. 'I'm sorry to have wasted your time – and mine.'

'It has not been a total waste of time for you, Mr Retallick. After all, you *have* obtained a promise of reparation for the loss of your goods. As for myself . . . ?' Sir Hercules Robinson produced one of his best, diplomatic smiles. 'I have thoroughly enjoyed your company. Perhaps the next treaty you persuade Lobengula to sign will be with Great Britain, eh?'

'My advice to Lobengula will be to steer clear of all treaties – not that he will need such advice. Lobengula once told me that white men always say one thing to his people and another to their own. Now he must realise that our written words are no more reliable. I'll give you a word of warning, Sir Hercules and it applies to Transvaal, Portugal, Germany – or any other country hoping to take advantage of Lobengula's inability to read, or sign his name. It's easy enough to concoct a treaty and find men ready to swear they witnessed its signing – but I suggest you remember that Lobengula rules a nation with close to forty thousand warriors who are itching for war. Push him too hard and that's what you'll get, treaty or no treaty.'

When Daniel left his office, Sir Hercules Robinson sat in deep thought for a long time. Then he pulled towards him a slim folder with the word CONFIDENTIAL stamped diagonally across the plain, buff-coloured cover. Opening the file, the boldly printed words on the otherwise plain fly sheet stood out in bold print.

'PROPOSAL TO DECLARE THE NATIVE PROVINCES OF MATABELELAND AND MASHONALAND BRITISH PROTECTOR-ATES.'

Inside were two long reports, both putting forward the arguments in favour of forming such Protectorates. One was signed by Cecil Rhodes. The other bore the stamp of Sir Sidney Shippard, K.C.M.G., Her Majesty's Commissioner for British Bechuanaland.

Raising the silver cap on a squat, glass inkpot, Sir Hercules Robinson dipped a quill pen inside and wrote in quick, neat words beneath the last report.

'I feel most strongly that implementation of the policies suggested here would involve the Government of Great Britain in a great deal of unacceptable expense. There is also a very real possibility that such a course of action would provoke Lobengula and result in him taking up arms against the British Government. Should this happen, the intervention of British troops would become inevitable. Other governments, with some justification, would no doubt suggest we were engaged in occupation, and not protection.

'I agree with both Rhodes and Shippard that British influence should extend north of the Limpopo River, but I believe it might best be advanced by the enterprise of a private company having proven assets. Such a company would, of course, enjoy the full support and encouragement of Her Majesty's Government.'

Sir Hercules Robinson read through his brief footnote. Satisfied, he signed his name.

There was only one company with sufficient assets to advance British influence in Lobengula's domain. That company was owned by Cecil Rhodes.

* * *

Daniel stepped from the train in Kimberley in the middle of a torrential downpour. He was tired, but had found the journey from Cape Town quite incredible. Sitting on the hard padded seat of the enclosed carriage, he had watched the countryside flash past the open window at what seemed to be a frightening speed. The six-hundred-mile journey had been achieved in only three days. When Daniel had first made the same journey in a slow, creaking ox-wagon it had taken an uncomfortable two months! Standing on the exposed platform, his saddlebags slung over one shoulder and a bedroll clutched in his hand, Daniel felt more alone and vulnerable than if he had been standing in the empty, scrub-filled bushveldt.

Aaron was not with him. He would not be returning to the Insimo Valley. The aged Jewish trader had been uncharacteristically quiet for many days before they were due to leave Cape Town. Finally, on the last night, he confessed that he wished to remain in Cape Town.

'I'm an old man, Daniel,' he said. 'I can't face that long journey northwards.'

'Nonsense!' Daniel was shaken by Aaron's decision. 'You'll enjoy every minute . . . you always do.'

'I might have fooled you, Daniel. I never fooled my own body. The thought of long hours in the saddle sets every one of my old bones groaning. I have only a few years left to me, my boy . . . . No, don't interrupt me. This isn't easy for me to say.'

There were tears lurking in Aaron's eyes and Daniel fell silent. He realised his partner had given the matter deep and careful thought.

'During the months we have been here I have been reminded of so many enjoyable things I had forgotten. A drink with friends who are old men like myself. Reliving shared memories. I've also visited the churchyard often. My wife is there, you know? Perhaps it's foolish, but I feel closer to her now than at any time since she died. I would like to end my days here – and take my place at her side when the time comes.'

Daniel did his best to hide the unhappiness he felt from Aaron. 'If you're really going to be happier here . . . but Matabeleland won't be the same without you.'

'You've been like a son to me, Daniel. I shall miss you too.'

He brushed a hand impatiently across his eyes. 'Agh! Such tears! I'm just a maudlin, foolish old man. Jacob! Jacob! Where do you keep your French brandy. I want to drink a farewell toast.'

'Mr Retallick? Are you Mr Daniel Retallick?'

Daniel came back to the present. A blue-uniformed African was standing on the station platform before him.

'I'm Daniel Retallick. Who wants me?'

'Sir Hercules Robinson sent word you'd be arriving, sir. You have a room booked at the Kimberley Club. I've been sent to carry your luggage.'

Perplexed, the uniformed African looked up and down the platform for the missing luggage.

Daniel shrugged his saddlebags higher on his shoulder and handed the bedroll to the African. 'This is all the luggage I have. I'm travelling on from here by horse and they aren't built to carry sea-chests.'

Daniel's first reaction was one of annoyance that the Cape Governor should have booked a room without saying anything to him. He might have refused the offer had the weather not been so appalling. As it was, he did not relish the thought of tramping the muddy streets of an unknown town looking for a room.

'Lead on, I'm with you.'

The African shook out a large, black umbrella. Holding it over Daniel's head, he led the way from the bleak, comfortless Kimberley Station, to the unashamed luxury of a club that catered for men who had gained great wealth from the nearby diamond diggings.

Daniel was too tired to eat. Going straight to his room, he lay on his bed and soon dropped into a deep sleep that lasted until the next morning.

He awoke to the sounds of the town stirring beyond the open window. After dressing and shaving, he made his way to the dining-room. Open to residents and non-residents, the Kimberley Club was a popular eating place for all who could afford the excellent food on offer. It seemed that every table in the place was full.

However, it was not many moments before a uniformed waiter asked Daniel to follow him. He was led to a table for two, strategically placed by a window to catch the scant breeze blowing from the rain-sodden hills.

The other seat at the table was occupied by a big man whose face bore a heavy moustache and a somewhat sorrowful expression.

Daniel nodded to his breakfast companion and would have been content to leave their acquaintanceship at that had the other man not extended a hand across the table. In a rather high-pitched voice, he said, 'Welcome to Kimberley, Mr Retallick. I'm Cecil Rhodes.'

Daniel had been half-expecting such a meeting. He knew Sir Hercules Robinson had not booked a room for him out of concern for a man he had met on only a few occasions. He took the proferred hand and looked at the other man with great interest. Cecil Rhodes was a legendary figure, both in England and in Africa, but there was little about his appearance to hint at such greatness.

'I believe you and I have a mutual interest, Retallick. Matabeleland – although in my case it would be true to say that Mashonaland interest me more.'

'Why?'

Daniel had observed in Cape Town that people indulged in conversational games, skirting around a subject without making direct reference to what they wanted to say. He had grown tired of their ways.

Rhodes was momentarily taken aback by Daniel's blunt question, but he was quick to recover. With a disarming smile, he said, 'You'll pardon me, but I'm not used to speaking to forthright men. Most of them say only what they think I want to hear – and they never ask me direct questions.'

The smile grew wider. 'I'll answer you equally directly. There are two reasons. The first is that there's gold in Mashonaland. The second, that I want to see Great Britain's influence extended north of the Limpopo River.'

Daniel shrugged indifferently. 'Substitute Germany, Portugal, or Transvaal for Great Britain and you're saying exactly the same as every other concession-seeker who squats on his haunches around Lobengula's camp fires.'

Rhodes leaned towards Daniel across the table, his smile gone. 'Compare me with any man who dances attention on

Lobengula and you're making as big a mistake as comparing Great Britain with any other country ... or persuading Lobengula to make a treaty with Transvaal and not with your own country. Why *did* you do that, Retallick?'

'Because Lobengula is a friend. I considered a treaty with Transvaal to be in the best interests of his people. Had they been honest with him I'm still convinced it would have been for the best. Trekkers are as thick as flies across the Limpopo. They're just itching to trek to Matabeleland. The only way to stop them is to call on the assistance of the Boers themselves. You can do nothing about them. The Cape is three months marching time from Matabeleland – even if Britain had an army to send. By the time they arrived a full-scale war would have broken out between the Boers and Lobengula's impis.'

Rhodes nodded. Daniel was talking a language he understood. Carefully weighing one option against another, Rhodes replied, 'What you say makes sense ... but if Lobengula had a treaty with Great Britain we could put a great deal of pressure upon President Kruger.'

'Pressure after the event would be too late. I want no war. I have a wife and four children in Matabeleland.'

'Ah yes!' said Rhodes. 'You run cattle on two hundred square miles of some of the finest country in Matabeleland. You also have a promising gold deposit on the land.'

Seeing Daniel's astonishment, the smile returned to Rhodes' face. 'It surprises you that I know about the gold? It needn't. Kurt Henkel found the gold on your land, what is it – seventeen years ago? That's close enough. Henkel now works for me. Don't worry, Retallick, your secret is safe. The last thing I want is a gold rush to the land occupied by the Matabele. War does nothing for share prices. I intend forming a company, Retallick. One to make the old East India Company assume the proportions of a village shop. You can help me, and so become part of one of the greatest enterprises of all time. You'll also be bringing the benefits of civilisation to the natives of whom you are so fond. At the same time you can ensure that their homeland remains intact. I'll also give you a signed undertaking that the carriage of all trade goods to and from Mashonaland will rest in your hands – and yours alone.'

It was impossible not to be caught up in the enthusiasm of

this man seated across the table, but Daniel forced himself to remember that Rhodes was a shrewd and ruthless business-man. He gave nothing away without ensuring he had a return.

'What am I expected to do to become part of this "glorious enterprise"?' Daniel asked.

'Persuade Lobengula to grant a concession giving me exclu-sive mineral rights to the whole of Mashonaland.'

Daniel laughed. 'You may not be squatting in the filth of Lobengula's kraal, Mr Rhodes, but you're a concession-seeker right enough. My guess is that Lobengula has had enough of signing pieces of paper held out to him by white men. He'll never agree. I value his friendship too much to try to persuade him.'

Daniel pushed his empty plate from him and stood up, 'You're wasting your time. Stick to Bechuanaland. You have the Commissioner and Chief Sekete Khama in your pocket there.'

'Sit down, Retallick.' Rhodes pulled a thick envelope from a pocket and pushed it across the table towards Daniel. 'I told you not to compare me with any other men you've known. Lobengula has already signed another piece of paper. Here it is. I suggest you read it before you refuse to go along with me.'

Daniel opened out the document and began to read, in-credulity increasing with every line.

The Chief Lobengula, ruler of the tribe known as the Matabele, suzerain of the Mashona and Manica tribes hereby agrees to the following. In order that peace and amity shall continue forever between Her Britannic Ma-jesty, her subjects and the Matabele people, Lobengula engages to use his utmost endeavours to prevent any rupture of the same. It is further agreed by Lobengula that he will refrain from entering into any correspondence or treaty with any Foreign State or sell, alienate, cede, or permit or countenance any sale, alienation or cession of the whole or any part of the said Matabele country without the previous knowledge and sanction of Her Majesty's High Commis-sioner for South Africa . . . .

The incredible document was signed with a large, somewhat shaky 'X' and the words, 'Lobengula, his mark' written alongside it. The document had been countersigned by three European witnesses. One of them was Farewell Loveday.

Daniel pushed the document back across the table to Rhodes. 'I don't believe it. This "treaty" virtually makes Lobengula a vassal of Great Britain and gives him nothing in return. There's nothing here to say that Great Britain will go to his aid if Matabeleland is invaded by the Boers.'

'There should be no need for such a clause. Now Lobengula has signed this treaty, Great Britain considers Matabeleland an area over which she has jurisdiction. Other nations will be warned off accordingly. You see, Retallick, diplomacy is always a stronger suit than violence. This document means that Lobengula cannot give any substantial concession to any national other than a Briton – and there is no company in Great Britain to match the resources of the company I'll form to exploit Mashonaland. I just made you a good offer, Retallick. I'll repeat it – once. Will you help me to get my concession? Remember, I *will* have it, whether you help me or not.'

'Then my refusal will make little difference to you. Now, if you'll excuse me . . . I'd like to put the smell of "civilisation" behind me before the day is out.'

Rhodes looked angrily at Daniel for a few moments, then he too stood up. 'You've just turned down an opportunity to become one of the richest and most influential men north of the Limpopo. You're a fool, Retallick . . . and I never give a fool a second chance.'

CHAPTER SIX

Daniel had been absent from Matabeleland for almost three months when the Greef brothers found their way to the Insimo Valley.

In a time and place where rugged individuality was the norm, Willem, Arne and Louis Greef, together with their father, Hermanus, stood head and shoulders above their fellows. Hermanus had made a home for his family in the remote hills of north eastern Transvaal. Shallow-soil crops fought a losing battle for survival around the primitive hut he built for them. When meat was needed they took their guns and hunted for it. Sometimes it was buffalo, sometimes the wild deer that roamed the wide valleys. Occasionally it was cattle owned by the few tribesmen who remained in the fastness of the hills.

There had been more tribesmen when Hermanus first reached here. Determined that their number would never pose a threat to the Greef family, he and his sons had culled them as though they were overstocked wild animals.

In their mountain stronghold, the Greefs and a few other families scattered about them, had little to do with the Transvaal Government. They neither knew, nor cared, for the ordinances published for the government of the country as a whole. The Greefs made their own laws. They paid no taxes, and no one dared venture into the hills to collect them.

On one occasion only did they bestir themselves for the benefit of their country. It was when the hated British had annexed the Transvaal and a 'people's army' of Boers rose and took it back again. Even then the Greefs were not so concerned with fighting for their homeland as taking up arms against the British. When the battle at Majuba Hill had been won, the Greefs turned their horses and went back to their home. Their departure was not regretted by their recent comrades. The Boers were hard fighters and showed no mercy in battle, but when white men threw away their guns and stood with hands raised it was accepted that they were surrendering. The Greefs did not take prisoners. Armed or unarmed, an enemy was an enemy until he had been killed.

These were the men who entered the Insimo valley from the low-veldt to the south east.

The three brothers rode close together along the valley, overtaken by a brief rainstorm that left water dripping from the wide brims of hats pulled well down, shielding their eyes. As they rode, steam rose about them from the wet horses and the hot, damp earth.

The Matabele herd-boys tending Daniel's cattle were at the far end of the valley, but the Mashonas working the early maize fields saw the riders and moved back out of sight among the whispering, sun-dried stalks of the tall plants.

The three Boer brothers saw the Mashonas. Indeed, their eyes missed nothing as they rode along, but their objective was the European-style house of Victoria, in prominent view further along the valley. From the direction in which they approached Insimo it appeared to be the only dwelling in the valley, except for the unfinished dwelling being built by Jannie Van Eyck.

When the brothers reached Victoria's home, they reined in cautiously, each man fingering the rifle he had slung across his shoulder. The house and outbuildings were clean and well up together. The Greefs were not always welcome visitors to such houses. They preferred to find tumbledown wooden shacks, where the occupants were not so fussy – or were amenable to pointed suggestion.

After a few moments of low conversation, Arne Greef swung down from his horse, handing his rifle to brother Willem. Arne was smaller than the other brothers and although none of the three men presumed to be smartly dressed, Arne's clothes were not quite so dirty as those of the others. Arne also knew some letters and was considered the smartest of the three.

Before Arne could raise his hand to knock at the door, it opened and Victoria stood in the doorway. Arne saw immediately that she was coloured and assumed she was a servant. 'Tell your boss there's some hungry travellers outside who'd appreciate a meal, and a place to sleep for the night.'

296

Arne Greef spoke in 'kitchen-kaffir', a mixture of English, Afrikaans and Bantu. It was fast becoming the *lingua franca* of those tribesmen of southern Africa who worked for white men. Victoria had learned the bastard language while she was in Tati, but the use of it here, when she was in her own house, made her flush angrily. She had seen the three men coming towards the house and knew they brought trouble, but her anger overrode caution.

'I'm the "boss" of this house. You'll find water in the stream coming down from the hill over there and I'll have meat sent to you. As for sleeping, you'll have to make do with the ground. There's plenty of it – outside the Insimo valley.'

Arne Greef stared at Victoria in disbelief. Then his thin lips parted in a mirthless grin and he turned to speak to his brothers, in Afrikaans. 'Did you hear that, broer? She's the boss-man here, and she's ordering us out of this valley.'

Louis, the youngest of the brothers and a simple giant of a man, sniggered. Willem, the bearded elder brother, scowled and said nothing.

Arne swung back to Victoria and his thin smile had vanished. 'No baster orders me and my brothers from anywhere. Who's the owner of this valley? Where is he?'

'It's owned by Daniel Retallick . . . .,' Victoria hesitated, Elvira and her children were in their house along the valley. Therese was with them. She would not send these Boers there. 'He's somewhere around. He never goes far.'

Arne Greef assumed that Victoria was living with Daniel, but he also knew by the way she had hesitated that he was nowhere around at the moment. The grin returned, wider this time.

'Well now, if your man's away you're going to have to entertain his guests yourself.' His gaze moved from her face to her body, kept slim from years of horse-riding. 'You'll know well enough how to do that, I don't doubt.'

From his horse, Willem growled in Afrikaans. 'If you're going to hump the bitch get on with it, man. Then she can get us some grub. I'm starving.'

Arne Greef saw instantly that Victoria understood what was being said. He grabbed at her as she reached for the loaded shotgun, placed just inside the door.

Victoria slipped from his grasp and took hold of the gun, but Arne Greef managed to grasp the barrel as she brought it up. The gun went off and Arne let out a howl of pain. He staggered backwards, deafened, his left ear bloody and ragged-edged — but he had the gun.

As Louis Greef leaped from his horse, Victoria ran inside the house. There was no time to try to bolt the door. The Boer brothers would have shouldered it open before she had the stiff wooden bolt across. Neither was there a place in the house to hide from them. She fled through the rooms at the front of the house to the kitchen. Running past the startled Mashona kitchen servant, she made her escape through the kitchen doorway.

Big Louis Greef was the first of the brothers to burst from the house. He howled in delight when he saw her running up the slope, heading for the broken rocks at the top of the hill. Louis ran after her, Arne behind him, cursing the blood that flowed from his ear. Meanwhile, Willem was still on his horse. He galloped past the two running men, legs and arms flapping as he urged the horse up the slope.

Willem Greef caught up with Victoria before she reached the cover of the rocks and drove his horse at her, knocking her sprawling to the ground. As she picked herself up, he rode the horse at her again. By now the two younger brothers had reached them and Arne gripped Victoria's arm. She cried out in pain as he twisted the arm, lifting her from the ground.

'I'll teach you to draw a white man's blood, you baster cow.'

He increased the pressure on the arm and she arched her body backwards in an effort to reduce the pain.

'Louis, get her clothes off.'

The big Boer leaned over her and gripping both shoulders of her dress he ripped it from her body. Then he reached out and touched her, his loose lips wet with spittle. 'Hey, Arne. She's got a great body, broer—'

'It'll do, but you'll need to help me if you want to do something with it—'

Before Arne could say more, Victoria kicked out, her foot catching Louis Greef in the groin. He fell back on the ground, howling in pain. But Victoria's respite was brief. Willem Greef leaped from his horse, rifle held in his hand. Striding to where Victoria struggled with Arne Greef, he swung the rifle butt against the side of her head. As she sagged unconscious in Arne Greef's arms, he let her slide to the ground.

Jannie Van Eyck had been concealed among the rocks along the valley when he saw the three riders, far in the distance. Jannie had found the lair of a leopard that had been bothering Daniel's herds of late. He was waiting for dusk in the hope of putting an end to its marauding. However, strangers were sufficiently unusual in the valley for him to abandon his task.

He had left his horse at Daniel's house and he called there first to tell Elvira of the visitors, and Therese rode homewards with him. Halfway between the two houses they heard the sound of Victoria's desperate shot.

Jannie Van Eyck had left his hunting rifle with a Matabele bearer. Looking back along the path, there was no sign of the Matabele. He was probably still talking with friends at the Retallick house.

Therese had a lighter, Winchester rifle in her saddle holster and reaching across, Jannie took it. 'You stay here until I've found out what's happening.'

'No, I'm coming with you.'

There was a great deal of Victoria's determination in Therese and Jannie knew better than to argue with her.

'All right – but stay behind me.'

Jannie Van Eyck dug his heels into the horse and took off at a gallop, Therese's horse pounding along only a length behind.

Jannie Van Eyck saw the group on the hillside before he reached the house and turned the horse to cut across the soft ground towards them. By now Jannie Van Eyck was close enough to see Victoria spread-eagled naked on the ground with two men bending over her. A third, bearded man stood looking on, a rifle cradled in his arms.

The two crouching men started up as Jannie slithered his horse to a halt. Clearing the saddle, he leaped to the ground, Therese's rifle clutched in his hand.

Pushing past the men he dropped to his knees beside Victoria. A moment later, Therese was at his side.

'Ma? Oh my God – what happened?'

As Therese cradled her mother, Jannie Van Eyck looked up and saw the coarse faces of the Boers. Suddenly he realised that this was not the result of some accident. He wished his father was with him . . . this was something that was beyond his youthful experience.

'She's all right,' said Arne Greef. 'We were enjoying a bit of fun together and it got a bit out of hand, that's all.'

'You're a liar,' Therese flared. 'who are you? What have you done?'

Arne Greef had recognised Jannie Van Eyck's uncertainty and had immediately written him off as a young lad who would cause the three brothers no trouble. Ignoring him, he reached out and gripped Therese's arm. 'You've got a bit more fire in you than your Ma, girl. You should have come along a bit sooner.'

Jannie Van Eyck straightened up and in a quick movement knocked Arne Greef's hand away from Therese. As he did so he caught the movement of Willem Greef's gun coming up. He dived to the ground and rolled away. As Willem Greef came in view he fired — but Victoria was quicker. She had regained consciousness a few minutes before and while all attention was focused upon Jannie she snatched up a single shot musket left on the ground beside her by one of the Greef brothers.

She fired a split second before Jannie Van Eyck's hurried shot went wide, but Willem Greef thought Jannie Van Eyck had shot him. He fell back in a sitting position, staring at Jannie in pained surprise. Then he removed one of the hands that was clutching his stomach and held it up, staring stupidly at the red blood that glistened on his fingers.

'He's shot me, Arne. The damned baster kid's shot me.' He gave a deep groan of pain. 'Aagh! He's set my blerrie guts on fire. Shoot him, Arne. Shoot the brat.'

Arne took a single pace forward but Jannie levered another cartridge into the breech of the Winchester and Arne Greef froze.

'You'd better get him out of here.' Jannie jerked his head nervously in Willem Greef's direction, without taking his eyes from Arne Greef. Louis Greef was also in his view, standing uncertainly a few feet behind his brother. Jannie pushed his elbows closer to his body in an effort to stop the rifle from shaking. He hoped neither of the two men facing him realised just how scared he was.

'Get him out? Kill him, Jannie. Kill them all,' Victoria screamed at him as Therese struggled to hold her.

Arne Greef licked his lips and looked pleadingly at Jannie Van Eyck. 'My broer's hurt bad, man. If we don't get help for him he'll die for sure.'

'You'll *all* die if Lobengula learns you're here,' Therese snapped as Victoria reached for her ripped dress and wrapped it about herself.

'Get him out of here,' Jannie Van Eyck decided. 'And don't stop until you're well clear of the valley.'

Arne Greef nodded to Louis and turned towards the horse that grazed nearby. Louis Greef bent down and picked up his elder brother as though he were a child. The movement caused Willem Greef to cry out in pain.

'Kill them, Jannie! If you don't you'll live to regret it.'

Victoria had picked up Willem's fallen gun. Now she threw it away again in disgust. It was a percussion model and in the fall the percussion cap had fallen and been lost in the grass.

Therese was shocked by her mother's determination to have the Boers killed, but the incident had taken Victoria back to her days, long ago, at Tati. She hated the Greefs with all the intensity of the hatred she had once had for Andreus Van Niekerk and the Australian miners who had abused her body.

Jannie Van Eyck followed the Greef brothers to their horses and slipped a heavy, large-bore elephant gun from its holster on Louis's horse.

'You can't send us off without guns,' Arne Greef protested. 'You might as well kill us here. With a badly wounded man and no guns we'll be a target for every thieving kaffir we come across.'

'Then you'd better keep clear of "thieving kaffirs" and everyone else on this side of the Limpopo. I'm still not sure I shouldn't be handing you over to Lobengula. You'd best get going before I change my mind.'

'We're going.'

Willem Greef was slung upon his horse by Louis. Sagging painfully, he rode away, his brothers supporting him on either side.

'Help me get Ma into the house,' said Therese with her arms about her mother. Victoria had sunk to the ground, overcome by a blinding headache that blotted out all thoughts of the Greef brothers.

'Some of the Mashonas are coming. Get the women to help with your Ma. I want to make sure those three leave the valley.'

'Jannie – take care,' Therese called after him and Jannie Van Eyck lifted a hand in acknowledgement.

At the head of the valley, the Greef brothers, Arne and Louis, bound Willem's stomach wound with a strip of his own dirty shirt. He was then transferred to the younger brother's horse and with Louis holding him in the saddle before him, they rode away from Insimo.

When Jannie returned to the house, Victoria was lying on the bed in her room, the curtains drawn to keep out the painful light. When Jannie looked in at her, she asked, 'Where are they? Where are those three Jaapies now?'

'They've left the valley. It's all right, they won't be back.'

'Won't they? One of them's badly wounded. Do you think they are going to go away and forget all about us? If he dies they'll be back here – with their friends. You should have killed them all – or let me do it for you. It's the only way with men like that. Let them live and you'll go in fear of them for the rest of your life.'

Victoria saw Jannie's confusion and she suddenly softened. He knew nothing of the life she had once led – and Victoria hoped neither he nor Therese ever would. She reached out her hands to both of them. 'It's all right, take no notice of me. I thank God you were in the valley. I wouldn't be alive now if it weren't for you.'

'I should have taken them to Lobengula,' said Jannie. 'But I wasn't sure—'

'It doesn't matter now,' lied Victoria. 'But until Daniel returns we'd better post armed Matabele boys around the house – Daniel's house too. They might try something there.'

She put a hand to her head, grimacing at the acute pain that had returned. 'You attend to that, Jannie. I think I'll rest for a while.'

*　　*　　*

Willem Greef died two days after arriving home. He was buried on Greef land, alongside the graves of his mother and the four Greef children who had not survived the rigours of Transvaal frontier life. He was laid in the ground in a rough coffin, constructed from planks of wood torn from the platform of an old trek-wagon.

At the shallow graveside, Hermanus, the bearded patriarch of his diminishing family, wept bitter tears at the loss of his eldest son. Then, no sooner had he and the two surviving sons set foot inside the dilapidated wooden shack than he knocked Arne to the ground with a blow that belied his sixty years.

Arne, bewildered, scrambled to his feet only to be knocked down again. He stayed on the floor, complaining bitterly at the treatment meted out to him, but a booted foot put a stop to his whining.

'Get out! You hear me, boy? Get out ... and you.' Hermanus jabbed a finger at his slow-thinking youngest son. 'You'll not sit here enjoying your brother's birthright while his killer walks and breathes. No one kills a Greef and forgets about it, d'you hear me? Get out, both of you and bring this boy back here.'

Arne and Louis Greef had told the old man that Willem had been shot by Jannie. They had said little about Victoria.

'I want to see the baster who shot my Willem and sent his two brothers scuttling away with their tails between their legs, like two scared mongrels. Bring him to me here.'

'But—'

'You want knocking down again? Bring him back, I say. Until you do I don't want to see either of you on this land. If you think maybe it's too much for the two of you then take the Pretorious boys with you – and the du Toits. God's teeth that should be enough to bring back one coloured boy. Get out now ... Go!'

CHAPTER SEVEN

The house for Jannie Van Eyck and Therese was nearing completion. The roof was on and the doors hung. It needed only the internal fittings and window glass. The glass was on its way by slow ox-cart from the Cape Colony.

Jannie and Therese visited the house most days. It somehow brought their wedding day closer and gave their marriage a feeling of reality. In here, Therese could make-believe that they were already married and she was mistress of her own home. She led Jannie by the hand from room to room, discussing yet again where they would place each item of, as yet, unmade furniture. It was a large house, but Therese was already finding accommodation problems.

The young couple were on one of their daily visits to the house when Therese stopped in the centre of the room that was to be their bedroom, and said, 'You know, Jannie. I think we should have had another bedroom built.'

'Another? We've got three. How many visitors do you expect us to have?'

'Well, there's your father. We'll need to keep a room for him, but I'm not thinking of visitors. I'm wondering about rooms for . . . the babies.'

'Babies?' The thought of children, his and Therese's, gave Jannie a strange feeling in the pit of his stomach. Family life was something he knew little about. From as far back as he could remember he had led a nomadic life with his father and, once the last of his half-sisters had married at the early age of fifteen, without the influence of a woman in his life. Jannie had never thought about it with any thought of regret. There had been something indescribably comforting about nights spent around a smoky camp-fire with the stars above and the sounds of the bush all round. Jannie Van Eyck had learned to enjoy the thrill of topping a hill and seeing a panorama of unknown land laid out before him. He had believed it to be as full a life as any boy could wish for. Yet, sometimes he and his father would spend a few nights in a house, or even a cabin in the hills, with a family. A husband, wife and children. On such occasions, Jannie's heart ached for something he had never known. The pleasures of family life. The feeling of *belonging* somewhere.

'. . . of course there'll be babies. At least as many as Daniel and Elvira.'

Jannie's astonishment was so genuine that Therese broke into a peal of amused laughter. Then she hugged him tightly to her. 'Oh Jannie! I do love you so much.' She looked up at him. 'Surely you'd thought about us having babies?'

Jannie grinned down at her. 'Of course . . . but I hadn't got as far as them actually being *born*.' He kissed her and, as she clung to him, he whispered, 'If we're going to have so many babies, oughtn't we to make an early start?'

His hands slid down her body and Therese let him have his way for a few minutes until she felt her need rising to meet his own. Then she gripped his exploring hands in her own and whispered breathlessly, 'Not yet, Jannie. Not now. You've been very good. You can wait a while longer . . . please. I want you too . . . very much. Don't make it difficult for me.'

Jannie's hands came up to hold her shoulders and she relaxed. 'I'll be worth waiting for, Jannie. I promise you.'

They left the unfinished house hand-in-hand, happy in the knowledge that each had so much to give the other. They had almost reached the horses when Jannie's keen, hunter's ears caught the sound of a snapping twig in some nearby under-growth. He knew instinctively that the sound had not been made by an animal.

The horses were still twenty paces away, their reins wrapped loosely about the lower branches of a Mopani tree.

The memory of the visit by the Greef brothers was still fresh in Jannie's mind. Squeezing Therese's hand so hard that she stopped her happy chattering and looked at him questioningly, he hissed, 'Act naturally, but walk faster. Someone's watching us from the bushes. When I say "Go", run for your horse and ride for the herd-boys' compound. Fetch them back here – armed. No questions now. Go!'

Therese sprinted for their horses. Startled, both animals drew up their heads and snorted, tugging at their reins. Therese unlooped the rein and leaped to her horse's back. Jannie stayed behind, keeping between Therese and the unseen watcher in the bushes until he saw her mounted. Now he too ran. He reached his horse just as big Louis Greef crashed from the bushes ahead of him and grabbed the animal's reins.

Jannie snatched his rifle from the saddle holster and, holding it in both hands, struck out at Louis Greef. The Big Boer uttered a single grunt of pain, then dropped to the ground.

The sudden flurry of activity frightened Jannie's horse. With empty stirrups flapping, it cantered away along the path. Jannie was given little time to curse his luck. No more than a hundred yards along the path, two riders emerged from the undergrowth and flanked Therese.

Jannie shouted and threw the rifle to his shoulder, but he dared not risk a shot for fear of hitting Therese as the horses swerved from one side of the path to the other. Eventually Therese was forced from the path and all three horses and riders crashed out of sight in the dense undergrowth.

The next moment he heard a shout from nearby and a bullet whined no more than a foot above Jannie's head. It cut through a leafed twig and sent it spiralling to the ground in front of him.

The urge inside Jannie to run to the spot where he had seen Therese forced from the path was overwhelming, but commonsense fought a winning battle. There were at least four men out there somewhere. One of them looking at him over the sights of a rifle at this very moment. He would be dead before he took half-a-dozen paces.

All these thoughts went through his mind in the fraction of a second. As he threw himself into the undergrowth beside the path, a second shot ricocheted from a tree beside him.

Crouching low, Jannie ran for the nearly completed house. The last twenty yards were across a clearing. He took it in a desperate sprint, waiting for another shot. It never came.

Vaulting through a window space, Jannie crouched beneath the sill, peering out, hoping to catch a glimpse of his adversaries. As he waited he checked his gun, wishing he had Therese's fifteen-shot Winchester. His gun was a very large bore, double-barrelled hunting gun. Both barrels were loaded, but the remainder of his ammunition was in a pouch on his horse.

'You in there—' The shout came from the bushes about fifty feet from the window where he crouched. 'We want you, not the girl. Come on out with your hands in the air and we'll let her go.'

The voice was Arne Greef's. Jannie had begun to suspect that the two shots had been no more than warnings. Now he was certain. The Greefs wanted him – and they wanted him alive! The thought gave him an uncomfortable prickly feeling at the back of his neck. But if it meant they would release Therese to get him . . . .

'Let her get on her horse and go. When I see her ride away I'll come out, not before.'

Jannie could just make out the sound of hoarse whispering, followed by a hastily stifled guffaw. Then there was the unmistakeable sounds of a struggle – and Therese screamed.

Jannie's knuckles turned white and his grip tightened on the hunting rifle. He raised his head to look over the sill and a well-aimed bullet splintered the woodwork of the window-frame, only inches away.

Jannie was helpless against the unseen besiegers, but less than half-a-minute later the same voice called again, 'You were too eager. *Now* you can look, but raise your head slowly and carefully.'

Jannie followed Arne Greef's instructions in time to see Therese pushed into view from the undergrowth. She had been stripped of all her clothes and Arne was holding her from behind, using her as a shield between himself and Jannie.

'You see this? This is what you should have been getting when that house of yours is finished. Now, do as you're told, or we'll show you what else you'll be missing – and my bet is that she'll be more lively than her mother was. Do you think you'll enjoy watching that?'

All the time Arne Greef was talking he was walking towards the house and now he was standing between Jannie and the place from which the unknown marksman had just fired at the window frame.

Jannie slid the barrel of his rifle over the sill and called, 'Now it's your turn to listen. I'll kill Therese rather than let you and your friends have her. This is a ten-bore hunting rifle with a hair trigger and it's pointing straight at Therese's heart. You can shoot me dead, but my finger will twitch just enough to send a bullet straight through Therese – and straight through you as well. Are you listening to me very carefully now?'

Arne Greef realised his mistake. His lips were suddenly dust-dry and he licked them nervously. 'You wouldn't kill her. You—'

Jannie drew back the hammer of one barrel and the click as it locked in place sounded to Arne Greef like the gate of hell being opened.

'Shoot, Jannie! Don't take a chance. Don't let them have me!'

Therese's shrill shout was all Arne Greef needed to reach a decision very quickly.

'Don't shoot! What do you want me to do?'

'Let her go – now.'

Arne Greef released Therese's arms and she took a step forward, unable to believe she was free. When she was quite certain she ran to the house and Jannie helped her through the window, the rifle still pointing unwaveringly at Arne Greef's heart.

'Hold this a moment – and be careful with that trigger.'

Jannie handed the hunting rifle to Therese while he pulled his shirt over his head and passed it to her.

The shirt did not reach to Therese's knees and hung in drapes about her body, but neither she nor Jannie were concerned with appearances.

Arne Greef still stood in the clearing in front of the house, hardly daring to exercise a muscle. He started nervously when Jannie Van Eyck called to him again from the shadows inside the house.

'Tell your friends to come out of hiding and throw their guns down on the path by the door. They'd better take it slow and easy. If they make me jump you're a dead man.'

'You heard him,' Arne Greef called over his shoulder. 'Come out and do as he says, *all five of you*.'

For a few long moments nothing happened. Then there came a stirring from the undergrowth. One by one, five men stepped into view, Louis Greef among them. Walking along the path leading to the house, they threw down their guns, then assembled self-consciously alongside Arne Greef.

'One of you go and fetch two of the horses here. You . . . the big man, you do it.'

Louis Greef looked to his brother and Arne Greef inclined his head.

The horses could not have been far away because Louis Greef returned only minutes later leading Therese's horse and another belonging to one of his companions.

'Go out to your horse and ride off,' Jannie said to Therese. 'I want to see you safely away before I leave the house.'

Therese looked as though she might argue, but Jannie said, 'Hurry, Therese. If they rush us we'll have no chance. I've got only two bullets in this gun.'

Therese scrambled awkwardly through the window. With the shirt flapping loose about her she ran to her horse.

Mounting the animal, Therese looked uncertainly towards the window where Jannie waited. Giving him a brief, unhappy wave, she galloped away along the path that led to the Retallick house and the compound of the Matabele herd-boys.

Not until she was out of sight did Jannie step into view through the window. He walked slowly to the horse that had been brought for him, his rifle pointing at the group of sullen Boers the whole while.

'Now move well away from those guns – as far as you can go.'

Jannie waited until they reluctantly shuffled to the edge of the clearing. Then he swung up to the saddle of the Boer horse. Kicking his heels in the animal's flanks, his elation escaped in a loud whoop as the horse leaped away.

The shout of victory died in his throat. The horse had hardly stretched out in a full gallop when there came the crack of a rifle, fired at point-blank range. Shot through the heart, the horse crashed to the ground, sending Jannie flying through the air over the beast's head.

The heavy rifle flew from his hand and, as Jannie staggered to his feet and looked about for the weapon, a grinning Boer stepped from the undergrowth behind him and knocked him to the ground with a blow from the gun that had brought down the horse.

* * *

Uiys Toblin had built a home for his family on a splendid farm a few miles to the north of Pretoria. Daniel made his way there from Kimberley, pausing en route to marvel at the vast gold diggings of the Witwatersrand. Here thousands of men from two dozen countries and many varied walks of life, dug deep down through the soil of the Transvaal, seeking the elusive ore.

Not all the miners worked for themselves. Many toiled for Cecil Rhodes – so many that Daniel was left wondering why Rhodes was so anxious to obtain a concession to search for more gold in Lobengula's territories. The more Daniel thought about the matter, the more convinced he became that mining was incidental to the grand plans Cecil John Rhodes had for the lands north of the Limpopo River. Daniel believed that if Rhodes gained so much as a toehold there he would somehow succeed in bringing the whole Matabele empire crashing about Lobengula's ears.

When Daniel reached the Toblin farm, he was delighted to find the Boer hunter, Jaconus Van Eyck there. After he had expressed his sympathy to Uiys Toblin's widow, Daniel told her and Van Eyck of his talk with Sir Hercules Robinson, and of the Governor's 'inquiry' into the death of Uiys.

Alice Toblin listened quietly until Daniel mentioned the pension Chief Sekete Khama had agreed to pay her.

'I'll have no blood money from the Bechuana – or from the British. They were responsible for Uiys's death, I'm certain of that. Paying me a pension won't give Uiys back to me. Not even the deaths of those who ordered his killing will do that – and, God knows, I want them dead!'

'*Ordered* his killing? Do you have any proof?'

'Proof? How do you obtain proof when so many lies are being told? *I* know who's responsible, but I don't want to talk about it anymore. Ask Jaconus. He knows, he was there.'

Choked with emotion, Alice Toblin fled from the room, greatly distressed. The Toblins had been a close and happy family. The death of Uiys, and the manner in which it had occurred, was a tragic blow to them all.

To Jaconus Van Eyck, Daniel said, 'Is what Alice said true – you were with Uiys?'

'I was with him.'

Jaconus Van Eyck spoke slowly and deliberately past the

large pipe that was a near-permanent feature of his weathered, bearded face. 'Half-a-dozen of us were on our way to Bulawayo to get Lobengula's permission to hunt, when we met Uiys coming down the trail. He was as excited as I'd ever seen him. When he showed us the treaty we knew why. We all agreed the treaty was more important than hunting, so we turned about and came back with him.'

Jaconus Van Eyck removed the pipe from his mouth and cradled the warm, wooden bowl thoughtfully in his hands. 'I suppose we were all hoping to be a part of history, as it were, and share in poor Uiys's glory.'

He replaced the pipe between his teeth. 'It brought very little glory – but a whole nest of trouble. We were halfway across Bechuanaland when up rode Chief Sekete Khama's brother and a bunch of mounted Bechuanas. He didn't seem pleased to see us. I got the impression right there that he'd been expecting to find Uiys on his own. Anyway, he ordered us to turn around and go back to Matabeleland. None of us was keen on doing that, so next he tells us we're to go along with him. That idea had even less appeal and we refused. Uiys told Sekete Khama's brother that the road through Bechuanaland had been guaranteed by the Cape Government, so he'd better have a very good reason for stopping us. Sekete Khama's brother got angry and the next minute he upped and shot poor Uiys. Then he and his men rode away, leaving us alone.'

Daniel frowned. 'He shot only Uiys and allowed the rest of you to ride away?'

'There was a bit of a fracas. One of the hunters got in the way of a bullet aimed at Uiys – but yes, that's about the way of it. Uiys was shot three times. He was the one they were after. There is no doubt of it.'

'Damn Rhodes and his scheming,' Daniel cried angrily. 'He's behind this – I'm sure of it – but it will never be proved. What I *do* know is that if I hadn't persuaded Uiys to sign a treaty with Lobengula he'd be alive today.'

Jaconus Van Eyck grunted noncomittally. 'I think Rhodes, or the British, really wanted to get their hands on the treaty. But Sekete Khama's brother became scared at what he was doing. He and his men rode off as though the ghost of Andries Potgieter was ofter them. Uiys lived for two days and before he died he gave me the treaty for safe-keeping. We buried Uiys alongside the road and I delivered the treaty to Pretoria myself—'

Daniel interrupted Jaconus Van Eyck. 'Before we go any further – are you *absolutely* certain it was Bechuanas who killed Uiys? It couldn't have been natives from Transvaal?'

Jaconus Van Eyck looked puzzled. He shook his head vigorously. 'They were Bechuanas. I know Sekete Khama and it wasn't the first time I've met his brother. Besides, why should anyone from here want Uiys killed? He'd just signed a peace treaty between the Boers and the Matabele – something the Transvaalers have been urging President Kruger to do for many years. Uiys would have been a hero when he reached Pretoria.'

'Perhaps the treaty didn't give Transvaal as much as Kruger wanted?'

Jaconus Van Eyck looked at Daniel, not understanding. 'What are you suggesting? That Uiys was killed by Boers and *not* by the British? That's ridiculous, Daniel. Why, nobody in Transvaal knew about the treaty.'

'If the British knew, then we must assume that someone in Transvaal knew too. Did you read the treaty yourself?'

'Uiys showed it to me before he died. It promised friendship and mutual co-operation between Lobengula and Transvaal—'

'Nothing about Lobengula committing his army on behalf of Transvaal in the event of war? Or throwing his country open to Boer hunters, travellers and traders?'

'Nothing at all.' Jaconus Van Eyck removed the pipe from his mouth. 'What are you saying, Daniel?'

'The copy of the treaty, allegedly sent out by the Transvaal Government, bore no resemblance to the one I helped negotiate between Uiys and Lobengula. I saw the copy that Farewell Loveday claimed was sent to Sir Hercules Robinson, at the Cape.'

'Then it's a forgery.'

'Yes – but who's responsible, Britain, or Transvaal? Someone will know in Pretoria. I'll go there and get the truth.'

'That's not a good idea, Daniel.' Jaconus Van Eyck spoke slowly and thoughtfully. 'I don't believe Uiys was killed by his own people – he was respected too much – but I don't doubt the government in Pretoria saw his death as an opportunity to alter the treaty to their advantage. They believed he was the only white man who knew exactly what the treaty contained – and who'd believe a kaffir if he complained he'd been cheated? Now you want to go to them and say *you* know the treaty's been altered? Think, Daniel. Only a few years ago they were slaughtering the British on the battlefield for the sake of our country. One more British death isn't going to break the heart of any Boer. Keep well away from Pretoria – and forget the treaty. I hear that Lobengula's repudiated it anyway.'

Reluctantly, Daniel was forced to admit that Jaconus Van Eyck was right. He had come as close to learning the truth concerning Uiys Toblin's death as any man ever would. Besides, he could change nothing now. Rhodes had come up with another treaty that gave Britain the lead over Transvaal. No doubt one treaty would cancel out the other and the interested countries would begin jockeying for position all over again. The only thing that was certain was that whoever won – Lobengula would be the loser.

CHAPTER EIGHT

Daniel rested for two days at the Toblin farm and the daily routine of life on a working cattle farm made him yearn for his own home in the Insimo valley. He had been away from home for six months and the Matabele winter had begun. It was time to be thinking of the next season's crops, and perhaps the formation of a new herd.

Then Daniel's plans received a setback. He, Jaconus Van Eyck and Alice Toblin were seated around the table, finishing lunch, when one of the Toblin servants came running to the room, eyes rolling in fright. He gasped out his news, not to Alice Toblin, but to Jaconus Van Eyck.

'Baas! Many men coming to the house from Pretoria. They carry guns. I think they look for the Ngesi.'

The servant used the native word for 'Englishman'.

The two men leaped to their feet and Jaconus Van Eyck looked through the window. Turning back, he smiled, 'They don't need to send a hundred men to arrest an Englishman — not even you, Daniel. Something must be happening. It's the Pretoria militia. They don't turn out as a rule for anything less than full-scale war.'

Outside the house the mounted commando stopped at the well in the yard to water their horses and Jaconus Van Eyck introduced Daniel to their commander, Major Peter Colenbrander.

The Boer commander shook Daniel's hand, then scrutinised him carefully. 'Daniel Retallick? I've heard of you — you're a trader, from Matabeleland. Is it merely a coincidence that you're in Transvaal at the same time as a Matabele army's crossed the river to raid our settlements?'

It was obvious that Daniel's surprise was genuine. 'I don't believe it! The last thing Lobengula wants is trouble.'

'I'll go along with that,' agreed Jaconus Van Eyck. 'Where did your information come from, Major. Someone's got it all wrong.'

'It's true enough,' replied Major Colenbrander. 'The reports have come in from too many people. I think you'd both better come along with us. You might be able to help us find out what it's all about.'

Major Colenbrander's commando was comprised of a hundred of the toughest men Daniel had ever seen. Heavily bearded men with well weathered faces, they carried their guns with the familiarity of men who knew how to use them well. Wearing heavy cross-belts packed with spare cartridges, each man was a walking arsenal. This was the type of force for which the Boers were to become justly famous in ensuing years. A mobile, hard-hitting commando, able to ride long distances, feed off the land – and hit the enemy hard when and where it was least expected.

On the way north riders were constantly intercepting the commando, bringing news of the progress of Lobengula's impis. It seemed the Matabeles had crossed the Limpopo River, marched swiftly inland for about ten miles, then turned south east. They were now heading for the mountainous region lying close to the lands claimed by the Portuguese.

No reports had yet been received of attacks on the Boer settlements along their route, but the northern Transvaal communities were in a state of near-panic. Tales of atrocities by the Matabeles and their Zulu kinsmen had frightened Boer children around countless camp-fires for many generations.

As riders came in and reported to Major Colenbrander, the commando constantly changed direction, to intercept the impis, but soon the messengers became unnecessary. The impis were moving fast, and in a straight line now, approaching the homeland of the Buvenda tribe.

Daniel thought that this tribe must be the target of the impis, although why Lobengula should risk incurring the wrath of the Boers by attacking such a little known and relatively inoffensive tribe was beyond his understanding.

As more information came in, Daniel found the cross-border incursion even more puzzling. This was no ordinary raid. The warriors were moving in two columns, indicating there were two impis, a fact borne out by the observation that the warriors of each column carried shields with differing impi colours. Reports put the total number of Matabele warriors at about four thousand men – outnumbering the Boer commando by forty-to-one.

By now the impis were in the heart of Buvenda country – yet not a single kraal had been attacked and not a Buvenda tribesman molested. Moreover, the few Boer farms in the area were being carefully by-passed by Lobengula's warriors.

Even Major Colenbrander now agreed that this was *not* a raiding party in the normal sense. The Matabele impis were after something particular, and they were wasting no time reaching their objective. On some days it was estimated that they were covering fifty miles between dawn and dusk.

When the commando eventually met up with the impis it came as a sudden surprise. Toiling up the side of a steep range of hills, they came out on the ridge – and saw the two columns of Lobengula's warriors moving across the undulating veldt beneath them.

'Jesus Cristus! Look at them.' The hoarse-voiced remark came from a young member of the commando. The Matabele made an impressive sight. There were not two but *three* impis, plus half of Lobengula's own bodyguard – the latter armed with modern, cartridge-firing rifles. The Boer estimate of four thousand warriors had been a conservative one.

The Indunas leading the impis were also very much alert. No sooner had the Boer horsemen topped the ridge than the impis merged into their traditional 'head and horns' battle formation and turned to meet the threat posed by the commando. The shields of the warriors formed a solid phalanx, a mile wide and at the centre of the battle line were the warriors armed with rifles.

Major Colenbrander began to look worried as the impis slowly moved up the slope towards his commando. They advanced, stamping their feet to the ground with every other step, and rattling heavy knobkerries on the taut hides of the cow-hide shields.

'If I've got to fight, *I'll* choose the battle-ground,' the Boer commander muttered. 'It won't be on an exposed hill-top like this.'

'I doubt if the Indunas want a fight,' Daniel said quickly. 'They're trying to frighten you away. Get your men to back away from the ridge. I'll go down and speak to them.'

'I'll come with you,' grunted Jaconus Van Eyck, gnawing at an empty pipe. 'Unless I'm mistaken, Gamba's regiment is down there. He came with me on a hunting trip to the Mazoe valley a few years ago. We're old friends.'

The news that Gamba had already re-established himself with the tribe came as a surprise to Daniel, but if he was indeed Induna of one of the impis, it was good news. Gamba and his family were deeply indebted to Daniel.

As Daniel and Jaconus Van Eyck rode slowly down the hillside, the advancing impis halted and their three Indunas stepped from the ranks and walked together to meet them.

The youngest Induna was apparently the one in charge of the mysterious expedition. Tall, even by Matabele standards, he carried himself with a proud bearing that bordered on haughtiness. He nodded his head seriously to Jaconus Van Eyck, but it was to Daniel he spoke first.

'Greetings, trader. You are far from home. I have yet to thank you for the lives of my family – and for persuading the King to accept me as husband for his favourite daughter.'

Daniel thought Lobengula had been wise to waste no time in placing Gamba at the head of one of his strongest impis. Gamba was a man born to command – and he possessed a deep sense of loyalty.

'You too are far from home, Gamba . . . and your presence angers the Amabhunu.' Daniel used the name by which the Matabele called the Boers. 'Why have you crossed the river?'

'You do not know?' Gamba was genuinely surprised. 'I thought that was why you and the hunter were here.' His expression changed suddenly and became one of grim anger. 'Then the men on the hill are not here to help you. They were sent to attack us. Had you not been with them there would have been a battle. *They* would not have asked us why we were here.'

'Why *are* you here?' Daniel repeated.

'Because of Lobengula's love for you, trader. The Amabhunu have twice raided your valley. The first time they attacked the Mambari woman – the one who lived in Khami when I was a boy.'

A horrified shock went through Daniel. Gamba was talking of Victoria.

'Was she badly hurt? What happened?'

Gamba shook his head. 'I don't think she was hurt,' he nodded to Jaconus Van Eyck. 'Your son drove them from the valley, hunter. But one was badly hurt.'

'Good boy!' Jaconus Van Eyck felt a sudden urge of pride but it was tinged with surprise. Jannie was a skilful hunter, but he was also a very gentle boy. So gentle that Jaconus had always been worried about him. He had believed that, faced with a situation where he must kill a man, or be killed himself, Jannie's nerve would fail him.

'You said there was a second raid . . . ?'

Gamba acknowledged Daniel's question with a quick nod of his head, but now he was looking only at Jaconus Van Eyck. 'The Amabhunu came again and this time they carried your son away with them.'

Jaconus Van Eyck's pipe dropped from his mouth and he made no move to pick it up. 'You're certain of this, Gamba? There's no possibility you've made a mistake?'

'None.' Gamba beckoned to someone in the ranks of his warriors and a young man trotted forward. It was Takwire, one of Daniel's senior herd-boys.

Takwire told the story of the two raids, adding a postscript of his own. 'Young boss Wyatt sent two herd boys to tell the King of the raids. He and I followed the trail of the Amabhunu to the river. We did not cross but waited until Gamba came. The young boss wanted to come with the impi, but Gamba sent warriors to take him back to Insimo.'

Daniel's own pride in Wyatt was lost in his concern for young Jannie Van Eyck.

'Do you know the names of the men who have my son?' Jaconus Van Eyck put the question in a gruff voice to Gamba.

'Yes, they are known to the Buvenda tribesmen. Their name is "Greef" and they live only a few hours march from here.'

'I know where they live – and I also know the Greefs. God help my Jannie.' Jaconus Van Eyck retrieved his pipe and tried to fill it with fingers that trembled uncontrollably.

'Perhaps they'll hand him over to the Transvaal authorities,' said Daniel with hollow optimism. 'When it's learned what happened at Insimo they'll let him go.' It sounded no more convincing now it had been said.

'Oude Baas Greef and his boys are what are called "Poor Whites" in the Cape. Here in Transvaal, where there are so many families with nothing, a "Poor White" is about as low as man can get. He has no one to look down on but kaffirs and coloureds. They'll know Jannie's coloured.'

Jaconus Van Eyck turned away abruptly and Daniel said gently, 'I'll go and tell Colenbrander what's happening.'

'Tell him also he can catch me up. I'm on my way to the Greef's home.'

Before riding up the hill to Major Colenbrander and the commando, Daniel suggested to Gamba that he and the impis should now return to Matabeleland, leaving the Boers to deal with the Greefs.

Gamba refused. He had been sent by Lobengula to punish the men who had raided the Insimo valley – Matabeleland – and bring Jannie Van Eyck back. If Gamba returned to Bulawayo unable to tell Lobengula of the fate the Greefs had suffered, he would be in disgrace once more.

Before Daniel was halfway up the slope to where Colenbrander waited impatiently, the impi were on the move again, jogging along after Jaconus Van Eyck in the mile-consuming pace they could maintain for hour after hour.

Major Colenbrander showed less concern for the events in the Insimo valley than in the continuing presence of the Matabele impis on Transvaal land, when Daniel gave him the explanation.

'I'll concede that they had some justification for crossing the Limpopo River in the first place,' he said grudgingly. 'But they should have reported what had happened to the nearest Burghermaster. Tell them to return to Matabeleland and leave us to deal with this matter.'

'They take their orders from their King, not from me, Major. Besides, they don't trust you. They want to see justice done.' Daniel pointed to the hunched figure riding ahead of the Matabele. 'So does Jaconus Van Eyck. It's his boy the Greefs have carried off.'

Jannie Van Eyck had a rough journey to the Greef homestead, deep in the fastness the Boers called the Spelonka Mountains. The Greef brothers were short of horses and Jannie was hauled along behind one of them, at the end of a long rope securing his hands to Arne Greef's saddle. At times he had to run to keep up with the pace set by the horsemen. If he fell he was dragged along, tearing clothing and skin until he was able to regain his feet and stumble after his jeering captors once more. At their infrequent stops he was subjected to constant taunting and an occasional beating. He was also kept short of food, forced to rely on the scraps the Boer brothers threw to him.

When the party eventually arrived at the Greef farm, Jannie Van Eyck was staggering along, as stiff-legged as a drunken man, his mind numbed by pain and fatigue.

As he stood swaying splay-legged at the end of the slack rope, his hands held out before him, Hermanus Greef came from the dilapidated timber shack and walked slowly around him, viewing Jannie's pitiful state with obvious satisfaction. To Arne, he said, 'So you've brought him back, eh? You've made him suffer a little?'

'He's suffered, Pa,' Arne Greef jerked on the rope. Jannie Van Eyck staggered and almost fell. 'He's come all the way from Matabeleland on the end of this.'

'Good!' Hermanus Greef's voice was thick with emotion. 'He'll stretch your rope still more when I've finished with him.'

Turning to Jannie Van Eyck, he said, 'You speak Afrikaans, boy?'

'Better than your two sons,' Jannie replied painfully.

Arne Greef tugged savagely at the rope and Jannie Van Eyck fell heavily to the ground.

Hermanus Greef kicked Jannie viciously in the ribs. 'Answer my questions and don't try to be clever to your betters, boy. You know why you've been brought here, eh?'

Jannie Van Eyck said nothing and his silence earned him another kick.

'You're the sort who never learns, boy. Too much to say when you'd do best saying nothing, and a closed mouth when you should be answering questions. All right, I'll tell you why you're here. My boys have brought you to me because you killed their brother – my eldest son, Willem. Nobody kills a Greef and lives to boast of it.'

Reaching down, Hermanus Greef took a cruel grip on Jannie Van Eyck's hair, lifting his head clear of the ground.

Glowering into his face, he repeated, 'No one, you hear me, boy?'

'I didn't kill him, I'm sure I didn't. I shot, but missed. He was shot by the woman he'd raped.'

'He's lying, Pa. He killed him. You know that. Willem told you so himself.'

'You hear that? Are you calling my poor, dead son a liar now? And what's this about raping a woman? My boys told me it was only some coloured bitch. Are you telling me they're all liars now?'

'She was coloured, Pa,' said Louis Greef.

'Of course she was – and so is this murdering . . . lying . . . little . . . no-good . . .' Each word was accompanied by a kick and Jannie was left sobbing in pain.

'What we going to do with him, Pa?' asked Arne Greef.

'Do? We'll make him suffer a bit. Then you and Louis can string him up to the baobab tree over by Willem's grave and leave him there to rot. It will serve as a warning to the kaffirs – and to anyone else who thinks of taking on the Greefs.'

Giving Jannie Van Eyck a final kick, Hermanus Greef stumped back to the rundown Greef shack.

The Greef boys, with their friends, the Pretorious and du Toit brothers, celebrated their return with the aid of cheap Cape brandy that left them lying on the ground when they fell in a drunken stupor. When they came round they were violently sick. Before they recovered from their excruciating hangovers, they repeated the process once more.

The orgy of drinking came to an end only when the cheap brandy ran out and Hermanus Greef's irritability exceeded his hospitality. Then the Pretorious and du Toit brothers tottered off to find their horses and set off in opposite directions to ride home.

Half-an-hour later, and ice-cold sober, the Pretorious boys were back, declaring to the disbelieving Hermanus Greef that the whole Matabele army was heading along the valley towards the Greef homestead.

'Matabele? What the hell you talking about? You boys still drunk? You'd better sober up pretty damn quick or your Ma will play hell with you.'

'We're telling you, Oude Baas. They're coming this way. Thousands of 'em. They must be after the coloured boy—'

'Then you'd better get him out of sight. Arne! Louis! Wake up and come out here, you good-for-nothing pair. There's work to be done.'

Hermanus Greef was still not certain the Pretorious brothers were telling the truth, but he was taking no chances.

He was too late. The Pretorious brothers had been so amazed at seeing the Matabele impis advancing towards the Greef shack that they had missed Daniel, Jaconus Van Eyck and Major Colenbrander's commando, riding ahead and to one side of the impis.

Suddenly they came into view and the Pretorious boys did not wait to see more. Turning their horses, they bolted along the valley, away from both impi and commando, leaving the Greefs to face whatever was to come.

Arne and Louis Greef had dragged themselves reluctantly from their beds. Now they stood in front of the sagging doorway, puffy-eyed and bad-tempered, glowering sullenly at the newcomers.

'Good day, to you,' Hermanus Greef addressed the three men who rode up to the shack. 'I'm relieved to see you,' he jerked a thumb in the direction taken by the Pretorious brothers. 'My neighbour's boys. They've had too much good Cape brandy. They thought you and your men were a Matabele raiding party.'

Hermanus Greef broke into a throaty laugh, but Major Colenbrander cut his amusement short. 'The Matabele impis are along the valley, scarcely half a mile away. They've been sent by Lobengula because you've been raiding inside his country.'

'Raiding? Me?' Hermanus Greef was not a quick-thinking man and he played for time, wondering where Major Colenbrander's interest lay. It was unthinkable that he should take the side of kaffirs, even Matabele kaffirs, against a white man. But Colenbrander was obviously a man of influence and authority. Hermanus Greef had never found a man of the major's standing sympathetic to his own views. 'I'm too old to go off raiding, Major. It's as much as I can do to get on a horse. Why, I haven't left my home for more than two years now—'

'Then it's your sons we should be speaking to,' Daniel cut in on the old man's prevaricating. 'They've raided my valley twice. The first time they attacked a woman. The last time they carried off Jannie Van Eyck.'

'Jannie's my son,' interjected Jaconus Van Eyck. 'Where is he?'

Hermanus Greef's eyes opened wide, 'You ... you're not Jaconus Van Eyck ... the hunter?'

'I am, and right now I'm hunting my son. What have you done with him?'

Hermanus Greef's throat suddenly felt very tight and dry. 'You've got it wrong, Jaconus. My boys have been to Matabeleland, yes. I admit that. They had some fun there too, they tell me. But their fun was with basters – coloureds, man. They know how to treat white women. I've taught them that, out of respect for the memory of their dear mother, God rest her soul. As for your boy – well, what would they want with the son of Jaconus Van Eyck?'

'My son, Jannie, is a "baster",' Jaconus Van Eyck rasped. 'I'm asking you for the last time, Oude Baas. Where is he?'

Daniel barely had time to register Major Colenbrander's startled expression at the news that Jaconus Van Eyck's son was coloured, for at that moment the Matabele impis emerged from the bushveldt.

As the commando milled about in confusion, Gamba issued his orders briskly. Within two minutes of their arrival, the Greef homestead was totally surrounded by four thousand Matabele warriors. As Gamba strode forward to join the group talking to Hermanus Greef, the warriors began rhythmically beating on their shields, a sound that quickly filled the air and struck terror into Arne and Louis Greef.

There were angry muttered protests from the men of the commando as Gamba arrogantly pushed his way between their horses to take his place with Daniel and the others. Gamba ignored them.

Pointing to Hermanus Greef, he said, 'Is this the man who hunts women and boys in our land.'

'No, he is an old man. His sons are the hunters.'

'Then we will take *them* back to King Lobengula.'

323

'Wait, Gamba. There is much talking to be done. First of all we must find Van Eyck's son.'

'My warriors have found him . . . .'

The conversation between Daniel and Gamba was in Matabele, but Jaconus Van Eyck understood enough to register relief at Gamba's words. The relief died when Gamba turned to him and Jaconus Van Eyck saw the sadness on his face.

'I am sorry, hunter. He hangs from the great tree behind the house, a rope about his neck.'

Jaconus Van Eyck's eyes closed and for a moment he swayed as though he would fall, but as Daniel took a quick step towards him he opened his eyes and the expression in them brought Daniel to a halt. Looking past Daniel, he said to the Induna, 'Show me.'

Inclining his head, Gamba walked away with Jaconus Van Eyck following.

'What was that all about? Where are they going?' Major Colenbrander moved to Daniel's side and looked after the departing men with barely concealed irritation. He did not speak the Matabele language. 'There's too much going on here that I don't understand.'

'Then let me enlighten you. Gamba is taking Jaconus to where his son is hanging from a tree. Murdered by your countrymen here, no doubt. When he comes back he'll expect to take the Greefs back to Matabeleland to stand trial before Lobengula.'

In the silence that followed Daniel's words, the rattling of Matabele war-shields sounded very, very loud.

Hermanus Greef broke in upon Major Colenbrander's troubled thoughts. 'You can't hand me over to kaffir justice. I'm a white man – a Boer, the same as you. All right, I had the boy hung, but he'd killed Willem, my eldest. How was I to know he was Van Eyck's son. He was a baster. You know voortrekker law, Major. You look after your own and expect help from no one. If you have trouble with kaffirs, or basters, you've got to stamp on it quick. If you don't you'll be murdered in your bed.'

'I wouldn't tell that to Gamba, if I were you. Your "voortrekker law" doesn't go down well in Matabeleland.'

Daniel looked at Major Colenbrander. 'The next move is up to you, Major. Your decision here is going to be an important one for future relations between Lobengula and Transvaal.'

'Perhaps – perhaps not,' Major Colenbrander looked angrily at Daniel. 'You've tricked me, Retallick. You and Jaconus. If I'd known all this was the result of a scrape between the Greef boys and some coloureds, I'd never have allowed things to go this far. I'd have ordered Lobengula's army out of the Transvaal Republic, double quick.'

There were murmurs of agreement from the listening Boers of his commando.

'What you see here isn't a tenth of Lobengula's army,' stated Daniel. 'Think of that before you risk upsetting Lobengula. Provoke a war and within six months there won't be a living soul for a hundred miles south of the Limpopo. Oh, I don't doubt you'd win in the end, you've got the guns that Lobengula lacks – but the cost of winning will be so high that you'll be unable to move across the Limpopo to follow up any success you might have. The British would. Your action will hand them Matabeleland on a golden plate. Ask yourself whether one murdering old man and his two vicious sons are worth such a price – and you'd better make up your mind quickly. Here come Jaconus and Gamba now.'

Jaconus Van Eyck carried the body of Jannie in his arms and Daniel had never seen such anguish on a man's face. As Jaconus laid his dead son on the ground at Hermanus Greef's feet, a few of the men in Colenbrander's commando removed their wide-brimmed hats out of respect. Most did not and Daniel's conviction grew that the Boers would never allow Gamba to take the Greefs back to Bulawayo.

'Look at him, Oude Baas. There's my boy. Look at him, I say!'

Hermanus Greef lowered his eyes to Jannie's body, then quickly looked away again.

'He took a fearful beating before he died, Oude Baas. Was that your work, or that of your boys?'

Hermanus Greef looked to Major Colenbrander for some sign of support, but the commando leader was not yet ready to commit himself.

'He . . . he fought us. He was a brave boy. I give him that . . .

he fought like a man. I'm sorry—' Hermanus Greef choked on his words.

'He was hardly eighteen years old, Oude Baas. A gentle boy. A good boy. I don't believe he killed your son. Killing a man just wasn't in him. Even a thieving, no-good son like yours.'

When Hermanus Greef made no reply, Jaconus Van Eyck spoke to Major Colenbrander. 'I'm making a formal complaint of murder against Hermanus Greef and his two sons. Will you take them in custody to Pretoria for trial?'

There was not a sound from the men about the commando leader as they awaited his reply.

Colenbrander knew whatever decision he made now would be criticised by someone. He chose the way that would be acceptable to the majority of those who rode with him, knowing that they represented Boer opinion.

'I'd like to take them in for trial, Jaconus, out of personal respect for you — but I must face the facts. The case would never reach a court and I'd be the laughing stock of Pretoria. This is voortrekker country – and the voortrekkers make their own laws. You know that – you've been one of them for most of your life. Why, it's not even certain this corner of the country belongs to us. Pretoria and Lisbon have been arguing about borders for months.'

Hermanus Greef's relief was evident and his face twitched in a nervous smile.

'Would your answer have been the same had my boy not had coloured blood in his veins?' Jaconus Van Eyck asked the question quietly.

'Yes.'

'There has been enough talking.' Gamba was one of the very few Matabeles who understood Afrikaans. He had been following the arguments of Colenbrander and Jaconus Van Eyck closely. 'Lobengula sent me to find the men who raided his country and attacked those who enjoy his protection. I have found them. I will take them back to Bulawayo now.'

Daniel translated Gamba's words for Major Colenbrander.

'Tell the Induna there are procedures to be followed in such cases. Lobengula should complain to the Transvaal Government. The matter will be looked into . . . but I must remind him it was Lobengula himself who tore up Toblin's treaty. He can't expect much sympathy from President Kruger.'

'That's right, Major. You tell this kaffir-boetje to take his broers back where they came from. We've fought for this country. No kaffir's going to come in and lord it over a white man. If you want some help you can count on me and my sons.' Hermanus Greef had regained much of his confidence after hearing Colenbrander's words.

'The Amabhunu did not listen to my words,' said Gamba, coldly. 'I was not asking him if I could take these men. I was *telling* him.' Gamba had earlier silenced the shield-beating, now he signalled with his hand and it began again, sounding even more menacing than before, and causing the Boer commando to look nervously towards their commander.

'For God's sake, Major. Don't back yourself into a corner. Sit down and talk to Gamba. You've got a hundred men's lives in your hands. Whichever way you look at it, the Greef's aren't worth such a price—'

Pale-faced, Major Colenbrander said stubbornly, 'My men knew what might happen when they volunteered to come out with me after the Matabele. There's an important principle involved in this.'

Daniel groaned. The last thing the situation needed was a man who was determined to write himself into the history of the Transvaal Republic. He appealed to Gamba.

'Back your warriors off while we talk about this. Lobengula didn't mean you to come here and start a war!'

'I have my orders, trader. These men must be taken to King Lobengula.'

'Damn your orders, Gamba, and your principles, Colenbrander. You're both talking over the dead body of my son as though he never existed at all. There *is* another way. *I'll* show you what it is.'

Jaconus Van Eyck strode the few paces to where his horse stood, loose-reined. A double-barrelled hunting rifle, twin to the one Jannie had owned, hung by its sling from the saddle horn. Jaconus lifted it down and, before anyone realised his intention, he swung around and fired. Once . . . twice.

The two Greef brothers were standing beside the cabin, leaning carelessly against the peeling bark of its wooden walls.

Jaconus Van Eyck's first shot knocked big Louis Greef back against the wooden wall before he pitched forward to lie on his face, arms and legs twitching in dying convulsions.

Arne made an attempt to run, but he had no sooner turned sideways than the second heavy bullet shattered his ribs, piercing both lungs before embedding itself in the wall of the shack. Arne fell back against the wall and slumped to the ground where he sat coughing up his life's blood.

As the second shot echoed back from the surrounding hills, the drumming of the Matabele warriors faltered and died. For a few moments the valley was hushed and still. The unnatural silence was broken by a howl of anguish that had an animal quality about it. The sound released an angry outburst from the Boer commando.

'Arne! Louis!' Hermanus Greef sank to his knees beside Arne Greef as his life bubbled away within arm's reach of Louis Greef's now-still body.

'Jaconus, man! That was sheer bloody murder.'

Jaconus Van Eyck pulled the empty cartridges from his rifle and thumbed two new shells in their place. After a quick glance towards the Boer commando, he slipped the strap of the heavy rifle over his shoulder. 'No, Major. It's voortrekker justice. You were telling me about it a few minutes ago, remember? You should be grateful to me. I've just saved your life – and the lives of your men.'

Turning his back on Major Colenbrander, Jaconus Van Eyck spoke to Gamba. 'You've done all that Lobengula asked of you, Induna Gamba. When you return to the King, tell him that the gun of his friend, Van Eyck, robbed you of the men you sought. I offer him no apology for avenging my son's death. Tell him that, Gamba. He'll understand.'

'I understand too, hunter. Better, I think, than your own people.'

Gamba called to his men and they responded to his words, shouting happily as they formed up in marching formation. Gamba was taking them home.

Before he left, Gamba turned to Major Colenbrander and spoke to him in passable Afrikaans. 'I say this to your face, so no man can say another used words that were not mine. I was sent to find the Amabhunu who had come to our land and attacked those who enjoyed Lobengula's protection. My King did not say, "It does not matter because those who were attacked were not Matabele." There is only one law in our land. Lobengula's words do not have two meanings: one for white, another for black. When I tell him what has been said here today, he will not be pleased.'

In a single sweep of his arm, Gamba encompassed all the men of the commando and Colenbrander himself. 'The road to Lobengula's kraal is no longer open for you and your people. There will be no hunting. No concessions. The days of friendship between our peoples are over.'

With great dignity, Gamba walked to the head of his warriors and gave the order for them to march northwards, taking the shortest route to the Limpopo River, no more than forty miles away.

CHAPTER NINE

When Wyatt and the Matabele trackers returned to Insimo with news that Jannie had been taken over the river to Transvaal, Therese had known she would never see him alive again. When Jaconus Van Eyck broke the news of Jannie's death to her, she accepted it with an outward calm that deceived everyone except her mother.

Jannie Van Eyck was buried in the tiny Insimo valley burial ground, beside the grave of Philippe, the one-time Pombeiro. It was here, during the simple burial ceremony for the boy who would have been her husband in such a short while, that Therese's composure cracked. Standing between the graves of the two men who had meant so much to her during her short lifetime, she suddenly broke down and, weeping inconsolably, was led away by Victoria.

Daniel quickly learned all the details of the two raids on the Insimo valley. He determined that before he left the valley again he would establish an efficient system of look-outs and armed guards. There would be no recurrence of the incidents involving the Greef brothers.

Jaconus Van Eyck agreed to remain in the valley and help Daniel carry out his plans. He knew it would be advisable to stay away from Transvaal until the killing of the Greefs was no longer a contentious issue there.

His decision was received with great relief by Elvira. Daniel would be spending many more weeks away from her, on his trading trips. After Jannie had been carried off responsibility for the valley rested with her. It was a difficult task. Both the Matabele herd-boys and the Mashona farm labourers resented taking orders from a woman.

Daniel's homecoming was heavily clouded by the tragedy of Jannie Van Eyck's death. There was uncertainty in the air too about the future of the Matabele kingdom. Despite all this, Daniel felt the anxiety and strain of recent months fall away from him. He was home again.

Late in the night after the funeral of Jannie, Daniel rose from his bed and made his way out to the verandah surrounding the house. Lighting a pipe, he stood gazing out at the valley, silvered by the light from a full moon. He had crept quietly from the bedroom, thinking that Elvira was asleep, but it was not many minutes before she joined him. Barefooted and wearing only a long, white nightdress, she slipped noiselessly from the house and he started as she slipped an arm about his waist.

'Is it so difficult to sleep by my side in a comfortable bed?' she whispered.

Daniel hugged her to him. 'It's what I've longed for more than anything else during the months I've been away. Every night when I laid my blanket down in some uncomfortable hollow in the bush, I hoped I might wake up and find myself back here, with you and the boys.'

'And your body has returned to us – but where are your thoughts, my husband?'

'They are here too, but they travel beyond today . . . this night. I'm wondering what the future will bring for Wyatt and Nathan, Adam and Benjamin. Lobengula is under tremendous pressure to open up his country to Rhodes and his friends. How can I prevent him from signing away the future of his people – and the future of our sons too? Wyatt will soon be a man. He'll want—'

Elvira's finger found his lips and pressed them closed. 'Shh! You praised Wyatt for behaving like a man when he and the herd-boys tracked the Boers. It was true, he did – but his pleasure at your words was that of a young boy. Let him be my young son for a while longer. Too many children have to grow up before their time. Poor Jannie was one.'

Daniel felt her tears warm against him and his arm tightened about her.

'Look out there, Daniel,' Elvira whispered fiercely. 'With so much beauty to be seen how can men's minds grow so ugly?'

'I don't know. Perhaps the Devil moved in while God was admiring the view – and I'm afraid of the same thing happening to Lobengula. If he's not careful he'll be so taken up with the presents and promises made to him by Rhodes and his agents that he'll not be aware he's sold the inheritance of his people.'

'Suliyana is concerned too. She came here with Lundi, while you were away. Spiteful kraal gossip had upset her. It's being said that Lobengula is twice the man his father was about the girth, but possesses only half his cunning. The truth is that drink is severely affecting his thinking. He now has a passion for champagne and brandy cocktails. A wagonload of drink was sent up for him from Bechuanaland, just before he signed the treaty with Great Britain.'

'I must talk to Lobengula about that. I'll need to go to Bulawayo in a few days time, to ask permission for Jaconus to remain at Insimo.'

'In a few days time it will be as though you have never been away – but tonight is a homecoming.' Elvira took his hand. 'Come to bed, my husband.'

Later, after Elvira had given Daniel the love she knew he needed, it was her turn to find sleep elusive. Although she had not admitted it to Daniel, she too was concerned about the future. Not only for her children – but for her husband. Suliyana had remained at Insimo for a week. During that time she had spoken honestly of matters that would have been dangerous to mention to a Matabele woman.

Drink was only one of Lobengula's problems, albeit the one that was most evident to other men. He could see his enemies growing stronger beyond the country's borders, while the Matabele fell further behind in both wealth and military strength.

The latest blow to fall concerned the Barotsi tribe, beyond the Zambezi River to the north of Matabeleland. Lobengula heard disquieting rumours that the Barotsi Chief, Lewanika, was contemplating a treaty with Rhodes and sent a senior Induna to investigate.

The Induna returned laden with presents from the Barotsi Chief . . . but the gifts made the Induna's news no more palatable. Lewanika had *already* granted a concession. Permission to prospect and mine for minerals had been granted to a private concession-hunter – who had promptly made for Kimberley where he sold it to Rhodes!

The news found Lobengula in a sober state and plunged him

in a state of deepest despondency. Matabeleland was now totally surrounded by lands to which the white men's influence had extended. Matabeleland stood alone.

The 'treachery' of the Barotsi – for this was how Lobengula viewed the concession, hit Lobengula particularly hard. For as long as the white men had been crowding his borders, Lobengula had always looked upon the road north as his ultimate escape route. If a white invasion came, Lobengula intended to emulate his father and retreat northwards, leaving the white men to fight over Matabeleland like greedy dogs over a bone. Suddenly this escape route had been closed to him. Now Lobengula knew without doubt that one day the Matabele would have to fight the white men. The ways of the two peoples were too far apart for them ever to stand side by side in friendship and the Matabele were too proud to submit to the protection of one of the European countries who coveted their land. They, like the whites themselves, were used to going their own way, taking the respect of others for granted.

It was a situation that gnawed at Lobengula's heart night and day. It became bearable only when he drank heavily. As a result, he drank heavily for most of every day.

All these things Suliyana told to Elvira who, in her turn, worried for Daniel. She knew how deeply committed he was to securing for the Matabele the right to retain their identity and independence. He would feel the impending disaster almost as keenly as Lobengula, and would become totally involved on their behalf. He could do nothing else. The Insimo Valley was Lobengula's tangible recognition of Daniel's commitment – and the Insimo valley was to be Daniel's legacy to his sons.

Daniel found Bulawayo unchanged. It was hot and noisy and smelly. Perhaps the grass-thatch 'beehive' huts sagged a little more than when he had left, but their ageing lines were blurred by the thick pall of dust that hung over the Matabele capital. Kicked up by the hooves of the great Matabele cattle herds, the dust was stained red by the rays of the setting sun.

Lobengula was seated by the 'indaba' fire – the fire around which the tribal officials conducted the business of the Matabele. Lobengula was drinking brandy from a wicker-clad jar, surrounded by the usual miscellany of Europeans. Concession-seekers and would-be hunters, they preferred the warmth and hospitality of Lobengula's fire to the lonely dangers of the bushveldt. Most of them had been here when Daniel left to go south – but he was quick to observe that there was not a Boer face among them. Gamba had kept the promise he had made to Major Colenbrander.

Lobengula boomed a loud greeting to Daniel. 'Welcome home, trader! You've been away far too long. Come, sit beside me and tell me about your journeys.' Lobengula looked about him at the noisy throng. 'No, we will go to my house, away from these noisy children.'

Struggling to his feet, the King leaned heavily on the shoulders of members of his bodyguard and preceded Daniel to the house. He was fifty-two years old now and age had dusted his hair with grey. He was also a very big man, taller and heavier than his father had been – and quite as unsteady on his feet.

Inside the hut he ordered one of his wives to put a light to the ready-laid fire, then stood unsteadily before the fireplace, warming his hands. Beaming genially at Daniel, he said, 'I hear your travels have taken you far, my friend?'

'Very far, Inkosi. I have spoken to the Governor in the Cape Colony, to Cecil Rhodes – and visited the family of my friend Toblin in Transvaal. I returned from there with Jaconus Van Eyck. I would like him to remain and work with me at Insimo. He is a good man. I will vouch for him.'

'He is also a brave man. Tell him I grieve for the son he has lost. He may stay.'

Lobengula eased himself into his large, leather armchair and exhaled his breath gratefully. Then he looked critically at Daniel. 'You have lost weight. Gamba told me of the troubles you and he had with the Boers. I do not like making enemies of white men, but the Boers can never again be the friends of the Matabele.'

'The great tragedy is, had Toblin not been killed the treaty would not have been altered and the Boers would have done the work Gamba set out to do.'

'You believe this? Do you think the Boers would have meted out justice as did your friend Van Eyck? Kill two white men to avenge the death of one who was neither of their people, nor mine?'

334

'I believe that if a Boer gives his word, it will be kept,' declared Daniel firmly.

'I accepted the word of your friend Toblin, but his countrymen twisted those words to suit themselves,' Lobengula reminded Daniel.

'There are always men at hand to take advantage of a situation. Both sides were quick to use Uiys Toblin's death. I've seen the treaty you made with the British, Inkosi. It's not a good one for your people.'

Lobengula scowled angrily. 'I signed no treaty with the British.'

Daniel could not believe the King was serious, 'I saw the treaty myself. It bore your mark – and that of Umnombati, and was countersigned by the Reverend Loveday. The British are using the treaty to warn off Transvaal, Portugal and the Germans.'

'If by signing such a treaty the white men would cease from pestering me I would happily sign. More than half my day is spent listening to their pleas.'

'A treaty must be carefully worded if it's not to arouse anger among others – unless it also guarantees that your battles will be fought for you. As things are, you've signed a treaty that gives you nothing. Britain can sit back while you wage war with your neighbours. Then, when you're all too weak to fight any more, they'll march in waving their treaty and take all they want.'

Lobengula tried desperately to pull his alcohol-dulled thoughts together – but failed. He roared angrily for one of his wives and a big, anxious-looking girl hurried in and dropped to her knees in front of the King.

'Go and fetch Umnombati.'

The junior wife momentarily forgot the awe in which she held her royal husband. 'Umnombati is a very old man. He sleeps—'

'Then wake him. Tell him his King wants him here now.'

The wife scrambled to her feet and fled from the room. Lobengula reached for the brandy flagon. It was empty and he threw it across the room in a fit of childish pique.

'You'll see,' he mumbled. 'You'll see, trader.' Suddenly struggling to his feet, spurning Daniel's hand, Lobengula made his heavy way outside, to where the men about the Induna fire were still drinking heavily. Here he took a brandy jar from one of the concession-seekers.

Umnombati arrived supported by two of his wives. He was now a very old man indeed, being well over ninety years of age. The flesh on his body had shrivelled away, leaving the wrinkled, leathery skin hanging on a skeletal frame.

The man who had for so long been the senior Induna of the Matabele nation raised a hand in a palsied salute to his King. Beside him his two wives also trembled, but they were unable to claim the excuse of age. They were scared. In their experience a man of Umnombati's status was not called from his bed in the night by the King unless he had incurred extreme royal displeasure. When such a thing occurred the whole family of the unfortunate man were likely to suffer whatever fate was meted out to the miscreant.

But there was no such fear in Umnombati, 'You sent for me, Lobengula. I am here.'

Lobengula grunted. 'The trader says he has seen a treaty signed between the Matabele and the British. It is a bad treaty, he says. Have I asked the advice of the Council of Indunas on such a matter?'

'The King of the Matabele is a King indeed. He does not consult with his Elders before doing that which he knows is right for the people.'

'No riddles, Umnombati. The trader says the treaty bears your mark too. I have said I signed no treaty. We await your words.'

Umnombati turned his face towards Daniel. 'The King has signed no treaty.'

Lobengula relaxed. 'There! I told you the truth. You should know by now that a King does not lie. His word can be believed by all men.'

Lobengula carried the jar of brandy to his lips and poured a frightening amount of the contents down his throat. When it was lowered to the ground, he said huskily, 'Go now. We will talk again, trader.'

Umnombati had been moved from his distant kraal to Bulawayo many years before. As befitted his age and position in the tribe, his hut was close to the King's house. Daniel walked with him and apologised for being responsible for having the old Induna brought from his bed.

'I am grateful that I can still perform a service for my King. But you are right, trader. It *is* a bad treaty for our people.'

'Then Lobengula *has* signed a treaty? But you said—'

'Would you have me call my King a liar before those who drink about his fire? To admit that the son of my great friend, Mzilikazi, was so stupid with drink at the time he did not realise what he was doing? The mark on the paper was made by a drunken man — not by a Matabele King. Lobengula has forgotten . . . so should all men.'

'The British won't let him forget, Umnombati.'

'If it were not this treaty it would be something else. The white men will squeeze the Matabele nation tighter, and tighter . . . and tighter still. One day they will feel it slipping from their grasp, like an over-ripe fruit. When that day comes there will be war. I think the Gods must have willed it, trader. So be it. Is it not better for a young Matabele warrior to die fighting for a nation that is still great and proud, than to live to old age with a white man standing between him and the sun?'

CHAPTER TEN

Elvira had not seen her father for some years and she was very concerned because there had been no news from him for many months. Daniel waited only until he was quite certain that Jaconus Van Eyck could run things at Insimo before announcing that the whole family would make the long journey to Sena.

The trip needed a great deal of planning. Daniel intended taking the proceeds of two seasons trading with him. Such a journey required the King's permission and Lobengula gave Daniel the road in late July 1888. The King also insisted on sending two hundred warriors along, turning the family trek into a major expedition. With a full dozen wagons drawn by slow-plodding oxen, it would be at least a month before they reached the home of Senhor Farrao.

But although it was a planning headache for Daniel, it was a great adventure for the four boys. Their excitement had reached fever pitch long before it was time to leave Insimo. Even Therese caught their mood and smiled happily for the first time since Jannie Van Eyck's death.

Therese was accompanying the Retallicks, mainly to help Elvira with the boys, but also because Victoria and Elvira agreed it would be good for her to get away from Insimo for a while. Therese spoke fluent Portuguese and should prove a great asset on the long journey through Mozambique.

The wagons and escort set off from Insimo on a wonderfully crisp and clear winter's day, with landmarks up to fifty miles distant standing out clearly against the sky.

All the Mashona workers turned out to wave them off as they left the house behind. Further along the valley, the Matabele herd-boys set up a continuous ululating cry that echoed from the rocky crags and startled their charges.

It was a good beginning for a happy trek that progressed without incident for the first two hundred miles. By then they were passing through an area abounding in cool, clear streams and spectacular, tumbling waterfalls.

One evening they camped early, in order to allow the boys to try their hands at fishing. There was no guard set. There were a few Manicas in the area, but they kept well clear of Lobengula's escorting warriors. Suddenly, a warning cry went up from one of the Mashona wagon drivers who had been exploring further along the valley where they had camped.

Immediately, the relaxed and carefree camp became a scene of confused activity. The Matabele ran for their spears and shields, and Daniel helped Elvira round up the boys. Lifting them to the dubious safety of a covered wagon, he snatched up his own rifle and ran along the narrow twisting valley after the Matabele escort.

The cry from the wagon driver had given the warning that armed men were coming. Suddenly, ahead of him, Daniel heard the knobkerries of the Matabele warriors begin beating against their long shields and he knew the information had been correct. Rounding a turn in the valley, Daniel's heart sank. The 'armed men' were riders – and there were almost as many of them as there were Matabele in the escort. As he watched they formed up with some semblance of order, rifles at the ready, in preparation for the attack of the Matabeles.

The warriors of the escort were armed only with the broad-bladed assegais. A battle would be a one-sided affair. A single volley would be sufficient to cut down many of the Matabele warriors and they would never get close enough to use their broad-bladed stabbing spears against mounted men.

Fortunately, the warriors were advancing in their customary slow and deliberate manner. Daniel was able to reach them and push ahead of their advancing ranks before either side took any positive action. He called on the horsemen to hold their fire. Much to his relief, a blue uniformed horseman broke from their ranks and a very young, fresh-faced Portuguese officer came to meet him.

'Who are you, senhor? Why do you bring an army of armed tribesmen to Portuguese territory?'

Ignoring the territorial claim, Daniel replied, 'My name is Daniel Retallick. My wife is the daughter of Senhor Farrao, Captain General of the North West District. We are bringing our children on a visit to their grandfather. The tribesmen are an escort provided for us by King Lobengula of the Matabele.'

The young Portuguese army officer's manner underwent a remarkable change at the mention of Senhor Farrao. 'My apologies, Senhor Retallick . . . but can you halt your warriors before there is a fight?'

The Matabele warriors were closer now, the short assegais already drawn back in readiness for battle.

'Get your men back out of the way – quickly,' Daniel snapped at the Portuguese officer. 'I'll need a few minutes to cool the warriors down. Don't come close until I call you.'

Jerking the reins of his horse, the Portuguese officer cantered back to his men and waved for them to follow him along the valley, away from the Matabele warriors.

Believing the soldiers to be running from them, the warriors howled in disappointment. They had not yet blooded their spears. There was not an Induna with them. Lacking his authority they would have broken ranks and pursued the Portuguese had Daniel not shouted them down, emphasising his words with a warning shot.

When he had their attention, he said, 'There will be no battle. The horsemen are Portuguese soldiers. They have come to escort my wife to her father.'

His words brought grumbles of disappointment from the younger warriors – the 'Mahaja', the unremittingly disgruntled young heart of Lobengula's army. Too young to have taken part in the fighting that marred Lobengula's accession to the Matabele throne, they listened enviously to the tales of battle, related about the camp-fires by older warriors. Each of them was eager for the day when he too would take part in a battle worthy of retelling again and again.

There would be no glory for them today, but Daniel did not breathe easily until the warriors lowered their shields and began chaffing each other in a slightly embarrassed manner, as tension eased.

Daniel called the Portuguese officer and took him to the wagons to introduce him to Elvira, Therese and the boys. The young Lieutenant's name was Carlos St Anna, a name with a familiar ring. Looking at him more closely, Daniel saw that the features of the young man closely resembled those of the officer he and Elvira had known so well before they were married.

'You are the son of Colonel Francisco St Anna?'

'*General* St Anna.' The young Lieutenant corrected Daniel proudly. 'You know him?'

'We both knew him very well. Your father commanded the garrison at Sena when I lived there. He was not very much older than you are now, in those days. He and my husband fought against the Pombeiros together,' Elvira smiled at Lieutenant St Anna, uncomfortably aware that Wyatt was staring at his father with undisguised hero-worship. He had been told little about Daniel's earlier days in Mozambique. Lieutenant St Anna also showed rather more deference to the man he had at first mentally dismissed as just another Englishman. Albeit one fortunate enough to be married to a prosperous and influential Portuguese of very good family.

Daniel was unaware of the rise in his status. He was more concerned with Lieutenant St Anna's open admiration for Therese. She was very aware of his regard, serving to increase Daniel's disquiet. Daniel's earlier years were so far removed from his present way of life that they might have involved another man – but there was one memory that Daniel could not forget. It concerned an incident that had occurred not very far from the valley where they now camped. He had ridden away from that spot on a blustery, grey day many years ago with Victoria beside him, doing his best to keep between her and the bodies that hung, wry-necked, from a tree beside the path. One of the dead men was Mariano, Therese's true father. He had been executed on the orders of Lieutenant Francisco St Anna ... father of the man who had just carried Therese's hand to his lips!

Daniel realised with a start that Lieutenant Carlos St Anna was speaking to him, 'You will be able to resume your acquaintanceship with my father when you reach Quelimane. He is now Commander-in-Chief of the army in Mozambique and his office is there.'

'But we're not going to Quelimane. We're on our way to Sena. To visit Senhor Farrao.'

'Forgive me! I was forgetting that news could not possibly have reached you yet. Captain General Farrao is no longer at

Sena. The Governor of Mozambique was recently recalled to Portugal. Senhor Farrao has been appointed Acting Governor, in his place. He is now, of course, at Quelimane.'

Now Daniel knew why the mention of Senhor Farrao had made such an impact on the young Lieutenant. Elvira's father had become the most powerful man in the ancient Portuguese colony of Mozambique.

Lieutenant St Anna insisted that the Matabele escort should now return to Bulawayo. He would escort them for the remainder of their journey, first to Sena, in the hope of finding a suitable boat to take them to Quelimane, and then downriver to the Portuguese port.

Daniel sent the Matabeles off with a message for Lobengula, commending the men on the manner in which they had performed their duties and they left well pleased with themselves.

The next night, Daniel and the Portuguese soldiers outspanned in yet another of the attractive, well-watered valleys which abounded in the Manica Mountains. As they sat about the fire Lieutenant St Anna told Daniel the reason why he was in the area. Acting Governor Farrao had sent him to remind the Manicaland Chiefs that their allegiance lay unequivocally with Portugal.

The Chiefs were anxious to assure Lieutenant St Anna that they needed no reminding. Living in great style only a few miles to the east of their lands was Manuel Antonio de Souza Gouveia, a Goanese landowner of mixed Portuguese and Indian parentage. His slave-trading links with the Arabs were extremely profitable and enabled him to maintain a large force of armed retainers. Because his vast estates bordered an area that was the subject of dispute with all those parties interested in Central Africa, the Portuguese bestowed upon him the title of 'Captain General of Gorongoza', charging him with the task of securing the loyalty of all Manica Chiefs in the disputed area.

The Portuguese authorities had made a good choice. Gouveia believed in rule by terror and his methods were terrifyingly effective. A Manica sub-chief complained to the Governor of Mozambique about the high taxes Gouveia was levying on his people. Captain General Gouveia's response was to send his private army to Manicaland to 'visit' the sub-chief. They returned to Gouveia's stronghold driving herds of captured livestock before them. Not one of the sub-chief's people remained on the lands that had been theirs for as long as men could remember. The Manica women and children were sold into a life of slavery. The men, together with the old folk, had their throats cut by Gouveia's mercenaries.

On the way to Sena, Lieutenant St Anna explained that it was necessary to make a slight detour, in order to call on Captain General Gouveia. He had some dispatches to deliver from the Acting Governor. Lieutenant St Anna spoke with the air of apologetic embarrassment adopted by all Portuguese of breeding, when they were forced to deal with Gouveia. To them, Gouveia was an 'animal', to be kept well away from cities and other places where civilised people gathered. At the same time, they recognised the need for such a man to act as a 'guard dog' along the uncertain borders of their territory.

Daniel had heard many rumours of Gouveia, the scourge of Manicaland. Yet, when the wagons creaked to a halt outside the huge, rambling, grass-thatched house on Gouveia Mountain and the Captain General came out to greet his visitors, the first sighting of the Goanese 'monster' came as a great anticlimax. Manuel Antonio de Souza Gouveia, was a small, insignificant man whose manners as a host could not be faulted. He bowed unctuously over Elvira's hand, and drooled over Therese. He was cooler in his welcome to Daniel, but that was only to be expected. Rhodes had done nothing to improve the already strained relationship between British and Portuguese.

When the Captain General learned of the contents of Daniel's wagons, his manner towards him thawed considerably and he asked if he might examine the ivory Daniel was carrying to the coast.

'Certainly. I wouldn't deny any man the opportunity to view the finest ivory in Africa,' Daniel replied, the trader in him coming to the fore.

Gouveia gave him a non-committal grunt, but when he had examined a sample from each of Daniel's wagons he showed much more enthusiasm.

'We have fine elephants here in Gorongoza too,' he said.

'But you are quite right, this is first-class ivory. What price do you expect it to fetch on the coast?'

Daniel named a price that was considerably higher than he would have asked from Senhor Farrao.

Gouveia shrugged. 'You *might* receive such a price, if you are prepared to wait for a buyer.' He then made an offer that was lower than Daniel's quote, but still higher than Daniel would receive from Senhor Farrao. 'I will pay you in gold. You can take it with you, or call here for it on your return.'

'I'll settle for a note drawn on a Quelimane bank,' said Daniel.

'As you wish. Then it is agreed?'

'It's agreed.' Daniel shook Gouveia's limp, pudgy hand. A deal concluded here suited him well. Senhor Farrao was now the Acting Governor General of Mozambique. He would not want to concern himself with matters of trade – and without the heavily laden wagons, Daniel and his party would be able to travel much faster across the unhealthy Mozambique plains.

Then Gouveia revealed some of the character that Daniel had expected to discover. 'The girl who travels with you – Therese. She is yours to sell?'

'She's not up for sale. She's the daughter of a friend.' Daniel wondered what Gouveia's approach would have been had he known she was also the daughter of one of the most famous rebels Mozambique had known.

'Ah! But you will have some influence with her? You could persuade her to remain here? It would prove very rewarding for you, Senhor Retallick.'

'Rumour has it that you've enough wives already.'

'I have *many* wives, Senhor. Enough . . . ? No, I think not.'

'Well, however many you have would be too many for Therese. She wants a one-woman man – and before you become too interested, I suggest you have a chat with General St Anna's son. I think he too has an interest in Therese.'

Daniel hoped the warning would deter Gouveia, but he determined to give Gouveia Mountain a wide berth on the return journey.

Later that evening, after a splendid meal, Daniel went for a walk about the grounds of the house, while Elvira prepared the younger boys for bed. In a quiet, enclosed garden that boasted a pool and a tiny waterfall, Daniel surprised a dark-eyed girl who looked to be part-Arab. He knew instinctively that she was one of Gouveia's 'wives'. She did not run away, as he thought she might. Instead, she stared at him with bold brown eyes. Then her tongue touched her upper lip briefly, and she gave him a smile that carried an unmistakable invitation.

At that moment a guard rushed from one of the buildings adjoining the garden and in angry Arabic ordered the girl inside.

Daniel smiled, remembering Gouveia's words. The Goanese Captain General might consider he could manage more wives, but Daniel doubted if they could be kept out of mischief.

To Daniel it had been no more than a harmless incident, quickly forgotten. But Gouveia had observed the brief encounter from the balcony of his house and there was no amusement in his expression.

Daniel's family-wagons and the Portuguese escort had hardly passed out of sight the next morning when swift punishment was meted out to the bold-eyed concubine.

She was dragged screaming from the harem to the same garden where her indiscretion had taken place. As she fell to her knees, sobbing and begging for mercy from the man to whom she belonged, the remaining ladies of Gouveia's harem were brought out. They were to witness the fate that would be theirs if they too forgot themselves and raised their eyes from the ground to look at another man.

Two men were also brought to the garden, their hands bound behind them. Slaves from the Sudan, they had been emasculated to provide Gouveia with harem guards. Their crime was twofold. First, they had allowed the erring concubine to slip past them to the garden. Secondly they had not reported the matter to their unforgiving master.

As the women of Gouveia's harem watched in horror, too frightened of the Captain General to avert their eyes, the woman and two men died, their throats slit by an Arab. The executioner was an Arab butcher, employed to kill animals in the special manner dictated by the religion of Captain General Gouveia's frequent Moslem guests.

CHAPTER ELEVEN

The visit to Gouveia's home had a strangely sobering effect upon the family party that had set off from Insimo in such high spirits. The Captain General of Gorongoza could not be faulted as a host, yet even the two youngest children had lapsed into unaccustomed silence in the somewhat sombre atmosphere of Gouveia's home.

Accompanied by Lieutenant St Anna's mounted escort they made fast time to Sena. Unfortunately, the only vessel available here was an ancient, open steam launch of about thirty-five feet in length. It had been at the fortified village for two months, having broken down en route to the garrison town of Tete, further upriver.

The launches master-cum-engineer was quickly located in a nearby native village and sobered up by St Anna's men. He grudgingly admitted that the engine of the launch *might* be repaired in a few days – given the services of a number of strong men, and a competent blacksmith.

The repairs in fact, took seven days and Elvira made the most of the time spent in her childhood home. She entertained neighbouring prazeros and proudly introduced her family to old family servants. When word went around that Elvira was at Sena, old friends came from miles away to admire the boys and tell Elvira how well married life agreed with her.

The children were in great danger of being thoroughly spoiled by the time the launch was repaired, but when Daniel heard the first wheezing strokes of the aged steam piston, he wondered whether spoiling his family might not be preferable to risking their lives on the Zambezi River in such an aged and decrepit vessel.

Indignantly, the owner of the steam launch assured Daniel that he and his vessel had been navigating the river between Tete and the sea for twenty-five years, and both were good for another twenty-five.

Much of the family's belongings had to be left behind at

Sena, for lack of room in the boat. In addition to Elvira, Daniel, the boys and Therese, Lieutenant St Anna insisted on accompanying them, with six of his soldiers.

Elvira shared Daniel's opinion of the old steam launch, but to the four boys this was the most exciting part of the long journey. The water in the river was low and, as the boat coughed and spluttered its way down-river, vibrating with every slow beat of the engine, it frequently ran aground. It seemed that soft mud banks abounded just beneath the surface of the sluggish brown water on every bend.

The engine of the launch had insufficient power to drag the vessel off the mud against the current, and it became the duty of Lieutenant St Anna and his soldiers to plunge into the water and heave the boat clear. During this operation, which occurred at least a dozen times each day, Daniel and Wyatt stood guard with their rifles, ready to scare away the crocodiles.

Once they had chugged past the sleepy, Portuguese village of Shupanga, the going became easier. The river widened out considerably and soon they were steaming easily through the mangrove swamps of the Zambezi estuary. Here they encountered a new hazard as the progress of the antiquated launch became subject to the ebb and flow of the tide.

There were many crocodiles here, and schools of hippopotami. Their great, water-polished bodies threatened disaster on more than one occasion when they bobbed to the surface of the water in the path of the launch. In the stillness of the night, when the boat's engine was silent and the occupants of the launch had bedded down in the bottom of the boat, lions and leopards could be heard growling and coughing among the lush undergrowth on the shore. The passengers slept with soldiers in the bow, amidst the carelessly stowed luggage, and Daniel and his family in the stern, behind the stacks of short, cut logs that fuelled the furnace of the launch.

There was little opportunity for romance in such a cramped and gregarious setting. Yet Lieutenant Carlos St Anna and Therese managed to make considerable progress. Unable to take long walks ashore, they were often to be seen sitting close together in the bow of the boat. Carlos St Anna would ostensibly call her attention to distant landmarks, or features on the river, using the opportunity to touch her, his head close to hers as she pretended not to see the object in question.

In the evenings the young couple would sit talking together in a low whisper, long after the other passengers in the launch were asleep. In this way they learned much of each others thoughts and hopes.

They were talking together on the night disaster struck the small party. It was the second night in the fetid mangrove swamp. The master of the launch had hoped to clear the unhealthy, mosquito-ridden area by dusk, but the craft had been able to make little headway against a strong tide. Tying up alongside the bank at dusk, the occupants of the launch ate a hastily prepared and unappetising meal. Then, with the exception of the young couple, they settled down to sleep, doing their best to ignore the persistent and irritating mosquitoes that abounded in the swamps.

Daniel felt he had hardly closed his eyes when he was awakened by the hand of Lieutenant St Anna. He sat up quickly, 'What . . . ?'

'Shhh! Listen.'

Daniel became aware of a sound that was like nothing he had ever heard before. At first he thought it was the roll of distant thunder, but it did not die away as did thunder. Instead the rumbling continued, growing louder with every moment that passed.

'What is it?' Daniel whispered.

'I don't know.'

The sound appeared to be coming closer. Beside Daniel the children began to stir.

'Wake the boatman,' said Daniel. 'Perhaps he knows . . . .'

The Portuguese boatman was already scrambling to his feet. In the moonlight, Daniel saw the man's abject fear as he hurriedly crossed himself.

'Madre Maria! A bore – a big wave. It is heading upriver. Get your family ashore – *everyone* ashore. Quickly! Make for the highest ground you can find. I must slacken off the mooring ropes or they will break and my boat will be lost.'

The passengers were already awake by this time and Daniel hurried to get them together. The huge wall of water, rushing upriver at twenty miles an hour made a deafening sound. Shouting at Elvira to follow him, Daniel snatched up the bewildered four-year-old Benjamin, who was beginning to cry. Stepping ashore, he reached back for Wyatt who was carrying Adam, his second youngest brother.

At that moment, the advance swell of the bore reached them, raising the level of the water by three feet. It took Wyatt beyond Daniel's grasp. Seconds later the giant wall of water struck. Daniel was bowled over and carried away, the sheer weight of the water threatening to crush him. He was flung against the rough clinker-planking of the launch, then tumbled end-over-end and carried upriver with the bore.

He was saved by a dense tangle of mangrove root, just when he feared his lungs would burst. Gripping tightly to the slimy, tangled roots with his free arm, he held on against the pull of the water, his other arm still tight about the limp body of Benjamin.

Just when Daniel felt his lungs could hold the air in them no longer, his head broke clear of the water and he was able to breathe again. Almost immediately, his feet touched bottom and he sank knee-deep in mud.

Benjamin was more dead than alive, but as Daniel floundered to the low river bank, the child began coughing and whooping as his lungs expelled water and sucked in air. Moments later Benjamin began to struggle frantically in Daniel's arms.

'It's all right . . . . It's all right, son. We're safe.'

Daniel's breathless attempt to calm his son was successful. Moments later father and son lay side-by-side on the bank, gasping in air together. Then, still breathless, Daniel rose to his feet and scooped up his young son. They had to find the others.

The deafening boom of the phenomenal tidal bore still filled the air, but it was receding. Somewhere along the river bank, Daniel heard a voice calling in Portuguese for help. Daniel squelched his way towards the sound, at the same time calling at the top of his own voice to Elvira and the remainder of the boys.

He found a soldier wedged in an uncomfortable, but not dangerous position among the roots of another mangrove tree. The soldier was easily extricated and new voices could be heard calling in the darkness along a hundred yard stretch of the river bank. When he heard Elvira's voice calling in answer to his own, he made his way towards her.

Elvira was close to the boat and Nathan was safe with her. They had been fortunate. The boatman had succeeded in slackening the rope at the bow of the steam launch — but not the stern rope. When the advance swell arrived, the launch was lifted in the water and slewed broadside on to the bore. With tons of water thundering down upon it, the boat was thrown on its side, spilling out the occupants. Elvira and Nathan clung to a part of the boat sheltered from the main weight of the tidal wave. The boat now lay on its side, securely wedged in the mud.

Wyatt and Adam were still missing, but as panic rose in Elvira, Daniel assured her they would be found. He squeezed her hand confidently, but he had spoken with more optimism than he felt.

'I'll help you to search.' Elvira was distraught. Wyatt was her eldest son and they had always been very close.

'You stay here. Wyatt's a sensible boy. He'll make for the boat as soon as he can and he'll expect to find you here waiting for him.'

Leaving Benjamin with his mother, Daniel set off upriver in the path of the bore. He occasionally met with soldiers making their way back to the boat, but he found no sign of either Wyatt or Adam.

Behind him, Daniel heard a cry as the boat was righted and, water-filled, floated low in the water. Beneath the boat was the body of a soldier, the first casualty of the freak tidal wave.

Daniel stumbled along the muddy bank, calling the names of his two boys and was soon joined by Lieutenant St Anna. Therese was safe. She had been hurried inland by the young Portuguese officer moments before the wave struck. Only the two boys and a soldier were unaccounted for and Daniel prayed that he would find the boys safe and together.

Lieutenant St Anna brought Daniel a rifle and cartridge belt, recovered from the launch locker. There were crocodiles and hippopotami here, both dangerous to an unarmed man.

Two hundred yards along the bank they met the missing soldier, limping his way back to the boat. In answer to their question he replied that he had neither seen, nor heard anything of the boys. He also informed them that there was a deep creek, extending a long way inland, only a short distance upriver. It could not be crossed in the darkness.

Ignoring this warning, Daniel and Lieutenant St Anna continued to search the bank until they arrived at the creek. The soldier had been right. It *was* impassable. As Daniel stood on the edge of the deep water he heard an asthmatic wheeze from a clump of reeds not twelve feet from where he and Carlos St Anna stood. There was also the sound of great teeth tearing at something and Daniel realised a crocodile was feeding in the darkness.

Querulously, he called, 'Wyatt? Adam?' There was no reply. Sliding back the safety catch on his rifle, Daniel sent a bullet crashing into the reeds.

There was a startled grunt from the ugly amphibian as it splashed into the water and glided away in the darkness. Fearful of what he might find, Daniel edged his way through the reeds, feeling the way with his feet. He had not gone far when the toe of his boot touched something that gave slightly. Reluctantly, Daniel reached down and touched the still form. It was the part-eaten carcass of a buck that had been caught up in the flood waters.

Daniel and Lieutenant St Anna traced the extent of the creek for more than half-a-mile before accepting that it would be impossible to cross on a rising tide. Returning to the mouth of the creek, they met soldiers coming to help in the search for the missing boys.

As the party trudged back towards the launch in a dispirited silence, the words of the late Mondoro of the Great House of Chiefs sprang to Daniel's mind, to add to his concern. He had said it would be left to Nathan to continue the family line. Was this the way Wyatt was to die?

There was no sleep for anyone during what remained of the night. The boat had to be baled-out and an effort made to assess the damage to the vessel. Daniel and Elvira worked together in silence, neither daring to put into words the fears that dominated their thoughts.

As dawn began to lighten the sky above the still-distant ocean, Daniel and the soldiers set off upriver once again. Few of them entertained any hope that the boys were still alive. Had they escaped from drowning, they would have had to contend with the night-hunting creatures inhabiting the dense thickets of the swamp. But no one questioned Daniel's determination to learn the fate of his two sons. They would search for as long as was necessary.

The creek they had encountered during the night was still deep, but wandering along its bank they reached a spot where the far bank jutted to within a stone's throw of their own. Here, Daniel and Lieutenant St Anna decided to swim across, leaving the remaining soldiers behind.

The undergrowth on the far side of the creek was very dense and it took the two men three hours to cover an estimated mile along the river bank. The flash-flood had claimed many animal victims along here. One dead buck was lodged twelve feet high, in the fork of a tree and they saw the bloated carcass of a hippo, swirling grotesquely downriver, four stubby legs pointing to the sky.

Another half-mile and Lieutenant declared that it would be useless to go on.

'To search further would be foolish,' he said sadly. 'I know how you must be feeling, Senhor, but you have a responsibility to the other members of your family. Soon the tide will turn again. What if there is another of these bores? We must be there to help them.'

In his heart, Daniel knew that St Anna was right. Nevertheless a stubbornness born of despair would not let him return to the launch without one last effort. Looking along the river, he pointed to a sharp bend, some three hundred yards distant. 'We'll go as far as the bend. Then we'll turn back.'

Wearily, St Anna nodded his head and set off behind Daniel, both men pausing every few yards to raise their hoarse voices in futile shouting.

They had covered almost three-quarters of the agreed distance when suddenly Daniel stopped and held up a hand to halt St Anna.

'Listen!'

The thick, damp undergrowth effectively muffled most sounds and the two men listened for a full minute without hearing anything. Daniel cupped his hands to his mouth and bellowed with all the power in him.

'ADAM! WYATT!'

Both men waited and the silence was as heavy as before — then they heard a faint cry.

'There! Did you hear it?'

'It might have been no more than an ape,' St Anna said doubtfully. 'Do not build your hopes too high—'

'An ape, be damned!' Daniel shouted. 'That was a child. I'm certain of it. WYATT . . . ? ADAM . . . ? Where are you?'

The reply was no more audible than before, but this time both men agreed that it came from well inland, and some way ahead.

Ignoring the creepers and thorns that tugged at him, Daniel fought his way through the undergrowth until he fell. Climbing to his feet, he called again.

'WYATT . . . ? ADAM . . . ?'

As the sound of his voice died away, Daniel's fingers dug into the palms of his hands and his lips moved silently in unfamiliar prayer.

'Pa . . . . We're here. We're here . . . .'

It was the voice of five-year-old Adam. As tears of uncontrollable relief sprang to Daniel's eyes, Lieutenant St Anna tugged at his sleeve. 'It came from this direction.'

Fifty yards further on, the two men came to a clearing. There, on the far side, perched in the fork of a tall tree were the two missing boys.

'Pa!' Adam wriggled delightedly in his brother's arms, but Wyatt neither released him, nor uttered a sound of greeting. Daniel's fears rose once again. Climbing the tree, he quickly learned the reason for Wyatt's peculiar behaviour.

Both boys were cut and bruised as a result of their experience in the river, but Wyatt had additional problems. Always susceptible to insect bites, he had spent the long dark night prey to the countless mosquitoes. Frightened of releasing the grip he had on his restlessly sleeping brother, he could do nothing about the blood-sucking insects. He was barely aware of the dawn's arrival, so swollen and tightly closed were his eyelids, and the face about them.

As if this were not enough Wyatt had swallowed so much salt water during the terrifying minutes he had been caught in the clutches of the bore, that it had affected his larynx. His voice no more than a painful whisper, he had heard Daniel calling long before his young brother. Unable to call out himself, he could not make his brother understand what he was trying to tell him.

When Daniel reached the two boys he had to prise Adam free of his brother's life-saving grip. Adam clung to his father desperately for a few minutes before being lowered to Carlos St Anna.

Bringing Wyatt down proved much more difficult. He had crouched in the tree, out of the reach of most wild animals for twelve hours. Blinded, he dared not move or shift the grip he had on his brother. Now he suffered from agonising cramp in almost every muscle.

When Daniel eventually brought him to the ground, the eleven-year-old boy clung to him as though he were still a baby and Daniel saw tears squeezing their way between the slits where his eyes were hidden. Wyatt was trying to speak and when Daniel brought his head close to his son's lips he heard his hoarse, almost inaudible whisper.

'I . . . was . . . scared, Pa. I was . . . scared.'

'Scared? No, son, not you. You're as brave a man as any I know.'

Choking back his own emotion, Daniel settled his eldest son more comfortably in his arms and set off to return the way they had come. He remembered the remainder of the Mondoro's prophecy: '. . . your first-born will prove himself truly a man.'

Daniel offered up a silent prayer to the Mondoro's Spirit God, Chiminuka. He asked him to accept Wyatt's brush with death as being sufficient to satisfy the prophecy and wipe the slate clean. . . . .

CHAPTER TWELVE

By the time the battered steam launch wheezed into the harbour at Quelimane, Wyatt had succumbed to a severe bout of malaria. Consequently, the reunion of the Acting Governor of Mozambique with his daughter and grandchildren became a desperate bid to organise doctors and other medical staff.

Within a few days, Daniel, Adam, and three of the surviving soldiers were also struck down with the same illness. To the Portuguese, it confirmed their widely held belief that the Zambezi estuary was so unhealthy as to be uninhabitable.

Daniel and Adam recovered quickly, aided by generous doses of quinine, but Wyatt hovered between life and death for three long weeks. Then, one morning, he opened his eyes and smiled at his mother. The fever was gone. For the first time in all those weeks, Elvira, gaunt with worry, felt able to leave his bedside.

From that day, Wyatt grew steadily stronger, but not until late October, when the family had been in Quelimane for two months, was he strong enough to leave the house. By now Daniel was anxious to return to Matabeleland, hoping to arrive there before the rains began in earnest.

Now it was Elvira's turn to spring a surprise. She and Daniel were talking in their bedroom, in the Governor's official residence. Busying herself re-arranging flowers in a great, windowsill bowl, she said, 'I think it might be better if we remained here until the rainy season was over.'

'Stay in Quelimane? There's work to be done at Insimo. Wyatt is well enough to face up to a slow journey home now.'

'Perhaps . . . but I think I am not.'

Daniel was puzzled and Elvira smiled at his confusion. 'It would be sad after presenting you with four sons if I should lose what I am quite convinced will be a daughter.'

Daniel's incredulity quickly changed to undisguised joy. 'You're sure . . . . ?'

Elvira nodded happily. 'I was certain before we had the

accident on the river. I said nothing then because I was afraid I might lose it . . . and you had enough to worry about with Wyatt.'

'Worry . . . ?' Daniel took Elvira in his arms and hugged her happily. 'I think it's wonderful news!' Smiling down at her, he asked, 'When will the baby arrive?'

'Early in March – and it *will* be a girl, I know.'

'Then we'll wait for her here in Quelimane. You'll have the best medical attention that's available. Now, let's go off and tell the good news to your father, and the boys.'

It was very hot in Quelimane during the rainy season. Hot and uncomfortably humid. The whole Retallick family spent a few weeks in the hills to the north of the city, but returned in time for the Christmas festivities.

For the four boys in particular, Christmas in Quelimane was a wonderful experience. It had always been a special time, a day for exchanging presents . . . a family occasion. But here, in Quelimane, in the heart of the Catholic Portuguese Colony, it became far more. They enjoyed the sight of streets of decorated houses, and were overawed by the pomp and beauty of the Christmas morning service in Quelimane's great church.

All of Quelimane's society was at the service. As he left, afterwards, Daniel found himself walking beside General St Anna. Ahead of them were Elvira, the boys – and Carlos St Anna, walking beside Therese.

'They make an attractive couple . . . but I remember seeing a face like that many years ago, when I too was a young Lieutenant. Am I mistaken, or is there Pombeiro in that girl?'

'There is, Francisco. Her mother is Victoria and the man she believed to be her father was Philippe. He died some years ago, a pardoned man.'

'I remember,' said General St Anna, non-committally. 'You say she *believed* him to be her father. Who is her *real* father?'

'I think you know the answer to that: Mariano.'

General Francisco St Anna allowed his breath to escape in a heavy sigh, 'The events of Vumba's kraal occurred almost twenty years ago. Has Victoria forgotten?'

Daniel shook his head. 'No, she has never forgiven you, or your countrymen.'

'Then there can be no question of marriage between Therese and Carlos?'

'Marriage? Are you serious?' Daniel looked at the well-dressed men and women leaving the church about them. 'Therese is a very nice girl, Francisco . . . but she is a Mambari — of mixed blood.' The use of the Matabele word had been automatic. 'Carlos is your son. Son of the General commanding the Portuguese army in Mozambique. Therese would never be accepted by your people.'

'You are mistaken, Daniel. This is Mozambique, not Mother Portugal. Here, I am a great soldier, with estates to match any in the land. In Portugal I am nobody. When I visit there you will find my name on no society guest list. Indeed, I hardly merit a salute from a non-commissioned officer. This is my home and here today I can see at least four women who are coloured — yet accepted by all. They, like all the other women, are dressed for the day. Tomorrow they will be in working clothes, kerchiefs about their hair, helping the workers in the fields. Judged not by colour, or breeding, but by the help they give to their husbands, and the manner in which they run their houses. *This* is the world to which Carlos belongs. It is to such a community he will bring a wife.'

Ahead of them, Therese laughed at something Carlos said to her and leaned towards him. Their hands met and held for a few moments, then fell away.

'I'll speak to Victoria,' said Daniel. 'But I promise nothing. She's a very determined woman.'

'If she were not there would be no daughter of Mariano to cast her spell upon my son. But you are going to be here for many months. I think it will be better if I send Carlos off on another expedition to the interior. The seasonal rains of Manicaland should be sufficient to dampen the ardour of the most passionate young man.'

After the excitement of the Christmas celebrations, life in Quelimane went on as indolently as before. The humid heat provided all the excuse the Portuguese needed to carry out only the minimum of work.

Then, one airless day in mid-January, Senhor Farrao sent a messenger to bring Daniel to his office.

When Daniel arrived, he found the Acting Governor pacing

the room, ignoring the perspiration that stood out on his red face. With no preamble, he strode to his desk, picked up a newspaper and thrust it at Daniel. 'Read this. It's that damned man Rhodes again. He and your Matabele King.'

The newspaper was an English language weekly from the Cape Colony. The headlines spread from edge to edge of the front page. 'RHODES OBTAINS EXCLUSIVE CONCESSION FROM MATABELE KING'. Beneath, in slightly smaller print, it added, 'Lobengula signs at last. Rhodes gets the lot.'

Daniel read on. The more he read the greater became his dismay. If the report were true it meant that Lobengula had given Cecil Rhodes a truly remarkable concession that gave him everything but the throne of Matabeleland.

Daniel lowered the newspaper, thoroughly bewildered. What could have happened to persuade Lobengula to grant such a concession – and to Rhodes, of all people? With his particular brand of ruthlessness, Rhodes would trample the Matabele into the ground.

'You think that is bad? The newspaper does not tell half the story. By the same boat I received a letter from the Portuguese Ambassador in Cape Town. He tells me Rhodes intends using the concession to commence mining in Mashonaland. I am protesting most vehemently, on behalf of my Government. Mashonaland is Portuguese territory. If Rhodes brings his miners there it will be an act of aggression against Portugal.'

Daniel had every sympathy with Senhor Farrao and could understand his anger, but it did not explain why the Acting Governor had sent a messenger for him.

'Because King Lobengula is your friend, you understand him. Why is he doing this?'

Daniel shook his head sadly. 'Lobengula is no longer the man I once knew. Certainly not the Jandu you met at Sofala. I don't think he is the man his people chose to lead them. He takes his own road now, helped along by brandy and champagne.'

But no matter how much Lobengula had changed, it seemed he still valued Daniel's friendship and advice. Before the month was out, a weary Induna, with an escort of only a dozen

Matabele warriors reached Quelimane, looking for Daniel.

The Portuguese soldiers, hastily called from the garrison barracks immediately surrounded the unfamiliar warriors and ordered them to surrender their weapons. The Matabeles knew nothing of what was being said and refused to give up their guns. An ugly situation was saved by Wyatt Retallick. He rode upon the scene and recognised the men as Matabeles.

His identification caused a great stir in Quelimane, where the Matabele were known only by rumour and exaggerated reputation.

Escorted by a rapidly increasing number of Portuguese soldiers, the warriors were brought to the Governor's office to await Daniel's arrival.

Daniel and Elvira were walking along the nearby promenade when the Acting Governor's messenger found them and they both hurried to Senhor Farrao's office.

Daniel recognised the Induna as a member of the Council of Indunas and treated him with a respect and warmth that did much to restore the Induna's bruised dignity. He had travelled far through a foreign land to reach this strange kraal where the houses were higher than the tallest Matabele tree. On the ocean beyond the town great creatures swam through the water belching smoke. It was a new and frightening world here. Not until he began talking to Daniel could the Induna overcome his awe and discharge the trust placed in him by his King.

'I have been sent by Lobengula to bring you back to him. The King has great need of you, trader. He has put his mark only on those papers given to him by white men he thought he could trust. Yet now it is said he has given away our country. This man Rhodes claims he may dig holes for gold wherever he wishes – even in the garden of the King. Lobengula has asked other white men to tell him the truth of this, but it seems the writing on the paper tells different things to all men. No two of them say the same thing. He needs you to tell him the truth of this, trader.'

'You've come a long way, Induna – yet you needed to journey only as far as Insimo. There you would have found a man who would not lie to you. Jaconus Van Eyck is an honest man.'

'He is all the things you say. Lobengula called for him when the Boers came to Bulawayo, demanding that their wagons be allowed to cross the country of the Mashona. They wished to seek new lands on the far side of the Zambezi River. Your friend sent them home again. Before they left they laughed in the face of Lobengula and said they would be back. Lobengula was so upset at this he has sent two Indunas to England, to speak to your Queen about the men who trouble him.'

Daniel found it difficult to hide his astonishment. 'Two Indunas have gone to England, to see Queen Victoria?'

'Yes, the missionary Loveday has gone with them – and the King sent Van Eyck to act as his personal interpreter. He thought it important that the Indunas be accompanied by at least one honest man.'

'Van Eyck's gone . . . ? Who's looking after Insimo?'

'The Mambari woman, Victoria.' The Induna came as close to a smile as any very tired man could. 'Lobengula sent an impi to guard your valley and help her with the work – she chased them away, firing a gun over their heads. She said they would eat more than they would earn for you.'

Daniel smiled briefly too. He had seen Victoria roused – and a Matabele Induna, scornful of a woman's ability to do a man's work was guaranteed to anger her.

'Please come, trader. You are Lobengula's friend. He needs you. He told me to tell you he is a blind bull surrounded by a pack of wild dogs. Now they are fighting among themselves, but the King fears that one day they will all rush in together and tear him and our country to pieces.'

'From what I have heard, Lobengula has already handed the country to them by giving Rhodes a concession.'

'Others say this too, but the missionary, Loveday, told the King that Rhodes is an important man. He said that if Rhodes is allowed to dig for gold he will drive all other white men away. The Commissioner from Bechuanaland also came to see Lobengula. He said it would please your Queen if Rhodes was granted a concession to dig for gold.'

Daniel sucked in his breath angrily. 'If men like Sir Sidney Shippard are mixed up in this, it's little wonder that Lobengula doesn't know which way to turn.'

'It is so, trader . . . and this man Rhodes has done nothing to chase away other white men. There are now more of them at Bulawayo than ever before. They bay like jackals about the fire.'

The Induna studied Daniel's face and read the indecision there. 'The King needs you, trader,' he repeated. 'My people need you.'

'You must go,' Elvira said quietly. 'Lobengula has done so much for us. The valley – everything we love – he has given to us.'

'But what can *I* do to help now?' They talked in English so that the Induna would not understand what was being said. 'It's too late to help him. I've told him time and time again to sign nothing. The moment I leave the country he scrawls a cross on the first piece of paper that's held out to him. As for sending Jaconus to England . . . !'

Daniel looked pointedly at the swelling of Elvira's body. 'Besides, there's the baby. I can't leave you now.'

'You will not leave me. I will come with you.'

Daniel opened his mouth to protest again, but Elvira reached a hand quickly to his lips. 'Please, let us not argue, Daniel. If we leave right away we will be home long before the baby is due. We *must* go. In your heart you know this. Lobengula is making a desperate plea to you for help. He believes, as do I, that you are the only one who can do anything for him.'

Daniel was not convinced that he would prove to be the saviour everyone was expecting, but Elvira was right. He could not refuse Lobengula's call. Whether or not Elvira accompanied him could be decided elsewhere.

To the Induna, he said, 'Come, I will arrange for you and your men to be given a place where you might rest. We will return to Bulawayo together.'

CHAPTER THIRTEEN

Senhor Farrao had grave misgivings about the family returning to Matabeleland at such a time and he did his best to dissuade them. That night, at dinner, he told them that all the news filtering from Matabeleland was bad.

'There is a very strong likelihood that Lobengula is no longer in control of the country,' he declared. 'I have it on good authority that the young warriors are on the verge of revolt.'

'The best authority on what is happening in Matabeleland is the Induna who arrived here today. Events may be moving too fast for Lobengula's liking, but there's nothing to suggest his leadership is threatened. The Mahaja are always complaining. They are young warriors – and young warriors want war. I've heard it all before. So has Lobengula. He and his senior Indunas listen to the wild talk of the young warriors and they smile. There is fire in the bellies of young Matabele men. They want to marry and raise families – but they can't do this until Lobengula grants them the right to wear a warrior's head-ring. Traditionally, this isn't done until they've proved themselves in battle . . . so they're anxious to fight someone. It's the way things have always been.'

'I hope you are right,' replied Senhor Farrao, gloomily. 'You will pay a high price if you are not.' The Acting Governor did his best to shake off his apprehension. 'But as you are determined to leave, I will do what I can to smooth your long journey. I have arranged for my own boat to take you upriver to Sena. I have also sent a runner to Captain General Gouveia, asking him to bring horses there. They will be faster than oxen for your wagons.'

Observing the look that passed between Daniel and Elvira, he added, 'I am aware of your feelings towards Senhor Gouveia. Unfortunately, he is the only man in the whole of the interior who owns horses.'

Senhor Farrao raised his own glass to them, 'What more can I say, except . . . go with God.'

* * *

The river voyage to Sena was pleasantly uneventful. The experience of Senhor Farrao's boatmen, a bright moonlit night and a flood tide all combined to take them through the worst of the Zambezi swamplands during the night hours, when the heat was not so unbearable.

At Sena they found that Gouveia had not yet arrived with the horses. They also learned they had missed Lieutenant St Anna by only two days. He had left Sena for his father's estates, a hundred miles upriver. Here he intended gathering militiamen to strengthen his small force of regular soldiers before moving on to Manicaland to remind the Chiefs of their allegiance to Portugal.

The realisation that she had missed Carlos St Anna by so short a time proved too much for Therese. The thought of perhaps never seeing the young soldier again made her realise how much he had come to mean to her. She had wanted to remain at Quelimane, believing he would soon return there, but Daniel insisted that she return to Insimo with him. He and Elvira had every sympathy with her, but they also had a responsibility to Victoria – and Daniel could not tell Therese of the objections he knew her mother would raise to a marriage with Francisco St Anna's son.

Therese left during the night on Senhor Farrao's sole remaining riding horse, leaving Daniel to fume at Gouveia's delay in reaching Sena.

It was another week before the Captain General of Gorongoza arrived, and the reason for the delay became immediately apparent. He and his men had been slaving. More than a thousand wretched women and children, yoked and tied, were herded to the far end of the stockade where they were closely guarded by men of Gouveia's 'army'.

Daniel's anger at the delay and its cause was shrugged off by the Captain General. This was Portuguese territory. What happened here mattered to no one but the Portuguese themselves.

It was no time to get into argument with one of Mozambique's most powerful men. Choosing a number of good riding horses, and taking along a guide, Daniel set off for the St Anna estates at Tete.

He arrived just too late to witness the wedding of Therese to

Carlos St Anna. Although arranged in a hurry, the marriage was no hole-in-the-corner affair. It took place in the small town's church, attended by friends and employees of the St Anna family.

The priest who had conducted the marriage made no apologies for his part in arranging the ceremony.

'A nice young girl who rides alone across a hundred miles of unknown country, to be with the man she loves deserves the blessing of the Church. Am I to say I will not marry them and allow them to go off and live together in mortal sin? No, Senhor Retallick. I say Mozambique has need of such spirited women. I told Carlos he had better marry her quickly, before some other young man came along and snatched her up.'

Therese stood beside her new husband and looked at Daniel with a mixture of defiance and happiness, coupled with a desperate wish for him to express approval of her marriage.

'Your mother is going to be very angry with me, Therese.'

'If she's ever had to make up her mind between doing something everyone else said was wrong – and losing her man, she will understand.'

Daniel thought of Victoria's love for Mariano . . . and later for his brother, Philippe. But Therese knew very little of her mother's early life. Victoria had worked very hard to ensure it remained a secret. Even so, Daniel knew she was not going to approve of this marriage.

To Therese, he said, 'I know Carlos has got himself a fine wife. His father will agree: We've already discussed it—'

Before he could say more, Therese flung herself at him. 'Thank you, Daniel. I *knew* you'd understand – you and Elvira. Please tell Ma . . . tell her I love her too. I *want* her to wish me well. It's just—'

'I know, Therese. She *will* understand, I promise you . . . but she'll probably never admit it to anyone. Go away now and write a letter to her. I'll take it with me.'

Pushing her away gently, he clasped Carlos St Anna's hand. 'Treat her well, Carlos. As soon as you're able, pay a visit to Insimo. You'll be made very welcome there . . . by everyone.'

Elvira shared Daniel's hopes for the young couple, but most of her thoughts now were for the life that was making its presence felt inside her. The delay at Sena had set back the plans she and Daniel had made, and brought the date the baby was due uncomfortably close.

Declining an invitation to spend a few days at Captain General Gouveia's mountain home, Daniel told the Goanese he was taking an easier route well to the south. It would take him through the long valley where the Rozwi Queen, uTshwebe, had her home.

'Why do you choose that particular route?' One look at Gouveia's face told Daniel that the question had not been asked from idle curiosity.

'uTshwebe is a friend. I arranged the marriage of her daughter to Lobengula, King of the Matabele.'

'Indeed? uTshwebe made a great many unwise alliances. She will make no more.'

'uTshwebe's dead?'

'Yes. I hope your friend Lobengula will not feel too distressed at the loss of one of his mothers-in-law. If he is, tell him Captain General Gouveia of Gorongoza may soon give him the opportunity of lodging a personal complaint. I am thinking of taking my army of four thousand men to receive an assurance from *him* that he acknowledges allegiance to Mother Portugal.'

Daniel laughed aloud at Gouveia's bravado. 'You'll need more than four thousand men. Lobengula has ten times that number – and none of them are slaves who will run at the sound of the first shot.'

Gouveia blinked when Daniel mentioned the strength of Lobengula's army, but he tried not to let Daniel see how much the information had impressed him. 'We shall see who will run.'

As the Captain General of Gorongoza rode away, Daniel was left with a feeling that he had just averted a foolhardy and bloody attack on Lobengula and the Matabele.

Travelling through the Manica Mountains, it became apparent that Gouveia had punished uTshwebe and her people ruthlessly. There were no signs of life in the hills for twenty miles about the deep valley and, when they reached the spot where the kraal had stood there was nothing left but a giant mound of ash covering the valley floor. The story of uTshwebe and the mystery of the scar she carried over her heart had passed into legend.

The valley had become a place of ghosts and shadowy memories and Daniel drove the wagons on, heading for less haunted country.

They were making good time now, although, after leaving the Manica Mountains, they crossed a narrow belt of tsetse fly country and lost four horses.

They were no more than sixty miles from Insimo when a large party of Mashonas began following them, running from the shelter of one rock to another along the ridges of the hills about them and hurling insults at the party.

Daniel fired a couple of shots in return, but they were warning shots only, aimed at persuading the Mashonas to keep their distance.

Not far ahead was a rolling plateau. Once there, the Mashonas would drop behind and the incident would be over. The Mashonas realised this too and a few of them hurried to get ahead of the wagons. Making their way through the tumbled granite boulders they reached a point as close as they dared to the wagons and their small Matabele escort.

Waiting until the leading wagon passed below, one of the Mashonas sprang to his feet and hurled a spear, running away without waiting to see where it fell.

The success of his throw exceeded all he could have hoped for. The spear smacked against the flank of one of the four horses harnessed to Elvira's wagon. Unhurt, but startled, the horse reared and shied. The sudden commotion frightened the other horses — and they bolted.

Elvira had the reins herself. She heaved back on them, trying to bring the horses under control, but there was no stopping them now. As they pounded along the valley, the wagon swayed and bounced alarmingly behind them. It had not been built to travel at such a speed. The four boys were in the wagon too and as they tumbled about, Wyatt fought his way forward until he too had a grip on the reins, adding his strength to that of his mother.

The horses had just begun to respond to the combined pull on the reins, when one of the front wheels of the wagon struck a large rock and splintered in a dozen pieces. The wagon tilted alarmingly. Then, accompanied by the screams of Elvira and the two youngest boys, it crashed on its side, Elvira falling inside and Wyatt being thrown clear. The weight of the wagon pulled the two rear horses to the ground and the leading horses slithered to a halt, to stand sweat-flecked, quivering with fright.

Daniel reached the wagon at the same time as the shaken but unhurt Wyatt. They both crawled inside the shattered wagon as native drivers from the other wagons ran to their aid and extricated the horses from a tangle of harness.

'Don't try to move,' said Daniel, as Elvira began throwing off the various items of clothing, cooking utensils and stores surrounding her.

'I'm all right,' insisted Elvira, to Daniel's great relief. 'Find the children . . . .'

Adam and Benjamin were howling noisily, but both boys crawled unaided from the rear of the wagon. Only Nathan remained in the wagon, amidst a pile of smashed boxes. He was clutching his arm, his face contorted in pain. Holding the limb up for inspection he said, 'I think it's broken, Pa—' with that, the nine-year-old boy fainted.

Wyatt and Daniel pulled Nathan from the wagon and an inspection of the arm revealed an irregularity, halfway between wrist and elbow. The bone had not broken through the skin and by the time Nathan regained consciousness, it had been splinted and tightly bandaged.

Daniel was confident the arm would heal satisfactorily, but he was far more worried about Elvira. She protested vehemently that she was well, but the attack and the overturned wagon had been a very frightening experience for her and, when she thought Daniel was not looking, he saw a grimace of pain cross her face.

The goods from the overturned wagon were quickly distributed among the remaining wagons and Daniel pushed on faster than before.

They reached the Insimo valley the following day, their arrival greeted by shrill howls of welcome from the Mashona women working in the fields, and cries of delighted greeting from the Matabele herd-boys.

Daniel drove hard for the house and not until she was

367

actually sitting in her own kitchen did Elvira finally admit that she felt unwell. When Daniel helped her to her bedroom, she sank on the bed with a groan of pain.

Panting heavily, she said, 'I think you had better find Victoria, quickly, my husband. I do not think our baby will wait any longer.'

Daniel shouted for Wyatt to ride off and find Victoria, but news of their return had already reached her. She rode up to the house before Wyatt had caught a horse.

Victoria took the news that Elvira was in labour with a typically efficient calm. She sent servants scurrying about the house, fetching and carrying. After a brief visit to Elvira she went to the kitchen to organise the things she was going to need – but all the time her eyes were searching for Therese.

When she did not see her, she put the question Daniel was dreading.

'I'm sorry, Victoria . . . it's a long story – but she's well, very well,' he added hastily to allay Victoria's sudden fear. 'She's married . . . eloped. But she's very happy. I went to see her—'

There was a loud crash as the large porcelain bowl Victoria was carrying slipped to the ground and smashed on the stone floor of the kitchen.

'Therese is . . . WHAT?'

'Married.' A cry came from the bedroom and Daniel took Victoria's arm. 'I promise you she is well . . . . Can we talk about it later. Please, Victoria, Elvira needs you.'

The cry from the bedroom was repeated. With a great effort, Victoria put the thoughts of her daughter to the back of her mind and hurried to Elvira.

The birth of Elvira's daughter was swift – and tragic. The child was born dead, killed by the accident that had hastened her arrival into the world.

Elvira grieved deeply. She had desperately wanted to give Daniel a daughter. Daniel was unhappy too. He blamed himself for not insisting that Elvira remain in Quelimane.

'I should have *made* you stay,' he repeated for the umpteenth time. 'Your father will say so too.'

'My father will say nothing. A woman's place is with her husband. He knows that as well as any man.'

Daniel was seated on the edge of Elvira's bed and she reached for his hand, fighting back her tears. 'Our baby was conceived in love, and she died loved. God will welcome her. Of that I am certain—'

Elvira's voice broke and Daniel held her to him until she slipped into a deep, exhausted sleep.

The baby was buried in the tiny cemetery, beside Philippe and Jannie Van Eyck. It was here too, beside the grave of her late husband, that Victoria came to read the letter that Therese had written to her. In the quiet of this place she finally came to terms with the knowledge that Therese was married to the son of Francisco St Anna, the man who had killed her true father. It was not easy, but once Victoria had made her decision a calmness came to her that would remain for the rest of her years. The ghost of Mariano had finally been laid. Therese had never known Mariano. She had thought of Philippe as her father, and had loved him. In return, Philippe had treated Therese as though she was his own daughter – and had loved her too.

Victoria would do nothing to destroy her daughter's happiness. Therese's father was buried *here*, at Insimo. Mariano had never been. Therese would receive her mother's blessing for a long and happy marriage.

CHAPTER FOURTEEN

The decision to send two senior Indunas to England had been made by Lobengula – but the seed had been sown by the Reverend Farewell Loveday!

For very many years Loveday had toiled in Matabeleland with little reward, either spiritual or monetary. He accepted that the conversion of the Matabele to Christianity would not be possible without a great deal of support, both inside the country and without. For this reason he approved of Rhodes' plans for settling the country. Loveday believed the European would bring with him Christian standards that the Matabele would ultimately accept.

Conversion of the Matabele was Farewell Loveday's first, idealistic aim. He had other ambitions too. Over the years he had seen men for whom he had obtained concessions grow rich on the proceeds of ivory sales. More recently he had carefully set the stage for the greatest coup of all, on behalf of the man who emulated the mythical Midas, turning all he touched to gold.

The exclusive mining concession granted to Rhodes was certain to make a number of new millionaires among the directors of the company being formed to exploit Lobengula's lands. Farewell Loveday had confidently expected to receive a substantial reward for his part in the great venture. Instead, he had been virtually ignored during the final stages of the lengthy negotiations, his place taken by three men sent to Matabeleland by Rhodes himself. When Loveday hinted he would like to be included among the shareholders of the new company, he was curtly informed that the shares were already fully subscribed.

It was clear that Cecil Rhodes' plans for Matabeleland and Mashonaland left no room for gratitude. Farewell Loveday decided to take steps to force the hand of the great man.

A few well-chosen remarks to Lobengula were sufficient to

set his plan in motion. Lobengula believed he had thought of sending his Indunas to England. But when they set off with Jaconus Van Eyck as official interpreter, Farewell Loveday was with them.

The news that the party was on its way to England to see Queen Victoria seriously alarmed Rhodes. He had gained a concession from Lobengula, but this was only the first move in his ambitious plans. He was aiming for a charter from the Queen for his company. With such a charter, backed by the might of Great Britain, a man could mould his own Empire. He would be a virtual dictator of all the lands at his disposal.

But the granting of such a charter was by no means a foregone conclusion. Already the Cape newspapers were eagerly printing stories that Lobengula was having second thoughts about his generous concession. Indeed, one or two smaller papers had published notices, purporting to be signed by Lobengula, repudiating the concession. The same newspapers also carried reports by knowledgeable hunters, expressing doubts about the reported extent of Lobengula's territory.

Such arguments and criticism mattered little to Rhodes. He was used to such outbursts of feeling against him – but he *was* concerned about Lobengula's motives for sending the deputation to London. He believed the Indunas must be carrying messages for Queen Victoria. If the two tribal elders reached England and fell into the clutches of the anti-Imperialist press, it might well spell the end of his carefully laid plans for Southern Africa. The Indunas had to be stopped.

Stopping the Reverend Farewell Loveday did not prove to be as simple as Rhodes would have wished. The Matabele missionary had served the great man for many years and was well aware of the extent of his considerable influence.

While the whole of the Bechuanaland Border Police were out scouring roads and paths, and even the wide wastes of the Kalahari Desert for the travellers, Jaconus Van Eyck was guiding them southwards, through Transvaal.

When the Bechuanaland authorities failed to intercept the Indunas, Rhodes realised they must have taken the Transvaal route. He mobilised the British Consul in Pretoria, and his own Company officials in that country, in a bid to locate them.

Rumour and counter-rumour came to him, but still the ill-assorted party eluded capture.

Then, one day, the London-bound group reached Kimberley.

Busy administrator though he was, Rhodes never ordered another to carry out a difficult task when it could be performed by himself. He sent for the Reverend Farewell Loveday.

The meeting took place in a ramshackle hut owned by Rhodes and located close to the Kimberley Club. It was furnished in a spartan manner, ill-suited to a millionaire, yet it was here that Rhodes carried out much of his work when he did not wish to be disturbed by the various activities and acquaintances to be found in the Kimberley Club. Rhodes also slept here on occasions on an ancient iron-frame bed in a corner of the room.

When Farewell Loveday entered the hut he expected to be greeted with an outburst of angry recrimination from the man whose interests he had served in Matabeleland for so long. Instead, Rhodes was the perfect host. In the rather bizarre setting, Rhodes behaved as though he were entertaining in a grand mansion. After pouring Loveday a drink, he enquired after his health, that of his family, the situation in Matabeleland – and then Loveday's journey, and the two Indunas he was escorting to London.

Farewell Loveday replied equally politely and it was Rhodes who was forced to breach the thin veil of affability hiding the real purpose of the meeting.

'You know, of course, that my concession for all the mineral rights in Lobengula's lands is an accomplished fact now? All the conditions have been met and the documents lodged with the British Government.'

Farewell Loveday took a steady sip of his drink. 'I too have a concession granting me mineral rights to a large section of Matabeleland. All relevant conditions of this have also been met – and it pre-dates your concession by some two years.'

'I don't believe you,' Rhodes said angrily.

Farewell Loveday shrugged. 'I'm quite confident that I can prove my claim to any interested party, and it so happens that both the Indunas travelling with me were witnesses to the concession.'

'Is this the only reason you are going to London? To prevent me from obtaining a charter? You are acting from spite, no doubt!'

'No, I am carrying a letter from Lobengula to Queen Victoria.'

'What does it say?'

'I think that is a private matter between King Lobengula and Queen Victoria.'

Rhodes looked at Farewell Loveday with renewed suspicion. 'I can prevent you from travelling. I have only to telegraph the Governor at the Cape and your natives will be stopped and sent back to Matabeleland, where they belong.'

'You can do that, Mr Rhodes, but there would be an awful fuss about it.' The Reverend Farewell Loveday was using his mildest missionary manner. 'I've already telegraphed the Governor to say we're coming. No doubt a great many members of the Church and the Native Societies will be at the station to meet us.'

Farewell Loveday stood up. 'Thank you for the drink. You know where to find me if you wish to speak to me again.'

Farewell Loveday left the untidy shanty and walked through the streets of Kimberley filled with an unusual exhilaration. He had taken on Cecil Rhodes, the most powerful man in Africa, and had successfully bluffed him, of that he was certain. Rhodes wanted nothing to cause even the slightest upset in his plans for a chartered company. He would send for Farewell Loveday again. If not here, then certainly in the Cape Colony. At that meeting, Rhodes would agree to whatever terms Farewell Loveday dictated. Rhodes would never forgive him, of course . . . but at least they would *both* be rich enemies.

Three days later the small party from the vast and sparsely populated land to the north of the Limpopo River stepped from the train to the bustle of southern Africa's largest and busiest city. In Kimberley, Farewell Loveday had groomed the Indunas for their foray into European social life by persuading them to adopt the white man's clothes, but neither Farewell Loveday nor Jaconus Van Eyck had been able to prepare them

373

for the revelation of European technology.

It began with the railway train. At first, the Indunas had viewed it with terror. Fear had turned to wonder when the train picked up speed and they had not been devoured by the fire-devils that lived deep in the heart of the engine.

When they reached Cape Town and viewed the ships, carriages and great houses, the Indunas realised they had much to learn about the ways of the white man.

Here in Cape Town, the Reverend Loveday suffered a minor setback to his plans. He had sent details of his proposed journey to the Governor, Sir Hercules Robinson, hoping to gain official backing for the Indunas. He should have known better. Rhodes had carried out his threat and telegraphed Sir Hercules.

The Governor refused to meet Farewell Loveday. He sent a message to say that although he was not able to prevent the small party from continuing their journey to London, the visit stood no chance of succeeding. Without his official backing the delegation would *not* be seen by Queen Victoria. Neither would any letters purporting to come from Lobengula be accepted by Her Majesty.

Farewell Loveday bullied, cajoled and pleaded until he finally arranged a meeting between the Indunas and the Governor. It was doomed from the outset. Sir Hercules Robinson demanded to see the letter from the Matabele King to Queen Victoria and wanted to know what verbal messages the Indunas carried. When neither was forthcoming, he dismissed the whole party from his presence. If they wished to waste time and money on an uncomfortable voyage to England they were at liberty so to do – but he would make quite certain the visit achieved nothing.

Rhodes had effectively demonstrated the power and influence he had in the Cape Colony, but Farewell Loveday was not beaten yet. The following morning he was waiting in the Governor's office when Sir Hercules Robinson arrived to begin the day's work. He had decided to show Lobengula's letter to the Governor.

It made startling and unexpected reading. Making no mention of Rhodes' controversial concession, Lobengula complained to Queen Victoria of Portuguese incursions in his country and spoke of Boers massing on his southern borders. He asked for the Queen's protection and, for the first time ever, set out the boundaries of his territories claimed by the Matabele nation. It took in not only the whole of Mashonaland but Manicaland too!

Suddenly, Farewell Loveday's mission to Britain took on a whole new meaning. With this letter entered in the official British Government records, it would add millions of pounds to the share value of any company which had Lobengula's concession.

Sir Hercules Robinson had the letter carefully copied, and three days later Cecil Rhodes arrived in Cape Town.

Rhodes went straight to the hotel where Farewell Loveday was staying. It was a different Rhodes from the ill-tempered man who had ridden rough-shod over Loveday in Kimberley. Today, Rhodes was friendly, benevolent ... almost apologetic. Of course Loveday *must* go to London. The delegation *would* be made official. Rhodes himself would see to this. As for the concession that Loveday himself held . . . .

When Cecil Rhodes left Farewell Loveday's room some hours later, the two men had agreed to merge their Matabele concessions, to their 'mutual advantage'.

Later that same day, Sir Hercules Robinson wrote to the Colonial Secretary in London, informing him that a mission from Lobengula would shortly be arriving in England. He requested that they be shown every diplomatic courtesy – and that arrangements be made for them to meet Her Majesty, Queen Victoria.

Unknown to any of the men who were celebrating their good fortune, there was another letter. Carried in a pouch strung about the neck of one of the Indunas, it never left his person. This letter was to be given only to the Queen of England. It complained to Her Majesty of those men who wanted so desperately to dig for gold in Lobengula's territories, that they lied and cheated in order to obtain concessions. He asked Her Majesty for her advice and her urgent assistance in keeping such men out of his Kingdom.

Had Rhodes known of the existence of this second letter he might not have been so eager to send the Indunas to London. In the long term, of course, the letter would make little difference to events in Africa. The letter carried by the Induna was a *personal* message from the King of Matabeleland to Queen Victoria.

The *other* letter was the one that would be passed through official channels and receive Government recognition. History would ignore Lobengula's personal plea.

Lobengula had displayed a lack of faith in Farewell Loveday, but his guile had been defeated by the subtle workings of the white man's protocol.

Lobengula's two Indunas were presented to Queen Victoria on 2 March 1889. On that same day, six thousand miles away, Daniel entered Bulawayo and was hurried into the presence of the King. Lobengula struggled to rise from his cow-hide throne and hugged Daniel as he would a long absent brother.

'It has been too long, my friend. Much too long.'

Holding Daniel at arm's length, Lobengula saw the strain of recent events on his friend's face and became momentarily struck with remorse. 'It sorrowed me to hear of the loss of your new-born child. It was fortunate it was only a girl child. However, Suliyana is sending your wife a gift—'

'Suliyana has cause for grief too. Her mother is dead, killed by the Portuguese.'

'Yes, word reached us from her people while you were away. I have sent a letter to the Queen of your country, telling her that the Portuguese are invading my lands and killing my people. I have asked for her help.'

Daniel winced, but Lobengula never noticed and continued, 'I would send impis against them myself, but the Portuguese live far away, and I have troubles close to my home kraal.'

'You certainly have, Inkosi. What's this concession you've signed with Rhodes?'

'I remembered your words and was careful what I said to the men belonging to Rhodes. We talked much before I made my mark. It was a good concession, when we spoke eye to eye. But writing words on paper seems to change them. They come back to the ears with a different meaning.'

'I had hoped you'd learned that lesson before I left. What on earth made you sign yet another concession?'

'The Induna Muvandi assured me that this was good for us. It offered guns – many guns, for the impis. I was told this man

Rhodes would give the Matabele much more than any other man.'

Daniel knew Muvandi, and liked him well. He was one of the few truly pro-European Indunas ... perhaps *too* pro-European.

'Rhodes will also *take* more than any other man in return,' retorted Daniel, grimly. 'Do you have a copy of this concession?'

Lobengula called one of his wives. She hurried away to return in a few minutes with a loosely rolled sheet of thick paper. As Lobengula unrolled the document, Daniel caught a glimpse of Muvandi. He was sitting impassively among a large group of fellow-Indunas, his eyes fixed upon the ground at his feet.

The concession began with a wealth of legal jargon, binding the signatories and their heirs and successors to the terms set out in the document. Daniel's eyebrows rose as he read of the gifts promised to the King. One hundred pounds a month, a thousand Martini-Henry breech-loading rifles, a hundred thousand rounds of ammunition – and a gunboat on the Zambezi River, or five hundred pounds in lieu!

But if the Rhodes faction was being uncharacteristically generous, the rewards the millionaire was gaining in return were truly stupendous. To Rhodes went complete and exclusive charge over all metals and minerals in Lobengula's domain, together with full power to do *all things he deemed necessary to win and procure the same.*

Daniel read the document through twice to ensure he had missed nothing. Lobengula watched his face anxiously.

'Is it true what men say, trader? Have I given away the lands of the Matabele?'

'Pretty well. You've given Rhodes great powers.'

'Does it mean Rhodes can send his men to come inside the King's kraal and dig for gold?'

'It does.'

'Even beneath my own house?'

'If that's where he thinks he'll find gold, yes.'

Lobengula's gaze sought and found the Induna whose advice he had followed in signing the treaty.

'Muvandi, friend to my father. Trusted Induna of my Council. You have betrayed the Matabele people.'

Muvandi rose slowly to his feet, his eyes still on the ground. As though in a trance, he picked his way through the seated ranks of his fellow Indunas until he stood before Lobengula.

'It is as my King says.'

'The light of day has seen enough of you and yours. Go!'

Muvandi raised his head now and met the King's anger with cool pride. 'I go, Inkosi, because it is your order, but I have served our people in the way I thought best. Bayete!'

With this last salute to his King, Muvandi turned away, pausing briefly before Daniel.

'Goodbye, trader. Today I am a dead man.'

These were Muvandi's last words. The Induna walked from the King's kraal, scorning the escort of jeering warriors who jostled him as he made his way to the place of execution. Daniel looked towards Lobengula, but the King had sunk back upon his cow-hide throne and was calling for beer to be brought to him. It would have been a waste of time for Daniel to plead for Muvandi's life. The King needed a scapegoat. Muvandi filled the bill.

Minutes later Muvandi had been clubbed to death by the King's executioners. It was only a beginning. For years the Matabele people had witnessed the ever-increasing encroachment on their lands by the white men. Many blamed Lobengula for not taking up arms against them. But no one dared air his opinion. The Mahajas, the young warriors, had been spoiling for a fight with the white men for years, but Lobengula had held them firmly in check. Now they vented their pent-up frustrations on the family of the man who had been publicly branded as the white men's tool.

All that afternoon and evening the Mahajas rampaged through Bulawayo, seeking Muvandi's many wives and children, slaying them where they were found.

As darkness fell and the effect of excessive beer-drinking took a firm hold on the young warriors, they cast their nets still wider. Anyone even remotely connected with Muvandi was hunted down and killed. Friends, servants, in-laws. All were targets on this bloody night.

When the sun rose again on Bulawayo, its rays fell on three hundred corpses, sprawling grotesquely where they had been slain. It had been the night of the Mahajas. Many of the white men who idled their lives away around Lobengula's fire heeded the warning. They were not welcome in the land of the Matabele.

Some 'asked for the road' that day. It was a request that was granted to them immediately. Others, less confident of the King's goodwill, simply saddled a horse and rode breakneck for the border. Their actions may have been dictated by panic, their fears premature, but the message spelled out by the slaughter was clear. The white man was not welcome in Matabeleland -- and the Mahajas, at least, were prepared to kill to keep them out.

CHAPTER FIFTEEN

In London, the two Indunas were taken to Windsor Castle to meet Queen Victoria. So impressed were the Matabele Elders with what they had already seen of London that they were fearful of meeting the ruler of such an incredible country. They cowered on the floor of the room where they waited her arrival, and nothing the palace officials or Jaconus Van Eyck said would persuade them to rise to their feet.

Eventually, the doors were thrown open and Queen Victoria entered the room. The two Indunas, peering childlike through their fingers at the most powerful ruler in the world were amazed. They saw a tiny woman who would not stand as tall as Lobengula's chest. What was more, she was smiling!

The Queen found the two men charmingly amusing, but insisted that they should rise to their feet to speak to her. With Jaconus Van Eyck interpreting, she asked them about their long journey, how they were enjoying Great Britain, then questioned them about their own families – and about Lobengula.

This was the moment for which the men had been waiting. The senior of the two drew himself up to the full height of a Matabele Induna and delivered the King's letter to her personally, in accordance with the instructions he had been given. In order that there should be no mistake, he had also learned the contents by heart. Now, through Jaconus Van Eyck, he told them to the Queen of Great Britain.

'King Lobengula sends his greetings. His body is well, but his mind is much troubled by those who come in your name, demanding that they – and they alone, should be allowed to dig for gold in his country. He begs you, as a great and wise ruler, to tell him what he should do?'

Queen Victoria was taken as much by surprise at the Induna's plea as were the officials about her. Without realising the full implications of her reply, she gave the Induna advice that, in any other circumstances, would have been perfectly sound.

'Tell Lobengula he should consider all such applications very carefully. It is not wise to put too much power into the hands of the man who comes first and exclude other deserving men. A King gives a stranger an ox – not the whole herd. Otherwise, what would strangers arriving at the King's house after, have to eat?'

It was a simply homily, but as Jaconus Van Eyck translated for the Indunas, he realised that the Queen's advice provided Lobengula with sufficient justification for withdrawing the Rhodes concession, thus blocking the millionaire's bid to gain a royal charter for his company. He smiled at the consternation among the officials.

Farewell Loveday was also aware of the implications of the Queen's words and his dismay was evident.

Fortunately for the fortunes of his company, Rhodes was himself in London. When Farewell Loveday repeated the Queen's words to him, Rhodes acted swiftly.

The Queen's untimely advice could cause trouble only if Lobengula received it in time to block the granting of a Royal Charter. While the Indunas were sent on yet another tour of military establishments, farms and impressive homes occupied by Company dignitaries, Rhodes telegraphed instructions to the Cape Colony. He ordered that all arms and money promised to Lobengula under the terms of the concession MUST be delivered immediately. In the meantime, he redoubled his efforts in England to have the coveted charter granted in the quickest possible time.

Rhodes worked hard and fast. Soon he had won over the vast majority of those opposed to the formation of a chartered company vested with almost unlimited power. Some he persuaded by charm. Others, who possessed particular influence, by the simple expedient of giving them a place on the board of the new company. His directors now included two Dukes and many other peers – one a son-in-law of Queen Victoria, prominent politicians and many of the country's soundest businessmen. Given time, the granting of a charter to such an august body was inevitable. But time was the one opponent Rhodes had not yet won over.

At the end of March 1889, the Indunas were close to exhaustion as a result of their strenuous programme and they announced that they wanted to go home. They had proved there *was* a Queen of Great Britain. She had given them a photograph of herself and a gold medallion to present to Lobengula. They had also been given the benefit of her wisdom. It was time to return to Matabeleland.

Not until the Indunas, Van Eyck and Loveday, were a day out from England did they discover that the ship on which they were taking passage had cargo on board for South America and would be calling there first. The Indunas would cross the Atlantic ocean twice before landing at Cape Town to begin the long land journey to Bulawayo.

It was August before the party returned to their homes after an absence of almost a year. They were received by the King and that night was spent in noisy celebration. Not until the sober light of day broke over Bulawayo did Lobengula have time to think about the words of the Queen whose photograph stared sternly but regally from the wall of his home.

'The Great Queen spoke wise words,' Lobengula repeated for the sixth time. Sprawled in his great, shapeless armchair, his chin sunk on his great chest, he spoke to Suliyana who busied herself repairing a hole in a faded brown trade blanket. 'The men who came from Rhodes lied when they said it would please the Queen if I gave him a concession.'

'But you *did* give it to him,' said Suliyana, brusquely. 'Just as you have signed others, in the past. It is being said by the Mahajas that all the lands won by Mzilikazi's spear are being lost by Lobengula's pen.'

'Who says this?' Lobengula roared, his head coming up. 'They will learn respect riding a stake—'

'There will be no names.' Suliyana bent low over the blanket and peered at her handiwork. 'One day you will need the young warriors to prove they can fight as well as they talk.'

After a long, brooding silence, Lobengula said gruffly, 'Do you think I have failed my people? Have I signed away the inheritance of our son?'

Suliyana put the blanket down slowly and gave Lobengula a look that was filled with sympathy . . . and love. 'You have done all that could be done. Mzilikazi would have gone to war

– and lost all. There is a time for all men. For the white man it is now. He is coming, whether or not he has his "concession". You might as well try to stop the sun rising as try to stop him. But, at the end of the day the sun sinks again. So it will be with the white man. All that you can do . . . all that any King might do, is to keep our people together. Ensure that when the white man's sun goes down there is still a Matabele nation. It will take much patience. You will need to fight our own people more fiercely than the white man.'

Suliyana carried the blanket close to her eyes for a final time. 'There is no other man who can do this. It is the duty of a King.'

'I wish I could be certain,' Lobengula rubbed a big hand wearily over his face. 'Sometimes I feel I have failed everyone. My father. My people. You—'

'Ah no! Jandu, the man I married, is no more. You are now Lobengula, King of the Matabele, and I am your Chief Wife. I have given you a son who will one day rule in your place. You consult me when you take a new wife, and you do not beat me. Because of these things I am respected above all women, even though I am not of the Matabele. You have not failed me, Inkosi. For as long as the Matabele listen to your wisdom you will not fail them either.'

After sitting in silence for some minutes, Lobengula struggled heavily to his feet and made his way towards the door. 'It is another day. I must take my place beside the indaba fire and listen to the problems of those who believe I have none of my own.'

Pausing beside Suliyana, he rested a huge hand lightly on her head for a brief moment. 'Have beer sent to me, wife. It is going to be a long day.'

His interpreting duties over, Jaconus Van Eyck returned to the Insimo valley. His arrival was warmly welcomed by Daniel and the Retallick family. The Boer hunter seemed tired and subdued, but it was not until Jaconus, Victoria and the Retallick family sat down to dine that evening that the reason for his reticence became known.

Jaconus Van Eyck told of the visit to the Queen at Windsor, and of her reply to the Induna's question. Daniel was jubilant. 'Then the troubles of the Matabele are over. The Queen of

England agrees with him. Lobengula now has all the justification he needs to repudiate this latest concession.'

Jaconus Van Eyck shook his head slowly and firmly. 'It's too late for that. Nothing Lobengula does will stop Rhodes now. The Royal Charter will be granted long before news of Lobengula's change of heart reaches the Queen. Besides, Lobengula has changed his mind so many times in the past that the British Government doesn't take him seriously any more.'

'They may not take him seriously in London, but Lobengula is King of Matabeleland. They'll *have* to take him seriously here.'

'No, Daniel. Rhodes is the man of the moment in London. He's the idol of the country and has the backing of the most influential men in the land. Britain will go to war if Lobengula tries anything. I realise it's unfair, but that's the way things are. Right at this moment, Rhodes can do no wrong.'

Jaconus Van Eyck fidgeted uncomfortably, toying with the knife resting beside his plate. 'I spoke to Rhodes in London before I left. He . . . he asked me to work for him.'

'What work could Rhodes possibly have for an honest man?' Daniel spoke with bitterness. 'He's got his concession . . . and it sounds as though he'll have his charter too. What more is he after?'

'He wants to occupy Mashonaland. Send in white pioneers to colonise the country.'

Jaconus Van Eyck's words left his listeners stunned.

'It sounds unbelievable, I know,' he continued, hurriedly. 'But Rhodes' plan makes sense. In London it's no secret that the Portuguese are out to grab as much land as they can before the borders of all lands to the north of the Limpopo River are fixed. It's equally certain that Boers from Transvaal are gathering, ready to grab a chunk of Mashonaland for themselves. It's the same old situation, all over again . . . only this time they've got to *do* something, or Rhodes will beat them to it.'

'Is Lobengula expected to sit back while white men divide up his lands between them?' asked Victoria, incredulously.

'It's too late for him to do anything,' said Jaconus Van Eyck. 'Yes, it's wrong. I know that . . . we all know. But every country with interest in this part of the world has its eyes on Lobengula's kingdom. Some are quite prepared to go to war to prevent the others from moving in. The Church is involved too, Daniel. Protestant, Roman Catholic, and Dutch Reformed. You know which is going to be best for the Matabele . . . . Lobengula has to get the best deal out of it that he can – and I think he'll get that from Rhodes.'

'Does this mean you've already made up your mind to work for Rhodes?'

'Yes.' Jaconus Van Eyck's manner was apologetic. 'I know you'll think me a turncoat, but I'm *not*. Hell, man, I'm almost as fond of old Lobengula as you are, but I reckon I can do more for him from inside Rhodes' organisation than outside. There's also a great chance for me to make something of my life from this. Rhodes is promising land and fifteen gold claims to every man who goes to Mashonaland with his column, together with whatever credit is needed to make a go of things.'

'Rhodes can afford to be generous with land that doesn't belong to him!' Daniel retorted angrily. 'God, Jaconus! You know the Matabele. Can you see them standing by and doing nothing while hundreds of white men march in and take over Mashonaland? They'll fight Rhodes and his "pioneers" every foot of the way.'

'That's what I told Rhodes. He doesn't agree. He says the concession gives him permission to mine anywhere in Lobengula's land – and to take whatever action he deems necessary to win ore and hold it. He says he needs a small army to do that and claims the authority is in the concession. All right, offering lands to those who go in for him is exceeding anything envisaged by Lobengula, but Rhodes has to keep men in the country somehow. If they leave, the Portuguese will move in. They're already fitting out an expedition to move into Mashonaland, from Mozambique. When I left London a very heated exchange was taking place between the governments of Britain and Portugal. Once Rhodes moves in he'll help to keep the Matabele and Portuguese apart.'

'The distance between Mozambique and Matabeleland has been sufficient to keep them apart so far,' retorted Daniel. 'This is just another of Rhodes' ploys, to justify his empire building . . . only this time he has the backing of Britain.'

'All eyes are on this part of Africa now, Daniel. It's a fever that's spreading throughout Europe. Either Britain gets a foot in the door, or another country will. That's the truth of it.'

'When are Rhodes' "pioneers" moving into Mashonaland?'

'Not until he has the charter. It will take some organising too. It won't be until next year, at the earliest.'

'Will you be staying at Insimo until then?'

'No, Daniel. Rhodes' original idea was to come straight through Matabeleland to Mashonaland. I managed to persuade him there would be far less chance of trouble if he kept his column well clear of the Mahajas. He wants me to go to Mashonaland with Selous and find a route for the pioneers that will take them as far as the Hunyani River.'

Daniel knew Frederick Courtenay Selous. One of the finest hunters to have found his way to Africa, he had brought ivory and skins to Lobengula in the past. In return, Selous had been granted permission to travel wherever he wished in the King's lands. Selous had stayed at Insimo on more than one occasion. Rhodes had employed two honest and skilful men as his scouts. Daniel hoped he would be as fortunate in the choice of the remainder of his force. Much would depend upon their level-headedness.

'You're free to leave whenever you wish, Jaconus. Until then you're a welcome guest in this house. You will be, whenever you pay us a visit – but I must tell Lobengula about Rhodes' plan. If he hears it from someone else he's likely to do something foolish.'

Abruptly, Daniel rose from the table and left the room. The Matabele nation was poised on the brink of disaster. Things were moving too fast. Unless he was able to slow them down the Matabele nation was doomed – and with its passing would go the life Daniel had carved out for his own family.

Daniel made his way to the stream not far from the house and sat upon a rock beside the tumbling water. He had once found gold here – the very mineral Rhodes claimed to be seeking, using it as an excuse to change the map of Africa. With a sudden chill of alarm, realisation came to Daniel that the concession gave Rhodes the right to seek gold in the Insimo valley – and Rhodes already knew it was here!

He heard the sound of footsteps on the path. A few moments later Elvira seated herself beside him. 'I knew this was where I would find you. It is where I come when things are troubling me. Wyatt does too, I have seen him.'

'A twelve-year-old boy shouldn't have troubles,' said Daniel, more gruffly than he intended, as she took his hand.

'He shares your troubles and mine,' replied Elvira softly. 'He loves us both. He loves this valley too. It is the only home he has known.'

'I know that. It worries me—'

'You are afraid this man Rhodes may change things for us?'

'The plans Rhodes has will change things for everyone. Us, the Matabele, the Mashona, Rhodes himself, perhaps – but most of all for Lobengula. He is fond of telling me how Mzilikazi was forced to move from Transvaal when the white men crowded the Matabele. Lobengula was a young boy at the time, but it's written on his memory as though it happened only yesterday.'

'Do you think he will move with his people?'

Daniel shook his head. 'He can't. The Mahajas will refuse to follow him. They will stay and fight to the death. Besides, Rhodes has his eyes on the country to the north too.'

Elvira was silent for a while, then she said, 'Perhaps the changes will be enough to keep the Matabele happy. If Rhodes brings them medicine and schools—'

'The changes will benefit only Rhodes and his men. For the Matabele it will mean the end of their way of life. They will never recover from the loss of freedom, and the shattering of their pride.'

'What will you do, Daniel?'

Elvira winced in the darkness as the tension in Daniel caused him unwittingly to squeeze her hand painfully.

'I've got to persuade Lobengula of the futility of fighting. It won't be easy, I would fight myself if I were him. Somehow I have to prevent the Matabele from scoring the one last victory they're ever likely to achieve in their short history as a nation. I'll tell Lobengula to allow Rhodes to take Mashonaland . . . even though my whole being screams out that Lobengula and his impis should drum Rhodes and his pioneers all the way back to the Cape Colony. The damnable thing is that neither Lobengula nor his people will ever understand my motives for stopping them going to war. They'll probably think *I've* sold out to Rhodes too.'

'Lobengula will know the truth – and so will I. You are an honourable man. Whatever you do, wherever you go, my love goes with you. It always has, my husband.'

Worried at the disappearance from the house of both his mother and father, Wyatt was coming along the path towards the stream when he saw them silhouetted together against the moonlit skyline. With the light-footed tread of a natural hunter, he turned and returned the way he had come. The situation in the land was causing both of them great anxiety, but while they enjoyed embracing in the moonlight, all was well at Insimo.

CHAPTER SIXTEEN

When Daniel reached Bulawayo, he found the Matabele King enjoying one of his rare sober spells, with its accompanying improvement in health. A Scots doctor, on a visit to Matabeleland had given Lobengula a morphine injection for gout and the pain had disappeared almost immediately. So impressed was Lobengula, that when the doctor insisted that he give up drinking in order to effect a more permanent cure, he had readily agreed. Daniel knew that the joyful sobriety would be of short duration, but he was happy to be able to take advantage of it now.

Lobengula's initial reaction to Rhodes' plans was one of great anger. As Daniel explained the full implications of the move to occupy Mashonaland, anger turned to despair.

'What can I do? How can I prevent this man Rhodes from stealing the land of my people?'

'You must do nothing, Inkosi. Even more important, you must prevent your Mahajas from doing anything.'

Lobengula eyed Daniel suspiciously. He trusted Daniel more than any other white man. More than any man – black or white, but could he really be trustworthy when he belonged to a race to whom lying, cheating and scheming came as naturally as breathing?

'You are asking much of me and my people. White men prepare to march into our lands and seize them, yet I must do nothing? The whole world will wonder what manner of man it is who rules the Matabele.'

'Those to whom such things matter will know you are a *wise* King. A ruler who has the ability to evaluate a very difficult situation.'

'Don't try to flatter me, trader.' Lobengula frowned. 'That is not the way to persuade me to do what you suggest. You should know this by now.'

'This is far too serious a matter for flattery, Inkosi. As I see it, you have two choices. You either allow Rhodes to take his men to Mashonaland – or you fight.'

'My Mahajas ... and many of their Indunas, would say there is no choice. We must fight.'

'If you fight, your impis *might* win the first battle, but it will be the last victory they will ever have. Rhodes can call on many men for help. They will come armed with Maxim guns – guns with which two men can fight as thought they are an army. If every one of your warriors fought as fiercely as though he were *ten* men, your army would still be beaten, just as Ceteswayo was beaten.'

Ceteswayo was a Natal Zulu King, the last of the true Zulu Kings. Disastrously defeated in their first battle with Ceteswayo's army, the British had returned to annihilate the Zulu's, removing for all time the threat they posed to European expansion in Southern Africa.

'Allow this to happen and you'll find Rhodes will not be satisfied with Mashonaland. He'll take Matabeleland too.'

Lobengula brooded morosely for many minutes. Then, the fire gone from his eyes, he looked up at Daniel. 'It is as you say. I am no longer a King, but a hunted animal. The hunters drum their shields behind and alongside me. There is only one way for me to go. I will send no impis to fight Rhodes' men, but I must keep the news from my Mahajas for as long as is possible. Only the most trusted members of my Council will know. In return, Rhodes and his men must stay well away from Bulawayo. If he comes into contact with my warriors I cannot answer for their actions. This is understood?'

'I think Rhodes is already aware of this.'

'This is too important a matter for there to be any uncertainty. I want you to go and find this man Rhodes. Tell him I am not pleased with what he is doing. I have never said white men could go to Mashonaland, but I will not make war if he keeps his men far from Bulawayo. When I learn his men are on their way to Mashonaland I will send my impis on raids to the north and west. Their paths will not cross that of his men.'

Daniel nodded his approval. 'Your decision is a wise one, Inkosi. You have given your people time they would not otherwise have. Use it to train your warriors in the use of guns Rhodes has sent to you. It might make him think twice before he takes advantage of the Matabele again.'

Lobengula nodded. 'Your words are the words of a friend,

trader. Go now. When you return, tell me what is in the heart of this man Rhodes.'

Cecil Rhodes was at Kimberley, celebrating the news that Queen Victoria had granted a charter to his British South Africa Company.

Daniel read the details of the charter in a Kimberley newspaper before going to visit Rhodes and he was astounded by the power it bestowed upon the company.

Bounded by Mozambique, Transvaal and British Bechuanaland, the charter stipulated no northern or western boundaries. Within this vast, ill-defined territory, Rhodes could 'assume powers of Government and administration, enact ordinances and maintain a police force.'

In other words, Her Majesty Queen Victoria had made Rhodes the dictator of a vast territory, twice the size of the British Isles, with expansion prospects not limited by the sea, or by prior claims.

It was an awesome mantle for any man to don, yet Rhodes was as cheerful and carefree as if he did not have a care or responsibility in the world. He was celebrating with brandy and champagne in the Kimberley Club, only a handful of close friends about him.

Rhodes recognised Daniel immediately and stood up to grasp his hand. In his high-pitched voice he called for a waiter to come and serve Daniel with a drink.

'Welcome to Kimberley again, Retallick. You've heard the news, of course? Yes, everyone's heard by now. Well, what are you doing here? Come to join my Company?'

There had been much time to think along the way and Daniel had devised a plan he hoped would secure the future of the Insimo valley, whilst achieving a guarantee for Lobengula of the route of Rhodes' column.

'No, Mister Rhodes, but I'll raise my glass and hope it brings peace and prosperity to all those who live and work in Lobengula's lands. I'm here to speak to you about your plans for Mashonaland.'

The transformation was astonishing. Rhodes' jocularity vanished. Before Daniel could say more he was hustled to a small room nearby. Slamming the door behind them, Rhodes rounded on Daniel. 'What do you know about my plans for Mashonaland? Who's been talking? I'll have no loose-tongued employees in my Company.'

'It's as well I *was* told, or the bones of your "pioneers" would have been scattered among the hills of your promised land. The British Government would be throwing your charter on their funeral pyre.'

'Don't try to stop me, Retallick!' Rhodes' high, effeminate voice was shrill with anger. 'I won't let anyone, or anything stop me now—'

'Stop you? Why on earth should I want to stop you?' Daniel took a sip of champagne and brandy from the glass that had almost been knocked from his hand in Rhodes' haste to remove him from the party in the club lounge. 'I'm here to offer you a proposition. You keep your men well clear of Bulawayo when they're on their way to Mashonaland and I'll persuade Lobengula to allow you through without trouble.'

Rhodes had already agreed to route his column of pioneers well clear of Bulawayo, but this was no guarantee that it would not be attacked. He looked at Daniel, evaluating his offer.

'You'll do this? Why?'

Daniel shrugged. 'My home is in Matabeleland. The last thing I want is war. If Lobengula's Mahaja go on the rampage, not even Lobengula will be able to control them.'

Rhodes frowned suspiciously. There was far more to this than Daniel had disclosed. 'No one wants war, Retallick. Not even Lobengula . . . but, all right, if you do this for me, what do you expect in return?'

'I want your company to forego all mineral rights in the Insimo valley.'

Rhodes stared blankly at Daniel for a moment, then enlightenment spread in a slow smile across his face. 'Ah yes . . . your personal gold mine.' He pretended to think. 'I'm not certain I can give you such an assurance, Retallick.'

Daniel placed his glass heavily on the desk beside him. 'Then I've wasted my time and yours, Mister Rhodes. The men of your column can expect Lobengula's impis to oppose them every inch of the way – and they'll be coming in force.'

Daniel strode towards the door, but Rhodes reached it first. 'You've ridden seven hundred miles to avert a war, and to secure a future for your family, yet you're ready to accept "perhaps" as a "no"? You have children?'

'Four boys.'

Cecil Rhodes grimaced in what might have passed for assumed envy. 'You're a lucky man, Retallick. *You* will never lie awake at night, wondering what is going to happen to everything you've worked for when you're dead and gone. You've got sons to continue your life's work. Part of *you* will live on through your boys. Surely you can spare me a few minutes of your time . . . for their sakes?'

Rhodes was mocking Daniel, he was calling Daniel's bluff and knew he would stay as long as it took to get what he had come so far for.

'For their sake I'll go much further. When your men try to enter Mashonaland they'll find Lobengula's impis waiting for them. I'll be there with them – and I'll have taught them to use your own guns against you.'

'I believe you, Retallick,' Rhodes sighed, then smiled. 'I had hoped to secure at least a share in the only confirmed gold find in Lobengula's country – but you've worked hard for all you've got, just as I have. I won't interfere with your sons' birthright. You ensure a troublefree passage to Mashonaland for my pioneer column and I'll have all mineral rights in your valley ceded to you and your family.'

'I'll need it in writing.'

'Of course. You'll have it by sundown.'

The meeting had become a business transaction, something Rhodes understood and was in the habit of conducting swiftly and conclusively.

He thought he now knew his man. 'Now, come and join my party. Help us celebrate the granting of my company's charter. It's an historic moment, Retallick. Come and be a part of history.'

'No thanks. Ask me again in ten years' time. If there's still cause for celebration then, *I'll* throw a party for *you* – and invite Lobengula along to enjoy it with us.'

News of the granting of the Royal Charter to Rhodes' company spread over southern Africa with the speed and heat of a bushfire. From the Zambezi valley, Lieutenant Carlos St Anna marched a sick and weary army deep into the heart of

Mashonaland. They passed through places where the tribes-men had not heard the Portuguese tongue since the sixteenth century, when the Monomatapa and his people suffered total defeat and years of subjugation and humiliation.

When his gallant little army was too ill to march another weary foot forward, Lieutenant St Anna planted the Portuguese flag on a low hill and proclaimed the Portuguese province of Zambo, encompassing much of Mashonaland and all Manicaland.

On his way through these almost empty hills and upland plateaus, Lieutenant St Anna flushed out a few prospectors from the Cape Colony who had somehow eluded Lobengula's impis. He ordered them to leave.

His actions brought strong protests from the British Government in London. One morning, Senhor Farrao's servant drew the curtains in the Acting Governor's Quelimane house and saw six British warships riding at anchor, no more than a cannon-shot offshore.

This was a time when the British Empire was still gathering strength. Portugal, on the other hand, was teetering on the brink of economic and political collapse. After a brief but acrimonious exchange of diplomatic notes between London and Lisbon, Lieutenant St Anna and his men were ordered to abandon their newly acquired province.

To the south, the Boer trekkers gathered yet again, determined that the Queen of Great Britain would not rob them of potentially rich trekking grounds by a signature on a piece of paper.

Rhodes hurriedly arranged a meeting with President Kruger, leader of the Transvaal Republic. Kruger entertained his own hopes of expansion. He wanted land to the east of his tiny Republic, in order to gain an outlet to the sea. Accepting Rhodes' half-promise of support in this direction, Kruger agreed to restrain the disgruntled trekkers.

It seemed that, for the moment, Rhodes had successfully defended his unborn empire against the threat posed by its neighbours.

Early in 1890, Rhodes' ambitions received an unexpected boost. It had been pointed out to the Colonial Office in

London that the Queen's advice to Lobengula's Indunas had brought the newly Chartered British South Africa Company close to disaster. Governmental steps were taken somewhat tardily to remedy the matter.

A letter from the Queen was sent out from England, explaining that the Chartered Company represented not one man, but many hundreds. It was a clumsy attempt to convince Lobengula that by granting the concession to Rhodes, he had acted in accordance with Queen Victoria's earlier, rather more honest advice.

As though aware that the letter might provoke a degree of scepticism in the Matabele King, the Government iced its unpalatable pill with an elaborate and colourful coating. The letter was sent from England with an escort of four officers of the Household Cavalry! They arrived at Lobengula's kraal in the height of summer, dressed in full ceremonial uniform.

Unfortunately, the letter was as clumsily worded as was the attempt to disguise its duplicity. It was open to a very wide interpretation.

Whilst the hot and uncomfortable cavalrymen performed elaborate sword drill for the benefit of Lobengula and his enthralled court, Farewell Loveday and other representatives of Rhodes toiled to rewrite the letter in order that it should set out their case in a manner more likely to impress the King.

No one ever knew whether Lobengula was more impressed by the letter, or the cavalrymen. Whichever it was, Rhodes had won yet again. The King dropped all objections to the concession.

1890 was to be Cecil Rhodes' most triumphant year. A Member of the Cape Assembly for many years, he was now made the Colony's Prime Minister.

All that remained was for his pioneers to move into Mashonaland and give him an empire that reached out for fifteen hundred miles from the Cape of Good Hope.

CHAPTER SEVENTEEN

The pioneer column set off from Kimberley on 6 May 1890 and by mid-June it was camping on the spot where Uiys Toblin had been murdered more than two years before.

When the column moved off from here, heading northwards, it made a brave sight. Two hundred pioneers with a hundred wagons and more than two hundred Bechuana natives were escorted by four hundred men of the company's newly-formed police force – many of its members drawn from the Bechuana Border Police. With spare horses, oxen, and goats belonging to the Bechuanas, the column extended for more than two miles and raised a dust cloud visible ten miles away.

Crossing into Matabele territory on 25 June, the column set a course that would take it diagonally away from Bulawayo. Passing to the south of the Insimo valley, the column then swung northwards and established a fort fifty miles from the Retallick home. It was close to the great ruins of the House of Chiefs, where once the White Mondoro had passed on the words of the God, Chiminuka. The new fort was named 'Fort Victoria', in honour of the British Queen who had bestowed her official blessing upon Rhodes' ambitious venture.

Daniel rode with Wyatt and Nathan to Fort Victoria late in August, when the company of police, left as garrison, had been there for a fortnight. Most of the British South Africa Company Police were living inside the wood and earthwork fort. A few more enterprising men had constructed wood and dacca huts nearby, staking a claim in what they hoped would be the first town of any size along the road between Kimberley and the new capital of Mashonaland, which was to be sited two hundred miles to the north.

There was plenty to excite the boys in and about the fort. They were allowed to examine two small artillery pieces and were given a brief but noisy demonstration of the fire power of one of the forts' Maxim guns, each capable of firing five hundred shots a minute. The fort also boasted a single Gatling gun. The ten rotating barrels were sufficient to keep a whole impi at bay – or destroy it if an Induna was foolish enough to press home the attack.

Daniel found much to interest him in his talks with the policemen manning the fort. Many of them were less than enthusiastic about Rhodes' much publicised 'pioneers'. They pointed out that the British South Africa Company Police taking part in the great adventure were being paid five shillings a day. It was a good sum, but less than the amount paid to the pioneers they were protecting.

When the roads and forts had been completed, the task of the Police would be to run the forts and ensure that the rough-cut roads remained open. Meanwhile, the pioneers would be disbanded, each man given six months' rations, a rifle and ammunition, and allowed to choose three thousand acres of land. In addition, he could register fifteen gold claims in his name.

Despite their jealousy of the pioneers, the men at Fort Victoria realised they had played a unique role in history. To a man, they were proud to be on the payroll of Rhodes' British South Africa Company.

The pioneer column reached its destination on 12 September. In the shadow of a steep-sided kopje, close to the source of the insignificant Makabusi River, the Union Jack was run up in 'Fort Salisbury'. The Chartered Company had arrived.

For a while, everything went exactly as Rhodes had planned. His pioneer column had reached its destination without incident. Lobengula's impis did not put in an appearance, and the Boers remained on their own side of the Limpopo River.

Less certain was the future reaction of the Portuguese. Talks held in London and Lisbon to establish a border between Mashonaland and Mozambique had broken down. The Portuguese thought the British brash and avaricious. For their part, the British were contemptuous of a decadent country, living on past glories and unwilling to face the facts of late nineteenth-century life.

While the politicians in Europe drew tentative lines on paper maps, those who rode between the weathered granite peaks of the disputed land played a very different game.

Guided by Jaconus Van Eyck, the men who were to administer Mashonaland on behalf of the company, went to Manicaland. Riding from one major kraal to another, they signed treaties of friendship with every Chief and Induna they found. The Administrators returned to Fort Salisbury well satisfied. As far as the company was concerned, Manicaland was securely under its jurisdiction.

They had reckoned without Captain General Manuel Antonio de Souza Gouveia. When news of what had happened reached his mountain stronghold, the Goanese half-caste mustered his army of slaves and set out for Manicaland. The Chiefs and Headmen needed reminding that they were vassals of the *Portuguese*, forbidden to make treaties with others.

Gouveia's methods were direct and absolute. Those Chiefs who admitted signing treaties with the British South Africa Company had their throats cut in front of their subjects. The Headmen of smaller kraals were forced to watch as Gouveia's bloody mercenaries pillaged their villages, raping women and putting men and children to death. Then they too suffered the fate of greater leaders.

Rumours of Gouveia's atrocities quickly reached the ears of Senhor Farrao in Quelimane, and Archibald Colquhoun, Rhodes' Administrator in Fort Salisbury. Both men were dismayed . . . but for differing reasons.

Of the two, Senhor Farrao's feelings were prompted by more humanitarian reasons. There had been disquieting reports of Captain General Gouveia's method of government before, but nothing approaching the present scale. He despatched his old friend General Francisco St Anna to Manicaland with orders to find Gouveia. The Captain General of Gorongoza was to be informed that the eyes of the world were upon him. Such barbarism as he and his men had practised in the past must cease. If it did not, international pressure would force Portugal to relinquish any claim upon Manicaland.

Archibald Colquhoun saw only that by killing off all the signatories to the company's treaties, Gouveia had made it very difficult for the British South Africa Company to prove its right of administration over the same territory. He despatched a force to bring Gouveia's campaign of retribution to a halt.

Captain Forbes and forty company police troopers made their way to the heart of the Manica Hills. Here they learned that General St Anna and Captain General Gouveia were visiting the kraal of one of the more important Manica Chiefs.

The small troop approached the site of the Chief's kraal quietly and cautiously. Such caution was well advised. A trooper, sent ahead to reconnoitre, returned with the news that the two men *were* in the kraal – and they had an escort that outnumbered the company troopers by at least ten to one.

The kraal was situated on top of a hill. St Anna and Gouveia were parleying inside, but the Portuguese and native troops were camped nearby, guarding the approach route.

Captain Forbes had been sent to Manicaland to stop Gouveia intimidating the local Chiefs. How he achieved this end was left entirely to his own discretion. Studying the Portuguese camp and the kraal on the hill beyond, he decided upon a bold move. Thirty of his men rushed the Portuguese camp and took the unsuspecting soldiers completely by surprise. They captured all the weapons, stacked with military precision, close to the cooking fires.

While this action was taking place, Forbes himself led the remaining ten troopers up the hill to the Chief's kraal. Grabbing St Anna and Gouveia, Forbes and his men backed away down the hill with them.

The Manica Chief's warriors danced alongside them all the way, making threatening gestures with their spears . . . but it was all a charade. The Chief was overjoyed to see the blood-thirsty Gouveia a captive in the hands of his enemies. The angry gestures of his warriors was no more than an insurance, should the Captain General of Gorongoza somehow manage to effect an escape.

There was to be no escape. The two high-ranking Portuguese officials were given horses and led away by their audacious captors.

General St Anna's silent but angry dignity contrasted sharply with the demeanour of Captain General Gouveia. Convinced that he was to be brought to justice for his many atrocities against the unfortunate tribes of Manicaland,

Gouveia begged for mercy, grovelling at the feet of Forbes whenever the opportunity presented itself.

Both prisoners were taken to Fort Salisbury, where their arrival caused great consternation. After a lengthy discussion between Administrator Colquhoun and his advisers, it was decided to send them to Cape Town, for eventual repatriation to Portugal.

Daniel learned of General St Anna's capture when a message reached him at Insimo. The General would be arriving at Fort Victoria early in December. He asked Daniel to meet him there.

The rainy season had started early and Daniel and Elvira set off for Fort Victoria in torrential rain. It made travelling difficult and river crossings were hazardous in the extreme. There were three rivers to cross along the route. At the second they were delayed for three days, the fifty mile journey taking them five days to complete.

They were afraid they might have missed St Anna, but the same difficulties in travelling had affected the party in which the two Portuguese prisoners were travelling. The old friends were reunited in the officers' mess at the fort.

Francisco St Anna had been deeply humiliated by the manner of his capture, but he knew there would be little sympathy awaiting him in Portugal. Crestfallen and haggard, he still managed to greet Elvira and Daniel with warmth and affection. After kissing and embracing Elvira, he held her at arm's length, looking at her with undisguised admiration.

'Ah, but you are a beautiful woman, Elvira. I should have married you myself before Daniel came along. You have grown more attractive with the passing of time . . . .'

Releasing her reluctantly, Francisco St Anna grasped Daniel's hand in both his own. 'And you, my friend? You are well?'

His hands dropped to his sides and some of the pleasure ebbed away. 'It is good of you to come and see me. I am sorry it has to be in such circumstances.'

'You are being well treated, Francisco? Is there anything you need?' Daniel put the questions in a bid to break the unhappy silence that fell between them.

'Anything I need? No, Daniel – at least, nothing you can give to me. My career is at an end. I return to Portugal in disgrace. An embarrassment to my Government. What can *anyone* give to me?'

'I'm sorry, Francisco. Perhaps things aren't as bad as you think. My father will do all he can to help you, you know this,' Elvira spoke optimistically, but she too knew the truth. She was Portuguese. General St Anna's shame at his ignominious capture would embarrass his country. He would never be forgiven for allowing himself to be captured without putting up a fight.

Francisco St Anna shrugged miserably. 'I am afraid that my shame will fall upon your father too. It is very sad. He and I have for many years asked the Government in Portugal for money to build fortresses in Manicaland. It was not forthcoming. We have asked for more soldiers, and for a rapid solution to the border problems. All these years – and nothing. Now your father and I must suffer for the incompetence of our Government.'

Turning to Daniel, General Francisco St Anna said, 'All governments seek others to pay for their own shortcomings, Daniel. This is the reason yours has allowed Rhodes to move into Mashonaland with his company. If he fails in his venture your Prime Minister will merely shrug his shoulders. It will have been the failure of a business venture, no more. It will have cost your country nothing at all. If Rhodes succeeds? Ah yes, then the outcome will be different. Rhodes will become a nobleman and your Government will take over the administration of the country from his company. It will become part of the empire of Great Britain.'

Daniel and Elvira spent the remainder of that evening trying to cheer up the depressed General, but without any noticeable success. Captain General Gouveia joined them for a while. He complained about his accommodation, the rigours of the journey – and the manner of their capture. He assured Daniel in a loud voice, that Metropolitan Portugal would demand a high price of the British for insulting the Captain General of the Province of Gorongoza. When it became clear, even to the insensitive Gouveia that he was held in contempt by Daniel and Elvira, he gave them a stiff bow and was escorted back to his sleeping quarters.

The following day the clouds temporarily rolled away and the troopers escorting the two Portuguese officials announced their intention of taking full advantage of the unexpected break in the weather and riding for the Bechuana border.

When his horse was saddled, and the escort waiting, General St Anna suddenly asked after Victoria.

'She's well,' replied Daniel. 'She misses Therese, of course.'

'Therese is a fine young girl. A good wife for my son. I think too that she will be a good mother, one day very soon.'

Elvira began to express her delight, but General St Anna had more to say to Daniel. 'My son does not yet know he is to be a father. He has been in the north, in Zumbo, for many months. I beg a favour of you. Get the news to him before he hears of my disgrace. Perhaps his mind will then be too full of thoughts of his unborn child to seek revenge for what has happened to me.'

The escort showed signs of impatience and General St Anna swung himself up to the saddle. 'I can accept with dignity all that has happened to me, but I fear my resolve would break if I were to lose my only son because of it. I send him my love . . . and love also for the grandchild I may never see.'

The capture of the two senior Portuguese officials was to be the last item of good news Cecil Rhodes received for a long time. Within a matter of only a few months, great cracks began to appear in Rhodes' dream of a brave new colony to add to the British Empire. It began with the onslaught of the rainy season. The skies above Mashonaland opened and it rained as never before in living memory. So much rain fell that new rivers burst forth from the mountain sides in roaring torrents, carving great fissures in the hillsides and flooding the valleys below. Rivers that were seldom more than sluggish brown ribbons of life, swept aside their banks and poured over the countryside in a swirling torrent of death and destruction.

The pioneers who had set up camp on rich, low-lying lands had to flee for their lives, many losing all their scant but precious possessions to the rising waters. A few huddled in what shelter they could find and sat the season out. Others left.

Those who had thought to find gold lying on the ground, waiting to be picked up, discovered that centuries of natives had been well aware of the value placed upon the yellow metal by Arab, Portuguese and others from across the seas. The land had been well prospected and mined. There *was* gold in the mountains of Mashonaland, but it would take experts to locate it, and a great deal of hard work would be expended in the winning. Disillusioned, many of these men left too.

Meanwhile, Britain signed an agreement with Portugal, 'freezing' the undefined frontier between Mashonaland and Mozambique. This did not prevent a remarkable outburst of public indignation in Portugal when General St Anna and Captain General Gouveia returned to their motherland. The two men were bitterly criticised for falling such easy prey to the invading army of Cecil Rhodes.

The wrath of the masses spilled over to include all things British. The embassy in Lisbon was wrecked, Britons were manhandled in the streets and posters adorned the walls of Lisbon, exhorting the populace to burn out the British. Students at Portugal's universities enlisted in a volunteer 'army', it's avowed intention to sail to Mozambique and liberate Manicaland. There was no shortage of brave young men, and subscriptions poured in to purchase arms and send the student army on its way.

While all this was happening, a 'Native Protection Society' in London published a series of articles sympathetic to Lobengula, criticising the manner in which Rhodes had dispossessed him of his lands. The articles told of a naive and innocent native who had been robbed of his birthright by a grasping adventurer.

It mattered not that only a year or two before, the same newspapers and magazines that now supported the campaign had printed horrific tales of the Matabele King's atrocities committed against his neighbours. This was the kind of campaign that sold newspapers.

Coupled with the persistent rumours that there was no gold to be had from Mashonaland, the increasing public sympathy for Lobengula caused the shares of the British South Africa Company to drop in value alarmingly.

Rhodes' troubles did not end here. Incensed by the manner in which Rhodes had taken possession of Mashonaland, a party of Boers announced that they intended trekking to Mashonaland, brushing aside President Kruger's plea to them.

Their leader was Jan Potgieter, the same man who twenty-three years before had led a Boer commando to the Matopos Hills to fight for Kanje against Lobengula.

Two hundred Boers gathered at a crossing place on the Limpopo River. Opposing them across the wide expanse of muddy water were no more than thirty British South Africa Company policemen. Had the policemen tried to prevent a serious attempt to cross the river they would have been blown out of existence by the large bore elephant guns carried by the Boers.

It was this scene that Jaconus Van Eyck saw when he came along the north bank of the Limpopo River, having ridden hard from the Bechuana crossing-place, many miles away. Jaconus Van Eyck had been to Kimberley and discussed the situation on the Limpopo with Rhodes. He was arriving with a possible solution . . . if only he could persuade the men of Potgieter's party to listen to him.

He arrived not a moment too soon. For days the Boers and the Company Police had faced each other across the river, the Boers occasionally taunting Rhodes' men. More than once when Boer sympathisers came visiting the trekkers, the taunts were accompanied by empty brandy bottles, which fell equally harmlessly in the wide Limpopo River.

Today was different. There was an air of excitement in the Boer camp, and far more activity than usual. Oxen were being inspanned, horses saddled, and surreptitious glances cast across the river. Grim-faced, the Lieutenant in charge of the troopers was deploying his men and giving them last-minute instructions in a low voice.

When the Lieutenant learned that Jaconus Van Eyck came direct from Rhodes with new instructions, he was relieved to hand over responsibility for the ugly situation to him.

Jaconus Van Eyck's first order was for the troopers to pull back to the shelter of the bush, more than a hundred yards from the river bank. The move brought a cheer from the intending trekkers. They thought they had scored a bloodless victory, but Jaconus Van Eyck soon enlightened them.

'You men . . . across the river,' Jaconus Van Eyck hailed them in Afrikaans. 'I've just come from Mister Rhodes. He has a proposition I am to put to you.'

'We don't care if you've just come from Jesus Cristus,' mocked Jan Potgieter. 'We're coming across.'

'Listen to what I have to say, Potgieter. Then, if you still want to cross you'll be welcome — on British South Africa Company terms.'

'We're not going to be dictated to by any Ruineck. Hell, we have as much right over there as Rhodes — more, in fact. You know that, Jaconus.'

'I'm not here to argue about rights. Rhodes has occupied Mashonaland with the backing of the British Government and by agreement with President Kruger. He says if you . . . any of you, want to come to Mashonaland you're welcome to ride-off farms for yourself, the same as his pioneers. All he asks is that you abide by company law.'

Jaconus Van Eyck's words provoked a stir of interest among the Boers, but Jan Potgieter remained scornful. 'Company laws are for Ruinecks. We're coming over, Jaconus. Don't try to stop us.'

Jan Potgieter kicked his heels in his horse's flanks, repeating the process until the horse reluctantly picked its way through the stones at the river edge and entered the dark brown water. One of the Boers, a rifle resting lightly on the saddle horn in front of him, followed suit. The remainder of the mounted men milled about uncertainly, waiting to see what would transpire.

When the two horses were chest deep in the river, Jaconus Van Eyck raised a rifle to his shoulder. Jan Potgieter was watching, but he kept going, expecting a warning shot. His companion had less faith in Jaconus Van Eyck's intentions and brought his own rifle up.

The crack of the shot echoed across the flat surface of the river. Shot through the head, the Boer's horse dropped sideways. The rider barely had time to kick his feet free of the stirrups before he too fell in the water. He came up coughing water . . . and minus his gun.

'Jaconus! What do you—?'

Jaconus Van Eyck's rifle cracked again. Potgieter's words were cut short as his own horse fell dead and he too was flung in the river beside his floundering companion.

Jaconus Van Eyck reloaded his rifle swiftly but calmly. Bringing it to his shoulder he fired yet again. A mortally wounded crocodile threshed the water in a death frenzy, twenty feet from the two men. Jan Potgieter and his companion shouldered each other out of the way in their frenzied haste to gain the Transvaal bank once more.

With one bullet in his gun, Jaconus Van Eyck waited tensely for the remainder of the Voortrekkers to make their next move.

Suddenly, one of the Boers laughed and the tension was broken.

'Hell, I never knew you could move so fast, Jan! That Krokodil could have been given a running start and still drowned in the wake you left behind. It was a pleasure to watch, man.'

The laughter spread among the others. Then the man who had made the remark called across the river, 'I'd like to cross the river, Jaconus. On British South Africa Company terms.'

'You're welcome. Make your way to Fort Salisbury and see the Administrator. He'll give you all the papers you need to file a claim. Any more of you coming across?

Less than a third of the would-be trekkers crossed the river to place themselves under the protection of the British South Africa Company. One of them was Jan Potgieter, who carefully avoided looking at Jaconus Van Eyck.

The numbers were sufficient to break the strength of the trekking party. As the tracks of their late companions' wagons cut a double furrowed track in the direction of Fort Salisbury, the remainder wheeled their wagons about and returned to the free and independent State of Transvaal, where laws were made by their own kind.

CHAPTER EIGHTEEN

Coming to terms with the Boer trekkers seemed to mark a turning point for Rhodes. Shortly afterwards, the Reverend Farewell Loveday solved the delicate problem of the Chartered Company's right to dispose of land it had not been given — and he did it with typical Loveday deviousness.

Farewell Loveday was deeply disappointed with the lack of spiritual progress in Matabeleland. The arrival of the pioneers in Mashonaland had made no impact on Lobengula's tribe at all. Loveday conceded that the process of civilising the Matabele could not be speeded up, but the thought that public opinion in Europe might possibly force the company to withdraw filled him with alarm. Missionary considerations apart, the Reverend Farewell Loveday had a considerable monetary stake in the success of the British South Africa Company's venture.

For many years a nondescript German had been trying to win a concession from Lobengula, with a notable lack of success. Now he was in Bulawayo once again and he was amazed when Farewell Loveday came to him with a proposition. The missionary would persuade Lobengula to grant him a major concession. In return, the German would immediately sell it to Rhodes. For this he would be paid a great sum of money, be given a substantial block of shares in the British South Africa Company, and allowed to prospect in Mashonaland.

Not unnaturally, the German jumped at such an unexpected opportunity. Ever since the all-embracing mining concession had been granted to Rhodes, the Europeans frequenting Bulawayo had been eager for the smallest crumb dropped their way. Yet here he was being offered the opportunity to join the man who had been given the whole loaf.

Lobengula was still unaware of the freelance missionary's total involvement with Rhodes and he shared many of his thoughts with the white man he regarded as a friend. His hatred of Rhodes now amounted to an obsession. When he had been drinking heavily, he became morose and bitter about Rhodes' trickery. Time and time again he declared that Rhodes was occupying Mashonaland illegally and his followers had no right to the land that had been given to them.

It was this argument that the anti-Rhodes campaigners were using. Rhodes himself was aware of the gaping loophole in the concession he held from Lobengula.

By playing upon Lobengula's hatred for Rhodes, Farewell Loveday convinced the King that if he were to grant a concession to someone else, specifically giving them the right to allocate farms, lay out townships and generally distribute the land as *they* thought fit, it would throw Rhodes and his company into utter confusion. The pioneers could be ordered to leave their farms and the Chartered Company would collapse.

Farewell Loveday's scheme worked better than he had dared to hope. Lobengula signed away his interest in Mashonaland on an evening when brandy and champagne combined with his burning resentment of Cecil Rhodes to cloud his judgement. By the time he was sober again, the concession was ten miles along the Kimberley road. The British South Africa Company now owned a concession to confound even Rhodes' most persistent critics.

Daniel received the news of Lobengula's latest folly with sad resignation. It was not yet known that the concession had passed to Rhodes' hands, but Daniel had none of the King's faith in the Reverend Farewell Loveday. He believed that the missionary would sponsor nothing likely to benefit the Matabele.

Daniel had little time to worry about the matter. Other things were happening that would involve him deeply.

In February of 1891, the Portuguese student 'army' arrived at the tiny Mozambique port of Beira. Ill-prepared and lacking even the basic training for an African campaign, they camped on the unhealthy marshland, inland from the port. Very soon malaria and dysentery struck their ranks, undermining morale if not enthusiasm. Determined to strike at least one blow against Rhodes, they appealed to the Portuguese army in Mozambique for assistance and were reluctantly given basic instruction in the art of war.

This was the news that Daniel and Wyatt were given when they passed through Fort Salisbury on their way to Tete to make good the promise Daniel had given to General Francisco St Anna.

The administrative capital of Mashonaland was a diverse conglomeration of huts and shanties. Some were built in the Mashona style, of mud and thatch. Others were constructed from locally-cut logs. Not a few incorporated planks of seasoned wood from pioneer wagons, broken up when the column reached its objective.

The disastrous rains of the summer had ended, but no supply wagons had yet been able to ford the still swollen rivers to the south. The men living in Fort Salisbury were short of food and clothing. In some cases men walked about bare-footed, their boots having rotted on their feet as a result of the unprecedented wet season.

Daniel and Wyatt stayed to take part in a hunt not far from the embryo capital. They flushed out a small herd of reedbuck and seven were killed. They also bagged two impala, a sable, an eland . . . and two elephant. It was enough to ensure that the small community would have full bellies for a week or two.

Tete lay in the Zambezi valley, two hundred miles north east of Fort Salisbury. The terrain here was different to that of the high, Mashonaland plateau. Game was plentiful, one herd of elephant they saw containing more than eighty of the great beasts.

Daniel enjoyed seeing so much thriving wild life, but he derived the greatest pleasure from the company of his son, and the opportunity to share the experiences of the journey with him.

Wyatt had a quick mind, and was a deadly shot with his Gibbs-Melford .450 rifle, but he much preferred to stop and observe animals rather than shoot them. There were times when Daniel was concerned that Wyatt's nature was far too gentle for the harsh environment in which they lived, but he consoled himself with the knowledge that the Matabele herd-boys held Wyatt in high esteem. They did not show such respect to any man, or boy, who did not meet with their very high standards. On this journey, Daniel quickly learned that his son was as much at home in the bushveldt as he was himself.

They reached Tete six days after leaving Fort Salisbury and received a reception that was more hostile than any Daniel had known during his travels in Mozambique. Tete was a much larger settlement than Sená and there were many more white faces here. For a while it seemed he and Wyatt might be sent back to Mashonaland. Not until he told them he carried a message from General St Anna to his family did they allow Daniel and Wyatt to proceed – under escort.

At the St Anna estate they were met by a delighted Therese. In her arms she carried a month-old baby son.

'Daniel . . . Wyatt,' Therese kissed each of them in turn. 'It's wonderful to see you—' Suddenly her expression changed and she looked at Daniel anxiously. 'There's nothing wrong? I mean . . . with Ma?'

'No, your mother is well and sends her love . . . to both you and Carlos – she doesn't know about this one yet.' Daniel placed a finger beneath the baby's chin. It pushed the tip of its tongue between pursed lips and began making noisy sucking noises. Daniel smiled, and then became more serious.

'I'm really here to speak to Carlos. I saw his father when he and Gouveia were taken through Mashonaland. He sent a message, urging Carlos not to seek revenge for his capture.'

All the happiness left Therese's face. 'I think you may be too late. I had a letter from Carlos a month after his father was taken. Carlos was *very* angry. Since then I have had two more letters. He seems to have thrown himself body and soul into raising an army to take back Manicaland for Portugal. I've written to him but I don't think any of my letters have reached him. I'm worried about him, Daniel. Upset too . . . he doesn't know about our baby yet.'

'Where's Carlos now?'

'The last letter came from somewhere along the Zambezi, well beyond Zumbo. But the messenger who brought it said he thought Carlos was going to cut through Mashonaland to the fort at Macequece before going on to Beira.'

Daniel frowned. 'If he's on his way to Beira he'll be going to aid the student army there. They've sworn an oath to chase Rhodes and his company from Manicaland.'

Therese looked at Daniel with wide-eyed concern. 'Will there be a battle?'

'I'd like to be able to say "no", Therese. But the Company Administrator at Fort Salisbury knows the students are on their way. He's sent reinforcements to Umtali with orders to prevent them from coming any further. I'll go there to see what's happening. I might prevent Carlos from doing something foolish.'

'I'm coming with you.'

'Impossible! Who'll look after the baby while you're away?'

Therese's chin came up in a defiant attitude that reminded Daniel she was Victoria's daughter.

'The baby will come with me.'

'It's out of the question. Wyatt and I will need to travel fast—'

'The St Anna horses are the best in Mozambique. I'll have no difficulty keeping up with you. My baby will be happy enough in a sling, in front of me.'

Therese looked at Daniel defiantly. 'Either we travel with you, or without you. I have more reason than you for wanting Carlos to remain alive. I doubt if he will take unnecessary risks once he has seen his own son.'

'She's right, Pa. I'll help carry the baby. It can't weigh very much.'

With Wyatt on Therese's side, Daniel capitulated. 'All right. We'll leave first thing in the morning. In the meantime someone will need to tend our horses. They've got a hard journey ahead.'

They set off escorted by a dozen mounted Manicas, armed with ancient flintlock muskets. At midday they struck the Luenha River, a tributary of the Zambezi, and followed it for a hundred miles to its source in the Inyanga Mountains.

Here they passed through the ruins of Chief Vumba's village. It brought back many memories for Daniel. Here he had found Victoria – and Sam Speke was buried nearby. Daniel tried to find the grave, but all traces of it had disappeared many years before. It was here too that Mariano,

Therese's true father had died. But the gallows' tree had long since been cut down for firewood and Mariano's daughter and grandson passed the spot with no hint of a ghost to haunt them.

There were few tribesmen in the hills now. Many of the Chiefs and Headmen had signed treaties with the British South Africa Company and, as a result, had received visits from Gouveia's slave-army.

Leaving the ruins of Chief Vumba's village behind, Daniel led the way through the Manica mountains to the isolated Portuguese fort of Macequece. Much to his surprise he found it occupied by troopers of the Chartered Company's police.

The troopers were piling up guns, general stores and great mounds of ammunition on the fort's parade ground and were in high spirits.

'Well .... We don't often see women in these parts — leastways, not an English woman!' The speaker was a young, sun-tanned Police Captain, the commander of the troop.

Daniel returned the Captain's greeting without enlightening him as to Therese's nationality. 'We didn't expect to see you here, either. What's happened? Where are the Portuguese?'

Contemptuously, the officer jerked a thumb in the direction of the coast, almost two hundred miles away. 'Gone. Ran like rabbits. Most of them while the battle was still on.'

'A battle?' Daniel looked to where Therese leaned wearily against her horse, surrounded by British South Africa Company troopers. The men, starved of any form of family life, were attracted equally by Therese and the young baby in her arms. 'Were there any casualties?'

The young Captain laughed. 'None ... unless you count Trooper Green. He found the Portuguese wine store and quite literally drank himself to death! They tell me there's only one better way to go.'

'How about the Portuguese? Did they suffer casualties?'

'A great many. I counted forty-nine bodies, and they carried many of the wounded away with them. Their tactics were quite unbelievable. They made no attempt to take advantage of cover. Our position was a few hundred yards from here and, before they broke and ran, they came on as though they were on parade! It wasn't a battle, we just picked them off. I didn't want a repeat of such slaughter, so I came to the fort to parley with them this morning – and found they'd scarpered! Just ran off, leaving everything behind them!'

Aware that Therese had extricated herself from the group of admirers and was advancing towards them, Daniel broke in quickly, 'A Portuguese officer – Lieutenant St Anna? He wasn't among the casualties?'

Therese had reached them now and, as the Captain turned to greet her, Daniel added, hurriedly, 'This is Lieutenant St Anna's wife and son.'

'Oh!' The Captain's manner changed abruptly and for a moment he looked embarrassed. 'I'm sorry. Yes, I'm afraid Lieutenant St Anna was a casualty.'

'NO! He's dead?' Therese's agonised cry brought a hush to the parade ground.

'Wounded . . . but rather badly, I'm afraid.'

Daniel discovered he had been holding his breath. He released it noisily.

'Where is Carlos now?' Therese's voice came out as a hoarse whisper.

'We sent him to Fort Salisbury. There are no doctors here, and without one—' The Police Captain looked at Therese's anguished expression and bit back the words he was going to use. 'He'll be looked after well at Fort Salisbury.'

'When did he leave?' Daniel asked.

'Two days ago. In a wagon.'

Daniel and Therese exchanged glances.

'I'll feed my baby, then we'll leave. We can travel a lot faster than any wagon.'

Therese, brought up among the Matabele, quite unselfconsciously pulled a milk-swollen breast from her dress and put the teat in her baby's mouth. As she walked through the gaping troopers towards her horse, Daniel would have followed, but the young Captain caught his arm and drew him back.

'Don't let that young lady build up too many hopes. I don't think her husband will survive the journey to Fort Salisbury.'

They caught up with the Chartered Company wagon carrying Carlos St Anna that same evening. It had travelled no further than the fifteen miles from Fort Macequece to the police fort at Umtali.

The four-man police escort decided to remain here when Carlos St Anna began dribbling blood. They considered that taking him to Fort Salisbury would be a wasted journey. Far better to let him die at Umtali and save them all the discomfort of a long wagon trek.

Although so seriously wounded, Carlos St Anna was conscious. When he saw Therese and the baby his eyes opened wide with joy and astonishment. It was doubtful whether he even saw Daniel and Wyatt. As the badly wounded young Portuguese Lieutenant struggled to speak to his wife, Daniel felt an emotional lump rise in his throat. It threatened to choke him. Placing an arm on Wyatt's shoulder, Daniel led him from the room, leaving the young couple alone with their baby son.

The Commanding Officer of the police fort, a florid-faced Captain had been standing in the doorway. He closed the door behind them and asked, 'What are your plans now?' Adding, apologetically, 'We're a mite short on accommodation — especially for women and babies.'

'We'll most likely stay here for a few days, until Lieutenant St Anna's a bit stronger. Then I'd like to take him to my home, in the Insimo valley. You've no objection?'

'None at all. He's not a prisoner . . . we're not even at war with the Portuguese. The whole business was too damned ridiculous for words, especially in view of this—' He dug into a breast pocket and pulled out a crumpled telegraph form addressed to the Company Administrator in Fort Salisbury. It was from the Governor of the Cape Colony. It stated that agreement had finally been reached between Great Britain and Portugal on the border dispute. It went on to set out a number of readings in latitude and longitude. Scribbled beneath them were the pencilled words, 'Fort Macequece — Portuguese. Fort Umtali — British.'

'So a lot of men have died for nothing,' said Daniel bitterly, handing back the telegraph message.

'Many more than we'll ever know,' agreed the Captain. 'Those Africans who fell victim to Gouveia — and the Portuguese Student batallion. I heard tell they were dying like flies in the Mozambique marshes. What a waste of bright young men.'

'A waste indeed,' agreed Daniel, looking to where Wyatt stood talking to some young troopers, only a few years his senior. Daniel hoped his son would never blindly follow any cause to such an inevitable end.

Daniel, Wyatt, Therese, Carlos and the baby left the Umtali fort the following morning. Therese would not stay a moment longer, declaring the fort to be unhealthy for a man with damaged lungs. Carlos travelled in the same wagon that had brought him from Macequece, and Wyatt drove. Therese, the baby safe in an improvised cot, was in the back of the wagon with her husband and did her best to protect him from the worst of the jolting they encountered.

The wagon had been loaned willingly by the Fort Umtali Commanding Officer. He would arrange to have it collected at some future date, when the Chartered Company had a police troop passing close to the Insimo valley.

They moved slowly, Wyatt picking his path carefully. Nevertheless, that night Carlos was restless and feverish and, when morning came, he was noticeably weaker.

After a hurried discussion on whether to carry on, or remain where they were for another twenty-four hours, Daniel said anxiously, 'Perhaps we should have left Carlos at the fort. The journey is proving too much for him.'

'He *couldn't* have stayed at the fort,' cried Therese. 'There was no one there who cared whether he lived or died. In fact, they were *hoping* for him to die. I could see it in the way they looked at Carlos . . . and at me. Here, he is with those who love him. His wife and child. His friends. If he dies—' Therese choked on the words. She began to cry softly, disturbing the baby who lay in her arms.

Daniel stepped forward to comfort her, but thrusting the baby at him, she fled to the wagon where Carlos lay restlessly sleeping.

They remained at this camp for two nights, but the condition of Carlos St Anna showed no improvement. At night it was cool in these mountains and the cold air made him cough. Each bout of coughing left his pillow flecked with blood. His fever was worsening too. Daniel believed the fever to be caused by the bullet, still lodged inside him, but the nearest surgeon was still many miles away, at Fort Victoria.

Then Daniel remembered that when he had come this way in company with Jandu and Suliyana, many years before, Suliyana had taken them to a hot springs that the Manicas claimed to have strong healing powers. It was hardly likely that the waters could heal a bullet wound, but the air about the steamy pools would be warm. Carlos would be more comfortable there.

They set off immediately and reached the springs the next day. Therese thought that a bathe in the hot, mineral rich waters would be good for Carlos, if only to remove the dust and perspiration of their travels.

Daniel, assisted by Wyatt, lifted the wounded man bodily from the wagon. As they carried him between them, Carlos cried out that he had an excruciating pain, high in his back. As the bullet wound was in his chest, Daniel thought the pain must have been brought about by the rough wagon ride. However, when Carlos was stripped for his bathe, Daniel saw a small lump, just above the right shoulder blade of the wounded man. Protruding from it was something that might have been a small piece of jagged bone.

Pointing it out to Therese, Daniel said, 'It could be that the bullet has passed through his chest and ended up there, damaging a rib.'

'What can we do about it?'

'*We* can do nothing. If only there was a doctor closer than Fort Victoria. An operation to remove the bullet might make all the difference.'

That night Carlos St Anna's fever worsened. By morning he was in a state of delirium, knowing nobody. Daniel deliberated for a couple of hours before making up his mind. He knew what had to be done, but had been reluctant to face up to the inevitable. He would have to try to find the bullet.

When he went to speak to Therese, he found her with Carlos, whose breathing was now very ragged. 'Someone's got to try to get that bullet out, Therese. Carlos may die in the attempt, but he *will* die if it isn't removed.'

Therese nodded. 'I know. You do it Daniel, please.'

The surgical 'scalpel' was a hunting knife, honed to razor-sharpness and heated in the red-hot ashes of the fire. With a white-faced Wyatt holding Carlos firmly on his side, Daniel poised, the knife held over the irregular lump on Carlos' back. He made a swift stroke, the knife slicing deep into the muscle of the wounded man's back.

Carlos cried out and began to struggle, but Wyatt held him tight. Then Therese began to speak softly to her husband and slowly he quietened. With the point of his knife, Daniel probed the wound and a sliver of bone was removed. He probed again, deeper and this time the point struck something hard – and slipped away.

Doing his best to stop his hand from trembling, Daniel eased the point of the knife further into Carlos' body. Carlos screamed with pain as Wyatt exerted all his strength to pin him to the floor of the wagon. Daniel prised upwards and at first thought the knife had lodged in another piece of bone. Then, with a suddenness that took him by surprise, the blunted nose of a long bullet from a .450 Martini Henry rifle came into view and clattered to the wooden floor of the wagon.

The operation was over.

Looking down at the bullet, Daniel's hand suddenly began to shake uncontrollably and he backed away, leaving Therese to dress the wound from which the bullet had been removed.

That evening, Carlos St Anna's fever subsided and he slept well. The next morning when he woke he asked for food, but neither Daniel nor Therese dared voice the elation they both felt.

They remained at the hot springs camp for four more days until, on the final evening, Carlos St Anna held his baby son in his arms for the first time.

When Therese returned to the Insimo valley with a baby and her wounded husband, it was as though history had thrown up a copy of Victoria's arrival, many years before. It could have been a difficult homecoming. Although she had sent a blessing to her daughter and Carlos St Anna, Victoria had believed she might find it very difficult to welcome the son of Francisco St Anna to her home. Now, the circumstances of their arrival, and the sight of the pale-faced, gaunt young man propped up in the wagon with her grandson in his arms, won Victoria over completely. One day the young couple would return to

Mozambique, but, until then, Victoria would do everything to make their stay with her a happy one.

Carlos and Therese were still at Insimo in August when Senhor Farrao arrived from Mozambique, accompanied by a mixed escort of Portuguese troops and British South Africa Company Police. The latter had been supplied by a startled Administrator, to whom Senhor Farrao had reported after riding unchallenged half the width of Mashonaland, from the Mozambique border.

Senhor Farrao was still the *de facto* Governor of Mozambique, but he had been recalled to Lisbon. He knew the summons was a prelude to his dismissal. His fall from favour had been inevitable after the defeat suffered by the student batallion at the hands of the Chartered Company's police.

Senhor Farrao had never been overawed by the importance of his position and he would not allow his imminent dismissal to destroy his outward composure. His only complaint was that the Portuguese Government could have dismissed him on the spot, permitting him to return to his estate at Sena without forcing him to suffer the perils and discomforts of a long return voyage to Portugal.

Although the story of his own downfall was distressing to Elvira, he had far grimmer news for Carlos St Anna.

Public indignation at the numerous setbacks suffered by Portugal in Africa reached a crescendo when students of the ill-fated 'army' returned to their homeland. Defeated in battle and decimated by malaria, the survivors stepped ashore broken in both health and spirit. Seeking someone on whom to vent their anger, the populace turned on the only available man who had held a post of responsibility in Mozambique. That man was General Francisco St Anna.

The unfortunate General was blamed for the lack of fighting spirit in the colonial troops. His accusers conveniently forgot that the battle had been forced upon the Mozambique authorities by the ill-trained and unprepared students from the mother country.

Stripped of his army rank, Francisco St Anna maintained a dignified silence while the populace howled for more blood. It was rumoured that the Portuguese army council were drawing up papers to have him tried for cowardice.

One day, after being stoned and reviled whilst walking the streets of Lisbon, Francisco St Anna returned to his home, placed the barrel of a loaded revolver to his temple, and pulled the trigger.

The newspapers reporting his death, carried on the same page an article written by a sympathetic student. The student told of the bravery of Francisco St Anna's son, who had fallen at the battle of Macequece, while leading the students in an assault upon the enemies' position.

Such was the fickleness of public opinion, the brief article was sufficient to have Francisco St Anna belatedly cleared of the charges that had driven him to self-destruction.

Posthumously restored to his former rank, General Francisco St Anna was given a warrior's funeral. Meanwhile, the Portuguese finally accepted that their great days of colonial glory were over. It had been a long, hard lesson.

CHAPTER NINETEEN

In the same month that Senhor Farrao arrived at Insimo, the Reverend Farewell Loveday left Matabeleland and moved to Fort Salisbury. It was a hasty departure, and the reason was not hard to find. Rumours had reached Bulawayo that the land concession Lobengula had granted to the German, at Farewell Loveday's insistence, had found its way into the hands of Cecil Rhodes.

Farewell Loveday had got away with much in the past because of his association with Mzilikazi, but he knew he had pushed Lobengula's patience too far on this occasion. It was time for the scheming missionary to seek the company of white men.

Loveday arrived in Mashonaland's administrative capital a wealthy man, although his missionary record was less than impressive. During the whole of his time in Matabeleland he could not claim a single convert to Christianity, and the bloody raids carried out by Lobengula's impis against his neighbours continued unabated.

In Fort Salisbury, Farewell Loveday found new and untried fields of endeavour in which to exercise his pastoral prowess. Wagon loads of whisky and dubious Cape brandy were arriving regularly – and the capital could already boast Mashonaland's first brothel, set up on the kopje, just outside town.

While Senhor Farrao was still at Insimo, a large impi passed through the hills north of the valley, on its way to punish a Mashona Chief with a kraal close to Fort Salisbury. This unfortunate Chief had refused to pay his annual tribute to Lobengula, believing that the white men who now occupied the land would protect him.

The mistake cost him his life together with the lives of his family and everyone else who happened to be in the Chief's kraal on that fateful day.

The raid, in Chartered Company territory, caused a furore in Fort Salisbury. Farewell Loveday's voice was raised louder than any other in condemnation of the bloody act. From the pulpit at the town's church he declared vehemently that Christian standards might only be taught to the Matabele with sword and gun.

The Administrator of Mashonaland lodged a protest with Lobengula about the raid, but he received short thrift. The Matabele King told him bluntly that he had said nothing when men of the British South Africa Company entered Mashonaland without 'asking for the road'. He had not complained when they built huts on land that was not theirs. He had even held back his warriors when they clamoured to be allowed to attack the white trespassers. But the white men must not imagine that such forbearance meant he had abandoned his subjects, the Mashonas, to the white invaders. They still enjoyed his 'protection' and would suffer his retribution whenever they offended him. If the white men had no stomach for Matabele justice, he declared, then perhaps they should leave the country?

Lobengula did not add that the ranks of his impis were full of generations of Mahajas who had never faced the guns of the white men in battle. They had not learned to respect their weapons and their tactics, as had their fathers and grandfathers. These young warriors knew only that the white men had invaded their lands and their King would not send them to war to win it back.

The Mahajas needed warfare. The whole structure of the Matabele nation was built around the impi. No young warrior would be accepted by a Matabele woman as a husband until he had 'washed his spear' in the blood of an enemy – and a Mashona who had not paid his dues to Lobengula was considered an enemy.

As if to emphasise his right of life or death over the unfortunate Mashonas, the scale of Matabele raids into their country gradually increased. Some of the farms pegged out by the Europeans lay directly in the paths of many of these sorties. Mashona farm labourers going about the business of their white employers were slaughtered as indiscriminately as their unemployed kinsmen in remote kraals and villages. It became increasingly apparent to even the most optimistic observer that a clash between whites and Matabele was inevitable.

*   *   *

In the Insimo valley, the Retallick family and those who worked there were strangely remote from the problems of the outside world. The distant rumbling of white discontent in Mashonaland and the frustration of Lobengula's warriors were far removed from them. For Daniel, the two years to mid-1893 were the best he had ever known. Wyatt was now sixteen years old and Nathan thirteen. Both were doing a man's work. Adam and Benjamin were younger, but they too enjoyed working with Daniel and their brothers in the fields and pastures of their valley home.

Daniel's proudest moments came at the end of each hard day's work. He sat his horse overlooking the Insimo valley, four sons at his side, and looked at what he had achieved in more than twenty years of work here. Along the valley herd upon herd of fat, healthy cattle grazed some of the best grass in the land. The Matabele herd-boys, almost as content as their charges, lolled in the shade of hill-top rock formations, or called out to friends in singsong voices that echoed from hill to hill.

On the slopes of the hills, Mashona workers cultivated acre after acre of tall maize. There was enough food here to meet the needs of both white settler and Matabele warrior. Daniel was friends with both.

It was lonely for the women in the valley, especially when Thérèse returned with her husband to the St Anna estates in Mozambique. Yet, had anyone suggested to them that there was another way of life, both would have scoffed at such an idea. In the fastness of this corner of Matabeleland, the residents of Insimo had discovered contentment.

The end of this settled and happy way of life was brought about by a tragically simple incident that took place on a mild April day in 1893, seventy miles away, close to Fort Victoria. Sometime during the day, part of the telegraph line linking Fort Salisbury and Fort Victoria with the Cape Colony was cut and a length of copper telegraph wire stolen.

A troop of British South Africa Company Police quickly discovered the culprits living in a nearby kraal. Brought to justice, they and their Headman, Gomella, were fined a large number of cattle as a salutary example to others. To the surprise of the District Administrator in Salisbury, Gomella paid his very heavy fine without complaint – indeed, with a remarkable readiness!

Not until he received a strongly worded complaint from Lobengula did the Administrator understand why. The cattle did not belong to the Mashona Headman. They were Lobengula's, sent to Gomella to graze on behalf of his Matabele overlord.

The cattle were returned to Lobengula with due apologies from the Chartered Company, but the incident did not end here. Gomella had given away the King's cattle. He had failed in his duty and had made Lobengula look foolish.

Early in July, a huge Matabele impi crossed the Shashi River, the unofficial border between Mashonaland and Matabeleland. The warriors descended upon the area about Fort Victoria, intent on teaching the Mashonas a lasting lesson. Gomella was captured and disembowelled in view of his terror-stricken family, then they too were hacked to death.

On previous occasions, such retribution would have been sufficient . . . but this was a large impi. Many of the Mahajas were unblooded. Determined to return to their homeland as men, they went on the rampage in a savage welter of bloodletting.

The Matabele killed Mashonas wherever they found them. For the first time, the residents of Fort Victoria witnessed at first-hand the handiwork of one of Lobengula's impis. They watched helplessly as farm labourers, house servants, and even the 'nannies' of white children were put to death by every means known to the unpractised but resourceful Mahajas.

In all this wild orgy of blood-letting, not one European was harmed, although many had belongings and livestock stolen. As they crowded inside the earthwork walls of the police fort with a handful of Mashona survivors, they clamoured for action from the Chartered Company's Police, demanding that the Matabele be driven away.

Meanwhile, their blood lust unsatiated, the impi sent their Induna to arrogantly demand from the Europeans that the Mashonas inside the fort be handed over to the warriors. The Induna thoughtfully promised that the Mashonas would be slaughtered well away from the river, in order that the fort's water supply might not be contaminated.

The Company Police refused to hand over the cowering Mashonas but, outside the fort, the Matabele terror continued unabated. Eventually, the Chartered Company Administrator arrived from Fort Salisbury with a large force of Police. Ordering the Induna to take his impi back to Bulawayo, the Administrator threatened to open fire on the Matabele warriors if they had not obeyed his order at the end of an hour.

When two hours had elapsed, the Administrator sent his men from the fort, to determine whether the Matabele had gone. On their way out of the town the troopers passed the mutilated bodies of dozens of Mashonas, men, women and children. By the time they caught up with the retiring impi they were in no mood to accept the Induna's protest that he was returning to Bulawayo, as ordered by the Company Administrator.

The Captain in charge of the troopers retorted that the impi was not moving *fast* enough. He ordered his men to open fire. About thirty Matabele warriors were killed instantly and the troop drove the remainder before them to the river crossing. Once there, they watched the Matabele warriors cross, then turned about and returned to the fort.

The impi passed through the Insimo valley on its way back to Bulawayo, still smarting at what they considered to be an unprovoked attack on them by the white troopers. Their Induna had been killed in the brief exchange of fire and they were now led by Nyamatakah, Lobengula's eldest son, the heir to the throne of Matabeleland.

Meeting up with Nathan who was out with some of the herd-boys, Nyamatakah imperiously demanded cattle for his hungry and dispirited men. Nathan replied that he would have to ask his father. Before he had even finished talking, some of Nyamatakah's warriors walked up to the herd and plunged their spears in two of Daniel's best milking cows. The remainder of the herd, many heavy with calf, panicked at the scent of blood and began running.

Nathan remonstrated angrily with the warriors, but when he attempted to draw his rifle, his arms were pinned to his side by Matabele warriors.

It was an ugly moment. It would no doubt have been much worse had Daniel not come along, attracted by the commotion. Seeing the warriors holding Nathan, he knocked their arms away and rounded on Nyamatakah.

'Has the son of the King become a thief? Has he taken to stealing the cattle of his father's friends?'

'I have not stolen. I asked for them . . . as a friend,' Nyamatakah replied, surlily.

'I told him to ask you, but his warriors started killing our best milking cows,' Nathan retorted indignantly.

'My men are hungry. We have travelled far.' Nyamatakah's anger matched Nathan's. This white man before him was no different to those who had attacked the impi without provocation. Nyamatakah would have killed Daniel – and every other white man and woman in the valley, but if he did he knew he too would die – and at the hands of his own father. This man was Lobengula's friend and was afforded his personal protection.

Daniel was aware of Nyamatakah's thoughts. He could also see this was an impi that had run into trouble and been badly mauled. Many of the warriors were nursing wounds inflicted by rifle bullets. From the direction in which they were travelling, those rifles would have been in the hands of white men.

'Your warriors may kill six of those cattle.' Daniel pointed to his beef herd, further along the valley. 'You will take them with you and make your cooking fires elsewhere. No impi has entered this valley since it was given to me by your father, before you were born. You are welcome here whenever you choose to come in friendship, but not when you travel with men who have blood on their spears.'

Smarting at the snub, Nyamatakah said angrily, 'One day the blood will be that of the white men. Then the Matabele will go where they please.'

The unpleasant incident in the valley might have been forgotten had not Jaconus Van Eyck arrived a few days afterwards. He gave Daniel details of the Matabele raid in the Fort Victoria area.

'This is only the latest in a whole series of incidents, Daniel,' he said when they were seated on the verandah, that evening as the sun went down beyond the hills. 'But it's brought things to a head. Something has to be done – and quickly.'

425

'This raid only lasted so long because Nyamatakah was in the impi,' explained Daniel. 'He was out to prove something and wanted to return home to act it all out in front of his father and the tribe. I've seen it all before, Jaconus. The warriors are never going to stop raiding, but I'll have a word with Lobengula.'

'It may be too late in the day for words. Rhodes has promised the settlers that he'll put an end to the raiding. He's called on them to form companies of mounted volunteers and is recruiting in the Transvaal. He's promising six thousand acres and gold claims to every man prepared to fight the Matabele to a standstill.'

The information shocked Daniel. 'He's doing WHAT? Why, an army of Boer mercenaries would commit more atrocities than a Matabele impi! Damn the man! He could almost have planned this whole business of the telegraph wire himself.'

'No, Daniel. Rhodes is genuinely concerned about the situation in Mashonaland. Many settlers are talking about leaving if the Matabele raids continue. He's *got* to do something.'

'Nevertheless, Rhodes is using this whole sorry business to his own advantage. Mashonaland hasn't fulfilled its promise. It's not the pot of gold he was led to expect. Now he's out to get Matabeleland. God, Jaconus! That man has no scruples at all. He'd sacrifice us all to get what he's after.'

Daniel had sprung to his feet and was pacing about as he spoke. Suddenly he stopped in front of Jaconus Van Eyck and looked down at him. 'All right, Jaconus, you're not making a social visit. What do you want me to do?'

'Nothing. As I've said, it's far too late to do anything. I'm here to suggest you take your family to Fort Victoria. They'll be safe there.' .

An expression of incredulity took over Daniel's face. 'Leave the Insimo valley and everything I've built up here? After all these years? Never. There's too much of me here . . . part of you too, Jaconus. Young Jannie's grave is still tended every week. No, I'm grateful to you for coming all this way to warn me, but I'm in less danger from Lobengula's impis than I will be from Rhodes' Boer mercenaries.'

*　　*　　*

In spite of his assurance to Jaconus Van Eyck, Daniel discussed the question of leaving the Insimo valley with Elvira, when they lay side by side in bed that night.

She listened in silence as he told her of the Fort Victoria raid by Lobengula's impi, and of Rhodes' preparations for war. Then, quietly she asked, 'What do you *really* believe is going to happen, Daniel?'

'Lobengula has never broken his word to us about anything. He told me we'll always be safe in this valley. I believe him.'

'Then there is nothing more to be said. I trust him too. We've faced trouble before and come through. We'll do the same again. This is where we have brought up our children and watched them grow towards manhood. They would not be happy anywhere else . . . and neither would I. We stay, my husband. The Insimo valley is our home.'

CHAPTER TWENTY

When Daniel went to Bulawayo, a week after Jaconus Van Eyck's visit to him, he found far more Matabele impis than usual encamped about the Matabele capital. None of the Mahajas attempted to interfere with his progress, but many hostile glances were cast in his direction.

It was a relief to reach Lobengula's house and have the King greet him warmly at the doorway, in full view of his people. But once inside, with the door closed behind them, the Matabele King launched into a fierce attack on Rhodes.

'Have you heard what his men did? They fired upon my impi. Shot my warriors. Nyamatakah was with them. He might have been killed!'

'There's likely to be a lot more killing, Inkosi. The men of Rhodes' company are angry about your raids. They say it's impossible to carry on normal life in Mashonaland while they continue.'

'Mashonaland belongs to me. I will do as I wish there. The Matabele have always raided the Mashona.'

'I know, but Rhodes and his company weren't there before. Can't you cut down on your raiding? Make an effort not to provoke him?'

Lobengula sat down in his battered old armchair wearily and one of his wives hurried across the room with a calabash of beer. Lobengula waved her away irritably.

'You think *I* provoke *Rhodes*, trader? I ask no more than that my people be allowed to live as they always have – no more than that.'

'Times are changing rapidly, Inkosi. The Matabele *must* change with them.'

'No!' Lobengula roared the word. His wives who were in the room rolled their eyes nervously at the anger of their King. 'Raiding is an essential part of the Matabele way of life. The prowess that the Matabele warrior learns on the raid makes him unbeatable in war. Our ways have made my people great.

If the impis of the Matabele can no longer march across the hills of their own land and listen to the wind singing among their spears they cease to be the Matabele. If it were not for this man Rhodes I would do as my father did . . . take my people, my cattle and belongings, and go north across the Zambezi. But Rhodes sends his men there too.'

Daniel felt desperately sorry for Lobengula, but he did his best to be practical. 'You would need to fight hard to conquer new lands. Such battles would leave you with a much weaker nation. You must try to make peace with Rhodes. It's your only chance.'

'I have tried to live at peace with *all* white men. All my reign I have tried. Can you tell me of one white man who has lost his life at my hands . . . or at the hands of my warriors? No, I have treated them as though they were my own sons. In return they show me nothing but ingratitude and contempt. Tell me, you are my friend, what more can I do?'

Lobengula was King of the Matabele. He represented life or death to hundreds of thousands of men, women and children. Yet he was a very lonely man. The duplicity of Farewell Loveday had hit him particularly hard. Lobengula had trusted him, spending many hours talking over his problems with him. Now there was only Daniel, and his visits were all too infrequent these days. The King sat in his chair, a picture of total dejection. In his heart he knew that war with the white men was inevitable . . . and he entertained few doubts about its outcome.

Resisting the almost overwhelming urge to place a comforting hand upon the King's shoulder, Daniel said, 'Try to hold your warriors in check, Inkosi. I'll go to Fort Salisbury. If there is anything to be done, I'll do it.'

'Thank you, trader. You alone among your people are a true friend. Go in peace.'

Lobengula hoped desperately that Daniel would succeed in averting war. All the same, he sent out messengers, recalling six thousand warriors who were at that moment raiding north of the Zambezi River. While he awaited their arrival, he deployed other impis along his borders and on all roads leading to the capital.

Returning to Insimo, Daniel collected Jaconus Van Eyck and Wyatt. He rode first to Fort Victoria, then northward along the pioneer road to Fort Salisbury. In both towns Daniel saw clear preparations for war. Men were going about their business with that peculiar cockiness they adopt when a battle is imminent. Part bravado, it was also an attempt to cover their fears.

In Fort Salisbury, Daniel was given a short and unsympathetic hearing by the Chartered Company Administrator. Daniel had hardly begun to explain the purpose of his visit before he was rudely interrupted.

'If you're here to discuss peace, Mister Retallick, then you're talking to the wrong man. I suggest you go back and speak to your friend, Lobengula.'

'I've just come from Lobengula. He doesn't want war.'

'His warriors *do*. I have received two reports only today of Matabele impis firing on British South Africa Company Police patrols.'

'Come with me and talk to Lobengula. Bring these reports with you. I guarantee that those responsible will be punished—'

'As far as I am concerned, *Lobengula* is responsible. I will carry out whatever action I deem necessary to punish him. If Lobengula is so anxious to avert war, tell him to come *here* and see *me*. I will listen to him, but only if he leaves his army behind in Bulawayo.'

As he left the Administrator's office, Daniel saw a large troop of well-armed men riding out of Fort Salisbury, heading south.

Wyatt and Jaconus Van Eyck were waiting for him. Jaconus nodded towards the departing men. 'They're on their way to join up with columns from Fort Victoria and Fort Tuli. That's not all. We've just come from the telegraph office. A mixed column of Bechuanaland Border Police and Boers is in the country and another is expected from the Cape within a few days.'

Daniel's anger and frustration spilled over. 'You tried to tell me this was the spontaneous reaction of the settlers to Lobengula's raids, Jaconus. You must know now that's nonsense. These preparations for war have been going on for weeks – probably months. Lobengula's raids on the Mashona are no more than an excuse for Rhodes to invade Matabeleland. I've said so all along.'

'There's something else I think you ought to know, Daniel . . . Rhodes is in Mashonaland.'

'Then why didn't he come to speak to me at the Administrator's office?'

'He's not in Fort Salisbury. He's camped at Chief Macheke's village.'

Daniel was puzzled. Macheke's village was about seventy miles from Fort Salisbury, on the track to Umtali and the Mozambique border.

'I don't believe it. Why would he be skulking there when all the action is being directed from Fort Salisbury?'

Then suddenly, enlightenment hit Daniel with all the force of a blow to his stomach. There was only one man who could effectively stop open warfare between the Matabele and the Europeans. That man was Cecil Rhodes.

The Governor in Cape Town would be fully aware of this. Sir Hercules Robinson had been replaced by Sir Henry Loch – and Loch was not a Rhodes Company man. If he learned what was happening, he might *order* Rhodes to put a halt to warfare between the forces of the Chartered Company and Lobengula – but only if he were able to contact Rhodes.

By remaining at Macheke's kraal, Rhodes had effectively cut himself off from all communications with the outside world. He could be ordered to do nothing. It was the final, carefully thought-out detail in his well-laid plans.

Daniel found Cecil Rhodes relaxing outside his tent on a hill overlooking the Macheke River. He showed no concern at the unexpected arrival of Daniel and Wyatt.

'Hello, Retallick. We're both a long way from home. Is this your son? He's a fine looking boy. Sit yourselves down and have a drink. What'll you have, eh?'

'I'd rather talk, Mister Rhodes. About ways to stop a bloody war.'

'War?' Rhodes was in a jocular mood. 'Who'd want to make war on such a lovely day as this?'

'Mister Rhodes, I'm pleading with you. You *have* Mashonaland. It became yours without a fight because Lobengula promised that was the way it would be, and he's a man of honour. Had he attacked when your pioneer column was crossing any one of a dozen rivers, he could have cut your men to pieces.'

'Of course he could. I knew that. But you told me he wouldn't. I believed you. In return I promised to make no claim on the Insimo valley. Neither will I. That means we are *all* men of our word. What more is there to be said?'

'A whole lot more, as well you know. Lobengula has done his best to remain at peace with Europeans, in spite of all the provocation he's received from your company—'

'Provocation?' Rhodes squeaked the word excitedly. 'Provocation, you say? That's ugly talk, Retallick. If anyone has been provoked it's my company. No sooner do we begin to make a go of things – acting within the terms of our concession, I would point out, than this . . . this SAVAGE orders his army here to kill all our workers, or send them scurrying to the hills, afraid to show their faces in the light of day. Sometimes they are gone for weeks. I can't run a company like this, Retallick.'

'The Matabele have always raided the Mashona. They see no reason to stop now . . . but, if you come with me to talk to Lobengula, he'll not only listen, he'll come more than halfway towards satisfying your complaints. He wants peace.'

Cecil Rhodes snorted. 'Then he's got a damned funny way of showing it. That's all I can say.'

'Come and talk with him. You might even find you like Lobengula. You're both big men – and both have much to gain . . . or lose. At least come to Fort Salisbury and call in your various columns until we've had time to discuss the matter.'

'I can't. I may have smallpox in my party. That's why I'm remaining here. We can't have that spreading through the country, can we?'

Daniel looked about him at the men of Cecil Rhodes' party, each of whom looked the picture of health. Those who had heard Rhodes' words were grinning openly.

Daniel turned back to Rhodes in desperation. 'Mister Rhodes, I've never begged anything from anyone before but I'm begging you now. *Please* come and talk to Lobengula.'

'I'll bear it in mind . . . when I come in to Fort Salisbury.'

Daniel's shoulders sagged as he conceded defeat. He walked away from Rhodes filled with bitterness. He knew the Macheke camp would not be broken up until the columns of armed Europeans were beyond recall. He would have been even more bitter had he known, as Rhodes assuredly did, that the value of shares in the British South Africa Company had leaped to a new high on the London market. News had been 'leaked' that the Chartered Company was expanding into Matabeleland.

'What will you do now, Pa?' Wyatt asked the question as they turned their horses towards Fort Salisbury.

'Telegraph to the Governor in Cape Town. I'll ask him to order the Mashonaland Administration to stop all aggressive action against the Matabele. Then I'll go back to Lobengula and get him to pull his impis back to Bulawayo, clear of trouble. I can think of nothing else at the moment.'

Unknown to Daniel, Lobengula had also decided to approach the Governor in the Cape Colony. He sent off three Indunas with a message to Cape Town. One of them was his brother. Escorted by the European who had taken on the task of running Daniel's Bulawayo store, the three Indunas got as far as Tati. Here, their escort left them and went off to find himself a drink. During his absence the three Indunas waited patiently until they were approached by a group of Bechuanaland Border Police, demanding to know their business. Within minutes a bitter quarrel had broken out. Two shots were fired, and two of the Indunas lay dead on the ground. Lobengula's brother was the lone survivor – but not for long. He fell ill with a mysterious sickness and died within a few days of his murdered companions.

When news of the three deaths reached him, Lobengula became angrier than any of his people had ever seen him. For a few minutes the overweight, self-indulgent sovereign became once again the Warrior-King his people had elected to lead them. Rising from his throne of animal hides, he seized a spear from one of his bodyguard. Drawing back his arm, he hurled the weapon high in the air, towards the distant skyline where the sun was climbing into the sky above Mashonaland.

Pointing to where the spear stuck quivering in the ground, Lobengula cried, 'My impis will follow the path of the spear until they meet with the white man. Then they will KILL! KILL! KILL! His feet shall trample our lands no more.'

The roar of approval that rose from the throats of the Matabele warriors sent creatures fleeing through the bushveldt two miles away.

It was war at last.

By the time Daniel and Wyatt reached Fort Salisbury, the first pitched battle between the Matabele warriors and the forces of the Chartered Company had already been fought only a few miles from Insimo.

Filled with a variety of emotions, Elvira and the three boys had watched the six hundred men of the Fort Victoria column ride through the Insimo valley on their way to war.

The boys were filled with excitement at the sight of so many horsemen. Elvira was dismayed at such tragic evidence that Daniel's mission had failed. Whatever the outcome of the fighting, things would never be the same for any of them again.

Elvira climbed the hillside behind the house with the boys, following in the wake of the column. From here they heard the first volley of rifle shots in the battle between the two opposing forces. Minutes later there came the steady and monotonous chatter of the Maxim guns as they poured bullets into the packed ranks of the Matabele army. When the screams of the wounded began to make themselves heard above the din of battle, Elvira took her children back to the house.

Safely inside, Elvira made her way to her bedroom and kneeled before a silver and mother-of-pearl crucifix. Here she prayed. She prayed for the Matabele and for Daniel too. She knew that part of him was dying in the fighting going on beyond the hill.

The battle ended in a decisive victory for the men of the Fort Victoria column. More than two thousand Matabele warriors were killed, such was the killing power of the Maxim gun. It was also an indication of the recklessly brave tactics of the impis. But even Lobengula's great army could not afford to sustain casualties in such appalling numbers.

When news of the battle reached Fort Salisbury, where

Daniel had been denied use of the telegraph because of 'war requirements', he and Wyatt rode for home as fast as their horses would carry them. At Fort Victoria they obtained fresh mounts and, accompanied by Jaconus Van Eyck once more, galloped home to the Insimo Valley.

All was well at Insimo, but a number of wounded Europeans were being looked after in the house, and twenty men of the Fort Victoria column had been left behind by their Commanding Officer to guard against a possible attack by wandering Mahajas who had fled from the battlefield.

There was news too of a second battle, fought closer to Bulawayo – but on this occasion the Maxim guns had succeeded in scything down only *one* thousand Matabele warriors.

That night Daniel and Elvira slept little. Daniel grieved for Lobengula and the loss of so many of his warriors. Beside him, in the darkened room, Elvira clung to him tighter.

'What are you going to do now, Daniel?'

'I must go to Lobengula. Somehow this slaughter has to be brought to an end. I'll try to persuade him to surrender to the Commander of the troops from the Cape. That way he'll become the Queen's responsibility and not Rhodes'. He might even be able to appeal to her and obtain an honourable settlement.'

'Will Lobengula listen to you?'

'He *must*. The whole future of his people depends upon what he does next. A wrong move now and the Matabele will no longer exist as a nation.'

'This means very much to you, my husband, I know . . . but I wish you were not going. I have a feeling . . . a deep, empty feeling in here.' She placed his hand on her breast.

'I must go, Elvira. Everything we have here we owe to Lobengula. He's been a very good friend to us. Now, more than ever before, *he* is in need of a friend.'

Elvira clung to Daniel and, when he slept with his arms about her, she wept as she had never cried before in all the years of their marriage.

CHAPTER TWENTY-ONE

Daniel rode off the next morning with Jaconus Van Eyck. Both Wyatt and Nathan accompanied them. Wyatt would have come anyway, but Nathan pleaded that history was being made all about them and he was seeing none of it.

Nathan was not so certain he enjoyed history in the making when they passed the site of the first big battle. The stench was appalling. Around the battlefield vultures waddled and flapped in uncomfortable awkwardness, so gorged they were unable to leave the ground. When the party stopped for a meal a couple of miles on, no one felt like eating.

They arrived at Bulawayo mid-morning the following day and discovered that all that remained of Lobengula's capital was a wide expanse of smouldering ashes. The forces of the Chartered Company were in camp nearby and as Daniel picked his way through the ruins of the once-great kraal, a man approached him. It was an Afrikaans blacksmith who had been employed by Lobengula, mainly to keep the guns of his personal bodyguard in working order.

The two men clasped hands and Daniel said, 'It's good to see you . . . but how did you escape from this?'

'I didn't have to. Lobengula sent for me. He told me he was setting fire to Bulawayo, but that I wouldn't be hurt. I wasn't.'

'Do you know where he's gone?'

'North, that's all I know. I wish I thought he'd make it to safety, but he's got Major Forbes and two hundred men on his tail.'

'What was his mood when he spoke to you? Do you think he'll run until he's across the Zambezi, or will he stand and fight?'

The blacksmith shook his head. 'You know Lobengula better than me. He doesn't want to fight . . . he never has, but he's got his best impis around him now and they're just as keen for war as Rhodes.'

Daniel glanced up at the sky, Huge, brooding clouds were

pushing up from the east, threatening the sun. 'The rains will be here soon. Perhaps they'll cool everyone's tempers.'

When Daniel returned to the horses he suggested that the boys should return to Insimo accompanied by Jaconus Van Eyck.

The boys protested vigorously. So did Jaconus Van Eyck.

'You're not heading north alone, Daniel. Half the men with Forbes are Boers. They'd all as soon kill an Englishman as a kaffir. No, I'm coming with you.'

In the end, Daniel agreed that they would all go on together, reassessing the situation if it appeared likely they might run into trouble. They set out immediately, following the broad trail left by Lobengula's fleeing nation.

It was not long before they began meeting small groups of Matabele, all heading back towards Bulawayo. These were stragglers who had been overtaken by Forbes. They had decided to return to the ruins of their city, rather than risk becoming embroiled in a battle.

Once Daniel saw a family he recognised as kinsfolk of one of Lobengula's Indunas. In reply to Daniel's questions they told him that the King had indeed gone northwards. So too had Forbes, although when he caught up with the King, the company man would no doubt wish he had not. The family would not elaborate, but Daniel was left with the impression that Forbes was being drawn into a trap.

After threatening for so long, the rain began to fall the following day. Large drops stung their faces as the two men and two boys followed Lobengula's trail.

They passed more refugees now. Significantly, they were all women and children. Then, on the bank of the river where there were signs that a great many people had made camp, Daniel found the charred remains of Lobengula's old armchair. Now he knew that the forces of Major Forbes must have been pressing close to the Matabele King when they passed over the river.

Daniel decided to make the river crossing immediately, for fear the waters would rise during the night and make the river impassable.

They gained the far bank safely, but had advanced no more than a hundred yards when they suddenly came upon armed

Europeans wearing the crossed cartridge belts favoured by Boer commandos.

After identifying themselves to the other men's satisfaction, Daniel was subjected to urgent questioning. 'What's it like on the other side of the river? Are there any Matabele over there?'

'Not unless you count women and children . . . . But what's happened? Where's Major Forbes?'

'Major Forbes is no longer in charge. If you want to speak to someone it had better be Commandant Graaf.'

The Boer outriders did not elaborate, but led them to an uncomfortable camp, about a mile ahead.

Commandant Graaf and Jaconus Van Eyck greeted each other by their first names and it was apparent by Graaf's manner that they knew each other well.

'Agh, man! This whole chase has been a bloody shambles from start to finish, eh? This "Major" Forbes couldn't lead a party of drinkers to a booze-up. I had to take over from him or we'd all be dead now. We've got a hundred and thirty men here, many of them wounded, and another thirty-four back there somewhere. God knows what's happened to them. We've fought the whole Matabele army most of the way here.'

'Well, once across the river you'll be clear of them,' Daniel assured the Commandant. 'But I'd get across quickly if I were you. We've had rain and the river might rise very quickly.'

'You've no need to tell me that,' said Graaf bitterly. 'That's how we lost touch with Allen Wilson and his men.'

Graaf raised his voice, shouting to his men to break camp. His exact words were, 'Get your butts off the ground and ride like hell out of here.'

The demoralised column rode away without Daniel once seeing Major Forbes, the official Commanding Officer of the column. But he was not given long to concern himself with the squabble between Graaf and Forbes. Half a mile along the trail they encountered a very large Matabele impi. A roar went up from the warriors and Daniel and the others backed away nervously, keeping their distance until Daniel recognised the tall Induna who ran from the ranks of his warriors to meet them. It was Gamba, Lobengula's son-in-law.

After exchanging greetings, Daniel told Gamba he was seeking Lobengula.

'Every white man there ever was is seeking the King.' commented Gamba drily. 'But you are his friend, trader. I will take you to him.'

As Daniel and the others led their horses beside Gamba, Daniel questioned the Induna about the progress of the war and asked whether he knew what Lobengula was hoping to do. Gamba's replies were evasive and noncommittal.

Late in the day they forded another river. The trail they were following now passed through an area of tall, green-leafed Mopani trees. The ground was soft underfoot and with Gamba's impi trailing some way behind, it was as quiet as a cathedral. Then, as they approached a clearing, visible some way ahead through the trees, Gamba tried to head them away, to one side of the clearing, but Daniel called him to a halt.

'Wait a minute . . . . Can you hear anything?'

In the ensuing silence they all heard the low drone of millions of tiny wings beating the air.

'Flies.' Daniel exchanged glances with Jaconus Van Eyck. Both men thought of the thirty-four men missing from Commandant Graaf's column.

Ignoring Gamba's plea that it was not good for them to go to the clearing, Daniel mounted his horse and urged the animal forward, closely followed by the others.

At the edge of the clearing, Daniel saw that his fears were realised. Reining in his horse he called back to Wyatt, 'Take Nathan back out of the way. There's no need for either of you to see this.'

Wyatt did as he was told without question, ignoring Nathan's protests.

Daniel slid from his horse and walked into the clearing, with Jaconus Van Eyck a pace behind him. The buzzing of the flies was aggressively loud here and they hovered in great clouds over a gruesome scene.

Daniel had found Allen Wilson and his men. Their naked bodies were piled in an untidy heap in the centre of the clearing. They were horribly mutilated, but Daniel was able to recognise two of them he had met in Fort Victoria. Jaconus Van Eyck had known them all.

Daniel found himself searching the recesses of his mind desperately for an appropriate prayer, but the words eluded him. Gamba had come silently to his side and he said quietly, 'They did not die alone, trader. Four hundred of my bravest warriors died with them.' Gamba gazed at the bodies and in a voice filled with respect said, 'Yes, these were men of men, and their fathers were men before them.'

Gamba had paid the men the ultimate compliment of a Matabele warrior, but Daniel left the clearing deeply distressed at the unnecessary waste of so many lives.

The next morning they met up with another Matabele impi. This one was much smaller than Gamba's, containing no more than a hundred men. The Induna in charge was Nyamatakah, Lobengula's eldest son. With him was his brother Lundi. They had been guarding a pass in the hills to the east while Lobengula passed by. Now they were on their way to rejoin him, frustrated that they had not yet been involved in any action.

Lundi grinned self-consciously at Wyatt, but Nyamatakah scowled when the Mahajas of Gamba's impi shouted of the many men they had killed in battle.

'I have not yet washed my spear in a white man's blood,' Nyamatakah said loudly.

'There is no need for such words before a man who is your father's friend,' snapped Gamba.

'It is not long ago that *all* white men claimed to be the King's friends,' retorted Nyamatakah. 'Now we are fleeing north. We will have a new land, and who knows . . . perhaps a new King. Remember that, Gamba. For now you can return to the Shangani River with your impi. Chase the white men back to where they came from. I will take the trader to the King.'

Gamba looked at Nyamatakah suspiciously, but the heir to the Matabele throne rounded on him angrily. 'That order came from the King. Go!'

'My brother likes to hear his own voice. He thinks he is King already.' Lundi spoke the words quietly to Wyatt, so that his brother would not hear.

All that day Daniel, Jaconus Van Eyck and the two boys travelled with Nyamatakah's impi, without the royal Induna saying a word to them. Towards the evening, Daniel edged his horse towards Van Eyck.

'I'm not happy, Jaconus,' he said, in a low voice that would not carry to the boys. 'Gamba was bringing us in a straight line, due north. Now we've swung away to westward.'

Jaconus Van Eyck nodded. He had noticed that Lundi too was uneasy and twice he had seen the royal brothers arguing.

That night they camped in an area of broken rocks, building their fire some way from the fires of the impi. Daniel ensured the horses were left saddled in readiness and the two men and Wyatt took turns in maintaining a guard. Wyatt had the last two hours of the night and drowsily he watched the colours of dawn begin to chase away the night shadows. He must have dozed off for a few moments, but woke suddenly to hear a voice whispering hoarsely in his ear, speaking Matabele.

'Wyatt! Wyatt! Wake the others. Go . . . quickly.'

It was Lundi.

As Wyatt shifted stiffly, Lundi added, 'Leave everything and go now. My brother means to kill you all.'

Wyatt shook the others hurriedly and as they came awake the low voices of Matabele warriors could be heard moving towards them between the broken rocks on the hillside.

Wasting no time, Daniel checked that they were all ready then signalled for them to sprint for the horses.

As they rose to their feet the Matabele warriors saw them and set up a howl that raised the hackles on Nathan's neck. It was a sound like nothing he had ever heard before. He made it to the horses but then hopped around frantically, one foot in the stirrup while his horse, startled by the suddenness of his arrival, pranced away from him.

Daniel gave him a heave from behind and, when Nathan was safely mounted, vaulted to the saddle of his own horse.

As they galloped from the shelter of the rocks, a small party of warriors ran in an attempt to head them off, but Jaconus Van Eyck fired his rifle from the saddle and one of the Matabele fell to the ground, the others hurriedly losing all enthusiasm for the chase.

Behind them the thwarted warriors began shooting wildly . . . and suddenly Daniel's horse stumbled. He was not certain whether it had been hit or if it stumbled on a piece of rock, but it was sufficient to bring the horse to the ground. Daniel just managed to shake his feet free of the stirrups before the horse rolled over.

The horse tried valiantly to rise, but one of its back legs was broken and Daniel snatched his rifle from the saddle holster and ran.

The others had seen him fall and gave him covering fire from about a hundred yards away. The Matabeles had also seen the incident and were running in pursuit. Some were brought down by the rifle fire, but there were many more to take their places – and they too were firing.

A searing pain burned through Daniel's left leg as a bullet struck him behind the knee. For a couple of paces he tried hopping, dragging the wounded leg behind him. The pain proved too great. Turning to face his pursuers, he fired twice, downing two warriors. Then he was forced to stop to reload.

The Matabele warriors who had been spread out across the hillside closed in upon him. Daniel snapped the breech of his gun shut and shot the nearest warrior. The second cartridge misfired. An assegai flashed down, sending Daniel staggering backwards. He fell and immediately another warrior stabbed down at him, pinning Daniel to the ground.

Daniel lay helpless, aware that he had been severely wounded. Strangely, he felt no pain now.

The knot of warriors about him parted and Nyamatakah stood above him. Quivering with excitement, Nyamatakah raised his assegai. As Daniel looked up at him, a hole suddenly appeared in Nyamatakah's chest and blood blossomed around it. A moment later Lobengula's son dropped dead at Daniel's feet.

The death of the Induna brought Daniel a brief respite. Then as the warriors began to howl in anger, Daniel heard Wyatt's cry.

'Pa . . . ! Pa . . . ! I'm coming . . . .'

Turning his head with difficulty, Daniel saw Wyatt galloping his horse towards him, elbows and legs flapping wildly, a look of anguish on his face.

'No, Wyatt! Go back, son . . . .'

The words were a despairing croak in Daniel's throat as his mind flashed back to the words of the White Mondoro, spoken on the hilltop fortress, high above the Great House of the Chiefs. *'I see a hand stretching towards you. . . . . It holds a spear . . . . There are many spears pointing at your people . . . .'*

'Wyatt, go back! For God's sake go back.'

A shot from point blank range brought down Wyatt's horse. It fell to the ground and lay with legs and head twitching. '*Your heart weeps . . . but the tears are not for yourself.*' Wyatt bounced up, running. Seeing no one but his father.

As Wyatt plunged into a flailing mêlée of arms and assegais, Daniel remembered another day, an older Mondoro. '*Your first born will prove himself truly a man . . . .*'

Miraculously Wyatt fought his way through the warriors before being hacked to his knees at Daniel's side.

'*. . . . Truly a man.*'

Wyatt died calling his father's name. Daniel managed to grasp his son's hand before the assegais of Nyamatakah's impi stabbed out his life too.

'*. . . The second son will carry your line.*' Nathan almost confounded the Mondoro's prediction, and Elvira came close to losing two sons that day. Sobbing with anger and grief, Nathan was kneeing his horse towards the impi when Jaconus Van Eyck snatched the reins from his hands and led him away from the place where his father and brother had died.

As the two horsemen galloped out of sight, Lundi looked about him at the bodies of his people . . . and those who had been his friends. Tears rolled down his face. They were for his friends. He did not look at his brother. After a few minutes, Lundi turned and took his place at the head of his late brother's impi and he set off to find Lobengula.

Behind him the clouds gathered, building up far away over the hills that surrounded Insimo. In the valley the wind bowed the heads of the tall maize plants as it ran ahead of the rain, and touched the blooded spears of Lundi's impi. '*The spears and the wind sing together . . .*'

The wind whispered a dirge through the mountains and woodlands of Matabeleland. It touched the hair of Cecil Rhodes as he left the telegraph office in Fort Salisbury, rustling the messages proclaiming victory clutched in his hand.

Lobengula never learned of the death of his friend. He died on the road north. Some say he was poisoned. Others plump for suicide. A few claim he died a victim of smallpox. One or two, those who had known him well, believed the loss of his father's nation broke his heart.

The Matabele King was never again seen by a white man after firing Bulawayo as a funeral pyre for the Matabele nation, and many refused to accept the stories of his death. For many years men claimed to have seen the last Matabele King in many remote corners of the African continent.

What can never be disputed is that the wind touched upon triumph and sorrow, victory and defeat on this stormy December day. It drew from them all the seeds of discontent and scattered them far and wide across the land, there to flourish and multiply. One day those seeds would burst forth in a blood-red harvest for all men, black and white to reap.

When that day came, the final prophesy of the White Mondoro, made to the last King of the Matabele would be fulfilled.

'One day it will be the Mashona who rule all the people who now bow before Mzilikazi. The sons of your sons, and those of others here will witness the fulfilment of my words . . . and they will remember.'